Acclaim for Tony Earley's

THE BLUE STAR

Selected by USA Today *and the* Christian Science
Monitor *as one of the year's best books*
A New York Times *Notable Book of the Year*

"Tony Earley delivers a rarity: a good story, told without
fuss or flourish, and with the assurance of someone who
knows what he's doing on every page. . . . Earley's novels
are the Shaker chairs of American literature. They're
well-made, sturdy tales that are stripped of excess and
postmodern gimmicks, and they just might last you forever." — Yvonne Zipp, *Christian Science Monitor*

"I galloped through the novel and relished every page. . . .
Earley's simple prose is always informed by Jim's good
heart. . . . *The Blue Star,* like its hero, is irresistible."
— Scott Turow, *New York Times Book Review*

"Tony Earley catches up with 'Jim the boy' in a beguil-
ing sequel that's never too good to be true. . . . Always
careful but never fussy, Earley writes prose so cadenced
and so acute that he bewitches his readers with an idyll
of boyhood so completely realized that we never want to
leave it." — Malcolm Jones, *Newsweek*

"Beautifully told, this old-fashioned love story is the
kind of fiction readers have come to expect from Earley
after his luminous, warmhearted first novel, *Jim the Boy.*"
— Patrick Sullivan, *Library Journal*

"When you've loved a novel as much as I loved Tony Earley's debut, *Jim the Boy*, the prospect of a sequel triggers an uneasy blend of anticipation and doubt. . . . I'm happy to report that Earley's *The Blue Star* works as a sequel and a lovely coming-of-age story that can be savored on its own." — Bob Minzesheimer, *USA Today*

"Mr. Earley's style remains endearingly airborne. . . . Jim the boy could have remained a boy forever. Mr. Earley's crystalline portrait of him as a ten-year-old brought up by a tenderly protective family needed no expansion or improvement. But here is a second, cloudier installment, and it brings Jim into contact with a new set of realities. Jim's adolescent joys (secretly fishtailing the family car on country roads), urges (his crush on Chrissie is full-fledged first love), and fears (*The Blue Star* is infused with signs of the coming war) are much more fateful. . . . Mr. Earley's disarming folksiness is intact, but the portents of his story are dark. Jim feels this shift as he senses that his real life is about to begin. He knows he has reached an age to make irrevocable choices. But for the moment, in the teenage time capsule that is *The Blue Star*, the future is only foreshadowing. Jim lives in a beautifully evoked state of suspended animation." — Janet Maslin, *New York Times*

"At the heart of *The Blue Star* is a good, old-fashioned love story. . . . Earley writes with the same lyrical simplicity that he employed in *Jim the Boy*, calling to mind his literary idol Willa Cather." — Porter Shreve, *Boston Globe*

"With the publication of *Jim the Boy*, *Granta* named Earley one of 'the Best of the Young American Novelists' and *The New Yorker* announced him one of the '20 best young fiction writers in America.' Often such praise proves more hopeful than accurate. *The Blue Star* confirms that the praise is spot on."

— Denise Gess, *Raleigh News and Observer*

"It's been seven years since novelist Tony Earley introduced readers to Jim Glass and his small North Carolina town of Aliceville in the acclaimed novel *Jim the Boy*. Now, it's a pleasure to report that Jim has returned as a young adult in Earley's quietly moving, elegiac sequel, *The Blue Star*. It's refreshing to see that Earley's writing has lost none of its elegant simplicity. What makes *The Blue Star* such a rewarding contribution to the coming-of-age genre is the author's skill in crafting a vivid and yet fully plausible interior life for his protagonist. And every character, from Jim's bachelor uncles to his ex-girlfriend Norma, contributes depth and richness to the story." — Harvey Freedenberg, *BookPage*

"*The Blue Star* is a very fine book, full of moments of humor and tenderness, prose so glassine you almost forget it is there. . . . In the main, the quietude and restraint of Earley's third-person narration, which isn't much different from Flannery O'Connor's or Mark Twain's, explains itself. . . . For that reason *The Blue Star* is, in more ways than one, a wonderful reminder of how we used to live." — John Freeman, *Minneapolis Star Tribune*

"The style and subject matter of Tony Earley's coming-of-age tale harkens back to the classic coming-of-age fiction of writers like J. D. Salinger and Harper Lee."
— Kate Vagnino, *Time Out New York*

"The deceptive simplicity of the matter-of-fact narrative inexorably draws the reader into this tender and true coming-of-age tale." — Margaret Flanagan, *Booklist*

"Plotwise, this is the narrative equivalent of ambling along a country road. Earley keeps things simple. . . . You take in what you see and savor it without giving it much thought. . . . There's an appealing sweetness to this story." — Carmela Ciuraru, *Los Angeles Times*

"Tony Earley and his novels of farm life in the '30s and '40s, *Jim the Boy* and a fresh delight, *The Blue Star*, herald a new nostalgia. . . . In Earley's expert hands that feeling becomes essential, elemental, and vanished."
— Bethany Schneider, *Newsday*

"We've waited a long time for a sequel to that story, and during those eight years, Jim the boy has grown into Jim the young man, the sort of person you'd expect from the first novel. He's decent and contemplative, concerned about others' feelings and his own shortcomings, suspended awkwardly between adolescence and adulthood. . . . The novel left me eager for the story of Jim's adventures in World War II."
— Ron Charles, *Washington Post Book World*

"*The Blue Star* packs a startling emotional punch."
— *Publishers Weekly*

"Inspired by the rural hamlet in which the author grew up, Aliceville is populated by modest people struggling to lead decent lives amid the historical upheaval of the Depression and World War II. . . . Jim's search to find himself — including a moral compass with which to navigate the larger world — speaks as much to contemporary experience as it does to life in the bygone era in which Earley's books are set."
— Bill Friskics-Warren, *Nashville Scene*

"Rewarding. . . . A sweet coming-of-age novel. . . . Earley fans can only hope they won't have to wait as long for the next installment of Jim, a boy who is becoming a man."   — Cristina Rouvalis, *Pittsburgh Post-Gazette*

"If you're looking for a good weep, score a copy of Tony Earley's *The Blue Star:* It has one of those happy endings shadowed by the possibility of tragic events just out of sight."   — *New York Observer*

"Earley has a sure touch with language. . . . The novel is filled with sharp detail and small dramatic moments rendered precisely. . . . *The Blue Star* leaves us hoping Jim will come home safely, to Chrissie, to Aliceville, and to the next novel about his life."
— Lynna Williams, *Atlanta Journal-Constitution*

Also by Tony Earley

Jim the Boy
Here We Are in Paradise
Somehow Form a Family

THE BLUE STAR

A NOVEL

TONY EARLEY

BACK BAY BOOKS
Little, Brown and Company
New York   Boston   London

Back Bay Books/Little, Brown and Company
Hachette Book Group
237 Park Avenue, New York, NY 10017
Visit our website at www.HachetteBookGroup.com

Originally published in hardcover by
Little, Brown and Company, March 2008
First Back Bay paperback edition, August 2009

Back Bay Books is an imprint of Little, Brown and Company. The Back
Bay Books name and logo are trademarks of Hachette Book Group, Inc.

Joan Brasher's interview with Tony Earley, which appears in the
reading group guide at the back of this book, was originally
published in March 2008 in *Vanderbilt View*.
Copyright © 2008 by Vanderbilt View. Reprinted with permission.

Library of Congress Cataloging-in-Publication Data

Earley, Tony.
    The blue star : a novel / Tony Earley. — 1st ed.
        p.   cm.
    ISBN 978-0-316-19907-0 (hc) / 978-0-316-00805-1 (pb)
    1. Teenage boys — Fiction.   2. Nineteen forties — Fiction.   I. Title.
    PS3555.A685B56 2008
    813'.54 — dc22   2007009921

                    10   9   8   7   6   5   4   3   2   1

                                RRD-VA

                PRINTED IN THE UNITED STATES OF AMERICA

For
The girls who live in the blue house

I got a pig home in the pen
And corn to feed him on
All I need is a pretty little girl
To feed him when I'm gone

Arthur Smith,
"Pig in a Pen"

In memory of
Gordon Kato
1961–2006

CONTENTS

Prologue

Book I: Indian Summer

Book II: The Secrets of Women

CONTENTS

Prologue

March 12, 1918

Lynn's Mountain, NC
Dear Zeno,

    It is a cold day up here, and though a few trees are start-ing to bud and a few brave wildflowers are coming up in the sunny places, I'm afraid it will never be spring again. There is still snow on the other side of the hollow and I don't think it will ever melt. I still feel awful about the fight we had last Sunday when you rode all the way up here on your white mule in the mud just to see me and you got so cold, and I wish that I felt different from what I said then but I still don't. I will never understand as long as I live why you do not want to do your duty and join up for the fight with our boys "over there." Boys from NC and this county are being blowed up and shot in the head by the Germans, even boys from this mountain, like poor Alfred Summey. You even rode by his house on that handsome white mule you're so proud of and saw that awful wreath on the door. Zeno, I thought I loved you with all my heart forever but maybe I don't anymore if I ever did, because I don't really know who you are. All the other boys I know have either been drafted already or have joined up or are getting ready to. Even Al-fred Summey's little brother William is raring to go fight the Huns and he is only twelve years old and he is afraid the war will be over before he can get to France and make up for his brother who was killed, and he just breaks my heart. Don't you feel awful, Zeno, when everybody else is doing their part and you don't do yours? If there was a dam about to bust and wash everybody's house away and you saw all your friends working trying to fix it, would you ride on by on that big mule and just tip your hat howdy or would you get down and help? Zeno, I don't think I can be married to a man who would just ride by that dam and let everybody else's house get washed away, especially when there are twelve-year-old boys begging to help dig. I don't know how you can live with yourself in these awful times and I don't know how you expect me to live with you either, the way things are. I intend to marry a man I can be proud of, and right now I just don't think I can be proud of you because of the decisions you have made. Everybody up here is already calling you a "shirker" and worse and they say your daddy paid and fixed it so your number wouldn't come up, and how do you think that makes me feel? Is riding up here pretty as you please when you know everybody you pass on the road hates you the only brave thing you can do? (I have heard people say that if you keep coming up in here anymore, somebody is bound to shoot you!) This is the hardest thing I've ever had to say in my life but it is the truth. If you had joined the army when everybody else did, I would have waited on you until the end of the earth, but I can't wait on you anymore. When I hear about somebody I can trust going down your way, I will send the ring with them. I cannot keep it anymore or wear it on my finger. I am very sorry and I hope that someday you will be able to see that this is right and forgive me in your heart.

Love always,
Nancy

November 21, 1941

Dear Jim

Hey old buddy I bet you never expected to hear from me did you? Have you started getting ready for baseball season yet? It'll be here before you know it so you better get in shape! Now that I'm gone I guess shortstop is all yours. You ought to be able to handle it after watching "the master" play it for three years straight. Ha!

I just got stationed on the USS California I guess you heard. It is the best ship in the navy. Where else would you expect me to be? Ha! You would not believe how beautiful Hawaii is. Is it cold there yet? Not here boy. I would bring a palm tree and the ocean home with me if I could. The food on the ship is "OK."

Hey Jim a little "birdy" tells me that you've been sniffing around Chrissie Steppe. As you know she's my "girl" but maybe you just forgot. Don't forget that I'm not dead I'm just in the navy! They're not the same thing! Ha! Anyway the last thing you want to do is make a sailor mad. Don't forget to cover the old "sack" like I taught you once the season starts!

Your friend,
Arthur Bucklaw Jr. USN

BOOK I

Indian Summer

At the Top

BECAUSE THEY were seniors and had earned the right, Jim and his buddies stood on the small landing at the top of the school steps, squarely in front of the red double doors. Every student entering the building, boy or girl, had to go around them to get inside. The boys pretended not to notice that they were in everyone else's way, and moved aside only when a teacher climbed the stairs. They had ruled Aliceville School for less than a month but now held this high ground more or less comfortably. The first few days of school, Jim had halfway expected some older boys to come along and tell them to get lost, but during the preceding three weeks, he had gradually come to appreciate that there were no older boys. He and his friends were *it*.

The school overlooked the town from atop a steep hill. Jim tilted his face slightly into the clear sunlight and tenderly considered the world below him. At the foot of the hill the houses and barns and sheds of Aliceville lay scattered around the town's small tangle of streets. Near the center of town the uncles' three tall houses stood shoulder to shoulder. (Jim lived with his mother and her oldest brother, Uncle Zeno, in the middle house. Uncle Coran and Uncle Al, who were twins, lived on either side.) Beyond the town itself, across the railroad track, the uncles' corn and cotton crops filled the sandy bottoms all the way to their arable edges; beyond the fields the neatly tended rows unraveled into the thick gnarl of woods through which the river snaked. The corn, still richly green, stood taller than any man, and the dark cotton rows were speckled with dots of bright, emerging white. West of town the engine smoke of an approaching train climbed into the sky.

Jim could not see Uncle Zeno or Uncle Al in the fields, nor Uncle Coran in the store, but he knew they were there, the same way he knew that when the time came to pick cotton they would not ask him to skip school to help. Just as he wondered what his mother was doing, Mama came out the front door of Uncle Zeno's house with a bucket and dipper and began watering the chrysanthemums blooming in the pots on the porch steps. She glanced at the orange bus from Lynn's Mountain as it turned off the state highway and ground its way up the pitched drive. Jim was glad she didn't look all the way up the hill toward the school. Had she seen him and waved, he not only would have been embarrassed, but he would also have been tempted to weep with some mysterious, nostalgic joy. The warm sunlight on his face seemed to remind him of something — but he couldn't explain what — and some vague but pleasant longing filled his chest. Already he could sense the end of these good days rapidly approaching, like a mail train filled with unexpected news.

"Hey, Jim," Buster Burnette said, "there's your mama."

Dennis Deane squinted as he looked down the hill. "What's she doing?"

"Daggum, Dennis Deane," Jim said. "You can't see a lick, can you?"

"I don't need to see," Dennis Deane said. "I've got an extra eyeball."

Everybody grinned, but nobody said anything. They all knew better.

Dennis Deane batted his eyes innocently. "Ain't you going to ask me where it is?"

Jim shook his head. "Ain't no way."

"Cowards," Dennis Deane sniffed. "The whole bunch of you." He cleared his throat. "Now, where was I?"

"The secrets of women," said Larry Lawter.

"Oh, yeah. Like I said, I know the secrets of women. I can make any female I want to fall in love with me."

"Bull," Buster said.

"I'm telling you," Dennis Deane said. "I'm the Large Possum. The King of the Squirrels."

"You're a nut is what you are," said Jim.

"The Head Nut," Dennis Deane said. "Twice as much for a nickel. Try me just once and you'll know why."

The bus grumbled to a stop at the bottom of the steps. The doors swung open and the students from Lynn's Mountain climbed off and curled around the front of the bus. In the distance the train announced itself at the state highway crossing with a long blast from its whistle. Jim wondered about the train because it was not one that was regularly scheduled. Like everyone else who lived in Aliceville, Jim knew the timetables of the trains and noted when they passed, even in his sleep.

"Prove it," Larry said. "What you said about women." He jerked his head toward the bus. "How about one of these mountain girls?"

"How about her?" Buster said, nodding at a freshman girl with green, shrewd-looking eyes who came around the front of the bus with her books clutched closely to her chest. A pack of third- and fourth-grade boys chattered by her and up the steps into the building. The girl did not look at the seniors on the landing, but Jim could tell she knew they were there.

Dennis Deane squinted again. "Who is it?" he asked. "What's her name?"

"Ellie," Buster said. "Ellie something."

"Okay," Dennis Deane said. "Ellie something. Watch and learn, boys."

When the girl reached the landing, Dennis Deane said, "Hey, Ellie Something." When she looked up, he closed his eyes and contorted his face into an enormous pucker. "Kiss me," he said.

Jim winced when he saw the stricken look on Ellie's face and stepped out of the way to aid her escape. She jerked open one of the doors and ran inside.

"You shouldn't have done that, Dennis Deane," he said, although, despite his better judgment, he laughed along with everybody else.

"I knew it wouldn't work," Buster said.

"Of course it worked," said Dennis Deane. "Ellie Something is now in love with me, although, bless her little heart, she would never, ever admit it. She's just too shy."

Otis Shehan and Horace Gentine climbed the steps and joined the group. The mountain boys were also seniors. "Howdy, men," Horace said. "How's it hanging?"

"Try it on her," Larry said, nodding toward Christine Steppe.

No, don't, Jim thought, but he didn't say anything. As far as Jim was concerned, watching Chrissie Steppe climb the stairway was the best part of the day. And because this information seemed valuable to him in some way he could not name, he had never told the other guys.

"Try what on her?" Otis asked. "I wouldn't try anything on her. That's Bucky Bucklaw's girl."

"I don't care if it's Franklin D. Roosevelt's girl," Dennis Deane said. "Hey. Chrissie Steppe. Kiss me." He squeezed his eyes shut and puckered up.

Chrissie stopped and her large, dark eyes blinked

slowly as she considered Dennis Deane. Her black hair reached almost to her waist. She shifted her books to her left arm.

Jim noticed that her right hand was balled into a dangerous-looking fist. "Hey, whoa," he said, stepping in front of her. "Don't hit him."

Dennis Deane flinched. "Hit me?" he said, without opening his eyes. "Is somebody about to hit me?"

Chrissie's shoulders rose and fell with her breathing. "I'm about to beat you all over this schoolyard, you little worm," she said. "I will not be talked to that way."

Dennis Deane covered his head with his arms and whimpered, "Don't hurt me, you big, strong, she-girl."

"He didn't mean anything by it," said Jim. "He's just a little, well, insane, is what he is."

"I've got an extra eyeball," Dennis Deane said. "Do you want me to show it to you?"

Chrissie turned away from Dennis Deane and stared levelly at Jim with what he took to be an expression of slight disappointment. "Are you his friend?" she asked.

"Sort of, I guess," he said. "More like his guardian. Something like that."

Jim caught a slight whiff of vanilla and wished she would step even closer. He felt himself beginning to smile and thought, wildly, *We're almost close enough to kiss.*

Chrissie did not smile back, but she opened her fist. "Well. You tell your little friend that I will not stand for *any*one talking to me like that. Ever. You tell him that if he talks to me that way again, I will beat him like a borrowed mule."

"Hee-*haw*," Dennis Deane said from behind Jim.

"Dennis Deane," Jim warned over his shoulder. "Shut *up*."

"I mean it, Jim Glass," Chrissie said.

"I know you do," said Jim.

"You tell him."

"I will."

Chrissie nodded once, turned on her heel, and pulled open the door. Then she was gone. Nobody laughed, although Jim wanted to. He felt wonderfully, inexplicably happy.

Dennis Deane stepped out from behind Jim and made a show of adjusting his shirt collar. He blew into his palm, checking his breath.

"Well," he said. "She loves me. Write it down in the big book, boys. Write it down."

"She was going to knock you out," Larry said.

"I should have let her hit you," Jim said.

"Don't mess around with that girl," said Otis. "I'm serious. If she doesn't beat your ass, then Bucky will when he gets home on leave."

"Bucky Bucklaw," Dennis Deane scoffed. "How am I supposed to be afraid of somebody with a name that stupid?"

Larry pointed down the hill at the long passenger train drawing a thick silver line through town. "Hey, look at that," he said.

The windows of the coaches were open, and men in uniforms, their shirtsleeves rolled up, were hanging out most of them. Soldiers. A whole trainload of them. Jim wondered what they saw when they looked at Aliceville, if anything would make an impression worth remembering; he wondered where they were going.

"Troop train," he said.

"What?" Dennis Deane said. "Has the train got soldiers on it?"

The bell rang. The boys picked up their books.

"You're blind as a mole," Jim said.

"I don't need to see," said Dennis Deane. "I've got an extra eyeball."

A History Lesson

AT THE start of fifth period Jim was already seated in history class when Chrissie Steppe walked through the door. She sat every day at the desk immediately in front of his. This was another, although brand-new, reason that Jim thought history his favorite subject. As he watched her make her way across the room, Jim slid his desk forward until it bumped against the back of Chrissie's chair. He opened his history book without looking at the page and pushed it forward until it, too, touched the back of her chair. He opened his mouth to say something as she approached, but she didn't look at him; he closed his mouth without ever knowing what it was he would have said.

When Chrissie sat down, she leaned forward, slid both hands beneath her hair at the base of her neck and flipped it away from her body over the top rung of her chair, almost hitting Jim in the face, so that she would not lean back against it. It spilled onto his open book just as he had hoped it would. He sat and gaped.

Chrissie's hair almost obscured the pages about the blockade of Wilmington during the Civil War.

Miss Brown — who had taught Mama and all three of the uncles and, so far as Jim knew, Moses and Aaron — shuffled into class before the bell rang and began calling the roll. She was tall and stooped and thin as a broom handle. She never waited for the bell to ring before calling the roll, no matter how often the students complained. She had spent most of her career teaching in two- and three-room schoolhouses without electricity and apparently either did not understand what the bell was for or simply refused to acknowledge its existence. When she reached Jim's name, he said, "Present," in a loud voice. He liked to say *present* instead of *here* because it aggravated his friends, particularly Dennis Deane, who said it was a teacher's-pet kind of thing to say.

The subject that day was the early European exploration of America, but Jim paid only sporadic attention. He studied instead, with a scholar's single-minded intensity, the way the light reflected off Chrissie's black hair. The day before, Jim had noticed that when the sun hit it just right, it sparkled with the deep colors of a prism hanging in the window of a science class. Today he wanted to see if he had imagined it. He studied it so closely that his eyes slipped out of focus and the scale of the room swelled in an instant and became immense around him; he felt suddenly microscopic, a tiny creature swimming in a drop of pond water. At that moment Chrissie's hair seemed to take on an infinite depth; it became a warm, rich space into which it suddenly seemed possible to fall and become lost. Off in the distance somewhere he heard Miss Brown say the word *conquistador*. She always trilled the *r* and added a long *a* sound to the end of the word, a pronunciation that made most of the students snicker. But Jim thought it sounded romantic and filled with adventure, an altogether fitting word for men who sailed across oceans and waded into strange jungles, searching for lost cities of gold. *"Conquistador,"* Jim whispered, adding the long *a*. He leaned forward almost imperceptibly and moved his head slightly in relation to the sunlight falling through the tall windows.

There.

The colors of the spectrum flared in Chrissie's hair with the hopeful radiance of undiscovered stars. Jim sat very still and held his breath, aware that he had entered a magical place where it would not be possible to stay. The colors and lights swirled around him in their private orbits. He was sure that he knew something about Chrissie Steppe that no one else knew, that maybe no one else in the world would ever know. He certainly doubted that Bucky Bucklaw, who was a lunkhead, knew about Chrissie's hair. The moment he thought about Bucky Bucklaw, however, the colors in Chrissie's hair blinked out, and the scale of the room spun back to normal. Jim found himself back in North Carolina, in Aliceville, at his desk in history class, his history book covered with the beautiful hair of a girl he barely knew, who probably didn't like him, anyway. According to Miss Brown, Ponce de León's men staggered through the swamps of Florida until they collapsed, their lungs filled with the mosquitoes they had no choice but to inhale. They never discovered the fountain of youth.

Jim sighed.

He opened his notebook and wrote "ROY G. BIV" in block letters at the top of a clean piece of paper. Then he wrote "RED ORANGE YELLOW GREEN BLUE INDIGO VIOLET." He looked at what he had written and realized it wouldn't be much help in studying for a history test. He forced himself to turn his attention to Miss Brown, who had moved from Ponce de León on to Hernando de Soto. Jim wrote "de Soto" in his notebook.

"We North Carolinians," Miss Brown said, "speak with justifiable pride about Sir Walter Raleigh and the Lost Colony, and about poor Virginia Dare, born on the hostile shores of the New World, never to be heard from again, but what we do not regularly speak of, perhaps because we are of English descent, is the expedition of the great *conquistador* Hernando de Soto into what is now North Carolina in the early fifteen forties, years before our beloved Raleigh was even born. Search in the history book on your desk all you like and you will find no mention of de Soto's expedition into the Tarheel State. Why is that? I do not know, children. Most of the decisions made in Raleigh have always struck me as illogical, if not arcane.

But, had history played out in a slightly different manner, this class today would be conducted entirely in
Spanish. And wouldn't you find that confusing?"

Miss Brown seemed to think this very funny. She
put her hand to her chest and snorted, her face red-
dening. "Oh, my," she said. *"Muy bueno."*

Jim wrote "#1" and "NC" in his notebook beside
the word "de Soto." This, finally, seemed to be a fact
worth remembering.

"Allow me to tell you a story," Miss Brown continued when she recovered.

Here we go, thought Jim.

"My maternal grandmother grew up not far from
here, near Tryon. Her family owned a small plantation, which, by the way, the male descendants of my
family have managed to squander over the years until
not a shred of it remains in our possession. Not a
shred, children. Be that as it may, my grandmother's
people owned a few slaves, no more than ten, I suppose, at any one time — this was only a small plantation, you see — but they owned a few. One of those
slaves, an old fellow named Big Walker, told my grandmother, when she was just a little girl herself, that,
when *he* was a young man on a neighboring plantation, he had plowed up a steel helmet and a fine
sword. The helmet and sword were, of course, Spanish in provenance, which would prove, incontrovert-
ibly, that de Soto passed not only through western
North Carolina but through *our* part of western North
Carolina. The helmet and sword were, naturally,

turned over by Big Walker to his master, in whose possession they remained until the War Between the States. According to my grandmother, when that gentleman went off to fight for the Confederacy, he reburied that helmet and sword, lest those artifacts be seized by Yankee foragers in his absence. Alas, he did not tell anyone where he had buried these treasures, and he did not return from the war to reclaim them. To my knowledge, they are to this day buried still beneath the soil of Polk County, waiting to be discovered yet again."

Miss Brown sighed theatrically. "To think," she said, "that I knew someone who knew someone who once held in his very hands a sword and helmet worn by a member of de Soto's army."

Jim held his pencil poised above his notebook, his brow furrowed. He wondered if any Spanish artifacts were buried in the uncles' fields but had no idea what to write down. Miss Brown rarely seemed to talk about anything that was actually *in* the history book. After almost a month of classes, he had no idea what she would put on their exams. She had yet to give them even a quiz. Jim decided to read the book, anyway, just in case. He glanced down at the book and wondered what Chrissie's hair smelled like.

"I have often wondered," Miss Brown went on, "how that helmet and sword came to be abandoned by their Spanish owner. For surely nothing could be more important to a soldier in a hostile land than his helmet and sword. Without them he would be defenseless against his enemies. Obviously, some great tragedy must have befallen him. The only plausible answer I can think of to such a perplexing question is that he was slaughtered by the Cherokee, whose ancestral lands the Spanish were at the time claiming for the crown of Spain. Miss Steppe, you are at least partially descended from the Cherokee, are you not?"

Jim saw Chrissie stiffen.

"I don't know," she said.

"Wasn't your father a Cherokee? That's what I have always heard. That would explain your lovely hair."

"I'm not sure. He never said."

In his notebook Jim wrote "INDIAN?"

"Perhaps he was only part Cherokee?" Miss Brown went on.

"Which part?" Dennis Deane asked, to a smattering of coughs and snorts, from across the room.

That's enough, Dennis Deane, Jim thought. He squirmed in his seat, cleared his throat, raised his hand, and asked, "Miss Brown, do you think de Soto and his army might have come through Aliceville?"

"That's an interesting question, Mr. Glass," Miss Brown said. "In the future, please wait until I acknowledge you before speaking."

"Yes, ma'am," Jim said.

"To answer your question, asked rudely though it may have been, I think it's entirely possible that de Soto's army passed through Aliceville, although, of course, it wasn't Aliceville at the time. If it had a name at all, it would have been some Cherokee name we could never hope to recall. Still, our river passes near Tryon, where Big Walker discovered the Spanish helmet and sword, and was de Soto following our river west, which seems to me a likely route, he easily could have passed this way. Isn't that something to think about?"

"Yes, ma'am," Jim said.

"Indeed, de Soto himself might have climbed this very hill to survey the surrounding countryside, for this is the only vantage point of any elevation nearby. Perhaps he saw our blue mountains in the distance and thought that surely there he and his men would find the cities of gold they sought."

Jim wrote, "gold?" in his notebook, then looked at the word "INDIAN?" and underlined it. Jim had heard years ago that Chrissie's father was a Cherokee, but he had forgotten it until that moment. Chrissie had gone to school in Aliceville until the third grade, when she moved with her mother and father to the deep mountains west of Asheville. From there they had moved on to Oklahoma. Jim didn't remember much about her, although she had been in his grade. Her hair had been very long even then, and she had been very quiet. His only vivid memory of her was of something that happened during recess just before she moved away. It was the last day of school in the old building, before the new building (the one in which they now sat) opened the next fall. Jim had seen Chrissie standing alone on the playground. Something about the way she stood by herself had made him

angry, and a sudden fury had overcome him. Without knowing why, he had rushed up behind her and
shouted, "Have a nice TRIP!" before shoving her
down. Chrissie had skinned both knees and cried,
but she had not told on him. Jim was never punished,
although he felt he had deserved to be, and he never
told her he was sorry, although he had been. He
didn't see Chrissie again until the first day of school
this year, when he had watched her walk around the
front of the bus from Lynn's Mountain and up the
stairs toward him. And, without knowing why, he had
watched for her ever since.

The rest of the class passed slowly while Miss Brown
talked about her extended family and the occasional
Spanish explorer. The afternoon had grown hot and
still, the air rapidly thickening with the smell of teen-
agers ripening against their will in the heat, an odor
poorly masked by vanilla extract and cheap perfume
and scented hair oil. Several of the boys were sound
asleep, their heads down on their desks. Dennis Deane
picked something off the tip of his chin and tried
to show it to the girl sitting beside him, who refused
to look.

Jim leaned back and stretched. He tapped his pencil on his notebook. He glanced over at Norma Harris, his old girlfriend, with whom he had broken up
during the summer. She was getting a head start on
her math homework, which filled Jim with contempt.
Norma was pretty, probably the prettiest girl in Alice-

ville School, but she was a know-it-all. A goody-goody and a know-it-all and a cold fish. Her yellow hair was exactly the same color as Jim's, and for that reason, and because they both made good grades, people had always assumed that they would go together some day.

And so they had.

But Norma had barely let Jim kiss her, and never for very long, and he had gotten tired of arguing about it. She had absolutely refused to climb into the rumble seat of his car to look at the stars. The night he finally broke up with her, Norma had said, "I can see the stars from my house, Jim." That, somehow, had been the last straw. Some girls were just *too* religious. *I can see the stars from my house, Jim.* He didn't want an easy girlfriend, just one that was easier than Norma Harris. The girl actually had a picture of Abraham Lincoln on the wall in her bedroom. Jim had never set foot in Norma's bedroom, of course, but he had glimpsed Lincoln from the hallway. Mama was still upset with Jim for breaking up with Norma, but he didn't care. He had decided that he liked black hair better than blond anyway, especially when it was long.

Why *was* Chrissie's hair so long?

Jim considered the possible reasons. Maybe she was a member of the Holiness church. Holiness women weren't allowed to cut their hair. But most of the Holiness girls Jim knew piled their hair into elaborate, impossibly tall hairdos and kept it in place with complicated arrays of hairpins and bows, or even nets. Jim wrote, "HOLINESS?" in his notebook underneath

"INDIAN?" but then crossed it out, hoping it wasn't true. Holiness girls were even stricter than Baptist girls. A Holiness girl probably wouldn't let you kiss her at all until you married her. And then you'd still be kissing a Holiness girl, and she'd tell you not to mess up her hair and she'd want you to go to church for six hours every Sunday, and three hours on Wednesday night. You'd probably have to sit beside her father while she sat with the women on the opposite side of the church and waved her arms in the air and shouted in unknown tongues. Besides, Chrissie just didn't *seem* to be Holiness. He drew another, darker line through "HOLINESS?" and put another question mark after "INDIAN?" Jim knew that Mama would throw a fit if he ever tried to date a Holiness girl and wondered if she would throw a bigger one or a smaller one if he tried to date a Cherokee.

Chrissie shifted in her seat, and the hair lying on Jim's history book moved slightly and became a small, glossy animal curled and napping in the sun. A muskrat, Jim thought. No, a mink. No, a small, black fox. A kit. Jim wondered if a kit fox would bite you if you tried to pet it. He placed his left hand on his history book and drummed his fingers. He slowly slid his fingers up the page toward Chrissie's hair. Chrissie shifted again. The kit twitched in its sleep, dreaming of green fields lush with mice. Jim stopped. He felt his heart stuttering beneath his skin. He pursed his lips and almost inaudibly whispered, "Shh." The kit remained still. He moved his hand up the slick paper, a line, a half line at a time, through the Yankee blockade at Wilmington. Only the bravest blockade-running captains, under cover of darkness, were able to bring desperately needed supplies into the besieged port. Jim raised his middle finger and inched his hand forward until his finger was suspended above Chrissie's black hair. He took a deep breath. He lowered his finger and touched her hair as gently as he knew how to touch anything. He had never felt anything so soft.

Norma

WHEN THE bell rang, ending the day, Jim took his time heading home. He wandered slowly down the hallway while his schoolmates swirled noisily from the classrooms, their feet pounding on the wooden floors; he sauntered down the front steps while the fleeing students parted into streams around him. One by one his friends climbed onto the idling buses or walked down the hill toward town. Once the schoolyard was empty, the buses folded their doors and one at a time pulled away. The Lynn's Mountain bus was the last to leave. Chrissie Steppe sat by Ellie Something near the front and didn't look out the window toward Jim. The bus eased down the drive and turned right onto the state highway. Jim watched it disappear from sight; he listened until the drone of its engine and, finally, the last, happy shouts of its passengers simply vanished from earshot. Aliceville School suddenly seemed a lonely place. Somewhere inside, a teacher laughed, a ghostly sound in the nearly deserted building. A stray breeze blew one of the classroom doors closed, and the bang echoed through the hallway.

Jim reluctantly started for home and only then turned his attention to Norma Harris, who waited for him underneath the tall pine tree at the top of the driveway. Every Tuesday and Thursday she visited Jim's house to work on a quilt that she and his mother had started the previous winter. And Mama insisted that Jim be a gentleman and walk Norma down the hill. After he broke up with Norma, he had been shocked that his mother chose to continue working on the quilt, and shocked that Norma even wanted to finish it. When Jim complained about Norma's visits, his mother only shook her head and stared at him as if he needed a bath.

Jim could tell that Norma was angry with him as he crossed the schoolyard. She had been mad at him more or less continuously since he had broken up with her. This school year their walks down the hill to Jim's house had not been pleasant. He walked past Norma without acknowledging her; she fell in beside him without speaking. Her heels scuffed on the pavement as they descended the hill, making a sound that Jim had once found endearing but that now simply irritated him; once he had thought that the worn-down heels of Norma's shoes were cute, but now he thought they looked shabby.

"Everybody knows we're not dating anymore,"

Norma said. "You don't have to make me stand by my-self like that. It's embarrassing."

"You know where I live," Jim said. "You don't have to wait on me if you don't want to."

Back when they were going together, Jim and Norma had walked down the hill holding hands almost every day. The teasing and needling spilling from the passing buses had simultaneously pleased and annoyed him. He had shouted at the boys hanging from the windows, but only halfheartedly; he had smiled proudly while his ears burned. In those days he occasionally let go of Norma's hand and tried to drop back a step just so he could watch her walk from behind. Watching her walk had made him want to grab her and kiss her over and over — although she wouldn't have let him if he had tried. Now he thought the way she walked made her look smug and bossy, the walk of a know-it-all, and he no longer wanted to kiss her. Jim could not understand how he could have loved Norma so much then and feel so differently now. His head seemed filled with memories belonging to another person, and he wished he could give them back.

"You act like it might kill you to be seen walking with me," Norma said.

"You act like you can't walk by yourself."

"When did you become so impolite?"

"Four score and seven years ago."

"Jerk," Norma said.

At the bottom of the hill, they had to pause at the

highway while three cars and a truck passed. The traffic seemed intentionally spaced to prolong their time together as much as possible.

When the last car went by, Jim bowed and extended his arm toward the highway. "After you," he said.

Norma lifted her chin and tossed her hair in response.

They crossed the road and cut through the fallow field that separated the highway from Depot Street, where Jim lived with his family. They walked on the path he had worn clean over the last eight years while walking to school. He saw his footprints from that morning, and some from the day before; he wondered, as he often had, why the path had never been quite straight. There was no reason it shouldn't be.

"I saw you today," Norma said.

"You saw me doing what?"

"I saw you playing with that Indian girl's hair."

Jim felt his cheeks go hot. "She's not an Indian," he said.

"She's half an Indian," Norma said.

"You don't know what she is."

"I know, among other things, that she's got hair like an Indian."

"So what? A lot of people have black hair. *Mama* has black hair."

"I know people call her daddy *Injun* Joe Steppe."

"Big deal," Jim said. "Uncle Zeno calls me Doc, but that doesn't mean I'm a doctor. Besides, so what if she is an Indian, or half an Indian, or whatever you said."

"Maybe she's not somebody you should get tangled up with, that's what."

"And you are, I suppose."

"Well," she said, "I *was.*"

"Why are we even having this discussion? Chrissie Steppe is not my girlfriend. She's Bucky Bucklaw's girlfriend. Everybody knows that. I've never said ten words to her in my whole life. I don't even know her daggum middle name, or anything else about her. So, why don't you just mind your own business?"

Norma stopped in her tracks. "Look at me," she said.

Jim looked instead at his shoes. They were dusty from the path through the field.

"Jim Glass, you look at me right this minute."

He looked up and watched Norma study his face as if she were about to spit on her finger and rub off a streak of dirt.

"Good Lord," she said.

"What?"

"You're in love with her."

"I am not."

"You are, too."

"I am not. I don't even know her. How could I be in love with her?"

"Then why is your face red?"

"I don't *know,* Norma. Because you're staring at me.

Because you're bothering me. Leave a boy alone, for gosh sakes, why don't you?"

Norma's eyes briefly clouded over. "I can't believe this," she said. "You break up with me and now you're in love with that . . ."

Jim almost smiled. He knew that Norma wanted to use a curse word, and also that she wouldn't.

". . . that *Cherokee.*"

Jim shook his head in disgust and turned toward home.

Norma grabbed his arm. "Jim," she said. "Listen to me. I know you won't believe this, but I'm telling you this for your own good. You should stay away from Chrissie Steppe."

"Why?"

"Because I've *heard* things."

"What things?"

"Things I can't tell you."

"You don't know any more about her than I do."

"I know that a nice girl wouldn't let her hair fall all over some boy's desk, and then sit there while he plays with it. Especially when she's got a boyfriend in the navy."

"It's just hair," Jim said. "It landed on my desk by accident and she didn't know it. I was moving it so I could read about Wilmington."

The shadow of a smile passed across Norma's face. "That's the most ridiculous thing I ever heard," she said.

"Just leave me alone, Norma."

Uncle Zeno's house had never seemed farther away. Jim stopped when he reached the front steps. Norma brushed past him and climbed onto the porch.

"Tell Mama I'm going out to the mill to see Uncle Zeno," Jim said.

Norma opened the screen door, paused for a moment, and turned around. "Marie," she said.

"What?"

"Marie. That's Chrissie Steppe's middle name."

What Strange Country

 *J*IM BACKED his Ford out of the shed behind
Uncle Coran's store and eased it around the side of
the building. He knew that Mama was more than
likely listening at the screen door to the manner in
which he drove away. Early on he had made the mistake of bragging about the power of the car's V8 engine, and since then, Mama regularly threatened to
take away his key. She religiously complained to anyone who would listen, especially the uncles, that a
Ford V8 was just too much car for a teenage boy to
handle. After all, she said, John Dillinger had driven
Ford V8s, and look what happened to *him.* Jim was
sure Mama talked about the gangster just to make
him nuts. Dillinger had been shot down coming out
of a movie; he hadn't been anywhere *near* a Ford V8.
And besides, whatever it had been that made John
Dillinger go bad, it had certainly not been his *car.*
Still, Jim drove with the decorum of an undertaker
within earshot of Mama.

 The dirt lot in front of the store was empty, and the

CLOSED sign hung from its wire on the doorknob. Uncle Coran occasionally closed early on slow afternoons, and Jim was glad he didn't have to talk to anyone just yet. He stopped at the edge of the state highway and made a show of looking both ways. He pulled delicately onto the road and shifted peacefully up through the gears until he reached the ridiculous Mama-mandated speed limit of thirty-five miles per hour. The car, a 1935 coupe the uncles had given Jim on his sixteenth birthday, was a dull, lusterless green, but Jim liked the color because he thought it gave the Ford something of a military look. He had dubbed the car "The Major," a nickname Uncle Al had eventually painted in white cursive letters just beneath the driver's-side window.

The intersection of the railroad tracks and the state highway marked for Jim the point beyond which he figured he was safe from Mama's nosiness. He kept the speedometer steadily on thirty-five as he approached the crossing sign and hit the railroad bed without slowing down. Jim bounced out of his seat toward the ceiling and savored the brief airborne sensation he felt in his stomach. Once across the tracks, he downshifted into second gear and pushed the accelerator all the way to the floor. When he popped the clutch, the resulting roar from the Major made him smile for the first time since fifth period. Soon Jim was traveling at sixty miles per hour, a mile a minute, pretty much the Major's top speed on level ground. He leaned forward to let the wind whistling through the windows cool the sweat pasting his shirt to his back. On both sides of the road, cotton rows clicked past kaleidoscopically, each revealing for a fraction of a moment the full secret of its carefully hoed length. The Major's tires hummed on the smooth concrete.

Although Jim liked driving the Major fast more than just about anything, he soon felt his anger at Norma gaining ground on his attempt to flee it. *"Jim,"* he said, mimicking Norma's voice, *"I know you won't believe this, but I'm telling you this for your own good. You should stay away from Chrissie Steppe."* He pushed the accelerator harder against the floorboard, but the Major refused to go any faster. He slapped the steering wheel in frustration.

"Daggummit, Norma!" he shouted. "Leave me alone!

"I can't believe this," he whimpered. *"You're in love with that, that Cherokee.*

"So what if I am?" he answered. "It's none of your damn business who I'm in love with."

Jim paused in his argument with the imaginary Norma. The Major slowed involuntarily. *I'm in love with Chrissie Steppe,* he thought, allowing himself to fully consider the possibility for the first time. He realized that the idea had been a shadow inside his head for so long that it had become familiar. Now, by attaching itself to words, it had taken on solid form and stepped into the light. "Hello," it seemed to be saying, "you know who I am."

Something warm inflated and rose inside his chest,

replacing in a single moment his ill temper with a growing elation. "I love Chrissie Steppe," he said out loud, realizing as he did so that the words were carrying him over some momentous boundary he had never known existed. Jim didn't know in what strange country this unexpected crossing landed him, or what dangers faced him, only that he found the vistas glorious to consider. He didn't know how it was possible that he loved Chrissie Steppe, only that he did. He didn't wonder whether Chrissie would, or even could, ever love him back. Nor did he think for more than a fleeting second about Bucky Bucklaw, floating on his lunkhead boat somewhere in the Pacific Ocean. For now, all that lay far below him. He leaned over so that he could see out the passenger window all the way to the top of Lynn's Mountain, which rose to the north and west of the highway. Chrissie lived up there somewhere, and for a moment he imagined her waiting for him, watching his tiny car inch along the road in the valley far below. He blew the horn as if she could hear it. Then he blew it again. He wanted to yell something to her, but couldn't bring himself to direct the words *I love you* toward the mountain. Not yet, anyway. Instead he yelled, *"Conquistador!"* which was the first word that came into his mind.

When Jim reached the Lynn's Mountain turnoff, he jerked the wheel sharply to the right and felt the Major's tires leave the pavement and scramble uncertainly onto the dirt road. He again downshifted into second and popped the clutch, but this time he winced, when the Major's engine bellowed in complaint. He had been going too fast to downshift and could have blown the motor. He let off the gas, cocked an ear toward the engine, and listened carefully. Once satisfied that the motor had not come unraveled, he stomped again on the accelerator and whipped the wheel to the left and to the right, joyously sliding through a short series of fishtails. Like most boys who did the majority of their driving on dirt roads, Jim liked to think that he could drive as well sideways as he could in a straight line. He slowed only when he approached the turnoff to Uncle Zeno's mill. Uncle Zeno understood that Jim, like most boys, was occasionally going to drive too fast, but he had also made it clear that he never wanted to catch Jim doing it. Jim looked wistfully in the rearview mirror at the thick cloud of red dust drifting in the Major's wake. He responsibly stuck his arm out the window, signaled a left turn, and pulled sedately off the road and into the yard of the mill, where, surprisingly, all three of the uncles' trucks were parked.

The mill was a wide, whitewashed building made of rough lumber, roofed with moss-covered oak shingles the uncles had split themselves years before. Across the front of the mill, MCBRIDE was painted in large, fading black letters. When Jim walked inside, he found the uncles sitting on straight chairs at the edge of the loft with their .22 rifles on their laps. A thin cloud of gun smoke nosed through the dust particles rising steadily toward the sunlit windows; the sharp smell of the burned powder blended oddly with the warm, sweet smell of ground corn.

"Halt!" Uncle Coran called out. "Who goes there?"

"John Dillinger," Jim said.

"Well," Uncle Coran said. "You know what happened to him."

"He got in trouble for driving his car like a knothead," said Uncle Zeno.

"You heard me coming?" Jim asked.

"People in Virginia heard you coming," said Uncle Al. "Did you blow the motor?"

"The Major's fine," Jim said. "It's going to take more than a little downshift to kill the Major."

"We ain't going to put a new motor in that car," Uncle Zeno said. "You remember that. Your mama would have all our hides."

"You won't have to."

"So make yourself useful," Uncle Coran said. "Go get your gun."

Uncle Zeno's gristmill, despite the best efforts of a sizable contingent of half-wild cats, was beset with rats. Jim had learned to hunt by shooting rats from the mill loft, and he had no idea how many he had killed over the years. He returned to the Major and pulled his .22 from behind the seat. He removed the magazine tube from the rifle, emptied the shells into his free hand, and put them in his pocket. Back inside the mill, he took another chair from around the stove, handed it up to Uncle Zeno, then climbed the steep, open stairs to the loft, carrying his rifle. Jim sat down beside Uncle Zeno, who passed him five rat-shot cartridges. Jim loaded the cartridges into the magazine, levered a round into the chamber, and set the hammer on half cock. He squinted down into the dimly lit machinery of the grinding room.

"Who's winning?" he asked.

"I think Zeno is," said Uncle Coran. "By my count, he's got four. Al's got two and I've got two."

Uncle Al snorted.

Uncle Coran pointed at a dead rat lying along the far wall. "That one's under protest," he said. "Al says they shot him at the same time."

"Tie goes to the runner," Uncle Al said.

"But I'm pretty sure Zeno shot him first," said Uncle Coran.

Uncle Zeno winked at Jim. "One more, Doc, and I'll be an ace."

"The score's three and a half to two and a half to two, and you know it," Uncle Al said. "One more and *I'm* tied for first."

Uncle Coran turned and stared at Uncle Al. "Allie, do you honestly think it's possible to kill *half* a rat?"

"You never could count," mumbled Uncle Al.

Uncle Zeno winked again at Jim. "Is Norma at the house?" he asked.

"Afraid so."

"Figured that's why you were here."

Jim leaned forward as his eyes became accustomed to the shadowy room. The sun drew soft yellow pictures of the streaked windows on the floor. Gradually, he was able to locate the rest of the rat corpses scattered around. The immobile humps had obviously once been alive and were now just as obviously dead. He quickly scanned the holes in the floor and along the baseboards where he knew the rats came into the mill but saw nothing moving. Outside he could hear the lazy groan of metal and the rhythmic *splash-splash-splash* of water falling as the great iron wheel turned.

"Norma and Mama are about to drive me crazy," he said.

"You stepped in that pile all by yourself," Uncle Zeno said.

"Daggummit," Jim said. "I didn't step in anything. I don't have to date Norma Harris if I don't want to date Norma Harris."

"Shh," said Uncle Al.

"Don't raise your voice," said Uncle Zeno. "And I'm not saying you do. I'm just saying a lot of people got their feelings hurt when you broke up with Norma, your mama included."

"Well, I don't see what the big deal is."

"The big deal is," Uncle Zeno went on, "that Norma *chose* you. You understand what I'm saying? She picked you *out*. She decided you were the only boy in the world for her, although I don't quite understand that."

"There's no accounting for taste," said Uncle Coran.

"But we were just *dating*."

"*You* were just dating, Jim. Norma was picking. And when she picked you, your mama picked her. Norma was going to be the daughter she never had. That's what that quilt was about."

"It's just a quilt," said Jim.

"That's where you're wrong, Doc," Uncle Zeno said. "You're wrong as you can be about that. I told Coran and Al when your mama and Norma started in on that thing, I said, 'Boys, that quilt's gonna bring a world of trouble. You mark my word.'"

"I still don't see what the big deal is," Jim said.

Uncle Zeno swallowed. "Norma was making that quilt for your bed, Jim, and your mama was helping her."

Jim frowned. "I already got a quilt," he said. "I got three or four quilts."

Uncle Al shook his head. "He ain't too bright, is he?" he said.

"Hush, Allie," Uncle Coran said. "Here comes the good part."

"Jim, you're not listening to me. For your *bed*, you big knothead. For after you and Norma got married."

"*Married?*" Jim said. "Who said anything about *married?*"

"Daggummit, hold it down," said Uncle Al. "You're gonna scare every rat in this country off."

"Who said anything about married?"

"Did you tell Norma you loved her?" Uncle Zeno asked.

Jim blushed and looked away.

"Did you?"

Uncle Al shifted uncomfortably. "I don't need to hear this," he said.

"I guess so," said Jim.

"Well, Doc, that's all she needed to hear," Uncle Zeno said. "Norma's a serious girl. Some girls run around with boys for fun, but Norma's not one of those girls. You tell a girl like Norma you love her, you better be ready to marry her because she's gonna piece you a quilt."

"I didn't ask nobody to make me no daggum quilt."

Uncle Coran suddenly raised his rifle. The contested rat was trying to drag itself along the far wall. When Uncle Coran pulled the trigger, Jim saw the orange muzzle blast lick out into the dim light. The percussive, splitting report was surprisingly loud inside the enclosed room. It always was.

"Ha!" Uncle Coran shouted. "That rat wasn't dead. *I* killed it. That makes the score three to three to two. Now I'm tied for the lead."

"Ain't no doggone way," Uncle Al said. "Ain't no doggone way you're counting that."

Uncle Coran stared at Uncle Al in disbelief. "Now you're going to tell me you killed a *third* of a rat?"

"Yes, that's exactly what I'm telling you."

"Well, a minute ago you said it was half a rat. Seems to me you're losing rat by the minute."

"Cheater," Uncle Al said.

"Cheater?" said Uncle Coran. "How do you figure I'm a cheater? That rat was alive and I killed it."

"Boys," said Uncle Zeno.

Uncle Al levered three shells out of his rifle onto the loft floor. "If that's how it's going to be, I quit," he said. "I ain't going to play in no rigged game." He laid his rifle in his lap and crossed his arms. The uncles sat and stared silently into space. After a while Uncle Al leaned over, picked up the shells, and loaded them back into his rifle.

Jim wanted to smile but knew better. "Why are y'all killing rats, anyway?" he asked.

Uncle Zeno turned toward him. "Did you see that troop train this morning?"

"Yeah. Me and Dennis Deane and them were standing on the steps."

Uncle Al shook his head. "Here we go again. Daggummit."

"I don't see why y'all are killing rats over a troop train," Jim said. "We're not fighting anybody."

"No, but we're getting ready to," said Uncle Zeno. "You just wait. If Hitler invades England, we'll be knee-deep in that mess."

"And don't forget the Japs are getting bowed up, too," added Uncle Al.

"I think we ought to invade South Carolina," Uncle Coran said. "I never did like it down there. The people are peculiar."

"But Roosevelt said he was going to keep us out of the war," said Jim.

"Yeah, I know what he said, but cotton prices have started up," Uncle Zeno said.

"Cotton prices? I don't understand. Isn't cotton going up a good thing?"

"Not necessarily, Doc. You've got to wonder why now, all of a sudden."

Jim thought. "Uniforms?"

"Uniforms. Tents. Somebody somewhere has already decided to do something they ain't told us about yet."

"Puttees," said Uncle Coran. "Don't forget about puttees."

"Puttees," said Uncle Al. "I *hate* puttees. Daggummit."

As it grew too dark to shoot, Jim left the uncles sitting glumly in the loft — before they could ask him to pick up the rats — and headed back to town. It was almost suppertime. On this trip he drove so slowly that he could hear the songs of solitary crickets rising along the shoulder of the highway as he approached, and falling away as he passed. The road and the surrounding fields lay in cool shadow but the top half of Lynn's Mountain still warmed itself in the sun. Jim pulled off the road for a minute and watched the evening advance toward the ridgetop. The air was so clear, the light so fine, that the shapes of the individual trees blanketing the upper slopes separated themselves from their brothers and stepped forward for Jim to count or admire. He picked out a tree and watched until the shadow line climbed past it. The great love for Chrissie Steppe he had discovered on the drive out had already been tempered by the uncles' war talk, and by the knowledge that he might be forced to leave her behind, maybe before he could tell her how he felt. He didn't know for sure where she lived — he thought it was somewhere near the Bucklaws — and even if he turned around and drove as fast as he could, it would be dark long before he got there.

When Jim reached town he parked the Major underneath the shed and walked slowly down Depot Street, beneath the blank windows of the school, toward home. Tomorrow morning he would stand on the landing with his friends, and Chrissie would step off the bus from the mountain. It wasn't much, but it was something. It was a start. He wiped his feet carefully on the back porch, dropped his books on the bench by the door, and stepped into the kitchen. After the cool of the evening, the room seemed almost unbearably hot from Mama's cooking. A big pot of pintos simmered on top of the stove; he opened the warming cabinet and found two pones of corn bread and a peach cobbler. Jim swallowed hungrily. He was very fond of pinto beans and corn bread, particularly with chopped onion and a big glass of buttermilk.

He found Mama in her bedroom. She had laid the quilt that she and Norma were making on top of her bed and was studying it critically.

"Decided it was finally safe to come home, did you?" she asked.

"That's about right," said Jim.

"We finished piecing the top today. What do you think?"

"I like it," he said, which was the truth.

The pattern of the quilt was called "Schoolhouse," although Jim thought the buildings Mama and Norma had pieced together looked more like houses or cabins than they did schoolhouses. They were cut so that they seemed viewed from an angle; one long side and one gable end of each were visible; each house had two doors on the long side and a yellow window in the gable; each roof had two red chimneys. The walls and roofs of each house were cut from different fabrics, mostly from printed flour sacks that Mama and Norma had collected or traded other flour sacks for, although here and there Jim recognized a piece of cloth from a dress that Mama used to wear, or one of his old shirts. The few pieces he didn't recognize had come from Norma's family. The houses were set onto squares of dark blue; the squares, separated by rich, red sashing, were arranged in five rows of four squares each.

Mama reached into her apron pocket and pulled out her pair of good scissors. When she sewed she wore small gold glasses on the end of her nose that made her look older than she was. She leaned over the quilt and snipped off a stray piece of thread that Jim never would have noticed.

"It looks like a town," Jim said, tracing a path along the background in between the squares. "The red looks like streets."

"I think so, too," said Mama. "That's what I like about it."

"Why are all the windows yellow?"

"That shows that somebody's home. They look too lonesome without a light on inside."

"Where do you live?" Jim asked.

Mama studied Jim for a moment before pointing to the third house in the second row. It had light blue walls of faded chambray. "Right there," she said, flushing slightly. "Do you know where that cloth came from?"

Jim knew but didn't say anything.

"From one of your father's shirts," she said.

She ran a finger over the fabric before suddenly smacking Jim three times on the arm, not quite playfully.

"Oh, daggum your fickle hide, Jim Glass. That's the last piece of that shirt I had."

"Ow," Jim said. "Nobody told you to put that cloth in Norma's quilt, now, did they?"

"I just feel like beating you half to death right now."

"Did they? Tell the truth."

Mama put her hands on her hips. "No," she said. "Nobody told me to use the last piece of your dead father's shirt in this quilt. Let's just say that because of the actions and words of a certain young man last winter regarding a certain young lady, I felt safe in making certain assumptions."

"Well, you know what they say about assuming, don't you?"

"Humph," Mama said. "There's only one *A-S-S* in this room right now, young man, and it's not me."

Jim laughed. "Where do I live?"

"I'm not sure you're still welcome in this town."

"Well, where was I going to live, before you ran me off?"

Mama pointed at a house in the third row, across the street from her own.

"Was Norma going to live there, too?"

Mama shook her head briskly and snipped at Jim with her scissors.

"You're trying my patience, mister," she said. "I'm warning you."

"You could always stop working on the quilt."

Mama rolled her eyes at the ceiling. "You don't have any idea why I'm doing this, do you?"

"No, ma'am," Jim said. "I don't have any idea."

"What I'm trying to do is let that poor girl escape this whole fiasco with a little dignity intact. But you probably can't understand that."

"I guess I can understand that," Jim said.

For a moment he felt a little bad about making Norma wait underneath the tree until all the school buses had passed. He resolved to do better. Maybe on Tuesdays and Thursdays he could hurry and get Norma down the hill before the buses finished loading.

The uncles clomped onto the back porch and stomped their feet on the mat.

"What were they all doing out at the mill?" Mama asked.

"Shooting rats," Jim said.

Mama frowned. "How come?"

"I think they were upset about that troop train this morning. They think we're about to get in the war."

"The president's going to keep us out of the war."

"What if he doesn't?" Jim asked.

"That's easy," Mama said. "I won't let you go."

BOOK II

The Secrets of Women

Call to Glory

*T*HE WEATHER was still warm — the days mild, the first frost still days or weeks away — but the world seemed bent on practicing for the coming winter. This morning the clouds resembled snow clouds, but instead of snow they produced a steady gray mist that absorbed sound and discouraged ambition. People all over Aliceville rose, stared out at the day, and lit fires they did not need.

Among the loafers smoking in the store, Uncle Coran tried to incite a disagreement about whether the precipitation falling outside was a heavy fog or a light drizzle, but he found no takers. Mama grew sleepy after the midday meal and left the dishes soaking in the sink. Uncle Zeno drove slowly toward New Carpenter with the idea of buying a new logging chain but, because he didn't really need a new logging chain, thought better of it, circled the courthouse, and drove slowly home. Uncle Al found himself sitting on a crate, staring out the wide door of the mule barn. He had no idea how long he had been there. He stood up and dusted off the legs of his overalls, even though he had put them on clean that morning and had done no real work to speak of.

Jim spent the day staring distractedly into the gloom. He paid little attention to anything that was said in his classes. When the bell rang ending each period, he moved on to the next classroom, took his seat, and stared again out the window. Each new window changed the perspective from which he viewed the world but did nothing to improve it. The mist had reduced the woods on the far side of the bottoms into mere suggestion. The trees were discernible only sporadically, like the memory of something pleasant that happened a long time ago.

The weather matched Jim's mood perfectly. He found it a good day to labor under the almost public burden of a not-quite-secret unrequited love. His friends, both the guys on the steps and the girls who pretended to be offended by their existence, had begun to tease him about Christine Steppe — which genuinely puzzled Jim because he had spoken of his feelings about Chrissie to no one, and certainly not to Dennis Deane, who these days, when the bus from Lynn's Mountain pulled up in front of the school, launched into a ridiculous, mincing recitation of "Jim and Chrissie sitting in a tree" that even Jim had to admit was funny. The only person with anything resembling direct knowledge about Jim's great "secret" was Norma Harris, and Jim knew that Norma was unlikely to have tattled. Complaining about Chrissie would have made Norma look bad, and besides, Norma was nothing if not discreet. (Had she been the kind of girl who worried less about public appearance and was occasionally indiscreet, Jim might not have broken up with her in the first place.) He didn't bother denying the accusations about Chrissie when they arose, because in each instance he secretly hoped that his lack of a denial would twist itself into a declaration by the time she heard about it.

And he counted on her hearing about it.

Because Chrissie had a boyfriend (even an absent one he neither liked nor respected), Jim believed he had to wait for Chrissie to confront him about the rumors before he could honorably tell her how he felt. He had no respect for guys who snaked away other guys' girlfriends, or attempted to, although he now longed for a loophole — such as Chrissie calling him out — that would allow him to become a snake without appearing to be. For her part, however, Chrissie showed little inclination to talk to him at all, let alone raise the question of whether or not he loved her.

When Chrissie didn't show up for Miss Brown's class, Jim sat up alertly for the first time all day. He scooted his desk away from hers, put his feet on the back rung of her chair, and stared at the door until he was sure she wasn't coming through it. He had seen Chrissie periodically throughout the day — in addition to history they had two other classes together, although their desks weren't close by in those classes — but now she had stepped out of the familiar track in which they all marched through the days. Jim knew that, not being outgoing and popular (like Norma), she wasn't the kind of girl who one of the teachers would have held out of class to paint posters or carry notes here or there, and he couldn't think of anywhere else she could be. He looked around the room when Miss Brown called Chrissie's name from the roll, but no one else seemed to be wondering where Chrissie had gotten to, nor care about the fact that he was wondering.

When Miss Brown told the class to open their books, Norma glanced up at him, tilted her head to one side, and sighed in commiseration at . . . what? The long day, the bleak weather, the heavy volume of English homework? Jim didn't know. But when she blushed and looked down quickly at her book, he knew that he had somehow responded to her friendly look with what had appeared to be a hostile one of his own. That had not been his intent. He had only been concerned about Chrissie, and facing an hour of Miss Brown's rambling without Chrissie at the desk in front of his, without her hair falling onto his history book, he would have welcomed any friendly gesture, even one that he might have regretted responding to later. He stared at Norma for a while, hoping to make up, but she did not look at him again. The weather naturally caused Miss Brown to forget about taxation without representation and drone on instead about the moors of England, which to Jim sounded more like a disagreeable family than a disagreeable place. In his notebook he wrote, "BEWARE THE MOORES OF ENGLAND!"

When the bell rang ending the day, he stood on the landing at the top of the steps and watched for Chrissie. But she did not appear among the stream of students who drained out the school and filled up the buses. When the Lynn's Mountain bus shut its doors and pulled forward through the mist, Jim felt a worry roll itself into a ball inside his chest. He knew that Chrissie had no other way up the mountain. As the bus passed his place on the steps and started down the drive, Ellie Something leaned out a window and yelled, *"She's sick. She needs a ride home."* Jim nodded and waved in response. Because of the nature of Ellie Something's news, he was only mildly irritated that even the freshmen of Aliceville School now seemed to know his business. He turned, and, without thinking, pulled open the door and strode into the building.

When Jim walked into the office, Mr. Dunlap, the principal, and Mrs. Murray, the secretary, were laughing about something, but they stopped when they saw him.

"Yes, Mr. Glass?" Mr. Dunlap said.

"I heard that Christine Steppe was sick."

"Yes?"

"And that she needed a ride home."

"You heard correctly, I suppose," said the principal. "Are you volunteering for the job?"

"Yes, sir," Jim said. "I have a car."

Mr. Dunlap and Mrs. Murray looked at each other. Mr. Dunlap winked and Mrs. Murray not very successfully stifled a smile. Jim felt his ears go red.

"Okay, Jim," Mr. Dunlap said. "Provided Miss Steppe is agreeable. I frankly didn't know how we were going to get her up the mountain." He pointed across the hall at the nurse's office. "She's resting in there."

Because Aliceville School didn't have a nurse on staff, the nurse's office was used infrequently — most often when the severe-looking woman from the county office showed up to check the heads of the poor kids for lice. The room held an ancient hospital bed, a beat-up steel cabinet, and a single, punitive-looking chair; in the corner lurked the rusting metal wastebasket that Mrs. Murray or one of the teachers unceremoniously thrust at sick children during moments of crisis. The only picture on the walls was a print called *Call to Glory*, torn from a magazine during the Great War, in which a nurse held the hand of a comatose doughboy while above them the soldier's spirit marched triumphantly up a sunbeam toward George Washington and Abraham Lincoln, who waited to greet him knee-deep in a radiant cloud. The nurse's office was — according to the story older students told to frighten first-graders — haunted by the ghost of a little boy who stuck a marble up his nose and accidentally sucked it down his windpipe.

Jim found the door slightly ajar. He tapped on it twice and slowly pushed it open. Chrissie lay curled up on the bed, facing the wall, her knees clutched to her stomach. He heard her moan softly.

"Christine?" he said. He was surprised at how soft his voice sounded.

Chrissie raised her head and looked at him over her shoulder. Jim saw her pupils widen.

"Oh, no," she said. "Get out of here."

"Chrissie?"

"Right now."

"I've come to give you a ride home."

She moaned again. "You've what?"

"Come to give you a ride home."

"Have you gone completely insane?"

"No," Jim said. "I've got a car."

She didn't respond.

Jim eased farther into the room. "The bus just left," he said. "How else are you going to get up the mountain?"

She didn't respond.

He drew the uncomfortable-looking chair away from the wall and placed it beside the bed. Sad gray light settled on the bed from the single window high up on the wall. Chrissie's hair lay spread in disarray on the white sheet. Jim hoped it wouldn't get tangled.

"Don't sit down," Chrissie said.

"Okay. I won't."

"Put the chair back."

"Okay," he said. "It's back."

"Is your car here?"

"No. It's down at the store."

"Go get it," Chrissie said.

Jim first jogged to the store and from the doorway told Uncle Coran that Mr. Dunlap had asked him to give a ride home to a sick kid. (As he told the story, Jim hoped it was close enough to the truth to keep him out of trouble. The loafers at the store — as Jim had hoped — kept Uncle Coran from quizzing him too closely; Mama would have demanded a fuller explanation and perhaps forbidden him to go.) When he stopped the Major in front of the school, one of the red doors swung open and Chrissie stepped out. Her skin looked unnaturally pale, and Jim thought that, were the nurse's office really haunted, *that's* what the ghost would look like. She walked down the stairs with the exaggerated care of someone navigating an icy sidewalk. Jim leaned over and pushed open the passenger-side door. Chrissie placed her books on the seat between them. Once she closed the door, she wrapped her arms around her abdomen, closed her eyes, and leaned against the window.

"Don't talk to me," she said. "I'm about to throw up."

"Okay, then," Jim said.

Not talking, however, was the last thing Jim wanted to do. Speaking privately to Chrissie at school was out of the question, of course, and running into her around town was unlikely because she lived on Lynn's Mountain. By Jim's reckoning, this might be his only opportunity to talk to her alone, ever. He could feel thousands of words, everything that he wanted to say to her, piled up behind his teeth, waiting for him to open his mouth so they could storm into the light.

Instead he said, "Here we go."

At the highway, he waited to let a single car pass, although he could have beaten it easily. Sitting at the stop sign in the Major greatly increased his chances of being spotted — and perhaps waved down — by Mama, but Jim wanted the trip to last as long as possible. He nervously watched the front door of Uncle Zeno's house and drummed his fingers on the wheel. The approaching car, an ancient Marathon, eventually clattered by. Jim pulled onto the highway behind it and shifted languidly up through the gears to a speed even Mama would have approved of.

At the railroad crossing he slowed the Major to a near crawl and bumped gingerly across the tracks. Chrissie still leaned against the window and he didn't want her to bang her head against the glass. But once he reached the turnoff to the Lynn's Mountain road, he couldn't resist downshifting and throwing the Major into a single lazy fishtail. (He suspected that Norma had secretly liked fishtailing, although she had always demanded that he stop.) Chrissie whirled on him angrily.

"What's the matter with you?" she asked. "Do you think that's funny? Are you trying to make me throw up?"

Jim slowed the car so quickly that it almost stalled and he had to downshift into first.

"No," he said. "No. I'm sorry. I wasn't thinking."

While Jim looked at Chrissie, her skin changed in an instant from a not-so-healthy-looking pale into a desperately unhealthy-looking gray. Sweat bloomed on her cheek and above her upper lip.

"Oh, no," she said, leaning forward and placing her head on the Major's dashboard.

"What?"

"Ohh," she moaned.

"Are you going to be sick?"

Chrissie sat up straight, looked around wildly, then lay back against the seat and tightly shut her eyes. "No," she said. "I'm fine. Keep driving."

She moaned again.

"Hold on," Jim said. He steered the car across the bridge over Painter Creek.

"Stop the car," she said.

"Right now?"

"Stop the car."

Jim jerked the wheel to the right, and before the Major even stopped rolling, Chrissie leapt out and disappeared into the thick rhododendron that lined the stream's steep banks. Jim didn't see how any creature could have vanished into a tangle of rhododendron so easily, especially a full-grown girl wearing a skirt. When he turned off the engine, he heard her crashing through the thicket toward the creek bed. He imagined that must be what a deer sounded like. Jim knew what rabbits and squirrels sounded like, but all the deer in his part of the world had been shot years before.

He sat behind the wheel until he heard Chrissie stop running, then he opened the door and climbed onto the running board. He cocked an ear toward the rhododendron and listened. The woods were quiet; at first he couldn't hear anything, save the indifferent murmur of the creek. Then, somewhere near the water, he heard Chrissie gag. He felt a tearing sensation, a great helplessness, rip through his chest. He ran around the car and squinted into the rhododendron, but he couldn't see her. More than anything, he wanted to help, but he had no idea what to do.

"Chrissie," he called. "Chrissie! Are you all right?"

She gagged again. When she finally answered him she sounded desperate. "Don't you dare come down here!" she said. "You stay right where you are!"

"Where are you?" Jim asked.

"I mean it!" Chrissie yelled. "I said no!" She started to say something else, but coughed and was ill again.

Jim moved to the edge of the roadside and looked for a way into the rhododendron. "I'm coming in," he said.

"No!" Chrissie screamed.

Jim fidgeted toward the thicket, but didn't move forward. "Okay," he called. "Ready or not, here I come!" (And would wonder for the rest of his life why he had said *that*.)

A rock sailed up out of the rhododendron and plunked into the road. "Damn you! I'll kill you if you take another step!"

Jim clapped his hands against the side of his head. He turned around in a circle. "But you're *sick*," he said. "You shouldn't have to be sick by yourself. Nobody should. Let me come down there."

Another rock flew up out of the trees. This one landed with a clank on the roof of the Major and bounced onto the road.

"Hey!" Jim yelled. "Take it easy on the car!"

"I'll kill you deader than hell, Jim Glass! So help me God. I'm warning you for the last time!"

Jim heard Chrissie scrambling around for another rock. He heard a hysterical-sounding giggle bubble up out of his mouth and wondered why Chrissie Steppe throwing rocks at his car made him feel like laughing.

"All right," he said. "Don't shoot. I give up."

While Chrissie climbed up out of the rhododendron, Jim surreptitiously examined the round dent on the roof of the Major and, to his surprise, found that it didn't bother him very much. In fact, he didn't care about it at all. When she appeared at the edge of the thicket, he took her hand and helped her into the roadway. Her hand felt cold and clammy, not at all the way Jim had imagined it would feel, but he was glad to be holding it, anyway. Chrissie still looked desperately pale, but much better than she had when she had run into the rhododendron. He opened the door for her. Before he closed it he removed his handkerchief from his back pocket and offered it to her. He had been carrying one only since he became a senior, but until that moment he'd found no use for it.

"You can wipe your mouth off with this," he said. "I haven't used it. I mean, it's clean."

Chrissie accepted the handkerchief and stared at it. "Thank you," she said.

Between the bridge and the valley at the foot of the mountain, the road halfheartedly trailed the creek through a range of short, rolling hills. Sometimes it dipped down through the laurel and rhododendron and ran just above the level of the water, but other times it climbed away, so that not even the ravine that carried the creek was visible. When it curved through the woods, the straight black trunks of the trees loomed somberly in the mist. A few yellow poplar leaves lay pasted to the roadway and softly hissed beneath the Major's tires; their sweet, melancholy smell affirmed the coming of the hard frosts and cold winds that would strip the trees bare. Jim opened his window a crack. He was afraid that the curves and the rise and fall of the road would make Chrissie sick again, so he drove very slowly.

"It's okay," Chrissie said. "It's over now. You can speed up."

Jim glanced over at her. Her color had almost fully

returned, and in general she seemed to be a different person, perhaps someone it might be safe to talk to.

"What do you think was the matter?" he asked.

Chrissie shook her head. "I'm fine now."

"Do you think it's the flu?" Both of Jim's maternal grandparents had died of the flu in 1918, and Mama had reared Jim to expect the worst regarding sudden illnesses.

"No, it's not the flu," she said.

"Maybe you just ate something that didn't agree with you."

Chrissie slapped her palms twice against her legs. "*Jim* . . . ," she said.

"What?"

"Listen to me. It's not the flu and I didn't eat anything that disagreed with me. Okay? *Now* do you understand?"

"I don't think so," he said.

Chrissie covered her eyes with her fists. She sighed deeply. "I'm only going to say this one time, all right?"

Jim nodded.

"It's my *P-E-R-I-O-D.*"

Jim mouthed the letters. When the letters bunched themselves into a word, he swallowed hard and stared straight ahead at the road. "Ah," he said. "Okay. All right. I see."

Chrissie looked away and stared out the window. They were passing a poor upland farm stacked precariously on the side of a red, barren-looking ridge.

The pasture was so steep it looked painted onto the hillside.

"Well," she said. "I don't see how they ever got grass to grow on the side of a bank like that."

They stared at the farm like pilgrims on reaching a site they had traveled thousands of miles to see.

"They used to have a white cow," Jim said.

"A what?"

"A white cow."

Chrissie started to laugh.

"Well," said Jim. "They did."

They settled into an embarrassing but not unwelcome silence. Jim was at least glad the subject had changed. He tried to think of something else to talk about, but before he came up with anything, he felt Chrissie looking at him. When he sneaked a look at her, her brow was dipped into a furious V.

"Promise me you won't ever tell a soul we talked about my you-know-what," she said.

"Trust me," Jim said. "You don't ever have to worry about that."

The Abandoned House

*T*HE NEXT farmstead they passed lay deserted. Stickweed and broom sedge and ragweed and small, scraggly pine trees loitered about the yard and pasture; the roof of the barn had fallen in, and a nest of poison oak vines, their leaves turning a bloody red, seemed intent on pulling the rest of the structure down. The front door of the house was open and the broken windows on either side of the door gaped at the road.

"I hate to see that," Chrissie said.

"What?"

"An empty house. Every day when the bus comes by here I want to get off and shut the door. I wonder why they left the door open?"

"I couldn't tell you."

"What do you guess it would rent for?" she asked.

"I don't know. It would depend on how much land came with it."

"Do you think the house is still good?"

Jim looked in the rearview mirror, but the house was already out of sight around the curve behind them.

"I think it had a tin roof," he said. "The house should be okay if the roof's all right. Are you looking for a place to live?"

"We're staying with my grandparents until Daddy gets back from Oklahoma," she said. "Then we're going to need a bigger place."

"Who's 'we'?" Jim asked.

"Me and Mama."

"What's your daddy doing in Oklahoma?"

Chrissie kept looking out the window. "Working," she said.

They crossed Painter Creek a second time and drove into the long valley that lay between the creek and Lynn's Mountain. The valley was one of Jim's favorite places. The road wandered through prosperous-looking farms with painted houses and clean fencerows and thick green pastures. The soil in the creek bottoms was rich and brown. In the distance the mountain seemed to angle downward and disappear, along with the road, at some magic, unreachable point.

To the right of the road, a thick bank of white clouds had lowered itself onto the top two-thirds of the mountain. The bottom line of the clouds was so straight it could have been drawn with a ruler, and nothing about them suggested movement. They seemed to have come to stay.

When Jim leaned over to look through the passenger window, he smelled the vanilla extract Chrissie wore as perfume. He found himself in no hurry to sit up straight. She still held his handkerchief in her lap and hadn't unfolded it. He had never wanted to kiss anybody so badly in his whole life.

"Look at that," he said. "Most of the mountain's gone."

"I like it when it gets like that sometimes," Chrissie said. "Everything looks different and spooky, and it's like living somewhere else. Sometimes you just want to live somewhere else. But it gets old after a while. Have you ever lived on a mountain?"

"Nope. I've always been a town boy."

"I like living up high as long as I can see the sun," she said. "We used to live on a mountain up above Tuckaseegee, but we were on the wrong side."

"What do you mean, 'the wrong side'?"

"The side facing north. You don't ever want to live on the north side of a mountain. You don't get hardly any sun that way. The south side's always better."

"How long did you live there?"

"Four years. Then we moved to Oklahoma."

"How'd you like it?"

"Oklahoma or the mountain?"

"The mountain," Jim said.

"It was all right," Chrissie said. "It was pretty and green during the summer, but it felt like it started getting dark in the middle of the day and it seemed to rain constantly."

"The wrong side of the mountain," Jim said.

Chrissie nodded. "And you really had to look out for

copperheads. They were everywhere. One day Mama found one in the potato hole."

"What else?"

"Well, during the summer it seemed like mold would grow on your shoes overnight. And in the winter it was just awful. It never got light and the wind blew all the time and it stayed so cold you never could get your feet warm."

"Sounds like you didn't like it at all."

"That's not true," Chrissie said. "We just didn't have a good house. I intend to have a nice house someday." She looked at Jim seriously. "Y'all have nice houses, don't you?"

The question seemed to hold neither envy nor resentment, so Jim nodded.

"They look nice from the school."

"What about Oklahoma?" Jim asked.

"I didn't care for it. It didn't have any mountains that I saw, so it never looked right to me. You just get used to looking at mountains. Then, in the spring you had to worry about tornadoes, and it was way too hot in the summer." She shuddered a little. "And they have scorpions out there. You have to shake your shoes out before you put them on. I hate a scorpion worse than a snake."

"You never struck me as the kind of girl who would be afraid of anything."

"I never said I was afraid. I said I didn't like scorpions and snakes."

Jim grinned. "So, how was your house in Oklahoma?"

"We couldn't keep the dust out of it."

"I've never been out west," Jim said, "but I want to go someday."

Chrissie shrugged. "I don't think you're missing much. Some people like it, though."

They crested a short rise and the school bus Chrissie had missed materialized up ahead as if it had been conjured. It moved broadside to them at the spot where the road and creek turned in unison and raced toward the wooded side of the mountain.

"Do you want me to run the bus down for you?" Jim asked.

"No. Slow down. I can't let anybody see me in your car."

"Oh."

"That sounded awful, I know," Chrissie said. "But that's not how I meant it. Things are just kind of complicated right now."

"With Bucky Bucklaw?"

Chrissie tossed him a sharp look but didn't say anything.

"So, what do you want me to do?" Jim asked. "We're going to catch it pretty quick once it starts up the mountain."

"I don't know exactly. I guess we need to stop somewhere and wait," Chrissie said. "If that's all right with you."

Jim slowed the Major. "Do you want to turn around and go look at that old house?"

"That sounds good," Chrissie said.

Jim stopped the car in the yard and cut the engine. The house seemed to be trying to disappear into the landscape. It had once been painted white, but it had long since faded to a gray slightly darker than the color of the day; the roof had rusted to the red color of the muddy driveway. The open door and broken windows looked ominous.

"Who used to live here?" Chrissie asked.

"I don't remember their names," Jim said. "Some old couple. I saw them a few times from the road, but we never stopped. I guess they must have died."

"Oh," Chrissie said. "That's sad. And I guess they must not have had any kids to take over the place."

"I guess not."

"Do you think we ought to go in?"

"Why not?" Jim asked. "Are you scared?"

Chrissie stuck her tongue out at him. "No," she said. "I just didn't want to be disrespectful."

Beside the house stood a black walnut tree already devoid of leaves, save for a few yellow stragglers clinging to the topmost branches. The upstairs window of the house was open to the weather, and one of the tree's limbs reached through it as if feeling around for the lock. Jim imagined that the house, or someone or something inside it, was listening to them as they approached, and he caught himself stepping through the weeds as quietly as possible, almost tip-toeing. He stopped on the top step and checked the soundness of the porch before venturing onto it. When Chrissie stepped onto the porch behind him, the boards creaked deliciously, and he felt gooseflesh scamper up his arms.

When he turned and looked at Chrissie, her eyes had warmed with excitement into some miraculous, glowing shade of brown, a color Jim had never seen before. For a moment he couldn't remember how to move his legs. He felt himself smile so broadly, so ridiculously, that he would not have been surprised had sunshine poured out of his mouth.

"What?" Chrissie asked.

"You look scared," Jim said.

"No, I don't."

Jim smiled again. "You're right. You don't."

The delicate segments of her irises seemed to have been cut from some impossibly fine glass, except that, as Chrissie's pupils widened in the shaded light of the porch, they changed shape while he studied them.

"Why are you staring at me?" Chrissie asked. "You look like a possum. All that grinning."

Jim pretended to take offense. "A possum," he said. "I don't look like a possum."

Chrissie giggled. "You're right," she said. "You don't."

At the threshold Jim pushed against the door, but

it had swollen into place against the floorboards. He stepped sideways through the opening into a dim, unpainted hallway that bisected the length of the house and stopped at what Jim guessed was the back door. On the right side of the hallway a stairway disappeared up into the shadows, and beyond the stairway stood a single doorway; on the left side two doors faced the hall. The shadows between Jim and the exit at the back of the house seemed to possess mass and bones; had Jim been a few years younger, he would have turned around and run as fast as he could. Chrissie stepped into the house behind him. She grasped the doorknob and pulled but could only move it two or three inches. The doorsill scraping against the floor of the silent house struck Jim as one of the loudest noises he had ever heard.

"What are you doing?" he asked. He noticed that he was whispering, so he forced himself to loudly repeat the question. He still thought he sounded scared.

"Houses know when people don't live in them," she said. "Did you ever notice that?"

"What?"

"Look at this door. It's rotten and it's all swelled up."

"I guess it got wet," Jim said. He checked the ceiling for water stains but didn't find any.

"It knows that nobody lives here anymore so it started rotting."

"That's crazy," Jim said.

Chrissie scowled at him impatiently. "Have you ever seen an old house that had fallen in?"

"Sure. Lots of times. So?"

"Well, have you ever seen a house that fell in while somebody was still living in it?"

Jim thought for a minute. "No. I guess not."

"Then, you tell me what that proves."

"I don't know what that proves."

"Yes, you do," Chrissie said.

She stepped past him toward the door opposite the stairway, which opened into what must have been the house's parlor. The walls of the room had once been papered with an old-fashioned pattern of pink roses on a pale background, but large strips of the paper had been ripped from the walls and now lay twisted about the floor. The shredded wallpaper shared the floor with the broken glass from the windows and the rocks that had broken them. The glass crunched underneath their feet. Jim kicked one of the rocks and it fled noisily into a corner. He looked through the windows and saw the Major obediently watching the house. He noticed that neither of them had shut their door all the way.

Chrissie found an old broom leaning in the corner and took a couple of halfhearted swipes at the floor. She called to Jim from across the room. "Look at the fireplace," she said.

"Somebody pulled up the hearth."

"Whoever it was, they were looking for money. I bet that poor couple wasn't even cold in the grave before somebody broke in here looking for their savings. Don't you think people are just awful?"

"We're in here," Jim said.

"But we don't have bad intentions."

He walked over and looked into the hole where the hearth had been but saw only the ground underneath the house. The hearthstone lay off to one side. It was a large piece of fieldstone that someone had roughly chiseled into shape. Jim studied it for a moment, then worked his fingers underneath it and slid it back into place.

"There," he said.

"Thank you," said Chrissie.

She squatted and ran her finger around the edge of a perfectly round hole, about the size of a silver dollar, cut into one corner of the hearth. "What do you guess this was for?"

Jim suddenly brightened with the answer. "Walnuts," he said. "There's a big walnut tree in the front yard. They used to put the walnuts into the hole and bust them open with a hammer."

Chrissie snapped her fingers. "That's it," she said. "That's it exactly. They sat here by the fire in the wintertime and shelled walnuts. Whose job do you think it was?"

"His," Jim said.

"Then she would put them into pound cakes."

"Whatever was left over. He ate most of them out of the shell."

"Well, then, I hope he was ashamed."

"He was."

When they left the parlor they tiptoed down the hallway, and Jim pushed open the door of the room on the right. The floor was covered in trash, with chicken bones and empty whiskey bottles and torn magazines and piles of old clothing; a man's single shoe, rotting and curled up at the toe, lay on a soiled mattress in the corner. The ticking of the mattress was almost entirely blackened by dark stains.

"Tramps," Jim said. "Tramps stay here." He thought about going to get his rifle out of the Major.

"Lost people," Chrissie said. "Lost people stay here. Just because somebody is lost doesn't mean you have to call them a tramp."

She moved past him into the room and with the handle of the old broom poked through the piles of trash.

"Are you looking for something in particular?" Jim asked.

"No. I'm just looking."

When she reached the mattress she stood staring down at it a long time. She jabbed at the shoe with the broom. When she turned around, Jim thought she looked a little scared.

"I have a bad feeling about this room," she said. "Bad things have happened here."

"Then, let's go."

Chrissie dropped the broom and tiptoed quickly across the floor. Jim shut the door securely behind her. He watched her carefully. If she had run for the car, he would have run, too.

"Say a prayer," she said.

"What?"

"Say a prayer. There are bad spirits in there and we don't want them to follow us when we leave."

"What kind of spirits?"

"Spirits of despair," Chrissie said. "Say a prayer to protect us."

"You say one."

"I'm going to say one for the lost people. You say one about the spirits."

Jim closed his eyes. At first he couldn't think of anything to pray, but then the words *Lord, in the coming months protect us all from the spirits of despair* whispered into his mind. The words puzzled and frightened him a little, and he tried to shake them out of his head. He never said them out loud. When he opened his eyes he saw Chrissie studying him.

"Amen," she said.

"Amen."

"Do you think we're safe here?"

Jim closed his eyes again and listened but heard only the silence of the empty rooms and the slightly urgent sound of his own breathing. "I think we're okay," he said. "I don't think there's anybody else in here. Are the spirits after us?"

"Not right now," she said.

Across the hallway they found the room that had

once been the kitchen. A black stovepipe poked out of the wall, and beneath the stovepipe lay a sooty tin fire mat. Jim studied the four deep indentations in the tin and pictured a fat stove squatting there, connected to the chimney by the pipe, a fire burning in the box, a pound cake with walnuts cooking in the oven; the fact that a stove no longer occupied the place where a stove so obviously belonged made the room seem strangely forlorn. An overturned wooden chair lay on each side of the fire mat. The strips of oak caning the bottoms of the chairs were busted downward. Someone had apparently forced a foot through each of the seats.

"Their chairs," Chrissie said. "They liked to sit by the stove."

She righted one of the chairs and perched primly on the edge of the broken seat. She pointed with her chin at the other chair. "You sit there," she said.

Jim picked up the chair and turned it so that its back faced Chrissie; he squatted across the seat and sat on the frame. He draped his arms across the back, and Mama would ask him later how he had gotten his shirt so dirty.

Chrissie watched him a long time, the look on her face unreadable. Then she dropped her chin to her chest and frowned.

"What did I do?" Jim asked.

"Old man," she said, "I can't believe you ate all the walnuts."

Jim blinked rapidly, then smiled. Once again he

felt sunshine pouring out of his mouth. "Old woman," he said in a gruff voice, "I didn't eat *all* the walnuts. I just ate *most* of the walnuts."

"You didn't leave me enough to make a cake."

"Well, I don't know what you expect me to do about it now. You know I flat love walnuts."

"I think you're a very selfish old man."

"Am I?"

Chrissie slowly nodded. "You only think about what you want. You never, ever think about what I want."

"But they were just walnuts."

"Not to me," she said.

"Chrissie . . ."

She started, or pretended to. "What did you call me, old man?"

"Ah," he said. "Old woman, I'm afraid I'm getting forgetful in my old age. Tell me, what did you say your name was?"

"Juanita Loretta Rebecca," she said.

"And what's my name again?"

She closed one eye, cocked her head, and carefully considered him. "Hernando Amos Grover," she said.

Jim laughed out loud. "Okay, then," he said. "If old Hernando Amos Grover goes and shells you some more walnuts, will you forgive him?"

Chrissie stared at him sadly. "Probably," she said. "I always do."

At that moment, whatever reserve and decorum that had held Jim in his chair, that for weeks had kept him from telling Chrissie how he felt, that had kept him from swimming to Hawaii and challenging Bucky Bucklaw to a fistfight, simply went away. He stood up and moved around the fire mat and knelt on one knee in front of Chrissie. Reaching into her lap, he picked up her right hand. He turned it palm upward and studied it the way he might have studied some book whose pages contained everything he needed to know in writing too small to read. When she didn't withdraw her hand, he placed it against his cheek. Now it was warm and dry and smooth. Jim closed his eyes. He felt on the verge of calamity, and he had never felt more wonderful in his life. When he opened his eyes and spoke, his voice shook and came out lower than he had ever heard it. "Juanita," he said, "you're the best thing that ever happened to me. I don't know what I would do without you."

"You're a crazy old man," she said softly, "saying a thing like that. If something happened to me, you know you'd just go off and marry somebody else."

"No," he said. "I would never do that."

"You would, too. You just love me for my pound cakes."

"That's not true," Jim said. "I love everything about you."

Chrissie withdrew her hand. One strong feeling after another moved silently across her face like the shadows cast by clouds. One moment she looked fierce, and the next she looked ready to kiss him, and the next she looked as sad as anyone he had ever seen. Jim couldn't tell from instant to instant what she might be thinking, so he didn't dare move. He had the distinct feeling that whatever was about to happen would be the first really important thing to happen to him in his entire life. Chrissie might tell him she loved him, and she might punch him in the eye. Either way, Jim was sure that the boy who left this kitchen would be an entirely different boy than the one who had entered it.

"Jim . . . ," she said softly.

"Shh," he said. "Hernando. Please call me Hernando."

Chrissie reached out with a finger, as if to brush the hair away from his forehead, but seemed to think better of it and dropped her hand into her lap.

"Jim," she said, "I think we need to get on up the road."

"Chrissie, can I kiss you?"

He watched as her chin first moved almost imperceptibly to the right, and then farther, with more assurance, to the left and back again.

"No," she said. "You can't."

Jim and the Beanstalk

*A*BOUT A third of the way up the mountain, the world disappeared. One minute Jim and Chrissie were traveling upward along a path Chrissie knew well and Jim knew somewhat: through open, second-growth stands of oak and maple and poplar and sweet gum muted by the drizzle and gathering fog; through rich hells of laurel and rhododendron, out of which carried the tumbling voices of creek branches and wet-weather springs too small for names; up slopes too steep for logging, where ancient pine trees of impossible girth and height still climbed out of sight. But the next minute, the cloud they had seen from the valley silently closed around them, and every landmark — every rock, bush, tree, and opening in the trees, every mud hole, bank, ditch, straightaway, and switchback — that marked the mountain as a place recognizable to them simply ceased to be. Jim slowed the Major and downshifted into first; he leaned forward until his chest touched the steering wheel, but he could see no more than a car length of road at a time unrolling ahead of them. For all he could tell, a car length of road was all that lay between them and falling off the edge of the world into the void feared long ago by sailors. He switched on the headlights, but the enveloping whiteness swallowed the feeble light the Major manufactured as easily as it had swallowed everything else. The windshield wipers also proved to be of little use. Jim felt a panicky sweat blossom in his armpits.

"I don't know about you," he said, "but I can't see a daggum thing."

Chrissie, too, leaned forward and squinted into the fog. "I can't see anything, either," she said. "You be careful."

"I'm going to."

They had talked little since leaving the abandoned house. Jim was still tormented by a desire to kiss Chrissie — for that matter, by an overwhelming, though still somewhat vague, longing to *possess* her in general — but surprisingly did not feel awkward riding in the car with her. Likewise, Chrissie seemed to find traveling up the mountain with Jim a perfectly pleasant way to pass the time. Though she had refused to kiss him, she had, however briefly, pretended to be married to him; that make-believe intimacy, and the make-believe years on which it was built, seemed to remain comfortably settled around their shoulders — even as they left Hernando and Juanita sitting in their broken chairs by their ghostly stove, forever arguing about walnuts.

"I've never been inside a cloud before," Jim said. "How about you?"

"Nothing like this. I've never seen anything like this in my life."

As long as Jim drove no faster than he could have walked, road enough to navigate continued to materialize before them. The switchbacks, however, proved to be especially frightening because Jim had to speed up in order to climb through them without stalling. But when he accelerated, waves of fog leapt angrily at the windshield and crashed against the glass, and the edge of the earth hurtled forward just inches ahead of the car's front tires. Eventually Jim began to feel disoriented and dizzy. The Major seemed balanced on top of a flagpole, or caught in the uppermost branches of a tree; Jim was afraid that the slightest misstep on his part would send them plummeting into space. He kept driving, but his neck and shoulders ached with tension.

When the switchbacks stopped rolling at them and Jim felt the road level out, he knew that they had driven out into the high, narrow valley that lay beneath the ridgeline of the mountain. A mailbox sprang into being suddenly on the right, and Jim had to swerve to miss it. More mailboxes, sometimes whole rows of them, appeared then at regular intervals, like sentries at the ends of the narrow, rutted roads that spilled down out of the deep hollows that creased the side of the ridge. And when the road rose again, Jim knew that they had reached the end of the valley, and that beside them, below the road, lay the bald from which — on a clear day — it was possible to see not only Aliceville but, farther away, the brick cotton mills that straddled the river at Roberta and Allendale and, beyond the mills, the hazy, patchwork country rolling away until at some point it mysteriously became South Carolina. Jim could feel the great empty space yawning to his left, although he could not see it, and the knowledge that it lay only yards away from where he drove made his heart leap like he had just dreamed he was falling. He stopped the car.

"Let's get out here for a minute," he said.

He climbed out but kept a hand safely on the reassuring bulk of the car. Chrissie walked around the Major and stood beside him — at a companionable distance, he thought, but not nearly close enough — and together they stared into the fog and imagined the world that lay beyond it.

"Look," Jim said. "You can see my house from here."

"I know."

"You mean you've looked for it?"

"I mean you can see a long way from here. And I mean I've seen your house."

Jim nodded. The air was perfectly still, but the fog was chilly on his face. He shivered and stuck his hands in his pockets. He didn't know what else to say. Hoping that Chrissie had viewed his house as more important than any other house visible from the mountain had been too much to hope for.

"I know what," Chrissie said. "Let's be really quiet and see if we can hear anything."

Jim let go of the Major and stood up straight. He cocked his ear toward the place where he knew the mountain fell away into the air. He closed his eyes, but that made him feel like he was falling, so he opened them again. Dead silence. He couldn't remember ever being anyplace where he couldn't hear anything at all. No wind blowing or dogs barking in the distance or Mama moving around in the next room or the low murmur of the uncles talking as they rocked on the porch. Nothing. He and Chrissie could have been the only living things left on earth, an idea that made him as happy as he could remember ever being — despite the fact that the noises that came to mind had always made him happy before. Eventually Chrissie took a deep breath and exhaled.

"I couldn't hear anything," Jim said. "Could you?"

"Nope," she said. "I feel like we just climbed the beanstalk."

Jim smiled. "You never know. Maybe we did."

"Now all we have to worry about is getting past the giant's house."

"Do you think he'd kill us if he knew we were up here?"

"More than likely," she said. "And then I think he'd eat us."

"I ain't afraid of no giant," Jim said. "I'll chop his head off if he messes with us."

"Well, *I'm* still glad it's foggy," Chrissie said. "You never know when he's watching. I'm going to walk up the road and count my footsteps, and you tell me when you can't see me anymore."

"You're not going to run off, are you?"

"Not right now. Just tell me when you can't see me."

Jim watched Chrissie walk off into the fog and listened to her counting slowly. By the time she counted to five, her outline began to grow indistinct, and by the time she reached twenty, she vanished entirely. The last thing Jim saw fade out of sight was the long, black stripe of her hair.

"There," he said.

"You can't see me anymore?"

"No. Can you see me?"

"There's sort of a dark place where your car's parked, but I can't tell what it is."

Jim squinted at the spot where he had last seen Chrissie and rubbed the gooseflesh on his arms. He felt suddenly heartbroken, and wished she would come back.

"Are you still there?" he asked.

"I'm still here."

"You looked like a ghost," he said. "You just disappeared."

"I feel like a ghost. Are you sure you can't see me?"

"I'm sure."

"Then you can ask me three questions."

"What?"

"You get to ask three questions when you climb the beanstalk. But only if you can't see the person you're asking."

"I've never heard that part of the story," he said.

"You just didn't have the right person telling it," she answered.

"Three questions aren't enough."

"But that's the way this story goes."

"Okay. Let me think."

"Number one."

"All right," he said. "Here goes. Number one. Are you an Indian?"

"Half," she said. "I can't believe you wasted a question on that. Number two."

"Number two. Do you get sick like that every month?"

Chrissie didn't say anything at first. "Yes," she said finally. "But only since we moved back to North Carolina, and only for a few hours at a time, and only on the first day."

"That's awful."

"I'll live. These aren't very good questions, Jim."

"I'll try to do better."

"Okay. Number three."

"Number three. Are you Bucky Bucklaw's girlfriend?"

"That's complicated."

"What do you mean 'complicated'?"

"That's four questions, Jim."

"Then answer number three."

"I don't know how to answer number three."

"It seems easy enough to me," Jim said.

"Well, it's not."

"Either you're going with Bucky Bucklaw or you're not going with Bucky Bucklaw. Which one is it?"

Somewhere up the road he heard Chrissie stomp her foot.

"Look here, Jim, I can't be your girlfriend," she said. "All right?"

"Nobody asked you to be my girlfriend," Jim said. "But why not?"

"That's five."

"Damn it, Chrissie," Jim said. "Will you please, please, please stop counting?"

"No more questions, Jim."

"But you didn't tell me what I need to know."

"Take me home," she said.

"I'm not taking you home until you answer number three."

"When you take me home, you'll know the answer to number three."

The road wound through the half dozen buildings clustered in the small village of Lynn's Mountain, though all Jim saw of it was the store and a handful of tombstones in the graveyard at the church. Chrissie pointed at the tombstones and smiled as they passed but did so without comment. Jim was pleased that they had apparently just shared something, even though he didn't know what it was.

"You can ask me questions if you want to," he said. "You climbed the beanstalk, too."

"How many questions?"

"As many as you want. I'm not stingy like some people I know."

"Why did you break up with Norma Harris?" Chrissie asked.

Jim winced and twisted in his seat. "I don't know," he said. "It just wasn't any fun, I guess. That's the main reason. Is that a bad reason?"

"I don't know if it is or not. Y'all seem like you belong together. You're both fair-skinned and your hair's the same color. You're both real smart and you seem a little stuck-up at first."

"Well, we don't belong together, and I'm not stuck up. Ask me another question."

"Why do you want to be my boyfriend?"

"What makes you think I want to be your boyfriend?"

"I'm not stupid, Jim," she said. "You play with my hair during history class. You stare at me all the time. And you came to give me a ride when you heard I was sick. That was a very nice thing to do, by the way."

"Thank you," he said. "You can feel it when I touch your hair?"

"It's attached to my head," she said. "Of course I can feel it. But you didn't answer me. Why do you want to be my boyfriend?"

Jim gripped the steering wheel tighter. Chrissie had

finally asked the question; he was going to step up and answer it truthfully, Bucky Bucklaw be damned.

"Because I love you," he said.

"Oh," she said, looking down into her lap. "I see."

"I've loved you since you got off the bus the first day of school."

"Now, wait a minute. That just sounds like something that boys say to girls."

"Well, maybe it was the second day."

"That's better."

"And I know I don't know you very well," Jim said. "So, you don't have to tell me that. I don't understand it, either."

"I wasn't going to say that. I think we at least ought to be able to love whoever we want to, even if it's not a good idea."

"Well, at least that's one thing we agree on, I guess."

That seemed to be the end of it. Jim had always imagined that telling Chrissie he loved her would lead to more discussion, but then again, he couldn't remember talking about love much with Norma, either. Maybe love was just one of those things it didn't take long to talk about.

Close by the roadside, a mountain of logs marked the yard of Carson's Mill, and from out of the fog they heard the banshee keening of the big saw blade. Jim noticed that Chrissie shivered at the sound. A little farther up the road he tried to see his friend Penn's house but couldn't find even the mailbox.

"Where does that Carson boy go to boarding school again?" Chrissie asked.

"Outside Philadelphia somewhere."

"I saw him around a time or two over the summer. He's handsome."

"He's got that bad limp, though," Jim said.

"That's not a very nice thing to say about somebody who's had polio. Especially when they're supposed to be your friend."

"You're right. I don't know why I said it."

"Yes, you do."

"Is there anything else you want to ask me?" Jim said.

"Did you know that my mama and your uncle Zeno almost got married?"

"What?" he said. *"What?"*

"They broke it off at the last minute."

"I never heard anything about Uncle Zeno even having a girlfriend, much less one he almost married. Why did they break up?"

"I don't know," Chrissie said. "Mama won't talk about it. She says it's ancient history."

"So Uncle Zeno had a girlfriend," Jim said. "My, my, my. Is your mama pretty?"

Chrissie briefly looked upward, studying some picture Jim couldn't see. "I don't know anymore," she said. "I guess she was at one time. Does it matter?"

"No. I guess not."

He drove through the ford on Painter Creek and crept the Major past the spot where his grandfather's house had stood. Jim had visited the old man only once before he died. In the fog there was nothing to see — the house had fallen in several years before — and nothing to hear, but Jim still felt uneasy passing by it. He pointed out the window.

"That's where my grandfather's house used to be," he said.

"You can still see the chimney from the road," Chrissie said. "It always gives me a bad feeling."

"You get bad feelings about a lot of things."

"There's a lot in the world to feel bad about."

"I guess I never thought that way," Jim said. "I think there's a lot in the world to feel good about."

"I heard your grandfather bought your grandmother from her daddy and treated her real bad. Isn't that enough to give somebody a bad feeling when they see his old chimney sticking up?"

Jim accelerated the Major slightly. "I didn't have anything to do with it," he said.

A mile or so past Amos Glass's place, the road switchbacked twice in rapid succession, then straightened out and continued upward toward the far western reach of the mountain. Soon they drove out into the apple orchards owned by Bucky Bucklaw's father, Arthur Bucklaw Sr. Save for the few apple trees crouched close to the road, Jim could not have said how he knew that they had driven out into open country; he knew only that they had.

"You turn to the right up here," Chrissie said.

"You *live* on the Bucklaw place?" Jim said.

"Yep."

"I didn't know that. I thought you lived just past it somewhere."

"Nope. We live on it."

"Huh."

"But it's only until my daddy gets here."

"When's that going to be?"

"I'm not sure."

Arthur Bucklaw Sr. had moved with his wife from the Casar side of the mountain to the Aliceville side thirty years earlier, where, much to the amusement of his neighbors, he purchased five adjoining farmsteads of almost unworkable steepness and immediately went to work setting out fruit trees. The sunny, southern slope of the mountain had proved ideal for growing apples, however, and Bucklaw Sr. had made what everyone agreed must have been a great deal of money, and this despite the Depression. Many of the people who had laughed at him now picked apples for him in the fall. The responsibility for rubbing people's noses in just how much money Bucklaw had made seemed to have fallen to his only son, Bucky. Jim thought that the uncles were probably worth more than the Bucklaws, but he had no way of knowing for sure. At least with Bucky graduated out of high school and off the baseball team and gone away to the navy, he didn't have to think about it so often.

After Jim turned off the main road onto the Bucklaw place, he drove down a narrow boulevard of huge packing sheds and barns that grew one at a time out of the fog like the palaces and temples of a ghostly city. He assumed they had been built, in typical Bucklaw fashion, within spitting distance of the road simply so they wouldn't be missed by visitors. Despite the hearty contempt Jim held for Bucky, the closer they drew to the Bucklaw house, the more nervous he became. Chrissie, likewise, slumped down in her seat, hiding from any Bucklaw who might magically be able to see her slinking past. The house, which occupied the top of a small knoll set back from the drive, was at least mercifully obscured by the fog.

"Slow down," Chrissie said. "You don't want to run over those dogs."

Jim had opened his mouth to say "What dogs?" when he suddenly found himself face-to-face with a nightmare constructed of sharp claws, large teeth, and hateful, pale eyes — two wolflike dogs who threw themselves at his window, apparently trying to chew through the glass. After a few horrifying seconds, the dogs vanished just as quickly as they had appeared, leaving behind an impressive layer of dog slobber and muddy paw prints on his window.

"Good Lord," he said. "What in the world was that?"

"Bucky's dogs," Chrissie said. "They're German shepherds."

"I'm glad I had the window rolled up."

"I would've warned you if you hadn't. They might've gotten in here and chewed you all to pieces."

"What about you?"

"Oh, they know me."

At Chrissie's direction, Jim pulled into a muddy clearing walled off by a thicket of scruffy-looking pines. He parked beside a decrepit Model T truck whose flatbed was constructed of mismatched lumber.

"We're here," she said.

When Jim cut the engine, he heard what sounded like an immense pack of hounds baying urgently somewhere close by. In the fog the noise seemed to come from all directions at once. He expected to see more vicious dogs, hundreds of them this time, loping out of the trees. He hesitated before getting out.

"What about those dogs?" he asked. "Are they going to chew me all to pieces?"

"They're penned up," Chrissie said, shutting her door.

"What are they?"

"Plotts mostly. Some blueticks. Mr. Bucklaw uses them to hunt bears."

"Bear dogs," Jim said. The uncles used their hounds to hunt raccoons. "How many does he have?"

"I don't know. Twenty or twenty-five, I guess. You're not allowed to pet them because they're bear dogs, so I don't pay them any mind. They smell bad, too. My paw-paw takes care of them for Mr. Bucklaw."

She led him up a narrow path into the pines. The dogs' voices ran in and out of the fog; they surged forward and retreated from every direction he turned. The baying grew louder and more urgent the farther he and Chrissie walked. He squinted up the path.

"Are you sure they're penned up?" he asked.

Chrissie smiled and took his hand. "Don't worry, Jim. I won't let them get you."

Up ahead he heard a door creak open. A man's voice yelled, "Hey! You there!" and the dogs fell silent on a single note. The door creaked closed.

"That's Paw-paw," Chrissie said.

They walked into another clearing and a house began to form itself out of the fog. It seemed to be misshapen at first — the house in a children's story where a troll might live — but eventually it sharpened into a dogtrot cabin whose sagging ridgepole dipped toward a covered passageway separating two log rooms. Chimneys of rough fieldstones plastered with mud rose unsteadily on either side of the house, just high enough to clear the roof. The roof was covered by ancient wooden shingles, patched here and there with flattened tin cans. Jim could see tiny slivers of light leaking from in between the logs of the walls. In the places where the chinking had fallen away entirely, someone had stuffed wads of old newsprint into the cracks.

A single hound Jim couldn't locate barked a sharp warning, and a door on the left front of the cabin swung open. A feeble column of orange kerosene light tipped across the yard, and the silhouetted shape of a stooped old man appeared in the doorway. The old man had only one arm; his right sleeve dangled emptily by his side.

"Who's out there?" he demanded.

Chrissie dropped Jim's hand as they stepped into the light. "It's me, Paw-paw," she said.

Jim had never known that Chrissie's family was as poor as this house revealed them to be; he felt immensely sad that she had to live in such a place, and he took an immediate, irrational dislike to the old man who stood before them. He needed to blame Chrissie's predicament on someone, and the old man was the only possibility to present itself so far.

"Where you been, girl?"

"I got sick at school. I missed the bus and had to get a ride home."

"Who's that with you?"

"This is Jim Glass," she said. "He's the one who gave me the ride."

"Jim Glass," the old man said. "I knew your granddaddy."

"Yes, sir."

"He was a bastard."

"*Paw-paw*," Chrissie said.

"Well, he was. No reason not to call a spade a spade."

Jim almost smiled. Amos Glass had been a bastard, but to Jim's knowledge nobody ever called him one until after he died.

"Jim, this is my paw-paw, Solon McAbee," Chrissie said.

"Nub," Mr. McAbee said.

"Excuse me?" Jim said.

"Everybody calls me Nub."

"Oh. Nice to meet you, sir."

"I can see you're wondering what happened to my arm."

"Oh, no, sir," Jim said.

"Paw-paw, you always do this," Chrissie complained.

"I wore it off playing the fiddle, is what happened," Mr. McAbee said. He opened the door wider and stepped to one side. "Y'all get on in here. You're letting all the fog in."

"This is the only time I'll ever be able to bring you up here," Chrissie whispered. "Look at everything close and you'll know the answer to number three."

Once inside, Jim studied the room intently. In the center of the floor the old man drew a chair from underneath a homemade table covered with an oilcloth and sat down. The wide pine planks of the floor had been worn thin and splintery, but they were swept clean. The walls were sealed with newspapers and pieces of cardboard tacked up by nails driven through old bottle caps. A large, rusting cookstove dominated the wall facing the door, and a black pot of greens bubbled on the stove. To the right, a small bed, made neatly with a worn but clean feed-sack quilt, lay along the wall beside a misshapen door Jim assumed opened into the dogtrot. A teddy bear slumped against the wall and stared into the room as if he could not believe his misfortune. On the left, two women sat on either side of the fireplace, although no fire had been lit inside it. One woman was old and shriveled and as dry-looking as an old harness. She had no teeth and her white hair was pulled back into a painful-looking bun. The other looked like an older, tired version of Chrissie, although her hair was brown, going to gray, and not black.

"Who's that with you?" the younger woman asked.

"Mama, this is Jim Glass," Chrissie said. "I got sick again at school and he gave me a ride home. Jim, that's my mama, Nancy Steppe."

"Hello, Mrs. Steppe," Jim said. "Pleased to meet you."

Mrs. Steppe nodded to him, expressionless, but didn't take her eyes off his face.

The older woman leaned over, picked up a tin can from the hearth, and spat into it. "Did anybody see you drive up in here?"

"Jim, that's my grandmother, Effie McAbee."

"Hello," Jim said.

The old woman nodded curtly at Jim and spat into the can again. Jim disliked her as instinctively as he had disliked the old man. She had the bright, appraising eyes of a small dog plotting to steal food from a bigger dog.

"The fog sure is thick out there today," Jim said to the old woman. "Nobody can see much of anything."

"It ain't that thick," Mrs. McAbee said.

"I knew your family, a long time ago," Mrs. Steppe said. "I trust everybody's doing well."

"Yes, ma'am," Jim said. "Thank you. Everybody's fine, about the same, I guess."

"Business doing good, I hope?"

Jim felt his face tighten. He had learned from the uncles a long time ago never to discuss the family businesses with anyone outside the family.

"We're doing all right," he said. "Things seem to be picking up."

"Picking up," mumbled the old woman.

"That's good," Mrs. Steppe said. "I imagine they must be awfully worried about you, driving around up here in all this fog. You should probably head on back. It'll be dark before you make it down the mountain."

Jim backed up a step. "Oh. Yes, ma'am. I guess I ought to be going."

"I'll walk you to your car," said Chrissie.

"Well," Jim said. "It was nice to meet y'all."

The old woman stared at him with her bright eyes. "Don't run off," she said.

"I need to get on."

Chrissie's mother's smile suggested she remembered something funny that had nothing to do with the current conversation. "You tell your people Nancy McAbee asked about them," she said.

"Steppe," said Chrissie.

"I'll do that."

"And, boy," said Mr. McAbee. "Whatever you do, don't let 'em make you take up the fiddle."

"I won't," Jim said. "Well, bye."

"Don't run over them dogs," the old woman said.

"I won't. I'll be careful. Y'all take care."

Chrissie took Jim by the arm and steered him toward the door. When he stepped outside he heard the old woman say, "If he runs over them dogs, there'll be a world of trouble."

"Hush, Mama," Chrissie's mother said. "He'll hear you."

Walking back to the car, Chrissie held on to Jim's arm with both hands. Her clinging to him didn't make him happy, however, because he could tell that she was unhappy.

"Hey," he said. "What's the matter?"

"Now do you know the answer to number three?" she asked.

"I'm not sure. Maybe. I think so."

"Then, tell me what you think it is."

"No. You tell me."

"All right," Chrissie said. "Number three. You see where we live."

Jim nodded.

"And you know who owns it."

"Bucky's daddy."

"Right. So, when me and Mama moved back here, Bucky just up and decided on his own that I was his private property. Before he went off to the navy, he told everybody up here I was his girlfriend. Now nobody else is allowed to talk to me."

"And you just let him?"

She let go and stepped away from him. "You're not thinking, Jim," she said. "My paw-paw's only got one arm."

"So?"

"So, what if I make Bucky mad and Mr. Bucklaw runs us off? What do you think would happen then?"

"I don't know."

"I'll tell you what would happen. We wouldn't have any place to live, and we wouldn't have any money, and nobody would hire my paw-paw because he's dead old and was stupid enough to get his stupid arm cut off in the sawmill, and then we'd be up the creek so far nobody would ever find us. We're poor as church mice as it is."

"You can't let them get away with that," Jim said. "You can't let Bucky do that to you."

"I don't have any choice in it."

"What do you mean you don't have any choice?"

"I mean that people with money can do just about anything they want to people who don't have money."

"That's not true. I don't believe that."

"You've always had money."

"You wait just a minute," Jim said. "My family's not rich, and nobody ever gave us anything. We've worked for everything we've got."

"How many houses does your family own?" Chrissie asked.

Jim didn't answer.

"How many?"

"Three," he said, "not counting the tenant house, but it's falling in."

"Three houses. And how many people live in those three houses?"

"Five."

"Five people in three houses," Chrissie said. "So, let me tell you something. I sleep in a *kitchen,* so don't you dare tell me you're not rich. *My* family doesn't have a pot to pee in, and I don't know where my daddy is or when he's coming to get us, and Mr. Bucklaw watches me like a hawk, and my mattress is made out of corn shucks and I can hear bugs crawling around in it, and then you drive up here in your dumb car with its dumb name like some kind of big shot and talk to me like I'm stupid and say, '*Oh, I'm not rich,*' and tell me that I can just break up with Bucky Bucklaw pretty as you please?"

Jim stopped walking. "Whoa," he said. "I'm sorry. Please don't cry. I just wasn't thinking."

When he reached out and tried to take Chrissie by the arms, she slapped his hands away. "Don't touch me," she said.

"Shh," Jim said.

"I mean it, Jim Glass. You can't put your hands on me just so it'll make you feel better. If you ever touch me again, I swear to God I'll knock those nice straight teeth of yours right down your throat."

"Listen to me."

"Don't you dare touch me. I'll kill you if you touch me."

"I won't touch you. I promise. Just listen."

Chrissie glared at him. "What?" she said.

Jim took a deep breath.

"I'm just sorry," he said. "I'm really, really sorry. I don't know anything about your life . . ."

"That's right, you don't."

"And I'm sorry if I acted like I did."

"Okay."

"And I'm sorry Bucky has got you so jammed up, and I'm sorry you don't have a nice house, because you deserve one, and I'm sorry you have a corn-shuck bed, and I'm sorry you got sick today, and I'm just awful sorry about everything, and I would change it all if I could so you wouldn't have to be sad ever again, because I love you."

Chrissie blinked, nodded curtly, turned, and continued down the path.

Jim fell into step beside her. "Why don't you ever say anything when I tell you that I love you?" he asked. "I've been telling you that all afternoon."

"I heard you," Chrissie said without looking at him, "and I think you're a very nice boy. But I also think you've never learned you don't get to have everything you want every time you want it."

"You make me sound like Bucky Bucklaw."

Chrissie shrugged. "You are like Bucky Bucklaw."

"I don't think that's fair."

"It's just the truth."

"Are you in love with him?"

"No," Chrissie said. "There's your car."

When Jim opened the door he noticed for the first time that the light was failing. It would be dark soon and he was a long way from home. Mama would be worried sick.

"Are you in love with me?"

Chrissie shook her head angrily. "Jim. Listen to me. If I lived somewhere else and had some different kind of life, I could lay around all day on my pretty bed and think about which boy I loved and which boy I didn't and then I'd dress up all pretty and write about it in my diary. But I don't live somewhere else, and this life is the only one I've got. I don't have time to think about things like that."

Jim slid underneath the wheel, slammed the door, and rolled down the window. "Have you kissed Bucky Bucklaw?" he asked.

"You're asking way too many questions."

"I'm not going to get mad. I just need to know."

"Bucky's kissed me," she said. "But I haven't kissed Bucky."

"What's the difference?"

"There's a difference."

"Oh."

"Do you know what I mean?"

"No."

Chrissie leaned in through the car window and kissed Jim so quickly on the lips he didn't have time to shut his eyes.

"Hey, wait a minute," he said. "I wasn't ready. Let me kiss you again."

She shook her head and backed away from the car. "Have a nice trip," she said.

*　　*　　*

Jim rolled up his window and drove carefully as he approached the Bucklaw house. He figured the dogs would be waiting for him to come back by and he didn't want to run over one of them, no matter how much he thought it was a good idea. He was still searching for the dogs, his heart racing, when the fog to his left began to brighten. The brightening condensed into the circular glow of a lantern, and as he drew closer, the form of a very tall man squeezed into being out of the light. Two large dogs sat on either side of the man, their bushy tails curled around their haunches. The man held up a hand as Jim approached; when Jim stopped the car, he tapped on the glass. Jim looked into the amber eyes of the panting dogs and rolled the window down less than halfway. The man leaned slowly over, held the lantern up, and looked into the car.

"Hey, Mr. Bucklaw," Jim said. "It's me, Jim Glass. I played baseball with Bucky."

"I know who you are," Arthur Bucklaw said. "What are you doing up in here?"

"Christine Steppe got sick at school today and missed the bus, so I gave her a ride home."

"You running a taxi service, then?"

"No, sir."

"Then how come you're driving a taxi?"

"I'm not driving a taxi. I just gave Chrissie a ride."

The upper lip of the dog on Mr. Bucklaw's right puckered slightly, exposing two long, curled fangs. Jim heard a growl bubble softly in the dog's throat.

"Easy, Jackson," Bucklaw said.

"Nice dogs," said Jim.

"They don't like strangers."

"No, sir."

"Did that girl ask you to bring her home?"

"No, sir."

"I ain't gonna have a bunch of boys sniffing around after that girl. She ain't in heat. You understand me?"

"Yes, sir."

"This is private property."

"Yes, sir," Jim said. "I know that."

Mr. Bucklaw rapped twice against the roof of the car. "All right, then," he said. "You best get on down the mountain, where you belong."

October 5, 1941

Aliceville, North Carolina
Dear Mr. Dunlap,

 I am writing to you today regarding my son Jim Glass's recent mission of mercy up Lynn's Mountain, about which I am not pleased. He did not return home until well after dark, by which time his uncles and I were beside ourselves with worry. (When he walked in the door, my brothers were preparing to drive up the mountain in search of him, expecting to find God knows what!) Once Jim learned that his Uncle Zeno had already contacted you and learned his whereabouts, he freely admitted that you had not asked him to take Christine Steppe home after she grew ill — as he had at first fibbed to his Uncle Coran — but that he had volunteered for the duty. (You may rest assured that he has since been punished for the lie, as well as for the adventure itself.) You, of course, had no way of knowing that I would have not allowed Jim to take that girl home under any circumstances. (Heaven forbid, what if he had run across her father?) That is why I am writing to inform you that should a like occasion arise in the future, Jim does NOT have my permission, unless you hear differently from me personally, to use his car to provide transportation to needy students, particularly if they live at the ends of the earth. Despite Jim's opinion to the contrary, I do not think that at seventeen years of age he is ready for the medical mission field. In fact, I am no longer convinced that he is even old enough to drive, and only the intercession of *his uncles has prevented me from throwing his car key into the river.*

I am,

Respectfully yours,
Elizabeth McBride Glass

Uncle Zeno and the
White Mule

JIM SLEPT late the morning of Big Day, a first
for him. Mama twice opened the door of his room
and stuck her head in. At the kitchen table Uncle
Zeno rattled his newspaper and cleared his throat
and set his coffee cup down in its saucer harder than
was absolutely necessary. When Jim finally opened
his eyes, sometime after eight-thirty, he smiled only
slightly at the noise his uncle was making and still
didn't get out of bed.

Instead he stared at the ceiling and listened to the
lonesome *shush* of cars passing on the highway. It had
rained off and on most of the night, and ordinarily
the threat of bad weather on Big Day would have worried him. But this year he had no desire to trudge up
to the school and walk the same hallways he walked
during the week, looking at the fresh Bible story
paintings taped to the walls, while the little kids who
had painted the pictures ran up and down, shouting
to one another, and the teachers who had made the

little kids paint the pictures snapped their fingers at them from the doorways as they ran by, and the parents of the little kids, decked out in their good overalls and Sunday dresses, the men with their hats in their hands, tiptoed up and down like they were coming in late to church and studied the pictures and introduced themselves to the teachers. And this year he had no desire to throw rings at hoops or baseballs at milk jugs or darts at balloons or footballs through holes in a wall, not even if girls from New Carpenter or Allendale were watching him do it. Most particularly he had no desire to ride the rides partnered up with Dennis Deane or — even worse — Mama or one of the uncles. This year he didn't want to go to Big Day at all. He had gone to sleep thinking about Bucky Bucklaw and was still thinking about Bucky Bucklaw when he woke up.

Jim had never liked Bucky, not even before Chrissie had moved back. For three years he had played second base while Bucky played shortstop, an injustice if there had ever been one. Bucky had been the kind of baseball player who blamed his glove when he booted a ground ball, or his bat when he struck out. During double-play situations, when he did manage to field a grounder cleanly, he had always run over and stepped on second himself, rather than toss the ball to Jim. And when his throws didn't arrive at first on time (which they never did), more often than not he had glared at Jim and told him to stay out of the way. (Coach Hamrick never said anything to Bucky about blowing all those double plays because he picked apples for Bucklaw Sr. in the fall — everybody knew that.) And now, as if claiming shortstop when he didn't deserve it hadn't been bad enough, Bucky had also claimed Chrissie, against Chrissie's will, and seemed to be getting away with it.

Since their one trip up the mountain the week before, Chrissie had all but stopped speaking to Jim. In history class she stood frowning in the aisle, without really looking at him, until he moved his desk back so that her hair wouldn't land on it. He waited for her every morning at the top of the steps in the vain hope that something had changed, but nothing ever did. He had, for all practical purposes, become invisible to her. Still, he believed that she loved him as much as he loved her — he could tell that by the *way* she didn't look at him — only she couldn't tell him she loved him because she would get in trouble. As a result, Jim carried around a knot in his gut that wouldn't unravel, and his dislike of Bucky had blossomed into a fine hatred. Sometimes he daydreamed about finding Bucky hurting Chrissie somehow and shooting him dead.

When Jim finally made it in to breakfast, he didn't eat much. The eggs tried to climb back out of his throat, the milk smelled sour, and even the biscuits didn't taste good.

"You're losing weight," Mama said. "Are you sick?" She leaned over and tried to put her hand on his forehead, but he moved out of her reach.

"I'm fine," he said. "I'm just getting in shape for baseball season."

Uncle Zeno folded his newspaper and put it down beside his plate. "You'll never grow hair on your chest if you don't eat more breakfast than that," he said.

"I've already got hair on my chest," said Jim.

"I meant another one."

"Humph."

"I think somebody woke up on the wrong side of the bed this morning," Mama said.

Jim glared at the eggs hardening on his plate.

"Ain't you going to Big Day?" Uncle Zeno asked. "Corrie and Allie are already up there."

"I doubt it," Jim said. "I might go up with Dennis Deane this evening for the dance."

"Come with me this morning and look at the pictures," Mama said.

"They could put the same ones up every year and nobody would notice," Jim said. "They're always the same."

Out of the corner of his eye he saw Mama cast Uncle Zeno a meaningful look.

Uncle Zeno slid his chair noisily away from the table. "Then let's me and you go for a ride."

"Where are we going?" asked Jim.

"To see a man about a dog."

At the stop sign on Depot Street, Jim couldn't help looking up the hill toward the school. Despite the weather, the crowd at Big Day seemed as big as it did every year. Uncle Zeno pulled slowly onto the road, into a creeping line of traffic, and pointed the truck toward New Carpenter. Jim watched the Ferris wheel spinning on the playground, but only a thin memory of the happiness and excitement he used to feel stirred in his chest. He was glad when they finally passed over the railroad tracks and into the countryside, where it wasn't Big Day at all, only Saturday.

Uncle Zeno cleared his throat. "Does Christine Steppe know how bad you're in love with her?"

Jim started, then smiled a little for the second time that morning. "What makes you think I'm in love with Christine Steppe?"

"If you were any more in love with her, we'd have to bury you."

"Being in love never killed anybody."

"You know that ain't right. Being in love is like getting run over. Sometimes it kills you and sometimes it don't."

Jim turned away from Uncle Zeno and stared into the ditch winding by.

"I don't want to talk about it," he said.

"All right, then. We won't talk about it."

"But she's a good girl, Uncle Zeno. I think she's about the best person I ever met."

"I never said she wasn't."

"And I know she loves me, too, but Bucky Bucklaw has told everybody that she's his girlfriend, even though she's not, and since her granddaddy only has one arm and works for Bucky's daddy, she can't go out with me, or Mr. Bucklaw might run the whole bunch of them off, and then what would they do?"

"I don't know."

"And I hate Bucky's guts. He's a terrible baseball player, and I'm sick of him assuming everything in the world belongs to him just because his name is Bucklaw, and I wish he would just, well, die."

"*Jim!*"

"But I *do*. I wish he would die and then I wish his sorry hide would burn in hell."

"You stop it right there," Uncle Zeno said. "That's enough. I don't ever want to hear you say that about anybody. I don't care who it is."

"But it's not fair, what he's doing to her."

"I don't care if it's fair or not. Wishing somebody dead is a terrible thing, a sinful thing, and wishing they would burn in hell is even worse. I want you to be a better man than that."

"But I'm not a better man than that."

"You have to choose to be a good man," Uncle Zeno said. "You have to choose every minute of every day. As soon as you don't, you're lost."

Jim didn't feel like listening to another one of Uncle Zeno's lectures about life, so he tried to head it off. "Fine," he said. "I'll choose to be a good man."

"All right, then."

They rode in silence for a mile or so, but Jim was still angry. "What do y'all have against Chrissie?" he asked.

"I don't know that we have anything against her," Uncle Zeno said. "She might be the best girl to ever come down the mountain. You just need to remember that when you get tangled up with somebody, you get tangled up with their whole family."

"What's wrong with her family? I met her folks. They just seem poor, is all."

"Oh, the McAbees are all right, I guess. Hard times just run 'em down after Nub got his arm cut off. It's Injun Joe that worries me."

"What's wrong with him?"

"He ain't worth killing, that's what."

"Now, how is what I said about Bucky different than what you just said about Chrissie's daddy?"

"I never said I wanted to kill Injun Joe. I just said he wasn't *worth* killing."

"And that's not sinful?"

Uncle Zeno stared resolutely ahead.

"Oh, come on, now," Jim said. "Don't be a hypocrite."

"All right, then, daggummit, Doc, have it your way. It was sinful. I shouldn't have said it. I'll repent for it after while, but that's between me and the Lord. Right now maybe I just want to enjoy it for a minute."

"I think I know why you hate him so much."

"You do, huh?"

"Chrissie told me that you and her mama almost got married."

"Is that right?"

"And I met her mama that day I took Chrissie home. She said to tell you hello."

"Well, wasn't that nice of her."

"And I bet y'all broke up because of Injun Joe."

"And how do you figure this is any of your business?"

Jim shrugged. "If Chrissie can ever figure out how to get out from under the Bucklaws, I'm going to try to marry her, which would make her parents my in-laws."

"You know her daddy's full-blooded, don't you?"

"So?"

"So Chrissie's half Cherokee."

"What difference does that make?"

"I'm just doing the arithmetic. Your babies would be one-quarter Indian. Is that all right with you?"

"It doesn't bother me," Jim said. "They'd still be half Chrissie."

"What if people talked?"

"Since when do we care about people talking? And surely you're not saying that all Indians are bad."

"I don't know nothing about Indians. I don't know if Injun Joe was trouble because he was an Indian, or if he was trouble because he was trouble, but he was already bad news the day he got off the train. I've only ever met one Indian, and he was a bad one. That's all I'm saying."

"That doesn't mean Chrissie's going to turn out bad," Jim said.

"Sometimes the apple don't fall far from the tree."

"And sometimes it does."

"You don't look for apples in a peach orchard, Doc."

"That doesn't make a bit of sense, Uncle Zeno. Is she an apple or a peach? And you never told me if I was right about you and Chrissie's mama."

Uncle Zeno never took his eyes off the road. "If I tell you how it was this once, will you not ask me about it again?"

"Just this once," Jim said. "That'll do."

"The first time I ever laid eyes on Nancy McAbee was at the brush arbor revival in 1916. They built the brush arbor up on the mountain because it was a little cooler than it was down here, and the revival lasted the better part of a week. It was always the second week in July, after everybody had laid their crops by, and people would come from all over. They'd load up in their wagons and head up the mountain and camp out and go to the meetings. They would have four or five preachers there at one time, so when one got wore out with preaching, somebody else could start in. There'd always be a bunch of people get saved or rededicated, and the preachers would take turns baptizing them in the creek, and you heard tell that sometimes when the weather was hot, people got rededicated just because the water was cold.

"That was the year Corrie and Allie and I sang. We had just won the Associational ribbon for the first time, and they asked us to come up and sing at the brush arbor. You should have heard Allie sing back then. He could sing alto pretty as any girl. He can still sing that high, but he won't do it anymore because people made fun of him. Now he'll only sing lead or tenor, as you know, and we don't win the ribbon because there's not enough space between his voice and mine, and you can tell him I said so. Anyway, we had a buckboard then with a hoop top on it, and we had a matched set of white mules named Caesar and Augustus, which you've heard tell about, and me and Mama and Daddy and your uncles and Cissy loaded the wagon and went up for the revival. Me and Corrie and Allie sang every morning and every evening at the start of the service.

"The first or second day of the meeting, I was up there singing, and I looked out in the pews and saw the prettiest little brown-headed girl I'd ever seen. You ever seen a chestnut-colored mare? Well, that's the color Nancy's hair was then. And you wouldn't believe how fair her skin was. So instead of thinking about what I was singing, I was thinking about who that little girl was, and how I could get to know her. This was right after Nub had got his arm cut off at the sawmill. He still looked awful and he was so weak he could hardly get around and they hadn't figured out yet how they were going to live and they came to the brush arbor to pray about it. At one of the services, I remember, we took up a love offering for them.

"One evening after supper, before they started the service, I was watering and brushing Caesar and Augustus down at the creek, and I looked up and saw

Nancy standing on the other bank. All of a sudden she was just there. I didn't even hear her come out of the laurel. When she saw me looking at her she said, 'Where'd you get them white mules?'

"I said, 'At the white mule store. Where'd you get them brown eyes?'

"And she said, 'At the brown eye store.'

"After that I acted like I wasn't going to say anything else. It was always my experience that girls liked you better if you pretended you didn't care anything about them. So I didn't even look at her. When she didn't turn around and go back in the laurel, I knew I was in good shape. After a minute she said, 'One of your brothers sings like a girl.'

"And I said, 'That'd be Allie.'

"She said, 'And he's got a name like a girl, too.'

"I just kept brushing whatever mule it was I was brushing.

"Then she said, 'What's your other brother's name?'

"And I said, 'Corrie.'

"She said, 'And that's a girl's name. Do you have a girl's name, too?'

"I said, 'My name's Colleen. What's yours?' Colleen was my mother's name, of course, but it was the first one I could think of.

"She thought about it a minute and said, 'Bill.'

"And I said, 'Bill, do you want to go walking with me after the service?'

"And she said, 'Colleen, that sounds good.'

"The funny thing about the meeting at the brush arbor was that a whole lot more courting went on up there than you might think. Men who might get their gun and shoot at you if you showed up on a Sunday afternoon in the bright sunshine and asked to speak to their daughter, for some reason up on the mountain would let you go walking with that same daughter after the evening service and it pitch-black dark. I figure it was because back then the roads were bad, and the only people you ever saw were the same bunch who lived in your settlement that you went to school with during the week and church with on Sunday, and most of them were already your cousins, anyway. It was just hard to find somebody to go out with. So, at the brush arbor, while everybody did pay attention to the preaching and the singing and the Holy Spirit came down and people got anointed and baptized, like a regular revival, a lot of boys and girls were looking for somebody they could marry. That's just how it worked. You might not believe it today, but back then boys and girls just couldn't wait for the lay-by time so they could get up to the brush arbor. And when you didn't have a girlfriend, you thought about the brush arbor all year long.

"That first evening, Nancy and I were holding hands before we got out of sight. I still remember how pretty it was. After you got away from the wagons a little bit, you could look back toward the camping ground and see all the campfires burning through

the trees and the lanterns hanging up over the wagons, and you could hear the mules stomping around
on their pickets and snuffling in their feed bags or
cropping on the grass, and you could hear the water
running in the creek. If you walked far enough down
the trail, you'd come out in the bald, where you could
see down in the valley. If you looked hard enough,
you might see a lamp or two burning way off in the
distance at some farmhouse or other, but mostly it
was just dark and still and quiet and up overhead was
the moon and the black sky and all the stars."

"Did you kiss her?"

"Of course I kissed her. And after I kissed her, just
that one time, I didn't care anything about any of the
other little girls I'd been courting down here. I'd liked
all of them just fine before Nancy came along, but
after I met up with Nancy, they just didn't interest
me none. We were going steady before the end of the
revival. The only problem, of course, was that she
lived up on the mountain, and I lived down here. I
had to work six days a week, so Sunday was the only
day I could see her. I'd get up before daylight and
saddle Caesar and ride up the mountain and get
there in time for preaching. Then I'd take dinner
with her and her mama and daddy. Of course, I always made sure I had a ham with me, or a chicken, or
a peck of potatoes, since I knew they couldn't afford
to feed me. Nub had got hurt at Rad Carson's sawmill.
They were running a load of ties one day the belt
broke and snapped his arm off about six inches above

the elbow. Radford felt awful about it, of course, and would've kept Nub on, doing something or other, but Nub felt like that was charity and went on his way. So, I made sure I carried food up there with me when I went to see Nancy. After dinner we would go walking, or sit by the fire if it was cold and pop popcorn or shell walnuts. Then I'd saddle up and ride down the mountain and get home after dark. It wasn't so bad as long as the weather was warm, but when it turned off cold or it was raining, it was a pretty doggone miserable trip. And if you think that road's bad now, you should have seen it then. During the week we wrote letters back and forth."

"When did Injun Joe show up?"

"Hold on, now. Nobody at our house wants to talk about Injun Joe and Nancy McAbee. And I don't want you talking about them to anybody else. You understand?"

"Yes, sir."

"All right, then. Injun Joe. One day, around the time of the brush arbor meeting where I met Nancy, he just got off the train. Nobody around here had ever laid eyes on him before that. He was from somewhere or other up above Cherokee, and he said he'd gone to college down in Raleigh but he'd got in some kind of fight and somebody or other had stole his money. It was quite a tale, and I don't know if there was any truth to it or not. He said he'd started out for home but didn't have the fare to make it all the way back to Dillsboro. He only got as far as Aliceville. If he'd made it to New Carpenter, we never would have heard tell of him. When he got off the train, he didn't have a dime to his name, and Daddy believed what he said and hired him."

"Chrissie's daddy used to work for us?"

"He didn't work for us long. We took him on as a hand, that was the only job we had, but Injun Joe didn't want to be a hand, he wanted to be the boss man. He'd only been here a day or two when he started coming up with ideas about how we could do this or that better than the way we'd been doing it for years."

"What's wrong with that?"

"Well, nothing, I don't guess, initiative's a good thing, but that's not what we were paying him for. We were paying him to work in the field, not tell us how we ought to run our mill or our cotton gin or rotate our crops or what kind of bull we ought to get."

"Were any of his ideas any good?"

"Sure, some of them were. I'll grant him that. Injun Joe was as smart a man as I ever met. He just didn't like his station in life. We noticed right off that he wouldn't have anything to do with the other field hands. He wouldn't even drink water out of the same jar they did. He always lined up to drink water out of our jar. And when dinnertime came, he wanted to come to the house and eat dinner with us. I've never seen anybody hate a black man as much as Injun Joe did."

"Did you let him come to the house?"

"We didn't quite know what to do, to be honest.

None of us had ever met an Indian. When he came to the house, he didn't go around the back, the way the field hands did. He just knocked right on the front door, which surprised us. Then when Cissy or who- ever opened the door, he didn't take his hat off. Mama thought that was awful forward."

"Did he quit?"

"No, we let him go. One day out in the field, we were picking cotton, and he said Abraham's son, Isaac, spit water on his shoe. Isaac's the one that moved to Chicago. I don't think you've ever met him. Now, Isaac might have spit on Joe, he had a temper on him, and maybe it was over the water jar, so I don't know. And it might have been an accident. Isaac said he didn't do it one way or the other. Whatever happened, Joe knocked Isaac down flat on his back and I fired him on the spot."

"Did you fire Isaac?"

"No. Abraham's people have been working here since slave times, and you give people who've worked for you that long the benefit of the doubt. Joe's just lucky I was there and Abraham didn't cut his throat."

"If you fired Injun Joe, how did he wind up mar- ried to Nancy?"

"After I fired Joe, he hated me as much as he hated a field hand. I guess he looked at me and saw every- thing he wanted but didn't have any way of getting, and he saw that I had taken a black man's part over his, in front of other black men. I always figured that he went after Nancy to get me back. But who knows?

Nancy'd been down to visit and had stayed overnight with us, and Joe'd seen her, of course, and maybe seeing her for the first time had the same effect on him that it had on me. I don't know. She was just the prettiest girl. After I fired him, he cleared his stuff out of the storeroom and took off. We figured he was going to walk back to Cherokee, but where he went was straight up the mountain. He worked for Rad Carson a while, but Radford didn't need a foreman any more than we did, he needed somebody to stack lumber, so he caught on with Arthur Bucklaw, working in the fruit trees. Joe said he'd gone down to Raleigh to study forestry, and apparently he had a way with trees and already knew how to graft and prune, and it wasn't long until he was Bucklaw's right-hand man. A lot of those apple and peach trees you see now up on the Bucklaw place Injun Joe planted. The apples have done real well, of course, but more often than not, frost gets the peaches."

"Back up," Jim said. "Did Injun Joe start courting Nancy while she was still your girlfriend?"

"I don't know if you could call it courting, exactly, he was way too smart for that, but he was always just . . . *around.* Nancy'd go down to the store on Saturday, and he'd be there. She'd be walking home from church with some of her girlfriends the Sundays I couldn't make it, and he'd pass them on the road and tip his hat. She'd be sitting on the porch stringing beans with her mama, and he'd just happen to pass by and stop in the edge of the yard and talk for a while.

If he found a bee tree, he'd bring them a comb of honey. It was all real innocent at first, nothing you could call him out on."

"Did you ever get in a fight with him?"

"No, sir. I did not."

"I might've had to fight him, if she'd been my girl-friend."

"I don't believe in fighting a man to keep him away from a woman. Either you can trust a woman or you can't. If you can trust her, nothing anybody can say is going to turn her head, and if you can't trust her, beating up every man who says howdy to her won't do you a bit of good."

"Didn't you worry about him, though?"

"Nah, although, looking back at it now, I obviously should have. As far as I was concerned, he was just some hothead Cherokee buck who didn't have two dimes to rub together. And I trusted Nancy. I never would have thought of Injun Joe as a rival in a million years. What put him over the top on me, though, was the war. The war was going hot and heavy then, and all you heard were people jawing back and forth about whether or not we were going to get in it, or whether or not we should get in it, or whose side we ought to get in it on, and then, in 'seventeen, of course, we got in it, and Wilson started up the draft. I registered, but they never called my number. And I didn't join. I thought about it and prayed about it and studied about it, and I just couldn't figure how I had a dog in that fight. I couldn't see how the king and his bunch

and the French and their bunch were any better than
the kaiser and his crowd. It seemed to me that everybody had just got bowed up for no good reason and
were going to get into it no matter what. I just couldn't
see how any of that mess had anything to do with
me or mine. I had too much work to do here. So I
didn't join.

"Of course boys from New Carpenter and Aliceville and up on the mountain did join, by the trainload, they just lined up to get in. Once we got in the
war, you'd read in the papers how the Germans were
raping nuns and hanging them from the church stee-
ples, and you'd read how they were marching down
the road with babies stuck on their bayonets, but it
didn't seem to me like much of it could be true. A lot
of people did think it was true, though, and it wasn't
long before most of the fighting-age boys around here
had either gotten drafted or joined up and gone off
to France. When I didn't go, and didn't go, people
started to talk. And when boys from here started getting killed, they started getting mad."

"At you?"

"At me. At Nancy. At Corrie and Allie and Mama
and Daddy. Your mama. All of us. Homer Ruppe was
the first one from here to get killed. He got his foot
hung in a ladder on the troopship going over and fell
and managed to break his neck before he even got to
France. It wasn't but a day or two after his folks got
notified that somebody wrung a chicken's neck and
threw it up on our porch. It seemed like people just

got mean all of a sudden. Most of the time you can live your whole life and the crowd won't even notice you, but once it singles you out, you can't get away from it. People are like a pack of dogs that way. They threw chickens up in the yard, we had a hound or two disappear, they put manure in the mailbox and threw a dead snake in the well, and somebody even painted a bad word on the side of the barn and we had to take off from work and paint over it. And it's all because I didn't join the army."

"You weren't a conscientious objector, were you?"

"No, sir. I was not. I was somebody who didn't get drafted. And not joining the service when I wasn't drafted was my Constitutional right. Injun Joe saw which way the wind was blowing, though, and he started to run me down bigger than any of them. Never to my face, I guess I would've had to fight him over that, but you'd hear tell down here how he was up on the mountain, flapping his jaws. Sometime along the way, he started running me down to Nancy, telling her how I was a coward, how I didn't care about my country, how I was going to let the kaiser march up the mountain and rape all the girls before I decided to do anything. I still rode up the mountain on Sundays to see Nancy, but I noticed that people up there stopped speaking to me after church and saying howdy when I passed them on the road, and I'd see them whispering when I went by. And it was hard on Nancy, I know it was. If I was the coward, then she was the coward's girl. She started asking me, wasn't I going to join the army, wasn't I going to join the army, was I afraid of the Germans, and this or that, and it finally got to be a hard place between us. We'd gotten engaged Christmas in nineteen seventeen, and the next March she broke up with me. Injun Joe joined up sometime in there, and with me out of the way he somehow talked Nancy into marrying him before he shipped out. One Sunday afternoon, they just walked down to the preacher's house. To this day I don't know how in the world he managed it.

"Then things just went from bad to worse. Coran and Al got tired of people running us down and throwing dead chickens in the yard, and as soon as they turned eighteen, they run off and joined the army without telling anybody they were going."

"I never knew Uncle Coran and Uncle Al were in the army."

"They weren't in it long. The war ended, thank the Lord, before they finished their training, but before they could get mustered out, most of the boys in their camp came down with the flu and they got quarantined. When they finally got out of quarantine, they started on home, but the flu beat them here. As you know, that's how Mama and Daddy died. The flu killed fourteen people in Aliceville that year. Later on, everybody said that Coran and Al were the ones who brought it here, but that was a bald-faced lie. Mama and Daddy were already on their deathbeds before their train even got here, and it's all wrote down in the Bible if anybody wants to see it. Of course, after all the funerals and the flu talk, Coran and Al couldn't even get a girl to look at them. Between that and me not going to the war and Mama and Daddy dying and us trying to figure out how to run things on our own, I guess that's how we all got set in our ways and ended up bachelors."

"Y'all could still get married," Jim said.

"Oh, it's nice to think so, I guess, but I figure that ship sailed off to France or somewhere a long time ago. Nancy McAbee was the only girl I ever came close to marrying."

"What did Chrissie mean when she told me she didn't know where her daddy was?"

"If I tell you, you have to promise you won't mention it to a soul."

"I promise."

"Because if this got out, it would bring hardship down on Nancy and that girl, and they don't need any more of that."

"I swear I won't tell anybody. What did he do?"

"He robbed a bank, and he shot a policeman. The law can't find him. That's why Nancy and Chrissie came home."

In New Carpenter, Jim sat in Uncle Zeno's truck and stared at the window of the hardware store. Most of what he could see in the glass was the reflection of the world behind him: the line of farm trucks sniffing out parking places; people scurrying between the awnings of the stores across the street as though it were still raining; the lettering on the store windows backward and foreign-looking. All he could see inside the hardware store were a display of canning jars and the occasional passing shadow of a clerk or customer. Uncle Zeno was in there somewhere, but Jim didn't know where. He had elected to wait in the truck rather than going in to gawk at the fishing plugs and the pocketknives and the dark, glamorous pistols. He thought he was getting a little old for that.

It seemed as though there were good reasons to be mad at all of the people in Uncle Zeno's story and — save Injun Joe and the people who ran down Jim's family — an equal number of good reasons not to be. He was disappointed in Uncle Zeno for not joining the army but simultaneously proud of him for continuing to ride that white mule up the mountain, even though the world had turned against him. It was easy for him to work up a satisfying case of contempt for Chrissie's mother but equally easy to feel sorry for her when he considered how hard her life had turned out. She had obviously picked the wrong man. And while her choosing Injun Joe had somehow locked Uncle Zeno into a permanent bachelorhood, it had also eventually led to Jim watching Chrissie walk around the front of the bus on the first day of school. If Uncle Zeno had married Nancy, Chrissie — if she had been born at all — would have been his cousin. He didn't know what to think about her lying to him about Injun Joe. He knew that if word got out, she would probably be hounded out of school, but he also wondered, now that she had proved she was capable of it, if she was lying to him about anything else. Maybe she really did love Bucky; maybe she just wanted to string Jim along for fun, or as a spare. No matter how Jim tried to follow the story in his mind, it never led to a satisfactory destination, only to a new place to begin thinking about it. Eventually the door of the store swung open and Uncle Zeno appeared with a logging chain looped over one shoulder. He threw the chain heavily into the bed of the truck before climbing into the cab.

"What's wrong with the chain you got back at the house?" Jim asked.

"Nothing, I don't guess. I just thought it might be handy to have a longer one."

"Do you still love her?"

Uncle Zeno reached for the starter, but paused. "Nah," he eventually said. "Let's go home."

Back in Aliceville, Uncle Zeno parked the truck in the yard. Jim got out and walked backward toward the porch. The sky had cleared slightly, and on top of the hill the rides spun in a thin sunlight that neither looked nor felt quite warm. A breeze had freshened in the north, and on it rode the manufactured screams of people pretending to be scared, the crazed hooting of the calliope, and the good carnival smells of sawdust and popcorn and engine exhaust and burned sugar. Jim closed his eyes and inhaled deeply, but just once, then turned his back on Big Day and

strode into the house. Mama's door was closed. Uncle
Zeno tiptoed down the hallway and out the back door.
Jim thought about going squirrel hunting, but the
woods seemed too far away and he dreaded the prospect of cleaning whatever he shot. He retreated into
his room and lay down on the bed and tried reading
the Zane Grey novel that had come in the mail that
week, but he put the book down as soon as the penniless cowboy protagonist fell in love with the raven-
haired daughter of the ranch owner. That happened
in all the books. He crossed his hands on his chest
and decided to think about baseball. When he opened
his eyes it was dusk outside and the uncles were talking around the kitchen table and Mama was calling
him to supper.

Dance Lessons

JIM WALKED up the hill toward the school with Dennis Deane. The breeze that had come up during the afternoon had blown the clouds off to the south before falling quiet at sunset, leaving the air chilled but pleasant, the stars close overhead. Up ahead the school building was dark, except for the tall gymnasium windows which threw light across the broad, sloping backs of the cars parked in the school-yard. In the distance Jim could hear the furious sawing of a fiddle, the *doom-Doom, doom-Doom, doom-Doom* of a bass, and the rumbling *choonk-Choonk choonka-choonk, choonk-Choonk choonka-choonk* of clogging square dancers. The band was a good one — Joe Doug Revis and the Cherry Bounce Boys, all the way from Whittier — but Jim had already decided that he wasn't going to dance with anybody, no matter what. Not pretty, rich girls from New Carpenter, nor wild mill-hill girls from the towns on the other side of the river, not even if they grabbed his hand and pleaded and tried to drag him onto the floor. The only reason he was going was so that everybody could see how miserable he was. And if nobody told Chrissie how miserable he was, the evening would be a waste of time.

Maybe, he thought, he should just forget about the dance altogether and go coon hunting. It wasn't too cold, the woods would be wet from the rain earlier in the day, and the dogs would be able to trail easily. He would have a hard time, however, dragging the uncles out of the gym and getting them to go with him. They didn't dance much, but they loved listening to a string band. And they hardly ever went coon hunting on Saturday night. They said it made them too sleepy during church the next day.

What Jim really wished was that he was going to the dance with Chrissie. They would dance for a while — only with each other — and when Mama and the uncles went home, he would drive her through the fields down to the river. On the way she would scoot up close beside him and he would hold her hand — except when he had to change gears. (Maybe, though, he could put his arm around her and work the clutch and she could change the gears.) At the river they would cuddle up in the rumble seat beneath a blanket and listen to the water and look at the stars. Chrissie's nose would be cold and he would feel it on his cheek when he kissed her.

Of course, Jim had never actually cuddled up with

a girl in the rumble seat of the Major, and his prospects didn't seem to be getting any better. Norma had steadfastly refused, and there was fat chance of getting Chrissie anywhere near his car. If he welded the rumble seat shut it wouldn't make any difference. He might as well sell the daggum car for all the good it was doing him. He looked over at Dennis Deane and disgustedly jammed his hands into the pockets of his jacket. Going to square dances with Dennis Deane was not how he had imagined spending his senior year.

"Tell me something," Dennis Deane said. "Why are we walking up this hill when you have a car?"

"Because the school is only three hundred yards from my house."

"But, Jim, it's a *steep* hill."

"Stop whining, Dennis Deane. I'm taking you home after the dance. Isn't that good enough for you?"

"Does that mean we're going steady?"

"Not hardly."

"Well, then I just might catch a ride home with somebody else."

"Who?"

"I don't know yet. I've cooked up a new secret saying to make girls fall in love with me, and I'm turning it loose tonight."

Jim waited.

"You wanna hear it?" asked Dennis Deane.

"Nope."

"Oh, come on."

"If I let you tell me, will you shut up?"

"I promise I'll never speak to you again as long as I live."

"Then you've got a deal," Jim said.

"Okay. You be the girl."

"I don't want to be the girl."

"Well, you can't be me, because you don't know the secret saying."

"I don't want to be you, either."

"Everybody wants to be me."

"No, they don't."

"Damn it, Jim, will you shut up for just one minute and listen to my secret saying? I need to practice it before the shooting starts."

Jim huffed but didn't say anything.

"That's better," Dennis Deane said. "You're a girl."

"I'm a girl."

"I walk up to you and I say, 'Hey there, Red Riding Hood, I'm the big, bad wolf.'"

Jim stopped in the road and stared at Dennis Deane. "That's it?"

"Of course not. Then I say, 'Do you want to see my long, bushy tail?'"

Jim shook his head and started again up the hill. "That's about the stupidest thing I ever heard," he said.

"Then how about, 'I'll huff and I'll puff and I'll pull your drawers down'?"

"That's even worse. Now you've got stuff from two different stories. It's not even the same wolf."

"Well, if you're so smart, let's hear your secret saying to make girls fall in love with you."

"Have a nice trip," Jim said.

"I don't get it."

"That's because there's nothing to get. If I had a secret saying to make girls fall in love with me, I wouldn't be walking up this daggum hill with you, now, would I?"

Dennis Deane was quiet for a few steps. "You just need to forget about Pocahontas," he said.

"I've asked you to not call her names," said Jim.

"She's Bucky Bucklaw's girlfriend, for God's sake. Don't you even wonder what kind of girl would go out with an idiot like that in the first place?"

"You don't know anything about it."

"And you keep saying that. Meantime, there's a whole gym full of *available* girls right up there, Jim, just raring to go. All you have to do is pick one out."

"Just raring to go, are they, Dennis Deane?"

"You know they are. Nothing makes a girl go crazy like square dancing. That's a scientific fact."

"I must've slept through that class."

"But it's *true*," Dennis Deane said. "All that clogging gets everything bouncing up and down and makes it all loosey-goosey and lovey-dovey."

"You belong in Broughton with the rest of the nuts."

"Just try it out, if you don't believe me. Ask somebody to dance. I dare you. You can even use my secret saying."

"Thanks, but no thanks."

When they reached the schoolyard, Jim threaded his way through the haphazardly parked cars and trucks with Dennis Deane close on his heels. The gymnasium windows were so brightly lit that the glare made it difficult for him to see where he was going.

"I can't see too good," Dennis Deane said.

"That ain't exactly news."

"What if we run up on Injun Joe out here in the dark?"

"We ain't gonna run up on Injun Joe."

"How do you know? I heard he might be anywhere."

"You don't know what you're talking about."

"Injun Joe?" Dennis Deane whispered. "Hello? Chief? You out here?"

"Cut it out," Jim said. "You're not funny."

He spotted a small group of grown men smoking up ahead and circled around to avoid them. Anybody hanging around the schoolyard during the dance was probably drinking, and anybody drinking would sooner or later be looking for a fight.

"You ought to be more worried about lintheads, anyway."

"I ain't worried about nobody," said Dennis Deane. "Lintheads. Injuns. Tall girls. Bring 'em on."

When they finally reached the front steps, it felt

like home base in some not particularly fun playground game against much older boys. From the
landing he turned and looked back across the schoolyard. With the light now at his back, it didn't look
scary at all.

Dennis Deane suddenly punched him on the arm.

"Ow. What was that for?"

"Daggummit, Jim. This is our last Big Day before
we graduate."

"So?"

"So just forget about her. Have some fun for once
in your life."

"Go show somebody your bushy tail."

"Oh, I'm planning on it."

Inside the gymnasium, the floor was ringed with a
crowd seven or eight people deep. The air was hot
and close, stale with cigarette smoke, even though the
tall windows were raised. The music — a reel Jim
didn't recognize — thumped and twanged over top
of the thunderous stomping of the dancers. Jim could
feel the floor spring beneath his feet in perfect time
to the song and wondered what kept it from falling in.
When he worked his way to the edge of the floor, he
found squares of dancers cutting needle-and-thread
figures on what seemed like every available inch of
open space. When the sharply amplified voice of the
caller sang out, "All join hands," the squares unraveled and formed into two large circles, one inside the
other. The circles slowly began to spin in opposite directions, a sight that never failed to impress Jim, no

matter what kind of mood he was in. When the circles got up to speed, they generated a breeze that felt cool on his face. The breeze carried the scents of denim and gingham and calico and hair oil and tobacco and sweat and perfume and hot breath all rolled into a single warm smell that seemed somehow manufactured by the music. Jim turned around to ask Dennis Deane if he could feel the breeze, but Dennis Deane had disappeared.

At the far end of the gym floor, the Cherry Bounce Boys frailed at their instruments on the small stage, beneath a printed banner bearing their name and an advertisement for flour. They wore white shirts and red string ties and matching white cowboy hats, except for Joe Doug himself, whose black hat, cocked just so, identified him as the leader. Romeo Paris was the caller. In front of the band he gripped the microphone with both hands and rocked back and forth and smiled broadly at the spinning circles he had conjured. He was a preacher from New Carpenter who called cattle auctions and square dances on the side. The uncles explained away his name and slightly scandalous avocations by pointing out that he was a Presbyterian. Jim tapped his foot along with the music but stopped as soon as he noticed. He didn't want anyone to think he was having a good time.

The Cherry Bounce Boys played the chorus through one more time and, on a signal from Joe Doug, ended the song on a shave-and-a-haircut, two-bits. The circles slowed and stopped and began to dissolve almost instantly, like smoke rings. Romeo Paris announced that the band was taking a break. The dancers, some of them still clapping, drifted past Jim toward the refreshment table and the door, their voices a happy buzz whose component parts were indistinguishable. Over there, Mama was leaving the floor holding on to Uncle Coran's elbow with both hands, laughing as he told her a joke. Mama loved to square-dance as much as anybody Jim knew but would do so only with him or her brothers. Over here, Norma was thanking Buster Burnette for the dance and trying politely to back away. Jim smiled bitterly. Buster had bad acne and was dumb as a rock and had no idea he was a charity case. Jim would try to remember to sic Dennis Deane on him Monday morning.

He was looking around for Ellie Something, to make sure she knew how unhappy he was so she could tell Chrissie, when he saw Chrissie walking toward him, escorted by an older guy he had never seen before. The guy was tall, with dark, slicked-back hair. He wore sharply pressed suit pants and a shirt and necktie and two-tone gangster shoes. His necktie had flowers painted on it. Jim felt instantly ashamed of the dungarees and high-tops and letter jacket he was wearing, the uniform he wore every single day of his life, which identified him as nothing more than a boy.

When the stranger put his hand in the middle of Chrissie's back to steer her through the crowd, Jim felt a sudden, sharp pain like a punch in his stomach. The guy was obviously Chrissie's *date*, not someone who had simply asked her to dance. She had ridden all the way down here in his *car* — a Pontiac, at least, judging from the looks of the guy, maybe even a Buick — and after the dance they would drive together all the way back up the mountain. Somewhere along the way, the guy would pull off the road into some dark spot and cut the headlights; Chrissie would turn to him and smile. Jim's soul flooded with hatred, not just for the stranger but for Chrissie. She had obviously lied to him about her predicament with Bucky Bucklaw just to get him off her back, and now this stranger was going to put his arms around her and kiss her, when Jim could not.

When Chrissie saw Jim she stopped for a moment and stared. Jim saw her eyes widen. He had caught her. He stared back at her with angry satisfaction, slowly shaking his head in disapproval. She turned and stood on her tiptoes and whispered something into the guy's ear, then turned and started quickly for the door near the bandstand on the far side of the gym. Before the guy followed Chrissie, he stared blankly in Jim's direction but obviously didn't know who or what he was looking for. "You're looking for me, chief," Jim said, but the crowd was too noisy, the stranger too far away, to hear him.

Jim watched them cross the floor and leave the gym together, then forced his way through the crowd and into the hallway. He heard Mama call after him, but he didn't stop. He thought he was going to be sick, and he knew that the restroom would be crowded. He banged open the door to the stairway and ran up the steps into the darkened hallway on the second floor. He ran past Miss Brown's room and kicked open the door of the bathroom, where he startled two young boys, maybe ten years old, who were leaning against the sinks importantly smoking cigarettes.

"Get out of here," Jim said.

"You ain't my daddy," the larger of the two boys said.

Jim felt himself shaking. He stepped forward and slapped the cigarette out of the kid's mouth.

"Get out of here now!" he yelled.

The boys clawed at the door in a panic as they tried to get away. Jim listened to them running down the hallway. He went into a stall and sat down on the toilet and shoved the heels of his hands into his eyes but could not stop seeing Chrissie turn toward the stranger inside the stranger's darkened car. The stranger stroked her hair. Jim got on his knees in front of the toilet and waited to throw up, but nothing happened. He couldn't get sick and he couldn't get better. He thought about praying but didn't want to humble himself, to anybody, when he hadn't done anything wrong. He was the one who had been lied to. Eventually he became aware of the dull percussion of the stomping dancers working its way through the floor. He got up and washed his face. From the mirror over the sink some stupid boy in a stupid jacket stared back at him. He trudged back downstairs and into the gym, even though it was the last place on earth he wanted to be. Sure enough, as soon as he shoved his way through the crowd, he spotted Chrissie happily dancing with her date. She laughed as she ducked and twirled beneath the guy's arm.

Jim spent the rest of the evening watching her. He watched her while she danced, the way her hair bounced and jumped from side to side on her back as she clogged, marking time to the music, a sight that twisted his heart like a rag. He watched her while she drank punch and talked with the stranger on the sidelines during the few songs they sat out. She glanced at him only occasionally, never long enough to see in his eyes how much he despised her. The stranger never looked at him at all. The Cherry Bounce Boys played what seemed like ten thousand songs. Romeo Paris called dance after dance after dance. He knew all the dances in the world. When Jim pushed up his sleeve and looked at his watch, he was surprised to see that it was only ten minutes until ten, and not the darkest middle of the longest night of his life.

Ellie Something tugged on his sleeve.

He leaned toward her so that she could hear him over the music. "Go away," he said.

"I need to talk to you."

"I don't want to hear it, whatever it is."

"I've got a message from Chrissie."

Ellie Something's cheeks and lips were flushed, and she stared at him intently. He raised his eyebrows and waited.

"Chrissie says, cut it out."

"Cut what out?"

"You know what."

"Tell Chrissie she can kiss my long, bushy tail."

Ellie Something looked startled. "What did you just say?" she asked.

"You heard me," Jim said. "Now, go away."

"No," she said firmly. "Chrissie's my friend and you're going to get her in trouble."

"How can I possibly get somebody like that in trouble? She's already a liar and a tramp."

"I'm not going to tell her you said that."

"I don't care what you tell her."

Ellie Something stomped her foot.

"I ought to just slap you silly," she said. "That boy she's with is Bucky's cousin, from over by Casar. The only way the Bucklaws would let her come down here to a dance was if that boy right there brought her. This is her senior year, too, you know, and this is her Big Day as much as it is your Big Day, and you stand over here like some kind of hotshot, staring at people like you know everything, when you don't know nothing about anything."

"Wait a minute," Jim said. "That's Bucky's *cousin?*"

"From over by Casar. He brought her all the way down

here as a *favor*. All Chrissie wanted to do was come to a dance before she graduated. Just one. Her daddy never would let her go to a dance in Oklahoma, and now she's got the Bucklaws to worry about. So the last thing she needs is you treating her like she's trash."

Jim stared darkly at the stranger. "I'm sick of the Bucklaws," he said. "I'm sick of them thinking they own everybody and I'm sick of them pushing people around."

"She's not crazy about them, either, you know."

"What kind of car does he drive?"

Ellie Something's eyes widened comically. She grabbed his sleeve and twisted it.

"No!" she cried. "Promise me you won't do anything! You'll get her in so much trouble. The Bucklaws might make her quit school and stay in that awful cabin, and then she won't be able to go anywhere ever again in her whole life. *Promise* me, if you love her as much as you act like you do, you won't do anything at all."

"Let go," Jim said.

"Promise me."

"All right, already. I promise."

Ellie Something patted the wrinkles on his sleeve. "Okay," she said. "Good."

"I just wanted to know what kind of car the jerk drove. That's all."

"Oh. Sorry. I thought you wanted to fight him. It's a black one, I think."

"It ain't him I want to fight," Jim said. "Will you give her a message for me?"

"I don't know. It depends on what it is."

"Tell her I said . . .'"

"That you love her?" She batted her eyes at him and giggled.

Jim blushed. "Oh, Lord, Ellie, *no.* Just tell her I said that . . . she looks nice when she dances."

"For such a stuck-up boy, you sure can come up with some sweet things to say."

"Cut it out," he said.

Norma and Dennis Deane appeared on his other side. "Jim," Norma interrupted, "we need to talk."

On the dance floor, Chrissie was waltzing gracefully with Bucky's cousin. Jim had never learned how to waltz, even though Mama had offered to teach him. He wondered who had taught Chrissie.

"I'm tired of talking," he said.

"You're gonna want to hear this," Dennis Deane said. "Hey, there, Ellie Something."

Ellie Something's face instantly went red. "Hey, there, Dennis Deane."

"Jim, this is *very, very, very* important," said Norma. She leaned around Jim and spoke to Ellie Something. "If you'll excuse us, please."

Ellie Something placed her hand on Jim's arm. "Don't worry, *Jim,*" she said. "I'll give you-know-who your message." Then she crinkled her nose at Norma and stalked off.

"What was that all about?" Norma asked. "Who's that nosy little girl delivering your messages to?"

"Nobody," Jim said.

"What were you two talking about, anyway?" asked Dennis Deane.

"*Nothing,*" Jim said. "I thought y'all said you had something important to tell me."

"We do," said Norma. She tilted her head toward the gym entrance. "Don't stare, but look over there and tell me what you see."

Jim moved his head slightly and looked toward the door. The kid whose cigarette he had slapped onto the floor was pointing in his direction. Gathered around him were eight or ten tough-looking guys in their twenties. Mill hands. They were all staring his way. The kid was talking a mile a minute.

"Uh-oh," Jim said.

"Please tell me you didn't slap that little boy," said Norma.

"I didn't exactly *slap* him," Jim said. "But I can see why he might be telling people that."

"I don't know what you did to him, but the little bastard's telling every linthead he can find that you slapped him in the face," Dennis Deane said. "Norma heard him out in the hall and came and got me."

Jim looked around wildly. "Are the uncles still here?"

"No," Norma said. "They left about an hour ago."

"So that makes you General Custer," Dennis Deane said.

"We've got to get you out of here," said Norma.

"How?"

"Door by the stage," Dennis Deane said. "Before they get organized and head us off at the pass."

"Dance with me," said Norma.

"Now?" Jim said. "Are you crazy?"

"No, silly. Waltz me over to that door."

"But I don't know *how* to waltz."

"You daggum better learn," said Dennis Deane.

Norma held out her arms. "Remember. It just goes one-two-three, one-two-three."

Jim sought out Chrissie and Bucky's cousin and watched them and silently counted. Then he looked over at the gym door. The kid was still talking and pointing. Jim had never seen so many lintheads in his life. Wasn't anybody working second shift?

"One-two-three, one-two-three," he said out loud.

"All right, all right," Dennis Deane said. "Everybody knows how to count. Now just count your way over to that damn door and run like hell."

Jim took Norma's right hand in his left and placed his right hand in the middle of her back. Norma smiled and blushed a little. She looked very pretty. What had he been thinking when he broke up with her? She wasn't *that* bad. He looked down at his feet, which looked huge and so far showed no inclination to start dancing.

"One-two-three," Norma said.

Jim rocked back and forth without quite going anywhere.

Norma giggled. "Stop moving your lips," she said.
"I'm counting."

"Count faster," said Dennis Deane. "Maybe skip some numbers."

"Move me out onto the floor," said Norma. "No. Left foot first. Good. Here we go. Here we go. One-two-three. One-two-three. Don't go straight toward the door, or they'll know what you're doing. But don't get us too close to them, either. They might grab you. And stop stepping on my feet."

He looked down. His feet didn't seem so much to be dancing as they did violently pursuing Norma's. "Sorry," he said.

"Stop looking at your feet," she said.

"I'm not. I'm looking at your feet."

"Well, stop it. You've got to watch where you're going."

"Norma, stop leading."

"I'm not leading," she said. "I'm just trying to keep you from running over somebody."

Jim turned Norma so that she was facing the door. "Are they coming?"

"No. But they're still talking to that little boy. Keep going."

He tried turning Norma again so that he could look for himself, but ran solidly into someone behind him. When he turned he found himself face-to-face with Bucky's cousin.

"Careful, there, friend," the guy said.

"Sorry," said Jim.

Chrissie looked furious. She stared angrily at Jim and mouthed the words, *Leave. Me. Alone.*

"Excuse me?" Norma said.

"Sorry," Jim said again, his face burning. "I'm sorry. Well, bye." He gave up trying to waltz and began pushing Norma more or less directly toward the door.

Norma tried to look back over her shoulder. "Slow down, Jim," she said. "Slow down. You've got to make it look good."

"I don't care how it looks," he said.

As they passed the bandstand, Joe Doug looked down at them and winked and touched his hat with his forefinger. Norma stepped away from Jim but held on to his left hand. She pushed open the door. On the landing outside, Romeo Paris was smoking a cigarette, which he hurriedly tried to hide in his palm when he saw them.

"Excuse us, Reverend," Norma said, starting down the steps.

"Where are you two running off to in such a hurry in the dark?" he asked.

"To see a man about a dog," Jim said.

"Pray for us," Norma called over her shoulder.

At the bottom of the stairs, still holding Norma's hand, Jim broke into a run. They sprinted around the corner of the building and into the schoolyard, where they crouched and ducked between the parked cars. With the light from the gym behind him, he had no trouble seeing and was able to pick a path through the maze at almost full speed. When they cleared the cars, they sprinted down the driveway toward town. They had a good head start, but Norma wasn't very fast. He couldn't tell over the sound of her shoes scuffing the pavement if anybody was chasing them. Below them, all three of the uncles' houses were dark. Everybody had already gone to bed. *Wake up,* Jim thought. *Wake up!* When they reached the bottom of the hill they crossed the highway without breaking stride. The road felt like the boundary of enemy territory, so he slowed and looked back over his shoulder. He didn't immediately see anyone, so he stopped altogether for a better look. He heard Norma panting beside him. He felt a pulse pounding in his palm but couldn't tell if it was hers or his. Nobody was chasing them. Jim felt strangely disappointed. A minute ago, he had been important enough for a posse of lintheads to want to kill him. Now he wasn't important at all. He should have stayed and fought, even if it meant getting beaten up.

"It worked," Norma said.

"Stupid lintheads," Jim said.

"That's an ugly word, Jim."

"Don't start on me, Norma."

"I'm just saying they can't help where they work."

"Yeah, but they can help being stupid," he said. He turned away from the school, dragging Norma behind him.

At Depot Street, they turned automatically toward Uncle Coran's store. When they were dating, he had

walked her home from his house by cutting between
the store and the building where Uncle Coran kept
fertilizer and feed. Norma lived on Raleigh Street, on
the other side of the cotton gin. As they passed the
shed where Jim parked the Major, he stopped and
pulled Norma toward him and wrapped his arms
around her and kissed her. When she started to say
something, he kissed her again. To his surprise, she
began kissing him back. She put her hand on the
back of his neck. He had forgotten how good the lilac
soap she used smelled on her skin and how soft her
lips were. She was a good kisser when you could get
her to do it.

He pulled her into the shed and opened the rumble seat of the Major. He helped her over the fender
and into the back of the car. He climbed in after her
and began kissing her again. Every time he started to
think about running away from the lintheads, every
time he remembered the look on Chrissie's face as
she told him to leave her alone, he kissed Norma
harder. And every time he kissed her harder, she
kissed him back. When he reached inside her sweater
and rubbed the front of her blouse, she did not stop
him. Back when they were dating, she would have
slapped his knuckles raw for even trying that. That
she would let him put his hand inside her sweater
now, when she knew he loved Chrissie, suddenly made
him sad. Whatever he had been trying to hold up by
kissing Norma collapsed on top of him. He stopped

kissing her and leaned back and stared straight up into the blackest blackness he had ever seen. He knew it was only the underside of the shed roof, but he imagined it was the sky, without form and void, the stars burned out for good. When he turned to look at Norma, he could see that she was looking at him, but he couldn't make out her expression, only the whiteness of her skin, and the two deep holes where her eyes should have been.

"Norma," he said. "I . . ."

"Shh," she said, placing her fingers on his lips. "Don't."

"But . . ."

"Please don't apologize to me, Jim. That would be the worst thing you could say to me right now. I know you don't love me."

"Then why . . . ?"

She shrugged. "Because I still love you, I guess."

Jim miserably shook his head. "Oh, Norma," he said. "You shouldn't love me."

"You don't get to decide that, Jim. If I want to love you, I can. It's really, well, none of your business who I love."

"Why don't you just find another boyfriend?"

"Because I'm going to college in the fall. I'm going to be a math teacher, Jim, and I'm going to marry somebody who doesn't live in this little-bitty town. I'm going to learn advanced algebra and geometry and I hope trigonometry and calculus. And I'm going to live in a big town, like Charlotte, or Greensboro. But not here, Jim. Not in Aliceville."

"But you were going to marry me."

"You're not going to stay here any more than I am."

"I guess so," Jim said. "But right now I can't think of anyplace in the world I want to be. Here included."

"You don't have to think about that now." She picked up his hand in both of hers. She inhaled through her nose and sighed deeply. "I know it doesn't mean anything to you, but right now I wish you would kiss me some more."

"I don't understand you," he said. "You always said no when we were dating."

"Well, I'm going to tell you a secret, Jim, just this once. Saying no is the only power a girl has in this world. A girl who doesn't say no doesn't have anything at all."

Jim nodded. Chrissie said only no to him, and she had all the power in the world; Norma saying yes just made him feel sorry for her. He helped her down out of the Major and walked her over to Raleigh Street. They didn't talk on the way. Norma walked with her arms crossed but she refused Jim's letter jacket. On her front porch they hugged awkwardly, patting each other's back, just as the porch light blinked on.

"Well," Jim said, "some things never change."

Norma turned toward the door. "And some things do," she said.

BOOK III

Unexpected News

Target Practice

DENNIS DEANE was acting strange, or at least stranger than usual. First, he missed an entire week of school, although the uncles reported seeing him riding his bicycle all over town. But whenever they asked him if he needed a lift somewhere, or why he wasn't in school, or, finally, on Friday, why he had been riding his bicycle around in circles all week, he pretended not to hear them. He just kept pedaling. Then, when Jim drove to Dennis Deane's house Sunday afternoon to pick him up, he found Dennis Deane crouched in the scraggly troop of malnourished cedar trees across the driveway from the Deanes' mailbox. Jim stopped and rolled down the window.

"What are you doing in there?" he asked.

"This used to be my secret hiding place," Dennis Deane said.

"I know. So, what are you doing in there now?"

"Hiding."

"You know I can see you, don't you?"

"Yeah, I guess so."

"So, who are you hiding from?"

"I can't tell you."

"Why not?"

"Are you alone?" Dennis Deane asked.

"What?"

"I said, are you alone?"

"Am I alone," Jim said slowly.

"Did anybody follow you out here?"

Jim frowned at Dennis Deane.

"Damn it, Jim, I ain't fooling around," Dennis Deane said. "I'm trying to keep a lookout here. Did you notice anybody following you?"

"The Lone Ranger," Jim said. "The Lone Ranger followed me. I think I lost Tonto, though."

Dennis Deane paused, apparently weighing his chances against the Lone Ranger riding alone versus his chances against the Lone Ranger and Tonto together. Finally he hurried out of the trees and into Jim's car. His hair was greasy and he didn't smell particularly good. He slammed the door, slid down in the seat, and put his feet up on the dashboard.

"Go," he said.

"Take your feet down."

"What?"

"I'm not driving anywhere until you get your dirty feet off my dashboard."

"There. You happy now?"

"You wanna ride over to New Carpenter?"

"I don't care!" Dennis Deane almost shouted. "Just stop jawing at me and go somewhere!"

Jim popped the clutch, steered the Major sideways, and spun a roostertail of mud all over the mailbox.

"What in the world's wrong with you?" Jim said. "You're acting like some kind of idiot."

Much to Jim's surprise, Dennis Deane jammed the heels of his hands into his eyes and fell over onto the seat. His head lay almost in Jim's lap; Jim shifted uncomfortably toward the door.

"Ohhh," Dennis Deane moaned. "I *am* an idiot. And I'm dead. I'm a big dead idiot."

"What's the matter?"

"Deader'n a doornail, Jim. Deader'n hell. Deader'n dead people."

"Why are you dead?"

"Because they're going to kill me."

"Who's going to kill you?"

"The hillbillies."

"What hillbillies?"

"All of 'em, Jim," Dennis Deane said. "All the hillbillies. They're probably coming down the mountain right now." He sat up straight and looked behind the car so earnestly that Jim glanced in the mirror to see if anyone was following them.

"Why are the hillbillies coming down the mountain?"

"Hey, that sounds like a joke."

"Dennis Deane . . ."

"They'll be riding six white horses when they come, the hillbilly bastards. You just wait."

"What did you do, Dennis Deane?"

"I can't tell you. Can we go to the river? We go to New Carpenter every Sunday. I hate New Carpenter. All the people are tall. Did you ever notice that? Even the girls. All tall." He lay down in the seat again and covered his eyes with his forearm. "Oh, God, I'm dead," he said.

"We can go to the river if you'll tell me why the hill-billies are going to kill you."

"Can I shoot your .twenty-two?"

"If you'll tell me."

Dennis Deane looked up at Jim with one eye from behind his arm. "How many shots?" he asked. He loved to shoot Jim's rifle, but he never bought shells. He didn't have a rifle of his own.

"Six," Jim said.

"Fourteen," replied Dennis Deane.

"Fourteen? You're crazy. Eight."

"Twelve."

"Ten," said Jim. "And that's all."

Dennis Deane shook his head. "You always were stingy," he said. "But all right."

Jim turned the Major around and drove back through Aliceville. Nobody seemed to be roaming the streets looking for Dennis Deane, which Jim duly reported. East of town, he turned off the highway and followed the two muddy tracks of the farm road through the uncles' walnut grove, across the branch, and around the edge of the corn bottom. The field was empty now, save for the shocks of fodder; the uncles and the field

hands had pulled the ears earlier in the fall. Brown
weeds scraped against the undercarriage of the car.
On the far side of the bottom, Jim parked the Major
and got his rifle and a box of shells from behind the
seat. Dennis Deane sat up and blinked and looked
around cautiously. He got out of the car and followed
Jim along the narrow path through the woods toward
the green smell of the river; they couldn't hear it at
first because of the noise they made walking through
the leaves. The day was cool, but the sun shone on the
large flat rock by the water. The river wandered in
from the west but at the rock turned decisively to the
south, as if it had received an urgent summons. The
water in the elbow was deep and solemn and quiet; in
the summertime it was a good place to fish and swim.
Jim watched an oak leaf bump against the rock but
catch again in the current; it spun slowly, then continued downstream. He watched it until he lost sight
of it in the sunlight glittering on the water.

"Now tell me," Jim said.

"Let me shoot the gun."

"How do I know you won't shoot the gun and then
not tell me?"

"Have I ever lied to you?" Dennis Deane asked.

"Well, yes, Dennis Deane. You have. A lot."

"So, I ain't gonna lie to you today."

"Ten shots," Jim said. "That's all."

He handed Dennis Deane the rifle. He searched
around in the underbrush until he found a dead limb,

which he broke over his knee into several pieces. When he stepped back onto the rock, Dennis Deane levered a shell into the chamber.

"You ready?" Jim asked.

Dennis Deane raised the rifle to his shoulder and squinted down the barrel. "I was born ready," he said.

Jim threw one of the sticks upstream and across the current so that it would pass them on the opposite side of the river from the rock. The first shot Dennis Deane fired at the stick didn't even hit the water, but he immediately levered another shell into the chamber and fired again. This time he managed to hit the water, but nowhere close to the target. As the stick floated past them, Dennis Deane fired the rifle as fast as he could work the lever and pull the trigger. The noise of the shots clapped down the river and echoed back toward them; each of the bullets hit the river with a *thoomp* sound; they sent up small geysers of white water. In between the reports, the spent shell casings bounced off the rock with tiny, almost musical *tinks*. Dennis Deane always shot the rifle as rapidly as possible. No matter how many shells Jim let him shoot, he never made them last.

"Eight," Jim counted. "Nine," he warned. "*Ten.*"

By then the stick was perhaps twenty yards downstream, and hard to see in the reflected sunlight. Dennis Deane kept the rifle to his shoulder and squinted harder.

"I said that was ten, Dennis Deane," Jim said. "Don't do it."

Dennis Deane pulled the trigger anyway. The report spat and clapped, and once again the shot seemed to miss the river entirely. The stick bobbed unharmed out of sight. Dennis Deane turned and smiled happily at Jim. A pale string of gun smoke moved out over the water and headed downstream.

"Eleven," Dennis Deane said.

Jim pulled the rifle out of his hands. "Daggummit," he said. "You always do that. You always lie to me. Always."

"Yeah, I know. I don't know why you put up with it."

"Maybe I won't anymore."

"Oh, don't get all huffy."

Jim shook his head.

"How many times did I hit it?"

"None," Jim said. "Two times you didn't even hit the water."

"You're crazy," Dennis Deane said. "I hit that stick eight times. At least."

"You might've hit the river eight times, but that's all. Actually, now that I think about it, you managed to hit the river nine times. But you never got close to the stick."

"Well, if that's how you want to be," Dennis Deane sniffed, "making yourself look big by making other people look small, then go right ahead."

"Don't try to change the subject, Dennis Deane," Jim said.

"What subject?"

"Why are the hillbillies going to kill you?"

The happiness that had come from shooting the rifle slid so quickly and completely out of Dennis Deane's eyes that Jim instantly regretted saying anything.

"Oh, God," Dennis Deane said, "I've got to sit down." He collapsed onto the rock and lay there in the sun with his eyes closed.

Jim stepped off the rock, leaned the rifle carefully against a tree, then returned and sat down beside Dennis Deane.

"What?" he said softly. "What did you do?"

"What's the worst thing in the world you can think of that could happen to you?"

Jim gave the question some thought. "I don't know," he said. "Your mama died?"

"Okay. What's the second-worst thing?"

"You got somebody pregnant?"

Dennis Deane jerked, then turned and stared at Jim, his eyes wide.

"Boy," he said. "You're good."

Jim felt his mouth drop open. "What? You got somebody pregnant?"

"One shot," Dennis Deane said. "Bull's-eye."

"Who?" Jim said. "I mean, *who?*"

"Guess."

"I don't know, Dennis Deane. You don't even have a girlfriend."

"Well, I do now."

"So, who is it?"

Dennis Deane hit his head three times against the rock. (The name was apparently lodged inside his brain and needed to be knocked loose.) But when he opened his mouth, no noise came out.

"You gotta tell me," Jim said.

Dennis Deane swallowed hard and rubbed his throat. When he finally spoke, his voice was barely audible over the sound of the current.

"Ellie Something," he said.

Jim leaned closer to Dennis Deane. "Did you say Ellie Something?"

"Yeah. Ellie Something. You remember that day on the steps before school when I said I could make any girl I wanted to fall in love with me? Well, it actually worked on her."

"You're kidding."

"That's what she told me. I didn't believe it, either."

"And then you got her pregnant?"

"Well, not right then."

"How? I mean, I know *how*, but where? She lives on the mountain and you don't have a car. And she's only a freshman."

"Big Day," Dennis Deane said. "Square dance. And apparently being a freshman doesn't have anything to do with it."

"But you went to the dance with me, and I talked to you in the gym. Where'd you go?"

Dennis Deane closed his eyes again. "Nurse's office."

"The nurse's office, Dennis Deane? You did it in the *nurse's office?*"

"Yep. The nurse's office."

Jim whistled. "Boy," he said. "The nurse's office. Man, you could've been expelled."

"Yeah, that would've been real upsetting," Dennis Deane said. He sat up and wrapped his arms around his knees. "I'm probably not even going to be alive to go to school tomorrow, and all you can worry about is the principal."

"Oh, never mind," Jim said. "You know what I meant."

Both boys sat and stared into the water.

"How come people don't fish in the winter?" Dennis Deane asked.

"What?"

"How come people don't fish in the winter? Today's a pretty nice day. How come people don't go fishing? How come we ain't fishing?"

"Fish don't bite in the winter."

"Don't fish eat in the winter?"

"I don't think so," Jim said.

"What about up north, where people go ice fishing? Those fish must eat."

"I didn't think about that."

"You ever tried it?"

"Tried what?"

"Fishing in the winter."

"Never have. You?"

"Nope. We ought to try it sometime."

"Okay," Jim said. He picked up a twig and flicked it toward the water. "So, what was it like?"

"What was what like?"

"You know, with Ellie Something. What was it like?"

"You don't know what it's like?"

Jim looked away from Dennis Deane. "I guess not. No. Not really."

"Huh," Dennis Deane said. "I always thought that you and Norma, well, that you were doing it and just not telling me."

"Lord, no," Jim said.

"How far'd you get? Third base?"

"Dennis Deane, I really don't want to talk about Norma."

"Second base?"

Jim blushed miserably but didn't reply. His recent, brief trip to second base with Norma didn't feel like anything he should brag about.

"First base?" Dennis Deane said in disbelief. "You dated Norma Harris *all that time* and you only got to first base?"

"Norma didn't like baseball," Jim said. "I don't want to talk about this anymore."

He noticed five pebbles resting in a small, bowl-shaped depression in the face of the rock. He wondered how the river had managed to pick them up when the water was high and deposit them so carefully in this one spot. He tossed them one at a time into the water. Then he stood and collected the shell casings that hadn't rolled off the rock and tossed them into the water as well. Then he sat back down.

"Do you think she's pretty?" Dennis Deane asked.

"Who?"

"Ellie Something."

"I guess so," Jim said. "Do you?"

"I guess I think she's kind of nice to look at. I know she smells good."

"Well, that's something."

"Do you really think she's pretty?"

Jim hadn't thought about Ellie Something one way or another, but he said, "Sure. Ellie Something's a pretty little girl."

"That's good," Dennis Deane said. "At least I didn't get no ugly girl pregnant."

"You never did tell me what it was like."

Dennis Deane frowned. "I don't really know how to explain it," he said. "It was different than I thought."

"Different better or different worse?"

"Just different different. You know how, when you're by yourself and you think about doing it?"

Jim nodded slightly.

"Well, I guess I never really thought about the girl being there."

"How can you think about doing it without thinking about a girl?"

"I mean, sure, you think about a girl being there, but Ellie Something, she was *really* there. You know what I'm saying?"

"No," Jim said.

"Okay, well, sex, I never thought about it being something girls were interested in. I guess I'd always just thought about it being something we did to them. I never thought about it being something they did to us. Does that make any sense?"

Jim pondered a minute. "You mean you're saying Ellie Something did it to you? Is that what you're saying?"

"Not exactly. I guess what I'm saying is that she did it, *too*. And I'd never thought about that before. You think about doing it, but you don't really think about the girl. You don't think about being *with* somebody like that. But then you're doing it for real and you realize that somebody else is there with you and you realize that you've got your britches pulled down and your butt sticking up in the air and they've got their britches pulled down, too, and you feel like you're going someplace together and it's kind of embarrassing, but it's fun at the same time. Although it don't seem that much fun now."

Jim nodded slowly. "Huh," he said.

"Then, there you go. That's what it was like."

"So, what happens now?"

"I don't know, but it ain't going to be good. She was going to tell her mama and daddy today after church. Then I figure they're going to come down here and tell Mama."

"Uh-oh."

"You ain't kidding about uh-oh," Dennis Deane

said. "I figure her daddy's got some kind of hillbilly posse rounded up by now. They're probably waiting for me at the house."

"Do you love her?"

Dennis Deane didn't say anything.

"Hey," Jim said.

"What?"

"Do you love Ellie Something?"

"I guess so. I mean, I think so. I mean I think about her a lot. I didn't used to think about her at all. What does that mean? I look forward to seeing her get off the school bus. Does that mean I love her?"

"As far as I know. Are you going to marry her?"

"Would you?"

"Marry Ellie Something?"

"Not just Ellie Something. Anybody. If you got somebody pregnant, would you marry her?"

Jim closed his eyes. He thought about Chrissie and imagined carrying her over the threshold to his room and laying her down on his bed. He imagined holding a baby with black hair and found that the prospect made him happy. A little girl. He opened his eyes.

"Yeah," he said. "I think I would."

"I figured you'd say that. You always were a goody-goody."

"I don't know what else you could do."

"But I'm too young to get married," Dennis Deane said. "Do you have any idea how immature I am?"

Jim laughed. "Yeah, I think I do. You're pretty dog-gone immature."

"You ain't fooling none there," Dennis Deane said. "I'm the most immature person I know. I'm practically *childish*."

"Are you going to marry her?"

"Yeah, I guess so," Dennis Deane said. "Can I shoot your rifle some more?"

"No."

At a point Jim hadn't noticed, the sun had dropped low enough behind the trees that the light had left the surface of the water. The river had taken on a leaden hue; the water in the elbow had darkened into a color approaching black. Though the tops of the trees still glowed in the flat winter sunlight, the rock on which they sat lay completely in shadow. Jim shivered and buttoned the top button of his coat.

"So, what are you going to do?" Dennis Deane asked.

"About what?"

"About Chrissie."

"Nothing," Jim said. "There's nothing I can do. All I've got to look forward to is graduating so at least I won't have to look at her every day. Maybe she'll move back to Oklahoma to live with Injun Joe and the rest of the Cherokees."

"Or something could happen to Bucky."

"Oh, yeah? Like what?"

"I don't know. You could always shoot him."

"I've thought about it," Jim said. "I probably would if I could get away with it."

Dennis Deane stood and picked up one of the sticks Jim had broken for target practice. "Well, why don't you shoot him?"

Jim stared at the stick in Dennis Deane's hand and started to grin. "Why not?"

"Sure," Dennis Deane said, waving the stick at Jim. "Why not?"

Jim retrieved his rifle from the bank and loaded the tube full of shells. He stepped to the edge of the rock and shouldered it.

"You ready?" Dennis Deane asked.

"Throw it out there."

Dennis Deane tossed the stick into the current on the far side of the river. "There he goes, Jim!" he said. "Don't let him get away!"

Jim sighted down the barrel. The stick turned in the current until it was broadside to the rock. As it nosed downstream, it began to pick up speed. Jim tracked the stick with the rifle and drew a bead on a spot in the middle of it.

"Hey, Bucky," he said. "Over here."

When they left the river, they met Uncle Zeno driving his truck toward them around the edge of the bottom. Uncle Zeno pulled the truck off the farm road and rolled down the passenger-side window.

Jim stopped the Major beside the truck. "What's going on?" he asked.

Uncle Zeno looked grim. "The Japanese just bombed Pearl Harbor," he said.

"What's Pearl Harbor?" Dennis Deane asked.

Bucky Comes Home

J IM HEARD the train stopping along the edge of his dream and, without waking, wondered why. Nothing ever stopped in Aliceville during the middle of the night. Then he heard someone pounding on a door, but he figured he would be okay as long as he didn't open it. He heard heavy footsteps moving toward the door and the rattle of a knob and the creak of a screen on its hinges and the indistinct murmur of two voices, one asking questions, the other answering, the voices speaking urgently, almost on top of each other. The screen creaked again and the door clicked closed and the footsteps — Uncle Zeno's, Jim recognized them now — grew louder as they moved down the hallway through the house in which Jim had begun to remember he lived. He heard Uncle Zeno open Mama's door and speak quickly to her, and he heard Mama throw back her covers. Her shoes scuffed against the floor as she slipped her feet into them. Jim, fully awake now, stared at his door until it opened.

"Get up," Uncle Zeno said.

"What is it?"

"Bucky's here."

Jim squinted at Uncle Zeno's silhouette. The light slanting past it from the kitchen hurt his eyes. "Here?" he said.

"At the depot. Get dressed. They're holding the train for him."

When Jim ran from his room, he passed Mama sitting at the kitchen table, the quilt she had made with Norma draped over her shoulders. Her eyes were red and wide, and she held both hands in front of her mouth. He burst through the screen door and leapt from the top step into the yard. The ground was frozen and his pants slapped icily against his legs as he sprinted beside the waiting train toward the depot. The boxcars, stilled in a place they weren't supposed to be, bore the premonitory oddness of an apparition; from the corner of his eye, as he ran alongside them, they seemed to move silently toward the destination from which they had been kept. The windows of the depot were dark, but Pete Hunt, the station agent, stood on the platform beside a man holding a lantern. Jim slowed and climbed the steps. Pete and the man with the lantern stared at him. He heard himself panting loudly and tried to breathe through his nose. To his left gaped the open door of a boxcar, but he didn't dare look inside it. He smelled wood smoke and wondered who else in town was awake at this hour.

"Jim here played ball with him," Pete said.

"That right?" said the man.

"Yes, sir," Jim said.

"He any good?"

From the street behind him Jim heard footsteps jogging toward the depot. Uncle Zeno had rousted Uncle Coran and Uncle Al. Their change and knives jangled in their pockets as they ran. "He played shortstop," Jim said.

"Best I ever saw," said Pete. "Boy had an arm like a gun."

Jim blinked at Pete. *A gun that couldn't shoot straight,* he thought, and instantly felt ashamed.

The man studied Jim's face. "Too bad," he said.

The uncles clomped onto the platform behind him. Uncle Zeno briefly placed a hand on Jim's shoulder as he walked into the lantern light.

"This ought to do," said the man. "Let's get him off."

Jim fell in behind Uncle Zeno and stepped from the platform across the narrow gap into the car. Uncle Al came in after him. Jim found himself standing alongside Bucky's coffin. Pete and Uncle Coran faced them from the other side of it.

The man stepped into the car last, and when he held the lantern up in the air, their shadows loomed crazily around the walls. "Here's your boy," he said — unnecessarily, Jim thought, because the coffin was the only thing inside the car. It looked like it had been nailed together in a hurry. A bill of lading was tacked to the lid and the word BUCKLAW swam up at

Jim before he looked away. The man placed the lantern on the floor behind him.

"Y'all smell that?" Uncle Al asked.

Jim gagged and put his hand over his mouth and nose.

"He's about ripe," the man said.

Uncle Coran backed up a step and looked around angrily. "Now, damn it," he said. "This ain't right. There ain't nothing right about this." When nobody disagreed with him, he stepped back up to the coffin.

"I kept the doors open the whole way. I tried to freeze him, cold as it is, but I guess it didn't work."

"You gonna make it, Doc?" Uncle Zeno asked.

Jim didn't think so, but he nodded.

"He's lucky he made it back home," the man said. "I heard they only shipped a few. Let's see if we can get him up."

Jim took a deep breath and held it and squatted and tried to work his fingers underneath the casket. He felt the box lift from Uncle Zeno's end, then Uncle Al's.

"Up," said Uncle Zeno.

Jim lifted and stood and the casket swung unevenly into the air. The weight inside it was shocking. It was, well, *dead.*

"I don't have a good grip," Pete said.

"Get one," said Uncle Coran, who stood next to Pete.

Jim realized that the wood beneath his right hand was damp, the wetness slick and icy. "Oh, God," he said.

"I know, Doc," Uncle Zeno said. "Don't drop it."

The six of them began to shuffle sideways toward the door. "Watch your step," the man said.

They carried the coffin to the far end of the platform and carefully put it down, first Jim's side, then the other. Everyone got their fingers out from underneath it intact. They stepped back and looked down at it. Nobody spoke. The man returned to the boxcar and retrieved his lantern and from the platform waved it in a bright arc at his side toward the engine. Jim stared at his right hand and considered wiping it on his pants, but he thought better of it.

Up ahead a bell began to ring lazily in the darkness. Jim heard a determined *chuff* of steam and then another, and the wheels of the engine began a slow, almost animate screech against the rails. As each car began to move, it pulled with a heavy clank against the coupling of the stationary car behind it, dragging its brother, groaning, into reluctant motion. The sound of the individual couplings clanking together galloped in succession away from the engine, car to car to car to car, growing louder as it approached Jim's position on the platform and softer as it ran away; in a second or two it leapt into the darkness beyond the far end of the train. And then the boxcars were moving smoothly, gaining speed, bracketed by thin slashes of darkness. The brightly lit caboose, when it passed, left them alone on the end of the platform in an exposed, unexpected quiet; as it drew abreast of the man with the lantern, he nodded toward them and touched the brim of his cap with his index finger and stepped nimbly onto the rear step of the car. He opened the door, walked inside, and closed it behind him. Jim watched the lighted window of the doorway until it passed out of sight around the bend. And then the train was gone. Jim stood with the uncles and Pete in the starlight on the platform. When the engine whistled at the crossing east of town, it already sounded far away.

Uncle Coran tapped the coffin twice with his toe.

"Now what do we do?" Uncle Al asked.

"I don't know," Pete said. "I can't keep him here. Not with him the way he is."

"We'll take him home," said Uncle Zeno. "Somebody run get the truck."

Jim scrubbed his hands in the kitchen sink until they ached in the cold water. He refused to say anything to Mama about what had happened. He was afraid that if he opened his mouth he would vomit. He changed his pants, even though he hadn't wiped his hands on them, rounded up an armload of old quilts, and ran back to the depot, leaving Mama on the top step, worrying questions into the air behind him. At the depot someone had backed the truck up to the platform, and Pete and the uncles had slid Bucky's coffin onto the bed. Uncle Zeno had tacked scrap pieces of two-by-fours around the base of the coffin to keep it from sliding. Jim hoped he wouldn't have to touch it ever again. Just looking at it made him wish he had scrubbed his hands harder.

"Boys, I'd be glad to at least make you some coffee," Pete said.

"We need to get on up the road," Uncle Zeno said. "Jim, you going with us?"

"Yes, sir."

"Then, who's going to ride in the back?" Uncle Al asked. "We can't all fit up front."

"I will," said Jim. He had shot Bucky. Nobody else knew that.

"You sure?" asked Uncle Zeno.

"Yes, sir. I'll do it."

"All right, then. Let's load up."

Jim walked from the platform onto the truck bed and maneuvered around Bucky's coffin, staying as far away from it as possible. Uncle Zeno stepped on behind Jim, and Jim handed him the quilts. When Jim sat down with his back against the cab and extended his legs, his feet hit the end of the casket. He immediately jerked them back.

"Go ahead and stretch out, Doc," Uncle Zeno said, shaking out and tucking the quilts one at a time around Jim. "You ain't going to bother him."

"Was that a joke?" Jim asked.

"I don't think so. If Bucky was in that box and you were kicking it, then he might raise up and ask you to quit. But Bucky ain't in there."

"Oh, yes, he is."

"No, he's not. What's in that box will be dirt by springtime. You warm enough?"

"I guess so. Not really," Jim said.

"Just stay hunkered down. Maybe Corrie or Allie will switch places with you when we come back down the mountain."

"All right."

"A box can't hold the spirit, Jim. Right now Bucky's sitting around the throne with the rest of those boys. You remember that."

"But I still feel like he's in there."

"People are always looking for ghosts in the grave-yard, Doc. But that's the last place they'd be likely to find one."

"I hope you're right."

Uncle Zeno stepped to the side of the bed and jumped off. "Unh," he said. "Ground's hard."

They drove toward the mountain beneath one of those winter skies that made Jim wonder why he didn't study it more, why he didn't bother to learn when and where the planets made their appearances, and the names of the constellations. So vivid and bright were the stars that the great mechanisms that moved them across the sky seemed almost understandable while remaining incomprehensible, like a familiar Bible story read aloud in a foreign language, or the ticking guts of a watch.

The night was bitterly cold. Jim looked at the stars until the pain of the cold air swirling over his face became unbearable, then he pulled the quilts over his head and breathed into his mittened hands. Eventually he at least stopped shivering. Underneath the quilts, he tried to figure out, through the motion of the truck, exactly where they were on the trip up the mountain, but he lost track soon after they crossed the bridge over Painter Creek. The curves invariably bent opposite to the ways he anticipated. The road fell in the places he imagined it would rise, and rose in the places he was sure it would fall. Several times he tried to think backward and remember the sequence of the curves and hills they had just traversed so he could align the template of his memory atop the map of the road he carried inside his head, yet the two never matched up. Jim could have been anywhere, but he discovered inside that disorientation a small measure of comfort. As long as the road beneath him moved randomly, he found it possible to imagine that its destination remained fluid. He wasn't on his way to the Bucklaws' after all, and the corpse of a boy whose death he had wished for wasn't lying inches from his feet. Bucky didn't even have to be dead. Chrissie and Bucky could get married, for all Jim cared. And when the truck finally stopped and he looked out from beneath the quilts, the war would be over and he wouldn't have to fight in it.

Eventually the growl of the engine withdrew to a great distance. Bucky rode on the front bumper of the truck, draped in a peacoat and holding on to his sailor hat, but he was too far away to worry about. Someone wearing mittens tenderly cradled Jim's face. He leaned into the hands, and breathed on them to keep them warm, and rubbed his cheeks against the scratchy wool.

"That feels nice," Chrissie said. "Your face is warm."

"I love you so much," Jim said.

"Oh, I love you, too, Jim. But do you know the answer?"

"What answer?"

"To number twelve."

"I didn't know we had any homework."

"It's due tomorrow, Jim. Now I have to go ask somebody else."

"No, wait," Jim said. "Don't go. I bet I can figure it out. Tell me the problem."

"Okay. There's these two trains," Chrissie said. "And they're going two different directions. We have to calculate the area."

"Of the trains?"

"Yes. It's a train problem."

"Are you sure you don't mean the volume? If you told me the dimensions of the cars and how many there were, I bet I could figure out the volume."

"No. The book says area."

"But I don't know how to do that," Jim said. "How do you calculate the area of a train? It's a three-dimensional object. Do you mean surface area, or what?"

"You're going to get us in trouble."

"No, I just want to marry you."

"I want to marry you, too, Jim, but you know I can't."

"Why not? We can ask Norma for the answer."

"No. Look what's behind us."

Jim lowered the quilt and peeked out over the top. He saw Bucky Bucklaw running easily in the distance behind the truck. His body looked solid, but it seemed to be made out of darkness. And as Bucky ran, the darkness peeled away in sheets, like ashes, or gauze, and caught the wind and billowed out in shreds behind him.

Jim pushed himself hard against the cab of the truck. He pulled the quilts up over his face but could still see Bucky running along the starlit road. And Bucky must have seen Jim watching him, because he waved and sped up and flew toward the truck until he was within arm's length of the bed.

"No!" Jim yelled. "Get away! Get away from me, Bucky. I'm not kidding around."

The darkness peeling off Bucky made a flapping sound, like newspaper, as the wind whipped it away. Jim hoped that Bucky would eventually blow away and disappear, but he didn't seem to be getting any smaller.

"What's the matter, old buddy?" Bucky asked. "Are you scared? Are you scared of me, now that I'm back?"

"I ain't scared of you," Jim lied. "I just want you to get away from me. That's all."

"Are you going to my house?"

"No. We're not going to your house."

"You are, too."

"No, we're not. I don't even know where your house is. We're going somewhere else."

"Where?"

"Somewhere. I don't know where. I'm not driving the truck."

Bucky laughed and pointed at Jim. "You're lying to me, you old hound dog. You are, too, going to my place. Hey. Watch this." He ripped a swatch of darkness about the size of a handkerchief off his left arm and held it up and let it go in the breeze. "Woo-hoo!" he yelled. "Did you see that? I've been doing that all night."

"Please go away, Bucky," Jim said. "I'll leave Chrissie alone. I promise I will."

Bucky leaned forward and placed both palms flat against the truck bed. "It's a little late for that, old buddy," he whispered. "There's a ladder in the well. Ask Daddy about it when you get there."

The truck started up the first steep grade of the mountain, and Jim tipped to one side and pitched forward and hit something solid with his shoulder. He knew instantly that it was Bucky's coffin, and that he would have to fight Bucky because he had collided with it. Bucky shouted and flew into the truck bed and covered Jim so thoroughly with darkness that Jim could neither breathe nor see. Jim screamed and punched and kicked but got tangled up and couldn't free himself.

"Get off!" Jim yelled, thrashing wildly. "Get off me, Bucky. I'll kill you! I swear to God, I'll kill you if you don't get off me!"

Then the darkness tore away around him, and Bucky's spirit exploded into a blast of angry, frigid air, leaving Jim on his knees searching for it in the quilts. He had killed Bucky all over again, and again wanted to bring him back. The truck stopped suddenly, sliding briefly on the gravel, and Jim rolled against the cab, banging his head. He grabbed it with both hands and curled up in a ball.

"Please leave me alone," he whimpered. "I didn't really want you to die."

"Jim!" somebody yelled. "Hey! Jim!"

Jim opened his eyes and saw the head and shoulders of a dark figure on the running board of the truck, looking at him around the back of the cab. For a second he thought Bucky had come back to fight him some more, but then he recognized Uncle Al.

"What the hell's wrong with you?" Uncle Al asked.

Jim sat up and looked warily at the coffin. He realized he was freezing and wrapped his arms around his knees. He began looking around, trying to figure out what had happened to the quilts.

"Bucky," he said. "Bucky was in here with me, and we were fighting."

"You say you were fighting with Bucky?"

"Yes, sir," Jim said.

Uncle Al glanced at the coffin before disappearing into the cab. Jim heard him say, "He says he was fighting with Bucky."

Uncle Zeno climbed out the other door and looked around the back of the cab. "You say Bucky was back there with you?"

"Yes, sir, but I guess it was just a bad dream."

"I reckon it was. What did he say?"

"I don't remember. He told me to leave Chrissie alone."

"Sounds like a guilty conscience to me," Uncle Al said.

"There's nothing wrong with my conscience," Jim said. "I haven't laid a hand on that girl."

"You want to ride up here with us?" Uncle Zeno asked.

Jim stood and began sorting out the quilts. "No, sir," he said.

Uncle Coran's head appeared beside Uncle Al's. "I'll ride back there, Jim," he said. "I ain't scared of no knothead ghost."

"You'd be afraid of this one," Jim said.

The uncles were quiet for a moment or two. "All right, Doc," Uncle Zeno finally said. "You get covered up again and we'll finish this job."

The Red Canoe

*J*IM DIDN'T go to sleep again the rest of the way up the mountain. He closely watched the road unrolling behind the truck and kept a wary eye on the woods in the dark places where the trees grew closest to the right-of-way, but he didn't see Bucky again. The fact that Bucky did not haunt Jim while Jim was awake more or less convinced him that he had dreamed the whole thing. The dream, however, seemed more real to him than anything he could think of that he knew for certain had actually happened. He tried to pull the quilts more tightly around himself, and he wondered if a ghost who appeared in a dream was considered a real ghost, or if you had to be awake when you saw it in order for it to count. Ghost or dream, Bucky had at least been on his way home, a destination Jim found hard to hold against him. Jim was quite sure that when he died, home was the one place, aside from heaven, he would want to go. He tried to tell himself that any ghost who would run all the way from Hawaii just to get back to North Carolina couldn't be all bad.

Once the road climbed through the switchbacks and into the valley at the top of the mountain, Jim noticed that most of the stars had dimmed to the point where he could no longer see them and that the sky had begun to brighten into the noncolor of the day when it's still deciding what it wants to be. Up the narrow tracks that climbed into the hollows Jim occasionally spied the sleepy glow of a kerosene lamp burning in a kitchen window. A solitary planet remained lit low in the sky and he found himself wondering if God had forgotten to blow it out. He wished once again that he knew enough about the stars and planets to say, Look, Chrissie, there's Jupiter, or Mars, or whatever it was, but he also knew, now that daylight was almost here, that he wasn't so interested in astronomy that he would go to the necessary trouble of learning about it. Many Varmints Eat Much Juice Saturday Unless Nobody Pays was the sentence Norma had come up with in eighth grade to help them memorize the names and orbits of the planets, and that was probably all he would ever know about the subject. Norma had recently gotten her hands on an old college calculus book and studied it at home for no other reason than that she loved math. Jim couldn't think of anything, other than Chrissie, that he cared about that much.

Uncle Zeno turned off the headlights around the

time they passed Penn's house, and by the time they reached the Bucklaw place, the first rays of new sunlight had climbed out of the valley, casting long, tentative shadows against the mountainside. Nothing in the landscape suggested that bad news had recently arrived here, or would ever come. The orchards rolled away from the farm road in prosperous formation, ridge after terraced ridge, all the way to the top of the mountain. The grass was combed white with frost. The fruit trees glittered like fountains whose water had sprung suddenly from the earth, only to freeze before it touched the ground. Jim began to wonder about Bucky's parents. How could anyone who lived looking onto a scene so precisely beautiful even imagine they might one morning see a strange truck coming up the road with their son's body laid out in the back? Uncle Coran had been right. None of this made any sense. Jim gently nudged the coffin with the toe of one boot. "Hey. Wake up, Bucky," he said. "You're home."

As they approached the house, Jim spotted the two German shepherds who had attacked his car back in the fall silently streaking toward the truck, their ears up, their bushy tails straight out behind them. He scrambled to his feet and threw his arms over the cab, ready to climb onto the roof. But when the dogs drew close they yelped and pulled up before reaching the road. They trotted in small, tight circles, their tails between their legs and bellies low to the ground, before loping away at an angle, looking back over their shoulders. Only later would Jim realize that the smell had stopped them.

The house was two stories tall, constructed of quartz fieldstone Bucklaw Sr. had pulled out of his orchards when he moved to this side of the mountain and cut away the timber. After all these years, the rocks still bore the orange color of the dirt from which they had been dug. In the yard, Uncle Zeno stopped the truck and blew the horn. Jim caught a glimpse of Chrissie wearing a white nightgown, framed in an upstairs window. He moved his hand to wave at her, but she disappeared so quickly he had the fleeting notion that she must be dead, too. Before he had time to wonder what she was doing here, the front door opened and Bucky's father stepped onto the porch. Mr. Bucklaw put on his hat and adjusted the brim and closed the door behind him. He stared for a long moment at the truck, his face expressionless, his breath billowing evenly from his nostrils in quick white snorts. Jim thought, *He's going to blame me,* and fought the urge to leap down and run.

Mr. Bucklaw came slowly down the stairs, never taking his eyes from the bed of the truck, and took four steps into the yard before he crumpled at the waist. He dropped to his knees and wrenched his hat from his head and began slapping the back of his neck with it. Jim held his hands over his ears. The uncles scrambled out of the cab and rushed to Mr. Bucklaw and pulled him to his feet. Uncle Zeno and Uncle Coran wrapped their arms around him so that he couldn't hit himself anymore, and Uncle Zeno crooned the same wordless, soothing noises he might have made to a spooked animal. Uncle Al worked the crumpled hat from out of Mr. Bucklaw's fingers. He looked down at the hat, then around for somewhere to put it; he tried to mold it back into shape before finally giving up and holding it awkwardly in front of himself, crown down, like an usher passing a collection plate. Jim jumped down from the truck but gave the uncles and Mr. Bucklaw a wide berth.

Only the uncles holding Mr. Bucklaw kept him from collapsing again onto the ground. "Ohh," he moaned. "Oh, sweet Jesus. I can't do this."

"Let's get him to the house," said Uncle Zeno.

The toes of Mr. Bucklaw's boots dragged the ground as Uncle Zeno and Uncle Coran helped him away from the truck. At the house the uncles lowered him onto the second step. He leaned forward until his chest rested on his thighs. "It's too hard," he said. "I just can't do this. It's too hard."

Uncle Zeno and Uncle Coran sat down on either side of him, without touching him. Uncle Al extended Mr. Bucklaw's hat. Mr. Bucklaw took it and flung it into the yard, almost hitting Uncle Al with the hat and Uncle Zeno with his arm. Uncle Al didn't go get it.

"I don't understand," Mr. Bucklaw said. "Where did you find him? How did you end up with him? All we got is the telegram they sent us. They ain't said nothing about when he was supposed to come home."

"He came on the train last night," Uncle Zeno said.

"The stationmaster got us up because we live right there. Nobody's sure where he came from."

"I would have come and got him," Mr. Bucklaw said. "He's my boy. I got a truck. I would have come and got him."

"We didn't think you ought to have to do that," Uncle Zeno said quietly.

Mr. Bucklaw rose upright and gaped at Uncle Zeno. "What am I saying?" he said. "You came all this way. You came all this way and it dark and brought Bucky home. I thank you. I'm sorry I didn't say that sooner."

The uncles all turned away. Jim rolled a small stick back and forth with his toe.

"Now what do I do?" Mr. Bucklaw asked. He gazed almost eagerly into each of the uncles' faces. "I don't know what I'm supposed to do."

Uncle Zeno spoke as softly as Jim had ever heard him. "You need to put him somewhere," he said.

"Put him somewhere," said Mr. Bucklaw. "I need to put him somewhere."

"Tell us where," said Uncle Coran.

Mr. Bucklaw looked blankly around the yard before pointing slowly up the steps. "In the house," he said. "I guess we ought to put him in the house."

"We might need to stop and think here for a minute," Uncle Zeno said.

"What?"

"He's not in too good a shape," said Uncle Zeno. "The body's not. You may not want to put him inside just yet."

"Oh, God," Mr. Bucklaw said. "Please don't tell me that." He tilted slowly, then listed and fell sideways onto Uncle Zeno. He began to cry with his face mashed against Uncle Zeno's arm. Uncle Coran took him by the shoulders and guided him back to vertical.

"Maybe we ought to put him on the porch for now," Uncle Zeno said. "I bet he would like it out here on the porch, where he could see."

"Oh, Jesus," Mr. Bucklaw sobbed. "The porch. I don't know. I don't know what I'm supposed to do."

The front door opened and Chrissie stepped outside. She was wearing Bucky's Aliceville letter jacket. Uncle Coran stood up and took off his hat.

"Side porch," she said to Uncle Zeno. "We'll put him on the side porch for now."

Mr. Bucklaw reached toward her. "Chrissie, I don't know what to do," he said.

"You need to come on inside, Mr. Bucklaw," she said. "You need to come inside and go see Mrs. Bucklaw. We'll take care of things out here."

Mr. Bucklaw nodded. Uncle Zeno and Uncle Coran lifted him to his feet. "That's Bucky's fiancée," he said.

"We're sorry for your loss, Miss Steppe," Uncle Zeno said, removing his hat. Chrissie nodded. Uncle Al cleared his throat and went after Mr. Bucklaw's hat.

"She's been staying with us and helping Mama," Mr. Bucklaw said, starting heavily up the stairs. "Chrissie, is Mama all right?"

"No, sir," Chrissie said. "She's not all right. She

looked out the window and saw who it was. You need to go upstairs."

Mr. Bucklaw left the door standing open behind him. Chrissie closed it, then walked to the edge of the porch and studied the truck. She bit her lower lip.

"Things haven't been too good here," she said.

"Here's his hat," said Uncle Al, handing it up.

"Thank you."

"What do you want us to do?" Uncle Zeno asked.

"Sawhorses," Chrissie said. "I guess we're going to need sawhorses."

"Jim will go get the sawhorses," Uncle Zeno said. "Where do y'all keep them?"

"Wood shop," Chrissie said, pointing back down the road. "Between the first barn and the big packing shed."

"Go get two sawhorses, Jim," said Uncle Zeno.

The wood shop was a simple frame building, sided with corrugated metal and open at one end. Just inside the opening sat a single worn-looking, split-bottomed chair, its legs half buried in wood shavings. A lantern was suspended from the rafter above it with a piece of baling wire. Hammers and mallets and saws and wood chisels and files hung neatly above a workbench at the opposite end. Another lantern hung above the bench. Along the wall to Jim's right a red canvas canoe rested on the sawhorses he had been sent to find. He drew his finger along the brightly varnished side of the canoe and looked inside. The frame was made of bent and polished ash, as gracefully formed and light-looking as the skeleton of a bird. The seats were woven of narrow oak splits into an intricate diamond pattern.

"Bucky built that," a voice said behind him.

Jim started at the voice, and again at the figure silhouetted by the white winter sunlight.

"I didn't mean to scare you," Chrissie said. She stepped into the building and off to the side, out of the glare.

"I thought you were somebody else," Jim said.

She wasn't wearing Bucky's letter jacket any longer but had on the plaid cloth coat she normally wore to school.

"It was hanging by the door," she said.

"What was?"

"Bucky's letter jacket. It was hanging by the door and I just put it on when I came outside. I was in a hurry."

"I didn't notice."

"Yes, you did."

"Okay, I did. But how did you know what I was thinking?"

"It wasn't hard. You wouldn't make a very good liar."

"So, what am I thinking now?"

Chrissie leaned forward and squinted slightly. "You're thinking, 'I don't care what she wears. She can wear whatever coat she wants to.'"

"That's pretty close," he said. He enjoyed a passing but powerful urge to kick wood chips at her. "You didn't tell me you and Bucky were getting married."

"I'm not exactly Bucky's — I mean, I wasn't — Bucky's fiancée."

"What does that mean? 'Not exactly'?"

"It means I kind of got promoted after Pearl Harbor."

"Well, you live in a nice house now," Jim said. "Congratulations."

"You think I like living here?"

"I don't know. Do you?"

"These poor people loved Bucky, Jim. Now they're just about crazy."

"I understand that part."

"Mrs. Bucklaw says she wants me around because Bucky loved me, but she's got me cooking and cleaning like a maid, except she ain't paying me. And that's about the sanest thing that's going on. I can't wait to get out of that house. It's too sad and strange."

"Did Bucky love you?"

"What? I don't know. I guess. He said he did."

"Did you love him?"

"I think we've already had this conversation."

"Do you miss him?"

"I'm just real sad about everything. I'm afraid he suffered. I'm afraid he was trapped in a fire and he couldn't get out and he knew what was happening. I can't go to sleep for thinking about it. And I'm afraid he's in the house. I'm afraid I'm going to see him coming in the door if I open my eyes. I know you hated him, Jim, but he didn't deserve what happened to him."

"No," Jim said. "You're right. He didn't."

Chrissie stepped closer. "He finished that canoe right before we moved back here. He said it took him almost a year."

"It's beautiful," Jim said, meaning it. "I don't think I could ever make anything like that."

"He said he wanted to cover it in birch bark, but the only birch trees he could find up here were too scrawny."

"Birch bark?"

"Bucky loved boats," Chrissie said. "And he loved Indians."

"Seems like I've heard that before."

"Don't be smart. There's a whole shelf full of books about Indians in his room that he studied long before he ever laid eyes on me. He was one of those white boys who liked to run around in the woods wearing moccasins. Did you ever do that?"

"Not much," Jim said. "I was usually a cowboy."

"Because you like to win?"

"No, because I had a cowboy hat and a pony. Why did you call Bucky a white boy?"

"Because he was."

"But you're half white."

"That depends on whether or not somebody's asking me to mop." Jim opened his mouth to speak, but

Chrissie held up her hand. "I can tell you're about to show your ignorance, Jim, and I'd just as soon you didn't."

"Your mama's white," Jim said.

"There. You went ahead and did it, anyway."

"What did I say?"

"Lift up that end of the canoe," Chrissie said. "We need to get these sawhorses to the house."

They walked slowly along the farm road through the orchards. Jim carried the stacked sawhorses over his shoulder. Chrissie didn't seem in a hurry to get back to the house. The morning was cold but calm, the sunlight weak but bright. It should have been a better day than it was.

"What's been going on at school?" Chrissie asked.

"Everybody's been talking about Bucky and the war. Horace Gentine and Buster Burnette have already joined the navy and gone off to basic training."

"I heard about it."

"We had assembly and prayer meeting every morning for Bucky because they didn't know if he was dead or not. At first it was just preachers coming in, but then kids started asking Mr. Dunlap if they could pray. The day school let out for Christmas, second period was almost over before everybody finished. There's a kid in the fifth grade who says he's called to preach, and I thought they were going to have to drag him off the stage."

"Did you pray for him?"

"No. I mean, not out loud. Everybody was looking at me to see if I would do it."

"But you did pray for him?"

"Yes," Jim said. "When I was by myself. After you told me that day why you couldn't go out with me, I started wishing that Bucky would die."

"Oh, no."

"And Pearl Harbor Day, before we heard, I was down at the river with Dennis Deane shooting my rifle, and I pretended to shoot him."

"That's awful, Jim."

"I know it is," Jim said. "I've been praying about it, but I don't feel much better."

"Maybe we'll all feel better one of these days."

"Maybe." He moved the sawhorses to the other shoulder. "Tell me something. I know you believe in spirits, but do you believe in ghosts?"

"Sometimes spirits can be ghosts," Chrissie said carefully. "And sometimes they're just spirits."

"What would you say if I told you I think I saw Bucky last night?"

Chrissie didn't stop walking, but Jim heard her inhale sharply. "I think I heard him coming up the stairs, but I was too scared to look," she said. "When did you see him?"

"Coming up here. I guess I went to sleep in the truck, and I dreamed he was running up the mountain behind us."

"Did he say anything?"

"He told me to stay away from you."

The corners of Chrissie's mouth flinched upward. "Well, that sounds like him."

"He said there was a ladder in the well. Does that mean anything to you?"

"The Bucklaws have got a pump, so I don't know if there's a ladder down in the well or not. I ain't going to slide the slab back and look, though."

"If Bucky had made it home, what do you think you would have done?"

"I don't know. I guess I would have married him," she said.

Jim thought then of Bucky guiding his red canoe down the river. It was warm, Indian summer, the woods yellow. Chrissie sat in the bow. Jim stood on the flat rock. The water was green and smooth. The canoe was going very fast. Bucky was taking her away from him forever. *Hey, Bucky. Over here.*

"I can't believe you," he said.

"Don't you start on me, Jim. Not today."

"I can't believe you would marry somebody you didn't love."

"I keep telling you, you don't know anything about me."

"I know about Injun Joe," he said. "I know he robbed a bank and shot a cop and you don't even know where he is."

Chrissie stopped and wheeled on Jim. She was crying now. "What did you just call my daddy?" she asked.

He watched a tear drop onto the front of her coat and sink darkly into the wool. He felt as if he had strayed too far in front of the line during a rabbit hunt. If he flushed a rabbit now, somebody was going to shoot him.

"Injun Joe," he said.

And there went the rabbit.

"That's it, Jim Glass," she said. "That's it. You just settled everything."

"Oh, yeah? Then, why did you even come down here just now?"

Chrissie pointed back the way they had come. "Look down there."

Bucky's German shepherds stood about twenty paces behind them, ears up, one in each track of the farm road. They were staring straight at Jim.

"I should have let them eat you," Chrissie said.

February 8, 1942

Lynn's Mountain, NC
Dear Zeno,

    Well, it is a new year here as it is there, and I hope it is better than the last one, although it does not seem that the war news will be good anytime soon and you have to wonder what is happening in the world. I know you must not consider getting a letter from me to be good news either, as it hasn't been in the past, nor have telegrams, and if you think I am writing to you today to ask you for something, then you are right, I'm afraid. Here it is. I have heard that Mr. Harris is going to be looking for somebody to cook and clean at his hotel, and I am writing to see if you would put in a good word for me for the job, as I need it. (You know for yourself that I am a good cook! And I'm still not afraid to work.) We are nothing more than a hardship and a worry up here on Mama and Daddy, who do not have anything other than the scraps the Bucklaws throw them, and besides, I need to get Chrissie away from Mrs. B. because she has not been right since Pearl Harbor and especially since the funeral and she is treating Chrissie like her daughter, but if Mrs. B. had a daughter, she wouldn't make her cook and clean all the time and not pay her. She has got her sleeping in the little room across the hall from Bucky's room and Chrissie does not get a wink of sleep because she says she hears Bucky going up and down the stairs in the dark all night, and I know you don't believe in spooks but I'm not going to say she is wrong, because many places on this mountain are haunted, as I know you have heard, because you hated riding that mule down the mountain in the dark! I am afraid that they are going to take her away from me. That is why I want to be a cook in the hotel. I have to figure that we will not see Joe again, and if he is not dead already, then they will sentence him to life in prison in Oklahoma for what he did when they catch him, which they will sooner or later, and now I have to figure out how to take care of the two of us without making her feel bad for taking more charity than we have already took. I am not asking you for charity this time, though, only a kind word in passing between two business men in the same town. (I know that your Jim used to go with Mr. Harris' Norma, so I hope he is not feuding with you!) I know you must think I am like an old dog following you around who you cannot run off even if you throw a stick and a rock at it, but I hope this is the last time I will ever have to ask you for anything or anybody else. Cooking and cleaning in a hotel for traveling men is not the job I would have picked out for myself but I made my bed a long time ago when I was young and silly and now I have to lie in it. (That sounds like a joke because I would be making up beds in the hotel but I did not mean for it to be!) It is honest work and Chrissie can stay with me in the cook's room and help me in the kitchen but not upstairs, as I will not let her go there or in the dining room or out on the porch, and I will be able to take care of us, and that is all I want anymore in this life and it is enough. Thank you for anything you might say to Mr. Harris about me, and if you don't choose to, I already understand because I know I don't deserve it, but Chrissie does. If I get the job and see you on the street I will say howdy but that is all, so you don't have to worry about that. I am as always

Fondly,
Nancy McAbee Steppe

The Girl on the Bridge

THE FIRST Sunday in March, Mama and Norma decided to give the quilt and a basket of food to Dennis Deane and Ellie Something as a housewarming present. Mama asked Jim to carry them over to Allendale, but Jim didn't want to go. Sure, he wanted to see the mill where Dennis Deane worked and catch up on things, but he didn't want to get anywhere near Ellie Something. She might be showing by now, and just the thought of her being pregnant made his face hot. He had never talked to a pregnant girl before, not that he knew about, and he had no idea where he was supposed to look. How could you possibly be in a room with a pregnant girl and *not* look? And he also remembered Dennis Deane telling him years ago that when girls got pregnant their breasts grew gigantic. If, by some miracle, he managed to avoid looking at Ellie Something's big belly, he figured there was no way in the world he could also avoid looking at her big breasts.

Ultimately, he went along just for the chance to

drive his car. Once the war started, Jim had had no choice but to park the Major. He wasn't happy about it, of course, but saw no way to circumvent it, or even complain about it, without seeming small. The last thing in the world he needed was for someone to see him driving around and throw Bucky's sacrifice in his face. Jim already had enough problems.

While Chrissie now spent weeknights with her mother at the hotel, and he occasionally saw her around town, the unwritten rules against speaking to her seemed only to have grown more restrictive since Bucky's death. The simple fact that he had even wanted to date the so-called fiancée of the fallen hero had somehow called his patriotism into question; somehow once being lined up *against* Bucky had automatically made him *for* the Japanese. So he had dropped the key to the Major into Uncle Zeno's hand without complaint. There was a war on, after all, and he couldn't drive without gasoline, simple as that. But Mama, who never went anywhere, had registered for *her* ration — just in case of emergency, she said, and giving a quilt to Dennis Deane and Ellie Something apparently qualified. Allendale was a fifteen- or sixteen-mile round-trip and Jim was tired of walking or riding a mule everywhere he went. So he agreed to drive. Mama sprang for two gallons of gas.

Jim checked the Major's oil and the air pressure in the tires, and he parked the car in front of the house. He thought about leaving the motor running, because it had been slow to start, but figured that at least one of the uncles would get all over him for wasting gasoline. So he cut the engine and went inside, where he found Mama and Norma working furiously on the quilt, which they had unwrapped and spread out on Mama's bed.

Mama, looking down her nose through her sewing glasses, was busy with her seam ripper, removing the scrap of blue chambray that had once belonged to the shirt owned by Jim's father, while Norma, perched on the side of the bed, whipped two small doorways onto a replacement piece cut from one of Uncle Zeno's red bandanas. Norma looked up and smiled brightly when Jim walked in. He was glad she didn't hate him anymore. He still didn't want to marry her, and never would, but at least now he hoped he would always know her. Mama simply looked sheepish.

"Oh, Norma," she said. "I am so sorry about this. I hope you don't mind me ripping this out." She lifted the piece of chambray away from the quilt and waved it feebly. "And look at it. It's just a scrap. I feel silly."

Norma hopped down from the bed and handed Mama the new red wall of the house. "There's nothing to feel silly about, Elizabeth," she said. "I know what that shirt meant to you."

Jim's nose wrinkled involuntarily, the way it always did when he heard Norma call Mama "Elizabeth." The uncles, and virtually everyone else in town, called her Cissy. Only Norma used Mama's given name.

Mama pinned the new piece against the dark blue background and tilted her head. "It's already a bit faded," she said. "It makes the neighborhood look a little trashy, but I guess it will have to do."

She and Norma threaded needles and, working shoulder to shoulder, began stitching the house back together. "It's funny I'm being so ungenerous about that piece," Mama said. "Jim, my husband, would have given us the shirt if we'd asked for it."

"Mmm?" Norma said. She was holding a straight pin between her lips.

"He was a kind boy," Mama said. "It seems so strange to me now to realize that he was only a boy the whole time I knew him. He was only twenty-three when he died."

Norma took the pin out of her mouth and jammed it into the cushion. "What else was he like?" she asked.

Mama glanced up and stared out the window, her needle poised in midair, the white thread taut beneath it, as if she was expecting her husband any minute.

"He was quiet," she said. "A little shy. He had a lovely singing voice, but you had to stand close to him to hear it. Not like my brothers — they're vain as peacocks about their singing and try to outdo each other until you can't hear anything else — but just a pretty voice, the kind that's pleasant to listen to in the evening. He sang all those old sad mountain songs that go on forever, like 'Barbie Allen.'"

"That sounds nice," Norma said.

"I don't know if I appreciated it enough at the time," said Mama. "He never sang directly to me, of course.

He would have found that too embarrassing. But he would sing when he knew I could hear him, and I wouldn't let on that I had listened."

Norma raised her eyebrows at Jim, but Jim pretended he didn't see her.

"And on Sunday afternoons, especially cold ones like today — this was after we were married and lived in that little tenant house — he would make me pies. His mother was sick a lot when he was little, and he learned how to cook for her. He made better biscuits than I did. He didn't use as much baking soda. My biscuits are pretty to look at, fluffy and all, but I've always suspected they were a little bitter."

"I like your biscuits," Norma said. "Mine are too hard and they tend to burn on the bottom."

"Poor boy," Mama said. "The uncles kidded him unmercifully about those pies."

Jim rattled the change in his pocket. "Are y'all ready to go?" he asked.

"Hold your horses, mister," Mama said. "We still have to quilt the new piece, but that shouldn't take long. You didn't leave the motor running, did you?"

The sky was low and gray and hard-looking — not the roiled, booming sky of early spring, but the bitter, set face of deep winter. A cutting wind from the west chased trash from the fields across the road and occasionally dashed a thimbleful of sleet against the windshield of the Major. Jim drove with his mittens on and the flaps down on his hunting cap. Mama and

Norma peered from above their scarves and turned-up coat collars like wary box turtles. In a week or two the trees would bud and the daffodils would bloom, but all that still seemed months, or even years, away. At least it wouldn't snow. Snow in Jim's part of the world always moved quietly up out of the south, and it was never this cold when it came.

"Who's that on the bridge?" Mama asked.

Jim had already identified the plaid coat and the long black hair blowing wildly below a red knit cap and scarf.

"That's Chrissie Steppe," Norma said. "Where in the world is she going?"

Mama clucked her tongue. "Why, she'll freeze to death."

"We have to give her a ride," Jim said.

"Where's she going to sit?" Norma asked.

"In somebody's lap, I guess," said Jim.

"And I suppose you want it to be yours."

"I'm *driving*, Norma."

"Y'all hush," Mama said. "We at least have to stop and see about her."

The steel bridge over the river was a single lane wide. When they drove onto it, Chrissie moved as close to the guardrail as possible, then looked over her shoulder and recognized the car. She was carrying a package wrapped in newspaper but tied with a fresh-looking white ribbon. Below the hem of her coat her skirt flapped around her bare legs, but at least she had on gloves. She waved by lifting the fingers of one hand from the package. Jim pulled off his hunting cap and shoved it into his coat pocket and stopped the Major beside her. Mama rolled down the window. Chrissie leaned over and looked inside, from face to face to face. As she studied them, only her eyes were visible above her scarf and beneath her cap. Jim could hear one of the guy wires on the bridge banging in the wind.

"Hello," Mama said. "Where are you off to on such a terrible day?"

"Allendale," Chrissie said, pushing her scarf down beneath her chin. "I've been meaning to get over to see Ellie and this is the first chance I've had."

"That's five more miles," Jim said.

"I'm hoping that once I get there, they'll know somebody headed back this way."

"It's a small world," Mama said. "That's where we're headed. To see the newlyweds. Why don't you ride with us?"

Chrissie considered the crowded front seat, and Jim saw the shadow of some mischievous, secret thought peering out through her dark pupils. With a finger she brushed a strand of hair away from her mouth.

"I couldn't," she said. "Y'all don't have room."

"Sure we do," Mama said. "Jim's going to ride in the rumble seat."

"I am?" Jim said. "But who's going to drive the Major?"

Mama giggled as she opened her door. "*I* am. Hop out. We'll let you use the quilt, won't we, Norma?"

Jim took the long way around the front of the car so he would have to walk by Chrissie on his way to the rumble seat. Mama shoved the quilt at him when she passed him on her way to the driver's side. She knew what he was up to.

Chrissie had to push the passenger-side door closed to make room between the car and the guardrail for Jim to get by. Jim stopped in front of her. There wasn't much room.

"Thank you for doing this," she said. "I was about to turn around."

"You're welcome," Jim said. "I'm glad to."

She looked down at the box in the crook of her arm. "It's just a cookie jar," she said. "It looks like a cat. Its head is the lid." She shielded her mouth with her free hand. "It was made in *Japan*."

Jim held up the quilt. "Mama and Norma pieced this for Ellie and Dennis Deane. It was made in Aliceville." He tried smiling at her.

She shook her head. "You know I'm still mad at you."

"I know."

"I expected better."

"Yeah. Me, too."

She frowned a little, looking at him. "Do you want my cap?" she asked. "It's awful cold."

It was obviously a girl's cap — it had snowflakes and happy snowmen knitted into it — but Jim nodded stupidly, hoping the bill of his hunting cap wasn't sticking out of his coat pocket.

"Thank you," he said. "That would be a help."

When Chrissie pulled off her cap and handed it to Jim, her hair popped with static electricity and began to levitate in the wind. She tried, with no discernible success, to pat it back down.

"I better get in," she said.

Jim plopped down into the rumble seat, pulled his hunting cap out of his pocket, and dropped it onto the floorboard. He looked over the side of the bridge. The river was dark and swift, metallic-looking, almost silent beneath the whip and yowl of the wind. He winced as Mama ground the gears, looking for first. The car bucked twice, then moved steadily forward and off the bridge. Jim pulled the quilt up over his head and — once hidden from view — Chrissie's cap down over his face.

Mill Hill

As the Major began to descend the steep hill across the river from Allendale, Jim pushed Chrissie's cap above his eyes and lowered the quilt from his face. The white, uniform houses of the mill village clung to the hillside opposite, strung together along muddy streets. Below the houses lay the ornate WPA bridge, complete with wrought-iron lampposts, that spanned the river and connected the two hills. The river here had been backed into near stillness by a dam wedged into the gorge downstream, and the four-story mill building loomed over the water as if studying its reflection. The mill's opaque windows glowed against the dim afternoon, although here and there black windowpanes lurked mysteriously among the mostly silver-painted glass. Slightly distorted by the otherwise imperceptible movement of the river, the reflection struck Jim as belonging to a structure grander than the cotton mill running a full Sunday shift that actually produced it — a citadel guarding an ancient port against Barbary pirates, or a castle in a brightly colored book, a jolly king raising a toast to his knights in the banquet hall.

As they crossed the bridge, the anxiety Jim had always felt as a baseball player entering Allendale to play the Spinners began reflexively buzzing in his gut. Allendale High had always whipped Aliceville School unmercifully, and — though he would never have admitted it — Jim suspected it was because boys who grew up in mill towns were simply tougher than boys who grew up farming. If you ever got a hit against Allendale, you knew that the next time you batted, the pitcher would try to stick one in your ear. Teams that managed to beat the Allendale nine routinely had to fight their way off the field and — if the game was played in Allendale — all the way to the bus. Jim figured that the only good thing to come from the school board's decision to cancel the baseball season was not having to face Allendale. He of course hated himself a little for being afraid of another baseball team, and for worrying that one of the lintheads from the dance might recognize him. When Mama downshifted into first for the pull up Mill Hill, the straining note of the Major's engine struck his ear as puny.

During the summer, when its houses were partially shaded by the chinaberry and locust trees that had found purchase on the hillside, Allendale, at least from a distance, presented to the world a face of superficial loveliness. But when the leaves were off the trees, as they were now, that same countenance revealed nothing so much as a regimented hardness of situation. To the right of the road a metallic glacier of trash worked its way down a deep, smooth-sided gully toward the river, while to the left each of the village streets opened in the moment the Major passed it onto what seemed to Jim an identical sad vista. The white-frame houses were all built from the same story-and-a-half plan; an identical shed dormer peered from the roof of each house into the backyard of the house immediately downhill from it. Each house was marked near the ground by a splattered red stripe of mud, and each was tethered by a wire to one of the black power poles sprouting up out of the hillside. Coal smoke spun into the air from each chimney, where, in the light wind still blowing, it unraveled into a gray haze that gathered close to the rooftops and moved aimlessly off. The yards and streets were connected by capillaries of what looked like cow paths, down which, three times a day, a fresh shift of workers spilled toward the mill, followed, once the whistle blew, by the previous shift trudging home. Nobody was about in the cold afternoon, however, and only the cold, round headlights of old cars stared back at Jim.

Dennis Deane and Ellie Something lived on Leila Street. Colonel Allen, who had built the mill and the village in 1901, had named the town after himself and the streets after his children, but the street signs had been knocked down long ago, leaving the names to be passed along by word of mouth. Leila, Dennis Deane had directed Jim on a postcard, was the sixth street up from the river. He hadn't bothered to tell Jim the names of the other streets they would pass, and, as Mama slowed to turn off the main road onto Leila, Jim thought that all the streets could have been named Leila for the difference it made.

Mama stopped the Major in front of the eighth house, which differed from the seventh house and the ninth house in only the spindly-looking staircase that climbed the outside wall toward a small landing and a low doorway cut into the gable. Jim folded the quilt as best he could while Chrissie and Norma tiptoed out of the street toward the unevenly placed steppingstones that wandered through the yard toward the front steps. They carried the food basket between them. Norma sneaked a look at Jim and from behind her mitten whispered something to Chrissie, who giggled and whispered something back to Norma. Mama walked carefully around the rear of the car. Jim stepped onto the fender and hopped down.

"Did you get too cold, honey?" Mama asked. "At least the wind died down some."

"I'll live," Jim said. He handed Mama the quilt.

"I hope we didn't get it dirty," she said. "Let's at least refold it before we go in."

Jim turned his back to Chrissie and Norma, who seemed to be having a private and mutually satisfying conversation in the yard. "So when did those two get to be friends?" he asked.

"I don't know," Mama said, handing him back two corners of the quilt and briefly raising her eyes to glance at the girls. "I didn't really get the feeling that they had ever been enemies. Maybe being stuck in the car together did them both some good."

"What are they snickering about?"

"I think they like your hat."

Jim snatched Chrissie's cap off and shoved it in his coat pocket. "And why are you grinning?"

"Nothing, really. I'd just forgotten what it was like to be a girl. I had fun."

"Did y'all say anything about me?"

"Of course we did. You know you're the only thing we ever think about."

"Really?"

"Sure. With us it's Jim, Jim, Jim. Twenty-four hours a day."

"All right. All right," Jim said. "Did you like her?"

"This isn't the time, sweetheart," she sang softly.

"Did you?"

"I think she doesn't have an easy life."

"So?"

"But you do."

"What does that mean?"

"It means I don't really have anything against her personally."

"And?"

"You should be careful what you wish for."

"Are you slowpokes coming?" Norma called.

"There. That looks much better," Mama said. "I wish we could wrap it."

As they approached the house, a black-and-white

hound stuck its head between two of the wooden front steps and snuffled loudly. Then it pulled its head back and disappeared into the shadows beneath the porch, followed seconds later by a moaning, theatrical howl. An unseen dog immediately across the street took up the call, followed by two farther down the hill. Soon, dogs were howling all over Allendale.

"Goodness," Mama said. "It sounds like the Blitz."

"This . . . is London," said Jim.

The front door opened and a short, round old woman appeared behind the screen. She put her hand on the latch but didn't open it.

"Y'all made the dog bark," she said.

Mama moved around Chrissie and Norma and spoke from the bottom of the steps. "Hello," she said. "I'm Elizabeth Glass, from Aliceville."

"Mrs. Tessnear."

"Good afternoon, Mrs. Tessnear. We're here to see Ellie and Dennis Deane."

"We don't like for them to have visitors."

Mama cocked her head slightly and touched her throat with her fingertips. "Oh. I'm sorry. I didn't know. Really?"

"Who is it, Ma?" a man's voice called from inside the house.

"It's for upstairs," Mrs. Tessnear said loudly over her shoulder.

"But they do live here?" Mama said. "Ellie and Dennis Deane."

"They do."

"And that staircase around the side of the house. Is that the way to where they stay?"

"The boys all work third shift," said Mrs. Tessnear. "They're in bed."

"What do they want, Ma?" called a second voice.

"I don't *know*. It's for up*stairs*."

"What does who want?" asked a third voice. "Is somebody here?"

"Up*stairs*. Up*stairs*, I said."

"Did Ma go upstairs?" somebody else called.

"Go to *sleep*," Mrs. Tessnear said. "All of you. Right now."

"My," said Mama. "How many boys do you have?"

"Seven."

"Are they all in the house?"

The old woman blinked suspiciously. "All except Ernest," she said. "Ernest ain't here."

"Ma? Why do they want to know about Ernest if they're going upstairs?"

"They didn't ask about Ernest."

"That staircase around the side of the house —" Mama said.

"What did you say about Ernest, Ma?"

"There ain't *nobody* said *nothing* about *Ernest*," Mrs. Tessnear almost yelled. "Go back to *sleep*."

"Ernest ain't here," a new voice said.

"Where'd he go?"

"I don't know. I just woke up and he was gone."

"Did he take the truck?"

"*Hush,*" said Mrs. Tessnear.

Jim heard someone hurrying down the outside stairway. Ellie Something peeked around the corner of the house before stepping onto the porch, her mouth agape. Jim immediately caught himself studying her breasts and just as quickly blushed. If she was showing, he couldn't tell. She crossed to the top of the steps and clapped her hands together underneath her chin. "Oh . . . my . . . goodness," she squealed. "Did all of you come to see *us?*" She ran down into the yard and violently hugged everyone, even Mama, whom she had never met, and Jim, who tried to get away. "Are those presents? Is that a *quilt?* And do I smell *chicken?* Oh, I can't believe how sweet you are to come all this way. Jim, are you cold? Your face is so red. Did you have to ride in the rumble seat?"

"The boys are in bed," Mrs. Tessnear said from the door.

"Yes, ma'am," Ellie Something said, turning her head to the side and speaking to the ground. "We know that."

"You know we don't like for you to have company."

"We have a right to have people come see us, Mrs. Tessnear. The boss man said so."

"I don't care what the boss man said. This was my house before you were even born."

"Well, we're sorry, but now we live here, too."

"I didn't have no say in that," Mrs. Tessnear said.

She stepped backward into the house and slammed the front door.

"You'd think she would be nice to me on a Sunday," Ellie Something said.

"Let's just go upstairs," said Mama.

Chrissie and Norma left the food basket on the bottom step for Jim to carry. He leaned over the railing so he could see around Mama and watched the girls as they walked up in front of him. Maybe Ellie Something's behind was a little bigger than it used to be, but Jim couldn't remember what it had looked like before. He didn't think he had ever looked at it. She had only been a freshman. Norma's waist and hips were curvier than Chrissie's, which somehow made him feel virtuous for choosing Chrissie over Norma. Not that choosing Chrissie had done him any good. Mama glanced back over her shoulder and he straightened up. On the landing, Ellie Something opened the door and extended her arm.

"Welcome to our home," she said.

Jim ducked into a long, unpainted room with a low bead-board ceiling whose pitch matched that of the roof. A cheap cookstove and a tiny sink dominated the room near the entrance. Beyond the stove, a narrow bed with an iron headboard lay partially hidden behind a chifforobe with a work shirt hanging from the door. The room was almost alarmingly hot. Dennis Deane, wearing an undershirt and owly horn-rim glasses, stood up from behind the table in the alcove underneath the dormer. The windows in the dormer overlooked the street, and Jim wondered why Dennis Deane hadn't come down to greet them.

"Well, I'll be," Dennis Deane said. "Look who's washed up on Leila Street."

"Oh, no," Ellie Something cried suddenly.

"What?" Dennis Deane said.

"This is just awful."

"What is? What's awful?"

"We only have two chairs, Dennis Deane. Where is everybody going to sit?"

"Chrissie and I will sit on the floor, won't we, Chrissie?" Norma said. "And so will Jim."

"And I can sit on the floor, too," Mama said. "I'm not as old as I seem. You and Dennis Deane take the chairs. This is your home."

"But why do *we* only have *two* chairs?" Ellie Something said. "Those awful Tessnears have probably got *eight* chairs down there. Maybe *nine*."

Dennis Deane looked a little frightened. He shrugged. "There are eight of 'em living down there. They gotta sit somewhere."

Ellie Something glared at Dennis Deane, then stomped her foot. Seconds later someone downstairs whacked the ceiling with a broom handle. She leaned over and stared angrily at the floor. "Ooh, you nasty old thing," she whispered.

"Ellie and Mrs. Tessnear get into it at least once a day," Dennis Deane said. "They're like two cats that way."

Ellie parked her fists on her hips. "Are you taking her side?" she asked.

"Oh, Lord, no, honey. Of course not."

"I'm just trying to make us a home here, Dennis Deane, and I don't have much to work with."

"I know you are, sweetheart, and I think you're doing a good job." He took the shirt down from the door of the chifforobe and rapidly began putting it on.

"Where are you going?"

"Me and Jim are gonna go for a walk. Wanna go for a walk, Jim?"

"Sure," Jim said. "I guess." He set the food basket on the floor.

"A walk?" Ellie Something said. "You're going for a walk? These people are our *guests*, Dennis Deane. They just got here and they brought us *presents*."

"Oh, I think they should definitely go for a walk," Mama said. "You see, our visit is kind of a surprise housewarming shower, and men would just get in the way."

"Absolutely," Chrissie said. "They should leave."

"The only reason we brought Jim," said Norma, "was because it was his car."

"And he didn't even drive it," Mama said.

"A *shower?*" Ellie Something said. "You're giving me a *shower?*" She covered her face with her hands and began to cry.

"Shh," Chrissie said, kissing Ellie Something on the hair and glaring dangerously at Dennis Deane.

Dennis Deane looked helplessly to Mama, who

winked at him and nodded toward the door. He stepped forward and placed his hand in the small of Ellie Something's back. "Hey, little stuff," he whispered. "Look at me."

"I don't want to look at you."

"Well, I can't say that I blame you there. I know I'm not the handsomest man in the world. But, if it makes you feel any better, I'm pretty sure I'm the handsomest man on Leila Street."

Jim saw Ellie Something's cheeks rise behind her hands in the direction of a small smile. She peeked at Dennis Deane over the tips of her fingers.

"We won't be gone long," he said.

"You promise?"

"I promise."

Ellie Something opened her hands and Dennis Deane leaned in and smooched her on the lips.

We're Married Now

$\mathcal{J}$IM AND Dennis Deane sat atop the large hump of granite protruding from the ground near the top of Mill Hill. Dennis Deane's glasses were pushed up on his forehead, and his hands covered his eyes. Jim thought that Dennis Deane might be crying, so he didn't look at him. He studied instead the names and dates and initials and hearts and curse words, some of them faded and ancient-looking, scratched on the cold gray skin of the rock. Because Jim didn't recognize any of the names or initials, and the dates held no significance, the curse words seemed to rise above the babble of their surroundings and fly in his face — which left him feeling vaguely picked on. It was like being laughed at by strangers for no discernible reason.

Below him, the houses of the village dropped toward the mill a terraced row at a time, trailing behind them backyards cluttered with coal piles and outhouses and roughly made chicken coops and recently turned garden spots; with fruit trees and beehives and small forests of tall poles blooming with purple martin houses made from painted gourds; with squat, black washtubs and clotheslines bobbing with gaunt families of dungarees and shirts and dresses and underwear. The houses didn't vary in shape, but somehow no two yards looked alike, as if another town had exploded nearby and the debris from the explosion had fallen randomly from the sky. Allendale from the front proclaimed its toughness with a single rigid face, but from the back it revealed instead a collection of tired private faces that Jim didn't think he was meant to see, particularly when a woman wearing little more than a slip appeared on one of the stoops and threw a pan of dishwater into the yard. Maybe that's why the rock he was sitting on cursed at him every time he glanced at it: he wasn't supposed to be here. He looked at his watch. He had been in Allendale less than half an hour and already wished he were somewhere else. He didn't know how Dennis Deane stood it.

Dennis Deane sniffed and drew his coat sleeve across his face and lowered his glasses onto his nose. "Ah, God, look at this place," he said.

"Do you know the names of the other streets?" Jim asked.

Dennis Deane closed his eyes and pointed down the hill. "Esmerelda, Honoria, Virginia, Eugenia, Cecily, Leila, Elspeth, and Garland."

"Garland?"

"The only boy. 'A nineteen sixteen graduate of Yale University, he loved his God and his country, and on the cruel battlefields of France willingly offered the frail vessel of his earthly body as a sacrifice for the propagation of liberty, July nineteen eighteen.'"

"Where did you read that?"

"There's a plaque beside the main gate. I walk by it every day."

"Does anybody still live in the big house?"

"Just Elspeth. The rest of 'em moved back to New Hampshire when the Colonel died."

Set at the end of an avenue of walnut trees near the high school, its first story obscured by overgrown box-woods, the big house had always looked haunted to Jim, although maybe its proximity to the ball field was what made it seem so scary.

"Have you ever seen her?"

"Who? Miss Allen? Nah. She only comes out at Christmas. Gives everybody a poke full of oranges. I'll get mine next year, I guess. I didn't get in the navy."

"You tried to enlist?"

"They said I didn't see good enough, not even with these handsome glasses."

"Where'd you get them?"

"An eye doctor comes to the mill every three months. Are you going to join up?"

"I already did," Jim said. "Did the mill pay?"

"Nah. They take it out of your check. Navy?"

"Army. I go in the day after my birthday. In June."

"I still know when your birthday is. What did your mama say?"

"I haven't told her yet."

"Boy," Dennis Deane said, "I wouldn't want to be there for that conversation."

"Me, neither," said Jim.

Jim hadn't wanted any part of the navy because there was nowhere to hide in the middle of the ocean. If the Japanese, or a U-boat, found your ship, you couldn't do a thing about it. Pearl Harbor had proved that. And even if you managed to get off your ship before it sank, you might still be thousands of miles from land. What were you supposed to do then? Besides, Bucky had been in the navy, and as far as Jim was concerned, that was strike three right there. He kept Bucky's letter from Pearl Harbor hidden in his underwear drawer. He didn't know what to do with it. Throwing it away seemed sacrilegious somehow, but keeping it never let Jim forget that Bucky, even though he was dead, had won in the end.

Jim had decided on the army during the train ride into New Carpenter the day he sneaked off to enlist. At least in the army there was a possibility you might get to fight in the woods, where Jim figured he would have a chance. The uncles said that country boys always made the best soldiers because they already knew how to hunt and shoot when they went in. Jim knew how to hunt and shoot. And if a squirrel couldn't

see him, as good as their eyes were, then, how could a
German? City boys, the uncles said, were always the
first ones to get shot. The trick was to not stand next
to one. Jim hoped that when his time came to fight,
the battle would be in the woods.

"Who would you rather kill," Dennis Deane asked,
"a German or a Jap?"

"I would just as soon not kill anybody, Dennis
Deane."

"Well, you've got one bullet. And there's a kraut
and a Jap running toward your foxhole. Who do you
shoot?"

"The German."

"How come?"

"He's probably bigger than the Jap. I figure, shoot
the big guy and fight the little guy."

"But what if the Jap was meaner than the German?"

"He would still be little."

"Man, if I could ever get out of this place, I'd love to
go to the Philippines and kill me some Japs. I bet I
could even shoot straight now. Have y'all been keeping up with it?"

"It sounds bad on the radio," Jim said, "but the uncles say that ol' MacArthur's going to be hard to
whip."

"They're all screwed. Even ol' MacArthur."

Jim felt he should probably argue the point about
MacArthur — the uncles would have — but deep down

he agreed with it. He didn't see how anybody was going to stop the Japanese, so he let it go.

"Are you scared?" Dennis Deane asked.

"Some, I guess."

"Have you told Chrissie?"

"I doubt she would care," Jim said.

"You might be right about that. She and Ellie write
letters back and forth, and apparently you did something to make Pocahontas awful mad."

"I told you not to call her that. What did she say
I did?"

"I don't really know. Ellie won't say. She says girl
stuff is private, and I'm inclined to agree with her.
I know way more about girl stuff than anybody
ought to."

"Do you like being married?"

Dennis Deane swallowed, then pushed his glasses
up and covered his eyes.

"Are you crying?"

"Go to hell."

Jim looked at his watch again. Then he listened to
it tick. He could feel the curse words on the rock trying to get his attention. He studied the purple martin
houses down in the village to see if any birds came
out of them. His butt felt frozen.

"I'm just tired, is all, Jim. Ellie cries all the time
because she misses her mama, and her mama won't
come see Ellie because Ellie got pregnant. *My* mama
comes to see us all the time and starts crying as soon
as she walks in the door. I don't really recommend

knocking up a fourteen-year-old, Jim. It just causes trouble."

"I wasn't planning on it."

"The only real good thing about being married is that we get to do it whenever we want to."

"Really?" Jim said. "You can do it with a pregnant girl?"

"Oh, boy. Are you kidding me? That's all pregnant girls *want* to do. They're like daggum wildcats. Ellie likes to do it late at night when all the Tessnear boys are on third. It makes the bed squeak and drives the old woman crazy. Did you know your face was red?"

"Now you go to hell," Jim said.

"We'll take that trip together," said Dennis Deane.

"Well, we've got a good start."

"But first you've got to promise me you won't ever tell anybody I talked about Ellie like that. We're married now."

Jim still felt a little squeamish about the idea of doing it with a pregnant girl and couldn't imagine who he would tell, anyway. "I promise," he said. "Let's talk about something else."

"Tell me about Bucky's funeral. I heard there were two or three thousand people up there."

"There were more people up there than at the Christmas parade in New Carpenter, if you can believe that. Cars were backed up from the Bucklaws all the way down to Penn's house. They made Bucky out to be some kind of big war hero."

"Well, you know, Jim, Bucky is kind of a big war hero."

"He was on a ship and somebody blew it up," Jim said. "How does that make him a hero?"

Dennis Deane whistled and looked away. "Dag*gum*, Jim," he said.

Jim searched out and stared at the nearest curse word. He had it coming. "I know," he said. "I've got to do better. Please don't tell anybody I said that."

"I won't, but, boy, I can't believe you still hate him that much. I mean, he ain't coming home."

"He might as well be. He wrote me a letter right before he died and told me to stay away from Chrissie."

Dennis Deane laughed. "Some people ain't even nice when they're dead, are they? What time you got?"

"Ten 'til three."

"We need to go before long. I gotta be at work at four."

"What do you do in the mill?"

"I'm a sweeper."

"What does that mean?"

"It means I sweep. You see the third floor? That's what I sweep, every night, from one end to the other."

"Do you like it?"

"It's the worst job in the mill. The broom's four feet wide and it weighs a ton and it just kills my elbows. They only make dumbasses and people they want to run off do it."

"Which one are you?"

"I'm a dumbass. Ernest Tessnear is the one they're trying to run off."

"What did he do?"

"I'm not sure. He says they got tired of him not kissing people's butts. He used to be the guard in the gatehouse on first shift. Now he's a sweeper on *third* shift. And they made all his brothers work third, too. It looks like they're trying to run the whole crowd off. At least they gave me second."

"Why didn't they just fire Ernest?"

"They think they're teaching the rest of us a lesson. They're gonna wind up with a union in here if they ain't careful."

"Why does the old woman hate y'all so much?"

"They used to have the whole house. The boss man moved us in after they got mad at Ernest. We're on the waiting list to get our own house, but it might take a while."

"Why don't the Tessnears just quit?"

"I don't know. The whole gang tried joining the navy when they made Ernest a sweeper, but none of 'em could get in. They're all deaf from working in the mill. Me, I stick spit wads in my ears."

He stood up.

"Jim, do you remember all those times when we were in school and I acted stupid?"

"That would be hard to forget, Dennis Deane."

"Well, I just want you to know that I *knew* I was acting stupid. It doesn't really count as stupid when you know. Deep down, I'm actually pretty smart. I just tried to keep it a secret."

"Everybody suspects that, except maybe the teachers. I think you fooled them pretty good."

"I knew that one day I'd have to stop acting stupid and go to work and get married and all that stuff, but *damn*, Jim, I didn't figure it would happen this soon."

"It happens to everybody, Dennis Deane. It happens to me in June."

"Then we must have done something *wrong*. I ought to have some stupid time left. I ain't even grown up yet. Hey, can you hear that?"

The breeze had quieted for the moment, and in the lull Jim heard the faint hammering clack of the looms inside the mill. From a distance it sounded like cicadas, or banjos playing something fast, a rain shower coming across a cornfield, something other than what it was. He couldn't believe it was audible from so far away.

"Do you know what we're making down there?"

Jim shook his head.

"Khaki twill. Miles and miles of it. That's all we're running. Three shifts, seven days a week."

"For uniforms," Jim said.

"Yep." Dennis Deane hopped down off the rock. "Hey, y'all might make the cloth for my uniform. Wouldn't that be something?"

"*'Y'all might make the cloth for* my *uniform,'*" Dennis Deane said in a whiny voice. "*'Wouldn't that be something?'*"

"What the hell's the matter with you all of a sudden?"

"There ain't nothing the matter with me," said Dennis Deane. "What the hell's the matter with you?"

March 14, 1942

New Carpenter, North Carolina
Dear Elizabeth,

    Regarding your recent letter, I must take exception. Although I understand your position as the mother of an only son, I don't appreciate being taken to task for doing my duty. You should know me well enough to know that I would never certify any young man as unhealthy when he is as healthy as Jim is, no matter how long I've known his family. It's no easy thing approving any mother's son for military service, particularly when those sons are heading off to a war that's shaping up to be as bloody as this one appears it's going to be, and I don't take the responsibility lightly. Don't forget that I brought most of those boys into the world, Jim included! Please know that I will pray for him as I pray for all the others. Unfortunately, that's the best I can do. Be proud of Jim for wanting to serve his country. Don't blame me because you raised him properly!

Sincerely yours,
Theodore Burch Twitty, M.D.

p.s. It's been a while since I saw you last. Come on in when you're through being mad at me and we'll have a look at you.

"Heroes of Mathematics"

by
Norma Harris

*M*R. D*UNLAP*, *beloved faculty, family, and friends of the class of 1942, I stand before you tonight not as one who has arrived at a destination, but as one resting momentarily, as at an oasis, at the beginning of a much longer journey. Although we have on this day completed our long march through the difficult grades of elementary and high school, we are also fully aware that we have simultaneously arrived at a point of embarkation beyond which lie the disparate roads that will carry us to our respective destinies. For those of us whose destinies lead us away from our small, but beloved, home, we pray that those same roads will someday lead us back again, back to those of you who have selflessly loved and raised and taught us, equipping us for our journeys. We are also fully aware that, because of the great struggle in which our nation is now engaged, the days of travel ahead will be for many of us fraught with danger and hardship, and that all of us will be asked to make sacrifices greater than we think we can bear. [DON'T LOOK AT J!] Two of our number, Buster Burnette and Horace Gentine, have already heeded the call to arms, and others will no*

doubt soon follow in their brave footsteps, and, lest we forget, those of us who remain behind will also be asked to
make contributions no less important. We, the Aliceville
School class of 1942, wish to assure you on this occasion
that with God's help we are ready to do our respective duties, be they here or on some desolate foreign shore.

It seems like only yesterday that as a little girl I stood at
the bottom of this very hill and watched this great hall of
learning rise from the earth. At the time it seemed to me a
miracle that such a gigantic building should suddenly appear in my tiny world. Today, however, armed with the education I received here, I look around this auditorium and
think instead of the skill and knowledge necessary to make
possible the construction that so dazzled my young eyes.
From the architect who designed the building to the lowliest
laborer, the individual abilities of each person involved were
crucial to the building's successful completion, just as the
individual abilities of each of us will prove crucial to our
nation's efforts in the struggles ahead. It was the great Greek
mathematician Pythagoras who said almost six hundred
years before the birth of Christ that "all is number," meaning that the great truths of Creation can be reduced to
mathematical absolutes. While Christ Himself proved Pythagoras's theory to be in error, I think we can now more
accurately state that "much is number." I ask you now to
gaze up at the majestic height of the ceiling above us and to
note the great distance between its supporting walls. [GES-
TURE.] It seems impossible that the ceiling does not fall in
upon us, yet it does not fall! We sit here tonight secure be-

neath it only because men who fully grasped that "much is number" used their considerable mathematical skills to build it in such a way that it would not fall. It was mathematicians such as Pythagoras and Euclid, the father of geometry, and Sir Isaac Newton, the inventor of calculus and discoverer of gravity, whose mathematical truths hold up the roof over our heads just as the democratic ideals of great leaders such as Washington and Jefferson and Lincoln support the enduring edifice of our republic. It was President Lincoln who said that "a house divided against itself cannot stand," and tonight we sit in this magnificent, undivided house of learning as citizens of an undivided nation, each of us one of a greater number committed to the preservation of freedom and liberty.

While the memories of the peaceful world in which we lived prior to December seventh remain vivid in our minds, I ask you to imagine another nation at peace, the ancient kingdom of Syracuse, on the isle of Sicily, in the year 213 B.C. In Syracuse at that time, there lived a mathematician and engineer named Archimedes. Archimedes was a peaceful man who was never happier than when solving a complicated equation or making a difficult proof. It was he who once leapt from his bath and ran naked through the streets of Syracuse shouting, "Eureka! I've got it!" when he finally figured out the solution to a particularly vexing problem — much to the surprise of his startled neighbors, I'm sure! It was also he who, while out for a stroll one day, gazed out to sea and spied the deadly warships of the Roman general Marcus Claudius Marcellus approaching Syracuse

*under full sail! The Romans had come to invade and enslave
the city in the name of the emperor! Though he was a peaceful man, Archimedes decided at that moment to use his
mathematical skills to help defend his beloved city against
the overwhelming might of the Roman invaders. First, using
the laws of optics, he constructed great mirrors of bronze
to reflect the blinding rays of the sun into the harbor and
to set fire to the Roman ships that dared venture too close to
shore. Later, after the Romans gained landfall, he invented
great machines of war to defend the walls of the city against
the relentless siege of the irrepressible legions. And when
the Romans finally breached the walls and sacked the
city, a legionnaire came upon Archimedes scratching one
final problem into the sand with a stick, no doubt an equation he would use to invent yet another machine to help
his countrymen. Archimedes didn't even look up from his
work as the legionnaire drew his bloody sword and cut off
the peaceful mathematician's head. It was Archimedes
who said, "Give me a lever long enough and a place to
stand and I will move the world." Though we did not ask for
the responsibility, we, the class of 1942, have by circumstance and necessity been asked to take up the lever before
us and move the world. You, beloved parents and teachers,
have given us a secure foundation, a place on which to
stand. Though we are but inexperienced youths, we understand that while we may not yet feel ready to move the world,
move it we must, from the regions of darkness into which
it has fallen, back into the light of freedom and peace. In
generations to come, history will judge us by how we re-*

sponded when our nation called upon us. So years from now, when the day of judgment is at hand, let it be said that when the sails of our enemies appeared in our harbor, we set to work and directed the glorious rays of the sun back upon them! Though we long for peace, let us build great machines of war, and build them well, if that is what we must do.

Already we have lost one of our own to our dishonorable and inscrutable enemy, one who as a member of the class of 1941 sat in this very room just a year ago, filled with his own hopes and dreams for the future. No one here on that night, myself included, would have dared imagine that because of treachery already under way on the far side of the globe this young man in the prime of his life had but little more than half a year to live. Let it be known that the class of 1942 has voted to honor Arthur Bucklaw Jr. by leaving the seat he occupied last year vacant, and I now draw your attention to it. [PAUSE. GESTURE.] As we remember Bucky, I would like to close with the immortal words of Abraham Lincoln, who offered these sentiments during the dedication of the National Cemetery in Gettysburg, Pennsylvania, on November 19, 1863, following another dark moment in our nation's history. Though perhaps familiar, they have never been more apt: "It is rather for us to be here dedicated to the great task remaining before us — that from these honored dead we take increased devotion to that cause for which they gave the last full measure of devotion — that we here highly resolve that these dead shall not have died in vain, that this nation under God shall have a new birth of freedom, and that government of the people, by the people, for the people, shall not perish from the earth."

Thank you and may God in His infinite mercy bless us all.

Injun Joe

*E*ARLY IN the evening Jim walked around the hotel and let himself in through the back gate. A dozen or so hens fussed over a yellow stripe of corn strewn from the porch, and he watched where he put his good shoes as he crossed the dirt yard. He still wore the black gown in which he had graduated — although he had left the cap at home — and he felt awkward and somber and ministerial and grown-up as he climbed the steps. When he peered through the screen he saw Chrissie seated at the enamel-topped table in the center of the dim kitchen, her hands crossed in front of her, her face tilted toward the small window above the stove. He watched her for as long as he dared before he tapped at the door. In the soft, slanted failing light she had seemed as beautiful as the Virgin Mary listening to the call of the Lord on a slick page in an old Bible, but as she turned toward him, her face lengthened and her hair dulled and dusky circles appeared beneath her eyes. The woman who stared back from the other side of the screen wasn't Chrissie at all, and the picture she occupied became almost too sad to contemplate.

"Come on in the house," Mrs. Steppe said.

"Thank you," said Jim. He still felt startled as he crossed the threshold and eased the door closed behind him.

"I figured you might be the first one to show up."

Jim didn't know what she meant by that, so he stood there and watched Mrs. Steppe watch him. He wished he had taken off the gown; and the necktie; and the shiny shoes. He wished he weren't holding a bottle of perfume wrapped in lilac-scented paper. He wished he were sitting on the porch at home with Mama and the uncles, watching people drive away from graduation. Uncle Coran or Uncle Al would say, "Good crowd this year," and Uncle Zeno would say, "Yep."

"I didn't mean anything by that," she said.

"No, ma'am."

"I just figured that you would come on by when you heard. You've always seemed to me like you'd be that kind of boy."

Jim wasn't sure what kind of boy that was, so he smiled and looked down at the package. He had been careful not to mash the bow.

"Y'all did hear about it over there, didn't you?"

"Yes, ma'am," he said. "We heard. I'm awfully sorry about Mr. Steppe."

"Yeah, well, Joe. It's been coming a long time, I guess, but it's nice of you to say that. Do you want to sit down a minute?" She placed her palms flat against the table and looked around the kitchen as if a new workday had sneaked up on her and had to be immediately subdued. "I've got half a pot of coffee left over from supper. Would you like a cup? It's still warm. We got an electric pot in the dining room, the hotel does."

Jim didn't particularly like coffee, but he was a high school graduate now, offering words of comfort to a woman whose husband had just died. By his reckoning this was the first purely adult situation he would handle on his own — an Uncle Zeno kind of situation — and coffee drinking seemed called for.

"Coffee sounds good about now," he said. "Thanks." He drew the chair at the end of the table and sat with his back to the door.

"How do you take it?"

Jim preferred that his coffee come with enough cream and sugar in it to make it stop tasting like coffee, but he answered, "Black." That's how he would have to drink it once he was a soldier. He pictured himself squatting around a campfire with other soldiers, drinking bitter black coffee from a tin cup. He hoped one of the other soldiers was his buddy. It would be good to have a buddy in the war. He wondered if it would be safe to sit around a campfire. Would the Germans see the smoke?

"Here we go," Mrs. Steppe said.

The coffee smelled better than he had imagined. The steam rising from the cup curled into the light falling through the window, and it seemed important to Jim that the steam climbing through the light be noticed, so he noticed it. Outside the window, the evening had begun to dim toward twilight, although the sun wasn't quite down. A chimney swift dove crazily across the small square of sky, and the bird's pale shadow blinked almost invisibly on the white tabletop and was gone. Jim noted that he saw both the bird and its shadow in the same instant, and that seemed important, too. He wrapped both hands around the cup and felt the heat creep up his forearms. The attendant beauty and sadness of the world suddenly seemed to him available for pondering in a way they never had before. He felt as though he had spent his life until this evening poised over an exam, waiting for the teacher to say, "Begin." Now he had begun. He took a slow sip of coffee but found that it tasted as bad as he had thought it would.

"You sure you don't want cream and sugar?" Mrs. Steppe asked. "I can get you some. It's no trouble."

"No. No, thank you," Jim said, placing the cup down on the saucer. Maybe the coffee would taste better once it cooled down a little. "This is good."

"I suppose I'll drink me a cup," Mrs. Steppe said. "It's not as hot in here as it was." When she returned to the table, she nodded toward the door standing slightly ajar across the room. "I guess you came by to see Chrissie, but she doesn't feel like receiving visitors this evening."

"No, ma'am. I understand," Jim said, eyeing the sliver of shadow visible through the crack in the doorway. "How's she doing?"

"Ah, about like you'd expect. That little girl sure loved her daddy. And he was good to her, in his way. I have to give him that, even now."

"And how are you doing?"

Mrs. Steppe's face dipped toward the tabletop. She seemed to be studying her hands. Some seconds passed before Jim noticed a tear flare in the light along her jawline and drop from the end of her chin.

"I'm so sorry," he said. "I didn't mean —"

She held up her palm and cut him off. She leaned down and dabbed the corners of her eyes with her apron.

"I'm fine," she said. "I just act a little stupid when people ask me how I am. I guess I'm not used to it. So, tell me, how was graduation?"

"It was nice," Jim said. "Norma gave a good speech." He instantly regretted mentioning Norma and hoped Chrissie hadn't heard. "It got hot in the auditorium before it was over, but we got through it."

Mrs. Steppe shook her head. "Joe, I swear to God," she said.

"Ma'am?"

"All that girl has ever wanted to do was be in school and be like everybody else and go to the dances and march down the aisle and get her diploma, and he figured out how to mess that up, too."

Jim sipped his coffee. It didn't taste any better.

"And I just can't believe that he was trying to come to her graduation," she said, her voice rising. "Did he think he could just march in big as life and sit down in the auditorium and nobody would notice him? Did he think he wouldn't get us in a world of trouble by pulling a stunt like that? Did he think we were going to up and go off with him, and him running from the law?" She picked up her coffee cup, then sat it back down in the saucer. "I give up," she said. "I don't know what he was thinking, and I don't guess I ever did."

Jim sneaked another look at the door.

"I think she's asleep," Mrs. Steppe said. "And she's heard it all before, anyway. I know I'm bad to get mad and wear Joe out. I don't guess I should, not in front of her, but I do. Most of the time I don't have anybody else to listen to it."

Jim began to sweat underneath his graduation gown. He wondered if he would spend the rest of his adult life not knowing what to say. If this was an exam, he wasn't doing very well at it.

"What did y'all hear about it over at your house?" Mrs. Steppe asked.

"We just heard that Mr. Steppe got killed in a car wreck. In South Carolina."

"In Chesnee," she said. "He was headed this way sure as the world. Were people talking about it up at the school?"

"Yes, ma'am," Jim said. "A little."

"I just bet they were."

"Nobody really knew anything, though. There wasn't much they could say."

"Did you know he was in a stolen car? Did y'all hear

that? Were people talking about that up at the school-house?"

"No, ma'am."

"I swear to God. That man. Stolen car. And it was a *Packard*, for goodness' sakes, like nobody on the road would notice an Indian driving a Packard."

"Were the police chasing him?"

"Not this time. He just ran off the road and crashed into a tree. They said he probably went to sleep. Ain't that something? Went to sleep and ruined somebody's Packard."

"I'm sorry."

"He never could do anything right."

Jim didn't know if he was supposed to affirm the remark or challenge it out of respect for the dead. So he sat very still.

"Maybe I can finally get me some sleep now, though. I figured all along he was going to come back this way. Every time I closed my eyes I dreamed he was looking in the window."

"Why were you afraid of him?" Jim asked before he thought. "Y'all were married."

Mrs. Steppe studied him, a slight frown of concentration and disapproval on her face. He had seen Chrissie look at him like that, and he was disappointed in himself that he apparently deserved it so often.

"You think married people don't get afraid of each other?" she asked.

Jim scratched at a small nick in his saucer. He had

gotten that one wrong for sure. "I don't know," he said. "I guess not. I haven't spent a lot of time around married people, I mean living with married people, so I can't say."

"Joe had a temper on him," Mrs. Steppe said.

Her tone and frown suggested that her answer contained everything Jim needed to know. He didn't know exactly what that was, of course, but maybe he could come back to it and figure it out later.

"Oh," he said.

"You know he robbed a bank."

"Yes, ma'am."

"You know how come?"

"No, ma'am."

She paused.

"There was this ranch for sale near where we lived in Oklahoma, but really what it was, was a dustbowl. Every time the wind blew, half of it wound up in Arkansas. Barns rotten, house falling in. You should've seen it. Anyway, one night Joe had a dream that the place had oil on it. He said he could see it underneath the ground, a whole lake of it, and he knew just where it was, and the dream was so vivid, he was convinced about it when he woke up. Absolutely convinced. I couldn't talk him down. He got like that sometimes. The only problem with his plan, of course, was that he didn't have any money to buy the ranch. Come to think of it, not having any money was always the problem with Joe's plans."

"So he robbed a bank?"

"That's what he came up with, yes. We didn't know none of this at the time, but he was going to rob a bank and buy that ranch and be the Cherokee oil king of Oklahoma. The bank he finally picked out was way out west somewhere, and the county it was in just had one bank and one cop. So who do you guess walked in while Joe was robbing that one bank?"

"That one cop?"

"The very one. Who naturally pulled out his gun and shot at Joe and hit the teller. Joe shot at the cop and managed to hit him in the foot. I know Joe wanted to kill him, but he couldn't even get that part right. Joe always did have bad luck with policemen."

"Then what happened?"

"The poor teller, he died, and the cop got crippled. Joe ran out the door, and we didn't hear from him again. That broke Chrissie's heart more than any-thing. Then, late one night, after they figured out it was Joe they were looking for, Chrissie came and woke me up, and there was a cross burning in our yard. It wasn't much of a cross, just a little dinky old thing, but still."

"A cross burning?" Jim said. "But you and Chrissie . . ."

"Joe ain't a white man," said Mrs. Steppe, "however much you might want him to be. And one white man was dead because of him, and another one was crip-pled. It didn't make any difference how white I was. And Chrissie was only *half* white. Soon as it got light, I took my egg money, and me and her hitched a ride into town and got on the train to come to North Carolina. We only had enough money that morning to get to Little Rock, but we started out."

"How did you finally make it all the way home?"

"I was able to get your uncle Zeno to wire us the rest."

Jim gulped his coffee and swallowed miserably. He had to be the worst adult on God's green earth. Uncle Zeno would have steered the conversation somewhere else long before Mrs. Steppe embarrassed herself. Mama would kill him if she ever found out he had asked such a dumb question.

"I just couldn't think of anybody else to help us," Mrs. Steppe went on. "I knew Daddy and Mama didn't have it, and I wouldn't ever ask the Bucklaws for anything if I could help it. You've seen how they think they own people. So, now we owe you instead. I haven't been able to pay it back yet, but I will. You can tell your uncle Zeno I said that if you want to."

"I'm sure he's not worried about it."

"He won't ever mention it to me, but I guarantee you he ain't forgot about it. The McBrides didn't get where they are by not worrying about their money."

Jim nodded. That was true enough.

"It was awfully kind of him, though. I wouldn't have blamed him if he'd said no."

"Does Chrissie know where it came from?"

"I'm afraid so," Mrs. Steppe said. "And I'm sorry about it. I know it would be better for her if she didn't know, but she does. The first time she laid eyes on you this year, she knew we owed your family money, and that ain't no way to start out in a new school. And I don't guess I should have told you just now. I don't know what I'm thinking anymore. I just can't stop talking."

"Can I ask you a question?"

Mrs. Steppe shook her head a little but said, "You might as well. I've told you everything else I know."

"Why did you marry Mr. Steppe?"

"Ah, I don't even know the answer to that one anymore. It seems like a thousand years ago. Because he was the prettiest man I'd ever seen, I guess, and because he could talk like nobody else I ever listened to. And he said he was going to live in California and grow orange trees and I liked the sound of that. California. Daddy had got his arm cut off and he owed people money because he couldn't work, and I'd hardly ever been off the mountain, and I'd never even rode on a train until I started going with Zeno, and then we only went to New Carpenter, and I thought, why not? Why not marry this handsome Indian and ride a train all the way to the Pacific Ocean, then get off and live there?

"At the time I was just so mad at Zeno for not joining the army. I stomped my foot and railed at him, but you know Zeno, he wouldn't budge once he made up his mind, so I broke it off with him. But that seems like a crazy thing to get mad about now, when you think about it, because all them boys got killed for nothing. Zeno was right about the whole thing. There wasn't any reason for that war. Of course, you never will know as much as you do when you're young, and I knew everything there was to know. You didn't join up because of Chrissie, did you?"

"Partly, I suppose."

She raised her coffee cup, then set it back down in the saucer.

"I don't know that that seems like a good reason, to be honest with you," she said. "There ain't never been a little girl worth getting killed over, no matter how pretty her hair is. And she never was impressed with Bucky for being in the navy, not like the Bucklaws. You'd of thought he was an admiral, the way they talked."

"They probably would have got me in the draft, anyway," Jim answered, his face hot. "Did Mr. Steppe join the army because of you?"

"I suppose," she said. "I had pretty hair, too, you know. He figured he could at least get one up on Zeno, and he did. And I figured I could hurt Zeno's feelings, and I did. Now, of course, Joe stayed in trouble the whole time for fighting with his officers — that man never could stand taking orders from anybody — but he did get a medal for being brave. He gave it to Chrissie a while back. She's got it squirreled away somewhere."

"That medal must've made you proud."

"I didn't care much by the time everything was over with. Joe always was bad to be mad at somebody, but when we started going together, at least he had *resolve*. You believed him when he said he was going to do some big thing. But then when he came back from France, he was just mad."

"What was he mad at?"

Mrs. Steppe smiled sadly. "Oh, I don't know, just mad, I guess. Did you know Steppe wasn't his real name?"

"No, ma'am."

"His real name was Owl. Joe Owl. Steppe was the name of a missionary teacher he had at the Cherokee school who helped him get his scholarship at Raleigh. Of course, Joe, being Joe, never made it to Raleigh. He got off the train at some town down east and got in a fight with some old boys who didn't like a red Indian trying to eat in their train station. Then, when he got out of jail, most of what little money he had was gone from his wallet, and when he contacted the school, they'd canceled his scholarship. The cops had left him only enough to buy a train ticket, but not enough to make it all the way back to Dillsboro. That's how come him to get off the train here. This is where Joe's money ran all the way out."

"But that's not right, them taking his money," Jim said quietly. "Couldn't he take them to court or something?"

"That's not the way things work in the world."

"It ought to be."

"Do you think you'd still think so much of Chrissie if her name was Chrissie Owl?"

"Probably. I believe so."

"No offense, but you might and you might not. Joe's mother, Chrissie's grandmother, didn't even know how to speak English. All she spoke was Cherokee. What do you think of that? How would you like introducing somebody like that to your mama, prim as she is?"

"I don't know. I don't think it would matter."

"Well, it does matter. God knows Joe Steppe had a temper and a short fuse, and enough pride for ten Indians, but he also never got a fair shake, not once, besides that scholarship, in his whole life. If he'd been a white man, I wouldn't be a cook in a railroad hotel, I'll tell you that right now. We'd be *in* California."

"Yes, ma'am."

"You know how come she wears her hair like that, don't you?"

Jim shook his head.

"For Joe. He asked her to."

"I don't understand."

"It makes her look like an Indian, but she's white enough to pass. He said they were playing a joke on everybody, Indian and white, because nobody could tell what she was. It was their little secret."

"I still don't understand."

"I don't either," Mrs. Steppe said. "And I'm not sure Chrissie does. It was Joe's joke. How do you like that pretty hair of hers now?"

"I think it's beautiful," Jim said, blushing. "And I don't care who her daddy is."

"Was," Mrs. Steppe said. "Her daddy was Injun Joe Steppe and he robbed a bank and shot a policeman and wrapped somebody's Packard around a tree. That's who my girl's daddy was, and here we sit."

"Yes, ma'am."

"Now I got to figure out how to get him back to Cherokee. Chrissie would never forgive me if I left him in South Carolina, and I just know he would haunt me if I buried him around here."

At that moment someone slowly climbed the porch steps behind Jim. He noticed for the first time that he could no longer see Mrs. Steppe's face clearly. The square of sky in the window had darkened into a deep blue. The screen bumped gently against its frame, and Jim felt a whisper of evening air brush against his neck. Someone tapped at the door and he was afraid to turn around.

"Why, Zeno," Mrs. Steppe said. "Come on in and sit with us. I've been telling your nephew here my life story, and he's been nice enough to sit still while I do it."

Uncle Zeno removed his hat as he stepped inside. "Evening, Nancy." He nodded at Jim. "Doc."

"Hey," said Jim.

"Nancy," Uncle Zeno said, "we're awfully sorry over at our place about your loss. Please accept our condolences."

"Thank you, Zeno. Please tell your family I appreciate that. I truly do. Would you like some coffee? I've got about half a pot left over from supper. It's still warm. Jim don't like it much, but I think it tastes all right."

"Coffee sounds good about now."

Mrs. Steppe pushed through the swinging door into the dining room. Uncle Zeno hung his hat on the chair opposite Mrs. Steppe's coffee cup and sat down. He motioned with his index finger for Jim to lean closer.

"Go home," he whispered.

"They don't have any money to get Injun Joe back to Cherokee," Jim whispered back.

"I said, go home, Doc."

Mrs. Steppe backed through the door into the kitchen. "All right, then," she said. "Here we go. You still drink it black, don't you, Zeno?"

"The blacker the better."

Jim stood up. "Thank you for the coffee, Mrs. Steppe," he said.

"Why, don't run off."

"I need to get on home. Mama's probably wondering where I am."

"Do you want me to give Chrissie that present?"

Jim had forgotten about the package sitting beside his coffee cup. "Oh, yes, ma'am," he said. "It's not much. It's just for graduation. And please tell her how sorry I am about her daddy."

"I'll do that. Thank you for coming by."

From the porch Jim looked back through the screen.

The dark outlines of Mrs. Steppe and Uncle Zeno faced each other across the table. Neither seemed to have anything to say. When Jim turned toward home, he had trouble seeing the steps in front of him, and he had to feel his way into the yard.

BOOK IV

The Blue Star

The Sunny Side
of the Mountain

*J*IM STOOD with the uncles in the front yard of Uncle Zeno's house. He wore a new gray suit and a sharp fedora and a fancy wristwatch, all birthday presents from the uncles the day before. Mama had given him the small leather suitcase, his initials stamped in gold between the latches, that now sat at his feet. He pushed up his sleeve and admired the watch — a proper soldier's watch, with luminous numbers and hands — without noticing what time it was. His old watch still worked fine, but the uncles had worried because it wasn't shockproof.

He glanced over his shoulder and studied the outline of the hat worn by his shadow. It looked strange to him no matter how he turned his head. Jim had never owned a real hat before, only baseball caps and hunting caps and the cowboy hat, red with white piping around the edge of the brim, he had favored when he was a boy. He felt like he was wearing a disguise, or someone else's clothes.

"You still look like a knothead," Uncle Zeno said.

"Sir?"

"It's a good-looking hat, but you still look like a knothead."

"A knothead wearing a hat," said Uncle Coran.

Jim wanted to respond in kind to the teasing but found that he could only swallow. He could not believe he was going away to places the uncles would not be. He didn't think he could find a hotel room that night in Charlotte without their help, much less find his way through a war.

Uncle Zeno patted him on the shoulder. "You look fair enough, Doc," he said. "All we ask is that you fill that suit all the way up."

Jim blinked. "Yes, sir. I'll try."

Uncle Al took the handkerchief out of his back pocket and blew his nose.

"Oh, Allie, don't start," Uncle Coran said.

"It's the hay fever," Uncle Al said. "And I ought to be able to blow my own daggum nose without everybody in town commenting on it."

"Boys," said Uncle Zeno.

Jim stared again at his watch so he wouldn't have to look at the uncles. This time he couldn't read the numbers. "What are we waiting for, anyway?" he asked.

"It's a surprise," said Uncle Coran.

"Just hold on," Uncle Zeno said. "Cissy will be along in a minute."

All four of them stared intently at the house. Mama finally raised one of the window shades in the parlor.

"Look. There she is," said Uncle Al, pointing. "There she is."

Mama climbed onto a chair and hung a white banner bordered by red on the nail Uncle Zeno had mysteriously hammered into the window frame that morning. In the center of the banner was a blue star. Jim couldn't believe his eyes. He didn't think he had done anything to deserve a blue star — he didn't even know if he would be inducted tomorrow afternoon or the morning after that — yet there it was, rocking gently back and forth in the window for everyone to see.

"Is that for me?" he asked.

"It's a service banner," said Uncle Zeno. "For our serviceman."

All three uncles pulled out their handkerchiefs and blew their noses.

"Oh, come on, y'all," Jim said. "Please don't do this to me."

"We've all got the hay fever," Uncle Zeno said. "And we need to get over it before Cissy gets out here."

Mama stepped down off the chair and pulled the shade without looking toward them. After a moment she pushed open the front door. Jim picked up his suitcase. It was time to go.

When Jim walked onto the platform at the depot with Mama and the uncles, a swarm of people enveloped him with noise and back slapping and teasing, for which he was grateful. Norma was there with her parents, and Dennis Deane had managed to borrow a car and scrounge enough gasoline to drive over with Ellie Something, and Pete Hunt glowered importantly up the track and studied his pocket watch and pretended nobody else was there, and even old Miss Brown and Mr. Dunlap had turned up to shake his hand.

Miss Brown wore a ridiculous hat covered all over with wax fruit. She placed her hands on Jim's cheeks and stared into his face. Her hands were surprisingly soft, and up close her eyes looked like those of a young person, which startled him.

"Remember the lessons of the *conquistadors,* young man," she said. "Do not let go of your helmet and sword, not even for a moment! Do not leave them lying about in Flanders Fields for someone else to find!"

"No, ma'am. I won't."

She leaned forward and kissed him soundly on both cheeks. "That is in the continental fashion," she said. "You will learn about it in France."

"Yes, ma'am," said Jim, wriggling loose. "Thank you."

Norma wrapped him in a fierce hug. Jim put his arms around her and closed his eyes and laid his cheek on top of her head. She would have been a good person to love, and he was sorry he didn't.

"You're my best friend," he whispered.

"Just come home," she whispered back.

Jim kissed her on the forehead and realized as he

did so that she had tilted her face toward him. They were acting in separate movies but had mistakenly wound up on the same screen. "Oh, Norma," he said, shaking his head. "I didn't mean —"

"It's okay, Jim," she said. "No use confusing everybody at this late date."

Ellie Something dove at him and he leaned forward at the waist so that their stomachs would not touch when they hugged. He looked at Norma over Ellie's shoulder.

"When I get back, you can teach me how to do calculus," he said.

"As if you would care."

"I'll write you," he said.

Ellie Something held him at arm's length and frowned. "Don't you make me name my baby after you," she said.

"I'll send my address to Elizabeth when I go to college," said Norma.

"What?" asked Jim.

"You heard me," said Ellie. "I'm naming my baby after Dennis Deane, and don't you forget it."

"That's me," Dennis Deane said.

"I don't think I could ever forget that," said Jim.

"My address in Greensboro," Norma said. "I'll give it to your mother when I know it."

"Unless it's a girl," said Ellie. "Then we're going to name her Thelma."

"Good," Jim said to Norma.

"Thelma," he said to Ellie.

"I guess I'll get out of your way, then," Norma said. "You've got all these other people to speak to."

"That hat makes you look like John Dillinger," Dennis Deane said.

"And we all know what happened to him," said Jim. He had always enjoyed that joke, but this time he felt the light leaking from his smile before he even finished the sentence.

"Oh, boy. I guess that's not too funny today, is it?" Dennis Deane said.

"No, but it'll be funny again the next time I see you."

"Just don't go to the movies in Chicago and you'll be all right."

"Did you hear that Dennis Deane got promoted?" Ellie Something asked. "He's a doffer now."

"That's great," Jim said. "What does a doffer do?"

Dennis Deane looked uneasily at the people crowding around them. "It's in the spinning room," he said. "I'll tell you about it next time."

"You got a deal."

"I'm not going to kiss you in the continental fashion, though."

"I'm glad about that."

"I'm not going to French-kiss you, either."

"Dennis Deane," said Ellie Something.

"I'm *especially* glad about that."

Pete Hunt shouldered in front of Dennis Deane. "Say, Jim," Pete said, "when you get to Europe, do you

think you could take some pictures of the train stations?"

Jim frowned at Pete. Not getting shot in Europe
seemed to him task enough. "I don't have a camera,"
he said.

"Well, I guess we need to be getting on back across
the river," said Dennis Deane, a little loudly, near
Pete's ear.

"Don't hurry. The train'll be here in a minute," Jim
said.

"Oh, forget I asked you to do that," said Pete. "I
don't know what I was thinking. I bet I could find a
book somewhere with pictures in it. I was just curious
about what they looked like."

"I'll see what I can do," Jim said.

Uncle Zeno tugged at his sleeve. "Excuse me, Jim,
sorry to interrupt, but I think you need to step into
the waiting room for a minute," he said.

Jim scanned the platform until he found Mama.
She looked okay. "Right now?" he asked.

"I think you probably better."

Jim stepped inside and closed the door. The shadows cast by his family and friends milled about indis-
tinctly on the floor around his feet, and the voices on
the platform withdrew to a great distance and ceased
having anything to do with him. Bright dust floated
upward in the light. No one was sitting on the single
row of seats facing the doorway, and the door to Pete's
office was closed. He thought he might be alone.

"Hello?" he called.

"Hello," said a small voice from the far corner.

Chrissie sat on the short bench atop the shoeshine stand. Jim didn't immediately recognize her because she had cut her hair. Now it fell just short of her shoulders, and she wore it parted on the side, held back by a single barrette. As Jim crossed the room toward her, she stood and looked down at him. Her eyes were puffy and bloodshot and the tip of her nose was bright red. He wanted to wrap his arms around her hips and hold his face against her belly.

"You cut your hair," he said.

Chrissie reached up and hesitantly touched the barrette.

"But I liked it the way it was."

She covered her face with her hands and sat back down.

"That's not what I meant to say," Jim said.

"It was, too."

"I don't know what I meant to say, but that wasn't it. I think your hair looks nice like that."

"You go to hell."

"But I do. It does."

"I don't know what I'm doing here," Chrissie cried. "I don't think I even like you."

Inside Jim's head two scraps of truth clapped into place simultaneously: one, she loved him — she wasn't happy about it, but she did — and she had come to tell him before he went off and got himself killed just

the way Bucky had; two, he had made her life harder
than it had to be from the day he had first noticed
her getting off the school bus. Now it would be a long
time before he could even start to make amends, if
that day ever came.

"Can I sit down?" he asked.

Chrissie slid over and made room but she didn't
look at him. Jim climbed up and eased onto the bench
while she sobbed quietly into her hands. He placed
his feet on the iron footrests and looked around the
waiting room — at the empty chairs, the dented spit-
toons, the black stove, the green, soot-blackened walls,
the print of Pikes Peak covered in snow, cut from some
ancient calendar before he was even born. It wasn't,
he realized, much of a place to leave from or, for that
matter, come back to. In the whole world only a handful of people even knew about his going, and once his
train left Aliceville, the strangers who heard it passing in the distance or waited on it at a crossing or
glanced up as it shook their houses would not know
that he was on it. And if that same train later carried
his body by in the opposite direction, they would not
know that, either.

"I don't even know what this old thing is doing in
here," Jim said. "I don't think Aliceville has ever had
a shoeshine man."

Chrissie didn't say anything.

"Back when I was a little kid, on rainy days I used to
come in here and make believe that it was a stage-

coach, and I would sit up here and pretend that I was driving it until Pete would run me off. I used to go all over the country."

"Could you take me somewhere?" Chrissie asked. She still hadn't looked at him.

"You would actually go somewhere with me?" he asked.

Chrissie drew a deep breath and nodded slowly.

Jim turned toward her and studied the back of her neck. He didn't think he had ever seen it before. It was lovely. He raised his hands, grabbing a set of reins. "Hold on, then," he said. "Yah! Get up!" He bounced up and down a few times and the bench creaked beneath him.

Chrissie lowered her hands and dabbed at her nose with the back of her wrist. Jim would have offered her his handkerchief, but it was already damp. She turned and looked at him seriously.

"Where are we going?" she asked.

"How about our place? Up Painter Creek. I think there's going to be a big stand of walnuts this year."

"I don't want to go back there."

"Why not?"

"Because you're going to leave me in that old house all by myself."

"But I would never do that."

"You're already about to."

That was true enough. He looked around quickly, a small panic flapping in his chest. "Then, how about that mountain over there?"

They gazed at Pikes Peak on the wall across the room.

"It looks cold," Chrissie said.

"We'll live on the sunny side," Jim said. "I'll build you a good house and I'll keep the woodpile tall and I'll buy you a new coat and I won't let you get cold ever again."

"Is that a promise?"

"It's a solemn promise."

"Do you think it will take us a long time to get there?"

"A while, I'm afraid. We might wear these horses out."

He could feel her staring at him, but he didn't dare look at her.

"Okay," she said finally. "Okay." She leaned toward Jim and rested her forehead on his shoulder. "Drive slow."

Jim slowly turned his face until his nose brushed her hair. He could smell the perfume he had given her for graduation. He closed his eyes.

"Then everything's settled?" he asked.

"Yes. Everything's settled."

"You'll wait for me?"

Chrissie sat upright, mashing Jim's nose in the process. "You should know that if I ever decide to love somebody again, I'm going to love them hard, and I'm going to love them for a long time."

"I could make do with that."

"Is that how you would love somebody if you decided you were going to love them?" she asked.

"Yes, ma'am," he said. "That's exactly how I would love them."

"You're really sure?"

"I'm really sure."

"Then, I've got something for you."

Chrissie reached into her skirt pocket and pulled out a tobacco tin, which she presented to Jim. He opened it and looked inside and shook out a long, thin braid of black hair, tied tightly on each end with red thread. Jim noticed that his hands were shaking, and he noticed that he had started to cry, but for the first time he also felt blooming inside his chest the certainty that he would make it home from the war. He would somehow make it back to Aliceville, and Chrissie would be waiting. Wherever he went after that, she would go with him. He reached up and took off his hat. He closed his eyes and leaned toward her, knowing as he did so that she would be leaning toward him.

The sound of the door jerking open startled him. "Jim!" Uncle Zeno cried. "Are you coming or not? The train's going to leave without you!"

"Oh, God," Jim said. "The train's going to leave." He hadn't even heard it arrive.

He clapped his hat on his head and leapt off the shoeshine stand and helped Chrissie down. He pulled her across the waiting room and out the door into an indecipherable swirl of shouting and crying and the dangerous, breathing proximity of the train. Some-

how he lost Chrissie's hand and found himself clutching instead the handle of his suitcase. People he
couldn't even see were pushing him toward the edge
of the platform, and he had the awful feeling that if
he got any closer to it, the train was going to eat him.
He looked around wildly because he had so much to
say to everyone that he should have said long before
now, but he didn't recognize a soul. Someone was
shouting his name in his ear and it was Mama and he
grabbed her and she weighed next to nothing. She
might have disappeared right then if he hadn't held
on to her. She kissed his face and both of his eyes over
and over and whispered in his ear, "Oh, Jim, I think
I'm going to die," and he squeezed her until he felt
her breath catch and whispered to her, "Nobody's going to die, Mama. I promise you. We're all going to
live for a long, long time." Then the uncles surrounded
him and kissed him unashamedly and he kissed them
back. Their beards were scratchy the way they had
been when he was little and their breaths smelled of
buttermilk and onions and he couldn't remember the
last time he had kissed them and he wished that he
had kissed them every single day of his life. One of
them said, "May the Lord bless and keep thee. May
His face shine upon thee," but he wasn't sure which
one it was. He had to tell them something important,
but Uncle Zeno said, "Don't worry. We'll see about
her while you're gone," before he even opened his
mouth. The conductor yelled, "All aboard!" from just
a few feet away and up the track a bell clanged evenly

and the engine snorted an impatient blast of steam. "Chrissie," he said, and suddenly her face was inches from his own and he kissed her and thought, *This is what my life tastes like,* and the knowledge was brand-new and it was the secret to everything and it thrilled him and he kissed her again and tried to remember it, but it wasn't enough. He would need to kiss her for years and years, and that wouldn't be enough, either. Behind him the conductor said, "Son, we gotta *go.* You've got to get on this *train*," and the engine chuffed, and chuffed again, and the drive wheels screeched against the rails and the couplings clanked and the car lurched behind him and he said, "I love you, I love you," and let go and turned away and stepped off the platform onto the moving train.

Reading Group Guide

THE BLUE STAR

A NOVEL BY

TONY EARLEY

A conversation with the author of *The Blue Star*

Tony Earley talks with Joan Brasher of the *Vanderbilt View*

Was it difficult to take the established (and beloved) character of Jim Glass and "age him up" for this sequel?

I guess the hardest part was convincing myself that I would not mess up *Jim the Boy* if I attempted to do that. *Jim the Boy* was received so well that writing about Jim again sort of seemed like a trap, and it was a while before I could convince myself it was OK to risk it.

How long did it take to write The Blue Star *in comparison to* Jim the Boy?

Both took a while. They happened the same way. I had the idea, wrote the first section, lost the scent, put it aside, and then spent a couple of years figuring out how to solve the mechanical problems that presented themselves. Once I figured those out, I finished the books fairly quickly.

Was it more difficult to write The Blue Star?

In some ways it was easier because I think I know more as a writer than when I was writing *Jim the Boy,* which was my first novel. So it would have been easier, except for worrying about ruining this character for people. I always figure out a way to make things harder than they need to be.

What is life like for Jim as a teen?

He's still in the same town, but life is different because he is in love with a girl he can't have. World War II is sort of looming in the background. In the first book he had just begun to sense that there is a greater world out there, and now that greater world is confronting him in ways he's not ready for.

Tell me about your writing process.

It's not a particularly pretty story. I drag myself to the office I have behind my house, filled with self-loathing. I write for a while and then drag myself back to the house, more often than not convinced that I've made whatever it is I'm working on worse. Occasionally there will be a day where it comes very easily — five or six or seven pages — but usually it is much, much slower than that.

So writing is a difficult process for you?

It is, but I also don't want to be too whiny about it. It's not like I'm working third shift in a factory. So maybe

4

I should say that writing is not so much grueling as it is challenging. And the fact that it's challenging is what I like about it. I like writing because it's hard to do well. And since doing it well is the only thing I allow myself to settle for, it's always going to be a bit like swimming upstream — but that's fine. The individual steps of the process may not always be fun, but finally completing the process is a great deal of fun.

I have heard you say that you share pages with your wife as you are writing. Do you still do this?

Yeah, poor girl. I come in from my office with new pages and sort of follow her around the house. She has great suggestions, but I don't want suggestions — I just want her to praise me. It is not in her nature to hand out empty praise, and rough drafts rarely deserve it, so I think my writing is probably as miserable for her as it is for me.

Do you prefer writing fiction to writing nonfiction?

Most of the nonfiction I have done has been personal, and I've lost interest in myself as a subject. As far as the actual process, writing fiction and writing nonfiction don't feel that different to me. Both are about setting artistic goals and finding a way to check those off and tell a story. It's all storytelling.

How difficult has it been to balance your teaching life with your writing life?

It is not always easy, but in general it's not much of a problem. I wrote most of *Jim the Boy* while I was teaching. The best thing about teaching is that the enthusiasm of my students often inspires me. To see that kid in class who is sort of wild-eyed about writing and wants to be a writer more than anything reminds me of what I like about writing in the first place. That kid always makes me want to go home and write something.

Do you ever have students who take your class because they want to become famous writers? What do you tell them about that?

Often, the really ambitious kids want to know how to get an agent or how to find a publisher or how to get into good magazines. I tell them that publishing is easy. Learning how to write is hard. Once they learn how to write, the other stuff will fall into place. But if they don't learn how, all of that stuff is unobtainable.

Will there be more books about Jim?

I think so. I'm sort of toying right now with the idea of starting another one.

Is it your secret dream to be chosen for Oprah's Book Club?

Any fiction writer who tells you that he or she does not occasionally secretly think about Oprah is not telling the truth. I'm just glad she started the book club. Now every time the phone rings, I think, "It could be her." It's not going to be, of course, but it could be. You never know.

What other projects are on your horizon?

I need three or four more short stories and I'll have another collection finished. These are a little darker than the Jim Glass stuff. At times, they take a turn that might or might not be supernatural, so they are a little stranger than the other fiction I have worked on.

Do you prefer the short fiction genre to novels?

If one could earn the same money writing short stories that one can earn writing novels, I would be a short story writer. When I write a short story, the process might last a month. When I write a novel, it could take me seven or eight years. I really, really love the form.

What are you reading these days?

When I'm teaching, I don't read much else. But when I do read for fun, I tend to read nonfiction. I'll read anything that has the word "storm" in the title. Storms, epidemics, plagues, hurricanes — I just find those fascinating.

Joan Brasher's interview with Tony Earley originally appeared in the March 2008 issue of *Vanderbilt View,* a monthly publication for the Vanderbilt University community. Reprinted with permission.

Questions and topics for discussion

1. At the beginning of *The Blue Star* it is revealed that Jim's uncle Zeno once experienced a failed romance with Nancy, the mother of Chrissie, with whom Jim has now fallen in love. How does this shared history influence Jim and Chrissie's relationship?

2. The book's title is derived from a banner displayed in the family house of those actively serving military duty. How does Bucky Bucklaw's departure for the navy on the eve of World War II affect Jim's feelings for Chrissie? How does it affect Jim's feelings about himself?

3. Even though Chrissie is engaged to Bucky and Norma is eager to be Jim's bride, Jim refuses to consider spending his life with anyone other than Chrissie. What do you think his motivation is? Is it true love?

4. Discuss Jim's decision to enlist in the army at the end of the novel. Were you surprised? Do you think Jim's decision was influenced by his uncle Zeno's refusal to enlist in World War I?

5. *The Blue Star* is very much a story about becoming an adult, and at one point near the end of the novel Jim thinks to himself that "he had to be the worst adult on God's green earth" (page 262). Do you

think this is a fair assessment? Why do you think Jim is so hard on himself?

6. Discuss the impact on Jim's life of the death of his father so soon after Jim was born. How do you think this has shaped Jim as he becomes an adult?

7. Like Tony Earley's previous novel, *Jim the Boy,* this story centers around the character of Jim Glass. Was Jim your favorite character in the novel? If not, who, and why?

8. What do you think the future holds for Jim, Chrissie, Norma, and Dennis Deane? How will Jim and Chrissie's final encounter affect their futures? Will Norma move on now that Jim has left Aliceville? And how will Dennis Deane cope with parenthood? What would *you* like to see happen to each of these characters?

About the author

Tony Earley is the author of *The Blue Star, Jim the Boy, Here We Are in Paradise,* and *Somehow Form a Family.* He lives with his family in Nashville, Tennessee, where he is the Samuel Milton Fleming Associate Professor of English at Vanderbilt University.

. . . and his previous novel

Tony Earley introduced the character Jim Glass in his widely praised first novel, *Jim the Boy,* available in paperback from Back Bay Books. Following is an excerpt from the novel's opening pages.

Breakfast

During the night something like a miracle happened: Jim's age grew an extra digit. He was nine years old when he went to sleep, but ten years old when he woke up. The extra number had weight, like a muscle, and Jim hefted it like a prize. The uncles' ages each contained two numbers, and now Jim's age contained two numbers as well. He smiled and stretched and sniffed the morning. Wood smoke; biscuits baking; the cool, rivery smell of dew. Something not quite daylight looked in his window, and something not quite darkness stared back out. A tired cricket sang itself to sleep. The cricket had worked all night. Jim rose to meet the waiting day.

Jim's mother opened the stove door with a dishrag. Mama was tall and pale and handsome; her neck was long and white. Although she was not yet thirty years old, she wore a long, black skirt that had belonged to her mother. The skirt did not make her seem older, but rather made the people in the room around her feel odd, as if they had wandered into an old photograph, and did not know how to behave. On the days Mama wore her mother's long clothes, Jim didn't let the screen door slam.

"There he is," Mama said. "The birthday boy."

Jim's heart rose up briefly, like a scrap of paper on a breath of wind, and then quickly settled back to the ground. His love for his mother was tethered by a sympathy Jim felt knotted in the dark of his stomach. The death of Jim's father had broken something inside her that had not healed. She pulled the heaviness that had once been grief behind her like a plow. The uncles, the women of the church, the people of the town, had long since given up on trying to talk her into leaving the plow where it lay. Instead they grew used to stepping over, or walking inside, the deep furrows she left in her wake. Jim knew only that his mother was sad, and that he figured somehow in her sadness. When she leaned over to kiss him, the lilaced smell of her cheek was as sweet and sad at once as the smell of freshly turned earth in the churchyard.

"Oh, Jimmy," she said. "How in the world did you get to be ten years old?"

"I don't know, Mama," Jim said, which was the truth. He was as amazed by the fact as she was. He had been alive for ten years; his father, who had also been named Jim Glass, had been dead for ten years and a week. It was a lot to think about before breakfast.

Mama put the biscuits she pulled from the oven

into a straw basket. Jim carried the basket into the dining room. The uncles sat around the long table.

"Who's that?" Uncle Coran said.

"I don't know," said Uncle Al.

"He sure is funny-looking, whoever he is," said Uncle Zeno.

"Y'all know who I am," said Jim.

"Can't say that we do," said Uncle Coran.

"I'm Jim."

"Howdy," said Uncle Al.

"Y'all stop it," Jim said.

The uncles were tall, skinny men with broad shoulders and big hands. Every morning they ate between them two dozen biscuits and a dozen scrambled eggs and a platter of ham. They washed it all down with a pot of black coffee and tall glasses of fresh milk.

"Those biscuits you got there, Jim?" said Uncle Zeno.

Jim nodded.

"Better sit down, then."

In all things Jim strove to be like the uncles. He ate biscuits and eggs until he thought he was going to be sick. When Uncle Zeno finally said, "You think you got enough to eat, Doc?" Jim dropped his fork as if he had received a pardon.

Uncle Zeno was Jim's oldest uncle. His age was considerable, up in the forties somewhere. Uncle Coran and Uncle Al were twins. Each of them swore that he did not look like the other one, which of course wasn't true. They looked exactly alike, until you knew them, and sometimes even then. Not one of the uncles found it funny that they lived in identical houses. Uncle Al and Uncle Coran built their houses when they were young men, but, like Uncle Zeno, they never took wives. Most of the rooms in their houses didn't even have furniture; only Uncle Zeno's house had a cookstove.

Jim's mother cooked and cleaned for the uncles. When she said it was too much, the uncles hired a woman to help her. Uncle Coran ran the feed store and cotton gin. Uncle Al managed the farms. Uncle Zeno farmed with Uncle Al and operated the gristmill on Saturday mornings. As the head of the family he kept an eye on everyone else. Occasionally the uncles grew cross with each other, and, for a few days, Uncle Al and Uncle Coran would retire to their houses immediately after supper. There they sat by their own fires, or on their own porches, and kept their own counsel until their anger passed. In general, however, everyone in the family got along well with everyone else; to Jim, the sound of harsh words would always strike his ear as oddly as a hymn played in the wrong key.

Jim patted his stomach. "That ought to hold me till dinner," he said.

"You ate a right smart," Uncle Coran said.

"Well," said Jim, "I am ten years old now."

"My, my," said Uncle Al.

"I've been thinking it's about time for me to go to work with y'all," Jim said.

"Hmm," said Uncle Zeno.

"I thought maybe you could use some help hoeing that corn."

"We can usually put a good hand to work," Uncle Zeno said. "You a good hand?"

"Yes, sir," said Jim.

"You ain't afraid to work?"

"No, sir."

"What do you say, boys?" Uncle Zeno said.

Uncle Al and Uncle Coran looked at each other. Uncle Coran winked.

"He'll do, I guess," said Uncle Al.

"Let's get at it, then," said Uncle Zeno.

A Day of Work

AFTER BREAKFAST Uncle Coran went off to open the store. Jim rode to the field in the truck with Uncle Zeno and Uncle Al. He stood on the bed of the truck and looked out over the top of the cab. He held on to his straw hat with one hand and the truck with the other. The world at that early hour seemed newly made, unfinished; the air, still sweet with dew, an invention thought up that morning. In the low places near the river, stray ghosts of fog still hunted among the trees. The state highway led directly into the rising sun; when the sun pulled itself loose from the road, it suddenly seemed very far away. The sky, in a moment Jim didn't notice until the moment had passed, turned blue, as if it had never tried the color before and wasn't sure anyone would like it. Jim giggled out loud for no reason he could think of.

Five field hands met them at the edge of the river bottom. The field hands were black men who lived in the woods on the hill behind the new school. They walked over without saying much and took hoes out of the bed of the truck. Jim grabbed the newest hoe for himself. Its handle was still shiny and smooth with varnish, its blade not yet darkened by rust. Uncle Zeno shook his head.

"Give that one to Abraham, Doc," he said.

Abraham had white hair. He could remember the day a soldier told him he was free. He was the father or grandfather of most of the people who lived on the hill. Jim did not want to give Abraham his hoe.

"I want to use this one," Jim said.

"I'll use this one here," Abraham said. He took the last hoe from the truck bed. Its handle was broken off about halfway down. All the other hoes had been taken already.

"That one's for Jim," Uncle Zeno said. He took the new hoe from Jim's hands. Abraham handed Jim the hoe with the broken handle. Jim knew better than to say anything else.

"Let's get some hoeing done," said Uncle Zeno.

"By dinnertime you'll be glad you've got that hoe," Abraham said. "It's nice and light."

Jim was still angry. "I'm ten years old today," he said.

"My, my," said Abraham.

Jim walked with the uncles and the field hands through the wet grass to the far end of the bottom. The grass soaked the legs of his overalls; the cloth was cold against his skin. The men fell out of line one by one and arranged themselves two rows apart. Each man would hoe to the end of one row and then back up the other. Then they would walk to the end of the line and take up two more rows. In this way they would hoe the whole field. Jim took up the two rows beside Uncle Zeno.

The corn was knee-high to the uncles, but almost waist-high to Jim. The field contained thirty acres. It would take several days to hoe it all. Then, after the hoeing was completed, Uncle Al would come back with the mules and the cultivator, and plow the middles of the rows. The field would then be free of grass and weeds; the corn could grow without competition. At the end of the summer there would be more to sell and grind into meal and feed to the mules.

Uncle Zeno stepped into Jim's corn row. Jim's cheeks flushed. He could feel the field hands watching him.

"You do it like this, Doc," Uncle Zeno said. "You put the blade of the hoe against the stalk and then pull it toward you. That way you don't hack the corn down."

"I know how to hoe," Jim said.

"Show me," said Uncle Zeno.

Jim chopped at a small clump of grass. The hoe blade bit cleanly into a cornstalk. The cornstalk fell slowly over, like a tree. Jim heard a field hand laugh.

"That's one lick," Uncle Zeno said.

Uncle Zeno had never whipped Jim, but Jim was always afraid that he might. Uncle Zeno kept a running count of the licks he was saving for Jim. He said he had them written down in a book. When Jim did something good, he said he erased a lick or two. Jim figured that most of the time he ran a lick or two short of break-even.

"It's this hoe," Jim said. The end of the broken handle was as sharp as the point of a spear.

Uncle Zeno got down on one knee and looked Jim in the face. "Jim," he said. "I ain't got time to argue with you about that hoe and listen to excuses. Do you want to help me, or do you want to go home?"

"I want to help you," Jim said.

"All right, then. Watch."

Uncle Zeno dragged his hoe sharply across the clump of grass Jim had missed. The grass came up cleanly, and he scraped it into the middle of the row.

"Now you do it."

Jim scraped up a small sprig of clover. "That's good," Uncle Zeno said. "That hoe works after all."

Uncle Zeno stepped back into his own row. The field hands and Uncle Al were already at work. Uncle Al was slightly ahead of the line. None of the uncles liked to be beaten at anything. Jim didn't like to lose, either. He decided he would beat Abraham to the far end of the field. Then after dinner Uncle Zeno would give the broken hoe to Abraham. Maybe Uncle Zeno would tell Abraham to go home.

Without looking up, Jim carefully scraped the ground clean around the first ten stalks of corn in his row. He piled the weeds and grass up in neat piles. At the tenth stalk, he ran into a clump of grass that was too tough to dig up with his hoe. He got down on his knees and pulled at it with both hands. It wouldn't budge. He stuck the sharp point of his hoe handle underneath the grass and pried at it. He pulled and pried at the grass until the roots finally came loose with a ripping noise. Jim hoisted the clump of grass into the air like a trophy, or a large fish. Its roots held a clod of dirt as big as a cat. He looked around to see if anyone saw him, but everyone was gone. He couldn't see anyone at all until he stood up. The uncles and the field hands were a hundred yards or more ahead of him, and moving away at a slow walk. Uncle Al was out in front of everyone else. Uncle Zeno and Abraham looked to be tied for second.

Jim turned and stared back at the head of his row. He could spit that far. He looked in the other direction at the end of the row in the distance. The woods along the river seemed as far away as the moon. The uncles, as far ahead of Jim as they were, had hoed less than a fourth of the way to the end of the field. Jim didn't see how he could ever make it to the end of his row, much less hoe the one beside it. He had started a journey he knew he could not finish. He felt a sob gather up in his stomach like a cloud.

That Jim felt like crying made him angry. He attacked the ground with his hoe as if he were killing snakes. He struck almost blindly at the morning glories and grass and clover, but in his fury chopped down another stalk of corn. The sob that had been waiting in his stomach climbed up out of his throat and hung in the air for a second, a small, inconsequential sound, heard only by him.

The uncles and the field hands were still moving away, hoeing as they walked. Jim was afraid he would get into trouble if Uncle Zeno found out he had chopped down another stalk of corn. He could not bear the thought of Uncle Zeno being mad at him. He got down on his knees and dug a small hole with his hands. He stuck the end of the stalk in the hole and filled the hole around it with dirt. Then he patted the dirt around the stalk so that it stood up straight.

Jim picked up his hoe and wiped his nose on the back of his arm. He wiped the back of his arm on the leg of his overalls. He felt calmer. He decided that he would hoe until dinnertime. He couldn't think of a way to get home until then, but he knew that Uncle Zeno wouldn't make him come back to the field after dinner if he didn't want to.

Jim threw a rock toward the place he had started work. He often threw rocks as a way of gauging how far away things were. He wanted to know how far he had hoed. The rock, however, was a little flat and light, and curved off short to one side. Jim hunted around until he found a better rock. Good throwing rocks were hard to find in the rich dirt of the river bottom. He threw four or five more rocks until he was satisfied that he had hoed farther than he could throw a rock. This seemed like progress.

When Jim picked up his hoe, he noticed that it was about the length of a baseball bat. He grasped the handle right above the blade and took a couple of practice swings. He found a suitable hitting rock and tossed it up in the air and swung at it with the handle. Strike one. The hoe blade made swinging the handle awkward. Jim struck out twice before he finally hit the rock. It whizzed off to the right. Foul ball. He hit three more rocks before he got in a satisfactory lick and turned his attention again to the weeds growing in the field.

Jim saw a rock at his feet that looked like an arrowhead. He dug it up with his hoe, but found that the rock was fat and round on the bottom; it only looked like an arrowhead from the top. Jim had found only one arrowhead on his own, but the uncles often brought him the ones they found. Uncle Coran was the best at finding arrowheads. He could hardly walk through a field without picking one up. When Uncle Coran was a boy, he had even found a stone knife. He kept it in a cigar box on the mantel in his bedroom, and wouldn't give it to Jim. Jim was afraid the uncles would pick up all the arrowheads in the bottoms before he got good at finding them, but Uncle Zeno said there would always be plenty of arrowheads to find. More turned up every time the fields were plowed.

Jim studied the rock in his hand closely. Maybe it had been the start of an arrowhead. He didn't think so, but he could ask Uncle Coran about it at dinner-time. Uncle Coran knew a lot about how the Indians had lived. Uncle Coran said that Indians had started their fires by hitting two rocks together. Jim scraped together a small pile of dry grass and found another good-sized rock. He held the rocks close above the grass and hit them together until sparks flew off. The sparks, however, did not ignite the grass. Jim could not understand how Indians had been able to start fires like this. Nor did he understand how Indians made canoes out of tree bark, or got close enough to deer to shoot them with bows and arrows. Jim often wished he were an Indian, but thought that being a cowboy would be easier. He couldn't walk in the woods without making noise, and he couldn't start a fire by hitting two rocks together. Cowboys at least got to use matches and guns, but they also had to ride bucking bulls. Jim didn't know if he would ever be brave enough to ride a bull. He began to think he would never be good at anything. The end of the field again seemed farther away than the last time he had looked.

Jim could smell sweat soaking his overalls. He touched the denim covering his thigh with the palm of his hand. The cloth was hot to the touch. Jim squinted up. The sun was small and white; the sky was devoid of color, empty even of clouds and birds. Jim tried to figure out what time it was by looking at the sun. He tried without success until he could no longer see. He could not remember ever being as hot as he was right then. There was a bucket of water in the truck, but Jim knew that you weren't supposed to drink from it until you had hoed back to the head of the field. The uncles did not believe in wasting steps. The uncles and the field hands had made the turn and were hoeing back toward Jim. They were still a long way off, but Jim knew they would see him if he went to the truck. Two drops of sweat trickled out from under Jim's hat, and he stood still to see where they went. One drop ran into his eyes, and the other trickled down his cheek. A gnat flew into his mouth. Jim spat it out. He took off his hat and waved it around his face, but could not make the gnats go away.

"What are you doing down there, Doc?" Uncle Zeno asked.

Jim jumped. He had not noticed Uncle Zeno's shadow cover the ground where he crouched. "I'm looking at this praying mantis," said Jim.

"Did it bite you?"

"No."

Jim had knocked the praying mantis off a corn stalk and chopped it in two with his hoe. He was poking at the two pieces with the sharp point of the handle.

"Praying mantises eat other bugs, Jim," Uncle Zeno said. "If you want to kill something, kill a grasshopper. Grasshoppers eat corn."

"Yes, sir," Jim said.

He covered up the two green halves of the praying mantis with dirt. He wondered if in killing it he had added another lick to Uncle Zeno's list.

"Well," said Uncle Zeno, "let's see how you've been doing." He walked back toward the head of Jim's row, looking at the ground. "You missed a lot of morning glories through here," he said, scratching at the ground as he walked. "They'll take over a field if you don't get 'em before they get up on the corn."

Uncle Zeno came to the cornstalk Jim had chopped down and stuck back in the ground. He stood and looked at it a long time. Then he pulled it up and turned around and looked at Jim. Uncle Zeno was extremely tall. Jim had never noticed before exactly how tall.

"What happened to this one here?" Uncle Zeno said.

"I don't know," Jim said.

"You don't know," said Uncle Zeno.

"No, sir," said Jim.

"You know it won't grow now."

Jim nodded.

"Then why did you stick it back in the ground?"

"I don't know," said Jim.

"You don't know."

"No."

Uncle Zeno held the corn stalk up like a scepter, as if seeing it better would help Jim answer his questions.

"Jim, this was just a mistake until you tried to hide it," he said. "But when you tried to hide it, you made it a lie."

Jim looked at the front of his overalls. He felt a tear start down his cheek. He snatched at it and hoped that Uncle Zeno hadn't seen it.

Uncle Zeno threw the cornstalk away from him as if it were a dirty thing, something to be ashamed of.

"Do you lie to me a lot, Jim?"

"No," Jim said.

"Should I worry about believing the things you tell me? I never have before, but should I start now?"

Jim shook his head. He wasn't able to say no again.

"What's the matter?" Uncle Zeno said.

"I don't feel good," said Jim.

"Are you sick?"

Jim shrugged.

"Go on home, then," Uncle Zeno said.

Jim looked down the row toward the river. He suddenly wanted to finish his work.

Uncle Zeno pointed in the direction of town. "Go on," he said. "If you're sick, you don't need to be out in the sun."

"I think I can make it till dinner," Jim said.

"No, you go on home and tell your mama you're sick."

Jim sent a small whimper out into the air between himself and Uncle Zeno, like a scout in advance of the protest that would follow.

"Go on," Uncle Zeno said.

From the edge of the road Jim turned around and looked back at the field. Uncle Zeno was hoeing the row Jim had abandoned. The field hands were spread out through the bottom. Uncle Al was still way out in front of everybody else. He was approaching the river for the second time that morning, working as if he would never stop.

Also by Tony Earley

Jim the Boy
A novel

"A radiant, knowing, pitch-perfect parable of childhood. . . . Mr. Earley may not have invented the coming-of-age novel, but he streamlines and reawakens the genre with this swift, lovely book." — Janet Maslin, *New York Times*

"*Jim the Boy* is a delight. A sweet, graceful novel that charms the reader with marvelous language, honest emotion, and authentic characters who are no less human, no less complex, for being sincere and straightforward, and good. . . . Tony Earley is a wonderful writer."
— Alice McDermott

"From its wistful retro cover to its epigraph from *Charlotte's Web*, Tony Earley's *Jim the Boy* puts us squarely in mind of young-adult classics like *The Yearling*. And though Earley clearly wants to nibble around the edges of the juvenile genre, this exquisitely wrought story exhibits a clear-eyed maturity, and an understated daring, rarely seen in the most cutting-edge adult fiction."
— Mark Rozzo, *Los Angeles Times Book Review*

"A dazzling first novel. . . . Concentrating on the small events that make up a life, Earley has wired together almost every one of these seemingly inconsequential moments. By the end of the book, the life of this boy and his family blaze at you like a whole town of lights."
— Malcolm Jones, *Newsweek*

Back Bay Books
Available wherever paperbacks are sold

Also by Tony Earley

Here We Are in Paradise
Stories

"Tony Earley does the practically impossible. . . . These stories are both incredibly funny and effortlessly convincing." — Louise Erdrich

"Tony Earley has a wonderful gift for deep observation, exact and wise and often very funny." — Ellen Currie, *New York Times Book Review*

"Each of Tony Earley's stories is like a little novel: fully imagined, fully realized. Like the dampkeeper in 'The Prophet from Jupiter,' he sees beneath the surface, the calm water of everyday lives, into the hidden depths of the soul, where giant catfish glide and whole towns are hidden, full of our unrealized lives, our untold stories." — Lee Smith

"At times quirky and always honest, *Here We Are in Paradise* establishes Earley as that rarest of talents: a writer of excellent short stories." — *Details*

"Earley writes with such a wise and confident hand. These stories are funny, sad, and wonderful." — Mark Childress

Back Bay Books
Available wherever paperbacks are sold

Praise for

APRIL 1865
by Jay Winik

"A superb piece of history. Jay Winik is a master storyteller with a remarkable tale to tell—full of tragedy, treachery, ambition, nobility, defiance, and courage."

—Doris Kearns Goodwin,
author of the Pulitzer Prize–winning *No Ordinary Time*

"Winik's book will make a useful introduction to a crucial moment in American history. . . . The story he tells is powerful." —*Washington Post Book World*

"Jay Winik writes with the elegance of Bruce Catton. . . . [He] makes a more compelling case than previous historians. . . . A fresh perspective in a field dominated by narrowly focused studies." —*Civil War Times*

"*April 1865* vividly re-creates the last days of the Civil War. . . . It provides a fascinating history lesson." —David Ignatius, *Washington Post*

"A fresh, intelligent recasting of the American story." —*New York Times*

"In no other month of American history did the nation experience such momentous events, and its people such wild swings of mood, from euphoria to despair, as in April 1865. Jay Winik's *April 1865* captures all the drama and significance in a fast-paced narrative full of larger-than-life characters. Here is a book that fully measures up to the importance of its subject." —James M. McPherson,
author of the Pulitzer Prize–winning
Battle Cry of Freedom: The Civil War Era

"Winik's sense of the dramatic and his vivid writing bring a fitting flourish to his thesis that April 1865 marked a turning point in American history. . . . This book is a triumph." —*Publishers Weekly*

"With great eloquence and authority, [Winik] slips in and out of the lives of the leaders and common people on both sides of the conflict, offering insights into their characters—and ultimately into the nation's soul." —*Philadelphia Inquirer*

"This book is a treasure. . . . Jay Winik is a masterful historian." —*Indianapolis Star*

"An engrossing narrative history. . . . Winik has a keen eye for the choices men on both sides made. . . . Vivid." —*The Weekly Standard*

"Jay Winik's book is an exciting and penetrating contribution to the literature of the Civil War. It is history as it ought to be written—well researched, and as readable as a novel." —Paul Johnson, author of *Modern Times* and *A History of the American People*

"Brilliant. A narrative that mixes compelling character, shrewd insight, and lovely, lyrical writing." —Geoffrey Norman, *American Way*

"Dramatic. . . . Moving. . . . These events have been the subject of countless books over the past century. . . . Historian Jay Winik has said it better than all his predecessors." —*Richmond Times-Dispatch*

"Impressive. . . . A fresh perspective. . . . This is a deeply felt book, patriotic in the most informed and fundamental way." —Thomas Mallon, *National Review*

"The last days of the Civil War come alive again in Jay Winik's marvelous *April 1865*. This is narrative history at its dramatic best. A gripping page-turner of a book in which you can almost smell the smoke and blood." —Douglas Brinkley, professor of history and director of the Eisenhower Center of American Studies at the University of New Orleans

"Eloquent and erudite, Winik sweeps beyond the bounds of traditional Civil War history for discourses on Thomas Jefferson, the history of guerrilla warfare, and the controversies of presidential succession. . . . Brilliant. . . . Jay Winik was destined to write this book." —*Providence Journal-Bulletin*

"Perceptive. . . . Thought-provoking. . . . Winik demonstrates convincingly the successful end of the American Civil War was neither simple nor inevitable. Winik gives us a primer on statesmanship." —*The Public Interest*

"With cinematic sweep and novelistic detail, Jay Winik reintroduces us to the thirty most momentous days on the American calendar. Winik is a superb storyteller, with a special gift for making the familiar seem fresh. *April 1865* is a book that will belong to the ages."

—Richard Norton Smith, author of
Patriarch: George Washington and the New American Nation
and director of the Gerald R. Ford Museum

"Gripping. . . . The main achievement of Winik's book is the way it succeeds in so vividly reminding us that in the end the fate of this society—and no doubt of every democratic society—must sooner or later hang on the ability of brave men to call on others to be as brave as they."

—Midge Decter, *Commentary*

The Peacemakers, by George P. Healy

As April 1865 approached, Lincoln conferred with his high command—General U. S. Grant, General Bill Sherman, who came up from North Carolina, and Admiral David Porter—aboard the *River Queen,* to discuss when and how the war would end. "My God!" Lincoln groaned. "Must more blood be shed?" Yes, said Grant. *(White House Collection, courtesy of White House Historical Collection)*

APRIL 1865

The Month
That Saved America

�֍

Jay Winik

HARPER ● PERENNIAL

NEW YORK ● LONDON ● TORONTO ● SYDNEY

HARPER ◉ PERENNIAL

A hardcover edition of this book was published in 2001 by HarperCollins
Publishers.

P.S.™ is a trademark of HarperCollins Publishers.

HarperCollins books may be purchased for educational, business, or sales
promotional use. For information please write: Special Markets Department,
HarperCollins Publishers, 10 East 53rd Street, New York, NY 10022.

First Perennial edition published 2002.
First Harper Perennial edition published 2006.

Designed by Brian Barth
Maps designed by Paul J. Pugliese

Library of Congress Cataloging-in-Publication Data is available.

ISBN-10: 0-06-089968-9
ISBN-13: 978-0-06-089968-4

06 07 08 09 10 ❖/RRD 10 9 8 7 6 5 4 3 2 1

For Lyric, my North and South, and East and West

CONTENTS

Maps

INTRODUCTION

A tlanta had been overwhelmed. Columbia had been surren-dered—and burned. Charleston had been abandoned. The peace conference at Hampton Roads had been fruitless. And the British and the French had refused to intervene. The Army of Northern Virginia, after striking its own harsh blows against the Union in the six bloodiest weeks of the war, from the Wilderness to Cold Harbor, had wriggled free of the enemy's clutches and fallen back, con-verging in a defensive position around Petersburg and Richmond.

Across the slim divide of the battered landscape lay Grant's swelling Army of the Potomac.

It was the Confederacy's direst crisis since the start of the war, vaster than the fall of Vicksburg, more terrible than the failure at Gettysburg, and more traumatic than the toll of Sharpsburg. This time, the South stood irrevocably alone. But as smoky light filtered off the James River below Richmond, a strange emotion prevailed throughout much of the Confederacy. It was, Southerners knew, not the first time in history that defenders had been pitifully whittled down into pieces by attacking legions, cut in half, starved, demoralized, enervated, and yet somehow had found the will to prevail. They still had four armies in the field, and man for man some of the finest fighting men in all of the history of warfare. Their guerrilla fighters and cavalry were second to none. Their lineage, they reminded themselves, was impeccable, stretching from the Jamestown colonists of 1607 to the Founding Fathers of 1776, and included George Washington himself. This kindled and rekindled their dwindling resolve. So did their prayers. And so did their own spirit— however waning.

And so fervent were they in their desire to earn their independence that after an extensive, protracted debate, they had even held out the promise of freedom to any black man who would fight for their cause.

Now, confronted by the dreaded prospect of losing all, they looked to their leadership, for another George Washington, a figure who could rescue the South. In these desperate times, after all the suffering and death, after the multitude of exhaustion and despair, such a man—or such men—was the Confederacy's final chance.

In the trenches of Petersburg, there was such a man, and across the Confederacy, there were such men. As a weary Abraham Lincoln, who had braced the Union when the blood was thick and victory seemed lost, so deeply feared, Robert E. Lee and the generals who looked to him for leadership, and a good many of the Confederate citizens who looked to him for guidance, were as aggressive as ever: not ready to give up, to give in, or to relinquish their Confederate identity burnished in the fires of war. This war was not over. Not by a long shot. And the implications for the peace to follow were profound.

It is the eve of April 1865.

⋇ ⋇ ⋇

Even today, what followed in the remaining days of the Civil War seems almost miraculous. April 1865 is a month that could have unraveled the American nation. Instead, it saved it. It is a month as dramatic and as devastating as any ever faced in American history—and it proved to be perhaps the most moving and decisive month not simply of the Civil War, but indeed, quite likely, in the life of the United States.

Too often, it is at a small red brick house in Appomattox, Virginia, on April 9, 1865—Robert E. Lee's fateful meeting with U. S. Grant—that the story of the Civil War stops. Yet this is a mistake. For one thing, the war was still not over; it could have lasted several more hard months, even years. For another, no period was more harrowing, or had so great an impact upon this country, as the days that followed Lee's surrender. Within six days, Abraham Lincoln was dead, the first-ever assassination of an American president. Never before or since in the life of this nation has the country been so tested as in this one week alone. Nor have so many tales of human drama and so many remarkable events— surrender and assassination but two among them—occurred with such breathtaking simultaneity and far-reaching consequences, within a simple span of some thirty or so days.

Indeed, the whole of April 1865 was marked by tumult and bloodshed, heroism and desperation, freedom and defeat, military prowess and diplomatic magnanimity, jubilation and sorrow, and, finally, by individual and national agony and joy. Consider a few unforgettable images: this one month witnessed the poignant, frenzied fall of the rebel capital at Richmond and its government on the run; Lincoln's unprecedented walk through Richmond the next afternoon, as the city still smoldered and burned and its newly freed blacks brushed him with their hands; one of the most savage battles of the war, fought along Sayler's Creek, and the daring—and daunting—prospect of the South forming guerrilla groups to press the conflict and bleed the North, with grave, long-term consequences. It saw Lee's defiant efforts to head south and reunify with General Joe Johnston, while fervently proclaiming "we must all determine to die at our posts"; the Army of Northern Virginia force-marching in a labored, hurried retreat, an unduly complicated effort marked by heartbreaking mistakes, remarkable stoicism, and near split-second decisions with cataclysmic results; Lee's reluctant yet dignified surrender to Grant at Appomattox, accompanied by Grant's equally dignified, and largely unprecedented, handling of his fallen foe, a masterful act that set the tone for the rest of the war and the peace to come. It glimpsed Lincoln's eerie premonitions of death just days before his own assassination, followed by the successful plot to kill the president and a near-successful plot— foiled only at the last moment—to decapitate the entire Union government, threatening the revival of more ruinous war. And while sporadic fighting continued in the South, the Union was plunged into near chaos as the first-ever presidential transfer of power in a crisis commenced, amid widespread hysteria and rage, with the inauguration of Andrew Johnson of Tennessee, an illiterate until age twenty-one, who had met with Lincoln only once since the inauguration. This one month also beheld an angry nationwide search for John Wilkes Booth, while intensive on-again, off-again negotiations were waged over a ten-day span to produce General Johnston's eventual surrender to William Tecumseh Sherman——as other rebel generals and would-be guerrillas in the Deep South, in the backwoods, and in the Far West watched, waited, and pondered their next steps. And, of course, it ushered in the start of the nation's reunification.

But even as the war climaxed to a close, there remained the most significant question of all——one that had consumed Abraham Lincoln, haunted him, kept him awake at night, and etched lines of worry deep in his face: not simply how to subjugate the Confederacy by force of arms, but, more importantly, how to reunite two separate political, social, and cultural entities that had been bitter military enemies just days before. There is "no greater [task] before us," Lincoln bluntly told his cabinet, or for that matter, before "any future Cabinet." In truth, this was the foremost challenge of April 1865. This accomplishment——two nations becoming one——perhaps among the most momentous of all time, makes the story of April 1865 not just the tale of the war's dénouement but, in countless ways, the story of the making of our nation.

❧   ❧   ❧

For historians, it is axiomatic that there are dates on which history turns, and that themselves become packed with meaning. For the English, it is 1066, the bittersweet year of the Norman conquest and the beginning of the most widely spoken language across the globe today. For the French, there is the powerful symbol of 1789, marking the dawn of liberty and equality, and, just as accurately, the stunning transition between the old order and modern French society. For Americans, one magic number is, of course, 1492, the year marking the discovery of America——

which is to say its Europeanization—or 1776, the American Declaration of Independence. But April 1865 is another such pivotal date.

It was not inevitable that the American Civil War would end as it did, or for that matter, that it would end at all well. Indeed, what emerges from the panorama of April 1865 is that the whole of our national history could have been altered but for a few decisions, a quirk of fate, a sudden shift in luck. Throughout this period, there were critical turning points, each of which could have shattered a fragile, war-torn America, thrusting the new nation back into renewed war, or, even worse, into a protracted, ugly, low-level North-South conflict, or toward a far harsher, more violent, and volatile peace, with unpredictable results. Time and again, things might have gone altogether differently. For instance, we are sorely mistaken if we believe that Lee had no options after the fall of Richmond or if we assume that his final retreat could have ended only in wholesale capitulation. Or, as opposed to what 200 years of smooth constitutional government may lead us to think, we would be equally mistaken if we believe that the constitutional provisions guiding the Union cabinet—as it prepared to hand power over to Andrew Johnson— were anything but awkward, uncertain, and exasperatingly unclear.

In truth, one cannot understand how the nation came together without seeing the element of choice and uncertainty, or what historians often call "contingency," that hung over every dramatic event in April: from the final military battles to the diplomatic meetings, from the weighty political decisions to the tense presidential succession, from the deep and drastic social dislocations in the South to the raw nerves and excitement in the North. History is not a random sequence of events, and never more so than here. In a sense, the story of April 1865 is not just one of decisions made, but also one of decisions rejected. Lee's decision concerning guerrilla warfare, with immense if not unforeseen ramifications, was one such decisive moment; Grant's choice to be magnanimous at Appomattox was another; and then, of course, there is the first-ever assassination of a president, Abraham Lincoln, itself an unthinkable event. In light of the panic and chaos that followed, crucial questions remained. Would Southern leaders seek to take advantage of this moment of fleeting weakness? Or find new spirit in the North's woes?

And would Northerners now flirt with government by cabinet, as they had when John Tyler succeeded William Henry Harrison? Or inch toward military or autocratic rule, as some, cabinet members included, feared? Or would they impose far harsher terms upon the South and the remaining Confederate soldiers? And finally, there are the subtle but powerful efforts not just of Lincoln, whose wisdom and foresight shine in these days as vividly as at any other time in his career, but also of high-ranking military men, North and South, to resist what one historian has labeled the "hoarse cry of vengeance," and instead do their part in peace, to help heal the country.

Ever since the founding of the republican experiment in 1776, the United States was still very much a fragile entity, and each generation was fearful of its prospects for survival. They knew that most republics throughout history had been overthrown by revolution, or had collapsed into dictatorship or civil war, or had succumbed to uncontrollable anarchy. The same fate, they feared, could be theirs. And their fears were hardly unfounded; history, then and now, is littered with bad endings. As Lincoln said, the Civil War was a time of "great testing." In many ways, never were the temptations or threats for an imperfect peace, or a time of unbridled enmity, or a protracted low-grade North-South conflict, or even the allure of dictatorship, greater than in the final month. Whatever may have followed later, in these most crucial of days, none of this happened. How this came about is an important, and neglected, story of America.

In the end, only after each such concatenation draws into focus does April 1865 come to be seen as not simply a crucial and coherent period of the Civil War in its own right, but as an essential cornerstone in the events that ultimately brought America together. To understand this is to grasp something precious: it is to see our country anew.

✴   ✴   ✴

This work is, of sorts, a labor of love, and a culmination of some two decades of reflection. I nearly wrote my doctoral dissertation at Yale, under the tutelage of Professor Bruce Russett, on a topic closely akin to this book. In the years that followed, my career was largely focused on thinking about war, military strategy, and U.S. national security policy, not simply in academic settings but in government, as an adviser to congressmen, senators, and two secretaries of defense. In contemplating contemporary U.S. policies and possible strategies for the future, I invariably sought lessons and guideposts from the past. However, what always struck me as the most vexing question was not simply the phenomenon of war itself, but of civil war, that most difficult of all wars, and the most formidable of all tasks: how to bring peace to countries in the wake of a civil war's bloody aftermath.

Some of my earliest—and greatest—impressions about civil war occurred firsthand. While a longtime adviser to the late congressman and defense secretary Les Aspin, and while a senior staff member with the Senate Foreign Relations Committee, I had the chance to witness up close a number of civil wars around the globe: Cambodia, the former Yugoslavia, Nicaragua, El Salvador. I walked in the Nicaraguan jungles; I rode in armored cars through the bloodstained streets of El Salvador; but perhaps most formative of my informal training about civil war, and still quite fresh, was what I saw in the strife-torn cities and refugee camps of Cambodia, the home of the Killing Fields and quite likely the worst example of civil war in the twentieth century. I spent much of 1989 and 1990 working to help quell a renewed Cambodian conflict, and our painstaking efforts produced tentative success: the civil war burned itself out, the dreaded bloodbath was avoided, and a genuine, albeit still frail, national reconciliation began.

And over the last decade, it is with a sense of sorrow that I have watched the outbreak or renewal of other civil wars across the globe, from Indonesia to the African continent, from Afghanistan to the republics of the former Soviet Union. Yet one should not mistake the malignancy of civil war as being simply a Third World phenomenon. The recurrence of bloody conflict in the Balkans, for decades an island of stability and economic activity in Eastern Europe, is vivid testimony to that fact, as is the lingering "Irish question," which has eluded resolution not simply for four years, but for a good two centuries. Such events tragically highlight an enduring rhythm of history. Far too many civil wars end quite badly, and beget a vicious circle of more civil war and more violence, death, and instability.

But these civil wars are not ours; ours, ultimately, was quite different indeed. Why? That question, and perhaps the lesson for the rest of the world, and certainly for us, is how a young and still embryonic America avoided the terrible and tragic fate that has beset so many other countries wracked by civil conflict, in this and previous centuries. Why this is so—and how—is also at the center of this book, and what further impelled me to write it.

Jay Winik
Chevy Chase, Maryland

APRIL 1865

PRELUDE

"A Nation Delayed"

S pring came slowly and laboriously to the mountaintop that year. The rain lingered, turning the paths and highways to mud, then the cold returned, hardening and freezing both. The redbuds threatened to blossom late, and so did the fruit trees and the dogwoods. The garden, too, was in need of tilling; the beds clamored to be cleaned and pruned. But most noticeable in the spring of 1865 was the silence.

There was still the same awkward corkscrew road, the same two-and-a-half-mile winding climb to reach the grand house perched solidly on the flat crest. But almost nothing else was the same. The clop of horses' hooves and the clatter of buggy wheels had all but died away with the home's first owner. Now, almost forty years hence, things had fallen into near ruin. The front steps were broken. The roses had run over into the walk. In every direction, cracked windows looked out not on its creator's dream of a bustling "Mecca of democracy," but on desolation. Inside, the once gleaming parquet floors were littered with grain, the once lively parlor now echoed with the bellow of cattle on one side and the squeal of pigs on the other, the once magnificent study was dust-filled, barren, and disconsolately quiet.

Everywhere, the quiet.

❧   ❧   ❧

It was not supposed to be this way. This was not what the twenty-six-year-old lawyer-planter, turned erstwhile tinkerer and *philosophe*, had imagined when he had staked his home high atop an inhospitable wilderness rise. It was to be his hermitage or retreat, and he intended to construct no less than his own little Zion. Only in the name do we find any requisite trace of humility; the young Thomas Jefferson decided to call it Monticello, meaning "little mountain."

In its very placement alone, Monticello was unique. By 1769, this swath of Royal Britain was already blessed with growing cities, all pulsing with commerce and industry and the sights and sounds of jostling humanity—farmers in muddy boots making their way to the taverns; blacksmiths fresh from the forge plying their wares; merchants standing beside makeshift stalls, shouting to customers to step up and inspect their goods; pamphleteers hawking their ideas; and newly arrived settlers wrestling with the particulars of their common lives. And, too, it was these cities, Williamsburg and Richmond, and New York, Philadelphia, and Boston as well, that were the intellectual spokes of the New World, redolent with the steady cry of politics and the slow building of civic lives, out of which an infant country would soon be formed. But not for Jefferson. "I view cities as pestilent to the morals, the health, and the liberation of man," he scoffed. To the little mountain, then, secluded and remote, he went. But above this barbarous bank, could it be done? Would it be done?

Not easily. Problems plagued every phase of construction. For a ten-year span, Monticello's well had insufficient flow to meet household needs; for two of those years, it was completely dry. There were troubles with the brickmaking, with the finished woodwork, with the oversized windows, and with the hardware. The chimneys were laid too low and billowed smoke back into the house; the fireplaces themselves gave out too little heat. Some rooms were so frigid, like his much-beloved tea and dining rooms (and even his study), that Jefferson lamented "the ink freezes on my pen." There were endless delays because of the lack of skilled labor, or the out-of-town labor, or the slave labor, or just plain incompetence. Despite many tries, his carpenter-columnist, Richard Richardson, could not get the columns of the swagger-portico straight. And there was the dome room, for its builders the most vexing part of the whole affair. Ironically, once it was completed, there was no way to heat it, nor was its staircase ever finished. The only access to the room was through a dark, cramped passageway. Stunning as it was, the room made no sense. It was never formally used.

Still, Jefferson continued to alter, improve, and remodel Monticello for the balance of his life, a full half century. (After spending five years in Paris as minister to France, the restless Virginian returned with a whole new conception in mind, and abruptly tore down most of what he had already built.) When he became president, key rooms had not even been plastered, the exterior was ravaged by neglect, the entrance was a cavern of raw brick, and the house that he had been putting up and tearing down for more than thirty years was no more livable than it had been at the beginning of the American Revolution. As one guest wryly remarked, "It is falling around their ears."

Was it worth it? Was Monticello the work of a beautiful dreamer, a visionary, a romantic, or an act of absurd, self-defeating conceit? Here, the house spoke for itself. When all was said and done, when the large tree trunks substituting for classical columns on the western portico were removed, when the last bit of exterior work was finally finished three years before Jefferson's death, Monticello stood there, a rare gem, a house unlike any other home in the country. A curious blend of elegant architecture and everyday practicality, of "whimsy" and "eccentricity," it was a house that arguably should never have been built, and yet it was already one of the great homes of the United States, if not the world. In size, opulence, and personality, the building was enormously deceptive, the modest exterior scarcely suggesting its luminous interior or its many rooms, thirty-three in all, or its vast size, over 11,000 square feet, or the myriad of interests housed within, from the cannonball clock in the entrance hall to the alcove beds. And most importantly, there was the political talk. Inside these walls percolated the ideas that had forged a country and would change the world. Whether the subjects were natural history or geography, matters of state or the human condition, the nature of man or the nature of government, Jefferson was an engaging host, and his guests— men like Madison and Monroe, Webster and Van Buren and the Marquis de Lafayette—reciprocated in kind. Their dinners reverberated, in

Jefferson's phrase, like "Greek colloquia," and all assembled hoped that here lay the seeds of a second Athens or, preferably, a new Rome.

But there was one hitch. Monticello, breathtakingly beautiful and blessedly impractical, embodied not just the ideas and aspirations of Jefferson, but his contradictions as well. And, by the same account, just as Monticello embodied the varied strains of Jefferson, so did the adolescent republic he had so assiduously labored to found. His disparate threads were woven not just through its vibrancy and its growth, but also throughout its very deep and real divides.

"It fell to the lot of one Virginian to define America," the great twentieth-century scholar C. Vann Woodward would note. And no less than Abraham Lincoln had already agreed, saying, "Jefferson was, is, and . . . will continue to be the most distinguished politician in our history." Yet, in more than one way, as the national fuse smoldered in the years running up to the Civil War, and in the anxious days leading up to the pivotal month of April 1865, that politician and that definition would be precisely the issue.

❦ ❦ ❦

Few men, even among the Founding Fathers, have brought such a rare combination of formidable energy and prodigious intellect to American life as Thomas Jefferson. Born into the Virginia aristocracy, he came from the same background as George Washington, was related to such great Virginia gentry families as the Randolphs and the Marshalls, and, with his melancholy but cool green eyes, his folded arms and intense gaze, had an imposing appearance, which, as Abigail Adams once noted, imbued him with a look "not unlike God." But it is his contributions to the nation that are most often recognized as monumental. During the seething decade between the Stamp Act agitation and the Boston Tea Party, many able pens and probing minds had set out constitutional solutions for British America's dilemma. Yet it was Jefferson, in 1774, who cut to the heart of the entire debate confronting the colonies in one brilliant treatise—*Summary View of the Rights of British America*, a distillation that crystallized and combined the primacy of individual liberty with the notion of popular sovereignty.

His finest hour came two years later, in 1776, after the first shots of civil war with the British kingdom had been fired. The Continental Congress appointed a distinguished committee of five to consider a draft declaration, of independence, "in case the Congress agreed thereto." Jefferson was named to the committee. Only thirty-three, and despite the fact that the other members included the redoubtable Benjamin Franklin and such eminent figures as John Adams, Roger Sherman, and Robert Livingston, Jefferson was made the chairman. He quickly rose to the task with his electrifying draft, produced in a handful of weeks, which was then adopted almost in its entirety. Its riveting sentence, with one crucial edit by Franklin—"We hold these truths to be self-evident, that all men are created equal, that they are endowed by their Creator with certain inalienable rights, that among these are life, liberty and the pursuit of happiness"—said it all. And the Declaration did more than rouse a fledgling rebellion or serve as a kind of national birth certificate. More than any other single document, it rapidly became the classic statement of America's purpose and enduring idea—and it would, of course, be drawn upon again in another turbulent time when Abraham Lincoln weighed the winds of approaching war, and again when he delivered the Gettysburg Address.

Yet for all his intellect, his ebullient, inventive, and surprising mind, Jefferson, who was elected to Virginia's House of Burgesses at the age of twenty-three, who would go on to become governor of Virginia, America's minister to France, its first secretary of state, its second vice president, and then twice its president, was a bedeviling grab bag of paradoxes that would cast an ambiguous shadow over his successors and the country for generations to come. He was a democrat, who boasted that he would "always have a jealous care of the right of election by the people," yet he disparaged "the swinish multitude" and vigorously opposed direct election of the Senate on the grounds that "a choice by the people themselves is not generally distinguished for its wisdom." He protested that he had no wish to form a political party ("If I could not go to heaven but with a party, I would not go there at all"), but in the 1790s he did just that. For years, he jousted peevishly with Alexander Hamilton over economic policies, yet he shrank from personal political controversy whenever it touched him. He lived in a deeply religious land, yet he detested clergymen all his adult life. He drafted the Declaration of Independence, yet not once did he himself give an exciting speech. A passionate idealist, he was a fervent hater, hating the speculators, hating the Federalists, hating the merchants, hating industrialists without distinction.

Still, he meant to practice what he preached. He derided royalty, variously disparaging Louis XVI as a "fool," the king of Denmark as "really crazy," the king of Prussia as "a mere hog in body as well as in mind," and, upon his election to the presidency, he scrapped the trappings of aristocracy of which George Washington had been so fond. Gone were the powdered wigs, the white coach, the dress swords, and the guards for the president's house. But if his plebeian principles were strong, his aristocratic appetites were infinitely stronger. In addition to the French wines he personally imported, the *Muscat de Riverside*, there were the blooded horses and costly mahogany forte-piano ("solid wood, not vineered [*sic*]"), the coats and shirts from Savile Row and the porcelain from Wedgwood and Doulton, the pâtés, the fine port and the thick hams, and the costly leather-bound books, some 15,000 volumes, to form a library without peer. And there was the debt. To subsidize his expensive tastes and lavish lifestyle, Jefferson borrowed money all his life, sold his own cherished library, and, astonishingly enough, died over $100,000 in the red. He even sought to sell his beloved Monticello to relieve his heirs of financial burdens, but, remarkably, there were no bidders. And for all his cosmopolitan ideas, after the presidency—and this stunning fact provides profound insights into the Southerners who would one day seek their independence—he never once left his home state of Virginia, not even to go to Washington or New York or Philadelphia, and, outside of his hideaway at Poplar Forest, never ventured much beyond the amiable confines of Monticello itself.

But among those conflicts that defined Jefferson the man was one that would ultimately cleave the nation that he had helped to construct. There was no greater champion of personal liberty than Jefferson, yet few men have reaped more from human bondage. The dark shadows of slavery penetrated every nook of Jefferson's long, illustrious life. Though he owned from 100 to 200 slaves, comprising some three generations of human souls, and bought, sold, and bred slaves his entire life, Jefferson despised slavery, cursed it (under his breath, that is), and in vain tried to curb it, both publicly and in his own personal sphere. Yet at every step, his distaste was marked by temporizing, indifference, hesitation. In his *Notes on the State of Virginia*, he bitterly denounced slavery in the harshest terms, arguing that it was not just an economic evil, which crippled "industry," but a moral one that debased the slave owner even more than the slave ("the most unremitting despotism on the one part, and degrading submissions on the other"). Indeed, he wanted no less than outright abolition, and few Northern abolitionists would ever argue more forcefully or more thoroughly against the "peculiar institution." But almost as soon as they were completed, Jefferson sought to avoid a wide circulation of his *Notes* because he didn't want fellow Virginians to read his scathing observations—only 200 copies were printed, and he refused to have his name embossed on the title page. He told John Adams that he hesitated to publish the volume altogether.

And though an emancipationist in theory, warning that slavery was "the dreadful firebell in the night," Jefferson never systematically pursued an end to its practice: not as governor of Virginia or as the reviser of its law code, not as secretary of state, not as vice president, not as a two-term president. Earlier in his career in Virginia, he boldly drafted a law for gradual emancipation, but then he never presumed to introduce it. Later, he included a blistering attack upon the slave trade in the Declaration of Independence, but it was struck out. He did not quarrel. Even in his twilight years as an elder statesman of America, when slavery underwent a terrifying acceleration in the South, he accepted the Southern contention that emancipated slaves could not live as free men in the Southern states, but with a twist: they should be expatriated to form a separate and independent country—in Africa, or the West Indies, or beyond the Mississippi—to which "we should extend our alliance and protection."

At Monticello, the story was no less complex. Upon Jefferson's return from Paris after a five-year absence, his slaves eagerly collected around his carriage at the base of the mountain, shouting and cheering, "kissing his hands and feet, some crying and . . . others laughing." There is every reason to believe that this affection was genuine. Two years later, Jefferson would mortgage all of them, men, women, and children, to pay for the ambitious, French-inspired renovation of his home. When strapped for funds, he even paid his hired workers in slaves, as he did with his carpenter, Reuben Perry.

The daily routine of Monticello was equally sobering. In running his plantation, Jefferson's overseer severely flogged slaves, and more than once Jefferson was seen angrily shaking the whip; at least once, he may have done the flogging himself. And while he publicly denounced miscegenation, it is now widely accepted that he had a black mistress at home, and fathered at least one of her children.

Perhaps most troubling of all, while many of Jefferson's own neighbors invoked his ringing phrases to justify the liberation of their own chattel ("the glorious and memorable revolution"), Jefferson never emancipated his own slaves—not in his lifetime, as did his young neighbor, Edward Coles, the future governor of Illinois, nor in his will, as George Washington did.

Yet if slavery was a thunderclap reverberating across Thomas Jefferson's world, his paradoxical views on the Union were just as earthshaking. For all of Jefferson's love of the United States—there was no fiercer patriot and ardent expansionist—his love of his home state ran even deeper: he referred to Virginia not just as "a nation," but also as "my country"; he described Virginians as "my countrymen" and for a time spoke of the United States Congress as "a foreign legislature"; he even called the Union a "confederacy." And it was this duality, above all else, that fiercely tugged at him all his life and, in turn, at the nation in the years before the Civil War.

All throughout the late 1700s, and as president, Jefferson relentlessly pushed to expand America; in an age of imperialism, he was perhaps the greatest empire builder of them all (in Stephen Ambrose's richly descriptive words, "his mind encompassed the [entire] continent"). From the start of the revolution, he conceived of the United States as one vast body stretching from sea to sea. In 1787, he was a principal author of the Northwest Ordinance, which helped bind the distant Trans-Appalachian region to the United States. Then, in 1803, he finalized the Louisiana Purchase. At the time, the United States was a minor country on Europe's periphery, with a population about equal to Ireland's. Now, this single gesture, which doubled the size of America, helped create the Deep South, and opened up an ever-expanding frontier, would lay the foundation for Jefferson's "empire of liberty." Here, civilization would brilliantly sweep across, from east to west, "like a cloud of light."

But what kind of civilization? What kind of America? When Jefferson took the oath of office as the third president of the United States, the fledgling republic was already a land of limitless opportunities and vexing contradictions: an expanding country, it was not yet a single nation; the first free and democratic society in the world since ancient Greece, it stood out as a utopia for the common man, yet the individual states were a cauldron of smoldering resentments and seething differences, and human slavery was not just tolerated, but sanctioned; a country born by an audacious act of rebellion and secession, it had already changed its form of government just twelve years earlier and was still in a fluid political situation. And as Jefferson and Americans looked westward, past the Mississippi to the Rocky Mountains, even to the Pacific, the perennial question remained whether one nation could—or even should—govern the entire continent.

On this issue, Jefferson was torn. Until his dying days, he regularly propounded local self-government above all else, supporting states' rights against the Union, county rights against the states, township rights against the county, and private rights against all. He pushed for the Tenth Amendment to the Constitution, limiting federal power in favor of the states. In 1800, he soberly warned that "a single consolidated government would become the most corrupt government on earth." At the end of his first term as president, when New England was darkly threatening secession ("scission") over his economic and political stances, Jefferson mourned it as an "incalculable evil," yet he answered tepidly: "Whether we remain in our confederacy, or break into Atlantic and Mississippi confederacies, I do not believe very important to the happiness of either part." And he added this: ". . . separate them if it be better." True to his divided nature and divided philosophy, he was himself of two minds.

Jefferson died in his bed at Monticello on July 4, 1826, at the age of eighty-three. On that very same day, the country, marked by a astonishing growth and breathtaking vibrancy, was celebrating the fiftieth anniversary of his Declaration. There was much to celebrate. But discord was also part of the new American landscape. America was writhing over slavery; over sectional conflict; over states' rights; and, above all, over its very national identity, bequeathed in no small measure by Jefferson's own ambivalent views. And with the benefit of grim hindsight, we know that these contradictions were only one of the more conspicuous links in a very long chain of American history.

It is more than symbolic that, by 1860, Monticello lay abandoned and largely in ruins, and that by April 1865, it had two owners, one a New Yorker, the other a Virginian, and was cared for by neither.

❧   ❧   ❧

More than three and a half centuries earlier, in April 1507, Martin Waldseemuller, professor of cosmography at the University of Saint-Die, produced the first map showing the Western Hemisphere, a *novo mondo* with a long snaking coastline. He called it "America," after the discoverer of the new continent, an appellation that belonged as much to Amerigo Vespucci, the Florentine merchant, as it did to Columbus. Like an enormous board game whose pieces were slowly being put into place, the science of geography would eventually give way to the science of government, and by the time the Founders gathered at Philadelphia in 1787, nationhood was beckoning. No words can capture the boldness of all this—America not just as a place on a Spanish map or one more distant outpost of the sprawling British empire, but an actual self-governing country. A country not to be forged by a thousand years of shared history and shared dreams, but to be conceived in the minds of a handful of men over a handful of months. With pluck, daring, iron will, and imagination, and a brilliance unsurpassed in history, the Founders would in turn beget the national idea, a country unlike any since the beginning of time.

But in the crucible of the occasion, fateful questions would linger: What would knit this country together? Was it to be one country and one nation—or perhaps two, or even several? And was it to last in perpetuity, or to be a brave and daring experiment in democracy that could yet founder?

The fragility of America as a nation from its very first days cannot be exaggerated. Unlike the Old World, America was not born out of ancient custom or claim, its people bound together from the shadows of feudal, marauding bands, emerging as a nation by the time they could primitively write their own history. Where in most countries a sense of nationhood spontaneously arose over tens of centuries, the product of generations of common kinship, common language, common myths and a shared history, and the collective ties of tradition, America was born as an artificial series of states, woven together by negotiated compacts and agreements, charters and covenants. It did not arise naturally, as in Europe, or China, or Persia, but was made, almost abstractly, out of ink and paper, crafted by lawyers and statesmen. Insofar as the early Americans had a nationality, they were for more than a century and a half British. In fact, it remains a curious twist of fate that America was at first Britain's idea; it was the British who finally persuaded the American settlers to accept some kind of distinct national identity. Significantly, even in 1776, their contract to become Americans—the Declaration of Independence—did not make them a nation. Indeed, the very word "nation" was explicitly dropped from it, and all references were instead to the separate states. Thus, the very heading of the final version of the Declaration of Independence described the document as "The unanimous Declaration of the *thirteen* united States of America," and the momentous resolution introduced in the Continental Congress on June 7, 1776, by Richard Henry Lee and seconded by John Adams, declared: "That *these* United Colonies are, and of right ought to be, free and independent *States*." As historian Daniel Boorstin has noted, "Independence had not created one nation but thirteen."

There is more than a measure of truth to this. Like the colonies that preceded them, these new states were as dramatically different from one another as they were from England; each jealously guarded its self-rule, its independence, and its sovereignty. Each meticulously gathered its own army, chartered its own navy, commanded military actions to protect its own interests, and oversaw its own Indian affairs and postal routes. Each had its own legislatures, its own functioning courts, its own taxes, and, in time, its own individual constitutions. And too often forgotten is this simple but telling fact: before independence, Americans were both British subjects as well as citizens of Virginia or Massachusetts, New York or Connecticut, or some other home colony. After independence, they were no longer Britons, but neither were they Americans; there was, as yet, no American country to which to attach their loyalties. And so they remained faithful, proud members of their sovereign state, Massachusetts, or Virginia, or Connecticut. To the extent there was an American national identity, it was unexpected, impromptu, an artificial creation of the Revolution—and secondary.

And for all its genius, the U.S. Constitution provided no resolution. Until this point, constitutions were not national codes, but national inheritances; they were not written down, but existed almost intuitively, the ethereal sum of a whole country's charters, statutes, declarations, informal understandings, habits, traditions, and attitudes. Yet for the United States, what had started out as an exercise to do little more than revise the existing Articles of Confederation—a loose system designed for the exigencies of the Revolutionary War—instead produced a far more audacious gamble, an entirely new body of laws: the Constitution. Nowhere on the planet had anything like it been devised; there it was, at once a central government with the authority to tax and to maintain an army, and at the same time, a republican government with its powers scrupulously divided among a president, a House of Representatives, a Senate, and a Supreme Court. But when it came to articulating America as one nation, the men at Philadelphia flinched. This was the one nut they couldn't crack.

The word "nation" or "national" appears nowhere in the Constitution. Unable to reconcile the gnawing tensions between the proponents of the states, the anti-Federalists, and the proponents of the new federal authority that would come into being, the Federalists, the Founders resorted to the more ambiguous phrase "the United States." (Even the very use of the word "federal," or "foederal," as it was more often written, was actually meant to describe a relationship resting in good faith, *foedus* in Latin being the cognate of *fides,* faith.) When it was all done, an elated George Washington recognized not just the historic import but also the precariousness of the whole enterprise; it was, he maintained, "little short of a miracle" that delegates from "so many different States" should have united to form a national government.

A national government, yes, but did it form a nation? That still fell a little short of anyone's miracle. Consider Washington's parting speech. He used the word "nation" in his Farewell Address, but only prescriptively: "The name of AMERICAN, which belongs to you in your national capacity, must always exalt the just pride of patriotism more than any appellation derived from local discriminations." This, of course, begged the question, was America a nation? Or was it simply a community of states? What is clear is that in the architecture of nationhood, the United States had achieved something quite remarkable; as historian John Murrin has succinctly put it, "Americans erected their constitutional roof before they put up national walls."

The result? With characteristic anachronism, and with the benefit of this ingenious contrivance, Americans had a country even before they had their nation. And, in turn, the Constitution did something quite unique in the annals of human history: it substituted as precisely that, a kind of national identity. "Americans are intellectually autochthonous," Gary Wills has stated, "having no pedigree except that of the idea." But in the ensuing years, America would not be able to escape the price for such genius—the price of hate and blood in the making of nations. That would be paid in the Civil War.

The seeds of discord were there long before the guns of Fort Sumter began firing. In the absence of a common national identity, they were always there.

✳　✳　✳

The generation that wrote the Constitution was obsessed by the specter that republican government would not survive across a vast domain. Tradition was against them. They were boldly obliged to repudiate a political axiom that had behind it the domineering authority of the renowned French philosopher Montesquieu (always the "great" Montesquieu). In the mid-eighteenth century, he had pronounced that a republic could function only in a small territory, and the thirteen original states together—even some of the larger states individually—were already considered too large. Geography, too, was against them. As Americans traveled farther south and trekked farther west, the wilderness and the rivers and the mountains rapidly created breathtaking differences: differences in lifestyles, differences in culture, differences in economics, differences in political outlook.

What did not change was the flip side of America's auspicious birth, the secessionist tradition, a tradition that was older than America, older than the Revolution itself, as old as the earliest colonial settlements. From the very start, the discovery of the New World had made secessions and withdrawals, separations and dissolutions, practicable across a full hemisphere, and, from its initial beginnings, American life comprised not just relentless growth but countless efforts to secede. The Pilgrims, of course, were the first self-proclaimed American secessionists, coming to Plymouth only after their failed effort to extrude themselves from England in the Netherlands. This was just the beginning. The colonies themselves expanded and in turn acquired their varied characters by secession: Roger Williams and Anne Hutchinson, separatist fanatics, were driven from their own Massachusetts Bay and founded Rhode Island. Thomas Hooker seceded to his Connecticut. Lord Baltimore enabled a group of Catholics to secede from English life into a community that—for a while at least—remained exclusively their own. William Penn provided Quakers with a refuge. And the American Revolution was itself a monumental act of secession. And on it went.

Nor did this pattern change after independence. Indeed, for some 200 years, the powerful secessionist ethos was characteristically American. By the 1780s, many, if not most, Americans solemnly believed the nation would inevitably divide into two countries, and, by 1794, they seemed to be right. As if to prove Montesquieu's dire predictions right, America suddenly appeared on the brink of splitting apart.

The first spark assaulting national unity pitted not North against South, over slavery, but West against East, over taxes. Frontier farmers, all across the land, revolted against Alexander Hamilton's dreaded whiskey levy. They lived in towns literally hewn from the wilderness and in constant jeopardy, if not from wild animals then from Indians. But one thing they wouldn't countenance was taxation without representation. They did far more than refuse to pay the infernal whiskey tax; they blithely shot at revenue officers who would collect it, they tarred and feathered federal officials who sought to change their minds, and they set fire to the homes of George Washington's hated representatives. Thus began the Whiskey Rebellion. In the weeks and months that followed, the rebels raised liberty poles bearing inflammatory slogans, passed out petitions of angry resistance, and formed urgent committees of correspondence modeled on their Revolutionary predecessors. Then, after a serious military encounter in July 1794 between frontiersmen and federal representatives, war fever swept the country. By August, the call went out and a clutch of Whiskey Rebels began to gather. Soon, they were 7,000 strong, dressed for war, hoisting a six-striped flag, whooping and howling and openly flirting with independence. The indelible rationale of their rebellion was the very same rationale of the Revolution—like the ocean that divided England from America and mandated that there should be two countries, the mountains that carved East from West cried out not for one, but two nations.

It didn't happen. To the banging of drums and tramping of the march, President Washington personally reviewed an army of volunteer troops hastily assembled to quell the rebellion. In late October, the expedition, led by no less than the famous soldier-politician Lighthorse Harry Lee of Virginia, converged on Pittsburgh. The imposing show of force worked. The leaders of the rebellion fled down the Ohio River, headed for Spanish Louisiana.

But, if the threat of secession had receded, it did anything but disappear.

Remarkably, the next alarum came not from settlers but from two of the very Founding Fathers themselves: Jefferson and Madison. Their Virginia and Kentucky Resolutions of 1798–99, authored (secretly) only a decade after the adoption of the Constitution, held that states in the federal union could nullify acts of Congress. By arguing that nullification was a "rightful remedy" in state and federal disputes, the two men thereby laid the political and conceptual foundations for national dissolution as well. The Resolutions were never tested, but they were a dangerous weapon indeed. If invoked, both could have been fatal to the ten-year-old Constitution and even to the very existence of the United States, for, if only implicitly, they had unmistakably affirmed a basis for secession—another remedy that Jefferson had also privately contemplated.

And it would not be long before the next blush of crisis.

Thirteen years, to be exact.

The ensuing controversy occurred during the War of 1812 against Great Britain, with the advocates of disunion coming from the North, in Federalist New England. Disgusted with the iniquity of "Mr. Madison's War," fed up with the folly of Thomas Jefferson's Louisiana Purchase as endangering the "world's last hope of a republik," fearing their own voice to be under permanent eclipse, New England exclusivists let out a resounding cry for unified protest. To the horror and disgust of Southerners—the Senate debates of the time vividly attest to this—New Englanders talked not just of a separate peace with Great Britain but, more ominously, of outright disunion itself. From the very start of the war, Massachusetts, Connecticut, and New Hampshire had flatly refused to send their militias to fight, and New England even went as far as to collude with the enemy by investing money in London securities and selling supplies to the British forces. As Thomas Pickering of Massachusetts summed up the bitter feelings of defiant New Englanders, there was "no magic in the sound of Union. If the great objects of Union are utterly abandoned . . . let the Union be severed."

By early 1814, that seemed to be a real possibility and a real danger. Massachusetts, with its socially conscious aristocrats and high-shouldered mansions, its fashionable upper-class enclaves and grassy residential squares, was on the verge of rebellion, and some, like the cleric Elijah Parish, were now urging New England to "cut the connexion with the southern states." At this point, the call went out from Massachusetts for a winter convention in Hartford, Connecticut. Ultimately, cooler heads prevailed that December, and the Hartford Convention did not urge secession as feared. It did, however, endorse the next strongest thing: nullification.

Nullification and secession would eventually lead first to approbation, then to separation, and, ultimately, to the nightmare of civil war itself. By the end of the 1820s and into the early 1830s, after the government had been in operation for more than forty years, the language of nullification and state sovereignty, and the notions of self-governance and regionalism, had become indelibly embedded in the American vocabulary. Thus, much like Jefferson, when many Americans spoke of the Union, however much they had come to love it, they spoke of "our confederacy," or more simply of "the Republic." The Constitution, however revered, was a "compact." The United States was just as often "the states United," or "the united States," or even "a league of sovereign states," and was invariably spoken of as a plural noun. The term "sovereign" was associated far more with the individual states themselves than it was with the "general government," and state legislatures took for granted their right to "instruct" their United States senators on how to vote on important legislation. As a consequence the road to Civil War was paved with civic bricks like nullification and secession.

Nor did the studied ambiguities of the Constitution do much to solve this cycle of secessionist threat and counterthreat. To be sure, the crucial question was raised: did the Constitution create a Union from which no state, once having joined, could escape except by extra-constitutional acts of revolution? Or did it create a Union of sovereign states, each of which retained the right to secede at its own discretion?

In the face of these incipient signs of sectional tension, Americans increasingly wrestled with this issue, but they quickly realized there was no clause in the Constitution that established the Union's perpetuity. Where the Articles of Confederation contended that "the Union shall be perpetual," the Constitution only spoke of "a more perfect Union"— actually, Charles Pinckney's draft resolution containing the provision "the Union shall be perpetual" was never even brought before the general body for consideration. Where the Constitution was framed in the name of "We the People," Article VII firmly declared that it would be ratified, "between the States." In the end, to the extent that there was a discussion about the perpetuity of the Union, there was no consensus. No less staunch a Federalist than James Madison wrote, "each state . . . is considered as a sovereign body independent of all others, and only to be bound by its own voluntary act. In this relation then the new Constitution will . . . be a *federal* and not a *national* constitution."

What did Americans make of all this? In truth, in the early nineteenth century the wording of the Constitution gave neither the believers in the right of secession nor the early advocates of a perpetual Union a decisive case. Hoping for the best, the Founding Fathers instead left the question of perpetuity to posterity, and the most common perception of the Union was that of Washington: America was "worth a fair and full experiment." And where for many the Union was much beloved, for many others, it was an experiment valued less for its own sake than as a means to certain desirable ends, namely the protection of the people's liberties and the defense of the country from enemies abroad. And there the tension lay.

Between 1830 and 1833, the pendulum of secession swung again, indelibly and seemingly permanently, this time to the South, to South Carolina, which demanded nullification and echoed the principles of regional self-interest and regional self-rights, with its effort to nullify the collection of federal tariff duties. This crisis was averted temporarily by Andrew Jackson's firm response and a compromise ingeniously proposed by Henry Clay. And, for a brief time, it appeared that Southerners and Northerners might still march together toward forging one nation. But with each passing year, the prize that many of the Founders had sought—Union—again increasingly seemed elusive, as the strains of secession hardened into a fierce debate that would at first consume the country, then divide it, and eventually plunge it into all-out war: over slavery.

From 1820 onward, throughout the next forty years, the country lurched from one tense confrontation to another—the compromises of 1820, 1833, and 1850, the prelude of the Kansas-Nebraska Act of 1854 and of the Wilmot Debates, the firebell of Nat Turner's rebellion and the Dred Scott Decision, the terror of Lawrence and Pottawatomie, the rhetoric of the Lincoln-Douglas debates and the publication of *Uncle Tom's Cabin*, and, last but not least, the spark of Harper's Ferry. Each constituted a powerful symbol that would transform the country's landscape, and exacerbate the unresolved contradictions from America's founding. Throughout this period, Congress would become, in many ways, little more than a Union-saving body, that and nothing more.

It would not be enough.

❧   ❧   ❧

By mid-century, nowhere were danger and expectation held in more delicate equilibrium than in America. The country had doubled its population every two decades, leaving it behind only Russia and France. It had extended its continental reach from coast to coast, and boasted a burgeoning merchant fleet worthy of challenging the leading nations of the Old World for global supremacy. It was a magnet for the hopes of countless immigrants—the English, the Irish, the Germans, the Jews, the Catholics, the Chinese—and for the dreams of Americans migrating along the new roads and new railroads into the ever-expanding western territories. With an almost religious zeal, Americans felt compelled to press on west, to settle and republicanize, to civilize and democratize. And of course, when the gold rush began, to make money. Studding the landscape with balloon frame homes and hand-hewn log cabins, traveling by oxen and Conestoga wagons, and horse and buggy, Americans were suddenly everywhere over the immensity of its spaces: Chicago and Rochester, Santa Fe and Missouri, Oregon and the Great Salt Lake, California and Texas. The country was developing an incipient national art, an inchoate national literature, a thriving rancorous press, and even a new national idiom. Though it was still a rural land—most Americans, as historian James McPherson points out, had no experience with the federal government other than through the U.S. post office—major cities were emerging in Boston, New York, Philadelphia, Baltimore, and, of course, Richmond. With its textile mills, foundries, and factories, there was even a new economic class, again typically American: "the middling class." After a brief sixty-plus years of history, then, Americans were filled with an astonishing sense of optimism and a glowing sense of destiny. Increasingly sophisticated and wealthy, America was envied and admired in much of the world.

But between the idea of equality enshrined in the Declaration of Independence and the notion of popular sovereignty, between the demands of nationalism and the intimacies of community, between the bumptious sense of manifest destiny of a growing nation and the hard rock of slavery, and above all else, between the dramatic struggle to forge a national identity and the emergence of distinct separate nationalisms across the great American expanse, stood an old and enduring tension in American life that refused to go away.

The convenient version of history forgets the unbroken link of secessionist threats emanating from the country's earliest days, just as it intimates that it was only Southerners who flirted with disunion in these perilous later years. Northerners did, too. While there is a sense that Daniel Webster did indeed speak for all the North when he thundered, "Liberty and Union, now and forever, one and inseparable," this is not so. Senator Walter Lowrie of Pennsylvania echoed the sentiments of many when he warned that if the choice was between the dissolution of the Union and extension of slavery, "I, for one, will choose the former." Or consider the words of a young John Quincy Adams: "I love the Union as I love my wife. But if my wife should ask for and insist upon a separation, she would have it though it broke my heart." And then later: "If the union must be dissolved, slavery is precisely the question upon which it ought to break." For his part, the prominent intellectual and clergyman Theodore Parker, who had no qualms about separation of the Union, argued that division was far, far better than allowing the poison of slavery to spread to the North.

In these final years, slavery was the primary wedge cracking the underpinnings of national union. But it was by no means the only wedge. Too often overlooked is that during the run-up to the Civil War, New Jersey, for its own parochial reasons, flirted with secession, as did California, which, with Oregon, considered creation of a separate Pacific nation. The Mormons in Utah fought a handful of bloody skirmishes with the federal government, and they, too, sought freedom. And just months before Fort Sumter, New York City—which on and off in its history alternately considered independence and even confederation with the South—again threatened secession. Even on the eve of the Civil War, some Americans, harkening back to the earliest days of the republic, back to the Whiskey Rebellion, back to the War of 1812, still were speculating about the country splitting into three or four "confederacies," with an Independent Pacific Coast thrown in to boot.

By the time the war came, a tortuous circle was complete. The delicate balance of America's paradoxes could no longer prevail. Indeed, in retrospect, it is little wonder that the country didn't break up earlier. The unsettled and unanswered questions that had gnawed at the country from the very beginning now had to be resolved, by force of arms. And as the Civil War entered April 1865, dire questions remained: Could at long last those national walls be erected to support the constitutional roof? And could a now bloody, exhausted, embittered America survive as one country?

❧   ❧   ❧

The dismal examples from the rest of the world were not encouraging.

To the south, the Latin American wars for independence had produced not one, not two, but some twenty-two separate nations from a few vice-royalties. With bewildering rapidity, these republics came and went, trapped for decades in a vortex of conflict and military repression. Nor was this simply a Latin American trait. Across the Atlantic loomed the specter of the French Revolution, the Terror, "the contagion," occurring as it did in the most advanced country of the day. France had been the epicenter of the Enlightenment: its science led the world, its books were read everywhere (Madison had Jefferson, then the minister to France, send him $220 worth of books on government and philosophy to read as the Founders undertook to craft the Constitution), its language was the tongue of aristocracies, and it was the most powerful country in all of Europe, if not the world. Yet revolution plunged France, and in time, all of Europe, into an ongoing cycle of terror and violence, the remnants of which plagued the continent for decades, like a recurring nightmare. No country was totally immune, from Denmark to Sicily, from Bohemia to Hungary. And the problems of France and Europe in many ways resembled those of the United States: the fundamental questions of nations and nationalities, the task of bringing the people into some kind of rational relationship with their governments, and some form of mutual and moral relationship with their sovereign states.

The Founders themselves were acutely aware of all this; indeed, they were haunted by it. The horror of France was anticipated even in the very design of the capital city, Washington, itself. Rejecting the plan to lay out the city in elegant rectangular blocks and eye-catching right angles as in Philadelphia, the designers ultimately employed the radial plan, filled with *ronds-points* or "circles." In their conception and execution, these circles were to provide stations for armed soldiers, allowing them to maintain full command of the streets in case of any popular civil uprising or prolonged mob violence. Unlike in France, there should be no barricades in Washington.

But the Civil War threatened to take the United States down a very different sort of road. As the European and Latin American examples glumly proved, it was *not* solely a matter of whether the North or the South won the war. As critical was the delicate matter of how the war would end and how the peace would be made. Would the country emerge united, one nation, Abraham Lincoln's fervent dream? Or would it remain fragmented, ever ready to disintegrate into petty, squabbling minor or fragmented republics, or become chronically vulnerable to anarchy and low-level violence, as was the dismal fate of many of America's European friends and Central American neighbors, and, more generally, of other republics throughout history, and even in our own most recent century.

The Civil War, then, in its final months was more than a struggle for the soul of America, or the survival of the republican experiment: it was a larger fight, once and for all, to construct the nation. It was in April 1865 that the outlines of the answer to this question would finally appear with clarity.

❧ ❧ ❧

As spring crept north across Virginia in 1865, Monticello, like America itself, now seemed more a monument to folly than a measure of grand design, more a finite experiment than a creation that could endure. Like so much of the country, it sat, rather uneasily, in no-man's-land. It was a house with two competing owners, one Northern—the estate of naval officer Uriah Levy—one Southern—the Confederate entrepreneur Benjamin Finklin; it was a home with two competing souls, John Winthrop's "city upon a hill" and Thomas Jefferson's Declaration of Independence; and it was an estate with two diametric visages, one the best of America, the shining idea of equality; one the darkest, the specter of slavery. But in a curious, deeply symbolic way, and, despite all the neglect, it stubbornly remained a provocative reminder of the spirit of the elusive nation, as a shrine, not entirely Southern or really Yankee, a place where visitors still came to pay tribute to Jefferson, and where people could recall the moral imperatives and sense of high purpose that had once seemed so clear and compelling to the Founders. And come they did. Even in the Civil War. Even on the eve of April 1865.

Indeed, as the crisis of the Civil War intensified, Monticello was frequently the tranquil eye in the hurricane. Confederate troops had overrun it in 1862, but they were content to leave it in the hands of the old caretaker, Joseph Wheeler. No significant battles took place near Jefferson's mountain. When Confederate John Bell Hood's Texas Brigade did pass through, they stood reverently on the front porch, "the sacred portals," and mused about "the famous statesman" and his "glorious memories." Over the next two years, on sunny days under the velvety sky, a few picnics were held on Monticello's lawns. On one bright autumn day in the fall of 1863, some convalescing Confederate soldiers even held a day of "gaiety," a mock tournament of "knights," most riding with only one arm, reins held in the teeth, dashing valiantly at the rings, with wooden sticks employed as lances. Periodically, Northerners came, too. Mostly, visitors, wherever they came from, ended up in the great dome room. Almost unused in Jefferson's day, it now boasted more than a thousand of their names written on its walls.

And while they left their signatures, bold or hesitant, many took away something else. Year by year, they chipped and chiseled away at Jefferson's tombstone, a five-foot memorial that, upon his wishes, simply enshrined him not as president but as the author of the Declaration of Independence.

In drawers and keepsake boxes and on parlor tables they preserved these pieces, as if there was something worth saving of the man and the country he had helped create. But as April 1865 approached, what would ultimately be saved, if anything, depended on a handful of men, one of whom was readying to take his place upon an inaugural podium in the Union capital of Washington, D.C., and another of whom was urgently riding into the Confederate capital of Richmond, Virginia.

Part 1

March 1865

I

The Dilemma

The bells rang that day in Washington. Wherever there were brick bell towers and whitewashed churches, wherever rows of bells hung in ascending niches, wherever the common people could crowd belfries to take turns pulling the ropes, the bells sang. Bells were part of the American tradition. Cast in iron, bronze, copper, and sometimes silver, they rang with a hundred messages: summoning Americans to Sunday services, marking the harvest and holidays, signaling the prosperity of planting, tolling the sadness of death, chiming the happiness of marriage, clanging warnings of fire or flood, or booming out the celebration of victory. Today, they rang with the hint of promise. It was March 4, 1865. Inauguration Day in the Union.

Abraham Lincoln had been at the Capitol since midmorning, forgoing a traditional celebratory carriage ride up Pennsylvania Avenue to sign a stack of bills passed in the waning hours of the lame-duck Congress. He was determined to make his own mark on them before the vice presidential swearing in, scheduled for noon. Cloistered in the Senate wing, tracing and retracing the letters of his name, Lincoln remained the very picture of exhaustion. His face was heavily lined, his cheeks were sunken, and he had lost thirty pounds in recent months. Though only fifty-six, he could easily pass for a very old man. He was sick, dispirited, and even his hands were routinely cold and clammy. And today, the weather itself seemed to be colluding with his foul and melancholy mood. That morning, heavy clouds moved over Washington, as they had the day before and the day before that, whipping the capital with blasts of rain and wind. Even when the rain let up, the ground didn't. The streets were a sea of mud at least ten inches deep. Still, the people came.

On the following Monday, the inauguration rush would include a grand ball for 4,000: they would waltz and polka to the beat of a military band; feast on an elegant medley of beef, veal, poultry, game, smoked meats, terrapin, oysters, and salads; finish with an astounding wartime array of ices, tarts, cakes, fruits, and nuts; and then retire for the evening with steaming coffee and good rich chocolate. But that was for official Washington, for Lincoln's loyalists and Republican Party functionaries. This Saturday was a day for all the Union. And like a great herd, the people were seemingly everywhere.

Their wagons ground to a halt underneath thickets of trees in the distance, and the thud and swish of their feet could be heard along Pierre L'Enfant's wide, radiating avenues. All along Pennsylvania Avenue, they converged, where the crowd stood at least six and eight deep on the crude sidewalks, around Fifteenth Street past the Treasury, where the stars and stripes hung from second-story windows, past Kirkland House and Tenth Street and the National Hotel, where a clutch of handkerchiefs fluttered and gawkers hung out their balconies, and up the steep slope to the Capitol, past the greening swatch of emerald lawns. At street intersections, military patrols formed a watchful guard. So did the Capitol police. Reporters and photographers crowded the stoops, ready to record the event for posterity. Flags waved; people cheered; and the band played. But mostly, the vast throng jostled for position by the east facade of the Capitol, newly capped by its gleaming dome and the towering bronze statue of Freedom, to be near, even to catch a glimpse of the president himself.

Finally, the presidential party moved from the Senate chamber out onto the platform. A roar of applause rose from the crowd as Lincoln made his way to his seat. It dipped and then mounted again as the sergeant-at-arms beckoned, and Lincoln stood, towering over the other men, and made his way to the podium.

As Lincoln rose and moved forward, a blazing sun broke through the gray haze and flooded the entire gathering with brilliant light. Above and below, the collective pulse quickened. ("Did you notice that sunburst?" the president later said. "It made my heart jump.") But whatever ominous portent that moment may have held, it was overshadowed by the more powerful drama of Lincoln's speech. Succinct, only 703 words, eloquent, and memorable, it was reminiscent of the Gettysburg Address, and at this crucial stage of the war, every bit as important. Summoning his waning energies, Lincoln began to read.

❧　　❧　　❧

As he rode into Richmond, Virginia, on that very same March morning, Robert E. Lee was met with none of the same fanfare. Slipping north from the trench lines ringing Petersburg, he must have felt that, on this particular day, Union troops would be loath to undertake any action. But he had a far more specific reason for journeying to the Confederate capital. Today, he harbored a single, daring plan to reignite the waning fortunes of the Confederacy, to somehow push the eleven states toward eventual independence. And he had come to confer with Confederate President Jefferson Davis, the insomniac head of the Southern government, who liked to wage war from his dining room, with maps unfurled and instruments scattered across the table.

Lee's ultimate calculation was as bold as it was simple: abandon Richmond and take his forces south to meet up with General Joe Johnston in North Carolina. Leave U. S. Grant, snugly ensconced in his City Point camp, holding the bag, minus the string. From there, they could continue the war indefinitely.

In the early, predawn hours, Lee had already vetted his options with General John B. Gordon, a shrewd, able warrior and one of his most trusted lieutenants. That meeting had proved to be an eye-opener. A Confederate courier, sent by Lee, had roused Gordon sometime around midnight, and it took the thirty-three-year-old two hours of hard riding in a bitter chill to reach the commanding general at his Edge Hill headquarters, outside Petersburg. There, as Union troops slumbered and

Washington celebrated, Gordon found Lee surrounded by a long table strewn with recent reports from every part of the army. One by one, Lee handed Gordon the papers to read. Lee, his face tight, already knew what was in them.

Despite a score of earlier tactical successes, the news was dismal. For nine months now, Lee's men had been living in a thirty-seven-mile labyrinth of trenches, stretching east of Richmond and southwest of Petersburg. Three times, in July, in September, and again in October, Grant had hurled his troops at Lee's Army of Northern Virginia, only to have them repulsed. In one instance, the battle of the Crater, it was an outright disaster for the Federals. What Grant had hoped in the early spring of 1864 would become a quick war of maneuver, open battle, and offense had instead become a prolonged siege. One surreal month after another, the two exhausted armies shadowboxed from their trenches. Throughout the summer and fall, the earthworks reverberated with abrupt, all-out attempts to break Lee's lines, sudden unexpected death, and round-the-clock sharpshooting. This pendulum of harassment was punctuated only by the tedium of the siege, which was hardly any more palatable. As winter set in, the coldest in memory, Lee feared that unless his thinly stretched lines could be reinforced, "a great calamity will befall us." Actually, the first great calamity was the plight of the men themselves. Despite Lee's efforts to secure food and clothing for his army, little was available. Scurvy, dysentery, and night blindness invaded the Confederate trenches. Simple cuts and small wounds refused to heal. The men lived with rats and lice, amid the stench of urine, feces, and even decaying flesh, staring up at the sky by day and often venturing out only by night. Morale plummeted. Eventually, driven by extreme hunger, assaulted by the biting cold, torn by letters from wives that movingly spoke of starvation and loss at home, deserters mushroomed, reaching a hundred a day during the severe freeze of February. His hands tied, at one point Lee exploded to his son Custis, "I have been up to see the Congress and they don't seem to be able to do anything except to eat peanuts and chew tobacco while my army is starving."

When the long, low fever of the Virginia winter finally abated, the situation for Lee's men was no less desperate. Day after day, silence was punctured by the sporadic signs of war: billowing clouds of dense, roiling smoke, stabbing spurts of gunfire, the steady roar of bursting shells, scattered debris that heaved and shifted with each hit, and disemboweled corpses flying upward and out of the trenches. This Lee could live with. But, as he shuffled field report after report in his headquarters at Edge Hill in early March, what now struck Lee was the destitution of his beloved army: there were no shoes, no overcoats, no blankets, and little food; men scrambled between the legs of horses for dung to sift for undigested corn. There was insanity, exhaustion, wounds gone gangrenous. And of course, there was Grant. At the most, Lee now had 57,000 men in his army; fewer than 35,000 were present for duty. Grant had, he believed, 150,000. Once reinforced by Sherman from the south and Sheridan from the west, Lee feared the Union commander would have 280,000. His calculations were not far off the mark; the Union had near endless resources—although not always the will to use them.

As the minutes had ticked by that night at Edge Hill, and after Gordon had read the reports, Lee asked him for his options. Gordon reluctantly concluded that there were three: make peace between the two sides on the best possible terms; retreat and join General Joe Johnston's forces in North Carolina; or stand and fight where they were. Of the three, retreat and peace were the most promising ones. Lee agreed. But as he set out for Richmond after that largely sleepless night, the peace option had already been foreclosed. Peace feelers had been tried twice that year, the first culminating in a full-fledged conference on U. S. Grant's steamer, the *River Queen*, anchored off Hampton Roads. There, Lincoln and his secretary of state, William Seward, had met with the diminutive Confederate Vice President Alexander Stephens and two other Confederate representatives. Ironically, it was the Northerners who would offer the South drastic concessions on slavery and immediate emancipation, but, to the Confederates, their remaining terms smacked of unconditional surrender. Stephens, who had served with Lincoln in Congress and appeared as small and misshapen as Lincoln did large and gangly, said, "Mr. President, if we understand you correctly, you think that we of the Confederacy have committed treason; that we are traitors to your government; that we have forfeited our rights, and are proper subjects for the hangman." Lincoln in turn responded, "Yes . . . That is about the size of it."

The second feeler had come from Confederate General James Longstreet and Union General Edward Ord. They had proposed a meeting of generals, led by Grant and Lee, to "come together as former comrades and friends and talk a little." Lee had conferred with Davis and subsequently sent a note to Grant offering to meet. Grant had wired Lincoln regarding the plan on March 3, exactly one month to the day after the failed Hampton Roads conference, and Lincoln had wasted no time in killing this new one. No meeting, he chided, "unless it be for the capitulation of Gen. Lee's army." So, on that March Saturday, as an exhausted and careworn Lincoln took the podium in Washington and a baggy-eyed Lee trotted through the streets of Richmond, peace looked quite dead indeed.

❧ ❧ ❧

The Abraham Lincoln who gazed out at the inaugural crowd stretching before him was a distinctively complex and often deeply conflicted man. Complex because the man who had pledged the previous summer in Philadelphia that the war would not end until its "worthy object" was attained, and "Under God, I hope it will never end until that time," had returned from Hampton Roads in February and suggested to his cabinet that the United States pay the insurgent Southern states $400 million—as compensation for their lost slaves—if they surrendered by April 1. The Union cabinet was unanimous in its rejection. And conflicted because the man who had affixed his name to the unequivocal words of the Emancipation Proclamation had also offered the Southerners the carrot of "compensated" and even delayed emancipation at that meeting, if they would only return to the Union. Now, on this newly minted afternoon, Lincoln seemed to need the power and the firmness of his chosen words as much as did the anxious audience standing before him, or as did the larger, expectant Union nation.

When he started to read from a single sheet of paper printed in two broad columns, the crowd pressed forward slightly, to catch every word; when he spoke, they nodded in silent affirmation; when he addressed his larger themes, they listened with deference, even awe; when he truly touched them, they burst into applause and even tears. Notably lacking from his speech, however, was any stinging attribution of blame for the war. "All dreaded it," his voice rang out—"and all sought to avert it." But one of the parties to the conflict "would *make* war rather than let the nation survive; and the other would *accept* war rather than let it perish. And the war came."

Strangely lacking, too, from the speech, after his brief first paragraph, was a reference to anything that he had said and done during the previous four years. His goal today was not to take political credit or to assign blame, but to send a heartfelt message—to the Union and the Confederacy alike. Neither side had expected the war to last as long or grow to such magnitude as it had, he observed philosophically. "Each looked for an easier triumph, and a result less fundamental and astounding. Both read the same bible, and pray to the same God; and each invokes His aid against the other." On the matter of slavery, he reproached but absolved the South of the ultimate blame: "It may seem strange that any men should dare to ask God's assistance in wringing their bread from the sweat of other men's faces; but let us judge not that we be judged."

What was the war's cause? "Somehow," he suggested, it was "slavery." And how long would the war last, the question that was foremost on everyone's mind? Here Lincoln wearily made no pledge. "Fondly do we hope—fervently do we pray—that this mighty scourge of war may speedily pass away." At the same time, he left no doubt of his intention to fight on—"if God wills that it continue"—until slavery was crushed and the Union was permanently reunited.

He saved his most soaring and trenchant words for the conclusion, the true heart and the indelible spirit of his speech: "With malice toward none; with charity for all; with firmness in the right, as God gives us to see the right, let us strive to finish the work we are in; to bind up the nation's wounds; to care for him who shall have borne the battle . . . to do all which may achieve and cherish a just and lasting peace, among ourselves, and with all nations."

Lincoln then turned to Chief Justice Salmon Chase, soberly took the oath of office, and ended with an emphatic, "So help me God!" Bowing his head, he kissed an open Bible, and then as he bowed again to the cheering assembly, an artillery salvo exploded in the wind.

❧ ❧ ❧

The Confederate White House stood several blocks from the state capitol. It was not even designed as a public building, but rather came into being as the private home of a wealthy Richmonder, who had installed in it the mid-nineteenth-century miracles of gas lamps and crude but serviceable plumbing. When the war came, he offered his house for the new Confederate president, replete with its flat front and rear-facing porch, designed to protect the family from the dust and mud and pungent smells of the street. But he was also something of a prudent patriot. In a revealing bit of symbolism, he sold his home to the established City of Richmond and not to the fledgling Confederate nation. Its current occupant, however, harbored no such qualms about the Confederate cause.

Jefferson Davis had used the failure of the Hampton Roads peace conference to rejuvenate Southern pride and nationalistic ardor, and the people had rallied accordingly, from Richmond and Mobile, from Lynchburg and Raleigh, and other cities across the Confederacy. One by one, once passionate critics had also risen up in support of Jeff Davis and the Cause. So, while resources were running scarce, will was, for the moment, growing stronger. New appointments, most notably Robert E. Lee's recent promotion to commander of all the armies, and administrative changes had also led Southerners to believe again that the war's tide might yet turn. And everyone knew that the Robert E. Lee who came to Richmond that March morning was not simply the man who commanded an army of men pinned down in their trenches, but was the Southern general who had driven McClellan off the Peninsula, stopped Pope at Second Manassas, hoodwinked Burnside at Fredericksburg, destroyed Hooker at Chancellorsville, and thwarted Grant in the Wilderness—all against overwhelming odds. And while Lee himself understood that the Confederate hegira was at a turning point, perhaps even nearing the end, the Southern general in chief still harbored hopes of staving off disaster.

This was, of course, vintage Lee: ever bold and invariably aggressive. Now, meeting with Jefferson Davis as Lincoln spoke of "malice toward none" and "charity for all," the two discussed the Confederacy's options. Peace between the two countries was dead. But another option loomed: withdraw from Richmond, retreat south and join Joe Johnston's army, and strike hard at Union General William Tecumseh Sherman. Lee would have to make the most out of this opportunity. But he also believed that he could rely on the unparalleled endurance of his men, their loyalty, their fight, their overwhelming will in the face of the worst privations. In fact, this was also the opportunity he had long been waiting for; for some time, the commanding general had wanted to be free of Richmond.

In January, Lee had secretly told congressional questioners that the military evacuation of Richmond would actually make him stronger than before. Richmond's fall, he confided, "from a moral and political viewpoint," might be a "serious calamity," but once it happened, he could prolong the war for a good two more years on Virginia soil. In truth, since the war began, precisely because Lee had been saddled with vigorously defending the nation's capital, he had been forced to let the enemy make strategic plans for him, to dictate far too much of the course of battle, and to determine the pace and time of combat. But, he added, striking a more hopeful pose, "when Richmond falls I shall be able to make them for myself."

To Lee, one of the most daring and offensive-minded of generals, a war of attrition had always favored the North. As a strategist, Lee chafed under the yoke of defensive tactics. "We must strike them," he had lamented. "We must never let them pass us again—we MUST strike them a blow!" Yet Lee also knew the harsh reality of the arithmetic of war. He no longer had any men to spare. "If it becomes a siege," he had gravely told his general, Jubal Early, "then it is just a matter of time." At last, the time had come for Lee to make his own plans.

Davis listened and did not flinch. Why not withdraw "at once"? he countered.

Lee explained that the army's horses were too weak to pull the guns and wagons through the thick March mud. But in two or three weeks, the roads would be passable. Then he could make his move. In the meantime, he would make the necessary arrangements.

And here the matter lay: with Robert E. Lee, at fifty-eight, an imposing figure with a strikingly dignified face and an honorable pedigree, who could endure disappointment and frustration with stoic reserve, but who would not accept defeat. And with Jefferson Davis, the austere, ascetic, grim-faced, and obdurate Confederate president, the once poignant nationalist and unremitting Unionist, who now lived for Southern independence, that and seemingly little more. They, every bit as much as Richmond, were the polar stars of the Confederacy, its very embodiment. And on this fateful day, their decision was made. With this new strategy in mind, they would continue to fight. With everything they had.

In Lee's words, they would "fight to the last."

*   *   *

Under the jubilant eyes of Frederick Douglass, who would be ushered into the White House later that evening at the request of Lincoln himself, becoming the first black man to be officially received in the nation's home, and under the watchful gaze of the dashing young actor John Wilkes Booth, who occupied a prime spot in the balcony above the president, Abraham Lincoln had formally begun his second term. Now he had both a war to win and a "nation's wounds" to bind. To some, like his congressional critics, these two elusive goals may have been flagrant contradictions, but to Lincoln, they were nothing less than the bedrock of his policies, the true, indefinable purpose of this war. There were, he knew, some propitious signs that the national bloodbath was at last moving toward its preordained conclusion. In February, Sherman's army had driven into South Carolina, like a tribe of thundering Mongols—and South Carolina, the queen state of Dixie, where the nightmare of secession and rebellion had begun, quickly fell. Civilians deserted their houses and fled their cities before Sherman's approaching hordes; then Columbia, the state's capital, lay in flames, incinerated, a smoking ruin, the victim of Sherman's men and chaos. Meanwhile, in the breadbasket of the Confederacy, the Shenandoah, Union General Phil Sheridan had cut a channel of destruction, wide and long, straight to the Rapidan River. And Grant's mighty Army of the Potomac was hunkered down around Petersburg, ready to drive into the heart of the Confederacy, into Richmond, into Robert E. Lee's vaunted Army of Northern Virginia itself.

But there were also reasons why Abraham Lincoln was the most "tired man" in the world. For nearly every Union success, he could still count a time when Lee had been within their grasp and yet eluded his generals. McDowell, McClellan, Meade, Pope, Burnside, Hooker; each foiled. And Grant, too, decried as a butcher, sending the boys in blue into rebel range like cattle to a slaughter, mauled in the Wilderness, and now pinned down in Petersburg. Certainly, there were, as Lincoln was well aware, indications that the Southern will to fight was waning, that the Confederacy was slowly coming to pieces. But there were also indications that the war could drag on for at least three more months of murderous fighting, perhaps even for another entire year, and, he bristled, how much more could the country take? And then finally, for Lincoln there was the unthinkable: the specter of Lee and his men slipping into the western mountains to wage a prolonged campaign of harassment. As much as any other scenario, this was now his greatest fear. The glory of a restored Union, he believed, must be built on more than butchery, revenge, and retribution. So in the spring of 1865, this, then, was his dilemma: the exigencies of the total war that he was waging against the requirements of reunification and the peace that he hoped to make. Never were two goals more incompatible.

Lincoln was so exhausted after the inauguration ceremonies that he took to his bed for several days. By March 14, he would feel so ill that he would conduct a cabinet meeting in his bedroom.

❧   ❧   ❧

In the weeks that followed, Lee refined his audacious plan. As soon as the opportunity presented itself, he would attack Grant's lines below the Appomattox River, seeking to disrupt and disorient the Union commander. In turn, that would free a portion of his troops to quickly join

The Plan:
Lee would hook
up with Johnston

Johnston and later to strike at Sherman. If his offensive failed, he would then abandon Richmond and Petersburg altogether, joining Johnston with his entire army. After a lightning march, he would hope to smash Sherman and then do what he did best—contest Grant in a prolonged war of maneuver.

As the first hint of spring crept north into Virginia, Lee's strategy had crystallized. After months of stalemate and tense confrontation, he had settled upon this: shock Grant with a sudden assault on Fort Stedman, a federal strongpoint just east of Petersburg. To be sure, given the tattered state of his troops, it was a daring act, but then again, Lee was always at his best when he was daring; his spirits would brighten, his deep black eyes would glow, his carefully cultivated control would give way to a flicker of emotion. Though federal forces outnumbered the Confederates by more than three to one, Lee had repeatedly demonstrated that his men could overcome far larger numbers. Though his army was ragged and exhausted, he would rally it. And though he was a consummate military realist, he was also possessed by a rare compass, a gambler's sense that military miracles were not to be mocked or eschewed. History had turned on a dime countless times before. So it could again.

The attack on Fort Stedman, employing deception, secrecy, surprise, would take place on March 25. It would be one of the most intricate and brazen assaults of the war.

If successful, some believed it would open up a corridor all the way to Grant's headquarters at City Point.

❧ ❧ ❧

If the capture of Fort Stedman was a hope, the abandonment of Richmond was now a certainty, its fate having been sealed along with Lee's plans. Yet Lee's plans, of course, begged the question: what about Richmond? To be sure, if ever there was a capital to be hesitantly relinquished by the Confederates and, at the same time, to be eagerly prized by the Union, it was Richmond.

From its earliest years, Richmond had been a city of opposites: simultaneously genteel and seething. It seemed to be a magnet for uprisings, either igniting them or squelching them. Before there ever was a city named Richmond, it was here, along the banks of the James, that Nathaniel Bacon had settled on a spit of land and in 1676 started the revolt that would carry his name. It was here, in St. John's Church, that another proud son of Virginia, Patrick Henry, lit an inchoate country on fire, exhorting rebellion in 1775, when he declared "give me liberty or give me death"—as Thomas Jefferson, in the audience, watched on. It was also here in 1800 that the slave Gabriel Prosser staged—ultimately in vain—a widespread black insurrection. And it was here, in 1832, that the House of Delegates shook a nation, hotly debating a bill to end slavery in Virginia, only to have it lose by seven votes—and, in a tragic twist, to have the state convention end by further tightening the shackles of bondage. But the divided nature of Richmonders also went only so far. For the most part, Richmonders were scions of the legacy of the first settlers in America, the 105 men and boys who landed in 1607 along the broad sweep at Cape Henry on the Virginia coast. Arriving aboard the *Sarah Constant*, the *Godspeed*, and the *Discovery*, they had already braved harsh, howling winds; mighty gales; and turbulent seas. Now they anchored amid the uncertainty of a new land. Cast in a sturdy English empirical mold of fair-mindedness, united by a common desire to better themselves financially and socially, they were largely a moderate people, wedded to the rites of hierarchy and patriarchy, pragmatic, and deeply steeped in tradition.

One of those traditions, of course, was governance. As early as 1619, the first colonists had set up a miniature parliament when they debated "the Dale's code." Within a decade, "sweating and stewing and battling flies," they had already developed a highly impressive legislative machinery, establishing the House of Burgesses—the first representative body in the New World. More than a century later, by the time the state capital was moved to Richmond in 1780, Richmonders had been proudly and defiantly rooted in the exercise of popular will and the rancorous give-and-take of democracy. In no small measure, they had helped to invent it.

As the capital of Virginia, Richmond also had a heritage of leadership unmatched on either side of the Potomac. It rightly laid claim to being the seat of the great Virginia dynasty, to being the "capital of the Mother of states and Statesmen," and to being the cradle of democracy; it proudly boasted the authors of the Declaration of Independence and of the Constitution; and it justly claimed America's first president. No one cherished the tenets of republican liberty more than Richmonders. To the extent that Richmonders were inclined to view Virginia first and foremost as their "country," and they did, it was also true that no one was more fervent in the defense of Union in the first years of the new American republic. Indeed, in 1812, when New England Federalists were threatening secession, it was Thomas Ritchie of the *Richmond Enquirer* who alone unleashed the most stinging criticisms, denouncing the "disloyal elements" who would "dash to pieces the holy ark of the Union of our country."

In the years leading up to the Civil War, Richmonders built a stunning city, a thriving hybrid of old-fashioned Southern gentility and newfangled urban enterprise. Day to day, Richmond was undergirded by a sharply drawn social structure: an overlay of the old Virginia gentry; an assortment of newcomers, working-class immigrants, Germans, Irishmen, and Jews; and a foundation of free blacks and black slavery. But cast among its seven picturesque hills, this urban enterprise hummed with remarkable vibrancy. Richmond and its suburbs were studded with handsome parks, grassy residential squares, tree-lined avenues, and imposing statues. Red brick town houses ranged in long rows on Marshall, Cary, and Franklin streets, their russet facades displaying a pleasing symmetry. Above, atop the hills, were mansions, belonging not just to genuine aristocrats but also to much of the new wealth, the prosperous bankers, the merchants, and the industrialists, who were vying with the planters for supremacy in the city. Down by the waterfront, the James River teemed with coastal and oceangoing vessels, ships that traded not only with the countryside and the North, but halfway across the world, with Britain and even the far corners of continental Europe. Meanwhile, day in and day out, the Tredegar iron works spewed black smoke; Richmond had the largest iron industry in all of Dixie. And looming over it all was the classical splendor of the capitol building, designed by Jefferson; the elegant governor's mansion; the beautiful city hall; and the intricate landscaping of Capitol Square.

By 1859, with its population of almost 40,000, Richmond was not the largest city in the South. Slightly smaller than Charleston, it had less than a quarter of New Orleans's population and even ranked behind Louisville, Kentucky. But it was surely unique. Unlike the Deep South, it was distinctly more diverse: with its commitment to public education, it had six public schools as well as a college for women; with its commitment to religious pluralism, it had thirty-three Protestant churches that were complemented by three Jewish synagogues, three Roman Catholic churches, a Quaker meeting house, and a Universalist church. With its four newspapers jockeying for attention, its political voice was often broad and remarkably lively. Not surprisingly, as the war came, few doubted that the city was anything but an impressive blend of rural provincialism and urban potential; its atmosphere of high breeding and noblesse oblige made it distinctly Southern, but its diverse economy, heterogeneous population, and moderate outlook gave it a lusty, cosmopolitan air that solidly fastened it in the mold of the larger United States—unusual in the antebellum South. And, in a young country still very much struggling with its national identity, Richmond and Richmond alone among the great cities could bask in the golden age of Washington, Jefferson, Monroe, and Madison, making it a trenchant portrait of the young American republic.

But when the guns of Fort Sumter sounded on April 12, 1861, and the North-South divide could no longer be papered over, the city was immediately transformed, siding with its longer Southern roots. Having helped create "the United States," it would now look to dissolve them. With "flushed faces," "wild eyes," "screaming mouths," and "jubilant demonstrations," Richmonders chose the Confederacy. And in turn, the Confederate States of America soon made Richmond the capital of their new nation.

It was a fateful decision. With the benefit of more than a century of hindsight, it is easy to doubt the wisdom of locating the Confederacy's capital in Richmond; for one thing, it was a strategic gamble, boldly putting the capital within ready striking distance of the Union. Accessible by water and only a hundred miles from Washington, it was especially vulnerable. And on the fringe of the new nation rather than at its center, it would have great difficulty extending its power over the vast hinterland of the huge, eleven-state Confederacy. But in the end, when the war came, the Southern politicians rapidly tired of Montgomery, Alabama, the site of the first Confederate capital, with its clouds of mosquitoes and its pitiful facilities. After some to-and-fro, Richmond was the logical, if not the only, choice.

The significance of this decision was not lost on the North. As quickly as July 21, 1861, Union soldiers under General Irvin McDowell marched southward to the cry, "On to Richmond." This was but the first of six massive offenses waged against the rebel capital. And from then on, Richmond would live under the menacing scythe of Union attack. Sixty percent of the war would be fought on Virginia soil.

After the guns sounded, Richmonders' pride in their heritage was a goad to forbearance. Still, the city could not escape the transforming burdens of being a capital in the eye of a war. In every corner, life was quickly punctuated by the residue of strife. Groaning under the weight of refugees and the new Confederate bureaucracy, the city was often blighted with soot, noise, and darkness. Its once peaceful streets became centers of a garish nightlife; thus came a rash of burlesque houses and saloons, all-night prostitution parlors, pawnshops, thieves, and fences. The streets themselves overflowed with trash, empty liquor bottles, squalor, and vagrants. And of course, there was the more tangible specter of war itself, the gnawing realization that Richmond was now on the frontier of the conflict, an inexorable dividing line between North and South. With a hostile force always at its back, each day, each month, each year, its residents faced the awesome prospect of being overrun by federal armies.

But socially conscious Richmonders refused to be cowed. Amid the ever-increasing stress of total war, they danced, laughed, and somehow thrived. "There is life in the old land yet," Mary Chesnut observed in 1864. "Go on good people," wrote the *Whig*, "it is better to be merry than sad." For three precarious years, Richmond survived on savvy and sacrifice, indomitable will and sheer tenacity. In the face of hardship, hunger, and disease, its women stoically visited the hospitals and darned socks. As scarcity, impressment, and inflation ravaged the city, crowds still cheerily frequented the theaters, threw merry shindigs, and entertained one another in private gatherings and with intimate games "of charades." When the roll of cannons and drum of musket fire could be heard in the distance, they stubbornly maintained their faith in Robert E. Lee, Jefferson Davis, and the Cause. And as the noose tightened, and mothers, wives, and children became "pinched by hunger" or were "dying from broken hearts," Richmonders somehow pressed on.

Was it all an element of self-delusion? Or stubborn patriotism toward their young country? Surely, it was a bit of both. In 1864, Richmonders could console themselves with this sobering fact: the Confederacy's mighty Army of Northern Virginia had frustrated the designs and military careers of five separate commanders of the Union's Army of the Potomac. Indeed, most citizens saw their capital as an "impregnable Gibraltar." And by 1865, if that winter had been particularly cruel, so had each previous winter. If morale was low, they knew that this was when Lee had always fought most brilliantly. In truth, each year and each spring, the war brought changes in Richmond's spirit, harboring rousing news of dangers and triumphs, from Fort Sumter, to Seven Days, Chancellorsville, the Wilderness, and Cold Harbor. But their bemused views of the privations of war were underpinned by a quiet confidence in a Southern victory. Grant had jabbed, bruised, and stretched Lee's lines. He had fought all summer and all winter, yet still Richmond had evaded him. Spring meant a renewed campaign for war, yet one more campaign in which Robert E. Lee might eventually prevail.

Ironically, the more Richmond's fortunes declined, the more indignities it suffered at the hard hand of war, the more it found salvation in its new Confederate identity. By the time the Petersburg siege began, Richmonders had endured martial law, quelled a seditious bread riot, and survived conscription; they had withstood impressment of property and servants, bureaucratic ignorance, and urban overcrowding; and they had survived startling underfeeding and horrendous casualties. And by this point, virtually every family, both the well-to-do and the humble, lived side by side with the shadow of death, as the graves of husbands, brothers, fathers, and sons littered the hillsides of the capital. In the spring of 1865, food was so scarce that many citizens were reportedly forced to eat dogs and even rats. Even this did not deter them. "We are all good scavengers now," quipped the redoubtable diarist J. B. Jones. "As long as we can hear a dog bark or a cat meow," roared preacher Ezra Stiles, "know that we will not surrender!"

Against all, Richmonders still rallied. In countless ways, this period represented some of the city's most stirring hours. "Once more," said one stoic Virginia maid, "we hugged to our bosoms the phantom of hope." In fact, the residents did more than that. While their comrades in Petersburg wandered through streets, ducking and dodging federal missiles, balls and social events in Richmond flourished as perhaps never before. It was an amazing sight. Starvation balls became the rage. So did weddings. Church attendance rose. Buoyed by an evangelical fervor, believers flocked to St. Paul's for daily services and searched to understand why God had chosen to punish them with such severity. They prayed for guidance and wrapped themselves in Scriptures telling of a wandering Israel, seeing the Jews as a prototype for their own nascent Confederate heritage. And more than ever, the first families held on to their Revolutionary War moorings as a way of bracing themselves for the trial now thrust upon them. Some also hoped that they were living through a second, "Southern" revolution.

One noted scholar, John Murrin, has remarked that the Confederate national identity in 1861 was actually far stronger than any collective American national identity alive at the time of the Constitution; there is more than an element of truth to this. And from then on, a new sense of nationality, at once Southern and Confederate, had gathered in volume and strength as Richmonders confronted one of the most daunting armies the world had ever known. The rejoicing, the partying, the riding high on a cloud of euphoria and wishful thinking, the atavistic remembrances of the Revolution, the mystical examination of the Jews, all were merely part of a swelling belief that they were indeed forming a new nation. Their unanimity may be overstated, but there was little doubt that they were now a people united by a sense of common culture and a flickering, but nonetheless real, national spirit.

Thus, Richmond was not, in the spring of 1865, what it was in 1861, or for that matter, in 1776. And like Richmond, much of the Confederate South had also changed. Hardened and toughened by the privations of war, the South now had a very different conception of itself, its identity, and its purpose and reason. Nothing so captured the extent of that change as a debate that had raged for months in the capital city and beyond, from the port of Charleston and the trenches of Petersburg, to the Tennessee backwoods and Louisiana bayous.

The question was simply this: should the Confederacy emancipate slaves and muster them into the ranks of Southern soldiers? Before the guns had sounded over Fort Sumter, it would have been an unthinkable suggestion, a heresy of the highest order. But now, four years later, the South was asking precisely this. Driven in no small measure by the Confederacy's own desperation; by its dwindling resources, deaths, and desertions; and by an enemy who seemed to have inexhaustible supplies of material and men, this debate would culminate in one of the most momentous decisions of the Confederacy's life and one of the most fascinating discussions in all of America's span. It would say much of what the South was and what it had become. The final debate would come to a head in March, shortly after Lincoln's second inauguration.

And for Union and Confederacy alike, its implications were astonishing.

❧ ❧ ❧

"About the last of August came in a dutch man of warre that sold us twenty Negars," John Rolfe, a Virginia colonist and soon-to-be husband of the Indian princess Pocahontas, recorded laconically in 1619. The first blacks to enter an English settlement in the New World—as indentured servants who could theoretically be freed in five years—their arrival marked the start of American slavery.

The "Negars" were landed at Old Point Comfort, a sandy wedge that divides the James River from the broad stretch of the Chesapeake Bay. In ensuing years, American slave ships from the Yankee ports of New England—the birthplace of the abolitionist movement—would become a common sight on the Atlantic Ocean. Slaves, bought in Africa for five pounds sterling, brought from thirty to ninety pounds in the West Indies, a sum that laid the footings for many a New England fortune. The colonies of Spain, Portugal, France, Holland, and Britain similarly became strongholds of slavery, and the institution flourished in the American North until

1780, when, beginning with Massachusetts and ending with New Jersey in 1804, the Northern states one by one abolished bondage. It was hoped that the Southern states would do likewise, especially in the Cotton Kingdom of the lower South, but there it stubbornly persisted. After Eli Whitney patented his famous cotton gin in 1794, plantations began to proliferate throughout the Cotton Kingdom—as did the corresponding rise in the demand for slaves. Over the course of 250 years, then, at first unwittingly, even reluctantly, slavery became so intertwined and intermixed with the fabric of the South—even though only one-third of Southerners owned slaves—that any assault on slavery was seen as an assault on Southern institutions, Southern values, and the very Southern way of life.

From the late eighteenth century onward, the ferment over slavery only grew. The North was increasingly stung by the contradictions of its own struggle against Britain and the South's enslavement of others ("the execrable sum of all villainies," in the defiant words of Reverend John Wesley), and slavery soon became a matter of deep conscience, particularly as the religious fervor of the Second Great Awakening swept the country. By the early to mid-nineteenth century, reform was in the air. Year after year, with evangelic fervor, antislavery advocates kept scratching away with their pens and opening their mouths for freedom for people of all colors. And year after year, Southern politicians and Southern leaders bitterly fought back. Here, of course, was a classic formula for eventual conflict. Where many in the North, notably the abolitionists, clamored for the eradication of slavery ("Shall not our Lord, in due time, have these Heathens also for his inheritance"), Southerners clung ever more tightly to what they saw as the most treasured creed of republican liberty—property rights, including slaves. Where the abolitionists, heirs of the Puritan notion of collective accountability, viewed slavery as the most heinous of all social sins, slaveholders stonily saw only economic ruin, social chaos, and racial war. Where abolitionists regarded slavery as evil against God's children, pure and simple, Southerners increasingly saw it as nature's positive good: the foundation for peace, prosperity, and racial comity. And where abolitionists preached slavery as a violation against the higher law, Southerners angrily countered with their own version of the deity, that it was sanctioned by the Constitution.

In the vortex of this debate, once the battle lines were sharply drawn, moderate ground everywhere became hostage to the passions of the two sides. Reason itself had become suspect; mutual tolerance was seen as treachery. Vitriol overcame accommodation. And the slavery issue would not just fade away.

Yet by 1860, after decades of outspoken cries against slavery, this "peculiar institution" had been banned by all the European colonizers, had been eradicated in virtually all of Latin America, and was widely condemned by the Roman Catholic Church. It thrived only in Brazil, Cuba, and, of course, the American South and its border states. But to many Southerners, slavery was so intermingled with life below the Mason-Dixon line—with their independence, their institutions, and their social order—that on the eve of the Civil War, they would defiantly maintain "freedom is not possible without slavery" and "we are either slaves in the Union or freemen out of it." When the war finally broke out, it was accepted with an insouciance and inevitability and even enthusiasm that is almost impossible to fathom today. Not surprisingly, once the South seceded and drew up a new constitution, unlike the Founding Fathers, it did not waffle on the matter of slavery. Eschewing the tepid evasions over bondage found in the U.S. Constitution ("persons held to service or labor"), the Confederate Constitution outright called a slave a slave, and guaranteed the protection of bondage in any new territory that the Confederacy might acquire.

By the spring of 1865, then, on its surface nothing seemed more ludicrous, or for that matter more treasonable, than to propose the arming of any of the 4 million slaves—approximately one-third of the South's population—to fight for their masters, let alone for their own emancipation. Indeed, after 1863, Jefferson Davis had denounced the North's Emancipation Proclamation and recruitment of slaves to fight for *its* side as "the most execrable measure recorded in the history of guilty man." But nothing was sacred anymore, and wars have a way of transforming things. And in the dismantling of this tenet, it would be Davis himself, along with Robert E. Lee and a number of other prominent Southerners, who would lead the way.

As early as 1861, however, some Southerners had already privately broached the matter of arming the slaves. "Our only chance is to be ahead of them [the Union]," mused eloquent and discerning Mary Chesnut in December 1861—"Free our Negroes and put them in the army." Early in the war, a few daring Confederate voices had even openly urged making slaves into soldiers, but these random suggestions were regarded as heresy. But after the fall of Vicksburg and the defeat at Gettysburg, more iconoclasts were prompted to join the fray, wondering aloud whether the Confederacy might also tap this reserve of manpower. "We are forced by necessity of condition," lamented one Alabama editor with striking candor, "to take a step which is revolting to every sentiment of pride, and to every principle that governed our institutions before the war . . . It is better for us to use the negroes for our defense than that the Yankees should use them against us." An editor of the *Jackson Mississippian* was even more blunt: "Such a step would revolutionize our whole industrial system . . . [but] We must . . . save ourselves from the rapacious North, WHATEVER THE COST."

In truth, Southern blacks had already been playing a vital role in keeping the Confederate war machine alive. Slaves were used in great numbers to work as military laborers, freeing white males to fight; they also doubled as workers on the home front. Often at great danger to themselves, Southern blacks loaded, transported, and unloaded supplies. In the midst of exploding bombs and enemy gunshots, they dug trenches, erected barricades, constructed fortifications, and repaired and built roads, railroads, bridges, trestles, and tunnels. In between, they cooked and served food. Amid the marches and the fighting, they did backbreaking drudge work, washed uniforms, shined boots, mended clothes and tents, and moved ordnance. And, staggeringly enough, in Louisiana, some well-to-do free blacks outright rallied to the Confederate cause. Caught up in the general Southern view that hostile Northerners were bound and determined to force their way of life on the South, and looking for a more dignified role, they were allowed to form regiments of free blacks, serving as home guards to protect their state against invaders. In 1861, moreover, several other groups of black Southerners also offered themselves as soldiers to the Confederate War Department, only to be turned down. When black men offered to fight for Southern planter and Davis adviser James Chesnut, if he would only arm them, he responded tentatively: "One man cannot do it. The whole country must do it." On this matter, though, the slaveocracy of the South was still too entrenched, and thus was content to dally, vacillate, and remain engrossed in other issues.

Not so with the North. Lincoln's stunning twin measures of the Emancipation Proclamation and the arming of African Americans did more than strike a blow at the institution of slavery. They helped spur an estimated 1 million slaves to escape to the Northern side and added hardy troops to the war-weakened Union ranks in the last two and a half years of the conflict. Indeed, at one point, the some nearly 180,000 black troops marshaled on the Union side were greater than the total number of men able to engage actively in combat for the Confederates. And in a number of important tests, the soldiers fought bravely. Witness the Fifty-fourth Massachusetts Volunteer Infantry, which attained permanent glory with its assault on Fort Wagner in South Carolina, or the First Kansas Colored, which won broad praise for two fierce engagements at Cabin Creek and Honey Springs in present-day Oklahoma. "I was never much for niggers," said one Wisconsin cavalry officer after the Cabin Creek engagement, "but beJesus, they are hell for fighting."

By 1864, one highly regarded Southern general, Patrick Cleburne, was carefully assessing these stark developments. Once an Arkansas lawyer and considered the best division commander in both armies, the Irish-born Cleburne openly informed his fellow generals that the South should follow the North's example. With his firm-set lip, his erect bearing, and his regal gaze, he was, by all accounts, a rather eclectic warrior: fearless in battle (he had already been wounded three times), forthright in manner, discerning in tactics (many called him the "Stonewall Jackson of the West"), and deeply passionate. He was also prepared to shake up the edifice of the Confederacy.

And he did. The Emancipation Proclamation, he argued forcefully in a January 2, 1864, "memorial" presentation to corps commanders in General Joe Johnston's western army, had provided the enemy with a moral prerogative that rationalized his attempt at conquest. It had, he charged, rendered the slaves his friends, eroded the South's own security, and united Europe against the Confederacy. Therefore, Cleburne warned, we are threatened with "the loss of all we now hold most sacred." He then put the matter squarely: "As between the loss of independence and the loss of slavery, we assume that every patriot will freely give up the latter—give up the Negro slave rather than be a slave himself." To save all that they cherished—"property, lands, homesteads, liberty, justice, safety, pride, manhood," he concluded that Southerners should transform the "dreaded weakness" of bondage into "a source of strength," adding that they should recruit an army of slaves and "guarantee freedom within a reasonable time to every slave in the South who shall remain true to the Confederacy." Cleburne's appeal was smartly tinged with realism: "Ever since the agitation of the subject of slavery commenced, the negro has been dreaming of freedom and his vivid imagination has surrounded the condition with so many gratifications that it has become the paradise of his hopes." It was also shrewd politically: "The measure we propose," he added, "will strike dead all John Brown fanaticism, and will compel the enemy to draw off altogether or in the eyes of the world to swallow the Declaration of Independence without the sauce and disguise of philanthropy."

As for the slaves themselves, he minced no words. Recalling "the helots of Sparta" who stood "their masters good stead in battle," and "those brave galley slaves" who had helped check the spread of Islam over Europe in the "great sea fight of Lepanto," he maintained that not only would slaves fight for the Confederacy under such incentives, but that they would fight "bravely." And Cleburne then went even further: freedom should not be granted just to slave soldiers but to the "whole race" that was loyal to the South.

Such words would have horrified antebellum society. Yet these were not the musings of a private diarist or of men retiring to the comfort of their brandies after a warm meal, but the thoughts of a much-respected officer on the front lines of the Confederacy's defense. In a remarkable departure from the past, twelve brigade and regimental commanders in Cleburne's division wholeheartedly endorsed his proposal. But if such replies were brave, they were also, at the time, calamitous. Most of the other generals eyed the proposal stonily, and their animosity toward it was palpable. It was "monstrous," "painful," and "startling," one division commander fired back, "revolting to Southern sentiment, Southern pride, and Southern honor." Another averred that it was "at war with my social, moral, and political principles." "We are not whipped, & cannot be whipped," boasted another. "Our situation requires resort to no such remedy." Touching on the very raison d'être of the Confederacy, the debate was inflammatory, hot, furious, and, on its surface, even seditious. Fearful that it would cause "discouragements" and "dissension," Jefferson Davis quickly stepped in and squelched the proposal, bluntly ordering the generals to stop even discussing the matter.

But in the face of the South's increasingly gloomy prospects, the matter would not rest. Nor was it just a Southern concern. Tellingly, there were those in the North, such as the prominent intellectual Ralph Waldo Emerson, who as early as August 1862 deeply feared that the Confederacy might preempt the Union and adopt emancipation first. In so doing, he believed that the South would appear before the world as the champion of freedom, gaining recognition from France and England, and putting the North in a disastrous position. Emerson's fears were hardly unfounded. Within months, in the South, the issue did indeed come under serious debate.

As early as 1862—and long before Patrick Cleburne's presentation—Congressman Warren Akin, speaker of the Georgia state legislature, and later a Confederate congressman, wrote, "It is a question of fearful magnitude." Yet Akin, a slaveholder himself, now supported enrolling slaves as soldiers with the promise of emancipation. In September 1863, the Alabama legislature followed suit, recommending just that. And this was just the beginning. By mid-1864, Southerners now recognized that they might well have to make a choice between slavery on one hand and independence on the other. In fits and starts, the furious debate continued. That September, Henry Allen, the governor of Louisiana, declared that "the time has come for us to put into the army every able-bodied Negro man as a soldier." A month later, the governors of six more states, meeting in a conference, urged "a change of policy" concerning the impressment of slaves for public service, "as required." However much this last clause may have constituted flaccid tiptoeing around the issue, the Rubicon had been crossed. The debate, bordering on flouting much of what the Confederacy stood for, became increasingly passionate. Then, on November 7, Davis cautiously moved a step closer to arming the slaves—although in parts of the South the idea was received with utter revulsion—proposing that Congress purchase 40,000 slaves for work as teamsters, pioneers, and laborers, with the promise of freedom after "service faithfully rendered." He declared that he opposed arming blacks at *that time*, but added tantalizingly: "Should the alternative ever be presented of subjugation or the employment of the slave as a soldier, there seems to be no reason to doubt what should then be our decision." And perhaps his most striking line was this observation: "The slave," he ruminated philosophically, "bears another relation to the state—that of a person."

But in November 1864, this was still too much for the Confederate Congress; they sat on their hands and didn't act on the president's request.

Yet the issue would not die. Within three months, the dreaded alternative that Davis had raised now confronted the South, ominously and imminently. "We are reduced," Davis acknowledged in February 1865, "to choosing whether the negroes shall fight for us or against us." In the face of the Confederacy's rising peril, the president had finally made his choice—and it was unacceptable to many of his comrades. Georgian Robert Tooms thundered that "the worst calamity that could befall us would be to gain our independence by the valor of our slaves . . . The day that the army allows a negro regiment to enter their lines as soldiers, they will be degraded, ruined and disgraced." The president pro tem of the Confederate Senate, Robert M. T. Hunter, asked skeptically: "What did we go to war for, if not to protect our property?" And Georgian Howell Cobb, one of the South's most powerful political generals, summed up much of the debate, fuming that "if slaves will make good soldiers our whole theory of slavery is wrong. The day you make soldiers of them is the beginning of the end of the revolution."

Others in high places, however, felt differently. In the weeks and days that followed, the matter continued to be debated endlessly in the Southern press and by Southern politicians, with perhaps the tensest confrontation occurring at noon on February 9, during a mass meeting at the African Church in Richmond, one of the rallies held in the wake of the failure of the North-South meeting at Hampton Roads.

Every seat was taken. After the armory band struck up the *Marseillaise* and the Reverend Moses Hoge said a prayer, Senator Hunter strode to the podium. One of the most powerful foes of Davis's policy, he used the occasion to reassert the fundamental belief in slavery. "And what is to become of the slave himself?" he boomed rhetorically. "Those best acquainted with the negro's nature know that perish he must in time off the face of the earth; for in competition with the white man, the negro must go down. The only hope of the black man is in our success." These were strong words, but they were also to be overshadowed by those of Secretary of State Judah P. Benjamin. Benjamin, a Jew and a Louisianan, was a fighter, a savvy debater, probably the closest confidant to Davis, and the most intellectually gifted cabinet member in the Confederacy. Today, he meant to score a few bruises of his own.

It was a pensive moment. Stepping to the rostrum, Benjamin, who personally favored that his government should issue its own Confederate Emancipation Proclamation, countered with a dramatic appeal for freeing and arming the slaves, neither mincing words nor wrapping himself in vague generalities. "What is our present duty?" he asked defiantly, and answered himself with the cry: "We want means! War is a game that cannot be played without men . . . Where are the men?" Then Benjamin declared, "I am going to open my whole heart to you. Look to the trenches below Richmond. Is it not a shame that men who have sacrificed all in our defense should not be reinforced by all the means in our power?" Next, he thundered, "Is it any time now for antiquated patriotism to argue a refusal to send them aid, be it white or black?" A voice cried out, "put in the niggers!" and cheers erupted. Benjamin continued: "Let us say to every negro who wishes to go into the ranks on condition of being free—Go and fight; you are free!" Now he asked, "What states will lead off in this thing?" A voice called out, "Virginia!" And Benjamin answered, "When shall it be done?" From out of the crowd, "NOW!" came the cry. "Now," Benjamin answered quickly. "Let your Legislature pass the necessary laws . . . You *must* make up your mind!"

As it turned out, the crowd did. Benjamin had scored a great victory, rousing the pews of several thousand to near unanimity; but he didn't carry the day in the legislative councils of Richmond. With the Confederacy's fortunes in limbo, some Southerners still didn't want to make up their minds, precisely because they knew this meant abolition, or, as one Virginia newspaper fumed, "the very doctrine which the war was commenced to put down." Indeed, for many, on the question of slavery or independence, the dogmas of the day were still too captivating; a number of Confederates preferred to lose the war rather than to win it with the help of their slaves. "Freeing negroes seems to be the latest Confederate government craze . . . [but] if we are to lose our negroes we would as soon see Sherman free them as the Confederate government," insisted one Southern woman. "Victory itself would be robbed of its glory if shared with slaves," protested a Mississippi congressman. It would, stressed the *Charleston Mercury*, mean "the poor man . . . reduced to the level of the nigger. His wife and daughter are to be hustled on the street by black wenches, their equals. Swaggering buck niggers are to ogle them and elbow them." "If such a terrible calamity is to befall us," sniped the *Lynchburg Republican*, "we infinitely prefer that Lincoln shall be the instrument of our disaster and degradation, than that we ourselves strike the cowardly and suicidal blow."

But converts were increasingly found in the unlikeliest of places. Among them, evidently, was Nathan Bedford Forrest, a former slave trader and one of the South's leading Confederate commanders. He was not the only one. Throughout February, soldiers in the Petersburg trenches flooded Richmond with petitions and letters, undermining the view that white soldiers would not countenance serving alongside blacks. "If the public exigencies require that any number of our male slaves be enlisted in the military service in order to [maintain] our government," wrote the 56th Virginia, "we are willing to make concessions to their false and unenlightened notions of the blessings of liberty." Henry Allen, the secretary of the regiment, noted that "the resolution" was passed "with great spirit" and "entire unanimity," adding that its companies came "from the most populous slave districts in Virginia" and its members owned "as many slaves as any other regiment." And it was not just Virginians. For its part, one Georgia brigade in Lee's army was adamant: "We care not for the color of the arm that strikes the invader of our homes." Lee's Texas brigade was equally adamant, calling on all to "lay aside prejudice" for "independence and separate nationality." And deeper south, the headquarters of the

Fifteenth Alabama Regiment echoed these same sentiments. Composed of "young men of good families" in both "position and property," they not only endorsed the proposal, but went a step further, chiding some members of Congress for being "tender-footed on this point."

But Congress was more than tender footed. In secret sessions, it was arguing the matter furiously and endlessly; some members sulked and complained, others wanted to plow ahead. And in turn, from the mud-ridden trenches to the editorial boardrooms of Southern newspapers, from massed town hall meetings to contentious backwoods churches, from the beer-filled taverns and smoke-filled drawing rooms, this imbroglio was now raging across the Confederacy. Reported Francis Lawley of the London *Times* in February: "The question of putting negroes into the ranks, long and vehemently debated and combated, not only within the walls of congress but also in the corner of every street and round every fireside in the South, is gaining manifestly in opinion." Gaining in opinion, yes. However, time was running out. And one man had not yet been heard from: Robert E. Lee.

Soon, though, Lee would be in the thick of it.

For months, wild rumors had been circulating that Lee ("a thorough emancipationist," in the words of one Lee ally) was in favor of arming the slaves. Indeed he was, but discreetly. As early as 1863, he had gingerly let it be known among elite circles that he—along with Jefferson Davis— wholeheartedly supported this measure. In other circles, he was far more blunt. For two years, though, he remained publicly hushed on the subject, even as he privately lobbied, pushed, and praised such an effort. Then, on January 11 (three weeks before the Union Congress passed the Thirteenth Amendment codifying the Emancipation Proclamation by the narrowest of margins, and after a contentious protracted debate), Lee wrote to Andrew Hunter, a member of the Virginia state senate, expressing his opinion that "we should employ them without delay" and without regard for "the risk of the effects which may be produced upon our social institutions." For weeks, however, this letter remained largely uncirculated. But as the debate continued, all of the Confederacy began to clamor for "anything emanating directly from General Lee." At one point, no less than Judah Benjamin directly appealed to Lee for his views. Now all eyes were upon him.

Finally, Lee relented. Actually, at this moment, he skipped nimbly through the corridors of Confederate politics. On February 18, the general in chief broke his silence with a letter to Congressman Ethelbert Barksdale, the congressional sponsor of a Negro soldier bill. "This measure was not only expedient but necessary," wrote Lee. "The negroes, under proper circumstances, will make efficient soldiers. I think we could at least do as well with them as the enemy." In fact, he added pointedly, "They furnish a more promising material than many armies of which we read in history." By any measure, these words were a staggering break from the past. Nor did he stop here. On the crucial question of emancipation, Lee did not equivocate: "Those who are employed," he wrote rather firmly, "should be freed. It would be neither just nor wise . . . to require them to serve as slaves."

The effects of Lee's declaration, quickly made public, were immediately electrifying. The *Mercury* derided Lee as "the author of this scheme of nigger soldiers and emancipation" and as "an hereditary federalist and a disbeliever [in] slavery." It added darkly: *"We want no Confederate Government without our institutions.* And we will have none. Sink or swim, live or die, we stand by them." Richmond's influential daily, the *Examiner*, went as far as sourly expressing distrust as to whether Lee was "a good Southerner; that is, whether he is thoroughly satisfied of the justice and beneficence of negro slavery."

But Lee had forever changed the debate, and most recognized it. The very same newspaper that had called into question his credentials, the *Examiner*, hastened to add: "the country will not venture to deny General Lee . . . *anything* he may ask for."

On March 13, the Confederate Congress emerged from a round of secret sessions to narrowly pass a bill to enlist black soldiers, a measure that had already been endorsed some ten days earlier by Virginia's General Assembly, at the prompt urgings of the governor, William Smith. An astonishing number of up to 300,000 black men were to be enlisted. On one critical matter, however, these legislatures hemmed, hawed, and equivocated: in deference to the Confederate constitution, they did not endorse emancipation. But Jefferson Davis himself settled the matter, calling for emancipation by bureaucratic fiat. His General Order Number Fourteen stated flatly: "No slave will be accepted as a recruit unless with his own consent" and he is to be conferred "as far as he may, the rights of a freedman."

In many corners of the Confederacy—although most certainly not everywhere—this declaration produced a near sea change. As Mississippi Congressman John T. Lampkin put it, "Slavery is played out." Congressman Akin's wife was even more emphatic: "Every one I talk to is in favor of putting negroes in the army and that *immediately* . . . I think slavery is now gone and what little there is left of it should be rendered as serviceable as possible." For her part, Mary Chesnut lamented, "If we had *only* freed the negroes at first and put them in the army—that would have trumped [the Union's] trick." In turn, military men rose to put the plan into practice. The Virginia Military Institute quickly offered to help secure and train black recruits. Soldiers also stepped forward, seeking to make history, like Private James Nelson, formerly of the Sixteenth Georgia Battalion. He volunteered to form a company of blacks. So did one Captain Thomas J. Azy. And similarly, so did Nathan Burwell, Esq. And so did the Forty-ninth Georgia of the Third Corps. And so did thirty of the largest slaveholders near Salem, Virginia, each of whom pledged freedom to his slaves in return for their service. Noted Colonel Willy Pegram, of Lee's army: "I understand that a large number of the best officers in the army are trying to get commands in the '*Corps D'Afrique*.'"

And in stark contrast to the North, which separated blacks and whites by regiments, Lee proposed to integrate Confederate regiments, with companies of white soldiers serving side by side with companies of black soldiers. By March 22, a Confederate soldier was heartened to glimpse a company of Negro troops encamped near his regiment. "I hope we will be able to accomplish something by the use of negro soldiers," he commented. This, of course, was now the question. Early in the war, some Southerners had asked pointedly: "could they [slaves] be induced to stand fire on our side?" And now it seemed they could indeed. "The only doubt in this case," Horace Greeley's *New York Tribune* warned its Northern readers, "is not whether the rebels mean to raise a negro force, but whether they have not already raised that force."

On March 24 and again on March 26, thousands of spectators and an impressive number of Virginia legislators jammed the grassy hills of

Capitol Square in Richmond to witness one of the rarest sights in all the South: accompanied by the stains of "Dixie," a new Confederate battalion made up of three companies of white convalescents from Chimborazo Hospital and two companies of blacks marched up Main Street to begin drilling together. The Richmond papers enthusiastically reported on the newly formed black company: in dress uniforms, black Confederate troops displayed "as much aptness and proficiency . . . as is usually shown by any white troops we have seen," boasted the *Dispatch*. For its part, the *Examiner* bragged about the "free blacks" who were recruits; it preened about their "remarkable" knowledge of "the military art," and it noted their "evident pride and satisfaction with themselves." These units became attached to Lee's own beloved Army of Northern Virginia; four days later, no less than Lieutenant General James Longstreet, one of the Confederacy's prized commanders, recommended that five black soldiers be promoted "to the positions of commissioned officers in the first negro organization raised under the late act of Congress."

In this light, it is a mistake, however, to see the final decision to induct and arm Southern slaves simply as a desperate last-ditch measure by a dying people, a pitiful deathbed conversion. In truth, it was the product not solely of haste but of an extended two-and-a-half-year on-and-off public debate throughout the Confederacy, and a four-year private debate. Some Confederates had been recommending it from the very start. To be sure, it was being done more for utilitarian reasons than for reasons of conscience. And there were a number of opponents, some quite vocal, and others who chose to remain silent. Nevertheless, it had, at times albeit reluctantly, the support of major figures and institutions: from General Lee to President Davis, from the Virginia Military Institute to newspapers like the *Dispatch*, from the Virginia assembly and common soldiers to slave owners themselves. The decision was ultimately also a testament to the abomination of the institution itself, which many Southerners only belatedly recognized. Moreover—and perhaps most importantly—in March 1865, neither the South nor the Union knew with certainty when or how the war might end. As the *Toronto Globe* wondered aloud, would the black soldiers be ready for "the next summer's campaign"? That was unclear. But whatever the war's outcome, the Confederacy had itself, by its own admission, now sounded the beginning of the end of slavery.

Indeed, having gone to war in good measure to preserve the "peculiar institution," and then having faced the doppelgänger of certain defeat against the specter of abolition, after considerable debate and soul-searching, the Confederacy's leadership effectively chose abolition. Henceforth, and they all knew it then in their hearts, slavery was forever dead, a fact pointedly made by General Longstreet, who wrote, "such a measure will involve the necessity of abolishing slavery *entirely*." Or as one Confederate soldier put it so trenchantly in March 1865, "slavery has received its death blow."

The significance of this could not be underestimated. In the end, what the Confederacy most cherished was its independence. And unwittingly, this produced a supreme irony: as April 1865 approached, the two sides, North and South, were closer on the issue of slavery than perhaps they had ever been since the founding of the republic, and yet it no longer mattered.

* * *

On Sunday, March 5, 1865, Robert E. Lee took his seat in the Lee family pew at St. Paul's Episcopal Church, just across the street from the Virginia State Capitol. The night before, he had paid a rare visit to his family on Franklin Street. Pacing silently in the parlor, his eyes fixed on the floor, he abruptly stopped and told his son Custis, with a hard edge to his voice: "Mr. Custis, when this war began I was opposed to it, bitterly opposed to it, and I told these people that unless every man should do his whole duty, they would repent it; and now . . ." Lee paused. "And now they will repent." But that next day after services, Lee bade his wife farewell, mounted his horse, Traveller, and rode back toward Petersburg, to do his duty.

If Lee was not giving up, neither were his men. "I do not think our military situation is hopeless by any means; but I confess matters are far worse than I ever expected to see them," Lee's aide, Walter Taylor, wrote. "No one can say what the *next week* may bring forth, although the calamity may be deferred for a while longer. Now is the hour when we must show of what stuff we are made." And Lee's men were resolved to do just that when the order came down from the commanding general to attack Fort Stedman.

Under a moonlit night on March 25, a 300-man assault force, wearing strips of white cloth across their breasts and backs for ready identification in the pitch darkness, prepared to probe the Federal lines. Behind them, lying silently in wait, gathered 12,000 infantrymen. Though other troops may have deserted, these soldiers, the veterans of Lee's proud Army of Northern Virginia, were determined to "resist to the death." For the last nine months, they had lived in the damp, cold trenches of Petersburg, angrily eyeing their foes just across the way. But in truth, their emotions were now more complex than that. The slow Petersburg winter had allowed the troops time to pause and reflect on their former countrymen—and the feelings were often a mixed set of not just hatred but of admiration and even begrudging friendship. Conflict along the northern end of the line— by the infamous Crater—was both rancorous and incessant, yet to the south, relations were far more cordial. Notes and newspapers were routinely passed back and forth; pickets exchanged gossip; and warnings of impending action often preceded hostilities. "Get into your holes, Yanks, we are ordered to fire," was one common call. Another time, a message wrapped around a stone was tossed into a Federal trench, which cautioned: "Tell the fellow with the spy glass to clear out, or we shall have to shoot him." Such feelings of mutual respect were reciprocated by the Federals. "They are a valuable people," wrote one Union officer, "capable of a heroism that is too rare to be lost." If officers—rebel or Yank—passed by, the soldiers cautioned the other side, firing weapons at trees or birds or nothing at all. But not this night. In the predawn darkness, Lee's men sought to use such feelings of comity to their advantage.

The first stirring of men had the Federal pickets on their feet. "What are you doing over there, Johnny? What is that noise? Answer quick or I'll shoot."

"Never mind, Yank," one rebel infantryman replied. "Lie down and go to sleep. We are just gathering a little corn. You know rations are mighty short over here."

"All right, Johnny; go ahead and get your corn, I'll not shoot at you while you are drawing your rations."

By then, the Confederates were in formation, prepared to charge. At the rear of the trenches, Lee himself mounted Traveller and took a position atop a hill. The sound of a single gun pierced the chill air, the order was given, and the surprised Yankees were quickly overtaken. Before dawn broke, the initial assault had stunningly succeeded; Fort Stedman was taken. Teams hacked through *chevaux-de-frise*. Then rebel brigades poured through the gap, and, after surging hand-to-hand combat, they soon occupied nearly a mile of Yankee trench systems.

But as the early sun began to climb, the Confederate forces proved pitifully inadequate. They faced a fierce Union counterattack, a converging fire so intense that it was likened to a "metallic storm" or a massing, dark "flock of blackbirds with blazing tails beating about in a gale." By eight o'clock, Lee's daring raid had sputtered, and by midmorning, the Confederates had been driven back with a terrible loss of 4,800 men. The attack had gained Lee nothing, nothing except the loss of a solid tenth of his command. And if there were one thing he could ill afford to lose at this point, it was precisely that. Yet, "as if incapable of exhaustion," noted Lee's personal physician, "Lee rode erect—and from his perch, never faltered or lost his cool." But as the reality hit that the assault had failed, and failed badly, even Lee could not mask the "careworn expression" lining his face. He knew time was running short.

"I fear now it will be impossible to prevent a juncture between Grant and Sherman," Lee admitted rather soberly the next day in his report to Davis. And that was not all. Lee also indicated that the dreaded moment had arrived; Richmond would soon have to be abandoned.

But for Lee, the unspeakable—surrender or defeat—had not arrived. He had foiled his enemies before when the odds were at their longest, and he planned to do so again. His goal was now singular: to quickly get west and then south—south to hook up with Joe Johnston, south to where he could maneuver more freely, south to where he could dictate the time and pace of warfare, south to a breathing spell.

And that was precisely what Lincoln and Grant were determined to prevent.

❧   ❧   ❧

At this stage, no other figure saw the crisis as clearly as Abraham Lincoln. On March 24, the Union president came to City Point, to meet with his highest lieutenants—General in Chief U. S. Grant, General William Tecumseh Sherman, and Admiral David Dixon Porter—to discuss exactly the core of that crisis: how the Federals would corner Lee. It was billed as a vacation. But he also wanted to be near the battle, to see with his own eyes the forces and the weapons, to read the wires, and to visualize the lines. He would stay a full two weeks.

There was an almost odd serenity to City Point, odd given that it was the military nerve center of Grant's mighty Army of the Potomac. Indeed, at first glance—with its row upon row of office buildings and warehouses; its repair sheds and its sanitary commission headquarters; its guest facilities and its dockworkers, stacking supplies, stacking provisions, stacking building materials—one could have mistaken City Point for a vast commercial metropolis rather than a crucial military outpost. But here at the confluence of the Appomattox and James Rivers, just twenty miles south of Richmond, the sights, sounds, and scars of war were never far away. At night, the lights of Grant's headquarters winked quietly on a nearby bluff, the telegraph hummed with the latest dispatches, and aides scurried back and forth administering the machinery of war. And below and beyond lay a hodgepodge of scenes, each a monument to the shifting cycles of battle: there was the hospital, with its 4,000 beds and growing; the gunboats coursing down the river, their whistles pealing in the air; and the clank and clatter of City Point's wharves themselves, where day in and day out laborers unloaded supplies, troop transports docked, and fresh new soldiers arrived. Across the James and off to the north, there were the neat, white tents and gray warehouses lining the Bermuda Hundred and, farther down, were the tree-lined banks of Malvern Hill, blackened by fighting early in the war. And below City Point, across the eastern front of Petersburg, were the Union siege lines, stretching mile after mile toward the south—nearly as far as Baltimore to Washington, D.C., by highway today or from suburban Rye to Manhattan, New York. And back around to the southwest lay Petersburg itself, with its cobweb of ditches and earthworks, strongholds and fortifications, strung along the earth, with Lee's men tenaciously dug in, and, of course, the headquarters of General Robert E. Lee himself.

So anxious was Lincoln that when he received word of Lee's failed attempt to break through at Fort Stedman, he rushed out to see the battlefield himself on that very same afternoon. From the inside of a slack, slow-rolling train, he gazed morosely out at the hideous mementos of war creeping by: fresh skeletons of army horses, trees splintered by military fire, flocks of crows and buzzards hovering over the fields. For Lincoln, it was a tragic reminder of the enormous cost of this war. In every direction, it seemed, obscenely mutilated corpses were being carted off for burial; at every vista lay denuded earth; and, at every point, there was no respite from the wounded, men of both armies, blasted and bloodstained and forsaken. Lincoln watched all this and grieved. Whatever exhilaration he may have felt about the morning's victory—and its auspicious portents for a quicker rather than a slower end to the conflict—was mitigated by a line of rebel prisoners that crossed his view, these exhausted, ghostly men, stumbling in their "sad condition." In all the war, Lincoln had witnessed nothing like this. He commented that he "had seen enough of the horrors of war," that he hoped this "was the beginning of the end."

The beginning of the end was exactly the topic of the two days of discussion aboard Grant's floating headquarters, the *River Queen*. It was, arguably, the most important meeting a president has ever held with his combat generals in the history of the country. Grant, now preparing to launch a final assault against Petersburg, assured Lincoln that the end was at last within reach. Sherman, the loquacious, hot-tempered redhead, agreed.

Lincoln desperately wanted to be convinced, but he could not shake his own overriding fears, that somehow victory would slip through their hands, that Lee would break away from Grant and lead his forces into North Carolina to join the remnants of the Confederate army under Joe Johnston, or else fight another great battle and escape south. Or worse still, that Lee's forces would melt into the western mountains to continue the war indefinitely. Nor did Lincoln's fears concern Lee alone. "Johnston," he bluntly told Sherman, might slip out of his grasp and "be off south with those hardy troops of his." He gloomily continued, warning the general, "Yes, he will get away if he can, and you will never catch him until miles of travel and many bloody battles."

Lincoln's lieutenants shared his foreboding. Grant would later describe this time as "the most anxious of my experience," confessing, "I was afraid every morning, that I would wake from my sleep to hear that Lee had gone . . . and the war [was] prolonged for another year." And Sherman, too, was no less tormented by this thought, wondering if whole segments of the Southern army would disappear into the hills and roam the countryside as marauding guerrilla bands.

Even as the days passed at City Point, and Lee remained dug in around Petersburg, Lincoln, sitting in the cramped quarters of the *River Queen*, envisioned that the two sides were headed for one final, murderous, decisive battle, an Armageddon of their own making. "Must more blood be shed?" Lincoln asked. "Cannot this bloody battle be avoided?" No, came the answer. Both generals thought not. Lee had foiled them before when the odds were longest. And, Lee being Lee, they curtly reminded Lincoln, there was likely to be "one more desperate and bloody battle."

"My God," Lincoln instantly interjected, "my God! Can't you spare more effusions of blood? We have had so much of it."

But in truth, the answer to that heartfelt question resided with the selfsame man who was doing the asking, Abraham Lincoln. Indeed, it had always been Lincoln's question to ask and answer. For the Union president, who had spent many months pondering this very subject, how the war would end was every bit as crucial as how it had been prosecuted. And its resolution hinged on the most delicate balancing act of the entire conflict: the potentially irreconcilable contradictions of the total war now being waged by Sherman and Grant directly clashing with his cherished notion of "Union"; the moral fervor over slave emancipation and suffrage colliding with the urgent practicality of quickly healing the nation; and the gnawing concern that these two great sets of goals could, in the final months and final weeks and final days, drift dangerously apart rather than unite in tandem.

In fact, if the United States were truly to be reunited as one nation, Lincoln believed deeply that the war must not conclude with wholesale slaughter, nor could it slowly dwindle into barbarism or inquisition or mindless retaliation. All, he felt, would bode ill. To unite the country anew, it must be marked by reconciliation, by the lubricants of civil order, by a rejuvenated sense of what Lincoln termed on the *River Queen* the "rights as citizens of a common country." For this reason, as Admiral Porter would later observe, Lincoln now "wanted peace on almost any terms."

Wringing his hands, Lincoln thus enunciated to Grant and Sherman what would become known as the *River Queen* Doctrine, offering the South the most generous terms: "to get the deluded men of the rebel armies disarmed and back to their homes . . . Let them once surrender and reach their homes, [and] they won't take up arms again." And, further, "Let them all go, officers and all, I want submission, and no more bloodshed . . . I want no one punished; treat them liberally all around. We want those people to return to their allegiance to the Union and submit to the laws."

It was farsighted and far-reaching and as eloquent as his inaugural, but its specifics were only enunciated among these few assembled men. There was no written doctrine, no formal démarche to the Confederates, and no public call for anything less than surrender on the most unconditional terms. And its execution would be not just in Lincoln's hands, but, most prominently, in the hands of his fierce fighting men. And for all of Grant's and Sherman's confidence, no one could—or did—know what would follow in the days to come.

❧　❧　❧

Throughout his war-torn presidency, Lincoln was pilloried by his critics across the political spectrum: he was derided as a "duffer," mocked as "a rough farmer," criticized for "ignorance of everything but Illinois village politics." And as he steered the Union around one obstacle after another, enduring generals who wouldn't fight and Northerners deeply opposed to "the niggers," Lincoln was often criticized by the press, scorned by Washington society, held up as the object of lofty condescension by Eastern sophisticates, even defied by his own military men. To his harshest critics, he appeared remarkably clumsy and inept. But the writer Harriet Beecher Stowe was surely more prescient in praising Lincoln as a leader of considerable force, less a mighty, bellicose man, a sort of unswerving Hercules, than a placid one, with the consistency and stamina of an iron cable, swerving this way and that in the storm of war and the swirling winds of politics, but always resolute in pursuing his "great end." She was right on all counts except one: Lincoln was not passive as much as he was a shrewd master of indirection, speaking in homespun homilies rather than rigid directives, temporizing with characteristic caution until the time came to act. Yet, as Grant set out for Petersburg on March 29 in what Lincoln hoped would be his general in chief's final, all-out push, Lincoln seemed to be suffering more than ever. His eyes filling with tears, he could only muster one feeble joke and a heartfelt goodbye: 'Goodbye gentlemen. God bless you all! Remember, your success is my success."

That evening, the president nervously roamed the deck of the *River Queen*, pacing back and forth, awaiting the latest development. It came shortly. As he stared off in the distance, a tremendous artillery barrage began near Petersburg, accompanied by the incessant crack of gun after gun. Through the darkness and the drizzle, Lincoln could glimpse flashes from cannons silhouetted against the clouds. And so, the last balancing act had finally arrived: weighing the lofty considerations of Union with the dreadful particulars of winning the war, the fear of ongoing chaos and conflict with the necessity for reconciliation. But first things first; Lee must be ensnared.

Anything could still go awry, and in fact it did. The weather took an ominous turn. The sky had darkened. Rain began to fall, hard. And while Grant triumphantly telegraphed to General Phil Sheridan, "I feel now like ending the matter . . . ," the "matter" remained, delayed by a vile spring storm that first banged incessantly on the roofs of depot warehouses, then turned clay roads into sheets of water, and finally bogged down all Federal advances in mud.

In the meantime, Robert E. Lee and the Army of Northern Virginia were doing anything but standing still.

PART 2

April 1, 1865

2

The Fall

In the early morning hours above the battle-scarred landscape of Petersburg, a thick, gray fog is lifting. It is April 1, 1865.

Three days of pelting rains are nearing an end. And Robert E. Lee, recently named general in chief of the Confederate Armies, commander of the Army of Northern Virginia, is grimly supervising the final plans for the rebel evacuation from his headquarters at Edge Hill. Amid the day's slow-growing chaos, this much is clear: for the South, nowhere are promise and peril held in more tantalizing equilibrium than in the lines around Petersburg. Where just three days earlier, Lee thought he had some ten to twelve days to evacuate his army, the latest developments convince him that it must be done immediately. The facts are bleak; this he readily knows. Nearly 1 million men of the North, drawn from a seemingly inexhaustible reserve, are in arms against no more than 100,000–200,000 men whom the South can effectively hurl into battle. His own army is presently outnumbered three to one, and it is just a matter of time—no longer measured in days but in precious hours—before General Grant unleashes his legions in an all-out assault designed to annihilate his battered, shabby units once and for all. Even the Confederate States of America is little more than a shell. The South's industrial and commercial potential is in shambles, and Richmond is on the verge of being taken. The proud lands of the Confederacy, at one time stretching some 750,000 square miles—from the lush green hills of Virginia to the marshy bayous and magnificent oak-filled woods of Louisiana, to the arid mesquite and chaparral plains of Texas, a landmass larger than all of France and England combined, as large as all of Russia west of Moscow, and double the size of the original thirteen United States—have pitifully shrunk to embattled pockets scattered throughout Virginia, North Carolina, Alabama, Florida, and Texas. All that is left is the Confederacy's spirit, and even that appears to be rapidly flagging.

Nevertheless, the commanding general's hardened armada of fighting men is more imposing than it appears—he has seen to that. While riding across the battle lines, his head held high, his eyes calm and probing, he has been making his elegant presence known seemingly everywhere, where it is dominant, unrelenting, uncompromising, and, most importantly, inspiring. And as for the plans of retreat, he has meticulously seen to them, too.

His Army of Northern Virginia will have to cross out of Petersburg on the north side of the Appomattox River if it is to elude Grant's clutches. So he has personally reviewed the order of evacuation, an inordinately complicated ordeal with little easy parallel in history, although its spirit is certainly worthy of the fabled treks of a Hannibal, or an Alexander the Great, or a Napoleon. A logistical and communications nightmare, it will require the unwieldy movement of four separate commands of men, in snaking lines that now extend over a breathtaking arc of thirty-seven miles; in advance, it will demand the harnessing of bulging trainloads of ordnance and the removal of huge cartloads of official papers and countless boxes of state documents that catalog the history of his army; and then it will necessitate the hasty stitching together of a vast array of 1,000 supply wagons, 200 heavy guns, and the roughly 4,000 horses and mules needed to pull them. All told, the supply columns alone will be strung out over a daunting thirty miles of road. And to avoid clogging the escape routes, as well as to hold a pursuing Union army at bay, all of this will have to be flawlessly coordinated, even as each one of these endless streams of men and material moves precariously from five separate locations toward their eventual reunion.

Virtually every key detail has been personally reviewed by Lee. He has fastidiously surveyed the ordnance stores and has directed a detailed examination of the bewildering roads, narrow bridges, and thickening terrain over which his men will escape. Already, he has carefully dispatched pontoons to shore up the dilapidated Genito Bridge—it was washed out by the rains—over which one retreating column must cross. And last, but not least, he has also overseen the critical plan of supplying the army he means to lead to safety—ensuring that 350,000 rations will be sent from Richmond to Amelia Court House, the designated point where his disparate retreating bands will finally join together, eat, and rest, before hastening their march southward toward the North Carolina state line and General Joe Johnston's army. Large or small, no aspect of this staggering 140-mile journey can be overlooked. He knows this, too. Unless carefully attended, each is potentially fatal to his cause. Therefore, as guns begin to thud and mutter in the background, the plans are patiently yet anxiously rechecked. Now, from his desk at Turnbull House, the commander is conferring with his engineers and carefully preparing the maps for his army's retreat—never allowing himself to openly speculate whether he or his troops will survive.

Yet, for Lee, yielding is out of the question. He has one single objective remaining, one single loyalty: it is a crusade, with his men of the Army of Northern Virginia and the Confederate flag marching lockstep together. "If victorious, we will have everything to hope for in the future," he wrote to one of his sons earlier in the year. "If defeated, nothing will be left for us to live for." His spirit remains unchanged. This morning, after quickly dispatching a note to Jefferson Davis bearing the news of imminent retreat, he vows to fight on.

So, too, he believes, will his men. He knows so much comes down to these men, the army he loves as much as the Confederacy itself. Already, theirs has been a story of enormous sacrifice and agony so excruciating that only those who have been pushed to extremes of human endurance can comprehend it. For some of the troops, their resolve—and even their sanity—have crumbled during the nearly ten-month siege of Petersburg. Others have succumbed to unspeakable starvation and sickness. Still others, among the living, are little more than emaciated sticks or hollow-cheeked wraiths: their flesh is covered with ugly red sores and ulcers; their gums are swollen; their teeth are falling out; their limbs and their muscles have dwindled to the size of twigs. Many are vomiting from excessive fatigue. A few are too weak even to rise, while others, barely able to stand, hobble bravely but feebly. But remarkably, most of the men—these are his strongest and the heartiest—somehow press on. This, despite the fact that they have no idea of the campaign's outcome. This, despite the fact that they do not know if they will live or die. This, despite the fact that all they do know is that they will have to fight on, and on, and on. The Army of Northern Virginia is not invincible; Lee is well aware of this fact. But man for man, it is as formidable as any army ever assembled. Even in their weathered condition, his veterans have secured the admiration of their enemy and all the world at large. And even now, they are not to be taken lightly. When the time comes, they will fight and fight valiantly.

But on this morning, as the rain slowly dies down and the slush roads begin to harden and the battle is once again about to open, the question nonetheless is, what drives these men still? Why do they continue? For Lee, the answer is both important and complicated; as their commanding general he knows this all too well. They might fight for flag and country, they might die for the Southern way of life, they might rebel against the tyranny and despotism of the invading Yankees. Yet at this point all would quickly evaporate were it not for the reverence in which they hold Robert E. Lee. It is his iron will that fuels their resolve; it is his single-mindedness that sustains their stamina; it is his leadership that nourishes their determination. He is the red and white thread that binds them together, and this responsibility is, in turn, his cross to bear.

It has not been easy. For days now, Lee has been suffering from a lethal combination of too little sleep, too little nourishment, and too much stress. He is not a young man, and now, at fifty-eight and under the unremitting strain of the last four years of war, he has aged considerably: his body has grown old and tired; unknown to most of the Confederacy, his mane of hair has gone gray; and he suffers from repeated bouts of angina, which he mistakenly believes to be rheumatism. Moreover, that winter, a nagging throat infection had sapped his strength. Yet remarkably, in the heat of battle, his energy does not flag. Too often, he has been tempted to lead a charge himself; already, in 1863, a Yankee sharpshooter grazed his cheek. But he does not fear death. Rather, he has always believed that there is no more noble end for a soldier than dying on the battlefield. "The fame of virtue," he penned in a letter earlier in the year, "is immortal."

Proud of his lineage—he is descended from two signers of the Declaration of Independence, and his father was a Revolutionary War hero, a favorite officer, and a close personal friend of George Washington himself— driven, singularly willed, quietly but fiercely ambitious, hot-blooded and bold, Lee is a man who lives within, possessed by a private vision that he shares with no one. Indeed, what so sets Lee apart from the other figures of his day is a hidden side to this seasoned general that would astonish many of his peers, let alone most fighting men of the twentieth century. Underneath that thick skin, he is a dreamer, quite probably the last great romantic of his age. In a time of budding modernity, newly minted political generals, and the burgeoning thrust of an entrepreneurial class, he is driven by an antique sense of honor nearly unfathomable by the standards of today, and even to the cynics of his era. It is both tempting and common to compare Lee to other generals, but this actually tells one little about the essence of the inner Lee or the secret to the magic that he casts over his men. More typically, he is compared with George Washington, his idol. But the better comparison is actually to the medieval knights and warriors of the past, like King Arthur, the mighty English *Dux Bellorum* who won twelve terrible battles against Saxon invaders from Germany before being slain in A.D. 539. Or the eleventh-century Castilian hero Rodrigo Díaz de Vivar, the frontier warlord whose story became the legend of El Cid. Or the fabled Richard the Lion-Hearted, the chivalric king of England, who waged a long crusade in the Holy Land; was captured in battle by Austria and the Holy Roman Empire; was later ransomed amid much fanfare; and who suffered a final, fatal wound fighting for his country in 1199. Indeed, the coda of the courtly knight, *chansons de geste*, melding humility with bravery, quaintness with toughness, personal loyalty with ruthlessness, and above all, a gentle heart with devotion to God, aptly fits the nineteenth-century Lee.

Yet, what matters at this point is that each and every decision he makes—small or large—will affect the life and very survival of his army, and in turn, the independence of the Confederacy. There is no longer any room for error. Day after day, the hair-trigger decisions have come with frightening rapidity. And day after day, as Grant's men have pushed, probed, and feinted, the action does not stop. So Lee is fastidious, precise, driving himself to the limit. With little respite, he moves quickly from task to task. There are the military matters: reinforce Ewell's flank, quickly shift Gordon's men to the left, now bolster Anderson's men on the right; there are the matters of administration: requisition 140,000 pounds of rations, lobby the Congress for more food, keep the president apprised of all major developments; there are the matters of intelligence: weed out Grant's spies, remember to double-check the viability of alternative escape routes, protect the vital Southside Railroad; and there are the matters of morale: hold the loyalty of his men, don't forget to maintain the élan of his own generals, now fasten the spirit of the Southern people, then deal with deserters. Day after day, night after night, the decisions go on and on. It seems endless, but the commanding general's intensity never wanes.

Now, however, the Union assaults have again begun in earnest, as he knew they would. This morning Lee wastes little time responding, rapping out the curt order to General George Pickett: "Hold Five Forks at all hazards." And he adds: "prevent Union forces from striking the Southside Railroad."

Lee has the latest battlefield reports, but at this point, he instinctively knows Grant's plans; he surely knows them in his gut. If his weakly held far-right flank at Petersburg should fall, then his entire retreat route from Richmond and Petersburg will be threatened. For four days running, Grant has been harassing and testing him, like the slow dénouement of a hard-fought game of chess, where one player must eventually succumb. Still, Lee has thus far checked Grant at every stage. On March 29, in a drenching downpour, General Pickett and two divisions of infantry already have had it out with the fierce little Union general, Phil Sheridan; there were heated skirmishes at Lewis's Farm near Gravelly Run and sharp fighting at the juncture of Quaker and Boydton roads. Lee's men held that day. On March 30, there were yet more skirmishes; this time, Lee's troops repulsed Sheridan's cavalry near a place called Five

Forks. On the last day of the month, hard fighting by Lee's forces, following yet another blinding rain, surprised—and again halted—the Federals at a ramshackle site called Dinwiddie Court House. Another tactical defeat for the Union. As of this morning, then, Lee's men have been defeated nowhere along the critical right side. And by this point, a frustrated General Grant has already quarreled with his chief of staff and lost his temper with Sheridan, and the momentary Union disarray has been labeled by one prominent Federal general as "confused and conflicting." But Lee is suffering under no illusions. With 10,000 Confederates now warily poised against more than 50,000 Federals on the western part of the line, he is well aware that the Union can afford temporary defeats.

He knows they will come again.

And they do. Grant's strategy has been transparent: to continue to move to the left and westward, forcing Lee to stretch his lines further. Finally, on this first day of April, the Union forces unleash a massive enveloping attack against Pickett's isolated forces at Five Forks. "A voice of doom was in the air," noted a Union general. Yes, but for whom? Sheridan's rapid-firing troops, storming on foot, attack head-on, buttressed by Gouverneur Warren's men moving against Pickett's left flank. Cussing and prodding and inveighing the infantry to hit ever firmer and move ever quicker, the diminutive Sheridan is relentless. But Lee's rebels are equally relentless, desperately and bravely fighting back. As Sheridan's men ram forward, Confederate infantry and cavalry defiantly dig in. Suddenly, out comes the cry, *"Hooray! Hooray! In Dixie land, I'll take my stand, to live or die in Dixie."* They are singing, "Dixie," and also "Annie Laurie," as though they were back in First Manassas. Earlier in the day, they have captured some Federal troopers. Hope against hope, they now seek to prevail.

This is hardly the first tight spot Robert E. Lee has been in. After other battles and on other retreats, following Antietam and Gettysburg, each time Lee has given his adversaries the slip. Around noontime today, his eyes gleaming, his face flushed with anticipation, Lee himself rides out to watch the developments firsthand by Burgess Hill.

By four o'clock, the initial reports are that his men may have checked the Federals once again. Across the Virginia hills, the tireless crack of enemy fire could be heard. Moodily, anxiously, he stares off in the distance, waiting for further news.

✸ ✸ ✸

At long last, as the full import of the day's events begins to take shape and meaning, the time of reckoning for Robert E. Lee has arrived. But if ever there were a man who could best the daunting odds currently arrayed against him, it was the aging general, the distinguished product not simply of one of the country's most impeccable pedigrees, but the seeming embodiment of America's very destiny.

Destiny. The word is large, but unavoidable. All his life, Lee was driven by, forged from, and, to an inescapable degree, haunted by a sense of destiny. By birth and inheritance, he was tied to the Union, to its creation and its preservation. Two of his ancestors, Richard Henry and Francis Lightfoot Lee, had signed the Declaration of Independence; his father, Lighthorse Harry Lee, was a celebrated Revolutionary War general, an ardent Federalist, and the soldier whom President George Washington handpicked to stamp out the 1794 Whiskey Rebellion, the young country's first major secessionist threat. And finally, it was none other than Harry Lee who had eulogized—and immortalized—Washington with the soaring phrase, "first in war, first in peace, and first in the hearts of his countrymen."

But if destiny called for the Union, so, too, did it sound for Lee's home state of Virginia. Indeed, Southern history ran equally deep in his blood: he was related to most of Virginia's first families, the Lees, the Carters, the Randolphs, the Fitzhughs, and the Harrisons. For more than a century, his family—as counselors and burgesses, as aides to the king and then as revolutionary soldiers, as planters and foreign emissaries— had played a leading role in the history of Old Dominion. His own father was at various times a member of the Virginia House of Delegates, a Virginia delegate to the Continental Congress, three times a governor, and then a Virginia congressman; in fact, former President Washington made a conspicuous show of publicly voting for candidate Lee. And Robert E. Lee was himself born at Stratford, a great brick home overlooking the Potomac, and one of the most famous estates in all of Virginia.

Destiny, however, stalked Lee in one other way: in the lingering black mark upon his family's name. In truth, Lee's background was far more mixed than Lee family legend would often have had it. For all his distinguished exploits, his father was also a compulsive land speculator who was desperately in debt, repeatedly in flight from his creditors, and, after the Revolutionary War, was jailed not once, but twice. He eventually (and recklessly) squandered his wife's fortune before abandoning his family for the West Indies, only to return five years later in the final weeks of his life, a sick and broken man, dying in Georgia, hundreds of miles from his Virginia home. Born in 1807, Robert was just six when Harry deserted his family. He never saw the elder Lee again.

Thus, while his family may have had an exultant family name, which it did; fine social graces, which it also did; and an impressive array of Virginia connections, including senators and presidents, which it did as well; in Robert's youth, it was left fatherless, nearly broke (the Lees lost Stratford and for a time did not even have a carriage), and its once pristine reputation was deeply soiled. (The family name would be further disgraced by Robert's oldest brother, whose adulterous exploits with his sister-in-law would earn him the sobriquet of Black Horse Harry Lee).

Despite their privations, Lee's mother made do, and so did young Robert. From his earliest years, Ann Lee raised him in genteel surroundings. She taught him to revere George Washington and to lead an exemplary life that would redeem the family's honor. Central to these teachings was emulating not simply Washington's dignity, but his meticulous practice of "Self denial and self-control." Ann read and reread Harry Lee's letters to the children, which, despite his own jaded example, constituted a keen primer on the Founding Father's philosophy: "Self command is the pivot upon which the character fame and independence of us mortals hang." And: "fame in arms, or art, however conspicuous, is naught unless bottomed on virtue." And: "A man ought not only to be virtuous in reality, but he must always appear so." Lee learned these lessons well, and they would stick with him all his life. (Years later, as a father himself, an older Lee would echo these words, telling his son

Custis, who was experiencing problems at West Point: "Shake off these gloomy feelings," "Drive them away," "All is bright if you will think it so," "Do not dream," "Live in the world you inhabit," "Make the best of things," "Turn [things] to your advantage." And he spoke of "strength," "fortitude," "industry," "resolve," and "courage." And he stressed, "I hold to the belief that you must act right *whatever* the consequences.")

When responsibility came, he rose to it. As a young man, Lee took over the management of the household (in the phrase of the day, he "carried the keys") and carefully tended to his sickly mother. He left her side only to attend West Point at the age of eighteen. The separation was not easy: "How can I live without Robert?" Ann Lee mourned. "He is son, daughter, and *everything* to me." And even his choice of West Point contained an element of duty and self-sacrifice. Unlike other colleges for young gentlemen, the education at the military academy was free. But Lee was an outstanding cadet, earning not a single demerit, and graduating second in his class in 1829. Cautious and thrifty, he actually saved from his meager pay at a time when most Southern cadets prided themselves on acquiring debts.

He continued to distinguish himself in the military: for his first commission, he was appointed to the prestigious Corps of Engineers; in the years that followed, he was breveted three times for valor in the Mexican War; he ably ran West Point as its superintendent; he effectively led the U.S. cavalry against the Comanche Indians; and he was the commander of the marines who put down John Brown's rebellion in 1859. By the outset of the Civil War, the fifty-three-year-old Lee was considered the most promising soldier in the country. Lee's mentor, General in Chief Winfield Scott, had already called his exploits in Mexico "the greatest feat of physical and moral courage performed by any individual." He further termed Lee a "military genius" and deemed him "gallant," "indefatigable," and "the best soldier I ever saw in the field." Scott even boasted that in the event of war, the U.S. government should insure Lee's life for $5 million a year.

Lee's social position seemed equally assured. In 1831, the young officer had married Mary Custis, the great-granddaughter of Martha

Washington, and through adoption, of George Washington himself. He thus became heir not only to Arlington, the grand mansion overlooking the Potomac that had belonged to Washington's adopted son, but to everything that Arlington stood for. At the age of twenty-eight, Lee—now the owner of the very china presented to the Founding Father by the Society of Cincinnati, now the guardian of the handsome hardwood bookcase that had once graced the president's office, now the conservator of the magnificent oil portraits hanging on Arlington's walls—had come full circle. His family name had been redeemed.

The Lee and Custis match was a wise, enduring, and, by most accounts, reasonably happy one. There were minor tensions: where he was organized, she was quite spoiled; where he was a masterpiece of understatement, and actually quite shy, she invariably insisted on being the center of attention; where he was refined and handsome, she was at once pushy and somewhat homely; and where he was not a habitual churchgoer by the standards of the day—Lee was not confirmed until age forty-six—she was a fervent, evangelical Protestant. Still, there was much they had in common: both shared considerable antislavery sentiments (he had described the institution in 1856 as "a moral and political evil"), and both were equally outspoken against secession ("the framers of our Constitution never exhausted so much labor, wisdom and forbearance in its formation if it was intended to be broken up by every member," Lee had lamented as late as January 1861). Both were also keenly ambitious. And despite long separations, his inveterate flirtations with other women, and her ill health—she was slowly immobilized by arthritis and confined to a wheelchair—each maintained an abiding love for the other.

But beneath the surface, Lee, ever the picture of moderation and restraint, was dissatisfied. He doted on his seven children, bestowing a pet name on each, but he fretted constantly over their futures and worried that they would never amount to much in life. He cherished the military, but, after years of service, grew tired of the constant intrigues, the backbiting politics, and the daily pettiness, leading him at one point to confide to his son, "I wish I was out of the army." And while he had already achieved considerable fame and glory in the field, he still craved a more active duty befitting a soldier, not postings that smacked of an administrator or bureaucrat. He brooded that the years were slipping by, that he was growing old, rusty, and unappreciated in the service of his country. He did get a field command, in Texas, overseeing the entire Southwest. But for a restless Lee, still eager not just for action, but for a chance to make history, chasing renegade Indians did little to satisfy him. Then came secession.

Once again, destiny was at his door.

One by one, the Southern states began to leave the Union, and, as war loomed, in April 1861, on the same day that Lee learned of Virginia's withdrawal, U.S. General in Chief Winfield Scott summoned him for an urgent meeting in Washington. It was here that a stunning offer was made, bearing Abraham Lincoln's seal of approval: command of the new Union army.

All his life, this was the one position that Lee had coveted. It offered him a chance to walk in the footsteps not only of his own father, but also of the father of the country, with a chance for military glory rivaling even Washington's. In the three tremulous hours that they spoke—of which no record exists—Lee not only declined, surely the most painful decision of his life, but he also resigned his commission from the army. However much this son of an ardent Federalist longed for compromise to save the Union, in the end, the permanency of birth and blood won out: "I cannot raise my hand against my birthplace, my home, my children," he told a friend sadly. And he explained, "Save in defense of my native state, I never desire again to draw my sword." But draw his sword he would. Five days later, Lee accepted an appointment as commander in chief of Virginia's military forces; three weeks after that he was made a brigadier general in the Confederate army. He did it for "honor," but with no illusions and the heaviest of hearts: "I foresee that the country will have to pass through a terrible ordeal," he warned soberly. But in the end, he never openly regretted his decision or its consequences: "I did only what duty demanded . . . and if it were to be done over again, I should act in precisely the same manner."

Would Lee be equal to the task? He was one of the best-known and most-watched men of his era, yet as the diarist Mary Chesnut, who watched him more closely than most, once asked, "Can *anybody* say they know the general?" And she was surely right. For a man of such immense discipline, he was filled with paradoxes: all his life, he had stubbornly adhered to the military chain of command, even when it galled him, except once; when he chose Virginia and the Confederacy over the Union. Austere, ascetic, devoted, he neither drank nor swore nor smoked, yet he delighted in such pleasures as music, dancing, and food, especially fried chicken. Forever faithful to his wife, he was a constant flirt with other women and maintained a sensuous and lifelong correspondence with several of them. Never self-righteous, he was a pious man, praying regularly and long. During the war, he resorted to firing squads to cut down on desertions (his father was more brutal; he had once beheaded a man), but he also freely pardoned guilty men. And despite his legendary self-control, his foul moods and his temper were equally well known. Finally, as much as any other general—including Grant, including Sherman, including Stonewall Jackson, and certainly including his hero George Washington—Lee had a true killer instinct; in battle, his audacity, his aggressiveness, his boldness, his intuition were second to none. Yet at the same time, there was a surprising and decidedly unusual feminine side to him: a sweetness, a benignity, a tenderness unthinkable in other great fighting men. Once, during the Petersburg siege, one of Richmond's citizens sent him a peach, the first he had seen since 1862. He had it hand-carried to his wife.

Physically, he was impressive—and again paradoxical. Nearly six feet tall with a powerful, imposing frame and a striking barrel chest, he nonetheless radiated beauty and grace, accented by his unexpectedly tiny feet (4-C) and a beautifully shaped mouth. His eyes could be large, sad, and brooding; at the same time, when he was angered, his cold stare was unforgettable. Women swooned over him; whenever he visited a barber, they invariably lined up for strands of his gray hair. In 1863, one Union girl, watching Lee pass her Pennsylvania home near Gettysburg, cried out: "Oh! I wish he were ours!" Similarly, when he was a much younger man, his fellow cadets at West Point had called him the "marble Model," and by his mid-fifties, when his head was at first tinged with gray, then white, he acquired the aura of a Homeric patriarch.

Dignified, humble, gentle, he invariably saved the best not for himself, but for the heat of battle and, most of all, for his men. And in turn, they idolized him. When he rode among them, they did not whoop or cheer, but rather stood quietly, in awe, removing their hats reverently. "I've heard of God," one Southerner remarked, "but I've *seen* General Lee." Even Stonewall Jackson, who generally rested his confidence only in the Lord, gave him unshakable support: "So great is my confidence in General Lee that I am willing to follow him blindfolded." Still, Lee struck some of his aides as rigid, inflexible, and, most of all, icy and aloof. But he also earned their admiration. "Ah!" one of his adjutants once rumbled, "but he is a queer old genius." His men called him affectionately "Uncle Robert," or "Marse Robert," or "Granny Lee," or "the King of Spades," and for those who knew him well, "Bobby Lee."

"Bobby Lee" never wrote his memoirs and rarely did he confide in others, even in his many letters; what mark he left of himself was largely on the battlefield. And as a military man, Lee was largely without peer. His genius, whether on offense or defense, was always the same, somehow turning adversity to his advantage. As the war ground on, Lee increasingly lacked troops, lacked resources, and lacked resourceful subordinates. But against enormous odds, he won great battles, halting McClellan's threat to Richmond, routing Pope at Second Manassas, destroying Burnside at Fredericksburg, and pummeling Hooker at Chancellorsville. He was at once a consummate military realist, coolly gauging his odds before going into battle; at the same time, he took chances as did no one else, gambling, probably rightly, that the South had few other alternatives. This, of course, led him to such maddening, even suicidal, escapades as taking on an army twice his size and actually dividing his own forces and then dividing them again, before concentrating his columns, as he did at Chancellorsville. It was a stunning victory. Or using the mountains as cover while again halving his army and thoroughly baffling the enemy, as he did at Second Manassas, achieving another decisive victory. It also led to his boldest risk of all, his desire to fight one great and grand climatic battle on Northern soil, which produced the disappointment at Antietam, the bloodiest day in American history, and culminated in an even greater disappointment, Gettysburg.

Was Lee a born warrior? It is certain that his faith in gallantry ran deep. It is not without significance that he reconstructed the family coat of arms and believed that the family was descended from the legendary

Scottish hero Robert the Bruce. Nor is it without significance that at West Point, he assiduously studied the campaigns of Napoleon—in his spare time. And he was most certainly at home with the fanfare of war: the striking of the colors, the rhythmic beat of the drums, the peal of the bugles, the raising of arms, the fixing of bayonets, the turning of the flank. Lee loved war as a profession, accepting bloodshed and destruction with an alacrity that civilians, and even many generals, would find hard to fathom. But it is not clear that he loved war itself. What he cherished was duty. Listen to his words: "It is well that war is so terrible," he once said, after *not* a defeat but a victory, "or we should grow too fond of it." And: "What a cruel thing is war. To separate & destroy families and friends. To fill our hearts with hatred instead of love for our neighbors & to devastate the fair face of this beautiful world." And: "My heart bled for the inhabitants . . . the women and children." Not a Grant, and most certainly not a Sheridan, could have ever uttered those words, but they come naturally from Lee. Indeed, where a Grant or a Sherman or a Stonewall Jackson could leave a swath of destruction in his wake, without openly shedding a tear, Lee never lost sight of the fact that it was a multitude of fellow human beings who were being destroyed. He never became detached toward death, and he could openly weep at the loss of one of his own men, as he did when A. P. Hill died. Indeed, while he was not an overly philosophical man—being a fighter rather than a talker—he was often astonishingly reflective, even eloquent, after the death of one of his own: "[the] loss of our gallant men . . . causes me to weep tears of blood and wish I never heard the sound of a gun again."

But one should never mistake this as a sign of vulnerability. As a soldier and a commander, Lee relentlessly went for the enemy's jugular. In truth, his face never brightened more than at the prospect of military success. Where other Confederate generals may have felt urgency, or even panic, in the swirl of conflict and the prospect of defeat, Lee felt challenged. Where, after setbacks, other commanders would have sunk into gloom, Lee tightly fixed his jaw and resolved never to quit. Throughout the war, he was beset by physical problems: sore throats, heavy colds, coughs, fever, elevated pulse, chest pain, back pain, arm pain, angina pectoris, lumbago, sciatica, extreme diarrhea (confining him to a cot), two sprained hands and broken bones in one of them (leaving him unable to ride for a month), and, predictably, exhaustion; he was also afflicted by constant anxiety ("day and night") and sorrow ("[it] is wearing me away"). But he never allowed any of it to slow him down or delay his campaigns. Always, he soldiered on.

With greater frequency, he insisted on riding out with his men, or leading them in a charge, flirting nearly each time with death. And as the war progressed, he increasingly salted his speech with the language of military offense, railed against not attacking ("We cannot be idle!"), and spoke fervently about "a battle of annihilation" that would erode Union morale, once and for all.

But as great a fighting man as Lee was, he had his flaws, with many of his virtues as a man becoming vices for a commander. As a general, he was not stern enough with his own men, unlike a Stonewall Jackson, who countenanced no deviation, or a U. S. Grant, whose orders were given as absolutes. Nor was he cruel enough. In contrast to a Sherman or a Sheridan, he refused to burn or plunder enemy property, or engage in selective assassination, declaring it "Unchristian" and "atrocious," even though the South could have greatly benefited from such tactics. For all his strategic genius and killer instinct, Lee ultimately led not by fear or fiat, but example. Thus, he found it difficult to dismiss incompetent officers, or to settle disputes over authority, or to discipline men who fell out of line; equally, he shrank from confrontation with his own subordinates, guiding them less by outright command than by suggestion, which, of course, proved fatal at Gettysburg.

And he was never much of a hater. Like Lincoln, more often than not, he called the other side "those people," rather than blindly labeling them "the enemy." When his house on the Pamunky River was burned to the ground and, later, his mansion at Arlington gutted (even the priceless Washington relics were stolen), he never evinced any bitterness toward the Yankees, still alluding to many of his former friends and companions in "the kindest terms." In 1865, when the grounds at Arlington were turned into a Union cemetery, perhaps the greatest insult of all, to him as well as to his family name, he issued not one word of protest, not one rebuke, not one bitter rejoinder.

Yet lying beneath all the reserve and dignity and nobility, Lee was a strikingly emotional man. He was fiery, fiercely competitive, at times impulsive, quietly ardent, and certainly passionate. But like his idol George Washington, he carefully controlled these emotions. Still, this passion was always there, just beneath the surface. You could see it in everything he did: in his subtle change of moods, the quick flashes of anger, the occasional hard stare of disapproval, and the sudden twinkle of his eye when pleased; you could see it in his little gestures of affection for his wife and his loved ones; and you could see it in the tears he openly shed at the loss of his comrades. But most of all, you could see it in his face once the battle began anew: Lee fought to win as no one else did. He sought victory until events wrenched it from him. Robert E. Lee, son of Lighthorse Harry Lee, child of Stratford, husband of Mary Custis, scion of the first family, and general in chief of the Confederate Armies, was not about to let destiny slip through his fingers.

U. S. Grant and the Union, of course, learned this the hard way, in 1864 at a place called the Wilderness. By far the six bloodiest weeks of the war, this campaign across a hundred-mile crescent was the crucial prelude to the Petersburg siege. And equally, it was the crucial backdrop to the Grant-Lee cat-and-mouse chase commencing in the first days of April 1865.

✳   ✳   ✳

It was in the early spring of 1864 that Grant had worked out a coordinated plan for the simultaneous destruction of the Confederate army, massing as much force in as many locations as possible. Sherman would strike out for Chattanooga and make a drive for Atlanta, and, as Grant instructed George Gordon Meade, who was to lead the Army of the Potomac, "Wherever Lee goes, you will go also." But this was typical understatement, for Grant himself would go there, too—to shadowbox, to fight, and, he hoped, to personally crush Robert E. Lee. He earnestly believed that the North could win the war in a matter of months—a month or two, to be exact.

As Grant assembled his hulk of a war machine over eight weeks, outfitted and armed it, and sent it thumping toward his foe, Lee lay in wait

The Standoff

Union
Confederate

Washington

MARYLAND

Chesapeake Bay

GRANT

Chancellorsville

LEE

Fredericksburg
Spotsylvania
May 8–19, 1864

Wilderness
May 5–6, 1864

Potomac R.

Rappahannock R.

GRANT

VIRGINIA

North Anna
May 23–26, 1864

Cold Harbor
June 3, 1864

Richmond

York R.

Appomattox R.

Petersburg

Petersburg Siege
June 1864–April 1865

Five Forks
April 1, 1865

James R.

0   10 miles

in the steaming green tangle of the Wilderness. There, Grant enjoyed a two-to-one advantage in troops, 115,000 contesting 64,000; but Lee knew the terrain. And if Grant wanted to force Lee into a showdown out in the open, Lee, too, was thinking offensively: his ally here would be the smoke-filled woods where he would seek to ensnare Grant, just as he had done to Hooker at the battle of Chancellorsville, fought some five miles from this very spot just a year before. It would be a defender's dream—one in which he hoped to turn Grant's drive into a welter of slaughter.

On May 5, the first hostilities began—along the same fords, the same somber gloom, the same swamp and swale that also told of the savagery of Chancellorsville. Here, shreds of flesh—it was human tissue—and shards of blackened bone now rose from half-finished graves; birds nested in hollow sockets of weathered skulls that bore silent witness to the previous year's fighting; and horses dug uneasily at decayed legs and arms still swathed in remnants of enemy clothing. Even the low shrubs seemed rotten with bloodstains.

The Wilderness began as did so many other fateful battles—with a chance encounter. But within hours, this battle became something radically different. Under the dense cover of the woods, a savage fighting ruled: soldiers could rarely see the enemy through the twisted expanse of scrub oak and pines. They fired blindly into the smoke and murk, shooting at adversaries and allies alike. By noon, the combat had descended into sheer chaos. Commands separated and scattered. Mistakes went unexploited. And the geometry of conflict was maddening; opposing pockets of men, lost or confused or confounded, were tangled along all points of the compass—and soon the compass was the only instrument by which commanders could find their regiments. Darker than the blackest night, beneath the canopy of smoke and trees, without even stars to steer by, the Wilderness was now plunged into what one veteran described as the "battle of the invisibles with invisibles." Explained another soldier, "It was a blind and bloody hunt to the death, in bewildering thickets, rather than a battle." As the fighting raged throughout the afternoon, men crawled feverishly on their bellies, groping their way forward as bullets sliced through the air like a thousand small scythes. Then, suddenly, exploding rounds of shells set the underbrush on fire, and, soon, the crackle of flames intermingled with the wild screams of men and animals roasting alive.

But the Federals kept coming, attacking and attacking, in wave after wave, never surrendering the advantage and never once allowing Lee a chance to maneuver. The fighting seesawed back and forth. By nightfall, a tenuous stalemate reigned, and men lay exhausted, resting fitfully on their muskets, mindful that their closest neighbor—"a biscuit's toss away"—might be the enemy. After 8 P.M., except for random, anxious gunfire and the moans of the near-dead and dying, it grew strangely quiet. But the lull was only momentary: the Federals had secured a crucial position for attacking Lee's right. Now they meant to make something of it; before dawn came, Grant ordered the assault.

Lee, too, had planned a dawn assault, but Grant beat him to the punch. In darkness, the hard-fighting Yankees drove the rebels almost a mile through the woods, and then burst right through the Confederate center, converging on a small clearing where Lee had his headquarters. As the peril grew, a red-faced and agitated Lee spurred his horse forward into the confused mass, even as Federals advanced on him, only 200 yards away. In a sense, for Lee this was lunacy. A year before, he had lost his most valued general, Stonewall Jackson, to friendly fire, just three miles away in this same tangled vine and underbrush. This very morning, another of his most vaunted generals, James Longstreet, would be badly wounded by rebel guns, shot through the throat and shoulder by his own pickets. But as a swirl of smoke suddenly surrounded him, Lee was oblivious.

When the smoke cleared, Lee eyed a score of ragged soldiers dashing forward. They were Texans. "Attention Texas brigade," the Confederate General John Gregg shouted, "the eyes of General Lee are upon you." One of those Texans recalled, "Scarcely had we moved a step when General Lee in front of the whole command, raised himself in the stirrups, uncovered his gray hairs, and with an earnest voice exclaimed: 'Texans, always move them.'" The four words filled the air like a bugle call. Glimpsing Lee, the men unleashed a wild cheer, and the Texans began to fight back stubbornly. "I would charge hell itself for that old man," cried one soldier, tears coursing down his cheeks, before he plunged into battle.

And charge they did. Of the 673 Texans who went forward, only 223 survived. Moreover, to the horror of the men, Lee stubbornly seemed intent on charging with them. "Go back, General Lee, go back!" shouted the Texans as they swept toward the Yankees. Lee ignored them and continued forward, as minié balls and bullets began to rake the brigade.

"We won't go on unless you go back!" they cried. Lee continued onward.

"Lee to the rear!" they shouted. "Lee to the rear!"

Finally, Lee did fall back, and the Confederates halted the Union advance. By day's end, spurred on by Lee, the Confederates and not the Union had prevailed, smashing Grant's right, seizing two generals and 600 prisoners, and coming close to cutting off the Union supply line. When night fell, the killing and dying continued. Brushfires raged through the Wilderness, consuming some 200 wounded men alive. It was like a scene from the depths of Dante: screams echoed through the forest, the wind screeched through the tops of flaming pines, and the gamy scent of charred flesh filled the air. One officer described that stretch of woods as an "unutterable horror." But for Grant, it was more than that: he had lost an astonishing 17,500 men in these two days alone. Late that evening, as men roasted and writhed and died unseen, the Union general hunched his shoulders, crawled into this tent, threw himself facedown on his cot—and wept.

Other times, after being thrashed by Lee, previous Union commanders had invariably stuck their tail between their legs, withdrawn, and retreated. But not Grant, not even as panic spread through his own headquarters. "Whatever happens," he assured Lincoln, "we will not retreat." He didn't; Grant kept coming.

In the ensuing days, the shadowboxing continued. At Spotsylvania, a dozen miles away, Lee's men quickly constructed an elaborate network of trenches, breastworks, artillery emplacements, traverses, and abatis to entangle attackers—the strongest such fieldworks thus far. Grant was left with two options: flank the defenses, or blast through them. He tried both. Both failed. Yet Grant felt that a spot the men called "the Mule Shoe" could be penetrated with a larger force—splitting the weak seam of Lee's army in two. "A brigade today," Grant boomed confidently. "We'll try a corps tomorrow."

At dawn, after a chill, ill-tempered rain had fallen, Grant hurled a full 20,000 men forward across a mile-wide front. The screaming bluecoats swarmed though the mist and drizzle in a crowded elbow-to-elbow mass and successfully burst through the Confederate trenches. The rebels quickly fell back and the Union men occupied their log breastworks. For Lee, it looked like a debacle. And farther down along the rebel line, another crisis was brewing; here, the fighting turned vicious, producing some of the most frightful combat ever fought on American soil. Along a few hundred yards of muddy trenches, the men slugged it out for hours in the endless rain. In an often frenzied, hand-to-hand contest, skulls were smashed with clubbed muskets; soldiers were slashed by bayonets thrust between the breastwork logs; arms and faces were cut to pieces; and the wounded were entombed alive by slabs of newly dead bodies, sinking down upon them. Blue and gray fired muskets muzzle to muzzle, and, when there were no longer any weapons, they feebly struck at each other with little more than battle flags. Joined in a grisly ballet of death, they hurled their empty guns like spears, reached backward for freshly loaded weapons, and continued firing until gunned down or bayoneted themselves. As one man fell, like Medusa's locks, another quickly sprang forward to take his place.

In previous battles, hand-to-hand combat like this had usually dissolved quickly, with one side collapsing and retreating. But today, both lines held. Soldiers stayed and stood their ground. The results were ghastly: Union flags intermingled with Confederate flags, Northern limbs with Southern limbs. Blood ran as thick and furious as the rain, turning the muddy trench floors red. And on this muck, the dead and wounded were crushed by the next wave of fighting men, surging forward, jabbing this way and that. The bullets sprayed with such ferocity that during one assault a thick oak tree behind Southern lines was cut down by a barrage of minié balls. This was, in historian James McPherson's words, an "atavistic territorial battle" that continued from early morning through the afternoon, into the night, for a full eighteen hours, in the cold, damp rain. It was called "Bloody Angle."

Meanwhile, back at the Mule Shoe, Lee's situation worsened. Grant's men had borne straight down and broken it, splitting the Confederate army in two. This was now a crisis of unconscionable proportions, and, as he had done six days earlier in the Wilderness, Lee personally started to lead his reserve divisions in a counterattack. Again the soldiers—this time Georgians, Virginians, and Carolinians—let out a thundering shout: "General Lee to the rear! General Lee to the rear!" One of Lee's most trusted lieutenants, General John Gordon, a rising brigadier from Georgia, called out, asking the men if they would fail Lee. "No, no, no," they roared back. "We'll not fail him!" Turning back to Lee, Gordon himself shouted, "You must go to the rear." Lee would not. Only when the troops surged around him, turned his horse, and pressed him back, did the rebel commander relent. But, galvanized by the general's presence, Lee's men rolled forward, and, by nightfall, the Confederate position was out of danger. Once again, they had repulsed Grant.

By the next morning, an eerie pall hung over the battlefield; around Bloody Angle, 11,000 casualties lay dead and dying. All told, the butcher's bill for Spotsylvania was 18,000 casualties for Grant, between 9,000 and 10,000 for Lee. From May 5–12, the Army of the Potomac had lost a staggering 32,000, a total greater than all the Union armies combined in any previous week of the war.

But still they came at each other.

The armies continued to fight for several more days at Spotsylvania—and each time, Lee countered Grant's moves. After six days, Grant had gained no appreciable ground; he had only added 3,000 more Union casualties. For Grant, the calculations were as simple as they were numbing; he had desperately wanted to lure Lee out into the open, where Union superiority in numbers and firepower could cripple him. But calculations were one thing, execution was another. And thus far, Lee had more than skillfully matched Grant at every move. Back in the North, a pall of gloom settled over the Union psyche. Grant was denounced as a "butcher." Northern morale sharply plummeted. The peace movement gained steam. And Northern Democrats glumly proclaimed that "Patriotism is played out" and derided Grant as little more than "a bull-headed Suvarov."

Still, Grant was relentless. "I propose to fight it out on this line," he memorably declared in one dispatch, "if it takes all summer."

Now, as summer approached, Grant's words seemed strangely prophetic. The two armies were locked in a sprint toward a junction named Cold

Harbor, near the Chikahominy River. As before, Lee arrived first and ordered his men to prepare for the blistering attack that he thought would soon come. But while Lee's men dug in, another disconsolate reality settled over the battlefield; the two sides were exhausted. There had been no respite from the fighting, marching, digging, and planning. There had been no rest. After other major battles, one side would invariably retreat beyond the nearest river, giving both a reprieve from the combat. But not this time. Union Captain Oliver Wendell Holmes observed, "Many a man has gone crazy since this campaign began from the terrible pressure on mind & body." He did not exaggerate. Two of Lee's commanders suffered brief breakdowns; Lee himself fell sick for a week. Grant's losses, which virtually outnumbered the strength of Lee's entire army, had left his own men demoralized. And there was talk. Even some of Grant's staff began to grumble about the terrible toll of this dismal campaign.

Yet Grant remained not just confident, but almost strangely invincible. "Lee's army is really whipped," he wrote back to Washington. "The prisoners we now take show it, and the action of his army shows it unmistakably . . . Our men feel they have gained the morale over the enemy and attack with confidence." Armed as he was, he could not fail. Wasting no time, Grant ordered an assault to commence at dawn, on June 3.

It would take place a mere nine and a half miles from Richmond.

But if the Union general thought his troops were invincible, they felt anything but. Grant had badly mistaken the severity of the beating that Lee had imposed upon them over the last four weeks. They had seen Lee in action before, and they knew what he was still capable of. As they settled down on the night of the second, hundreds quietly pinned slips of paper with their names and addresses to their uniforms so that their bodies could be identified after the battle.

The bugles blew at 4:30 A.M. the next day, and 60,000 Union men rose up. In the dim, gray light, the rebels were waiting.

When the word "fire" was uttered, the ground itself began to "seethe." Along a seven-mile front, row upon row of blue uniforms came forward. From their trenches, the Confederates greeted the dense mass of attackers with a coordinated round of firepower. The Federals kept charging. The very volume of sound itself seemed unprecedented, combining the "fury of the Wilderness musketry" with "the thunders of the Gettysburg artillery superadded," in the words of one soldier. For Grant, it was an unmitigated bloodbath. Union men fell like dominoes, and Grant suffered some 7,000 casualties that day—most of them in the first eight minutes of battle alone.

The battle's horror was compounded by its astonishing speed. Across some five acres, the dead and wounded now lay thickly arranged in tidy little pyramids spread along the Confederate front. Then, by early afternoon, the earsplitting roar ended; there was only silence, and Grant privately admitted defeat. When talk began of mounting another assault, even his officers would have no more of it. "I will not take my regiment in another such charge," a Union officer protested, "if Jesus Christ should order it!"

The battle of Cold Harbor soon became a sullen test of wills between Lee and Grant. For three days and nights in this maze of swamps, streams, and hills, the two badly bruised armies glared angrily at each other. "An easy stone's throw away," neither commander was willing to tacitly concede defeat by asking for a truce to collect the wounded or bury the dead. As the sun beat down mercilessly, corpses exploded in the heat, and an unendurable stench hung over the battlefield. Men were forced to put makeshift masks over their faces to ward off the stifling smell. Some stuffed green leaves up their nostrils. Grant sent two letters asking that unarmed litter bearers from both sides be allowed to collect the casualties. Each time, Lee insisted upon "a flag of truce." Meanwhile, the cries and moans of the men grew weaker and fewer and more desperate—even as sharpshooters from both sides took deadly aim and fired at their hapless targets. Eventually, on the evening of June 7, four days after the fighting had ceased, Grant relented, tersely writing to Lee: "The knowledge that wounded men are now suffering from want of attention compels me to ask a suspension of hostilities for sufficient time to collect them." Having won not just the battle but the test of wills, Lee now agreed. When Union litter bearers made it onto the field, of the thousands of blue-coated troops they found, only two were still alive.

In the thirty days since Grant had first fired upon Lee in the Wilderness, his Army of the Potomac had lost 50,000 men. That same army had lost only twice that—100,000—in all the previous three years of war. A good many of his finest and bravest had fallen; far many more—another 100,000 alone in just that year—had refused to reenlist. Lincoln, stunned, soon pronounced that the "heavens are hung in black." Across the North, Grant's critics only raised their voices further and included the first lady: "Grant is a butcher and not fit to be at the head of an army," Mary Lincoln protested. "He loses two men to the enemy's one. He has no management, no regard for life." Added one Union man, "We were all quick to criticize McClellan's . . . fear of the Army of Northern Virginia," but "anyone that has seen that army fight and march would, were he wise, proceed . . . with caution and wariness knowing full well that defeat by such an enemy might mean destruction." Said another critic, "It is foolish and wanton slaughter." And even a gloomy Lincoln asked, "Why do we suffer reverse after reverse?"

There was, of course, a haunting irony here. While it was Grant himself who had bellowed to his men on the second night in the Wilderness, "Oh, I am heartily tired of hearing about what Lee's going to do. Some of you always seem to think he is suddenly going to turn a double somersault and land in our rear and on both of our flanks at the same time . . . Try to think what we are going to do ourselves, instead of what Lee is going to do," it was now Grant who had been taught the lesson. He would never be so bold or foolish as to underestimate Lee and his men again.

As one of his top generals, George Meade, observed pointedly: "I think Grant has had his eyes opened."

❧   ❧   ❧

But Grant refused to stand idly by. Nor did he make the traditional river retreat to rest. After Cold Harbor, under the evening shroud, Grant disengaged his army, led his men out of the fortifications, cleared the Chikahominy, leaned toward Richmond, steered left, and then marched swiftly to cross the James. There the Union army went: thirty-five miles of wagons and artillery, 4,000 cavalry, 3,500 head of cattle, and 60,000 infantryman, marching warily over the 2,100-foot-wide river. It took four days for the last man to reach the other side. In the chronicle of modern warfare, it was certainly an awesome sight, but, more than that, it was a stunning change in plans. (Lincoln thought so, too, telegraphing Grant: "I begin to see it. You will succeed. God bless you. A Lincoln.") Grant's new prize was to be Petersburg—a key communications center—and to its north, Richmond, the Confederate capital and the "promised land." And, when he could eventually force Lee out into the open, the Army of Northern Virginia itself. This time, however, his plan was more cautious. He would smother the famed mobility of Lee's army by settling down, if necessary, into precisely what Lee wanted to avoid: a dreadful siege.

Some nine months later, long after the summer had come and gone, the war was still raging, and the siege was still in place. But on April 1, 1865, the day that the battle of Five Forks began, a now confident Grant—like Lincoln—nonetheless knew better than to underestimate his vaunted foe and the ragged but hardy veterans that he still faced. Never again would there be a Cold Harbor or a Wilderness. Never again would he speculate that Lee was beaten. And here, perhaps at last, Grant had something in common with his wily and ruthless foe: as Lee's men hurled themselves forward at Five Forks, sounding the shrill yip yip of the rebel yell, Lee was equally resolute that he would not be beaten, either.

❧　❧　❧

But on April 1, by seven o'clock that evening, amid the budding trees and blooming daffodils, Five Forks was turning into Lee's first disaster since the campaign had commenced in the Wilderness. At long last, a coordinated assault by the Federals had worked; they had not only crumpled Lee's right flank and seized the Five Forks area, but they had almost encircled Petersburg south of the Appomattox River. Of even greater consequence was the fearful toll that the fighting of March 25 and April 1 had taken on Lee's army. He had now lost a solid fourth of his men.

For his part, Grant sensed opportunity. When he received news of Sheridan's victory, he bluntly announced, "All right," then ordered a frontal assault. It opened just after midnight on April 2, with a massive bombardment, hundreds of guns shelling the rebel trenches. Then, in a thickening fog, the infantry attack began at 4:45 A.M.—all along the Petersburg lines. It was the most massive attack since the start of the siege. It would unleash eighteen hours of continuous fighting.

As Grant's army prepared to approach, Lee was in his headquarters, conferring with two of his closest lieutenants, Generals Longstreet and A. P. Hill. His demeanor was calm, but not so his body; he felt unwell, exhausted, and he had barely slept. It was 4 A.M.

Abruptly, his door sprang open.

An aide rushed in, shouting that the road outside was filled with wagons and teamsters. Lee quickly wrapped a dressing gown around himself and moved to the front door. Peering through the dim light into the darkness and the gathering mist, he could make out only hazy, distant objects, silhouettes of skirmishers visible to the southwest. Were they retreating Confederates? Or advancing bluecoats? It was impossible to tell.

Lee ordered a courier out, but it was General A. P. Hill himself who ran to his horse and rode away at a gallop. Pausing momentarily, Lee hastily munched on a biscuit—probably his only meal for the day—and then hurried to dress himself. Finally, in the slow-growing light, he could make out the color of the men's uniforms: blue. They were coming. And coming fast. And his headquarters, Turnbull House, was directly in the line of the Federal advance.

Lee raced to the saddle, as the steady murmur of guns rolled up toward the house from both the south and the east. He was still surveying his forces below when a small group of horsemen approached; one was bearing Hill's horse. The general had ridden straight into Federal stragglers and had been shot dead, right through the heart. "He is at rest now," Lee pronounced hoarsely, his eyes welling with tears, "and we who are left are the ones to suffer."

As the sun rose, however, Turnbull House held; for now, Lee's own situation was secure. But while the telegraph chattered with urgent dispatches—to John Breckinridge, to Jefferson Davis, to General Richard Ewell—even that was about to change. While Lee dictated a fateful message to the secretary of war: "I advise that all preparation be made for leaving Richmond tonight. I will advise you later, according to the circumstances," Federal shells came lobbing into the grounds around Turnbull House. Moving outside, Lee was still dictating another dispatch when his headquarters received a direct hit; dust and splinters flew through the roof, everything was covered with debris, and a fire began to roar inside. The telegraph was hurriedly dismantled. Lee's immediate concern, however, was not Federal gunners, but murderous Federal troops themselves—three brigades' worth—now charging up the hill. Ordering six cannons to be deployed in the house's garden, he immediately assumed control, personally issuing the command to fire. Loaded and ready, rebel batteries held back the first push forward, and then a second. But eventually, Lee could no longer repulse the advancing invaders—there were far too many of them. Experience dictated a quick withdrawal, lest his own party be cut off. Yet even now, Lee himself was the last man to leave the guns. Mounting Traveller, he dashed away at a gallop, while behind him, Turnbull House was feverishly burning to the ground.

"This is bad business," Lee muttered acidly, making his way toward the inner fortifications of Petersburg. And the Union push was relentless: a fresh shell struck perilously close, barely missing the general and killing a nearby horse. As the ground shuddered, Lee flashed a cold stare in the direction of the bestial corpse now splayed below his feet. Then he turned eastward and rode off.

His determination now—or rather his hope—was that the city's inner defenses would hold until evening, when, under the cover of darkness, his army could more easily slip away. But by the afternoon, even that goal was in peril. Sheridan had seized the last railroad in Petersburg, and the blue infantry had smashed through Confederate lines southwest of the city. The rebels fought desperately—with their muskets and, when ammunition ran out, with their bayonets—as they slowly fell back. Soon, Lee was somberly informed that there were not enough men to reinforce his troops at the vital Forts Baldwin and Gregg. His ensuing instructions were as stark as they were simple: the soldiers must fight it out where they were. They did.

As old men and shoeless boys as young as fourteen stubbornly sought to hold the lines for Lee ("Surrender," the Federals called; "We'll see you in Hell first," came the Confederate reply), he and his staff finalized the plans for retreat. The one stumbling block seemed to be the Confederate government in Richmond. Late that afternoon, Lee received Davis's brooding reply, saying that "to move tonight will involve the loss of many valuables, both for want of time to pack and of transportation." Reading this, the general's much-vaunted discipline cracked. He abruptly tore the paper to shreds, saying hotly that he was sure he had given Davis "sufficient notice," and sent a testy response to Richmond: "Your telegram received. I think it is absolutely necessary that we should abandon our position tonight."

And then he added: "I have given all necessary orders on the subject of the troops, and the operation, though difficult, I hope will be performed successfully."

Lee's new destination lay to the west, a hard forty-mile march away. It was called Amelia Court House. And here, in an extraordinary cataract of events, a simple bit of fate would unalterably change history—although neither Lee nor Grant knew it yet.

❧   ❧   ❧

Aboard the *River Queen*, after a diet of sleepless nights, Abraham Lincoln was hovering between anxiety and exhilaration. Inside his cabin, as guns boomed in the distance, he stood hunched over his table spread with huge military maps, moving red and black pins around to follow the rapidly changing battle. Already, after Five Forks, he had been presented with some captured Confederate flags. "Here is something material," he rejoiced, "something I can see, feel and understand. This means victory, this *is* victory." Even Grant, too, had begun to believe. From inside the rebel fortifications, he exulted in his current triumph over Robert E. Lee, quietly writing to his wife that this was "one of the greatest victories of the war." But the North's long-awaited victory was nonetheless marred: even as Richmond and Petersburg stood poised to fall, the ultimate prize evaded Grant. Under the cover of darkness, Lee had once again escaped, stealthily crossing the Appomattox River and forging westward—for respite, for Johnston, for food, and then for more fight.

It was now a race.

❧   ❧   ❧

April 2, 1865, began in Richmond with the steady tolling of bells that awoke a slumbering city. It was Communion Sunday.

Most Richmonders arose as usual, unaware of the dire situation unfolding below the James. They were soon to be enlightened. For weeks now, in the early morning quiet, every sound had held a poignant meaning: the rumbling of wagons indicated heavy loads being hauled to the Danville rail line; the roll of cannons meant another skirmish by Petersburg; the anxious tread of feet signified faithful soldiers, young boys as well as older men, heading to man the breastworks around Richmond. Not a day went by in which danger signals didn't flare. Not a night passed in which disaster didn't stalk the town. But during these bleak moments, Richmonders coped. Hope and religious ardor—and the understandable unwillingness to face disaster—provided their sheet anchor. So did their newfound Confederate identity. Life continued, and stubborn optimism managed to prevail. In fact, it did more than that; amid the trials of war and privation, Richmonders had steadily continued their bold experiment in local Confederate government. Even in their waning days, they met to wrestle with the particulars of their common lives and their young country: the unpaid gas bills, the complaints about the Shockoe Hill burial ground, the quarterly reports from the city measurer of wood. Debate was intense, petty factionalisms and rivalries often intruded, but somehow faith persisted in their beleaguered way of life. Indeed, as late as April 1, the City Council convened an urgent session to approve funds for the Richmond Soup Association and the Male Orphan Society. Yet unknown to them, by the next day, their way of life was to abruptly change.

It wasn't apparent at first. The clouds of the evening were gone—and this morning, a hazy sky obscured the bursting of shells in the distance; a light breeze muffled their sound. And to the extent that Richmonders had heard guns before, they had been much nearer than today. This in itself meant nothing. By all apparent lights, it was a balmy day of Sabbath calm, with few absolute signs of the ominous portents to come.

As they did every other Sunday, under a now blazing sun, thousands of Richmonders strolled to church. For some time now, the wooden pews and the ministers' voices had been a favorite spot for many, a refuge from the sterner realities of the Civil War or a sturdy brace from which to confront the Confederacy's historic challenges. To the long-suffering

Richmonders, their churches were a fortress of sacrifice and prayer. While they didn't intervene in Confederate politics—actually, they reinforced them—they did exert historic prerogatives as the nation waded into troubled waters and delivered a rousing message: with God's help, we will prevail. Whether with pageantry and pomp, or simple hymns and psalms, theirs was a cool, consoling ritual in the eye of the storm. For their devout and dutiful communicants, the churches remained faithful custodians of the people's dreams. And if the pulpit were a place from which ministers inveighed against the enemy—or exhorted the flock—such priestly activism was hardly unique in history. As was typically the case, the passion, the commitment, the words reflected those of the people themselves.

The church of choice for Richmond's elite was St. Paul's Episcopal. Relatively new (built in 1845), today it was crowded with distinguished worshippers: mourning women, neatly attired in black; elderly men suited in gleaming blue; solemn government officials; and here and there assorted officers, resplendent in their Confederate uniforms. And of course, in pew number sixty-three was Confederate President Jefferson Davis, wearing a natty dark wool suit, a crisply pressed white shirt, and a traditional black tie.

Not a pew was empty. The choir sang "Jesus, Lover of My Soul" and the rector, Dr. Charles Minnigerode, his accented voice filled with robust timbre, intoned back: "The Lord is in His Temple; let all the earth keep silence before Him!" Richmonders were sticklers for clerical tradition, and Minnigerode, the tiny German immigrant, soberly obliged them: with his thin lips, high forehead, and aquiline nose, he cut a striking figure in his formal regalia. Addressed as "Your Eminence" or "Your Excellency," the intensely pious Minnigerode was in his own way a legendary figure in Richmonders' affections. With them, he had weathered numerous crises before: peering out with his Hessian eyes, folded hands, and bent head, he was unflappable in his priestly calm. This morning it would be needed.

As shafts of dusky light filtered in through the large windows on the serene gray walls and stained oak and rosewood pews, he moved on to reading Zechariah 2:20: "The Lord is in his Holy Temple," he beseeched.

"Let all the earth keep silence before Him." But it would have been just as appropriate if he had invoked "Gethsemane," the garden to which Jesus withdrew on the evening before the Crucifixion and the chilling code word for Christ's agony. That image, of course, is a grim one: Christ humiliated, Christ scourged, Christ bloodied and pricked by thorns. And by the time a military messenger eased through the door, it could well have been an apt metaphor for Richmond. Once Minnigerode's invocation was finished, the sexton hurried up to Davis and handed him a sealed envelope. Inside was an urgent telegram. Nearby congregants watched "a sort of gray pallor creep over his face" as he read the message from Lee—a moment forever frozen in the annals of the Confederacy. Then Davis rose and quickly walked down the aisle. A few staff members and couriers soon followed the president, but the bulk of the congregation remained in their seats. For these, the well-bred and well-to-do, manners forbade them from making an overt show of concern. So, too, with Minnigerode. But the circumstances threatened to betray even him; the reverend, who had always felt more comfortable in his native tongue, German, than in his adopted English, struggled to maintain his composure. His English steadily grew more "frantic," but he nonetheless managed to finish the service. His eyes filled. Then he explained Davis's abrupt departure.

Such attempts at serenity were not found at the rest of Richmond's churches. At the Second Presbyterian, Reverend Moses Hoge was in mid-sermon when a messenger delivered him a note. "Brethren," Hoge said, looking up, "trying times are before us . . . but remember that God is with us in the storm as well as in calm." Then, in a voice trembling with emotion, he bid his flock a qualified farewell: "We may never meet again. Go quietly to our homes, and whatever may be in store for us, let us not forget that we are Christian men and women, and may the protection of the Father, the Son, and the Holy Ghost be with you all." At this, the vast throng surged to its feet and quickly exited.

Outside, stacks of government documents were piled up on the sidewalks by government offices. They were burning.

The exodus had begun.

❧   ❧   ❧

Rumors flew. Word of the slow, bleak truth spread throughout the seven hills, and, by afternoon, most of Richmond knew that the city would have to be abandoned. Acceptance of the disaster began fitfully, accompanied by a sickening feeling of emptiness. Then came the initial panic. Railroad cars on the Danville line were hastily packed with boxes of official papers and more than $500,000 in gold and silver—gold eagles, gold bars, gold bullion, gold nuggets, and gold ingots; Mexican pesos; fine foreign currency; and gold plate and jewelry—while government officials tried to secure household goods and get reservations on the James River Canal packet boats for their families. It was generally assumed that the Confederate government had made adequate plans for evacuation. But events that afternoon told a different story. Church prayer services were canceled. For the next several hours, depositors stormed banks, and soldiers lugged wheelbarrows of Confederate specie onto the lawns of Capitol Square to light one of many fires set during the day. An official evacuation announcement was finally made, around 4 P.M., and it was at that point that any remaining veneer of calm broke.

Richmonders now fled.

Excited families, hauling their personal wares, began to run toward railway stations seeking passage westward. Frightened columns of refugees set out along the canal towpath, toward Lynchburg. Following behind, servants carried bundles to trains, and horses and their masters began plodding to all points west. As the city emptied, the streets were increasingly choked with humans, beasts, and all manner of wagons, carts, and rickety contraptions on wheels, anything to carry them to safety. From one road to the next, the pavement rumbled with the signs of incipient despair; and soon, the gathering night shook with sounds of desperation: screaming, swearing, wailing, and the dreadful howls of animals being whipped, perhaps the most unearthly sound of all.

Once dusk dropped steadily over Richmond, for those unwilling or unable to flee, a different kind of night began. "Into every house," recalled one young woman, "terror penetrated." The more prosperous residents who stayed behind quietly retired inside their homes, lowering blinds and sealing shutters, anxiously waiting. Women, preparing for the worst, stitched valuables into small cloth sacks and strung them under

their hoop skirts. Pistols were placed at the ready. People sat i
silence, loath even to speculate about what would happen ne
pense was nearly unbearable, and it kept on, hour after hour.

For his part, a grim-faced but calm Jefferson Davis continued working in his office while his executive papers were packed up. Then, shortly before 5 P.M., he straightened his desk—not wanting the Federals to
think him sloppy—and departed alone for the Confederate White
House. His wife and children had already left the capital on a train
bound for Charlotte, North Carolina. Around seven, after sending a
favorite armchair to Mary Custis Lee with a note saying that he hoped
it would ease her arthritis, Davis climbed into a carriage and headed for
the railroad station, a freshly lit cigar clenched between his teeth.

Hundreds were jamming the depot before Davis even arrived, and it
was here, in the midst of the Confederate flight, that the Richmond
slave trade came to its own ignominious end. A trader, with his coffle
of fifty chained slaves, sought in vain to convince a soldier to allow him
to board a crowded train. With a bayonet, the soldier barred him until
the trader unlocked his $50,000 worth of property in the street and let
them go.

Davis, his cabinet, and other government officials were scheduled to
depart at 8:30 P.M., crowded aboard a ramshackle train, each car poignantly labeled: "War Department," "Quartermasters Department," "Treasury
Department." But it was not until eleven that Davis at last bade farewell
to Richmond, as the train pulled away, jerking and clacking toward
Danville, Virginia—the new capital of the CSA.

The burden of government now fell to the city authorities. The
mayor and a citizens' committee were authorized to meet the Federal
army and arrange a peaceful surrender. As the minutes ticked by, the
city was laced with frustration and fear. Hard questions arose. What
loomed largest in the minds of those remaining was, who among them
would be made public targets of Yankee vengeance? There was talk of
prison and the hangman's noose for treason. Many ardent secessionists, like Reverend Hoge, chose to flee. But at this moment, the city
faced an even more immediate challenge: the near-impossible task of
maintaining order.

After nightfall, the military and the militia prepared to carry out their instructions. Destroy all weaponry; torch all commodities, including the vast tobacco warehouses; get rid of all liquor. As the evening faded, they complied. A few artillerists dumped cannon into the James, to join the handful of Confederate naval vessels being scuttled. It was the liquor, however, that went first—with unforeseen but dismal consequences. Around midnight, at the well-intentioned order of the City Council, the militia turned to Richmond's stores of whiskey, bashing in some 300 barrel heads and pouring thousands of gallons into the gutters. It was a grave mistake.

Shifty looters quickly followed, scooping up what they could from the streets and even lapping up the remnants like animals prowling along the curbs. Enlivened by the spirits, the melee began in full force. Prisoners, who had escaped from abandoned jails, began sacking everything in sight: food stores, jewelry stores, dry goods shops, warehouses, abandoned town homes. Elsewhere, the dispossessed left their dank saloons, whorehouses, and dilapidated tenements to join in the free-for-all, looting, fighting one another, even helping themselves to what remained of food for the army. Soon, a swelling mob—first in the tens, then in the hundreds, then in the thousands—ruled the night. In the words of one resident, it was "the saddest of many of the sad sights of the war—a city undergoing pillage at the hands of its own mob, while the standards of an empire were being taken from the capitol." Said another: "Dismay reigns supreme."

Now there were no guards, no policemen, nothing to stop the wholesale destruction. The rule of law was abandoned. That night, one citizen explained, "the devil was loosed."

But not everywhere. In the dark—the city's gas lines had been shut off—a few residents simply straggled to the sidewalks to watch as the last of their military defenders, the proud Army of Northern Virginia, swung southward over the James. They reassured themselves that the fight was anything but over; Lee would still carry on. Yet even this comforting interlude was short-lived. Under a pale, descending moon, a new terror now struck: fire. The second series of orders were to destroy the tobacco warehouses. In the depths of night, it was done; the initial flames began, innocuously, with thin wisps of bluish smoke curling upward from the doomed windows of these embattled buildings. But then they quickly raced through the dry, fragrant leaves and began to scale the walls and roof. From that moment on, no one knew exactly how the fires spread. Soon, however, entire buildings were ablaze.

Then a stiff southerly breeze began to blow.

The flames widened and lengthened and finally began to leap from one building onto the next. On many streets, the lights from the fires were now bright enough to read one's newspaper—or Bible.

The closer the flames came, the bigger they began to grow. Nor was this simply illusion. Like a funeral pyre, the blaze rolled up from the waterfront, hissing and sparking and crackling. The old colonial timber undergirding much of Richmond didn't help; it made the fire insatiable for more. Suddenly, in building after building, plaster dust came down. This was soon followed by a series of thunderous crashes as charred beams buckled and split. Walls began to break. The air was abruptly filled with flying brick and broken glass. And then came the earsplitting sounds of whole structures collapsing into rubble, crushed like paper bags. People began to wonder if they would be buried alive, or burned, or if their corpses would be recovered. And they were now running, stumbling, and crawling, dragging what few belongings they could out on the street. One woman was startled when her building literally "shook" and "quivered," and from nowhere, a brick came crashing through her window; she was convinced that the Federals were shelling Richmond. An elderly black man, in his small home on Second Street, was not so lucky. He died when another brick came hurtling through his rooftop and smashed his temple. So did a small black girl, whose faded dress was covered in red, caked with blood. And, too, an elderly gentleman at the American Hotel, who stubbornly refused to leave. His life ended, instantly, when a collapsing wall smothered him.

In successive thrusts, the flames now spread. The few volunteer firemen who responded to calls found their fire hoses chopped to pieces by vengeful, pillaging mobs. So block by block the smoke, the heat, and the ash climbed, unimpeded.

Meanwhile, out on the James River, the last of the Confederate navy had abandoned their ironclad warships for wooden gunboats. Following orders, the metal ships had been packed with surplus artillery shells and then set to burn. The sailors were inching their way upriver under the fiery glow when the water, the city, and its seven hills suddenly shook and the sky exploded with tens of thousands of loaded combat shells and projectiles from the National Arsenal. "The earth seemed to writhe as if in agony," one citizen noted fitfully, "the house rocked like a ship at sea." This blast was uncontainable: it shattered plate-glass windows blocks away, and that was only the start. Doors of houses were ripped off their hinges, chimneys spontaneously caved in, and the atmosphere was thick with the odor of smoke and heated air and burning brick. This blast was in turn followed by consecutive explosions that consumed three ironclads run aground on the James. Shells from the ships arced into the sky and returned to earth a fiery rain of debris. From their windows, Richmonders watched "those silent awful fires" lap along their streets. Wrote Mary Fontaine, "All like myself were watching them, paralyzed and breathless."

Up to now, there had been no letup from these hideous scenes. Nor would this change. Wholly unanticipated, the Confederate shells, now exploding in full force, would continue to do so with clockwork regularity, for four hours running, minute after minute, hour after hour, bombarding the city. All told, 100,000 shells would go off, driving Richmonders to distraction. The deafening sounds—worse than an enemy siege—would have a powerful effect on everyone who heard them; few who lived to tell the story would ever forget it. And not everyone would live. At the city almshouse near the river, scores of paupers had fled to a nearby hill. But as the hours passed, eleven of them, weak and shivering in their nightshirts, ignored warnings and returned inside, in search of blankets and better clothing. While some were simply climbing the front steps, the arsenal exploded, without interval or warning. There were no fire squads to come to their rescue; no good Samaritans to help them. The explosion engulfed them. No one survived.

Then came another grim symbol of the night's events. At Fifth and Main, residents watched, in dumb horror, as the spire of the United Presbyterian Church caught fire, swaying and tottering for some sixty minutes, until it fell, finally, and was no more.

In the last horrid moments before light, the city seemed almost suspended in an eerie, unnerving stillness. And as dawn came, Richmonders realized that all the routine noises and customary sights that had for so long been an integral part of their Confederate lives—the incessant clanking of workers by the wharves, the rumbling of soldiers on foot and the constant ringing of bells, the clatter of official carriages and the high-pitched whistles of naval vessels, and, of course, the long brick skyline adorned by the stars and bars flying aloft—had changed, absolutely and seemingly forever.

❧   ❧   ❧

With numbed, blank looks, more and more people, exhausted and frightened and heartbroken, picked their way outside. Before their very eyes, whole streets had seemingly disappeared. And against the strange, shimmering glow in the sky, the wreckage of thousands of lives could now be revealed in vivid detail: the broken tables and chairs, the shattered dishes and scorched silver, the blackened tools and melted dolls, and the bonnets, everywhere the bonnets, strewn about on the sidewalks.

Unknown to them, miles away in the distance, Richmond itself had disappeared, its hills and spires shrouded in smoke.

For those who had succeeded in getting out in the nick of time, or who were uninjured, or who were fortunate enough to have a comfortable roof to sleep under, there was the incredible agony of remembering what they had seen, and not knowing what would become of others. And for those remaining, the worst horror was what the next few hours would bring. All that could be done was to wait.

The sun rose, and the city's vistas were chilling. The fires still burned. Everywhere were broken houses, charred buildings, and dead animals lit by the infernal glow. Old businesses, fine hotels, elegant residences, newspapers, restaurants, all were destroyed by the indiscriminate inferno. True, many buildings still stood, a number of them the most handsome in the city. St. Paul's Church, for instance, was singed and blackened, but ultimately escaped burning, if only barely. So, too, the Executive Mansion, the oldest continually occupied governor's residence in America: its house and kitchen both caught fire several times, but were saved at the last second by hand brigades working frenetically with buckets. Much of

Richmond, however, was not so fortunate. Some twenty blocks lay in waste, a smoking, simmering ruin, forever thence to be known as "the burnt district." And the Mayo Bridge—the very last one standing—was jammed with tar-filled barrels in anticipation of its own approaching apocalypse. One officer, a South Carolinian, posted near the abutments, watched as the Confederate troops steadily trudged south. Finally, shortly after dawn, he rode over to the engineer who stood by, waiting, touched his hat, and reported: "All over. Goodbye."

Then he ordered: "Blow her to hell."

Within an hour, the Confederacy's greatest indignity would begin: Richmond would be occupied territory.

❧ ❧ ❧

"A single blue jacket rose over the hill," recorded one Richmonder, standing transfixed with astonishment at what she saw. Then another sprang up and another—"as if rising out of the earth." It was just shy of 7 A.M.

Outside the city, Union troops were moving, slowly but painfully, fear in their faces, in single file. The ground was so densely covered by enemy land mines that the soldiers were adhering to a little path marked out by wooden sticks and pieces of red webbing attached, which the Confederates, in their haste, had forgotten to dismantle.

But beyond the minefields, scores of Union troops, including the all-black Twenty-fifth Corps, were racing up the turnpikes and across unplanted fields to be the first to enter Richmond.

And racing to meet them in a rickety carriage flying a white flag was a well-dressed eighty-year-old man bearing the seal of the city and this terse message: "To the General Commanding the United States Army in front of Richmond: . . . I respectfully request that you will take possession of [the city of Richmond] with an organizing force, to preserve order and protect women and children and property. Respectfully, Joseph Mayo, Mayor."

Thus began what one Union soldier penned, "A day never to be forgotten."

❧ ❧ ❧

However breathtaking the sight of Union columns advancing on Main Street may have been for the North, for Richmonders, it was devastating. The long lines of artillery and cavalry moved, in the words of one Confederate, "like a serpent through the streets." Surrounding the troops was what Major General Godfrey Weitzel, the Union commander in charge, would later call "a yelling, howling mob" of drunken residents, white and black, pillaging or bent on saving some little piece that remained. Weitzel plowed through the crowd up to Capitol Square. There, the scene was horrific, a calculus of squalor, despondency, and terror.

The refugees were the worst sight. In the square itself, by the stately Old Brick Bell Tower, several hundred families had gathered beneath the hurling cinders, heated air, and flying pieces of burning wood. The elderly, the sick, women cradling infants, some holding young children by the hand, the rich and the destitute alike, all gaped in astonishment at the choking smoke, the flames now roaring out of control, and most of all, at the incoming Yankees. Evicted by the fire, these people were now homeless and penniless, left only with a few household items: a bit of bedding, cooking utensils, heirlooms and tintype photographs, a single bureau or chest, or even a sofa, gathered in haste and piled senselessly on the grass. But the Armageddon was not yet over. All around them, burning buildings threatened to collapse on both sides. Many did, falling into grisly heaps. By day's end, the initial estimates of damage could be tallied up: 900 homes and businesses destroyed; hundreds more badly damaged; at least fifty-four blocks, virtually all gone. Richmond's charming enclaves, in ruins. In many cases, even old-line Richmonders could no longer tell which block was which. Now the refugees huddled and wept on the open lawn, with scared, hungry children; it was, said the Union commander, a sight that "would have melted a heart of stone."

And even as more Richmonders stumbled up to the grassy flanks of the square, they could hear the ominous sound of military men maneuvering on the adjacent streets around city hall, the thud of enemy feet on the pavement, the sharp commands ringing in the spring air. At exactly eight o'clock, the Confederate flag that had fluttered above the capitol came down and the Stars and Stripes was run up. "My heart sickens with indignation to think that we ever should have loved that flag," wept one woman. Another lamented, "We covered our faces and cried aloud. All through the house was the sound of sobbing. It was as the house of mourning."

While Union regimental bands played "Yankee Doodle" and "The Star Spangled Banner" and black and white troops marched up Main Street, most citizens quickly retreated to their homes, peering through drapes pulled tight. "We tried to comfort ourselves by saying in low tones . . . that the capital was only moved temporarily," one resident told herself, ". . . that General Lee would make a stand and repulse the daring enemy, and that we would win the battle and the day. Alas, alas, for our hopes."

In the days that followed, some women did venture forth, masking their emotions with exquisite politeness or barely restraining them behind clenched teeth. For hours, these women, ominously swathed in black as a sign of their mourning, drifted aimlessly through the streets of their ruined city—avoiding the gaze of Yankees, avoiding the United States flag, avoiding the dreaded blacks, now freed, coming their way on the sidewalk.

"Anything would be better," cried one woman, "than to fall under the United States again." Bitterness lay as thick as the smoke and ash.

Reporters struggled mightily to capture the pathos and mystique of a fallen Richmond for their Northern readers. Wrote one *New York Times* correspondent: "Richmond is indeed most beautiful—in spite of the hideous ruins . . . left behind. It is a magnificent capital, both old world and new . . . I can scarcely record its [splendor] . . . built like a miniature Rome, upon a number of little hills." Strolling through Richmond at twilight, a reporter for the *New York World* put it this way: "There is a stillness, in the midst of which Richmond, with her ruins, her spectral roofs . . . and her unchanging spires, rests beneath a ghastly, fitful glare . . . We are under the shadows of ruins. From the pavements where we walk . . . stretches a vista of devastation . . . The wreck, the loneliness, seem interminable . . . There is no sound of life, but the stillness of the catacomb, only as our footsteps fall dull on the deserted sidewalk, and a funeral troop of echoes bump . . . against the dead walls and closed shutters to reply, and this is Richmond. Says a melancholy voice: 'And this is Richmond.'"

The North wisely sought to ease the pain of its occupation. Though martial law reigned, Union mechanics worked overtime to get the railroads functioning, a phalanx of Federal work parties cleared the streets of debris and quelled the fires, and Yankee "grocer confectioners" provided rations for starving Richmonders. Nonetheless, relations remained tense, and, despite the Union's benign rule, few signs were auspicious for reconciliation. "It is ultimately impossible for the people of the South to embrace the Yankees," editorialized the Richmond *Whig* on its last day of Confederate publication, "Even to recognize them as fellow creatures. An acre of blood separates [us] . . . "

In the days to come, that acre would widen. It would challenge Abraham Lincoln every bit as much as did the Confederate armies that still eluded him.

✳   ✳   ✳

As white Richmond retreated behind shutters and blinds, black Richmond spontaneously took to the streets. From the moment Union troops entered the city—*"Richmond at last!"* black Union cavalrymen shouted—crowds, the skilled and the unskilled, household servants and household cooks, rented maids and hired millworkers, jammed the sidewalks to catch a glimpse of the spectacle. No longer enslaved, they thrust out their hands to be shaken or presented the soldiers with offerings: gifts of fruit, flowers, even jugs of whiskey. Federal officers riding alongside promptly reached for the liquor bottles and smashed them with their swords. But the crowd was undaunted. Just a day earlier, they had been prohibited from smoking, publicly swearing, carrying canes, purchasing weapons, or procuring "ardent spirits." Yet now, to the sounds of "John Brown's Body," they jubilantly waved makeshift rag banners; to the tune of the "Battle Hymn of the Republic," they enthusiastically hugged and kissed the bluecoats. For hours, ignoring the furnacelike heat and the smoke-choked air, they lingered in the dusty streets as Federal soldiers passed, bowing and giving thanks ("de Yankees at last has gone and cum!"). In the late morning, when black troops marched in lockstep ("majestically and proudly defiant," in the words of an onlooker), they danced with unimpeded joy. And most of all, they praised God, shouting "hallelujah." Recalled one Connecticut soldier, "Our reception was grander and more exultant than even a Roman emperor . . . could ever know."

Indeed, for the slaves, who had long eavesdropped on parlor conversations or passed along snippets of war news gleaned from a trip to the store or post office, or who had listened month after month for the sounds of Federal shells and wondered how long the Confederacy would last, this was surely "the day of jubilo." What had been foretold in hundreds of secretly worded spirituals sung at dusk on thousands of plantations across the South had now finally come to pass.

The euphoria was difficult for either side to fathom. Said one white Richmonder, "Our servants were completely crazed. They danced and shouted, men hugged each other and women kissed . . . Imagine the streets crowded with these people!" A Union soldier seemingly concurred. The former slaves, he also wrote, were "completely crazed." In these early, heady moments, it was as if the Richmond heavens had been turned upside down.

Not completely. For a number of the city's former slaves, the full implications of freedom were still unclear. "All I know, it don't take no passes now to go around no where," one black man told a Northern reporter. It didn't matter. The newly freed men and women would soon understand this: finished were the days when women and girls would be tied to one another by ropes wound like harnesses around their necks; never again would black men and boys wear heavy iron collars linked by a thick chain, their wrists cuffed behind their backs; no longer would Negroes be taken to large wooden blocks to be blithely auctioned off as property, just as farmers routinely sold cows, pigs, and horses. And never again would their condition resemble "one grand menagerie where men are reared for the market like oxen for the shambles." Or, as one freed man put it, prosaically yet elegantly, "Bress God, the nigger's free. No more hoeing of corn for dis poor child, and no more lashes from dat cruel overseer."

The feeling was not, however, entirely monolithic; for a complex host of reasons some free blacks and former slaves readily identified with the Confederacy. Bound by time and familiarity and even affection, not all black servants openly reveled in their changed circumstances; some even stayed with their former masters. "I'm gwine to town to hunt my young mistress," said one, "I'd risk my life to git her from dem terrible Yankees." But in the same breath, many openly gloated. "Hello, massa, bottom rail on top dis time!" became the familiar saying. And in one far more telling instance, a "committee" of three former slaves bluntly informed their former owner that they were "free"—although they "would work" if paid in "federal greenbacks."

In these stirring, emotion-packed hours, there were also tender moments that transcended the high politics of emancipation and the gritty realities of a war that was still under way. Most memorable perhaps were those that involved the reunion of families wrenched apart by the slave trade. For many years, Virginia's Negroes had been eagerly sought along the Georgia and Mississippi frontiers. Between 1830 and 1840, no fewer than 117,000 Virginia slaves were sold to other states, often cruelly separating families: father ripped from son, mother torn from daughter, brother taken from sister. And a special sense of anguish was reserved for those Negroes snatched by the most insidious freebooter of them all, the kidnapper. But as Richmond fell, parents were reunited with sons and daughters alike. In one heart-stopping case, a mother rejoined her son, who had been missing for a staggering two decades. She wept: "This is your mother, Garland, whom you are now talking to, who has spent twenty years of grief about her son." The son and former slave whom she had found on the streets of Richmond was now the regimental chaplain of the United States Colored Troops.

Among the many reporters from Northern newspapers who sought to record the sights and sounds of this newfound freedom was one who was himself a searing symbol of the day. Writing under the nom de plume "Rollin," he was actually T. Morris Chester, who sat at a desk in the former Confederate Capitol penning his dispatches to the *Philadelphia Press*. Of all the reporters now jostling about in Richmond to chronicle events for posterity, he was unique; unusually cultured and urbane, he had been educated at elite schools in the rustic hills of Vermont, read law in London where he hobnobbed with British abolitionist circles, was filled with dash and bravado, and would at one time even be received by the czar of Russia. Calling America his "home," he would also enigmatically emigrate for a time to Liberia. But on this day, he was in the former citadel of the Confederacy, and with his keen eye for detail and his passion for ending slavery, he neatly captured the emancipationist's feelings with a stentorian voice few others could muster. He jotted, "Seated in the Speaker's Chair, so long dedicated to treason . . . I hasten to give a rapid sketch of the incidents which have occurred." And then: "Richmond has never before presented such a spectacle of jubilee. What a wonderful change has come over the spirit of Southern dream."

T. Morris Chester, of course, was the son of a former slave and the only black correspondent for a major daily paper in the North.

❧   ❧   ❧

The next day, April 4, brought an equally stunning sight. While General Grant was off in hot pursuit of Lee's army, President Abraham Lincoln, in a high silk hat and long black coat, landed at Rocketts in the early afternoon and, accompanied by a naval guard of ten sailors, six in front, four in the rear, set foot on Richmond's vaunted soil and began the nearly two-mile walk up the hill to Capitol Square. But even four long years of continuing war had not prepared the lanky president for the unprecedented reception he was to receive along a simple one-mile stretch. Out came a sound: "Glory to God!" It was a black man working by the dock. Then again: "Glory to God! Glory! Glory! Glory!" Leaving their squalid houses and their tar-paper shacks, an impenetrable cordon of newly freed blacks followed Lincoln down the rubble-strewn streets, starting with a handful and swelling into a thousand. "Bless the Lord!" they shouted, "The great Messiah! I knowed him as soon as I seed him. He's in my heart four long years. Come to free his children from bondage. Glory hallelujah." And Lincoln replied, "You are free. Free as air." "I know I am free," answered one old woman, "for I have seen Father Abraham and felt him."

One of Lincoln's aides asked the mass to step aside and allow the president to proceed, but to no avail. "After being so many years in the desert without water," a man said happily, "it is mighty pleasant to be looking at las' on our spring of life." Weeping for joy, they strained to touch his hand; dizzy with exultation, they brushed his clothing to see that he was real;

fearing that it was only a dream, they wiped their tears to make sure they were in fact looking out upon his face. Moved, Lincoln ignored his bodyguards and waded deeper into the thickening flock. One black man, overcome by emotion, dropped to his knees, prompting the president to conduct a curbside colloquium on the meaning of emancipation. "Don't kneel to me," said the president. "That is not right. You must kneel to God only, and thank Him for the liberty you will enjoy hereafter."

And then Lincoln declared, "Let me pass on. I want to see the capitol."

As the party wound its way deeper through the tattered downtown streets, columns of smoke ominously billowed into the sky. Several buildings were still aflame, and Lincoln's security men peered nervously at every window for would-be assassins. All around them was a strange, almost macabre quiet. There had been no official welcoming party to greet the chief executive of the United States, and now the crowds studying him from their windows did so in silence. There were no calls, no cheers. At one point, Lincoln's bodyguard, scanning the buildings, thought he saw the glint of a gun from a second-story window. Instantaneously, he stepped in front of the president.

Lincoln pushed on, fanning himself in the lingering heat, while hundreds of white Richmonders, cloistered inside, continued to fix their gaze on the president.

A cavalry escort took him the last few blocks to the rebel executive mansion, now a Union military headquarters. Inside, a "pale and utterly worn out" Lincoln wandered around the deserted rooms. And then, a mere forty hours after Jefferson Davis had left it, the president of the United States asked for a glass of water and sat down in the first-floor study of the president of the Confederate States—while Union troops broke into cheers. "Thank God I have lived to see this," Lincoln had muttered earlier in the day. "It seems I have been dreaming a horrid dream for four years, and now the nightmare is gone."

But not yet, and Lincoln knew it. Indeed, he would comment that his anxieties were so great that all he cared about was not how the Confederates were subdued, but "that the work was perfectly done." Still, he wasted no time in laying the groundwork for eventual reconciliation. For one thing, the occupation of Richmond was not to be a repeat of Sherman's march to the sea, nor of Sheridan in the Shenandoah. Here, in the heart of Virginia, the most important state in the Confederacy, Lincoln saw to it that restraint was the watchword. The military stubbornly prohibited the use of offensive words or insulting gestures; there were no reports of Union rapes or burnings, no break-ins, no sacking of houses. When Mrs. Robert E. Lee, who was too stricken by arthritis to flee and thus remained in Richmond, suggested that the soldier posted on her doorstep, a black man, was "perhaps an insult," she was promptly given a new guard, a white from Vermont, and had her household offer him meals on a tray. By design, Lincoln came "as a peacemaker," noted his escort, Admiral David D. Porter, "his hand extended to all who desired to take it." Porter hoped that Richmonders would see that Lincoln was not "a monster," that there were "no horns or hoofs," and that there was "less of the devil about him than . . . in Jeff Davis."

But the national nightmare was still far from over. As far as Lincoln could tell, the bloodshed could go on for months, even longer, if not on an organized battlefield, then on deadly guerrilla terrain. His morose fears, so deep and ubiquitous, had not yet been addressed. He surely didn't want a repeat of the Wilderness swings.

He wanted Robert E. Lee.

❧ ❧ ❧

"I have got my army safely out of its breastworks," Robert E. Lee told an aide as he began to swing west to Amelia Court House, "and in order to follow me, the enemy must abandon his lines and can derive no further benefit from his railroads on the James River."

On April 3, if Lee was disheartened, he was certainly not beaten. Freed of the yoke of Richmond, of maintaining his men in miles of dismal trenches, he was determined to rescue the South's battered and bloodied sons. For every mile that they crossed, Grant's supply lines would lengthen, and Lee's, toward Danville, would shorten. And now he was also relying on his old ally—the Virginia countryside—to help him escape. It would work like this: each mile that his army advanced westward was a little denser, a little more precipitous, a little more hostile to the invading army. Though his men and his horses were tired, they would reach Amelia Court House by the next day. Though Grant had the inside track to Burkeville beyond Amelia—his arc would be nineteen miles shorter than Lee's—Lee's men had a one-day jump on the Federals. And though Grant's cavalry was somewhere out sniping at the left flank of Lee's army by the night of the third, Lee's men were in surprisingly good spirits. For one thing, they were certain of this: once at Amelia, they could rest, catch a bit of sleep, and most importantly, eat a solid meal before moving on. And as they marched away from their trenches, Lee's hardy veterans, reassured by the imposing presence of their general in chief, were no less hopeful than he.

War, for victors and losers alike, is invariably about a series of contingent "ifs." The only thing certain about war is its uncertainty and unpredictability, as the master military theorist Karl von Clausewitz has reminded us. And, time and again, history has borne out Clausewitz. The English unexpectedly stymied the French at Agincourt. Napoleon succumbed to zeal in his long winter march on Russia, and suffered dearly as a result. The Mexican general, Santa Anna, fell prey to overconfidence against a makeshift army of Texans and paid the price for it. After an eighty-year siege, the Dutch republic held off a far stronger Spanish enemy and finally gained its independence. And, of course, even George Washington had suffered defeat after defeat, in New York and New England, in Georgia and South Carolina, before eventual triumph. The "if" now for Lee, given that his men were subsisting on the meagerest of rations, was that everything depended on a speedy and uninterrupted retreat. Lee's pace was unrelenting. Groping forward at an astonishing clip of twenty-one miles per day over rough and unforgiving terrain, Lee had some reason for qualified optimism. Indeed, on this day, while Richmond still smoldered and Union soldiers cheered, a curious, even mystical spirit, half of elation, half of frenzied, unconquerable faith, spread through the Confederate ranks.

And to those men watching Lee, sitting erect on his horse, looking anything but demoralized, the general exuded good humor—and seemed confident that Johnston's army was within reach.

3

The Chase—and the Decision

To the contemporary mind, it is difficult to contemplate the westward march of the Army of Northern Virginia and just as difficult to step outside all the history that has come after. In contrast with military campaigns across the most recent century, an extended troop march appears to be almost an anachronism. Today, great military machines race across terrain in high-speed tanks and armored personnel carriers or, more and more, jet overhead by cargo plane, unless they are poorly equipped or take to the ground for surprise, or because the battlefield has collapsed around them. They do not march on foot, and, if they do, they certainly do not expect grand victory. It is perhaps no accident that one of the most famous military marches of the twentieth century was neither a strategic retreat nor a tactical feint, both of which were part of Robert E. Lee's stock-in-trade, but something very different, a journey into captivity known as the Bataan Death March, made over ten days and seventy-five miles by 36,000 already defeated American servicemen in the Philippines. Even now, Bataan, where upward of 10,000 men died of thirst, exhaustion, beatings, torture, or beheadings, is a march that skews and defines much of the modern military imagination.

But Robert E. Lee was not of a twentieth-century mind. The marches he knew were not Bataan, but heroic efforts made by indomitable men like Hannibal, Alexander the Great, and Napoleon, for whom the distinction between military genius and reckless insanity was often measured by the razor-thin line of success. People must have thought Hannibal especially crazy, setting out from Spain with 40,000 men and an ungodly number of elephants to traverse two hazardous mountain ranges—the Pyrenees and the Alps—and a deep, rushing river, the Rhone, and to endure landslides, blinding snowstorms, and attacks by hostile mountain tribes; they thought him crazy, that is, until he did it in fifteen days and swept down upon the unsuspecting Romans. And even Napoleon's ill-fated march was less a cautionary tale than an object lesson, for when the 600,000 French forces lunged into Russia, it was the retreating Russians who had simply faded away in front of them, drawing the overconfident French ever farther into a harsh and unforgiving land. Now Lee and his veterans, some 35,000 men, had a roughly 140-mile march to make and a solid twelve- to twenty-four-hour lead; and, like the wily Russians, if necessary, they, too, could seek to melt away from Grant's legions of material and men. To be sure, Lee understood the odds, but ever the gambler, hadn't he bested them before? Hadn't he gotten to Cold Harbor first? Then, hadn't he held Richmond and Petersburg longer than most would have imagined? To leave Grant behind now would almost certainly enshrine him among history's great commanders and tacticians. But it would all come down to fate and execution. And as April 3 dawned, the signs of progress were still promising.

It was happening like this: four broad columns of troops had poured out of the trenches and fortifications around Richmond and Petersburg and were anxiously streaming toward Amelia Court House, which lay below a river bend. Almost unnoticed among the miles of stars and bars—it was pitch black—was Lee himself. Atop Traveller, he had posted himself at a fork in the road, and, for hours, man and horse directed traffic, until the last of the troops had filed past. Three of the contingents were to cross the Appomattox River en route to Amelia; the fourth, already south of the river, would simply continue west. Once they reunited, they would quickly eat, rest, and regroup, then turn south, to Danville, and then across the North Carolina border, to Joe Johnston. After they reached Amelia, moreover, the route would likely favor Lee's men. Union troops, in February, had themselves already probed a number of these backcountry roads and declared them "the worst possible." It was, of course, on these familiar roads that Lee and his army were now marching.

This is not to say the obstacles weren't considerable. By day, they fled along packed roads and stubby rural cut-throughs that necessitated traversing swollen, difficult streams and scaling high, sloping ridges. Sometimes the roads were open and expansive, but other stretches were far less hospitable, winding through uncut acres of scrub brush and pine that tore at and scratched their skin, their passage so narrow in spots that a single artillery wagon could barely slide past. Where they could, the men stepped around rocks and ruts. Where they could not, they simply went over or through them. At night, with little sleep and even less respite, the men continued to march under the cover of darkness. On and on, hour after hour, from hilltop to hilltop, for the better part of two solid nights and one continuous day, they struggled to keep their lead. By April 4, they were dirty, unwashed, mud-splattered, exhausted, and, most of all, desperately hungry. Their bread was gone, and so was their meat. Still, after months of languishing in the trenches, their morale and élan were surprisingly strong; and at the thought of food in Amelia, so were their spirits. And, too, they were comforted by this: once replenished, their lead over Grant solidified, they would complete their dash to safety. So what mattered now was each new stride, each new landmark, bringing them closer to the 350,000 rations they expected at Amelia Court House, and taking them a step farther away from Grant's huge force, eagerly trailing behind. Under the blanket of stars and into the blistering heat of midday and back again under the shelter of night, the men rushed ahead.

But U. S. Grant was not so forgiving. Already, there were signs of growing peril. In the rear of the retreat, low-level skirmishing raged like an ongoing battle; at Sutherland Station, the fighting was so fierce that a nearby house had to be requisitioned for a makeshift hospital, its doors ripped off their hinges to serve as stretchers for the wounded. The next day, the battle grew down the road, at Namozine Church, where Federal cavalry set upon trailing rebels. Lee's own riders repulsed the enemy, but not without a price. A number of rebels were cut to pieces, and while Grant's men had been stung, they were hardly vanquished; regrouping, they prepared to plunge ever deeper into Lee's lines. But the bulk of Lee's forces were still well ahead, and Federal cavalry was not Federal infantry; the latter would always be slower in coming. Indeed, Lee and his staff even felt comfortable enough to accept a leisurely dinner invitation from Judge James Cox at his house, Clover Hill. But with Grant's forces in pursuit, the commanding general didn't want to press his luck; thus, he did not stay the night, instead hurrying forward to make the Appomattox crossing. By morning, he expected to be in Amelia.

Once more, however, there was trouble. Lee's plans had called for his vast columns of men and material to cross over three separate bridges; but one of them, Bevil's Bridge, was washed out; at another, Genito Bridge, the materials to shore it up had never arrived. Lee improvised: in the first case, three separate corps—Gordon's, Longstreet's, and Mahone's—were densely wedged onto a single bridge; for the second, the Confederates found a nearby railway pass that they neatly planked over. These delays, costing the Confederates in manpower, in stamina, and, most precious of all, in ticks of the clock, held up the completion of the crossing until the following evening. But they were hardly fatal. For now, the rebels continued to retain their lead; there was little reason to believe this would change.

Managing the retreat, the stoic Lee himself made it across the Appomattox only on the morning of April 4, at 7:30 A.M. Like his men, he had scarcely slept since leaving Petersburg and Richmond. But this morning, his hopes—and theirs—rose at the stirring thought of the relief waiting for them in Confederate boxcars on the Danville line at Amelia. Here would be the sorely needed rations. Several hours later, around midday, Amelia itself came into view—a sleepy village of unpaved streets, with houses neatly tucked behind tumbled roses and weathered fences, and a few small shops converging around a grassy square. Lee raced ahead. His overarching interest was not the scenery but the rail line, where he would find the waiting commissary stores—and the much-needed food.

Upon locating the boxcars, he ordered them to be opened.

This is what he found: 96 loaded caissons, 200 crates of ammunition, 164 boxes of artillery harnesses. But no bread, no beef, no bacon, no flour, no meal, no hardtack, no pork, no ham, no fruit, no cornmeal. And no milk, no coffee, no tea, no sugar. Not one single ration. Lee was stunned. Ammunition, but no food? He was coordinating a massive retreat, holding his army together, keeping the Union at bay while maintaining almost a day's lead on the brunt of Grant's men. And as he had carefully planned, his troops were successfully reuniting at Amelia. But now, a mere administrative mix-up—over food, no less—threatened to do him in. In that one torturous moment, Lee was speechless. Yet standing there, staring at the wrong train, he could not mask the "intense agony" written all over his face. Even as he straightened his broad shoulders, the catastrophic news had shaken the commander to his very depths.

Well it should have. Lee knew that the implications were as staggering as they were immediate. His men had left Richmond and Petersburg with only one day of rations. That day had come and gone, and much more hard marching lay ahead of them. If the army wasn't fed, it could literally starve. Already, weakened men and animals were slowly dropping in their tracks. But to eat now meant halting the march to find food—which meant squandering his priceless lead over Grant. And in either case, there was no guarantee that he would secure food—that day, the next, or the next after that.

Wars can turn on such seemingly minor things: a clerk's careless error, a five-minute delay in sending a communiqué, or a failure to have one clear order reconfirmed. But near-fatal errors had played unexpected roles in history before. Great men—and certainly great generals—find ways to overcome obstacles, rather than find excuses to be thwarted by them. They may command, but they may never complain—even when luckless. And somehow, they move on. So it was for the resolute Lee; halting was out of the question. Nor was this mere soldierly vanity or military stubbornness. Lee knew, too, that if fate and luck had betrayed him here, they might well do the same to his foe. Anything could still happen: given time and "the worst possible" roads, Grant could stumble, or get overconfident, or succumb to sloppiness. Or like A. P. Hill, he could suddenly fall prey to an errant bullet; or like Stonewall Jackson, he could fall victim to friendly fire in the heat and smoke of a skirmish.

But now, Lee's first priority was his army. The general wasted little time, quickly giving the bad news to his division commanders and then writing out an appeal to "the Citizens of Amelia County" in which he called on their "generosity and charity" and asked them "to supply as far as each is able the wants of the brave solders who have battled for your liberty for four years."

Then he waited.

❧   ❧   ❧

From afternoon well into the night, thousands of hungry men, their bellies growling, converged upon the little town, all bewildered by the lack of food. But that evening, as Lee rode past the Second Corps, the troops let out a lusty cheer, throwing up their hands, shouting and waving. It was a small signal, but an important one nonetheless. His men may have lacked food, but they certainly still had heart; these veterans were hardly giving up. But as they fell asleep once again on empty stomachs, Lee well knew that heart alone would not allow them to continue.

As dawn broke on April 5, he received his answer.

The situation was ugly. The citizens of Amelia County had already been cleaned out by Confederate impressment crews and the exigencies of war. Lee's forage wagons came back virtually empty: there were no pigs, no sheep, no hogs, no cattle, no provender. And there would be no breakfast that morning for the men. Growing increasingly anxious, Lee knew that his only option now was to rouse his army and begin a hard, forced march toward Danville—where a million and a half rations were stored. It was 104.5 miles by railroad; four grueling days by foot; but, he calculated, this time could be whittled down to only one day if rations were rushed forward by train to Burkeville, a mere eighteen miles down the line. Lee dispatched an order by wire. Would it work? Just as he could no longer wait in Amelia for rations, no longer could he wait for an answer. With the buffer of the Appomattox River gone and crucial hours lost, Grant's men were now dangerously closing in. There was no time to waste.

It was, in fact, worse than Lee realized. Lee and his generals already knew the price that Union raiders had been exacting with their slashing hit-and-run strikes along the rear of the retreating Confederate lines. So stinging and furious were the Union assaults that the rebels could not stop even to bury their dead. But they had at least been confined to the rear. Now, however, some seven miles northwest of Amelia Court House, Federal cavalry had destroyed Confederate supply wagons arriving from Richmond. And they had not simply absconded with the material; they had ignominiously burned it, leaving behind charred wrecks that littered the ground. The Union was drawing closer.

Lee hastily mounted Traveller and immediately ordered his men to move toward Burkeville. It was early morning, April 5.

A cold hard rain began to fall over the empty Virginia land.

❧   ❧   ❧

Sometime after one o'clock that afternoon, Lee learned that the race had tightened. Just outside Jetersville, itself a ragtag town consisting of little more than a collection of weathered wooden houses scattered alongside the rail line, Union cavalry had beaten the rebels to the punch; earthworks were blocking the retreat path like a dam; battle flags had been raised; and well-fed bluecoats were peering over the lines. Dug in, "thick and high," the Federals were waiting.

Earlier, one of Lee's key lieutenants, General James Longstreet, had already sought to dislodge them; convinced that it was only cavalry in the way, he briskly attacked. It was indeed Federal cavalry, he discovered, but with one crucial difference: Sheridan's horsemen were now backed by two Federal corps strung out between Lee and North Carolina. The road of escape—through Burkeville—had been cut off.

Lee, however, would not be denied. At least not at first. Riding down the retreat line, he cast a sidelong glance, lifted his field glasses, and gazed out at the freshly dug Union fortifications. His latest plans thwarted, he wasted no time in licking his wounds. For several tense moments, he considered one last massive and final assault, in which his men would be faced with winning a crushing victory or dying heroically with their flags down. But however tempting, such thoughts were ultimately built on vanity and shifting sands, and Lee knew it. The Union troops were too well entrenched, and his army was in no condition for an all-out battle. So, instead, Lee quietly opted to set his men back in motion, again. This time due west, for Lynchburg.

Thus was delivered what many regimental commanders considered to be "the most cruel marching order" that they had ever given.

✴   ✴   ✴

To grasp the full horror of the march it is necessary to make it yourself. The landscape constantly changes: open fields are exasperatingly punctuated by high hedges and dense windbreaks that are impossible to see through or over or around. On the other side, they seamlessly merge into swamps, or dense, claustrophobic woods, or undergrowth so thick as to be a second forest, all but impassable; or, conversely, they run into long, muddy tracts, known euphemistically as Virginia quicksand.

Once more, Lee pushed his men to the outer limits of human endurance. "I know that the men and animals are exhausted," he bluntly told one of his generals, "but it is necessary to tax their strength." And remarkably, once more, they complied. Wagons bounced along the rutted roads, and the ground burned beneath soldiers' aching feet. Damp from the day's rain, their senses numbed from too little nourishment, they stumbled along with scarcely a word of complaint. But by now, they were fighting a second struggle, this one from within. The dreadful consequences were inevitable: without food and deprived of sleep, the body begins to feed on itself, consuming vital muscle, raping invaluable tissue, robbing itself of what little energy is left. At the precipice of bare sustenance, thoughts become woozy; some experience a light-headedness, others even hallucinate. And with each hour, the situation worsens: initiative is deadened, and judgment becomes impaired, giving many the mental capacity of a small child. The elements, too—the sun, the wind, and the rain—become merciless. So does thirst. Limbs struggle to obey the simplest motor commands, and each step is like hauling oneself up a mountain. Yet somehow, Lee's men inched forward.

How did they do it? After Amelia, what sustained them? In part, they rose to their feet because there was no other option; to be left behind was perhaps to be captured. Or to die. But this is at best an incomplete explanation. A better one is that these were also now the hardiest of Lee's veterans; like their leader, they, too, were nourished with an iron discipline, even as they were fueled by the last legs of adrenaline. Like Lee, these men were not quitters. And foremost, also like Lee, they believed not only in their commanding general but in their cause. It is a staggering fact that of the several thousand Confederate soldiers taken prisoner by the Federals after the battle of Five Forks on April 1, not even a full 100 would swear the oath of allegiance to the Union. Even when promised release and safe passage home, they refused, bitterly cursing those "cowards and traitors" who would raise their hands or sign their names.

But unless they ate, moving at this grueling pace, their life expectancies could be measured in days and, for some men, in mere hours. As they marched, the Army of Northern Virginia tore branches off trees, fitfully gnawed at wild buds, or even peeled and ate the bark itself. Every sudden halt saw a new round of men, like dim, purgatorial souls, pitifully sink to their knees or senselessly wander off in search of food or the restful escape of a long, deep sleep. Artillery mules collapsed, forgotten, in roads turned liquid by the rain; wagons slid into muddy ruts and abruptly halted, sunk axle-deep and waterlogged, too heavy for the malnourished horses to pull them. They were summarily abandoned. And weary men discarded their weapons so as to have only themselves to drag along. In every direction, the dead—men, mules, and horses—began to litter the roadside. Dense columns of smoke rose from exploding vehicles, and shells burst after being touched by flames. "It was now a race for life or death," one soldier concluded. Indeed it was.

Following alongside, Lee learned from two captured Federal spies that the Union was gaining ground. He pushed his men that much harder.

❧   ❧   ❧

Nighttime fell. It didn't matter. Morning now seamlessly intermingled with evening, darkness with sunset, breakfast with dinner, the fifth of

April with the sixth, two hours with eight hours, eight hours with sixteen hours, and eventually, twenty-four hours with forty hours. Hungry, with barely one night of rest in three days, many of the men wandered forward in a giddy, phantasmagoric state, slipping in and out of sleep and confusion as they walked. The evening was little better: as the long, black night wore on, more troops fell by the wayside; they would halt for a few moments' rest, and fail to rise, their dazed eyes gazing haplessly at Lee's line, still lumbering west. One commander pronounced it an evening of "gloomy silence."

Actually, it was more than that. At this point, marching for yet another night under the cover of darkness, the retreat had become a confused, tangled skein. Always in the western direction, at various points the passage led northward, southward, and for brief spurts, paradoxically eastward, now often following the longer route rather than the shorter one. Little streams suddenly posed formidable obstacles; flimsy pole bridges often had to be repaired, consuming invaluable hours and energy; jagged rocks, fallen branches, and even small stones tripped up weary and blistered feet. The men moved on with sad glances and few words. And to complicate matters, since Deatonville, there were not enough roads leading west to absorb the tens of thousands of soldiers and hundreds of guns and wagons. A network of parallel roads had collapsed into one single dirt lane; here, men and wagons and animals, moving at a testudinal pace, were thickly sandwiched in between, like debris trapped in a narrow, sluggish stream. And most ominous of all for Lee, the approaching high hills and thick pinewoods—daunting for the hardiest of men—now favored Grant's offensive, and not his retreat.

It was, in one historian's words, "just the setting for a military tragedy."

The toll itself began to wear on Lee. Still outwardly calm, his face nonetheless looked "sunken," "haggard," his resolution waning. In truth, though, it wasn't. For one thing, as far as he knew, the essential fact of his retreat had not yet unalterably changed; he still harbored hopes of dropping down to North Carolina, beyond the Roanoke River. For another, there was suddenly the prospect of food to spur his men on. That afternoon, he had learned that more than 80,000 rations of meal and bread—and even such delicacies as French soup packaged in tinfoil along with whole hams—were definitively waiting in Farmville. Nineteen miles away.

So it was in that direction that the Confederates picked up their step and began again, in one long, snaking line, to move.

✻ ✻ ✻

For his part, Grant was wasting no time; this was the opportunity that he had hoped for. But, summoned to Jetersville by Phil Sheridan, the Union commander now flirted with potential disaster. With only a handful of staff and fourteen cavalry, he took off through hostile country, riding for sixteen miles in the dark along unsecured roads. This meant that for several hours—some twelve times longer than at the start of Cold Harbor, perhaps more than four times as long as it took for A. P. Hill to be killed—he was out of contact not just with his own commanders, but with most of his army as well. However, even as Lee's luck seemed to turn against him, Grant's seemed to be holding. Sheridan's cavalry and three infantry corps continued to race alongside the retreating rebels, bludgeoning them with sledgehammer blows and quick, in-and-out lightning attacks that heightened panic and fatigue. Fueled by the prospect of victory, the Federals had at long last begun to show a fighting spirit that had been sorely lacking since the Grant-Lee slugfest began almost a year before: gone were the shock and dread of another Wilderness or Cold Harbor; no longer did they fear seeing "the elephant" of battle. It showed in their very stamina: Union men, despite their own obvious exhaustion, now seemed incapable of straggling, some handily marching upward of thirty-five miles per day. And it showed in their fighting, too. Accordingly, once safely at Jetersville, Grant caught the first scent of victory. It was, however, just that: a scent. After the carnage of the last year, he knew better than to take Lee for granted.

"Lee's surely in a bad fix," he announced. "But if I were in his place, I think I could get away with part of the army." Then he added tantalizingly, "I suppose Lee will."

That, of course, was precisely what he wanted to avoid. Meeting with Sheridan and Major General George Meade, he now reiterated his central plan. He did not want to follow Lee; he wanted to get ahead of him. Playing for keeps, this time Grant refined his stratagem. At dawn the next day, April 6, he dispatched Sheridan on a northwest swing—no longer aimed at Lee's rear but intended to move ahead of him, directly positioning the hot breath of Union armies against Lee's face. For good measure, he ordered another infantry corps to join the push in the rear, completing the pincer movement.

✦ ✦ ✦

But by all accounts, there was still fight in the half-starved rebels yet. Even Grant himself recognized this. "There was," he later acknowledged, "as much gallantry displayed by some of the Confederates in these little engagements as was displayed at any time during the war." Nor did he overstate. Sweaty, exhausted, and famished beyond belief, even now, the fleeing Confederates were in no mood to capitulate. As one crusty Confederate, a Yale man, jauntily sneered: "Over sir? Over? Why sir, it's just begun. We are now where many of us have longed to be. Richmond gone, nothing to take care of, footloose, and thank God, out of these miserable lines. Now we may get what we have wanted for months—a fair fight in open field. Let them come on, if they're ready, and the sooner the better." Come they did. On April 6, after Deatonville, after the Confederates had turned right at a fork in the road, along a cold, obscure stream called Sayler's Creek.

The skirmishing at Sayler's Creek, across three separate battle sites that would eventually merge into one, began early that day and mounted as the sun climbed. At Hillsman House, a little Revolutionary-era farm home high atop a bluff—it sits there still—a Confederate matron frantically passed out ashcakes from her basement to starving soldiers, until her house was quickly overrun by Federals. The battle itself began in earnest by the first brush of afternoon, when two dangerous gaps appeared in Lee's lines, in the middle and near the front. Deadly Federal horsemen, swinging sabers and led by the dashing, yellow-haired general, George Armstrong Custer, rushed in through the holes. Soon, three Union corps had cut off a quarter of Lee's army; their guns shattered the unearthly silence of the rolling hills. A row of artillery batteries followed, decking Confederates who had been lingering in the dank and muddy swale. "I had seldom seen a fire more accurate nor one that had been more deadly," one rebel noted. Off-balance from lack of food, dazed by lack of sleep, the rebels were at first stunned, then, as one Confederate put it, they "blanched," and finally, they were "awe-struck."

Sheridan wasted no time in capitalizing on their diminished state. "Go through them!" he shouted angrily. "They're demoralized as hell."

Not completely. At the sight of the Yankees, they rallied. Rebel batteries swung into position, anchored their lines, and trained their barrels on the advancing Federals, while infantry crouched and pointed muskets at the enemy. It was only a prelude to fighting that would outdo much of the rest of the war in its savagery. One Union soldier recorded it this way: "The bullets began to fall as hailstones around us." Then: "the bullets fell thicker and faster." Then: "the leaden missiles were as thick as mosquitoes." Then: "came the horror of stepping on the wounded." And then: "When I felt a dull blow in the neighborhood of my left hip, I realized I was shot."

The slopes were now rife with the smell of powder and smoke and cries of terror. After the methodical rebel order of "Fire!" the line of advancing bluecoats wavered and broke. The first crisis was apparently over. But then, without warning, the conflict degenerated, and the insensate killing began. Vaunted rebel discipline collapsed, and the hollow-eyed Confederates sprang to their feet with empty muskets, starting after the retreating Yankees. Catching up to the Federals, they became entangled in vicious hand-to-hand combat. Men struck one another with bayonets, flogged one another with the butts of guns, and flailed at one another with their feet. "I well remember the yell of demonic triumph with which that simple country lad clubbed his musket and whirled savagely upon another victim," observed one commander. And that was merely the beginning. Grabbing one another with dirt-sodden fingers, callused, sweaty hands, and sharp fingernails, they rolled on the ground like wild beasts, biting one another's throats and ears and noses with their teeth. Blood oozed freely. So did tempers. Even officers lost their cool and dispensed with their guns, fighting with swords and, when they no longer worked, with fists. Astoundingly, in this jumble of conflict, they were no longer battling one another over territory or vital military advantage or even tactical gain, but out of sheer impulse: they were killing one another over battalion colors.

For five hours, other parts of the line in this desperate struggle were littered with scenes of comparable fury. "They clubbed their muskets, fired pistols in each other's faces and used the bayonet savagely," noted an astonished Federal. Observed another, "One Berkshire man was stabbed in the chest by a bayonet and pinned to the ground as it came out near his spine. He reloaded his gun and killed the confederate who fell across him." As the wild melee grew, men accidentally killed their own. "I saw a young fellow of one of my companies jam the muzzle of his musket against the back of the head of his most intimate friend, clad in a Yankee overcoat, and blow his brains out," recalled a surviving Confederate.

Explained another simply: "I never before got into a fight like this."

But the Yankees kept coming, and the battered rebels, their assaults increasingly uncoordinated and disjointed, could not keep up the ferocity. They tried and failed and tried and failed. The bloody reverse was swift and incalculable. By day's end, they were overwhelmed; the dead lay so close and dense that bodies had to be dragged away to let a single horse pass. It was the South's worst defeat of the entire campaign. All told, Grant's army had captured an astonishing 6,000 rebels—Lee's son Custis and the one-legged General Richard Ewell among them—and destroyed much of their wagon train. Adding up the killed and wounded, Lee had lost up to 8,000. Lee himself felt the sting of defeat sharply. Late in the afternoon, he rode out to a high ridge overlooking the battlefield. Sitting on Traveller, on this small rise, the general found the sight astonishing. Lee was a badly shaken man.

"My God!" he cried out, watching his vanquished men lurch across the chaotic edges of shifting skirmish lines. "Has the army been dissolved?"

Bill Mahone, the tall, bearded general, was there, riding at his side. Deeply touched, he took a moment to steady his voice, then quickly offered words of encouragement. "No general, here are troops ready to do their duty."

As Mahone and his men drew into a line to hold back the Federals, Lee's temper again flared; he, too, was drawn to the fight. Leaning forward in his saddle, he snatched a single battle flag, to rally fresh troops as well as retreating men. On this day, it was no idle gesture. Earlier in the fighting, one flag bearer had been brought down by an artillery shell, only to have his brother grab the standard and promptly be shot through the head. Another Confederate quickly reached for the colors and also fell. So did a fourth. And so did a fifth, until the flag was firmly planted by a sixth in a low bush. Now it was Lee who sought to cheat fate. Riding past Mahone's assembled troops, he held the flag staff high in one hand. At the top of the rise, he stopped and waited. The wind caught the flag, and it snapped and curled around his silver mane, flapping about him and draping his body in Confederate red. Mahone's men fell deathly silent, and then this collective hush was punctuated by a scattered, spontaneous cry emanating from the frenzied survivors stumbling back: "Where's the man who won't follow Uncle Robert!"

Engaged and erect, Lee clutched the red silk flag as the sun gently set over the slaughter at Sayler's Creek. By now, he must have felt close to total despair. During the course of the war he had forged a mighty army in his own image, waged titanic battles against the enemy, and helped hold together a fledgling nation. Yet now, every hope had died glimmering. Barren, horrid, in the collective memory of the Confederacy, this one day would be forever known as "Black Thursday."

But Lee's desolation was ironic—for his actions to come in the next fearful, brooding thirty-six hours, every bit as much as those of the last four years, would enshrine him in immortality.

❧　❧　❧

With a dusting of snow flurries softening the Virginia land, the North smelled blood. After Sayler's Creek, Phil Sheridan tersely wired Grant:

"If the thing is pressed, I think that Lee will surrender." When Lincoln read this, his melancholy spirits soared.

Lincoln bluntly telegraphed to Grant: "Let the *thing* be pressed."

❧   ❧   ❧

It was now April 7. But Lee refused to be vanquished.

Indeed, the early morning actually looked promising. Lee's remaining forces had again crossed the Appomattox River to arrive in Farmville, where the first rations of the march awaited them. While the food was dispensed, campfires were hastily built; bacon sizzled; and corn bread was devoured. The other piece of good news—or so Lee believed—was that once nestled on the north side of the Appomattox, his army could finally steal some breathing room; the swollen river was too high to be forded by Union infantry, and he had ordered the bridges behind them burned. His troops, at last able to eat and rest, still had two options: try again to turn south toward Danville, or set out for Lynchburg and the sheltering protection of the Blue Ridge mountains. But in choosing to cross the Appomattox, Lee had also made a deeply controversial, if not flawed, decision: he had opted for a longer route rather than a shorter one.

Meanwhile, at his headquarters, Lee paused to speak with the secretary of war, John Breckinridge, who had ridden out on horseback from Richmond. The fact that Breckinridge, among the last of the Confederates to leave the capital, could have reached Farmville with such relative ease underscored the still limited control that Grant's armies had over the Virginia land. The two conferred, and then Breckinridge set out for Danville and Jefferson Davis. The next day, he would wire Davis, informing him of Lee's plans. But Breckinridge, himself a military man, would add one somber conclusion: "The situation," he noted, "is not favorable."

It would seem like an understatement by then. For just as quickly as rations were being handed out, a new threat loomed from the east. Inexplicably, one of Lee's generals had neglected to blast High Bridge— a massive steel and brick structure spanning a floodplain half a mile wide, at a spectacular height of 126 feet. Frantically riding back, an officer finally torched it, but the delay was fatal; a hard-marching Federal column reached the accompanying wagon bridge in time to stomp out the flames. Now there was no river between Lee and Grant's lead troops; indeed, the distance separating them was barely four miles. With Union soldiers approaching, Lee's army stood nearly naked to assault. Enraged, the general must have felt the sickening sense of déjà vu at yet another mishap with dismal consequences—he was forced to quickly withdraw his men from Farmville and recross the Appomattox to escape the threat, even as Union cavalry drew so close that fighting broke out in the town's streets. The priceless supply train quickly rolled away, while thousands of starving soldiers, who had not yet drawn their rations, watched in agony. Bedlam followed; haversacks still open, muskets in hand, men turned and raced across bridges that were already lit and burning.

Once more, Federal and Confederate soldiers clashed. But now, the shards of Lee's army successfully fended off the Union, smashing the bluecoats along both their front and their flank, even taking some 300 prisoners, including a Union general—all under the direct eye of Lee himself. This time, the rebels inflicted more casualties than they suffered—in fact, the Union had lost some 8,000 men in just the last week alone—and by moonlight, the road west to Lynchburg now beckoned.

"Keep your command together and in good spirits," Lee reassured his son Rooney. "Don't let them think of surrender."

And he concluded: "I will get you out of this."

❧　❧　❧

Grant, fast on Lee's heels, thought otherwise. Arriving in Farmville that afternoon, he took pen to paper and decided it was time to communicate directly with Lee. The note complete, he ordered Brigadier General Seth Williams, his inspector general and special envoy, to carry it under a flag of truce to the Confederate lines. Williams and an orderly set off across High Bridge, reaching rebel lines in darkness. There, they were met with a hail of gunfire from Confederate pickets that killed the orderly.

But an hour later, at 9 P.M., Williams again displayed the flag. This time, the letter was received.

❧　❧　❧

Lee was handed Grant's communiqué about ten o'clock, while he and Longstreet were conferring in a small cottage. Snatching the paper, he opened it himself.

Headquarters Armies of the United States
April 7 1865—5 P.M.

General R.E. Lee,
Commanding C.S. Army:

General: The results of the last week must convince you of the hope-lessness of further resistance on the part of the Army of Northern Virginia in this struggle. I feel that it is so, and regard it as my duty to shift from myself the responsibility of any further effusion of blood, by asking you the surrender of that portion of the C.S. Army known as the Army of Northern Virginia.

Very respectfully, your obedient servant
U. S. Grant, Lieutenant-General,
Commanding Armies of the United States.

Lee studied this silently, and then without a word or change in expression, passed it to Longstreet. Longstreet read the message and handed it back, with two additional words: "Not yet."

Lee agreed, but he also concluded that "it must be answered." He rose and, without summoning his secretary, personally composed his response to Grant. Thus began perhaps the most extraordinary correspondence the country has ever witnessed.

7th Apl '65

Genl
I have recd your note of this date. Though not entertaining the opinion you express of the hopelessness of further resistance of the Army
of N. Va.—I reciprocate your desire to avoid the useless effusion of
blood, & therefore before considering your proposition, ask the terms
you will offer on the condition of its surrender.

Very respy your obt. Servt
R. E. Lee, Genl

Lt Genl U. S. Grant
Commd Armies of the U. States

If Grant was blunt, Lee was being cagey. While he was willing to probe,
to see what terms might exist for some honorable conclusion, like a general settlement, he was still unwilling to give up, let alone to surrender. Never
was this more apparent than on the morning of April 8, as the frantic retreat
continued. Having already consolidated his remaining troops under two
commands, Gordon in the advance and Longstreet in the rear, he said of
Grant, rather testily, "I will strike that man a blow in the morning."

Actually, this day's retreat, despite three consecutive all-night marches, was the easiest of the six. The sun shone warm; the ground lay fresh;
there were signs of budding trees and new green grass, and, here, there
were few of the ugly marks of war upon the land. But if this was an
omen, it was a false one. That afternoon, Lee was approached by an officer, on behalf of several in the command, about the possibility of surrender. His response was at once abrupt and chill.

"Surrender?" he thundered coldly. "I trust it has not come to that! We
certainly have too many brave men to think of laying down our arms.
They still fight with great spirit whereas the enemy does not."

More soberly he continued, "besides, if I were to intimate to General
Grant that I would listen to terms, he would at once regard it as such

an evidence of weakness that he would demand unconditional surrender"—Lee then paused—"And sooner than that I am resolved to die. Indeed, we must all determine to die at our posts."

In hindsight, these words read like a quaint anachronism, but on April 8, they would shape the tense back-and-forth in the life of these two armies and the country at large over the ensuing hours and the following day.

✦   ✦   ✦

As the Unionists, following behind, retraced Lee's steps, the scene was a harsh testimony to the toll of war and to the wretched condition of Lee's army. Everywhere, the road was littered with remnants and ruins— discarded cannon and battery wagons, shivering horses so weak that they could scarcely lift their heads when touched, abandoned forage wagons, and ragged mules starved to the bone. And, too, there were the signs of desperate men: deserted muskets were randomly thrust in the mud, haversacks hung limply from tree limbs, and empty canteens were strewn about. Farm carts jammed with household wares were stuck in boulder-strewn roads. In the mad chase to catch up with Lee, however, they were ignored, as were the dead Confederate bodies. Only the exhausted and sullen rebels lying by the roadside or wandering aimlessly in search of food merited attention and were rounded up.

✦   ✦   ✦

Shortly before dusk on April 8, as he dismounted to make camp for the night, Lee received a second letter from Grant. Grant stated that "peace" was his "great desire," and the only condition that he demanded was that the officers and men "be disqualified from taking up arms" until exchanged. Unknown to Lee, Grant had labored more than six hours to compose this reply, and, in a tactful combination of diplomacy and insight, he suggested that Lee could be spared the humiliation of surrendering in person, that a surrender could in fact be conducted by officers whom the Confederate general could propose to "designate."

But Grant had sorely misread his opponent. With his army still march-ing roughly parallel to the Appomattox, Lee would hear nothing of it. As audacious in diplomacy as he was in war, he responded with the sug-gestion to Grant that they meet to explore a general peace discussion—a proposal similar to his unsuccessful effort in early March. Indeed, what is perhaps so remarkable about this letter is that, of all the senti-ments it reflects, despair and surrender are not among them.

Genl

I received at a late hour your note of today. In mine of yesterday I did not intend to propose the surrender of the Army of N. Va.—but to ask the terms of your proposition. To be frank, I do not think the emer-gency has arisen to call for the surrender of this Army, but as the restoration of peace should be the sole object of all, I desire to know whether your proposals would lead to that and I cannot therefore meet you with a view to surrender . . . but as far as your proposal may affect the C.S. forces under my command & tend to the restoration of peace, I shall be pleased to meet you at 10 A.M. tomorrow on the old state road to Richmond between the picket lines of the two armies.

The letter was sealed, and the courier dispatched. It was a bold gamble. Grant would not buy it.

❧   ❧   ❧

But for all Grant's confidence, and for the vast disparity between the two armies, one well-fed and abundantly armed, the other malnourished and its numbers pitifully whittled down, Grant clearly could not shake his own doubts about the ever-elusive Lee. At the day's end, with no response from Lee, he collapsed with a severe migraine. By the time Grant received Lee's second dispatch, he had been trying to soothe himself with mus-tard plasters on his wrists and neck and with hot footbaths. Nothing worked. The anxiety was killing him. Now, under a soft midnight sky, with a bright, nearly full moon overhead, Grant sat up on a sofa in a comfortable frame house, abandoned by its occupants, scanned Lee's letter, then handed it to his chief of staff to read aloud. The aide was furious at Lee's brash response, but Grant just coolly shook his head.

Then the Union commander said more ominously: "It looks as if Lee still means to fight."

❧   ❧   ❧

It was as though Grant read his old foe's mind. With enemy artillery roaring in the background, that night Lee and his weary lieutenants gathered around a campfire in the woods near Appomattox Court House. In the distance, they could see the faint glow of Union fires ringing the rebel army. The Confederates were almost entirely surrounded, outnumbered nearly six to one, with little food, little hope of resupply, little prospect for immediate reinforcement. But there was still the distinct prospect of escape, especially if those fires were of cavalry, not infantrymen. And before the opportunity slipped away, Lee hoped to turn the momentary lull to his advantage. Six straight days of Lee's relentless march westward had not dimmed his audacity, his remaining men's courage, or his desire to avoid surrender and somehow salvage victory. He devised another plan for breaking through the enemy lines: his men would attack as soon as possible, attempting to slice a hole through Grant's slumbering army, and if successful, they would resume the march southward. General John Gordon, one of Lee's most daring officers, was chosen to lead the breakout. And, if necessary, there remained a fallback position: they could make their way to the Blue Ridge mountains, where, Lee had once said, he could hold out "for twenty years."

Before dawn on April 9, in the pitch black, the advance was to begin. It was Palm Sunday, the day that marked the start of the Holy Week and Jesus' arrival in Jerusalem. Neither the day nor its significance would have been lost on Lee or his men.

❧   ❧   ❧

At four o'clock that morning, one of Grant's aides entered his room to wake him, but it was empty. The commanding general was already up and dressed, and was found outside in the waning darkness, pacing furiously, clutching his aching head in both hands. The throbbing migraine had not abated. Gingerly, the aide suggested that a cup of coffee might do some good. Grant took his suggestion. The coffee helped, but only somewhat. The business of war, however, would not wait, and Grant finally set about answering Lee's most recent letter. He was "anxious for peace," he wrote back, his head still pounding, and hoped that the war might yet be settled without "the loss of another life." But the ten o'clock meeting would "lead to no good," he stressed. "I have no authority to treat on the subject of peace."

As the fighting commenced and further chaos and confusion beset the battle lines, Grant's letter would not reach Lee. That is, at least not in time.

❧ ❧ ❧

At 5 A.M., just beyond Appomattox Court House, the momentous day began in earnest. A fog hovered over the landscape like a thick, sprawling ghost; the rolling hills soon echoed with the staccato rattle of artillery; and the Sunday stillness was again shattered by the piercing cry of the rebel yell. Gordon's men fought with a special fury. They drove Federal cavalry from their positions, captured several guns, duly cleared the road of bluecoats, and then swept forward to the crest of a hill. Suddenly, below them, concealed in the woodlands, lay the inexorable logic of the mathematics of war: a solid wall of blue, some two miles wide, was advancing—two Yankee infantry corps, with two other Union corps closing in on Lee's rear. Quipped one soldier at glimpsing this awesome sight: "Lee couldn't go forward, he couldn't go backward, and he couldn't go sideways."

Three hours later, around 8 A.M., a courier from Gordon hastily carried the apocalyptic message to Lee. "I have fought my corps to a frazzle," he wrote. "And I fear I can do nothing . . . "

Thus the ominous choice was finally set before Lee: surrender or throw his life on one last murderous fight—Lincoln's feared Armageddon. Lee summoned General Longstreet, who brought Mahone and Lee's chief of artillery, the twenty-nine-year-old brigadier general, E. Porter Alexander. All were expecting a council of war. Instead, the discussion turned to surrender. When a moment of vacillation came and an opening occurred, Alexander, one of the most talented and innovative men in Lee's command, took it. Pleading with his chief not to give up, Alexander saw another recourse: a third option.

"You don't care for military glory or fame," he protested, "but we are proud of your name and the record of this army. We want to leave it to our children . . . a little more blood more or less now makes no difference." Instead, Alexander suggested a Confederate trump card, in fact, the specter most dreaded by Lincoln, Grant, and Sherman: that the men take to the woods, evaporate into the hills, and become guerrillas. "Two thirds" would get away, Alexander contended. "We would be like rabbits or partridges in the bushes," he said, "and they could not scatter to follow us."

A veteran of Fredericksburg and Gettysburg, Cold Harbor and Petersburg, Alexander was so valued by Lee that Jefferson Davis once noted, he is "one of a very few whom Gen Lee wd [would] not give to anybody." Thus, Lee was listening carefully to his aide. There were no more miracles to be performed, but there were indeed certainly still options. And this option—guerrilla warfare—was not one to be lightly ignored. During the Revolutionary War, Lee's own father had fought the British as a partisan. Moreover, on April 4, a fleeing President Jefferson Davis had issued his own call for a guerrilla struggle. Yet it was Lee's judgment—and not Davis's—that would be most decisive. ("Country be damned," roared former Virginia Governor Henry Wise to Lee. "There *is* no country. You are the country to these men!") Alexander was already prepared to take to the bush rather than surrender—and so, he later indicated, were countless other men. In fact, that very morning after Gordon's breakout failed, some cavalry had already slipped away; two elite artillery units had destroyed their gun carriages and headed toward the hills; and hundreds more infantry had vanished into the empty, largely unsettled countryside.

At that very moment, in fact, the rest of Lee's men were looking to their commanding general for a signal, to tell them what he wanted them to do.

Robert E. Lee paused, weighing his answer, the question of guerrilla warfare ricocheting around in his brain. No less than for Davis, the momentous step of surrender was anathema to him. Here, surely, was seduction. And in this fateful moment, while he considered his response— both what he would decide and what he would reject—the aging general would alter the course of the nation's history for all time. It would constitute perhaps Lee's finest moment ever.

❧ ❧ ❧

Throughout the years variously referred to as "guerrillaism," or "guerrilleros," or "partisans," or "Partheyganger," or "bushwhackers," guerrilla warfare is and always has been the very essence of how the weak make war against the strong. Insurrectionist, subversive, chaotic, its methods are often chosen instinctively, but throughout time, they have worked with astonishing regularity. Its application is classic and surprisingly simple: shock the enemy by concentrating strength against weakness. And as Mao would one day explain, "The strategy is to pit one man against ten, but the tactic is to pit ten men against one." Countering numerical superiority, guerrillas have always employed secrecy, deception, and terror as their ultimate tools. They move quickly, attack fast, and just as quickly scatter. They strike at night—or in the day; they hit hard in the rain, or just as hard in the sunshine; they rain terror when troops are eating or when they have just concluded an exhausting march; they assault military targets, or, just as often, hunt down random civilians. In short, they may hit at the rear of the enemy, or at its infrastructure, or, most devastating of all, at its psyche; the only constant is that they move when least expected, and invariably in a way to maximize impact.

And as military men have often learned the hard way, guerrilla warfare does the job. By luring their adversaries into endless, futile pursuit, guerrillas erode not just the enemy's strength, but, far more importantly, the enemy's morale as well. Every American, of course, in the final third of the twentieth century saw just how effective guerrilla warfare is. They watched it be turned against them with frightening success in Vietnam. But neither has America been its only victim. An astounding number of other world powers, large and small, have been humbled by guerrilla war in the past century alone: at the turn of the twentieth century, the heavily outnumbered Boers in South Africa would stave off the mightiest force on the globe, the British empire, for a full four years. The Algerians used guerrilla tactics with devastating success against the far more powerful French; Castro handily deployed them in Cuba; the Khmer Rouge employed them to come to power in Cambodia; the PLO exploited them for over three decades in the West Bank of Israel; and, just as notably, against enormous odds the Mujahadeen managed to humiliate the Soviet army in Afghanistan. Robert E. Lee, of course, knew about none of this. Nor did he need to. Far from being simply a phenomenon of the most recent century, the awesome pedigree of guerrilla warfare runs back to the earliest days of human combat. Much of this he would—and in fact did—know about.

The list of effective guerrilla wars since mankind's earliest days is a long one. Five hundred years before the coming of Christ, the ceaseless harassment and lightning strikes of the nomadic Scythians blunted the efforts of the Persian king, Darius I, to subdue them; then, three and a half centuries later, the Israelite Judas Maccabeus waged successful guerrilla operations against the Syrians. In Spain, no less than the Romans (after suffering a number of humiliating defeats) required several long centuries before they could finally surmount the hit-and-run tactics of the Lusitanians and Celtiberians. Much later, in Wales, the English conquest succeeded only in 1282, after some 200 years of stubborn, acrimonious struggle and the widespread use of encastellation—covering the country with small strongholds—which presaged the blockhouse arrangements of ensuing centuries. By the time of the Civil War, even as the emphasis remained on large armies and full-scale battles (as one Prussian general put it, "the small war was swallowed by big war"), guerrilla efforts were well established as a viable mode of warfare. By then, the French ominously referred to guerrilla battle as a war of extermination requiring *"un peu de fanatisme"*; General Baron de Jomini, a Swiss military man and the most widely studied theorist in the mid-nineteenth-century world, warned in his famous work, *Précis de l'art de la guerre*: "National wars are the most formidable of all"; and European statesmen, eyeing the growing nationalist passions sweeping across the continent, agreed, speaking direly of guerrilla warfare presaging the *"bellum omnium contra omnes,"* or "the war of all against all."

The actual word "guerrilla" came from the Spanish insurgency against France in the early 1800s, a conflict Jefferson Davis frequently referred to. In 1807, while Napoleon's mighty legions were mired down in Spain, the great general once grumbled in a fit of pique that this guerrilla war was his "Spanish ulcer." And firsthand, he watched his ulcer grow, as regional bands seemed to spring up everywhere. As one observer at the time noted, "the priest girded up his black robe and stuck a pistol on his belt," "the student threw aside his books and grasped the sword," "the shepherd forsook his flock" and "the husbandman his home." Spurred on by small victories, the bands quickly multiplied and began attacking with greater conviction and fury than ever before, until at one point, guerrillas were largely responsible for containing three of Napoleon's armies. Remarkably, Napoleon met similar tragedy against poorly fitted yet equally determined guerrillas later on, in his ill-fated invasion of Russia. This, too, was of course well known to Lee and Davis.

But these were, by no means, the only widely known examples of guerrilla war. Equally familiar to nineteenth-century Americans were the Thirty Years War and French Religious Wars; the experience of Frederick the Great in Bohemia; of Wellington in Portugal; the partisan war against Revolutionary France in the Royalist Vendée; the Netherlands against the Spain of Philip II; Switzerland against the Hapsburg empire; the Polish uprisings in 1831 and 1861; and the nineteenth-century struggle of Caucasian tribes against their Russian invaders. At the same time as the Civil War was ending, in South America the tiny country of Paraguay was waging a fierce struggle against a triple alliance of Brazil, Argentina, and Uruguay, whose combined population outnumbered its by thirty to one; it would hold them at bay for six years. And then, of course, there was the most honorable example of them all, the American experience in employing guerrilla tactics against the British in the War of Independence. Using muddy roads and swollen streams to their advantage, American guerrilla heroes like Colonel Francis Marion, known as the "Swamp Fox"; Thomas Sumter; Andrew Pickens; and General Nathaniel Green harassed the European battlefield trained-and-bred British. And beginning with the "Liberty Boys" in Georgia, who first stole gunpowder from a British ship in 1775, the American insurgents had not shied away from employing guerrilla tactics in battle, in historic engagements like Kings Mountain and Cowpens, and then Guilford Courthouse—which British General Lord Cornwallis labeled "truly savage" and which another British general forlornly spoke of as "that sort of victory which ruins an army."

For his part, West Point graduate and former U.S. secretary of war Jefferson Davis was aware of much, if not all, of this illuminating past. Now, in April 1865, with his government on the run, he was thinking precisely about such things as a war of extermination, a Confederate ulcer, a national war that ruins the enemy. In short, guerrilla resistance.

The day after Richmond fell, Davis had called on the Confederacy to shift from a static conventional war in defense of territory and population centers to a dynamic guerrilla war of attrition, designed to wear down the North and force it to conclude that keeping the South in the Union would not be worth the interminable pain and ongoing sacrifice. "We have now entered upon a new phase of a struggle the memory of which is to endure for all ages," he declared. ". . . Relieved from the necessity of guarding cities and particular points, important but not vital to our defense, with an army free to move from point to point and strike in detail detachments and garrisons of the enemy, operating on the interior of our own country, where supplies are more accessible, and where the foe will be far removed from his own base and cut off from all succor in case of reverse, nothing is now needed to render our triumph certain but the exhibition of our own unquenchable resolve." He concluded thus: "Let us but will it, and we are free."

In effect, Davis was proposing that Lee disperse his army before it was finally cornered. Years later, Charles Adams, the grandson and great-grandson of two presidents, remarked balefully, "I shudder to think of what would happen" if "Robert E. Lee [was] of the same turn of mind of Jefferson Davis . . ." But was he? From a military point of view, the plan had considerable merit. The Confederacy was well supplied with long mountain ranges, endless swamps, and dark forests to offer sanctuary for a host of determined partisans. Its people knew the countryside intimately and instinctively and had all the talents necessary for adroit bushwhacking, everything from the shooting and the riding, the tracking and the foraging, the versatility and the cunning, right down to the sort of dash necessary for this lifestyle. Moreover, given that most of them would be battle-hardened and well-trained veterans, arguably an organized Confederate guerrilla army could be among the most effective partisan groups in all of history. For its part, no longer opposed by major concentrations of military regulars, the Union army would then be forced to undertake the onerous task of occupying the entire Confederacy—an unwieldy occupation at best, which would entail Federal forces having to subdue and patrol and police an area as large as all of today's France, Spain, Italy, Switzerland, Germany, and Poland combined. Even in early April 1865, the Union had actually conquered only a relatively small part of the physical South—to be sure, crucial areas for a conventional conflict, like Nashville, New Orleans, Memphis, and, of course, the crown jewel of Richmond—but all would be largely meaningless in a bitter, protracted guerrilla war. As the Romans had found out 2,000 years earlier, cities could become useless baggage weighing down the military forces, what the ancient commanders memorably called "*impedimenta.*"

In moving to occupy vast stretches of land defended only by small, dispersed forces, Grant's strategy of exhaustion would be turned on its head. Consider the nearly insuperable difficulties that he would face: up to that point, no more than roughly a million Union men had been in arms at any one given time. But confronted with a guerrilla phase, the Union would not be able to demobilize its armies, which is always problematic for a democracy, then and now. Wartime conscription would have to continue, with all its attendant political difficulties and war-weariness. Even granting the North's theoretical ability to put more than 2 million men under arms, it would be unlikely that the Federals could ever pacify, let alone manage and oversee, more than fragmented sections of the South against a willful guerrilla onslaught. Rather than having a restored United States, in time, the country could come to resemble a Swiss cheese, with Union cities here, pockets of Confederate resistance lurking there, ambiguous areas of no-man's-land in between. The cities would no doubt be firmly in Union hands, but as the days marched on, they, too, could become like embattled garrisons, where organized violence and chaos were always a real possibility. Even the North would not be safe. Indeed, in a likely harbinger of things to come, in 1864, a ragtag group of twelve Confederates, without horses, plus ten lookouts, and financed by a mere $400 in cash from the Confederate secretary of war, had crossed the Canadian border, plundered three Vermont banks, stolen $210,000, and turned the entire state into chaos. From New York to Philadelphia, and Washington to Boston, then, potential targets would abound: banks, buildings, businesses, local army outposts, and possibly even newspapers and statehouses. All were vulnerable, threatening to turn these cities into nineteenth-century versions of Belfast and Beirut. Under such a scenario, month after grinding month, even year after year, who would feel under siege: the victorious Union or the hardened guerrillas?

Across most of the South, the situation would be even more daunting. In Charles Adams's famous warning, "The Confederacy would have been reduced to smoldering wilderness." As in virtually all guerrilla wars throughout time, the Union forces would have little choice but to station outposts in every county and every sizable town; they would be forced to put a blockhouse on every railroad bridge and at every major communications center; they would be reduced to combing every sizable valley and every significant mountain range with frequent patrols. With Lee's army and other loyal Confederates—by some historians' estimates, there were still up to 175,000 men under arms who could be called upon, and virtually all agree that there were still large combat-ready forces to be mustered—dispersed into smaller, more mobile units, they could make lightning hit-and-run attacks on the invading forces from safe havens in the rugged countryside and then invisibly slip back into the population, only to reappear at a later date with renewed strength. Their molestations need not be constant or even kill many people; they need only be incessant. Terror would be the watchword. All the Union could do would be wait . . . and wait . . . and wait. And to the extent that they carried out counterinsurgency measures, they could well have found what many occupiers invariably learn: rarely do such tactics work, and in most cases, they only turn the local populace against them. As Marx would later comment on the French guerrilla experience, it would be like "the lion in the fable, tormented to death by a gnat."

The military balance would be almost meaningless. In truth, more frightening to the Union than the actual casualties it might suffer would be the psychological toll as prolonged occupiers, the profound exhaustion, the constant demoralization. Where would the stamina come from? There would be no real rest, no real respite, no true amity, nor, for that matter, any real sense of victory—only an amorphous state of neither war nor peace, raging like a low-level fever. In fact, recall this: success thus far had actually come to the Union only in the nick of time; prospects for Northern victory had seemed dim as recently as August 1864, largely because Northerners had grown weary of the war. In truth, the Northern home front had nearly crumbled first—by April 1865 an astounding 200,000 men had already deserted the Union army—and was saved only by the captures of Mobile and, more importantly, of Atlanta, which paved the way for a presidential reelection victory that Lincoln himself had, just weeks earlier, judged to be an impossibility. In fact, it was only the heartening prospects of sure and relatively sudden victory that had sustained the Federals to this time. In a guerrilla war, however, all bets would be off. The North, deprived of the fruits of closure, deprived of the legitimacy that all victors invariably clamor for, would at some point reach a moment of reckoning: how much longer would the country countenance sending its men into war? How long could it tolerate carrying out the necessary mass executions, the sweeping confiscations, the collective expulsions? At what point would it deem the agonies and cruelties of a full-scale guerrilla war, which would inevitably pervert its identity as a republic, to be no longer worth it? And when would the war become so unpopular that it could no longer be continued? We know what the French once said of a comparable experience. As its columns sought to put down the guerrilla resistance of Abdelkader in North Africa in 1833, one urgent dispatch to King Louis-Philippe stated sadly: "We have surpassed in barbarity the barbarians we came to civilize." It is hard to imagine Americans willing to pay this price for Union.

But could the South in fact carry it out? Grant and Sherman certainly had no doubt about the Confederacy's ability to wage protracted guerrilla war—it was their greatest fear. At one point, Grant himself ruminated, "To overcome a truly popular, national resistance in a vast territory without the employment of truly overwhelming force is probably impossible." As it was, the Union never had any systematic plans to cope with such an eventuality—all of Grant's efforts were principally designed to break up the Confederacy's main armies and to occupy the main cities. And what patchwork plans they did have had failed and failed them dismally in the more limited guerrilla war fought in Missouri. As General John D. Sanborn, who served under Grant's command, would later admit: "No policy worked; every effort poured fuel on the fire."

Lincoln, too, was equally concerned, and he, as much as anyone else, understood the toll guerrilla war could take on the country. On the Missouri guerrilla conflict he lamented, "Each man feels an impulse to kill his neighbors, lest he first be killed by him. Revenge and retaliation follow. And all this among honest men. But this is not all. Every foul bird comes along, and every dirty reptile rises up." Some of Lincoln's aides put it even more fearfully. Said one, guerrilla warfare is "the external visitation of evil."

Before the Civil War even began, guerrilla activity had already made its mark on the North-South conflict. On May 24, 1856, John Brown and five other abolitionists brutally murdered and mutilated five Southern settlers at Pottawatomie Creek in Kansas (Brown had read Wellington's *Memoirs* and, after personally inspecting fortifications on European battlefields, came to fancy himself a leader of guerrilla forces). Day after day for over two years, dueling bands of Free-Soil abolitionists and proslavery marauders burned, robbed, and killed in an effort to drive the other from "Bleeding Kansas," a grim dress rehearsal for the Civil War to follow. By the time war erupted in 1861, many on the bloodstained Kansas-Missouri border were already veterans of irregular warfare.

And once the war started, across the Confederacy, Southerners quickly took to guerrilla tactics. One partisan recruiter proclaimed, "It is only men I want . . . men who will pull a trigger on a Yankee with as much alacrity as they would on a mad dog, men whose consciences won't be disturbed by the sight of a vandal carcass." Such recruiters found their men in abundance. Sam Hildebrand roamed the woods of southern Missouri slaying scores of Unionists; Champ Ferguson tormented the Cumberland in Tennessee, knifing, mangling, and bludgeoning luckless Federals whenever he encountered them. Before he was eventually captured—he was summarily hanged—Ferguson personally extinguished over a hundred lives. In the swamps of Florida, John Jackson Dickison outmaneuvered, outfought, and outfoxed the bluecoats; and anarchy literally reigned in Unionist Kentucky, where brutal guerrilla bands led by Ike Berry, Marcellus Clark, and scores of others sprang up across the state. Whatever draconian measures the Union instituted, including confiscation of property and executions of five guerrillas for every loyalist killed, accomplished little. Adding insult to injury, guerrillas often shrewdly fooled Union military leadership. At one point, the partisan Jesse McNeil slipped into Cumberland, Maryland, and in a daring raid captured two Union generals, Benjamin Kelly and George Crook, narrowly missing two future presidents in the process, Congressman-elect James A. Garfield and Major William L. McKinley. (Incredibly, this was not the first time Union generals had been snatched.) And of course, there was the redoubtable chief of the Cherokee Nation, Stand Watie, whose exploits in major battles and in hit-and-run skirmishes alike made him a Confederate military hero, and eventually earned him the honor of an appointment as a Confederate brigadier general. A veteran of eighteen major battles and a multitude of smaller skirmishes, Watie and his Indian forces waged fierce guerrilla warfare along the Arkansas River valley. Among two of his most stunning victories was the capture of the federal steamboat *J. R. Williams* on June 15, 1864, and then, in a daring nighttime raid with his brigade of 800 Indians, the bold seizure of a Northern supply train carrying $1.5 million worth of Union supplies—food, clothes, boots, shoes, guns, medicine, mules, and ammunition—at the second battle of Cabin Creek in September 1864.

In fact, some of the Confederate's guerrillas became legendary, feared not simply in the North, but known internationally on both sides of the Atlantic. Of these, John Mosby was among the most dashing and prominent. Pint-sized, plucky, and daring, he was a bit of a Renaissance man. He read Shakespeare, Plutarch, Washington Irving, and Hazlitt's *Life of Napoleon*, and his words and writings were frequently sprinkled with passages from the classics. The twenty-nine-year-old had been expelled from the University of Virginia—he shot a fellow student—yet he later finagled a pardon from the governor, and then, of all things, took up the law. At the outset of the war, he was actually opposed to secession and was an "indifferent soldier" at best; though after joining Jeb Stuart's cavalry, he proved himself to be a fearless courier and cavalry scout and, when he raised a company of his own under the Partisan Ranger Act of April 1862, a remarkable guerrilla leader. His fame rapidly spread with such exploits as the capture of a Northern general, Edwin H. Stoughton, in bed with a hangover—a mere ten miles from Washington, D.C., in March 1863. "Do you know who I am?" bellowed the general, upon being so indiscreetly interrupted. Mosby shot back: "Do you know Mosby, general?" Stoughton harrumphed: "Yes! Have you got the rascal?" Mosby: "No, but *he* has got *you!*" (Mosby completed the humiliation by brazenly retreating with his prisoner in full view of Federal fortifications.) Operating on horseback at night, with stealth, surprise, and celerity, he soon earned the sobriquet of the "Grey Ghost," and the romance surrounding his exploits brought recruit after recruit to his doorstep. In turn, he was sheltered and fed by a large and sympathetic population in northern Virginia, which served as his early warning network—and his refuge. Never amounting to more than a thousand men, Mosby's partisans were confined to small platoons of several dozen. But they mauled Union outposts with such effectiveness and a whirlwind fury that the regions stretching from the Blue Ridge to the Bull Run mountains were quickly dubbed, by friends and foes alike, "Mosby's confederacy." Union supplies could not move through his territory unless well protected, and even then they were likely prey.

The destruction Mosby inflicted upon Union lines was considerable, and he was detested accordingly. Various strategies were employed— without success—to subdue him. One plan called for an elite team of sharpshooters to shadow Mosby until he was either caught or destroyed. It failed. Another promised massive arrests of local civilians in Mosby's confederacy and a wholesale destruction of their mills, barns, and crops. This, too, was done, but also failed. While Mosby still roamed freely, a frustrated General Sheridan, whom Mosby relentlessly foiled in the Shenandoah Valley, once thundered about the restless guerrilla: "Let [him] know there is a God in Israel!" Finally, Grant ordered that any of Mosby's men who were captured should be promptly shot. And in autumn of 1864, the yellow-maned General George Custer obliged, capturing six men and executing them all. Three were shot, two were hanged, and a seventeen-year-old boy was dragged bleeding and dying through the streets by two men on horses until a pistol was finally emptied into his face—while his grief-stricken mother hysterically begged for his life. But the Union's hard-line tactics collapsed when Mosby began (albeit reluctantly) hanging prisoners in retaliation.

Three times, Mosby was wounded; once, he was given up for dead—Union newspapers even carried his obituary. But by April 1865, Mosby was still very much back in action; he had already provided Lee with valuable information, had been honored by the Confederate Congress, and had become a constant irritant in draining Union strength and confounding its campaign strategies. Yet Mosby was hardly the only guerrilla who inspired such Northern outrage—and was ready and waiting to be tapped by Lee. The hard-bitten cavalryman Nathan Bedford Forrest had pummeled the Yanks so many times that he was known as "the Wizard of the Saddle." An enraged Sherman, who tangled with Forrest far too many times for his own taste, once called him "the most remarkable man our Civil War produced on either side." Sherman later ordered an expedition to hunt Forrest down, "to the death, if it costs 10,000 lives and bankrupts the treasury." Now Forrest and his men were still at large. Another dreaded guerrilla and a model to many was John Hunt Morgan, a flamboyant thirty-six-year-old Kentuckian, whose manner joined the spirit of Mosby and the killer instinct of Forrest. Well-groomed and genteel, the laconic Morgan unleashed his self-raised brigade of sturdy, nimble Kentuckians early in the war, first making a name for himself in July 1862 with a stunning 1,000-mile raid in twenty-four days through Kentucky and middle Tennessee that netted him 1,200 prisoners and stockloads of supplies in the tons. Morgan made life a festering hell for his enemies. In August, he turned up again in Tennessee, blocking the railroad to Nashville by pushing flaming boxcars into an 800-foot tunnel, causing the tunnel to collapse. As part of an overall guerrilla force of 2,500 rangers, Morgan helped pin down an advancing Federal army of over 40,000 men, by fading in and out of familiar hills and a friendly population, brilliantly burning, destroying, tapping and tearing down telegraph wires, and then retreating back into the mountains. As Sherman observed, "every house is a nest of secret . . . enemies." Later, Morgan was captured and imprisoned in an Ohio penitentiary, only to make a spectacular tunnel escape. Eventually, he was killed in 1864, but this hardly ended the North's woes. By 1865, partisans swarmed across the Confederacy like locusts in ancient Egypt.

But if ever there was a question about the Confederacy's ability to wage guerrilla war in April 1865, or the likely consequences of such a nationwide conflict, it was answered by the mere mention of one word: Missouri.

❧   ❧   ❧

Throughout the Civil War, Missouri was labeled "the war of 10,000 nasty little incidents," but it was much more than that. On one level, it was the very embodiment of the Civil War itself: a conflict-ridden slave state that didn't secede, a state deeply divided in loyalties, a state with an ill-formed identity. On yet another level, as it descended into full-scale guerrilla war, Missouri became a very different creature altogether, less a reflection of what the Civil War was and more a mirror for what the Civil War could become. It became a killing field.

Missouri also produced the most bloodthirsty guerrillas of the war. Topping the list was William Clarke Quantrill, a handsome, blue-eyed, twenty-four-year-old former Ohio schoolteacher. A close second was Bloody Bill Anderson, whose father was murdered by Unionists and whose sister was killed in a Kansas City Union prison disaster. Among their disciples were young men destined for later notoriety: Frank and Jesse James, and Coleman Younger. And there were countless other lesser but no less notorious lights.

In early 1862, Quantrill and his band of bushwhackers launched a series of strikes into Kansas that all but paralyzed the state. Then, in 1863, the revenge-minded Quantrill set his sights on a new target: Lawrence, Kansas. One would be hard-pressed to find a place more thoroughly despised by Quantrill and his comrades than Lawrence. It functioned as a Free-Soil citadel during the 1850s, then as a haven for runaway slaves, and, during the war, as a headquarters to the Redlegs, a band of hated Unionist guerrillas. Early in the morning of August 21, Quantrill and his

400 bushwhackers—including Frank James and Coleman Younger—struck. At 5 A.M., Quantrill and his men silently made their way into town. Then the killing began. With a triumphant yell, Quantrill began shouting, "Kill! Kill! Lawrence must be thoroughly cleansed . . . Kill! Kill!" For the next few hours, his fierce and sweaty long-haired men, unshaven and unwashed, rumbled up and down the streets of Lawrence, looting stores, shops, saloons, and houses. They systematically rounded up every man they encountered and then torched the town. By day's end, the deed was done. The city lay in ashes; 200 homes were burned to the ground. Over 150 innocent civilians, all men and young boys, had been murdered in cold blood.

The event shocked the entire country and captured the attention of the world. Thousands of Federal troopers and Kansas militiamen quickly pursued the bushwhackers, but by the next day, they were safely nestled in the woodlands of Missouri. The Federals swiftly retaliated, issuing the harshest order of the war by either side against civilians, known as General Orders Number 11. Almost as ruthless as the Lawrence raid itself, it was designed to strike at the heart of the guerrilla's power—the support given them by the civilian population. As one officer put it, the order was carried out "to the letter." Four whole counties were quickly depopulated; virtually every citizen was deported; their crops and their forage were destroyed. So were their homes, which were burned. There is no final list of how many innocent people died in the process—although some estimates suggest it surpassed the carnage in Lawrence. Nor is the list of total refugees in this mass exodus fully complete. In one town, the population dwindled from 10,000 to a mere 600. But what is complete is this: few of these refugees returned before the war's end. Many never did. When it was all over, these Midwestern counties lay like a silent wasteland, dotted by chimneys rising above the charred debris of blackened farmhouses.

Thus escalated the vicious cycle of retaliation and revenge. For the next six weeks, Quantrill and the partisans skirmished. Yet despite a massive sweep through the woodlands of western Missouri by Federal cavalrymen, Quantrill escaped. He and his men knew the countryside personally, and friends and relatives provided them with shelter, fresh horses, and timely warning in case of pursuit. In a telling instance of the relative ease with which guerrillas operated, Quantrill himself spent much of the time in comfort, neatly residing at a house near Blue Springs with his mistress, Kate King. On October 6, his gang again struck with considerable fury, overcoming a Federal wagon train at Baxter Springs. They mauled and killed eighty-five men, including the band musicians and James O'Neal, an artist for *Frank Leslie's Illustrated Newspaper*. So great was the wave of disgust over this bloodletting that news of the guerrilla war in the West actually supplanted—temporarily at least—the clash of armies in the East. Even Confederate generals were dismayed at the wanton carnage. Noted one high-ranking military man in Richmond, "they recognize the life of a man less than you would that of a dog killing a sheep."

At one point, a desperate Union, unsure of how to deal with the guerrillas, went as far as consulting Francis Lieber, the famous legal scholar. Lieber's message was hardly reassuring. While distinguishing between "regular and irregular partisans," he grimly likened the guerrilla war to the Thirty Years War and the religious wars in France. And he coined a most ominous phrase: "Where guerillas flourish," he noted, they create "a slaughterfield."

The slaughterfield was destined to grow even worse. The Union soldiers hunted the guerrillas like animals, and in return, they, too, eventually degenerated into little more than savage beasts, driven by a viciousness unimaginable just two years earlier. By 1864, the guerrilla war had reached new peaks of savagery. Robbing stagecoaches, harassing citizens, cutting telegraph wires were everyday occurrences; but now it was no longer simply enough to ambush and gun down the enemy. They had to be mutilated and, just as often, scalped. When that was no longer enough, the dead were stripped and castrated. In time, even that was insufficient. Then the victims were beheaded. And even that wasn't enough. So ears were cut off, faces were hacked, bodies were grossly mangled. Soon, Quantrill and his men rode about wearing scalps dangling from their bridles, as well as an assortment of other body parts—ears, noses, teeth, even fingers—all vivid trophies attesting to their latest victims. In one massacre, a Quantrill chieftain calmly hopped from one body to another, plundering his prey. Altogether, he stepped on 124 corpses. In another massacre, those who surrendered were clubbed to death, and others were pinned to the ground with bloody bayonets, their entrails spilling onto the ground. Wounded men were actually far luckier; they met death more quickly. Why? Their throats were slit. Those waiting were the least lucky. They were forced to watch until their turn came. Only later were they then bloodily killed. "The war has furnished no greater barbarism," wrote one horrified Union general. Said another, these men are "heartless and merciless fiends."

Nor did it end there. All order broke down. Groups of revenge-minded Federals, militia and even soldiers, became guerrillas themselves, angrily stalking Missouri, tormenting, torturing, and slaying Southern sympathizers. Ruthless reprisals and random terror became the norm, and the entire state was dragged into an incomprehensible and accelerating whirlpool of vengeance. New and no less bloodthirsty gangs of bushwhackers rose up, led by George Todd, John Thrailkill, and others who roved virtually unchecked, baiting Federal patrols—and murdering them; harassing the locals—and terrorizing them; and bringing all affairs in Missouri to a halt. Routinely, trains were stopped and attacked. So were stage lines. Steamboats, too, were not safe, coming under repeated sniper fire. To run the gauntlet on the Missouri, pilots started to request—and received—a thousand dollars for a single trip to Kansas. Petrified, Unionists ran, abandoning their houses and their farms, and converging on fortified towns—actually, by now they were garrisoned—which were reduced to nothing more than isolated enclaves in a sea of death. For their part, soldiers were pinned down at their posts in a countryside dominated by guerrillas, their men as much hunted as hunters. The lawlessness continued. As did the carnage. Every two or three days, a new corpse would be found floating in the river. "The very air seems charged with blood and death," wrote one Kansas City editor. Indeed it was.

Missouri was something that had never been witnessed before on American soil. And the Union was almost utterly unable to cope with the ongoing terror. Federal policies were at once muddled, incoherent, and ineffective. A collective sociopathy reigned in Missouri: the very fabric of all civil society was torn apart; all morals disintegrated. Both sides snapped. And the true victims, of course, were the civilians. Squeezed between the two warring parties, civilians became not just anxious spectators but unwilling participants. In a war without fronts, boundaries, and formal organization, the divisions between civilians and soldiers/partisans almost totally evaporated. Those who sheltered the guerrillas, and there were many of them—anti-Union farmers, their wives, even their children regularly spied for the guerrillas—placed their lives in peril. So did those who collaborated with the Unionists. Unsigned notes were ominously pinned to doors, "You are a damn Yankee. Leave . . . or your life will forfeit." They got the message. So did those whom the Union pressured.

It was not unheard of for civilians to undergo a torture ritual at the hands of one or the other or even both sides. A favorite tactic was a barbaric kind of repetitive hanging. One father, as his family watched helplessly, was strung up three times—and only on the last try was the deed done. Another's son was walked to the noose some seven times before he met his untimely fate. And there was torture by other means. Toenails would be pulled off, one by one. Knives would be thrust into bellies—but only partially. Houses would be burned. And on and on and on. To survive, people cheated, lied, acted duplicitously, and bore false witness against their neighbors—anything to appease the other side. In time, whole communities were torn apart. Neutrality became impossible. In the words of historian Michael Fellman, it became a "life of secret impeachments, divided loyalties, and whispered confidences."

Every bit as ominous, as one observer noted: "The enemy was everywhere and everyone." Guerrillas dressed as Union men, and Union men as guerrillas. And just as often as not, Missourians had no idea who was terrorizing them. Was it the friendly Virginian down the road? The drunken Kentuckian who ran the local grocery? A furtive stranger? A Union man—or a bushwhacker? Soon, townsfolk couldn't trust their own neighbors, not even those they had known for years. The smallest tic in speech came to mean something ominous; the slightest arched eyebrow would be feared; and so, too, in this pervasive atmosphere of paranoia, were one's own very senses. Union troops fared little better. In most instances their deaths came at the hands of some unseen sniper. So they, also, trusted no one; all civilians were seen as enemies. As such, many were wrongly robbed, tortured, maimed, and, of course, killed.

As time wore on, ever-greater numbers of people fled—to Texas, Colorado, California, Oregon, Idaho, even Tennessee. By 1864, most rural

Missourians had become refugees, inside or outside the state. For those stalwarts who stayed, a form of psychic numbing took over. "We hear of some outrage every day," blithely confessed one Missourian. Wrote the *Kansas City Journal of Commerce* in 1864, even before the worst of it: "East of us, west of us, north of us, south of us, comes the same harrowing story. Pandemonium itself seems to have broken loose, and robbery, murder and rapine, and death run riot over the country." One Union general said it perhaps most poignantly: "there was something in the hearts of good and typical Christian[s] . . . which had exploded."

❧ ❧ ❧

In Richmond, the Confederacy was watching these events carefully. Early in the war, in an attempt to tap the growing discontent behind enemy lines, the Confederate government had legitimized guerrilla organizations with the Partisan Ranger Act of April 1862. Yet ironically, as time went by, and even as the roaming guerrillas tied down Union troops and Union energy that might have been employed elsewhere, a number of Confederate authorities found the guerrillas' methods distasteful. To the chivalric Southerners, war was about noble sacrifice; it was to be gentlemanly and Christian, and there was an aristocratic code of honor to be adhered to. Typically, when most rebel generals thought of guerrillas, they thought of Mosby. But when it came to the guerrilla war in Missouri, a number of high-ranking Confederates found their methods repugnant. It was one thing to kill Yankees in battle; it was another thing to bushwhack and kill innocent civilians.

As such, Richmond's official policy was of two minds: it found guerrillas distasteful, dishonorable, offensive to the civilized sensibilities of the South, yet it willingly exploited or turned a blind eye to the guerrillas nonetheless. Moreover, there was some public support. As the *Richmond Times Dispatch* editorialized in 1863, "Let the guerilla system be thoroughly carried out . . . Let's exact an eye for an eye and a life for a life." By 1864, however, because of the heightened numbers of atrocities committed by bushwhackers in the West, as well as the penchant for plunder that virtually all guerrilla bands displayed, powerful Southern voices eventually called for repeal of the Partisan Ranger Act. They argued that irregular warfare was barbaric, too often uncontrollable, even injurious to the cause. Finally, in early 1865, the Confederate Congress revoked the act and the government ended its sanction of all partisan groups, with two notable exceptions: Mosby's rangers in the north, and McNeill's partisans in western Virginia. Robert E. Lee himself had come to harbor considerable doubts about the bushwhackers, and was instrumental in the Congress's decision.

Yet on that fateful morning of April 9, 1865, Lee had two very different faces of guerrilla war to consider: the first was the face of a Mosby and a Morgan—and should he authorize a full-scale guerrilla conflict, such exceptional cavalrymen as Nathan Bedford Forrest, along with so many other of his loyal soldiers. Beyond that, there was the shining example of his own Carolina ancestors against the British Lord Cornwallis. Or, alternatively, there was the anarchic, scarlet-stained face of Missouri. In all likelihood, a guerrilla war countrywide would be a combination of the two, and, even at this late date, it could likely have an awesome impact: total conquest could be resisted, until, perhaps, attrition and exhaustion would lead the North to sue the South for peace.

❧   ❧   ❧

Political genius, Otto von Bismarck once instructed, entails hearing the far-off hoofbeat of history and then rising to catch the galloping horseman by the coattails. The difficulty, of course, is that one may hear the wrong horse or leap after the wrong horseman. Was this to be Lee's fate? In his time, he had arguably been justified in choosing his state over his Union. He had surely been right about countless battles, from Chancellorsville to the Seven Days battle, from the Wilderness to Cold Harbor. He had equally been right, however belatedly, about inducting slaves into the Confederate army with the promise of emancipation. However, for all his strategic acumen, he had not been right about the ability of the South to win its independence outright, whether through a war of maneuver and attack, or through prolonged attrition while hoping for foreign intervention. Lee was sophisticated enough to know that the drum of history rarely beats for the men on the losing side in wars. Few achieve lasting greatness. Fewer still are venerated in civic halls and schoolkids' history lessons. Thus, it was here that

Lee was confronted with one last chance, one last opportunity for vindication. If he were somehow to succeed with guerrilla warfare, his place in history would be assured. The temptation must have been vast; no one should think otherwise. Moreover, it must be added that Lee himself was not always a model of absolute consistency. Throughout the war, a number of his key views evolved; in 1862, for instance, when the Confederacy rightly feared that Richmond might be overrun, Lee, with tears in his eyes, angrily told Jefferson Davis, "Richmond *must* not be given up; it *shall* not be given up!" By 1865, however, he was thinking exactly the opposite.

So as a sleep-deprived Robert E. Lee—now unable to move west, or south, or east, only north, the very last direction he wanted to go in— listened to one of his most trusted advisers in the cool early morning hours of April 9; hearing Porter Alexander out, he was doing some quick calculations in his head about the effect that generations of bushwhacking— guerrilla warfare—would have on the country. Lee, however, principled to the bitter end, was thinking not about personal glory, but along quite different lines. What is honorable? What is proper? What is right? Likely recalling Missouri, he quickly reasoned that a guerrilla war would make a wasteland of all that he loved. Brother would be set against brother, not just for four years, but for generations. Such a war would surely destroy Virginia, and just as surely destroy the country as well. Even if it worked, and perhaps especially if it worked. For Lee, that was too high a price to pay. No matter how much he believed in the Cause—his daring attempts over the last nine days were vivid testimony to that—there were limits to Southern independence. As he had once said, "it [is] better to do right, even if we suffer in so doing, than to incur the reproach of our consciences & posterity."

But Lee, more so than most other generals, also shunned making political decisions. He was uncompromising about the unique American ethos of respecting the primacy of civilian leadership to make judgments about affairs of state. Yet this was surely a weighty political decision if ever there were one. If he were to surrender his troops, it would be *against* the advice of Jefferson Davis, *against* the advice of his civilian authority. But on that Palm Sunday morning of April 9, he forged ahead.

❧ ❧ ❧

Suppose, he told Porter Alexander, that "I should take your suggestion. The men would be without rations and under no control of officers . . . They would be compelled to rob and steal in order to live. They would become . . . bands of marauders, and the enemy's cavalry would . . . overrun many sections they may never have occasion to visit.

"No," said the old commander. "We would bring on a state of affairs it would take the country years to recover from."

He continued his counsel to Alexander: "Then, general, you and I as Christian men have no right to consider only how this would affect us." We must, he stressed, "consider its effect on the country as a whole." Finally, Lee said, "And as for myself, you young fellows might go bushwhacking, but the only dignified course for me would be to go to General Grant and surrender myself and take the consequences of my acts."

Thus did Robert E. Lee, so revered for his leadership in war, make his most historic contribution—to peace. By this one momentous decision, he spared the country the divisive guerrilla warfare that surely would have followed, a vile and poisonous conflict that would not only have delayed any true national reconciliation for many years to come, but in all probability would have fractured the country for decades into warring military pockets, or as Tom Wicker has deftly put it, ensured, "the Vietnamization of America." Nor is it idle to speculate that even at such a late date such a mode of warfare might well have accomplished what four years of conventional war had failed to do: cleave North from South.

❧   ❧   ❧

None of this, of course, is to say that Lee made his decision without an inner struggle. For several days now, Lee had been vacillating among ending the hostilities, waging last-ditch attempts at escaping, and dying at his post. Just that morning, gloomily staring off into the distance, into the lifting mist, he had cried out, "How easily I could be rid of all this and be at rest! I have only to ride along the line and all will be over." But as Lee weighed honor and glory against duty and will, the latter trumped the former. He had already told his immediate staff with a heavy heart: "Then there is nothing left for me to do but to go and see General Grant, and I

The Chase

VIRGINIA

Richmond

Bermuda Hundred

Petersburg

Five Forks
April 1, 1865

Evacuation
April 2-3

April 4-5

Amelia C.H.
April 5, 1865

Appomattox R.

Sayler's Creek
April 6, 1865

April 7

Richmond & Danville RR

Lynchburg

April 9

Appomattox Station

Union
Confederate

0   10 miles

would rather die a thousand deaths." Poignantly, while tears and grief enveloped his men, he would add, "it is our duty to live."

At ten o'clock, Robert E. Lee promptly presented himself for his appointment with the Union commander. Dismounting, he stood tall under a flag of truce and, for the first time ever in his long career, in full view of Grant's army. But a new concern arose. With good reason, one of Lee's aides feared that another attack was in the offing; at that very moment, intermittent firing was heard off in the distance. And when Federal couriers finally arrived, there was no Grant, only his letter asserting that the morning meeting between the two "would lead to no good."

Lee carefully scanned the message, reflected for a few moments, and told his military secretary, Lieutenant Colonel Charles Marshall, the grandnephew of the renowned Supreme Court jurist, "Well, write a letter to General Grant and ask him to meet me to deal with the question of the surrender of my army, in reply to the letter he wrote me at Farmville."

With that one succinct sentence, Lee had now accepted Grant's terms. Marshall handed the letter to a Federal officer and told him the message required a "suspension of hostilities." No, was the answer. That could not be. An attack had already been ordered and the officer didn't have the authority to stop it; nor could a message be gotten in time to Grant.

Lee still stood under the flag of truce. The Federal soldier requested that he withdraw. Instead, Lee began writing—again—to Grant.

9th April 1865

General,

I ask a suspension of hostilities pending the adjustment of the terms of the surrender of this army, in the interview requested in my former communication today.

Very respectfully, your obt. Srt.
R. E. Lee Genl.

Once more, Lee was warned to leave immediately; he now stood directly in the path of an oncoming Federal advance. With blue columns a mere hundred yards away, the scene was a farrago of confusion and potential danger. His tired face set, jaw locked, soft eyes expressionless, Lee eventually mounted Traveller and rode back to his own rear guard. Finally, shortly after eleven o'clock, word came that the Union had authorized a cease-fire. Once again, Lee mounted his horse and made his way to the front, where he penned his third letter of the day to U. S. Grant.

> Hd Qrs A N Va
> 9th April 1865

> General:I sent a communication to you today from the picket line whither I had gone in the hopes of meeting you in pursuance of the request continued in my letter of yesterday. Maj Gen Meade informs me that it would probably expedite matters to send a duplicate through some other part of your lines. I therefore request an interview at such time and place as you may designate, to discuss the terms of the surrender of this army in accordance with your offer to have such an interview contained in your letter of yesterday.

> Very respectfully,
> Your obt. Servt.
> R. E. Lee
> Genl

For this scion of the first family of Virginia, these were undoubtedly moments of soaring anxiety and deep depression. From that day on, everything would be different. No longer would he be considered a noble Confederate patriot or a revered Southern George Washington; instead, he would be ignominiously known as a failed revolutionary and, to many in the North, an abettor of treason. Already, when he rose to dress that morning, he had donned his full general's uniform, including a fine red silk sash, a gleaming jeweled and engraved sword, and a pair of handsome thread gloves. "I have probably to be General Grant's prisoner today," he later explained to his men, "and I thought I must make my best appearance." And as the morning wore on, he increasingly feared the harsh terms that Grant might impose.

But what exactly did that mean? Lee himself left no lasting record, although we do know that as he rode with Longstreet around midday, he talked about the possibilities for some time, often mumbling in half sentences and fragments. While he at first thought that Grant might give "good terms," he was now clearly growing anxious. Indeed, beyond anticipating becoming the North's prisoner, he had no real way of knowing what would happen once the two sides met.

And what Lee did know at that moment about other failed revolutionaries could not have been terribly reassuring. In fact, on its face, much of Western history—a world with which he was closely acquainted—now seemed to conspire against him. King Charles I was beheaded in the English Civil War, the precursor to the American Revolutionary War, and to some extent, this Civil War as well. During the French Revolution, their version of the American Civil War, the young leader Robespierre led thousands of the French aristocracy— the *ancien régime*—to the guillotine, until his own neck met the blade. Lee had just rejected guerrilla warfare out of his sense of being a good "Christian." But throughout centuries of European Christendom, a history in which Lee was well steeped, the bodies of rebellious, treasonous men and women were routinely tied—or sometimes outright nailed—to the stake, and slowly roasted alive. The more fortunate— not those who begged for their lives, most knew better—were merely beheaded. Nor were the well-bred aristocracy, the refined nobility, the high-minded priests and much-beloved generals—men of Lee's lofty station—spared when treason was suspected or proven. In their case, the punishment was severe and quite public: nobles, archbishops, bishops, princes, dukes, margraves, and military men were routinely drawn and quartered, after which their reeking, bleeding cadavers, cut into four parts, were put on public display to rot as a warning for all who contemplated rebellion. More recently, the famed general Napoleon had met a far more merciful end, though one that would hardly have seemed attractive to Lee: this general, emperor, and one-time national hero was banished to the distant Atlantic island of St. Helena to live out his final years in ignominy. So, too, did numerous others meet death or exile after the revolutionary tide of 1848 that swept the entire European continent. In short, bloody executions and harsh revenge were as ordinary then as they are considered extraordinary today.

And in America? Across this troubled landscape of retribution, there was again not necessarily much in the way of consolation for Lee. Lee had the unique distinction of being the man who had captured John Brown, the revolutionary abolitionist, at Harpers Ferry. Brown was summarily hanged for treason. And while Lee rode Traveller to meet Grant, his own aides shared his unspoken anxiety. Upon surrender, the men feared they could be summarily marched off into confinement camps as prisoners of war. Porter Alexander later confessed that he expected all of them to be paraded through the streets of the North, humiliated, hooted at, disgraced. And, of course, there was the grim example of the fate of Bill Anderson, the rebel bushwhacker who was killed in the most horrible way: his head was cut off with an ax by revenge-minded Unionists and mounted atop a telegraph pole for all to see. And on this day, though Lee remained unaware, the fall of Richmond had already brought a spate of stinging calls for revenge, a grisly, thundering, roaring refrain, chanted and chanted again in an ever-rising crescendo, coming from New York, Boston, Philadelphia, Chicago, and, of course, Washington ("Burn it! BURN IT! *LET HER BURN!*" they cried about Richmond. On treason: "Treason is the highest crime known in the catalogue of crimes, and for him that is guilty of it . . . I would say death is too easy a punishment!" On Jefferson Davis: "HANG him! HANG him! Yes, I say *HANG* him twenty times!" On the Confederates who had graduated from West Point: "Those who have been fed, clothed, and taught at the public expense ought to stretch the first rope!" On those who had lifted their hands against the North: "Treason must be made odious; traitors must be punished and impoverished! . . . I would arrest them, I would try them, I would convict them, and I would hang them!" On pardons: "Never! *Never!*" And on Lee himself, a chorus cried: "*Hang Lee!* HANG Lee! *HANG LEE!*").

Indeed, the *Chicago Tribune* had recommended just that.

But as Lee waited anxiously, another man was riding furiously toward the surrender. Lee had no idea what he looked like, no idea whether his eyes radiated warmth or anger, no clue as to whether they were filled with reconciliation or with retribution. But this man, a man alternately known by many names—as "Victor," after King Victor Emmanuel II of Italy, or "Ulyss," after the great Greek figure, or "Tex," to his boyhood chums, or "Lyss," to his close friends, or "Dudy," to his wife, or "unconditional surrender," for his war achievements, or, most notoriously, as the "butcher," by his own people, for his indifferent ability to send wave after wave of men into battle to die—would today decide Lee's own fate and that of his men.

And now, on a spring afternoon at a small stagecoach stop, U. S. Grant, who had earlier made no bones about his intention to punish Lee and his army, would take on a most unlikely new mantle: statesman.

4

The Meeting

Now, at last, with Lee making his way to surrender, the hour has struck for U. S. Grant. It has been a long time coming. He has been waiting not just for many, many months, but for several years; it has been an excruciating journey. In the service of his country, he has hurled his men into battle like giant hunks of fresh meat, knowing that everything depended upon the force of arms; he has endured slander and calumny when the situation seemed hopeless to nearly everyone except himself and Abraham Lincoln; he has embodied an icy resolve to see this war through when the Northern voices of accommodation were at their greatest; and even in the grimmest of hours, when Northern defeat seemed possible, when there appeared to be no other choice but to make an imperfect peace with the Confederacy, when the sheer costs of war no longer seemed worth it, the inscrutable Grant looked up and somehow always saw victory.

In countless ways, Grant couldn't have been more different from the adversary who was now preparing to throw himself at his mercy. Where Lee was tall and stately, Grant was stubby and rumpled. Where Lee was a mature man who had already lived most of his life—he was fifty-eight—Grant was actually quite young, an astonishing mere forty-three. Where the patrician Lee was in many ways an American of the

eighteenth century, closer in spirit and outlook to the Founders, the plebeian Grant was decisively of the nineteenth century, tied to the dynamic strings of the future, to the capitalists, the Unionists, the speculators,
the doers, and, in time, to the political functionaries and party men.
Where both men were cunning and ruthless in war, Lee, the warrior,
however fierce in battle, was actually tender in human relations, passionate with his loved ones, florid in his Southern speech. Grant, by
contrast, was sensitive, but never showed it. He was crisp in demeanor
and crisp in spirit, speaking in blunt, lean sentences, barking out incon-
trovertible orders in his soft musical voice, never indulging, publicly or
privately, in excessive sentimentality, almost never doubting or second-
guessing himself. Lee disciplined his emotions; Grant repressed them—or
drank. Lee had a sublimely romantic quality about him: he was a figure
who gave his men heroic visions of what they were and what they
could become, was a testament to sweet humor and loyalty and duty and
the ultimate virtue of action, and was a true tragedian who understood
his own appeal to his followers. Grant was cut from a very different cloth.
He was in many ways the quintessential utilitarian, a man less of the
refined South, or the elite East, for that matter, than of the gritty West
(he talks "bad grammar," one Grant aide slyly quipped, but "talks it naturally"), a man fired by a deep-seated conviction and a confidence that
could belong only to someone who had failed in life time and time
again, until midway through the Civil War when he found what he knew
was somehow his destiny. And this—by dreary force of deeds in war
rather than sheer charisma or some indefinable presence—was how he
inspired his men, his army, and his president.

Yet if history was now beckoning for Grant, it hadn't always. Just
four years earlier, Grant had been an unsuccessful soldier turned shabby, insolvent Midwestern civilian, known only for the persistence of his
failures. Little in his family background or early career suggested he
would amount to much. In fact, his name wasn't even U. S. Grant; it was
Hiram Ulysses. He did come from a solid American pedigree—his
ancestry dated back to Matthew and Priscilla Grant, a Puritan couple
who arrived in 1630 aboard the *Mary and John*. Back then, the Grants were
affluent and prestigious members of colonial society—that is, until

Noah Grant more than a century later was killed in the French and Indian Wars. The family fortunes quickly declined, and the third Noah Grant (Ulysses' grandfather) was later jailed in a debtors' prison. Grant's father, Jesse, did a bit better, running a successful tannery in Point Pleasant, Ohio, and later becoming the local Whig mayor of Georgetown. As a boy, Hiram Grant was a curious mixture of insecurities and talents. He was withdrawn in public and tongue-tied around people, yet he was wonderful around horses, riding them with grace and alacrity. The vile stench of his father's tannery was one of his earliest—and more formative—memories. Ironically, it imbued him with a profound distaste for blood, and for most of his life he would refuse to eat any type of meat that wasn't fully charred. Moreover, of all things, it was cruelty to animals that sent him into a wild rage. It also gave him a horror of dirt. As a general, he was so fastidious—some might argue prissy—that he lugged around in his headquarters a collapsible rubber bath.

Using his influence, Jesse Grant got his short, scrawny son a congressional appointment to West Point in 1839, trusting that the army would provide him with some direction and earn him a solid living. It didn't. At the military academy, Grant discovered that a clerk had mistakenly written down his name as "Ulysses Simpson Grant," and, instead of insisting on a correction, the insecure Grant just shrugged his shoulders and submissively accepted it as his own. He was an unremarkable cadet ("a military life holds no charms for me," he lamented, "and I had not the faintest idea of staying in the army even if I should be graduated, which I didn't expect"), who read romantic novels rather than study hard, could never quite keep in step with the rhythm of marching or compare with the stylish demeanor of the more refined Eastern and Southern boys, and actually prayed that a resolution introduced in Congress to abolish West Point would pass. Contrary to his worst fears, though, he did graduate, but only a lackluster twenty-first in a class of thirty-nine, and he later failed to get the cavalry duty he so ardently wanted. His only real enthusiasm seemed to be for riding—and watercolors. His friends called him "Uncle Sam Grant," then "Uncle Sam," then "Country Sam," and finally, just plain old "Sam."

While he believed that James Polk's Mexican War was "wicked," and "one of the most unjust ever waged by a stronger against a weaker nation," he did his duty nevertheless. He fought bravely as a regimental quartermaster, at one point riding through enemy fire (likened to "a hailstorm") to bring ammunition to his men. In 1848, he married Julia Dent, the sister of his West Point roommate and the daughter of a Missouri slave owner. They would have three sons and a daughter. Subsequently, the army dispatched Grant to a Pacific station without them. He was sickened and secluded, and it turned into a disaster; he could not even earn enough money to send his family west. His fortunes quickly slid: a grocery venture collapsed, and so did a plan to raise potatoes. His savings started to waste away. While he had taken the oath as a Son of Temperance, he began to drink heavily, usually on two- or three-day sprees. In 1854 it cost him dearly; caught drunk on duty, he was faced with the prospect of resigning or being court-martialed. Grant took the lesser of the evils, quit in disgrace, and went back east to rejoin Julia and work a piece of land that his father-in-law gave him.

In a sarcastic swipe at the wealthy families who gave their homes noble-sounding names, he betrayed his lingering insecurities, calling his place "Hardscrabble Farm." Hardscrabble it was: even when he used two slaves to help with the work, he could not make a go of it. Poverty now stared him in the face, and he appealed to his father for financial assistance. He was rebuffed. Business suited him no better. He tried his hand at bill collecting, then real estate, and even hawked firewood on the St. Louis streets from his boxy wagon, still wearing his faded blue army overcoat. All failed. One Christmas, he was reduced to pawning his gold watch and chain to buy family presents. Eventually, before he hit rock bottom, his father bailed him out, giving him a job clerking in his leather store in Galena, Illinois; Grant's older brother was his boss. There, he amiably passed the time, analyzing politics with his pal John Rawlins, keeping the store books, and collecting his modest check ($800 a year). By all accounts, he was slovenly, unsoldierlike, a man of little reputation and little promise, hardly the stuff of which gladiators are made. Then came the war.

Grant, a staunch Unionist, quickly reenlisted. He wrote to the secretary of war politely asking for a command; his letter was never opened. Nor did the army itself see fit to give the returning officer a post—George McClellan deemed himself much too busy and much too important even to see him. Finally, his own governor appointed him as a colonel of a volunteer regiment—"the worst in Illinois." Grant never looked back. He triumphed in a little battle at Belmont, Missouri, then another one at Fort Henry, then a magnificent one at Fort Donelson, all while other Federal generals were being thrashed, one after another. Soon, Grant was promoted to brigadier general and became a Northern hero—his picture even appeared on the cover of *Harper's* magazine. In truth, he hardly looked heroic. Or all that much like an up-and-comer. Hearkening back to his bitter West Point years, he still disliked uniforms, liked military marching bands even less, and boasted he could recognize only two tunes: "one was Yankee Doodle, and the other wasn't." But for all his unpretentiousness, he also shrewdly reinvented his persona, smartly trimming his beard, giving up his pipe for his trademark cigar, and calmly whittling on a stick while battles were in progress. And he had retained his old innate genius for reading maps.

But all was not smooth sailing. Despite the watchful eye of his old neighbor and newly appointed army chief of staff, John Rawlins, Grant would on occasion backslide and take to the bottle. And when his army was caught by surprise at Shiloh in 1862 and suffered fearful losses, Grant was ignominiously labeled a "drunk" and branded an "incompetent." It was said he fed men heartlessly into "the sausage machine of battle." Ohio even disclaimed him, asserting that he had been born in Illinois. The tide of public opinion now turned sharply against him. Marat Halstead, editor of the influential *Cincinnati Commercial*, wrote that "General Grant . . . is a jackass in the original package. He is a poor drunken imbecile . . . Grant will fail miserably, hopelessly, eternally." Charles Dana, sent by Lincoln to spy on Grant, despite coming to like the general, was ultimately not a whole lot more charitable: "Not a great man," he reported, ". . . not original or brilliant . . ." (though he acknowledged that Grant was "sincere," "morally [great]," and "gifted with courage that never failed"). Eventually, A. K. McClure, the influential Republican leader and Pennsylvania magazine publisher, went to Lincoln and clamored for Grant's head. "I can't spare this man," the president protested. "He *fights*."

And fight Grant did, becoming the hero not just of Donelson but of Vicksburg, one of the most important strategic Northern victories, which helped cut the Confederacy cleanly in two, and of Chattanooga, and then becoming the first man to hold the rank of lieutenant general since George Washington. But when Grant again suffered frightful losses to Lee in the Wilderness and at Cold Harbor and the mortification of the Crater at Petersburg, new calls for his head arose. Plainspoken, detached, cool, the no-nonsense Grant nonetheless continued to plug away. He was rarely a man for small talk, or, for that matter, the cut and thrust of military politics or public opinion, but he was savvy enough to cultivate his most important constituency of one: Abe Lincoln. "I think Grant has hardly a friend left, except myself," Lincoln observed, adding, but "what I want is generals who will fight battles and win victories. Grant has done this and I propose to stand by him." Like Lincoln (and Lee, for that matter), Grant believed in taking risks. Also like Lincoln, he believed in attacking the enemy's army, rather than passively maneuvering to capture places. And like Lincoln, when the chips were down, he quietly thumbed his nose at the opposition and kept his eye on the goal.

And that goal was always to crush the enemy. In a thousand little ways, it seemed as though Grant was fated to fight this civil war. In battle, what galled Grant most was indecision. Once, an aide asked if he thought he was always right. "No!" Grant ripped back. "I am not, but in war anything is better than indecision. *We must decide.* If I am wrong we shall soon find it out and can do the other thing. But *not to decide* . . . may ruin everything." He was never a whiner: he didn't plead for reinforcements, seldom did he lapse into excuses, and he almost never argued with his colleagues; in the end, what mattered most was doing the job. And as his soldiers were disemboweled by Lee's men, blown into fragments, writhed with agonizing wounds, or were slowly roasted to death, Grant was unchastened. For Grant, casualties of war were no primitive aberration. Conflict, not amity, was the way of the world and, regrettably, the way to peace. He intuitively understood this. One of the harder questions about Grant, so often called the butcher, was whether he secretly enjoyed war too much. In fact, he was no lover of the panoply of war, of the bugles, the drums, the battle flags. And while he took terrible loses in such deafening stride, as though he were little more than a seasoned broker calculating the Wall Street markets or a farmer warily eyeing the weather, he often stayed away from the battlefield itself so that his compassion would not sap his resolve. For Grant, this battle, this fight, this war, was prosaically called "the business." The description is apt. One observer put it best, saying of Grant: his "expression [is] as if he had determined to drive his head through a brick wall, and was about to do it." Noted another: "Grant may possess the talisman."

Of necessity, generals inhabit the political world as much as the battlefield, but Grant had the good sense not to let his fame go to his head. His star rose and fell—and rose and fell again. In March 1864, this short, round-shouldered, "scared looking man" charmed official and social Washington—the refined diplomats, the busy socialites, the inquisitive clerks, the gossipy matrons, and the war-weary senators—as did no one else in the Union, including Lincoln himself. In the words of one awed congressman, Grant was "the idol of the hour." But this love and adulation were fleeting, and, at least then, he seemed instinctively to know it. His job was to prosecute the war, not to let newspaper clips go to his head, and, once his mind was made up about how to fight this war, he would not budge. Thus his famous line: "I will fight Lee if it takes all summer." Thus his guiding maxim, articulated after Shiloh: "I gave up all hope of saving the Union except by complete conquest." Thus his stoic proclamation in the Wilderness campaign: "Whatever happens, there will be no turning back." Grant had a kind of built-in shock absorber that permitted him in life and in war to survive the setbacks, the defeats, the humiliations, and, of course, the heartbreaking number of deaths. One cannot help but be struck by his tenacious resolve, his detached yet tightly focused energy, his unwavering determination and gritty pugnacity. But none of this is to say he was indifferent. Peel back his shy, composed demeanor and you find a core of cold steel. But there is little doubt that beneath the outwardly calm exterior that he projected to the world, he suffered from profound anxiety: the signs were all there. It wasn't just the episodic binge drinking, but the unbearable migraine headaches that necessitated chloroform treatments, the sleeplessness, the physical illnesses that manifested considerable emotional strain. Still, he knew what he wanted. In the hundreds of war photographs of Grant, you can glimpse multiple expressions and many sentiments, but one: he never looks defeated.

This couldn't have been easy, even for a man of Grant's iron disposition. Perhaps the most poignant and telling moment of Grant's generalship was that fateful evening in the Wilderness after Lee's massive drubbing. If ever there was a turning point in the war, it was this: Grant the "butcher" retreating to his tent, falling facedown on his cot, and apparently bawling like a baby. Then, the next morning, he got up to face the battle, again.

Five other Union generals had already seen their fates and their futures destroyed—McClellan's twice—by the fierce general in gray confronting them. And however much twentieth-century military analysts may point out that, as a percentage of his army, Grant did not necessarily lose that many more men than Lee, the indelible reality was that the losses of his army were colossally huge—more men, in fact, than Lee had in his entire army at the time. That spring evening, as Union men died and moaned in the maze of swamps and streams and hills, and as Grant was sunk in gloom, he now clearly stood alone. Mired in despair, he had to ask himself, how many casualties were enough? For even as hardened a man as Grant, one must wonder, could this have been anything other than the decision of a lifetime? What did he do? He reached deep within himself and found the inner mettle not to become the sixth casualty of Robert E. Lee. He would press on, he decided, as fateful a decision as any he made until that time, the siege of Vicksburg included. Even after Cold Harbor, an assault he "regretted more than any" he had "ever ordered," there would be no turning back, no retreat, no sign of weakness. The crucial question, of course, during that summer of 1864 was not what policy to pursue toward the South, not what to do once the war was won, but whether it would be won at all. But to his everlasting credit, as he fought "that enemy" who, in his words, repeatedly demonstrated "Herculean deeds of valor," Grant never considered that it could be otherwise.

Yet on the morning of April 9, 1865, when the first of Lee's letters reached him as he rode along the river on his way to meet Sheridan at Appomattox, his migraine still pounding away at his brain, an even harder set of questions was raised. What terms would he impose upon Lee? How did he intend to prosecute the settlement? Would the man who had found his way only in war know how to navigate through the equally treacherous terrain of surrender and peace? If all the world knew about what was in Grant's head, it would now find a very different side of this general, what was also in his heart.

In no small measure, no greater question had ever gripped the country during these four years of war. Most civil wars, in fact, end quite badly, and history is rife with lessons that how wars end is every bit as crucial as why they start and how they are waged. The beginning of the end would now be decided at Appomattox Court House.

✷ ✷ ✷

Earlier in the year, in March, after Lee had felt Grant out over the general issue of peace, Lincoln had bluntly sent Grant a clear, uncompromising order: "*I* will deal with political questions and negotiate for peace. Your job is to fight." Nonetheless, on this day Grant would evince a deft political and diplomatic touch, even as he appeared apolitical. And if it were Lincoln's fervent desire to press the conflict harshly while then making a gentle peace, it fell to Grant to make good on that promise. Hindsight should not obscure the potential minefield that Grant was walking into as Lee's correspondence was handed to him that morning. With a cigar in his mouth and quiet satisfaction on his face ("the pain in my head seemed to leave me the moment I got Lee's letter," Grant noted), he read Lee's letter and handed it to his aide, Rawlins.

"You had better read it aloud, General," Grant averred. His voice dipping with emotion, Rawlins complied, and a delicious shudder swept through their ranks. But when Rawlins finished, Grant fell silent.

His countenance now inscrutable, he immediately sat down on a grassy bank and composed his reply:

> April 9, 1865
> General R. E. Lee, Comd.g C.S.A.
>
> General, Your note of this date is but this moment, 11:50 A.M. rec'd., in consequence of my having passed from the Richmond and Lynchburg road to Farmersville & Lynchburg road. I am at this writing about four miles West of Walker's Church and will push forward to the front for the purpose of meeting you. Notice sent to me on this road where you wish the interview to take place.
>
> Very respectfully, your obt. Svt,
> U. S. Grant,
> Lt. Gnl

The ultimate fate of nations is often measured and swayed not by large events, but by tiny ones, small, symbolic gestures that shape men's passions, assuage or incite their fears, and quell or inflame lingering hostilities for years to come. On its own, it would be ludicrous to claim that John Brown's raid caused the Civil War, just as it would be nonsense to assert that Lincoln's election was anything more than a proximate cause. Such events are catalysts, sparks, symbols that ignite a series of chain reactions on the much longer, more rutted road to war. But, by the same token, there are also moments that can act as catalysts for peace. Whatever fears Lee may have harbored that morning about Grant's terms, the Union general's first gesture was astonishingly conciliatory—and farsighted. Having defeated the gallant Army of Northern Virginia, U. S. Grant was letting his vaunted foe, Robert E. Lee, choose the time and place of his surrender. However seemingly insignificant, it was a remarkable act that, like Grant himself, spoke simply yet clearly: the North may defeat the Confederate armies, it may strip away their guns and remove their cannons, but, if Grant was going to have anything to do with it, it would not also destroy their dignity.

Grant, normally so calm in war and composed in a crisis, later confessed that he was rather nervous about finally meeting Lee, and he now spurred quickly forward to the impending rendezvous. He would have to ride sixteen miles. For his part, an exhausted Lee, awake since well before dawn, lay under a nearby apple tree and took a short nap. By all accounts, he still hadn't eaten a morsel of food. He was exhausted, stunned, and, even more so, depressed. This would be the worst ordeal of his life, but he felt a solemn obligation to perform it just the same.

Stirred within the hour by Grant's staff officer bearing the Union general's request, Lee raised himself up, promptly scanned it, and quickly dispatched an aide to find a suitable meeting place for surrender.

❧   ❧   ❧

As the blazing yellow sun climbed high overhead, the winding country lanes in the rural stillness of Appomattox couldn't have appeared less suited to capturing the smoldering moment about to take place.

Told to find a suitable house where Lee could meet with Grant, Lee's aide found instead a drowsy village with broad grassy flanks, a small thicket of tall oaks and broad pine trees, a single unnamed street, and an erratic pathway meandering from and around the town center. Though Appomattox Court House had been a county seat since 1845, it was hard to envision much happening in this remote southside Virginia town comprising twenty or so simple structures quietly hugging the land: a half-dozen clapboard hutch houses, several small stores, a once busy tavern, the courthouse itself, and one handsome red brick home. Since 1819, Appomattox had been best known as a way station for travelers on the Richmond-Lynchburg Stage road, where the weary made do at the Clover Hill Tavern and guest house. (One can imagine it still as a place where Southerners lounged in the summer heat, where riders tilted back a cool lemonade or a shot of spirits at the bar, or where locals played a raucous game of cards—but not as the epic site where the Army of Northern Virginia would surrender.) By 1865, though, the area had become known as "a bare and cheerless place."

Lee's aide rejected the first house he was ushered into as too "dilapidated." Instead, he settled upon the home of Wilmer McLean, freshly built in 1848, bringing a fitting symmetry to battle and surrender. In 1861, McLean had lived near Manassas Junction, on the fields where the battle of First Manassas, or Bull Run, was fought. His house was a Confederate headquarters until a shell came roaring into his kitchen. A year later, McLean retired to Appomattox to flee from the seemingly permanent emergency of the Civil War, taking up residence in this neat and tidy brick house with its weathered hitching fence, its sweeping covered porch, and its sturdy facade. Now the war seemed to be waning—and remarkably enough, in his own living room. For a few moments, the only sound was the thump and swish of feet trotting up the worn wooden steps of his home. Lee's aide, Charles Marshall, went in, followed soon thereafter by one of Grant's aides, and then Lee himself. Lee, resplendent in his magnificent crisp gray uniform and with his engraved sword at his side, sat down in the parlor at a small wooden table, inside enemy territory, and, in painful silence, waited.

Half an hour later, at 1:30 P.M., came a new sound: the trot of Union horses.

⊁ ⊁ ⊁

With his queer, stumbling stride, U. S. Grant entered. He was swordless, dressed in a private's muddy shirt, his boots and trousers were splattered with mud, his cheeks were pink, his blue eyes clear, his hair dark. For the first time in nearly two decades, in this square, somewhat cramped room, the two generals would see each other in the flesh, face-to-face. On this day, there would be no rituals, no pageantry, no excessive ministrations. Rather, it would be their destiny to dictate the fate of their two armies—and set down the outlines for what would one day again become their common country.

Lee rose to his feet. The two men shook hands, and then they took their respective seats, eight feet apart. About a dozen of Grant's staff officers positioned themselves quietly around the parlor, a room that now pulsed with hidden excitement, awaiting the dazzling piece of theater about to be played out, even as it was suffused with Lee's private anguish. For his part, Lee's face revealed nothing. "What General Lee's feelings were, I do not know," Grant would later write. "As he was a man of such dignity, with an impassible face . . . his feelings . . . were entirely concealed from my observation." Interestingly, it was Grant, however, not Lee, who exhibited nervous tension, even a sense of awe at the occasion, as he did his best to put Lee at ease with a friendly overture. "I met you once before, General Lee, while we were serving in Mexico, when you came over from General Scott's headquarters to visit Garland's brigade, to which I then belonged. I have always remembered your appearance, and I think I should have recognized you anywhere."

"Yes," acknowledged Lee, "I know I met you on that occasion, and I have often thought of it, and tried to recollect how you looked, but I have never been able to recall a single feature."

The conversation momentarily lagged, but then Grant continued nervously to chat ("Our conversation grew so friendly," he recalled, "that I almost forgot the object of our meeting"), until Lee finally interrupted him.

"I suppose, General Grant, that the object of our present meeting is fully understood," he said quietly. "I asked to see you to ascertain upon what terms you would receive the surrender of my army."

Grant replied, "The terms I propose are those stated substantially in my letter of yesterday, that is, the officers and men surrendered are to be paroled and disqualified from taking up arms again until properly exchanged, and all arms, ammunition, and supplies to be delivered up as captured property."

Lee nodded. Whatever he felt at that exact moment, Grant's words would have eased his worst fears of the morning. "Those are," Lee now said, "about the conditions I expected would be proposed."

"Yes," Grant reassured him, "I think our correspondence indicated pretty clearly the action that would be taken at our meeting; and I hope it may lead to a general suspension of hostilities and be the means of preventing any further loss of life." Grant continued on this theme, happily talking of the future, of reunion and the prospects of peace. For his part, Lee said nothing, perhaps feeling uncertain, even slightly stunned. From West Point, through his thirty-six years of military service, Lee had become intimately acquainted with all the arts of war, save one: surrender.

But after a bit, the Confederate general found his voice and interrupted again. "I presume, General Grant, we have both carefully considered the proper steps to be taken, and I would suggest that you commit to writing the terms you have proposed, so that they may be formally acted upon."

"Very well," Grant said, "I will write them out."

❧   ❧   ❧

Grant, lighting not his trademark cigar but a pipe, directed that his order book be laid before him. He began writing steadily, halting only to glance at the sword on Lee's side. After conferring with his secretary about the terms as written—including some editing here, some clarification there—Grant then rose and, rather than have an aide deliver it, personally handed the book to Lee. Only several feet, it was, ultimately, a journey of timeless consequence.

The order book passed from Grant's hands to Lee's.

Now, Lee brushed aside the two brass candlesticks and some other items that were on the table, then took the book before him and opened it. With all eyes on him fixed in an almost reverential gaze, it became time for Lee to master his own nerves. He fidgeted, pulling his spectacles out of his pocket, withdrawing his handkerchief, carefully wiping his glasses. He fidgeted some more, suddenly crossing his legs and just as suddenly making a show of unconsciously adjusting his spectacles.

Then, the fidgeting ended and he began to read—attentively, slowly, carefully. This was no mere parchment or paper, that he knew all too well; it was a veritable exchange of the crosier of authority, the words that would eventually rewrite the rules and the realities of a new country.

Appomattox C. H., Va.
Apr. 9th, 1865
Gen. R. E. Lee,
Comd., C.S.A.

Gen.
In accordance with the substance of my letter to you of the 8th inst. I propose to receive the surrender of the Army of N. Va. On the following terms: to-wit:

Rolls of all the officers and men to be made duplicate. One copy to be given to an officer designated by me, the other to be retained by such an officer or officers as you may designate. The officers to give their individual paroles not to take up arms against the Government of the United States until properly . . .

Lee paused, abruptly looked up to Grant, and said, "After the words 'until properly,' the word 'exchanged' seems to be omitted. You doubtless intended to use that word—"

"Why yes," Grant said, surprised (in fact, these words "until properly" were themselves added only belatedly). "I thought I had put in the word 'exchanged' . . . "

"I presume it had been omitted inadvertently and, with your permission, I will mark where it should be inserted."

"Certainly," Grant replied. Lee felt around in his pocket for a pencil. One of Grant's aides, Horace Porter, supplied one. Nervously twirling and tapping his pencil, Lee read on:

(exchanged) and each company or regimental commander to sign a like parole for the men of their commands. The Arms, Artillery, and public property to be parked and stacked and returned over to the officer appointed by me to receive them. This will not embrace the side arms of the officers, nor their private horses or baggage. This done each officer and man will be allowed to return to their homes, not to be disturbed by the United States Authority so long as they observe their parole and the laws in force where they may reside.

Very respectfully,
U. S. Grant,
Lt. Gn.

For the first time since the meeting began, Lee's expression brightened. Now the terms were fixed in writing, and they were as generous as could be expected. His men would not be penned as prisoners of war; they would not be paraded ignominiously through Northern streets; and, most importantly, they would not be prosecuted for treason. Looking over to Grant, he said, somewhat warmly, "This will have a very happy effect upon my army."

Now it was Grant who wanted to move things along. "Unless you have some suggestions to make in regard to the form in which I have stated the terms, I will have a copy of the letter made in ink, and sign it—"

For one brief moment, Lee seemed frozen, and hesitated slowly. He was searching for the right words. "There is one thing I should like to mention," he interjected. "The cavalrymen and artillerists own their own horses in our army. Its organization in this respect differs from that of the United States. I should like to understand whether these men will be permitted to retain their horses."

Lee's reference to the armies of the two countries apparently startled some of the Federals—to the remarkable, almost surreal scene, it inject-ed a piquant note of Civil War reality—but an unfazed Grant didn't miss a beat in responding. Indeed, in a gentle way, he would now make it clear who was dictating the terms to whom. "You will find that the terms as written do not allow this, only the officers are permitted to take their pri-vate property."

Lee's eyes again painfully scanned the second page of the surrender document. "No," he said sadly, his face subtly registering disappointment, "I see the terms do not allow it; that is clear."

It was an awkward moment, and Grant clearly sensed that his next words carried authority far beyond this room and far beyond the seem-ingly minor subject they dealt with. What followed next, in all its sim-plicity, was one of his boldest strokes: "Well, the subject is quite new to me," he explained. "Of course I did not know that any private sol-diers owned their animals; but I think we have fought the last battle of the war—I sincerely hope so." Presuming that most of the men were "small farmers," and would need their horses "to plant a crop," he added, "I will arrange it this way"—Lee was listening carefully—"I will not change the terms as now written, but I will instruct the offi-

cers I shall appoint to receive the paroles to let all the men who claim
to own a horse or a mule take the animals home with them to their
little farms."

"This will have the best possible effect upon the men," Lee immediately answered, now returning Grant's gracious gesture with the words
the Union general wanted to hear. "It will be very gratifying and will
do much toward conciliating our people."

The surrender was promptly given to Grant's aide, Ely Parker, who
borrowed ink from Lee's secretary to copy it. Marshall, Lee's aide, in turn
borrowed paper from Grant's staff to write out the Confederate general's reply.

> General: I have received your letter of this date containing the terms
> of surrender of the army of Northern Virginia as proposed by you—
> As they are substantially the same as those expressed in your letter of
> the 8th instant, they are accepted—I will proceed to designate the
> proper officers to carry the stipulations into effect—

> Very respectfully, your obedient servant
R. E. Lee
General

> Lieutenant-General U. S. Grant
> Commanding Armies of U.S.

Lee had one bit of additional business he wanted to conclude with
Grant. Explaining first that he had more than a thousand Federal prisoners whom he could not feed, he added glumly, "Indeed, I have nothing for my own men." Without hesitation, Grant proposed sending
rations for the 25,000 men across the lines. Was that enough? he asked.
"Plenty," Lee said. "An abundance, I assure you."

After the two men had signed the preliminary papers, Grant proceeded to introduce Lee to his staff. As he shook hands with Grant's
military secretary, Ely Parker, a Seneca Indian, Lee stared for a

moment at Parker's dark features and finally said, "I am glad to see one real American here." If this account is true, Parker responded to the general, "We are all Americans."

As the completed letters of surrender were being copied, Grant again rushed to fill the silence, this time explaining why he was not wearing his dress sword (in fact, years later, Grant would admit to being embarrassed at wearing "no sword [and] dirty boots"). When the letters were ready, the acceptance, hand-signed by Lee, was given to Grant's secretary. Then Lee somberly shook hands with Grant, gave a courtly bow to the other officers in the room, and left.

By now, a crowd of anxious sightseers was clustered around the front porch to catch a glimpse of the Confederate general. His face flushed a deep crimson, Lee emerged onto the porch, carrying his hat and gloves. Here he paused, put on his hat, and slowly drew on his gloves, absent-mindedly gazing out into the field beyond. Once, then twice, then a third time, he unconsciously balled his left hand and pumped the fist into the palm of his right. Still seemingly oblivious to his surroundings, he auto-matically returned the salute given to him by the Union officers crowding around the porch, then descended the stairs. Now, as if drawing him-self back from a daze, he glanced deliberately in one direction and then the next. Not seeing his horse, he called out in a half-choked and more than half-tired voice, "Orderly! Orderly!" The horse was brought around. The general smoothed Traveller's forelocks as the orderly fit the bridle, then with a slow, exhausted tug, pulled himself on the horse, letting out a long deep sigh, almost a groan. By then, Grant had walked out on the porch, too, and as Lee rode past him, their eyes met. Each silently lifted his hat to the other. On the porch and in the yard, countless other Federals also returned the gesture.

In no small measure, this one poignant moment captured the spirit of Appomattox more than the words ever written about that day. But this didn't stop the participants from trying to give voice to the event, includ-ing Grant himself. "I felt sad and depressed," Grant later explained of this moment, "at the downfall of a foe who had fought so long and valiantly, and had suffered so much for a cause, though that cause was, I believe, one of the worst for which a people ever fought."

Two of Grant's aides put it thus: "This will live in history," one wrote. Another commented, "Such a scene only happens once in centuries . . . "

❧   ❧   ❧

Euphoria quickly spread through the Federal camp. General Meade, both arms in the air, shouted with all his voice: "It's all over boys! Lee's surrendered! It's all over now . . ." The air was quickly blanketed with whatever the men could hurl: hats, boots, coats, knapsacks, cartridge boxes, shelter tents, shirts, canteens, and haversacks. Huge bearded men embraced and kissed like schoolgirls. Grown men cried. Sobs and moans filled the valley. Bands struck up "Old Hundredth," "The Star Spangled Banner," and "Marching Along." And then Federal artillery started to fire salutes. All this, however, irritated Grant. He knew there would be plenty of time for rejoicing, but today was not it. He sternly ordered them to stop.

"The Confederates were now our prisoners," he later explained, "and we did not want to exult over their downfall."

For one thing, Grant was acutely aware that on this day, what had occurred was the surrender of one army to another—not of one government to another. In this sense, Meade was distinctly not correct: it wasn't yet "all over." The war was still very much on. There were a number of potentially troubling rebel commanders in the field. And there were still some 175,000 other Confederates under arms elsewhere: one-half in scattered garrisons and the rest in the three remaining rebel armies. What mattered now was laying the groundwork for persuading Lee's fellow armies to join in his surrender—and also for reunion, the urgent matter of making the nation whole again. Thus, it should be no great surprise that there was a curious restraint in Grant's tepid victory message passed on to Washington.

Dated 4:30 P.M., April 9, and addressed to Secretary of War Stanton, the message simply stated: "General Lee surrendered the Army of Northern Virginia this afternoon on terms proposed by myself."

❧   ❧   ❧

Robert E. Lee had done his duty and, however heartbroken, was prepared to do his duty still. Having devoted himself to winning the war, until the bitter end, he was now beginning the transition to an equally fervent commitment, reuniting the two halves of the divided country. As he slowly rode back to his camp, some fifteen minutes away, advance soldiers began to shout, "General, are we surrendered?" Lee struggled for words to express his sense of despair and came up short; he was speechless. But soon, two solid walls of men began to line the road, and when he came into view, they began to cheer wildly. At the sound and the sight, tears started to roll in the general's eyes, and his men, too, began to weep. "Each group began in the same way, with cheers, and ended in the same way with sobs, all the way to the quarters," observed one Confederate. Disheartened, bearded men collapsed on their knees, covered their faces, and wept like children. When Lee raised his head and waved his hat in his hand, the stoic reserve of officers also broke down, and they sat on their horses and openly cried aloud. With their commander gently riding by, men drew their hands sadly over the sides of Traveller, while one old rebel called out, summing up the feeling of all the men, "I love you just as well as ever, general."

But not all the soldiers cheered in defeat. One private fell to the ground and shouted, "Blow, Gabriel, blow! My God! Let him blow! I am ready to die!" Another muttered darkly, "No Yankee will ever shoot us . . ." A private swore he would never be surrendered and, shouldering his knapsack, readied to leave for North Carolina to join Joe Johnston. And one of Lee's generals and a prominent former Virginia governor would soon remark, when asked about reconciliation, "There is rancor in our hearts which you little dream of. We hate you sir!" But with his eyes fixed on a line between his horse's ears, his gaze straight ahead, his cheeks still damp with tears, Lee was determined to curb such sentiments. In a day marked by simple eloquence and simple touches, Lee ended with one that more than equaled all the rest: upon his return, a crowd of weeping soldiers was waiting in front of the general's tent. When Lee arrived, he paused thoughtfully, then spoke up. "Boys," he told his men, "I have done the best I could for you. My heart is too full to say more."

But, before he turned and silently mouthed, "Good-bye" and "God bless you all" and then disappeared into his tent, alone, he uttered this: "Go home now, and if you make as good citizens as you have soldiers, you will do well, and I shall always be proud of you."

Before dusk settled, a light drizzle began to fall on the land.

❧   ❧   ❧

The question that forever must be asked is this: how did a general, who declared we must all be "prepared to die at our posts," and men, who, in their final battle at Sayler's Creek, clawed and charged and even bit their enemy with a pure, savage fury, then lay down their guns and begin to open their hearts to the other side? In retrospect, there seems to be an air of inevitability about the three hours in the Wilmer McLean house in Appomattox and the process it set in motion, a belief that all this seemed so natural, the gracious meeting of two generals, a surrender conducted smoothly, without a touch of rancor. And there is a pervading sense that the reconciliation that followed was near flawless, that the men were gabbing maniacally with each other, emptying their guns and unshouldering their holsters, backslapping and laughing, suddenly racing headlong toward a peaceful coexistence. To be sure, late that afternoon, Union soldiers drifted into the Confederate camp, and soon knots of blue- and gray-clad men dotted the hills around Appomattox Court House; bullets were indeed replaced by backslaps, the rebel yell with a hearty Southern drawl, war fervor with the first hints of war nostalgia, unbridled hatred with nascent relief, and, by the next day, West Point mini-reunions were even breaking out at the McLean farmhouse. But all this is deceiving, of course, a view arising conveniently out of hindsight.

Appomattox was not preordained. There were no established rules or well-worn script. If anything, retribution had been the larger and longer precedent. So, if these moments teemed with hope—and they did—it was largely due to two men, who rose to the occasion, to Grant's and Lee's respective actions: one general, magnanimous in victory, the other, gracious and equally dignified in defeat, the two of them, for their own reasons and in their own ways, fervently interested in beginning the process to bind up the wounds of the last four years. And yes, if, paradoxically, these were among Lee's finest hours, and they were, so, too, were they Grant's greatest moments.

But we also delude ourselves if we think the process initiated at Appomattox was the summary end. Indeed, it was but the beginning of a long, arduous, and still tenuous course.

One that could still veer off track in the weeks ahead.

✣   ✣   ✣

The next day, it was still raining when Lee issued his final order to his troops, known simply as General Orders Number 9.

> After four years of arduous service, marked by unsurpassed courage and fortitude, the Army of Northern Virginia has been compelled to yield to overwhelming numbers and resources. I need not tell the brave survivors of so many hard fought battles, who have remained steadfast to the last, that I have consented to the result from no distrust of them. But feeling that valor and devotion could accomplish nothing that would compensate for the loss that must have attended the continuance of the contest, I determined to avoid the useless sacrifice of those whose past services have endeared them to their countrymen. By the terms of the agreement officers and men can return to their homes and remain until exchanged. You will take with you the satisfaction that proceeds from the consciousness of duty faithfully performed, and I earnestly pray that a Merciful God will extended to you His blessing and protection.
>
> With an increasing admiration of your constancy and devotion to your country, and a grateful remembrance of your kind and generous considerations for myself, I bid you all an affectionate farewell.

For generations, General Orders Number 9 would be recited in the South with the same pride as the Gettysburg Address was learned in the North. It is marked less by its soaring prose—the language is in fact rather prosaic—but by what it does say, bringing his men affectionate words of closure, and, just as importantly, what it doesn't say. Nowhere does it exhort his men to continue the struggle; nowhere does it challenge the legitimacy of the Union government that had forced their surrender; nowhere does it fan the flames of discontent. In fact, Lee pointedly struck out a draft paragraph that could have been construed to do just that.

Of almost equal import that day was a surprise message delivered to Lee at ten that morning. Grant was waiting at the Confederate picket lines. Lee immediately rode out to see him.

Once again, Grant sought to use Lee's influence to induce the surrender of other Confederate armies, and in so doing, Grant believed that he was on a mission from Abraham Lincoln. In their crucial City Point meeting on the *River Queen* in late March, and as recently as a week earlier in Petersburg, Lincoln had expressed his wish to let the South "down easy." His goal was a true Union, not a victorious North harshly punishing a vanquished and treasonous foe. Grant thus sought to push his former antagonist into the politics of dissolving the Confederacy, even asking (when he surely could have demanded) if Lee would go to Washington to meet with Lincoln. Well versed in war, Grant was pressing the tactics of peace; the entire Confederacy would look to the slightest gesture, to every word, every motion that Lee would make. Grant realized that even for a defeated General Lee, his fame eclipsed his rank. One statement from the aging patriarch could sway the entire South in the crucial weeks and months to come. But Lee, the military man, demurred, saying that such moves were impossible; he could not formally urge other surrenders without conferring with civilian authorities, namely President Davis.

Still, Grant's pleas were not in vain. Equally significant, Lee did pledge to do this: he would, he said, devote "his whole efforts to pacifying the country and bringing the people back to the Union." That was good enough for Grant. He promised he would carry Lee's message to Lincoln, immediately.

❦   ❦   ❦

If the spirit of Appomattox was codified on paper on the ninth, and reinforced between the two commanding generals on the tenth, it was enshrined in the memories of the fighting men on the twelfth. That day marked the formal surrender of Lee's army.

Above all, this surrender defied millenniums of tradition in which rebellions typically ended in yet a greater shedding of blood. As Henry Steele Commager and Samuel Eliot Morison properly remind us, one need only recall the harsh suppression of the peasants' revolt in Germany in the sixteenth century, or the ravages of Alva during the Dutch rebellion, or the terrible punishments inflicted on the Irish by Cromwell and then on the Scots after Culloden, or the bloodstained vengeance exacted during the French Revolution, or the terrible retribution executed during the Napoleonic restoration, or the horrible retaliation imposed during the futile Chinese rebellion in the mid-nineteenth century. And of course, in our own time there are the incalculable horrors of the Russian, Nazi, and Spanish revolutions and civil wars, and, both in and outside the industrialized world, the more recent bloodstained retribution in Cambodia, Yugoslavia, and Rwanda.

But on this April day in 1865, there was instead the formal stacking of arms and the last, somber folding of battle flags. Men were not hanged, they were saluted; they were not jailed, they were honored; they were not humiliated or beaten, they were embraced. Some of this was by design; much of it occurred totally spontaneously. All of it mattered.

It was Grant who had insisted upon a formal surrender—one that the participants would never forget—although, in typical fashion, he ordered that it be kept simple. The two sides met along the stage road at the eastern edge of the village. Behind them stretched rolling farmland, groves of trees, and grass-covered hills. The Union officer in charge of the ceremony was Joshua L. Chamberlain, the fighting professor from Bowdoin College in Maine, who had won a Medal of Honor for his valor at Gettysburg's Little Round Top. Now a brigadier general, he had been wounded twice since then and was still in pain from a bullet that had almost killed him during this final campaign. Leading the 28,000 or so Confederates was Major General John B. Gordon, one of Lee's hardest fighters, who had been shot through the face and wounded four more times during his service to the Confederacy, and who now commanded Stonewall Jackson's old corps. This was the last Confederate advance of the Army of Northern Virginia, and it was carried out with stunning precision. Chamberlain would never forget it: "On they came, with the old swinging route step and swaying battle flags . . . crowded so thick, by thinning out of men, that the whole column seemed crowned with red . . . In the van, the proud Confederate ensign . . . Before us in proud humiliation stood the embodiment of manhood; men whom neither toils and sufferings, nor the fact of death nor disaster nor hopelessness . . . could bend from their resolve; standing before us now, thin, worn, and famished, but erect, and with eyes looking level into ours, waking memories that bound us together as no other bond . . . "

Without having planned it—and without any official sanction—Chamberlain suddenly gave the order for Union soldiers to "carry arms" as a sign of their deepest mark of military respect. A bugle call instantly rang out. All along the road, Union soldiers raised their muskets to their shoulders, the salute of honor. "At the sound of the machine-like snap of arms," Chamberlain recalled, "General Gordon started . . . then wheeled his horse, facing me, touching him gently with the spur so that the animal slightly reared, and, as he wheeled, horse and rider made one motion, the horse's head swung down with a graceful bow, and General Gordon dropped his sword-point to his toe in salutation." And as he did, the veterans in blue gave a soldierly salute to those "vanquished heroes"—a "token of respect from Americans to Americans."

Gordon ordered his men to answer in kind, "honor answering honor." And then, Chamberlain wrote, "On our part not a sound of trumpet more, nor roll of drum; not a cheer, nor word, nor whisper or vainglorying, nor motion of man . . . but an awed stillness rather, and breath-holding, as if it were the passing of the dead."

The formal surrender continued for seven full hours, encompassing not just some 28,000 men, but over 100,000 pounds of arms, munitions, and colors that had been carried across some of the bloodiest battle lines. Chamberlain described it thus: "As each successive division masks our own, it halts, the men face inward toward us across the road, twelve feet away; then carefully 'dress' their line . . . They fix bayonets, stack arms; then hesitatingly, remove cartridge-boxes and lay them down. Lastly—reluctantly, with agony of expression—they tenderly fold their flags, battle worn and torn, bloodstained, heart-holding colors, and lay them down . . . "

And finally, he added, from his own heart, "How could we help falling on our knees, all of us together, and praying God to pity and forgive us all!"

❧   ❧   ❧

Yet, for all the promise of this day, as the Army of Northern Virginia slowly disbanded and began heading home, dire questions remained. Would the spirit of Appomattox infuse the rest of the tattered Confederacy, still prepared to fight and die for the Stars and Bars? Would Lee's rejection of guerrilla warfare prevail over Davis's embrace? Would the Confederates, some of whom were already scattered throughout the country like "partridges and rabbits," take to the hills in an organized manner and fight, for weeks, months, or years? Or would they now follow Lee's example and become "good citizens"? Would a last "apocalyptic engagement" still be fought in the deeper reaches of the South, with more lives lost, more men killed? And could the country finally become reunited, a true Union, at long last not simply a loose collection of states, but a nation?

These were hardly idle concerns, as a weary Abraham Lincoln in Washington well knew. One stubborn fact still clung fast: the war was not quite over; two state capitals remained in Confederate hands. Lee had surrendered only a fraction of the Southern soldiers under arms, and daunting obstacles remained. Even Mary Custis Lee had this to say: "The end is not yet. Richmond is not the Confederacy. General Lee is not the Confederacy." In truth, there was still Joe Johnston's army in North Carolina that had to be subdued, and a host of other extant smaller armies: Richard Taylor's, spread across Alabama, Mississippi, and eastern Louisiana; E. Kirby Smith's, just west of the Mississippi; the forces of Colonel John S. "Rest-in-Peace" Ford, in Texas; and the Indian armies in the far West, under Brigadier General Stand Watie. And there were still John Mosby in Virginia and Nathan Bedford Forrest, his men scattered across Mississippi, Alabama, and Tennessee, and an array of other smaller guerrilla groups. And of course, there was the Confederate government on the run. In a sense, Lincoln knew that final victory would come in a matter of time. But then, time could be a bitter enemy as well as a good friend. How much longer would it be? One week? Three? A month? Six months? Throughout history, such brief time spans have been long enough to form military alliances, declare and win wars, unseat dynasties, plunge countries into unmitigated chaos, or abruptly shift the momentum of entire conflicts themselves. Indeed, there was one more sobering fact: the grim aphorism that in matters of war and peace, the actions of one man alone could radically alter the whole constellation of events, that history could abruptly shift and turn, that the euphoria and inevitability of one day could dissolve into tragedy and disaster by the next.

Which was precisely what would happen.

PART 3

April 15, 1865

5

The Unraveling

I think we are near the end at last," Lincoln cautiously told his secretary of state when the sun had set on the events of Palm Sunday, April 9, 1865.

Outside, the people were far less restrained. Fruitful and teeming with hope, the North had already been celebrating heartily since the fall of Richmond. That day merited a whopping 900-gun salute. After Appomattox, 500 guns again boomed throughout the city, shattering windows across the way from the White House in Lafayette Square and sending a thrilling shock wave down the streets. The people themselves, from Georgetown to Capitol Hill, Judiciary Square to Center Market, Negro Hill to Swampoodle, Rock Creek Park to the fine estates of Harewood and Kalorama in the far-off suburbs north of Washington, have been "delirious with joy." For the better part of this week, the jubilation has been everywhere: bonfires burn on every corner, flags snap festively in the wind, normally dour men stomp their feet and wave their arms, children scamper about, chanting and cheering. Where Richmond is a dreary welter of burned-out buildings, dank boarding-houses, and scattered debris, of recalcitrant Southerners and occupy-ing soldiers, Washington reeks of one endless round of festivities: lawn fetes, bazaars, wild saloon gatherings, smokers, parties, torchlight parades, and theatricals. And most of all the people are hungering for speeches, above all, from the president. "Speech!" a crowd of some 3,000 cries out at the White House on Monday evening. Then once more: "*Speech!*"—as though it were a simple one-word cheer, an antiphon, echoed and reechoed by the beaming, tearful, exultant Unionists who rejoiced in the ecstatic evidence that their sacrifices had not been in vain. But Abraham Lincoln curiously puts them off, instead promising to deliver an address on Tuesday night. Oddly enough, only Lincoln, in his exhausted condition, seems strangely immune to the intoxicating glow of impending military victory.

But why? Since the stunning news of Appomattox, he should be relishing the splendid vindication of sticking to his guns over the last four years, of finally twitting his enemies and his critics, and huddling with his aides and closest friends in enjoying the moment. To be sure, there has been a striking change in his mood since Lee's surrender. For those who have seen him in the past few days, he "is like a different man," "his face is shining," his conversations are "exhilarating," his whole appearance is "marvelously changed." But others notice something else: he is still so exhausted that one newspaper, the *New York Tribune*, urgently pleads that "his energies must be spared" if he is to complete his second term. And, to some, he is almost at loose ends. He hasn't been sleeping well, troubled by insomnia and haunted by bizarre and ghoulish dreams. He is afflicted with fierce headaches. He is thirty pounds underweight. One evening, aides notice that he is grave and pale, even visibly disturbed. Mary Lincoln observes how "dreadful solemn" he is. And he is beset by dark thoughts. Earlier that week, along the James River near City Point, he and Mary had strolled through an old country graveyard. "You will survive me," he inexplicably muttered to her. "When I am gone, lay my remains in some quiet place like this."

Ironically, though, it is one of his own dreams in particular that has most unnerved him. One evening this week, Lincoln pulls Mary aside, as well as several others in the White House, and confesses, "I had [a dream] the other night, which has haunted me ever since." His morose tone is too much for the first lady. She cries out, "You frighten me! What is the matter?"

Lincoln pulls back, suddenly recoiling. He says faintly that perhaps he had "done wrong" in even mentioning the dream. But then, strangely enough, he continues, frankly admitting, "somehow the thing has got the better of me."

What is it then? Mary asks urgently. What has so gotten possession of him?

Lincoln again pauses, then begins. "About ten days ago, I retired very late," he says. "I had been waiting for important dispatches from the front. I could not have been long in bed when I fell into a slumber, for I was weary. I soon began to dream." As Lincoln is speaking, his tone shifts, becoming at once sad and solemn. "There seemed to be a death-like stillness about me. Then I heard subdued sobs, as if a number of people were weeping. I thought I left my bed and wandered downstairs. There the silence was broken by the same pitiful sobbing, but the mourners were invisible. I went from room to room; no living person was in sight, but the same mournful sounds of distress met me as I passed along. It was light in all the rooms; every object was familiar to me; but where were all the people who were grieving as if their hearts would break? I was puzzled and alarmed. What could be the meaning of all this?

"Determined to find the cause of a state of things so mysterious and shocking, I kept on until I arrived in the East Room, which I entered. There I was met with a sickening surprise. Before me was a catafalque, on which rested a corpse wrapped in funeral vestments. Around it were stationed soldiers who were acting as guards; and there was a throng of people, some gazing mournfully upon the corpse, whose face was covered, others weeping pitifully: 'Who is dead in the White House?' I demanded of one of the soldiers. 'The President' was the answer; 'he was killed by an assassin!' Then came a loud burst of grief from the crowd—"

"That is horrid!" Mary cries out this time. "I wish you had not told it."

"Well," Lincoln declares calmly, "it is only a dream, Mary. Let us say no more about it."

There is a moment's hesitation. The room falls silent. Guests accustomed to Lincoln's humor don't know what to say. For his part, Lincoln can now see that his listeners are just as frightened as the first lady. He rushes to fill the void with a light, reassuring, almost frivolous tone. He jokes to his bodyguard, big, strapping Ward Hill Lamon: "For a long time you have been trying to keep somebody—the Lord knows who—from killing me. Don't you see how it will turn out? In this dream," he continues, announcing in jest, "it is not me but some other fellow, that was killed. It seems that his ghostly assassin tried his hand on someone else."

Lamon says nothing. Nor does Mary.

Lincoln grows serious for a moment, then murmurs, his voice probably a near whisper: "Well, let it go. I think the Lord in His own good time and way will work this out all right."

❧   ❧   ❧

But in the chill, early morning of Good Friday, April 14, Lincoln wakes refreshed, around 7 A.M., and in a good mood. It is a rare occurrence, and he takes it as a good omen. Last night there were no nightmares, no haunting visages, no frantic worries about ending the war and negotiating the foundering shoals of Reconstruction. True, there has been a dream, but this time it is a heartening one, in fact, the one that has come to him before on the cusp of other major military battles. He had it on the verge of Antietam and Gettysburg, and also Vicksburg and Fort Fisher, all-important Union victories. In it, he is on a phantom ship, a "single, indescribable vessel" that moves with "great rapidity" through the water, racing toward a "vast" and "indefinite shore." To Lincoln, rising on this day, it signals good news. He feels that it augurs Joe Johnston's surrender in North Carolina, thereby removing the most powerful Confederate army remaining in the field, and making another large-scale rebel assault almost impossible. It speaks of peace to come. And it fills him with a visible blast of optimism.

Before breakfast, he lights the fireplace in his office. By the time he has finished his morning meal—dining cozily with Mary and then joined by his son Robert—and makes his way to an 11 A.M. meeting with Grant and the cabinet, he is in "great spirits," appearing more "cheerful and happy" than many of his secretaries had ever seen him. It is infectious; Mary Lincoln will even note that these last few days have been "the happiest of her life." And Lincoln is determined that the mood will not abate.

Thomas Jefferson, by Charles Willson Peale. (*Library of Congress*)

Lincoln's second inauguration, March 4, 1865, in which he called for magnanimity toward the South. (*Library of Congress*) The third president of the United States, Thomas Jefferson, one of Lincoln's heroes, cast a wide shadow over both sides of a war-torn nation. Jefferson was painted in 1791, while he was secretary of state.

Robert E. Lee. (*Library of Congress*)

They squared off in the bloody Wilderness Campaign and then settled down to a protracted siege. Grant called this period the "most anxious" of his experience and every morning worried that "I would wake up from my sleep to hear

U. S. Grant. (*Library of Congress*)

that Lee had gone." For his part, Lee was thinking anything but surrender. "We must all determine to die at our posts," he thundered.

THE CONFEDERATE DEBATE OVER
ARMING THE SLAVES

Confederate general Patrick Cleburne, an early and eloquent proponent of freeing and arming the slaves. (*Library of Congress*)

The prominent Northern intellectual Ralph Waldo Emerson openly worried that the Confederates might free the slaves first. (*Library of Congress*)

Secretary of State Judah P. Benjamin, Davis's closest adviser, favored a Confederate Emancipation Proclamation. (*Library of Congress*)

Mary Chesnut wished the Confederacy had moved first, thereby "trumping" the Union's "tricks."(*Museum of the Confederacy*)

Confederate President Jefferson Davis, an early supporter of arming the slaves, waited far too long. (*Library of Congress*)

The goal was former slaves fighting side by side with their masters. Here Andrew Chandler (*left*) poses with his servant, Silas Chandler. (*Private collection, courtesy of Museum of the Confederacy*)

Currier & Ives print of the fall of Richmond, on the night of April 2, 1865. (*Library of Congress*)

Mobbed by the city's blacks, Lincoln entered Richmond on April 4. "You are free," he told them. "Free as air." Denis Malone Carter's beautiful painting is, however, vastly exaggerated; virtually all white Virginians stayed behind shuttered windows. (*Chicago Historical Society*)

Richmond citizens frantically huddle in Capitol Square as their city burns. (*Battles and Leaders of the Civil War, vol. 4*)

THE FATEFUL DECISION:
GUERRILLA WARFARE OR SURRENDER

Brigadier General E. P. Alexander (*left*) counseled Lee to wage guerrilla warfare, saying, "We would be like rabbits and partridges in the bushes." (*Library of Congress*)

Colonel John S. Mosby (*center*), a feared partisan. (*Library of Congress*)

"Bloody Bill" Anderson (*right*), William Quantrill's second in command and later his replacement, was one of the most ruthless guerrillas on American soil. (*State Historical Society of Missouri*)

This poignant painting by George C. Bingham depicts the chaos in the border counties of Missouri, a response to the ongoing guerrilla conflict, General Orders No. 11, and martial law. (*Library of Congress*)

Painter Louis Mathieu Guillaume interprets the moving April 9 surrender of Lee to Grant inside the McLean House at Appomattox. In truth, the two generals did not sit at the same table. (*National Park Service*)

The surrender of the Army of Virginia, "honor answering honor," April 12, 1865, shown here in Ken Riley's vivid painting. (*West Point Museum Collection, U.S. Military Academy*)

Lincoln, meeting with his cabinet on April 14, declared that there was "no greater task before us" than resolving the final details of the war and its immediate aftermath. This engraving is from Francis B. Carpenter's huge oil painting, completed in 1864, portraying the first reading of the Emancipation Proclamation. (*Library of Congress*)

John Wilkes Booth,
actor and assassin.
(*Chicago Historical Society*)

The utter weariness of an anxiety-ridden Abraham Lincoln in the war's final days is hauntingly depicted in Alexander Gardner's famous print, said to be the last ever made of Lincoln. (*Library of Congress*)

Just as Secretary of State William Seward is viciously stabbed five times, Lincoln is shot and killed at Ford's Theater, Washington, D.C. *(Ford's Theater)*

The manhunt begins. *(Library of Congress)*

Andrew Johnson, widely derided as a "drunk" and shunned by official Washington, escapes untouched and is sworn in as president the next day. *(Library of Congress)*

A bereaved Union mourns. Here, New York's City Hall is draped in black bunting, with flags at half staff, as 160,000 mourners accompany the hearse down Broadway. *(Library of Congress)*

Irascible William T. Sherman, thinking back to his meeting with Lincoln and Grant at City Point, now worried that the country was perilously drifting into "anarchy" and "further civil war." More than anything else, he "dreaded" the thought of Joe Johnston's army breaking up into small guerrilla bands. (*Library of Congress*)

General Joseph E. Johnston, the head of the last remaining Confederate army in the East, was told by Davis to retreat and fight on. He refused, instead meeting with Sherman at Bennett House for a third time, where they concluded Johnston's surrender. (*Library of Congress*)

The surrender at Bennett House had none of the majesty of Appomattox—but it was crucial to the war's end. (*Library of Congress*)

Swathed in black, Richmond ladies drift through the streets of their now ruined capital. (*Library of Congress*)

White refugees with their possessions lashed to a single wagon. (*Library of Congress*)

Newly freed blacks—the next generation of citizens. (*University of Virginia, Special Collections Division*)

Mounds of fresh earth and crude headboards testify to the recent burials, April 1865. (*Library of Congress*)

For some Unionists, vengeance was to be the order of the day, as depicted in this lithograph, *Freedom's Immortal Triumph*. *(Library of Congress)* But this vision conflicted starkly with the generous spirit of Lincoln's postwar philosophy, as captured by the 1865 Kimmel & Forster lithograph, *The Last Offer of Reconciliation*. *(Library of Congress)*

Today, Good Friday, will certainly not be spent in morbid contemplation or prayer at the New York Avenue Presbyterian Church listening to Reverend Phineas D. Gurley, or simply more fussing and fretting over the war. Today, he wants something that will make him laugh. So this evening he plans to take Mary to see the eccentric English comedy *Our American Cousin*. It stars the famous English actress Miss Laura Keene, in her very last performance. He and Mary intend to go with General Grant and his wife, and the papers will officially announce their plans.

The comedy is playing at the Tenth Street theater, between E and F streets. At Ford's.

❧ ❧ ❧

In the meantime, a far more powerful drama is under way as the cabinet meeting commences. It has been simmering beneath the surface for months, and now Lincoln will confront perhaps his greatest challenge yet: to subdue the Confederate forces once and for all, while at the same time laying groundwork for the peace to follow. In short, the complex and demanding matter of a postwar America, of reintegrating the South into the Union and forging the nation anew. He calls it Reconstruction. A word that more adequately captures his spirit, however, is "reconciliation."

Only then, he feels, can he achieve the true Union that he spoke of so eloquently at his second inaugural. Even if there are no more feverish battles—and until Johnston actually does surrender he cannot be sure of this—further low-level fighting and bloodshed could prolong the bitterness, and in turn could tempt the Confederates to take to the countryside and continue the war in some manner. This must be avoided at all costs.

He believes deeply that the rebels must be able to return to their homes and see more than "desolation," see more than a "hated rule" of the North; somehow, he asserts, they must be enjoined to "accept citizenship" in the Union again. Could they? He does not have a rigid blueprint for this, but he does have a distinct vision: there has to be a speedy return of the Confederate states into the Union on the most generous terms. "Civil government must be reestablished as soon as possible," he has already instructed his navy secretary, Gideon Welles. "There must be courts, and laws, and order—or society would be broken up . . . [and] the disbanded armies would turn into . . . guerillas."

And he is equally determined to undertake the process of restoring the rebellious states to "their proper practical relationship with the Union." Thus, there must be, as he lectures his cabinet, "no persecutions," "no bloody work after the war was over," no expectations that he would "take part in hanging or killing these men, even the worst of them." Thus, he castigates those in Congress who "possess feelings of hate and vindictiveness," and has tartly stressed to the young French nobleman, Marquis de Chambrun, his "firm resolution to stand for clemency against all opposition." Thus, while he strolled through a smoldering Richmond and was asked by the commanding general in charge, General Godfrey Weitzel, how the defeated Confederates should be treated, he offered this homespun instruction: "If I were in your place, I'd let 'em up easy, let 'em up easy." And thus his choice to make a private—and unannounced—stop at the home of an old Richmond friend and Confederate general, George Pickett, the man who had led the infamous Gettysburg charge. There, he fondled Pickett's baby in his arms and whispered to the child, as the astonished mother curiously looked on, "Tell your father I will grant him a special amnesty—if he wants it—for the sake of your mother's bright eyes and your good manners."

After four bloody years of reaching for the Confederacy's jugular, Lincoln's humanity is unchanged. This avatar of total war is a staunch advocate of a soft peace, a generous peace, a magnanimous peace, just as Grant has carried out at Appomattox. It is his *River Queen* Doctrine writ large. So passionately does he feel about this matter that he will direly tell his cabinet today, in no uncertain words, there is "no greater or more important [issue] before us, or any future Cabinet" than Reconstruction.

That, too, was Friday, April 14.

❧   ❧   ❧

Yet Reconstruction is complex, it is nuanced, and, to later generations, almost wholly baffling and prone to being misunderstood. The popular conception is that Reconstruction was to commence at war's end. This is untrue. Actually, for Lincoln, it started not as a task to be implemented upon victory, but as a tactical measure of war itself. Since the conflict began, he had to prevent the border states themselves from slipping into rebellion (Delaware and Kentucky, for instance, still practiced slavery), seek to peel away shaky parts of the Southern coalition, govern sectors freshly captured from the South, and prevent occupied territories from falling back into the hands of "our enemies." In all this, he was convinced that one of the surest means to undermine the Confederacy was by setting up loyal regimes in Southern areas almost as soon as they fell under the control of Union armies. Already, he had made piecemeal attempts to do exactly that, reorganizing Federal-occupied Louisiana, Arkansas, and Tennessee, establishing military control there, then helping them to set up antisecessionist governments loyal to Washington and committed to emancipation. In this regard, however, he was thinking far less about the status of the South after the war—although to some extent he hoped his reconstructed Louisiana would be a showcase for how the North and South could be reunited—than about measures to stop the fighting.

But by April 1865, the hard questions could no longer be dodged. Now the end of the war was in sight but the country remained divided, both in spirit and in fact. When the guns fell silent, then, what was to be done with the victory? Lincoln fretted. The matter was as vexing as the war itself.

For Lincoln, Reconstruction was not so much a policy as a process. While he had outlined a specific plan in 1863 for restoring states back to the Union—a state could be readmitted if 10 percent of the captured voting population was willing to take an oath of loyalty to the Union and allegiance to the Emancipation Proclamation—his approach varied depending upon the circumstances and exigencies of the moment. Flexibility was the watchword. Promises of amnesty, discussions of gradual emancipation, matters like black suffrage were all up for debate.

And debated they were. For all his ministrations about Reconstruction, many of Lincoln's Radical Republican critics on Capitol Hill and elsewhere—those who wanted no compromise on the issues of black suffrage, black civil rights, or a harsh treatment of the South—were at best indifferent to his views and, at worst, outright hostile to them. And they included some of his own cabinet members as well. Here, the abuses and intrigues of Washington were unrelenting.

In fact, more often than not, Lincoln and his Republican colleagues were at each other's throats. He had his plans; they had theirs. For starters, there were the broad philosophical questions. Was the Confederacy to be treated like a conquered, treasonous nation, a hodgepodge of nameless, shapeless territories to be carved up and remade, *lex talionus* ("an eye for an eye"), as the Radicals believed? Or would it return, as an equal part of the United States, Lincoln's view, in which some rebels would be innocent and others, a far smaller number, perhaps guilty of crimes? Then there were the questions of government. Who would make the crucial decisions about Reconstruction? Congress? (It thought so.) The president and the executive? (Lincoln was adamant.) A special body to be established? (A compromise.) And there were, of course, the unending skirmishes over specifics. How would the guilty be distinguished from the innocent? On what timetable? Under whose supervision? And, naturally, what about the former slaves?

But the nub of the matter was largely this. The Radicals wanted to recast the entire social structure of the South, while Lincoln was principally looking to reincorporate the rebellious states back into the Union fold, absent slavery. Where they wanted full suffrage for blacks, he was far more tentative (the black vote still did not exist in most of the North), favoring the vote for "very intelligent Negroes" and black soldiers— although in saying this, he was the first president ever to announce that he favored any form of Negro suffrage. Where they were looking to divide up the estates of the defeated planters, giving each black family "forty acres and a mule," Lincoln still toyed with ideas on how to compensate the whites for their loss; more than ever, he was thinking about the painful transition that the Confederacy would have to make from a slave society to a free society. And where the Radicals vented progressive opinions on everything from school integration to social equality between blacks and whites and interracial marriages, Lincoln frequently remained mum. To be sure, he supported the Freedman's Bureau to protect blacks from exploitation by their former masters. But to Lincoln, these other matters were, in his own words, nothing but "pernicious abstractions," fanciful hypotheticals that only obscured the larger, more crucial issue of a search for peace.

So, time and again, Lincoln straddled an uncomfortable middle. It was precarious, it was awkward, and it was probably inevitable. While he did not share the conservatives' desire to put Dixie back into the hands of the planters and commercial men who had dominated before the war, neither did he subscribe to the Radicals' belief that the only true Unionists in the South were the blacks. Though he was politically isolated, often besieged between extremes, and even the underdog, his longer-term goal nonetheless remained fixed as a rock: end the war and revive the Union. Which meant rebuilding and restoring the conquered South while maintaining the loyalty of white Unionists, protecting black freedoms, and controlling a rebellious white majority. It was an escape act worthy of Houdini. And the problems were endless. No surprise, Reconstruction was repeatedly thwarted by continuing feuds and mired in endless delays, leading Lincoln to complain, "We can never finish this, if we never begin it." Never was this more true than by April 1865, as a dismal impasse had been reached altogether.

True, there were fleeting moments of cooperation. He and the Radicals had happily collaborated on Lincoln's boldest stroke, the historic Thirteenth Amendment abolishing slavery forever. But as it happened, the partnership largely dissolved after that. In Congress alone, Lincoln clashed with his friend, the dapper New Englander, Senator Charles Sumner; he jousted with the churlish representative, Thaddeus Stevens; he maneuvered against the blunt Ohioan, Congressman Benjamin Wade. The slurred epithets shouted against him were fierce. The hostility was often implacable—and seemed to grow daily. On Lincoln's attempts to get newly elected representatives from Union-occupied Louisiana and Arkansas seated in Congress, Marylander Henry Winter Davis fulminated, "When I came to Congress ten years ago, this was a government of law. I have lived to see it a government of personal will." When he sought to recognize a transitional Unionist regime in Louisiana, the radical abolitionists Wendell Phillips and George Luther

Stearns organized a protest against him, and Lincoln was widely labeled "a dictator." When he pursued his Louisiana plan nonetheless, Senator Wade and other liberals were no less cutting, castigating it as Lincoln's "seven months' abortion." And when Lincoln argued that the military could help establish a civilian regime in Louisiana, for safekeeping until it became a free and democratic state, pleading, "We shall sooner have the fowl by hatching the egg than by smashing it," Senator Sumner frostily snapped back, "The eggs of crocodiles can produce only crocodiles." In the end, Congress stymied all of Lincoln's cherished plans for restoring the occupied Confederate South, prompting the *New York Herald* to wryly note, Sumner has "kicked the pet scheme of the President down the marble steps of the Senate Chamber."

But, in truth, it was not just Sumner. Indeed, on February 3, 1865, when Lincoln met with the three Confederate commissioners at Hampton Roads, he had held out the carrot of compensated emancipation to the South—$400 million for the Confederate states—if only the rebels would cease their resistance to the national authority by April 1. Yet the equivocation of the Confederate commissioners was nothing compared to the stinging reply from, of all places, his own cabinet, which unanimously rebuffed him. Reeling from their vehemence, he bowed his head, folded up his papers, and chortled sheepishly, "You are all against me." His sentiment was understandable. For when the Radical Republicans weren't sticking their finger in Lincoln's eye, the conservative Republicans, and Democrats, and some of his own senior officials, like Postmaster General Montgomery Blair, were, criticizing his Reconstruction policies for surrendering to the "nigger" vote and succumbing to "radical" influences.

To his credit, during these tension-ridden months, Lincoln was always too much a politician to personalize things; he knew he needed the powerful Senate barons, the Sumners and the Wades, and he remained able to differentiate between mere glancing swipes of their criticisms and fatal blows. Yet the toll it took on him was often evident, in the deep lines crevassing his face, in the thick black rings that framed his eyes like a somnambulist's dark pouches, in his cold and clammy hands, and in his many bouts of depression.

But Lincoln, always itching for progress, kept plugging away. He didn't dally, he didn't vacillate, he didn't become engrossed in minor matters or get bogged down in rigid ideology. Nor was he impatient, arrogant, or unfeeling. When he visited Richmond on April 3, he made another bold stab at hastening the war's end, meeting with the rebel assistant secretary of war, John A. Campbell. Even then, Lincoln desperately feared more bloodshed, and he had calculated that if Virginia withdrew from the Confederacy and made a speedy peace with the Union, her example might mobilize the rest of a ravaged South to follow suit. He promised Campbell that he "would save any repenting sinner from hanging" and, more significantly, tentatively authorized the rebel legislature to convene and help disband Virginia's troops and send them home. In the ensuing days, however, when word of his actions leaked out, his cabinet again howled in protest, Secretary of War Edwin Stanton and Attorney General James Speed in particular. This was heresy, they argued strenuously, tantamount to recognizing the rebel legislature as a legal body. Lincoln had thought he might at least get the support of his secretary of the navy, Gideon Welles. He didn't. Welles, too, objected in the strongest terms. Flabbergasted, the president was at first overly defensive about his actions, feebly contending that he had only authorized the "gentlemen who have *acted* as the legislature," and denying that he ever intended to recognize them as "a rightful body." He further protested that he was only trying "to effect a reconciliation as soon as possible" and he shouldn't "stickle about forms," provided he could "attain the desired result."

But with his entire cabinet again arrayed against him, he buckled, meekly admitting he "had perhaps made a mistake." On April 12, he revoked the order.

❧   ❧   ❧

But perhaps never were his anxieties about Reconstruction and the waging of peace more apparent than on Tuesday, the evening of April 11.

It is a paradoxical sight, for signs of celebration in the Union capital are everywhere. Despite a thick mist outside, the four corners of the city are illuminated: high atop its hill, the new Capitol dome is brilliantly lit and visible for miles; 3,500 victory candles shimmer beautifully in the windows of the Government Post Office; not to be outdone, 6,000 glow along the Patent Office. Across town, the high, stately mansions of the rich and the powerful shine with gas lamps and fine candles, while eastward, the broken shanties of Negro settlements and the poorest alleys are proudly lit with the flickers of simple homemade tallow. Far off in the distance, across the blackened Potomac, Robert E. Lee's home, Arlington, blinks like a million dazzling fireflies in the night, ablaze with colored candles and exploding rockets and the voice of thousands of ex-slaves singing "De Yar ob Jubilo." And in the city's epicenter, hundreds of people gather on the White House lawn, clogging Pennsylvania Avenue and filling the streets. Drunk and exuberant, they are waving banners and singing songs, and, in call after call until their voices are hoarse, they summon the president once and for all to give a rousing, glorious speech about Union victory.

Finally, Lincoln steps to the second-floor balcony window to cheers that surge and break and surge and break. Standing in the darkness like a ghostly apparition, with a lone candle held by an aide, he carefully begins to read his prepared text, which he has labored over in the last day. It is to be, the crowd expects, a thundering speech, one that will be locked forever triumphantly into the Unionist memory. Instead, however, it takes a most puzzling twist.

"We meet this evening, not in sorrow, but in gladness of heart," he opens, adding, "The evacuation of Petersburg and Richmond and the surrender of the principal insurgent army, give hope of a righteous and speedy peace"; thus, he quickly reminds the audience that the war is not yet over. Promising a day of "National thanksgiving," he goes on to explain that the country will now face the trial of "the re-inauguration of the national authority," a task "fraught with great difficulty," all the more so because of a "small additional embarrassment." What is it? That "we, the loyal people, differ among ourselves as to the mode, manner, and means of reconstruction."

The audience, once buzzing with animation, soon falls silent, even restive. This is a frustrating, peculiar address; not a stem-winding speech but more the musings of a president obsessed with the "knotty problems" of Reconstruction. It is a defense—and a turgid plea, and they take it like a song sung off-key.

Lincoln continues: "Unlike the case of a war between independent nations, there is no authorized organ for us to treat with. No one man had authority to give up the rebellion for any other man. We simply must begin with, and mould from, disorganized and discordant elements." At great length, he then addresses his Republican critics, noting that they have already excoriated him for the interim state government that he has created in Louisiana, and are especially unhappy that blacks have not been given the vote (on this very day, in fact, Chief Justice Salmon Chase labels this act "criminal"). That may be so, but Lincoln explains that he personally prefers that "very intelligent" blacks and black "soldiers" should be given suffrage. Still, he protests, isn't it wiser to accept Louisiana with all its imperfections and "improve it"? Now he cajoles the crowd: there is much to commend Louisiana for already. It has a constitution that outlaws slavery, that grants blacks economic independence, that provides public school benefits equally for both races, and that empowers the legislature to enfranchise Negroes if it so chooses. "Grant that [the colored man] deserves the elective franchise," he says, "will he not attain it sooner by saving the already advanced steps toward it, than by running backward over them?" Moreover, he duly reminds his listeners, if his Republican critics reject Louisiana, they reject one more crucial vote for the Thirteenth Amendment outlawing slavery.

The mist changes to a drizzle, and soon it thickens into rain. By now, the tedium of the speech—it is actually somewhat pedantic and inelegant—drives some listeners off, one by one. Others shuffle their feet uneasily, recoiling at his mention of allowing blacks to vote.

Lincoln then holds out an olive branch to his political adversaries. He notes that he is willing to meet them halfway; he is willing to be flexible about Reconstruction and work with the Congress (in fact, this is little more than political maneuvering; he intends to sidestep them altogether, privately asserting: "I think it providential that there are none of the disturbing elements of that body here to hinder and embarrass us"). His plan for Louisiana is one plan ("*a* plan"), but not the "only plan" for reconstructing the other Confederate states. He is willing to retune and alter, fix and adjust, depending on the specific needs and circumstances of each state. "As bad promises are better broken than kept, I shall treat this as a bad promise, and break it, whenever I shall be convinced that keeping it is adverse to the public interest." But, he cautions, "I have not yet been so convinced."

Stressing that this situation is far from resolved, he closes with a mysterious caveat: "In the present *'situation'* as the phrase goes, it may be my duty to make some new announcement to the people of the South. I am considering, and shall not fail to act, when satisfied that action will be proper."

This final cryptic message again befuddles the crowd. Does it mean he will announce universal suffrage? Amnesty for all rebels—his City Point Doctrine? A proclamation putting the entire South under military rule? As a puzzled murmur rolls through the audience, this question is left unanswered. Lincoln himself withdraws, again ghostlike, into the White House. Meanwhile, the crowd gives him only the most perfunctory applause. In truth, they are disappointed. They were hankering for a stirring oratory, a triumphant speech about the success of the Union armies, about the glorious sacrifices of Gettysburg, Cold Harbor, and Mayres Heights, about how their years of suffering had been proven right and were thusly being rewarded. They are not interested in the nagging problems of Louisiana, or the particulars of Reconstruction more broadly. Tonight, they are even less interested in the president's dilemmas with Congress. Much of the crowd has already signaled its boredom and wandered off. Many others remaining fumed when Lincoln suggested limited Negro suffrage—both foolish and fanatical, they felt. To these people, and they were a considerable number, the country's troubles were Lincoln's doing—not the South's. Of these, one member of the audience, an actor by trade, feels particularly strongly, growling to his companion: "That means nigger citizenship! Now, by God, I'll put him through."

Back inside the White House, Lincoln is not just once again exhausted, but "very anxious" about the cool reaction of the crowd. He is hardly any more reassured when he learns that the Radicals, whom he sought to reach out to, have overwhelmingly rejected the compromises he offered in the address. One Boston journalist blasts him for his "backwardness" and argues that it "will be wicked and blasphemous for us as a nation to allow any distinction of color whatever in the reconstructed states." For his part, speaking for the Radicals from the Hill, Senator Sumner sternly agrees. "Alas! Alas," he protests. By failing to adopt "a just and safe system" of Reconstruction—to wit, one that enfranchises all freedmen—the president is only promoting "confusion and uncertainty in the future—with hot controversy."

And to make matters worse, within his own cabinet there is also continued opposition. Salmon Chase, his chief justice, for one, is unhappy that Lincoln is unwilling to endorse "universal suffrage."

❧ ❧ ❧

However, Lincoln is no mood to allow these temporary setbacks to thwart him, and by the time he meets with his cabinet three days later, on this morning of April 14, he intends to revisit the critical issue of postwar peace. "This is the great question before us," Lincoln announces, "and we must soon begin to act."

For three hours across a green-topped table, they thrash the matter around. Once the war is over, Lincoln wants to establish normal commercial relations with the former Confederate states as soon as possible. The cabinet agrees. The executive agencies should resume their traditional functions in the South: the Treasury Department would proceed to collect revenues; the Interior Department would set its surveyors and land and pension agents to work; the Postmaster General would reestablish mail routes. This, too, meets with cabinet approval. Lincoln also informs his cabinet that he has given up on the idea of temporarily working with rebel legislatures—his Virginia proposal—acknowledging that he had "been too fast in his desires for early reconstruction." But he hastens to add that the reorganization of these states must not be directed from Washington. "We can't undertake to run State governments in all these Southern States," he says. "Their people must do that," even if "at first some of them may do it badly."

There is a discussion about the appointment of military governors who would govern under martial law until civilian rule is reestablished. It is largely accepted that an army of occupation may be needed at first.

Stanton recommends that Virginia and North Carolina be combined into a single military department, while Navy Secretary Gideon Welles strongly disagrees, saying that it would obliterate state boundaries. Lincoln agrees with Welles. He instructs Stanton to revise his proposal, making separate plans for Virginia and North Carolina. There is little doubt that Virginia occupies an important position in Lincoln's vision of the future Union. "We must not . . . stultify ourselves as regards Virginia," he stresses, "but we must help her."

Lincoln decides to defer the other, more contentious matters of Reconstruction, like suffrage. But on one issue he is again adamant: there would be no war trials, no hangings or firing squads. As for the rebel leaders? His response is both emphatic and by now legendary. "Frighten them out of the country, open the gates, let down the bars, scare them off," he says, waving his hands as if he were herding sheep. And contrary to his public pronouncements, Lincoln indicates that he is glad Congress is not in session to impede and impair their work—they have eight months to get the "Union reestablished" before "Congress comes together in December." What concerns him most about Congress is not their motives, which he labels "good," but their "feelings of hate and vindictiveness." This, he makes clear, can have no place in the future of the nation.

Finally, the discussion drifts to the military situation. After Grant briefs the cabinet about Appomattox and the situation with Sherman in North Carolina, Lincoln comments on his dream last night about the phantom ship and the good news it surely prophesied.

"I think it must be from Sherman," Lincoln says hopefully. "My thoughts are in that direction as are most of yours."

❧　❧　❧

Though he does not know it yet, Lincoln's premonition is closer to right than wrong. William Tecumseh Sherman is about twenty miles above Raleigh, North Carolina, when he receives a message from General Joe Johnston requesting a truce to discuss terms of peace. Sherman is delighted, replying, "I am fully empowered to arrange with you any terms for suspension of hostilities between the armies." He adds that he hopes to extend to Johnston the same generous terms that Grant had given to Lee. The two commanding generals arrange to meet each other on April 17, between the Confederate position at Hillsboro and Sherman's headquarters.

It will take two days for telegraph messages to get from Sherman's headquarters to Washington, but there is little doubt that this news, above all, will be a delight to Lincoln. It would mark the virtual end at last. Lincoln is so eager to hear the news from North Carolina that he has already trudged over to the War Department in the morning. But there was nothing. On this evening, after dinner, he will make a second quick trip, but there will still be no news from Sherman.

After the cabinet meeting, Lincoln is too busy for lunch, munching on an apple instead. He returns to his office, where he deals with the endless drudgery of the executive office: the constant stream of petitioners, the never-ending interviews, the pile of papers to be signed. Already he has had conversations with the speaker of the house about the status of California and the Western territories; a chat with the postmaster of Detroit; a conference with a Maryland senator about a patronage matter; an audience with his newly appointed minister to Spain; and an interview with a Mississippi riverboat pilot whose cotton has been confiscated by the Confederates. He also meets with his vice president, Andrew Johnson, for the very first time since the day of the inaugural.

At three o'clock, he breaks away from the press of activities to take a romantic carriage ride with Mary. It is now chill and blustery outside, and they huddle close together as the carriage bumps and rolls through the streets toward the Navy Yard. Lincoln is finally able to relax a bit, exuding uncommonly good spirits. You seem "so gay," Mary tells him, so "cheerful—almost joyous." "And well I may feel so," he says, thinking ahead. "I consider *this* the day the war has come to a close." Then, in a tender, conciliatory voice, he recalls the biting private troubles that they have experienced over the last four years, "We must both be more cheerful in the future; between the war and the loss of our darling [son] Willie, we have been very miserable."

They talk about the future, about the years ahead and what they will do when Lincoln's second term is over. Unlike other presidents, such as George Washington, who was sixty-five at the end of his presidency, or Jefferson, who was sixty-two, or Jackson, who was seventy, Lincoln, at fifty-six, is still a relatively young man with the prospect of a long life ahead of him. There will be, he says, travel: to Europe with their sons, and perhaps even a visit to the Holy City in Palestine, which he had always wanted to see. There will be a journey out west, past the Rockies, and on to California, land of booming gold and silver mines. There will be a return home, to the practice of law; as he once said to his partner, William Herndon, "If I live, I'm coming back sometime, and then we'll go right on practicing law as if nothing happened." And there will be the farm they might buy along the Sangamon. His spirits are so high that Mary laughs, "Dear Husband, you almost startle me with your great cheerfulness." He tells her, "I have never felt better in my life."

Sometime after six, they return to the White House for an early dinner. Mary now complains of a headache and is inclined to stay at home. Lincoln, too, is tired, but says he needs to "have a laugh over the country cousin" and doesn't want to go to Ford's alone. In any event, if he were to remain in the White House, he explains, he would get no rest—visitors would hound him all throughout the night. Indeed, a congressman, Isaac N. Arnold, is coming up unannounced to the White House at this very moment, and will be turned away by the president. "I am going to the theater," Lincoln will tell him. "Come and see me in the morning."

After dinner, on his second trip of the day to the War Department, Lincoln notices some quarrelsome drunkards in the street. Should Crook, his bodyguard, accompany him to the theater? Lincoln says no. He makes nothing of it, but then quietly tells Crook that there are men who want to take his life, and that if it were to be done, it would be impossible to prevent it. Returning to the White House, Lincoln charms Crook with a heartfelt smile. "You've had a long, hard day's work, and must go home." They part at the portico of the White House, as Lincoln calls out not his familiar "good night," but a more formal "good-bye" and saunters up the steps.

The one question for Lincoln is who will accompany them to the theater. Earlier in the day, Grant begged off, muttering that he and his wife had plans to visit their sons in Burlington, New Jersey, and were catching an early train. Remarkably, Grant and his wife are the first of thirteen people who will turn down Lincoln's invitation, including a number of visitors who have called upon him this morning: Governor Richard J. Oglesby and General Isham Haynie, both from Illinois; Schuyler Colfax, the House speaker, and his wife; William Howard, the Detroit postmaster; William Wallace, the governor of Idaho Territory, and his wife; War Secretary Edwin Stanton and his wife; Thomas T. Accrete, chief of the telegraph bureau, and his wife; and even the Lincolns' son Robert, who says he is too tired. Finally, Mary secures a handsome young couple to accompany them, the ebullient Major Henry R. Rathbone and young Clara Harris, his stepsister and fiancée, and also a friend of the first lady's and the daughter of Senator Ira Harris of New York.

Delayed by last-minute visitors, Lincoln and Mary hop into the presidential carriage some fifteen minutes late, leaving around 8:15. Lincoln is wearing his customary black overcoat, his high silk hat, and white kid gloves, and Mary is clad in a smart low-necked gray silk dress and matching bonnet. As the carriage slips out into the street, its large wooden wheels groaning and creaking, and makes its way to Senator Harris's place, gaslights flicker spookily in the streets. The sky is overcast, and it is so foggy out that as the Lincolns drive on, they can barely see through the moist air and wandering evening haze: pedestrians become mere silhouettes; buildings disappear altogether; and it is nearly impossible to make out what lies beyond the next corner. Only Lincoln's personal attendant and the coachman are riding with them; Lincoln's guard for the evening, John F. Parker, has already gone ahead. The carriage pulls up to the theater at 8:30; "This way to Ford's!" a barker outside is crying. "This way to Ford's!" The performance has been under way for twenty minutes. So the two couples quickly hurry inside, Mary squired on Lincoln's arm, the attractive Clara Harris on Rathbone's.

With the president leading the way, the two couples ascend the winding stairway and cross over the dress circle at the back of the first balcony. The theater is jammed with assorted Washington dignitaries, an array of generals and admirals, leading journalists like *New York Times* publisher Henry J. Raymond, and well-dressed Washington socialites. When they spot the president, the audience rises to its feet and gives him a standing ovation as the orchestra promptly strikes up "Hail to the Chief." The presidential party sweeps around the back row of chairs, passes through a door and down a short hallway to the state box. There is more cheering. The president acknowledges the applause with a slight bow and slides his tired frame into a comfortable upholstered rocking chair, specially provided by the management. Mary sits beside him, and Rathbone and Clara to their right. The front of their box is adorned with an eclectic jumble of celebration: vivid patriotic colors, the Union treasury flag, and a fine handmade, gilt-framed portrait of George Washington. Below, Harry Hawk, the male lead, improvises: "This reminds me of a story as Mr. Lincoln used to say—" The audience claps and breaks out into a hearty roar. Mary soon rests her hand on her husband's knee and nestles close. "What will Miss Harris think of my hanging on to you so?" she later whispers. Smiling, he replies, "She won't think any thing about it."

As the play continues, Lincoln's guard, John Parker, slips off from his post in the hallway outside the state box. Distinguished largely for his incorrigibility and incompetence, he will either watch the play from the gallery or exit for a quick drink. Left behind is the White House footman, Charles Forbes, who will also grab a quick drink during the intermission. Nobody notices the small peephole carved in the door.

The comedy continues. It is about a conniving Englishwoman, Mrs. Mountchessington, who is thoroughly certain that Asa Trenchard, an American bumpkin, is actually a rich Yankee, whom she is determined to entrap as a husband for her daughter Augusta. The play weaves a mixture of melodramatic and farcical scenes, and the audience falls into one round of laughter after another. When the actors strike a mirthful chord, Mary applauds giddily, calling Lincoln's attention to the funniest lines. For his part, the president is more reserved; he does not clap, but from time to time, he does laugh heartily. At one point, he apparently feels a chill, and rises just long enough to put on his overcoat. It is unclear whether he ever fully relaxes; but it is also clear that he is trying to lose himself in the play's odd-duck humor.

During the third act, Lincoln slips his hand into Mary's. At this point in the play, the horrible truth about Trenchard has been revealed: he has given away his inheritance and is "church mouse poor" and most certainly is not fit for Mrs. Mountchessington's daughter. She angrily dispatches Augusta to her room and denounces the American for his ill-manners and for being an awful social boor. "I am aware, Mr. Trenchard, that you are not used to the manners of good society, and that alone will excuse the impertinence of which you have been guilty." She, too, makes an indignant exit, leaving Asa alone on the stage.

At roughly 10:07, outside the presidential box, an official-looking envelope is delivered to the White House footman, Charles Forbes; it is from S. P. Hanscom, a Lincoln ally and editor of the *National Republican*. Forbes takes it in to the president, then returns to his position.

It is now five minutes later; this time Forbes inspects a gentleman's calling card. A moment passes, and then the guest's hand is upon the door. There is no latch. He gives it a push, and it opens quietly, to reveal a full view of Mary and Lincoln snuggling close. "Don't know the manners of a good society, eh?" Trenchard cries out on stage to Mrs. Mountchessington. Watching this, Mary Lincoln is now smiling beautifully. And anticipating the punch line, Lincoln leans forward, with his chin cradled in his right hand and his arm resting on the balustrade. Mr. Trenchard continues: "Well, I guess I know enough to turn you inside out, old gal—you sockdologizing old man-trap . . ." The crowd bursts into laughter and a round of applause, punctuated only by the lone, muffled sound of an otherwise loud noise, like a violent clap of hands, or the crack of wood, or perhaps a firecracker.

Lincoln's arm jerks up convulsively. For a single terrible instant, nobody moves in the state box. Mary and Clara are frozen in their seats. Clara's dress, her hands, her face are saturated with blood. Then pandemonium breaks out. The audience, now looking around, wonders what is happening. Is it part of the play? Another improvised scene?

Softly, a blue-white smoke drifts out of the presidential box.

Suddenly, a man jumps from the state box onto the stage. He is immediately recognizable to most everyone there. He is the actor John Wilkes Booth.

At that selfsame moment, the air is rent with a heartrending, incomprehensible shriek.

And then come a woman's words, shouted at the top of her lungs: "The President is shot!"

❧   ❧   ❧

Thus begins the choreographed decapitation of the Union government in Washington. No other attempt this bold has ever been carried out, before or since. As Lincoln slumps forward, the entire theater is enveloped in mayhem. People begin yelling hysterically, pushing one another into aisles, even rushing for the exits in fear that the assassination of the president might be the signal for a general massacre. They are not far from the truth. It is 10:15, and John Wilkes Booth's shooting of the Union president is but one of three coordinated assaults scheduled to take place at this very moment across the city. In addition to Lincoln, the vice president, Andrew Johnson, is to be murdered. If both the president and vice president are incapacitated, the secretary of state will—according to the laws of the day—call a meeting of the electors the following December, a full eight months away, to elect a new president and vice president. And so William Seward, the secretary of state, is also targeted. In the ensuing chaos and disorder that would surely follow, Booth reasoned, the Confederacy would be poised to take advantage, perhaps winning its independence yet.

Shortly before 10:15, the second attack does take place, at Seward's elegant brick home at Lafayette Park, just across from the White House. It begins with the otherwise innocent ring of the doorbell.

❧   ❧   ❧

A tall, broad-shouldered, handsome man, nicely dressed, with a fine voice, and his hat pulled down over one eye, steps into the hallway, informing the servant that he has medicine for Mr. Seward, and has been instructed to deliver it personally. (A week earlier, Seward had been severely injured in a carriage accident, and was suffering from facial lacerations, a fractured jaw, and a broken arm, and was lying in his bed covered with bandages, his neck awkwardly fixed in a steel brace.) The servant explains that the secretary is to see "no one," but the man talks his way past him. However, when he runs into the secretary's son Frederick, in the upper hallway, the scheme appears to go awry. Here, the man is met with skepticism. Heated words are exchanged. Agreeing to leave, the man suddenly pulls a revolver out of his coat pocket and fires. By some quirk, it fails to go off, but he is unfazed. He violently pistol-whips Frederick's head with the gun, shattering his skull and leaving him in a pool of blood.

The man immediately pulls out a large Bowie knife and rushes upstairs to Seward's room. This time he encounters Seward's daughter and renders her unconscious with a single powerful blow. A male army nurse now stands in his way; he, too, is quickly dispatched. The assassin slices his brow with the knife and knocks him senseless.

Then, in the dimly lit room, he sees the secretary for the first time, lying immobilized and ailing. He raises his knife and thrusts again and again at Seward's face, looking to slash his jugular. Occasionally, there is—or must be—a loud clang, as the knife's edge pounds against the metal neck brace. Seward's throat is cut on "both sides." His right cheek is nearly "severed" from his face. Three times, his neck is stabbed. Moments later, the bloodstained secretary tumbles helplessly from the bed to the floor.

Another of Seward's sons, Augustus, rushes into the room. He is stabbed seven times. The army nurse has managed to pull himself to his feet, stumbles forward, and seeks to wrestle the man to the ground. The man stabs him four times.

The assailant then runs out the front door, encountering a State Department messenger who has innocently walked into the carnage. Without hesitating, the man pumps the knife straight into the messenger's chest. "I'm mad," he shouts. "I'm mad!"

He rushes out the door, into the night.

Left behind, lying ominously on the floor, are the telltale signs of assassination: the man's slouch hat and the defective pistol. Seward's bandages are running with a fresh trail of crimson. His son Frederick, with two holes in his head, is already sinking into a coma. All told, the assailant leaves five casualties behind him: the most people ever targeted by a single American assassin. Unknown to any of the victims at the time, Booth's accomplice, this hulking man who has turned Seward's home into a war zone, is a shifty, low-browed Alabama native who was wounded at Gettysburg, deserted, and later rode with John Mosby, leaving under clouded circumstances. He is alternatively known as "Lewis Powell," or the alias "Lewis Paine" or "Lewis Payne," or yet another alias known as "Reverend Wood."

But whatever his name, he will now never be forgotten.

❧   ❧   ❧

A few blocks away, at Twelfth and Pennsylvania, the assassination of Vice President Andrew Johnson is set to take place at the same time. All seemed ready. That evening, an unsuspecting Johnson had eaten a leisurely meal in the dining room of the Kirkwood House. Afterward, he and Leonard Farwell, the former governor of Wisconsin, share an amiable chat. Finally, Farwell announces: I am going to the theater at Ford's. Would you like to come? Johnson declines. He prefers to read in his room, then turn in. By ten o'clock, the gaslight is flicked off, and he is asleep in Suite 68, unaware that the third-floor room above houses his designated assassin, George Atzerodt. Atzerodt is a German immigrant and a carriage maker who, in his spare time, ferried Confederate spies across the Potomac. In his room lie the nefarious implements of conspiracy, kidnapping, and murder: a bankbook, coiled rope, and two carbines hidden between the mattress and the bedsprings. But tonight, he opts for a Bowie knife, sheathed at his side.

At 10 P.M., he enters the barroom of the hotel. In fifteen minutes, he is to carry out the relatively straightforward plan: knock on Johnson's door and sink the knife deep into the vice president's heart.

But at the last moment, Atzerodt gets cold feet. The would-be assassin instead wanders out into the streets and spends this night of mayhem and murder in a local tavern, nursing his nerves and getting drunk. Still, lead conspirator John Wilkes Booth has in fact anticipated a possible problem with Atzerodt. Earlier in the day, around 3:30, he had already visited the vice president's residence, Kirkwood House, and left a short note for Andrew Johnson. "Don't wish to disturb you," he slyly scribbled. "Are you at home? J. Wilkes Booth."

The note was no doubt intended to throw suspicion on Johnson. While by some twist of fate, Johnson and Lincoln had met that day in the White House for the first time since the inauguration, it was well known that there was little love lost between the two men. Since Johnson would be in line to assume the presidential duties upon Lincoln's death, the note could be interpreted to mean that Johnson was in league with the conspirators.

In either case, in the coming days, it would surely add to the confusion.

❧　❧　❧

In the next terror-stricken half hour, the secretary of war, undressing himself, is told the president has been shot and Seward has been murdered. Within hours, drums are rolling, bugles sound, and the cavalry plunges into the city. Washington is now filled with military patrols who will pound throughout the streets on the lookout, as guards stand tense watch outside the homes of all top government officials. When word of the multiple attacks seeps out, the Northern capital is immediately stunned, paralyzed by the series of vicious attacks. Urgent rumors quickly sweep the city. There is widespread fear that the Confederates are trying to disrupt the Northern government with a series of carefully planned assassinations. People are literally afraid of being killed in their beds. Others fear that in the middle of the chaos, rebel spies will torch the city. Martial law is quickly declared. Sometime after midnight, Grant, who could have also been shot in Ford's Theater, will be ordered to return immediately to Washington to defend the capital. By next morning, an overly distraught Mrs. Seward, weeping, will tell Senator Sumner, "They have murdered my husband! They have murdered my son!" By noontime that next day, the secretary of war will even send a dire note warning General Sherman: an "assassin is on your track."

The Night of Horrors

Mrs. Surratt's Boarding House
Where the conspirators frequently met

Patent Office

Herndon House
Conspirators' last meeting place

National Hotel
Where John Wilkes Booth stayed

Ford's Theater
Where Lincoln was shot

The Petersen House
Where Lincoln Died

Grover's Theater

The attack at Secretary of State Seward's House

Kirkwood House
Vice-President Johnson's residence

State Dept.

Treasury Dept.

Willard Hotel

The White House

I STREET

H STREET

G STREET

F STREET

E STREET

C STREET

B STREET

CANAL

NEW YORK AVENUE

PENNSYLVANIA AVENUE

LOUISIANA AVENUE

OHIO AVENUE

6th STREET
7th STREET
8th STREET
9th STREET
10th STREET
11th STREET
12th STREET
13th STREET
14th STREET
15th STREET
17th STREET

0   1/8 miles

Clearly, at first blush Booth's plans to sow chaos have more than worked. The ugly seed of assassination appeared to be falling on fertile ground. In the meantime, all attention in the beleaguered Northern capital turns to saving Abraham Lincoln. On whom so much depends.

❧ ❧ ❧

Lincoln. Abraham Lincoln was an American original. His genius is unquestioned. His niche in history—and it is a large one—is secure. And so is his place in our affections. It is hardly possible to talk about the North's effort to win the war—and just as importantly, to secure a compassionate peace—separate from Lincoln. There was always something lofty, something different, something special about the tall, lanky president.

He emanated a kind of parochial grandeur, itself rather unique in this country's annals. To be sure, there were many domineering men in Lincoln's time, whose own fame frequently eclipsed his: Czar Alexander II and Otto von Bismarck, Prince Metternich and Benjamin Disraeli, Giuseppe Garibaldi and Auguste Comte. And domineering women, too, like Queen Victoria. But in our day, Lincoln now seems to rise above, a looming hero somehow residing on a different moral plane. As is the case with many historic figures, it is futile to expect consistency in his genius, and he abounds with contradictions. But they served him well: he was a politician in the crudest sense of the term, but at the same time a man of moral stature; he was a genuine intellectual, but also a man of uncommon street sense; he had no executive experience whatsoever, and only the most modest preparation for the highest office in the land, but when the country was suddenly confronted by the mightiest challenge since its auspicious birth, he somehow managed to ascend to the occasion. He was a figure who could give heroic life to what the Union was and, just as importantly, to what it might become. And perhaps most strikingly, he was a leader of such inexhaustible magnanimity and vision that by April 1865, he could put himself in a position of finally rescuing not just the North's depleted and bloodied young men, but in his own distinct manner and his own distinct way, those of the South as well.

None of this was apparent in the beginning of his life. None of this was so starkly apparent, for that matter, until perhaps that single instant when Lincoln's arm abruptly jerked and his head slumped while a bullet lodged in his brain, and he waged the last, most desperate fight of his life. In truth, from his earliest years, Lincoln was always a riddle of quirks and impenetrable eccentricities. The *New York Times* even called him "peculiar." Yet from those earliest years, it seemed as though the stage of his life was always set for high drama—if not towering tragedy.

❧   ❧   ❧

"Everybody in the world knows Pa used to split rails," Lincoln's little son, Taddie, used to say. Certainly, Lincoln was hardly the first politician to be born of humble origins, nor the first to mine them. But few have matched his meteoric rise and fewer still have retained such deep links to their beginnings. Even when he had tasted the pinnacle of political success, Abraham Lincoln remained a self-made man, a middle–American man. Or so goes the standard Lincoln yarn. But unlike a George Washington, he did not need a Parson Weems to make his life a legend, for it was Lincoln himself who first authored his own tale—one that he acted out with great fervor. And it is in Lincoln that one finds that rarest of events, the nexus where legend and life often, though not always, meet.

"I was born and have ever remained," he explained in his first campaign speech, "in the most humble walks of life. I have no popular relations or friends to recommend me." Thereafter, his theme became: "I presume you all know who I am—I am humble Abraham Lincoln." His self-derogation was real: "My poor, lean, lank face." So was his simplicity: his clothes were invariably out of season or fashion; he referred to himself as "A" and greeted visitors with "howdy"; he stuffed notes in his pockets and stuck bills in a drawer; and his two most memorable speeches— at Gettysburg and his second inaugural—together total fewer than 1,000 words. He always insisted that he came from nowhere, telling his biographer, John Locke Scripps of the *Chicago Tribune*, that his early life could be condensed into a single sentence, "The short and simple annals of the poor." This much was quite true. He was born in a log cabin in Kentucky, where his father had even done a stint on the Hardin County slave patrol, and spent his early life on a succession of frontier farms as his family, like thousands of others at the start of the nineteenth century, chased their futures west. His father knew enough to sign his name—though scarcely more than that—so it was his mother who taught him to read. But she died when he was nine. After that, he largely taught himself; he had one year of formal schooling.

In the years that followed, the elder Lincoln, Thomas, hired his own son out for wages, until Abe was finally able to work for himself. In the backwoods of Kentucky, Indiana, and Illinois, and also along the Ohio and the Mississippi rivers, Lincoln grew to be unusually tall—six foot four, 170 pounds—and learned a myriad of trades: rafting, carpentry, boating, forestry, butchering, brewing, distilling, plowing, storekeeping, and, naturally, rail splitting. But he would shrewdly turn these modest beginnings into political assets later on. As local settlers once gibed, he was a "wild, harumscarum kind of man, who always had his eyes open to the main chance."

That main chance came first in education. Lincoln's innate intellect was apparent from his earliest years. He borrowed a copy of Kirkham's *English Grammar* and struggled to master his own tongue. He devoured the great works of history, literature, and biography and delved into a host of others: Gibbon, Paine and Volney, *Robinson Crusoe* and Aesop, *The Pilgrim's Progress* and Weems's lives of Washington and Franklin. Most importantly for his later career, he was inspired by Thomas Jefferson, Henry Clay, and Daniel Webster, three giants of American politics and history. Constantly seeking to improve himself, he practiced "polemics," recited poetry, and taught himself mathematics; yet while he was a voracious reader, he was not an instinctual but a political one. Thus, when his law partner tried to interest him in the works of Darwin, Spencer, and other literary writers, he scoffed that it was "entirely too heavy for an ordinary mind to digest." He had little interest in fiction and, surprisingly, not much more in history or biography. When he did read, he read aloud, because it enabled him to "understand [things] better." And for his larger edification, he relied on more than simple book learning.

Accordingly, despite his modest station in life, he traveled a fair bit, which gave him keen insights into his country that many of his later, more refined colleagues sorely lacked. This, of course, in itself says something about Lincoln. Travel throughout much of America was difficult and usually expensive, and the majority of Americans knew little about the state of society beyond the nestled confines of their own towns, let alone their region. Senator Charles Sumner never once set foot in the South; Jefferson Davis visited New England only once. Yet Lincoln rafted down to New Orleans and worked his way back on a steamer; all told, he visited the South several times, and unlike most Northerners, knew it and knew it well. Physically, he was a strong man: once, he lifted a barrel of whiskey from the floor to the counter; another time, as president, he grabbed an ax and began chopping wood, to the utter astonishment of the gawking Union soldiers who watched him. He was flat-footed and stoop-shouldered, with a peculiar gait, until he decided, for effect, to stand tall, holding his head high and regal; the trademark stovepipe hat only accentuated a stature that was already outsized.

But underneath all this, he was ridden with profound emotional swings, less up and more down. Early in his career, mortified by the humbling anonymity of Congress, he returned home and became brooding, withdrawn, beset by the specter of death and obsessed by his own anxieties. Overcome by a terrible fit of melancholy "so profound" (the characterization is Beveridge's) "that the depths of it cannot be sounded or estimated by normal minds," he called it the "hypo," or "hypochondria," or his "tired spot," even writing an essay on suicide: "I may seem to enjoy life rapturously when I am in company. But when I am alone I am so often overcome by mental depression that I never dare carry a penknife." Perhaps to balance this, he became a genius at storytelling, often addressing complex political situations with a simple quip, a revealing tale, an illustrative homily, even a smutty story. More often than not, storytelling was his broadsword; satire his rapier—and it always had a point.

He had his run of bad luck. He set up a store, which failed, then set up as a postmaster, but was unable to make a living at that. When a circuit court issued a judgment against him for overdue notes, the sheriff attached his personal possessions, even his horse. Then his store partner died. Forced to shoulder the hefty $1,100 burden of remaining debt, Lincoln spent fifteen years paying it off. His first lady friend, Ann Rutledge, died suddenly, of an attack of "brain fever." His first love, Mary Owens, turned him down. Later, like many an ambitious politician, he eventually did marry well, joining with Mary Todd, who came from an aristocratic and educated Kentucky family. But from the start, the relationship had a bit of the quality of an arrangement. Mary, plump and witty, cultured and French-speaking, knew politics and knew ambition; she had picked Lincoln out as destined for the White House: "Mr. Lincoln is to be president of the United States some day. If I had not thought so, I would not have married him for you can see he is not pretty." For his part, Lincoln once quipped about Mary: "For God, one 'd' is enough, but the Todds need two." In fact, the marriage almost never took place; Lincoln, insecure about his lack of pedigree and shunned by her family, at first begged off. But the thirty-three-year-old Lincoln and the twenty-three-year-old Mary eventually did tie the knot. Still, Lincoln's bad luck continued into their marriage. They had four sons, and two died tragically, including their much-beloved Willie, who passed away of a fatal illness in 1862 while Lincoln was president. It nearly broke both their hearts.

The marriage was a curious one, and in countless ways, the two couldn't have been more different. He loved humor; she had none at all. He grew up on dirt floors; she was served by slaves and attended finishing school. She was neat and fastidious; he was rumpled and disorganized, both at home and at the office. She insisted upon servants; he often did not file and would not keep a clerk. And if he was disconsolate, she could also be nasty and difficult. Acrimony, too, frequently crept into the Lincoln home. More than once she drove him from the house in anger, at least once while brandishing a broomstick; another time, she chased him down the street while waving a knife. Yet there was a deep root of tenderness in their marriage, and over time, she came both to understand his awkwardness and to respect his righteousness. In turn, he relied on her, far more than is often credited by history. When he repeatedly failed in his quest for Congress, she pushed, prodded, and propped him up; absent that, the depressive and often distraught Lincoln might well have quit. It is equally likely that without her, the presidency might also have eluded him. For his part, he attempted to behave decently toward her. And he loved her, affectionately naming her "my Molly," fussing over her as "my child wife" and "my little woman." Once she was in the White House, beset by her own deep and near-debilitating moods and disappointments, it was clear that she understood the inner Lincoln as did no one else around him. And this was a two-way street. His familial empathy no doubt helped imbue him with equal empathy for the South: no fewer than four of her brothers and three brothers-in-law fought for the Confederacy; two were killed in battle. (Although during his presidency, she would fall under the spell of her good friend Senator Sumner and become a far more ardent advocate of abolition than her husband.)

By way of a profession, Lincoln was a self-taught lawyer and a successful one at that, earning up to $5,000 a year by the 1850s, but law *per se* never held much appeal for him. Politics did. Not the Jacksonian Democrats of his father, which he rejected, but the new roads, central banking, and protective tariffs of the National Republicans and Whigs. From the start, Lincoln saw his role as a champion of the budding middle class. "Republicans," he memorably put it, "are for both the man and the dollar." He gave his first stump speech at nineteen, and the pleasant taste stayed with him long after that. "Politics were his life, newspapers his food, and his great ambition his motive power," his law partner Herndon wrote. At twenty-three, only seven months after coming to the little Illinois community of New Salem, Lincoln was already running for office. He lost. But contrary to the way he liked to tell it, success soon came to him; two years later, in 1834, Sangamon County sent him to the lower Illinois house. From this time on to the end of his life—except for the years between 1849 and 1854, when his political prospects were at their lowest ebb—he was either campaigning, serving in office, or out on the stump for other office seekers.

But, ultimately, it was not through Lincoln's middle-class mantra or his fiercely partisan Whiggery that he would make his lasting political mark. It was slavery: human bondage and human servitude. By some combination of design and fate, the slavery issue would not let Lincoln stray from public life, not let him fade into obscurity, not let him rest.

❧ ❧ ❧

Lincoln legend has it that at the age of twenty-one, on his second trip to New Orleans, he saw a handsome mulatto girl being sold on the block at the slave market. It was then that "the iron entered his soul," and he swore henceforth that, if he ever got a chance to, he would hit slavery and "hit it hard." The authenticity of this tale is suspect; but what is not suspect are the sentiments that haunted him: the image of the strutting slave owner, of the degraded young woman, of the utter scorn in which slavery held freedom. Time and again, from then on, his personal insights about slavery were deep and penetrating. Slavery was a dangerous, slippery slope, he contended, not simply an affront to freedom, not simply as an affront to democracy, not simply corrupting the South, but corrupting human relations everywhere. Consider this Lincoln musing: "If A can prove, however conclusively, that he may, of right, enslave B, why may not B snatch the same argument, even proven equally, that he may enslave A. You say A is white and B is black—is it *color* then, the lighter having the right to enslave the darker? Take care—by this rule, you are to be slave to the first man you meet, with a fairer skin than your own. You do not mean *color* exactly? You mean the whites are intellectually the superior of the blacks, and therefore have the right to enslave them? Take care again—by this rule you are to be the slave of the first man you meet, with an intellect superior to your own."

But Lincoln's private hostility to slavery belies another significant record, that of public vacillation, even accommodation. And here lies one of the great questions about Lincoln the politician versus Lincoln the principled leader. In political life, Lincoln was careful never to step too far ahead of prevailing opinion; he frequently calculated and fudged; his explanations were often wry and not always convincing; and he was not above pandering and manipulating, both facts and opinions. Yet because he was always cautious and instinctively conservative, his public actions concerning slavery invariably stand in bewildering contrast to his keen insights into—and his equally keen onslaughts against—pro-slavery arguments. Thus, despite his opposition to the peculiar institution, Lincoln outwardly maintained that slavery was destined to gradually disappear on its own, a victim of its own internal contradictions and of historical progress—and, in this sense, he was like a number of Southerners, including his political and intellectual idol, Thomas Jefferson, who tolerated the institution while quietly holding their noses.

It would prove to be a chimerical hope, but that realization would come to him only much later and after no small measure of public evasion: "I hold it a paramount duty of us in the free States, due to the Union of the States, and perhaps to liberty itself . . . to let slavery of the other states alone. While, on the other hand, I hold it equally clear that we should never knowingly lend ourselves . . . to prevent slavery from dying a natural death . . ." This fence-sitting bore a peculiar fruit. As a lame-duck congressman ("I was a nobody," he reminds us) in 1849, Lincoln got his first chance to take a crack at the institution he so reviled, drafting a "Bill to Abolish Slavery in the District of Columbia." It was to be enacted by local referendum, but the politician in him led Lincoln to soften the blow, adding a section that required municipal authorities of Washington and Georgetown to provide "active and efficient means" of arresting and restoring to their owners all fugitive slaves escaping into the District. In effect, the bill sought to split the difference between the two extremes of slave owners and slaver haters, but in seeking to offend nobody, Lincoln only ended up offending everyone. As soon as his plans were made public, all support for the measure vanished. The bill failed— yet when the House took it upon itself to debate the morality of slavery nonetheless, Lincoln sat by, mute and silent. He spent the next five years in much the same state, back in Illinois, practicing law, unhappily watching events pass him by.

It was the pugnacious "Little Giant" Stephen Douglas who, in 1854, opened the door that let Lincoln back into public life. Early that year, Douglas unveiled the Kansas-Nebraska Act, which put the question of extending bondage in the new territories to a majority vote. Watching the debate unfold, Lincoln saw a chance for himself. Now it was to be on the back of slavery that this failed one-term congressman would seek to rehabilitate his political fortunes; but here again, his moral zeal sometimes wrestled uneasily with his political pragmatism. Initially, Lincoln took great pains in all his speeches to emphasize that he was not an abolitionist, nor was he advocating political or social equality for blacks: he merely opposed extending slavery into the new territories. He knew all too well that most of his supporters were not only *not* abolitionists, but were outright Negrophobes, who did not want to live or work alongside blacks, free or slave.

But he could not equivocate for long. On May 29, 1856, his moment descended. Called upon to deliver the adjournment speech at the convention inaugurating the new Illinois Republican Party, Lincoln now staked everything in kind. Discarding his usual timidity, he finally made good on his much earlier promise to hit slavery and "hit it hard." It was the best speech of his life, a stunning oration so mesmerizing that reporters ceased scratching away, and, for some time, it was "lost." Actually, the only existing version of the speech is not verbatim. Even his close friend and legal partner, Herndon, a prodigious notetaker, gave up after fifteen minutes, throwing "pen and paper away," swept up "in the inspiration of the hour." "It was," he remembered, "hard, heavy, knotty, gnarly, backed with wrath."

Lincoln's gambit paid off. Within months, he became a champion of the new Republican Party; his golden opportunity soon followed in the senatorial election of 1858. He was pitted against Stephen Douglas, and the famous, worldly, and vain Douglas proved to be the perfect foil. Determined to make a national reputation for himself, Lincoln taunted and pressed and connived Douglas into a series of public debates, the sole topic of which would be slavery, from which Lincoln reasoned that he had nothing to lose and everything to gain. Douglas took the bait, with the Senate seat the ultimate prize. In the short term, it turned out, Lincoln was wrong; not so in the long term.

From August to October, the verbal jousting began. There were seven encounters held from one end of the state to the other, and each was a grand event in itself, preceded and accompanied by bands and music and processions, with huge crowds numbering upward of 10,000. Over these three months, both drew blood and bled themselves, and in the end, Douglas won the seat in Washington. But Lincoln, once the darkest of dark horses, had won a prize he coveted equally, having now been transformed from a minor state politician into a budding national figure.

It was heady stuff, and Lincoln didn't stop there. Denied the Senate, he brazenly sniffed a chance for no less than the presidency itself. He pounded away at the same theme over and over: if a halt was not put some-where upon the spread of slavery it would become nationwide—"one uni-versal slave nation"—and then only the "poor white men," who would lose wages and jobs to slave workers, would suffer. Yet even as he hammered away at his moral issue, Lincoln the moralist still wrestled with Lincoln the politician. In seeking to appeal to abolitionists and Negrophobes at the same time, he was often caught in embarrassing contradictions. (In Chicago: "Let us . . . declar[e] that all men are created equal," then in Ottawa: "We *cannot* then make them [blacks] equals.") But his ultimate goal was not intellectual consistency, but strategy, namely, the challenge of how to meld old-line Whigs and antislavery men into one potent political party. By hammering home the issue of the alleged plan to extend slavery and the dangers it would inflict upon the country, he was able to create a histori-cally unique amalgam of political forces under the same tent: abolition-ists and Negrophobes, high-tariff men and low-tariff men, former Whigs and embittered Democrats, immigrants and Know-Nothings, German tip-plers and Maine-law prohibitionists. It was nothing short of masterful, and this coalition would soon sweep him into power. But not yet.

In the months that followed, Lincoln hit the lecture circuit. He gave speeches in half a dozen Midwestern states, and, for the first time, he spoke in New York, where he was a big success. His stinging message about slavery was now repeated by his political rivals as well as his allies. He pointed out again and again that if anything was wicked, slavery was wicked. The country had outlawed the exportation of slaves from America, and even Southerners did not dispute that. It had prohibited the impor-tation of slaves from Africa, and neither did Southerners dispute that. He pointed out that in the South, it was not the slave who was treated as a social pariah—in fact, he was often regarded as a member of the family—but the slave dealer himself. So then, didn't the South, in its heart, know that slave dealing and thus slaveholding were wrong? Why else did Southerners routinely manumit? "Why," asked Lincoln, "have so many slaves been set free, except by the promptings of conscience?" And in reply, he was told, "You are like Byron, awoke to find himself famous."

And soon, Lincoln was back home in Springfield when a telegram arrived informing him that he had been nominated for president at the

Republican National Convention in Chicago ("TO LINCOLN YOU ARE NOMINATED"). Then, on November 7, 1860, at 2 A.M., the telegraph rapped out this startling news: Lincoln was now elected president of the United States, having defeated his main opponent, none other than the little Democrat, Stephen Douglas.

But in a grim sign of what was to come, the vote carried with it an ominous message. The nation was woefully divided. The dynamic of the election itself was unlike that of any other ever held. Lincoln had managed to win the necessary electoral college, getting a handy 180 votes, and carrying all but one of the free states. But this was misleading: he won only because it was a four-way race, and the Southern vote was split among two other candidates who had denied Douglas the chance to run as the only true "national candidate," an appeal that he had nonetheless tried to make. On the popular vote it was truly a squeaker: Lincoln got only 39.9 percent. His opponents—when totaled up—had defeated him by 2,815,617 votes to 1,866,452. And more revealingly, in ten of the Southern states, Lincoln did not receive a single vote. In fact, in these states the Republicans did not even bother to field a ticket. In the remaining five slave states, mainly in the Upper South, he received a pitiful 4 percent of the popular vote.

There was a price to pay for such a split election—and for the reputation Lincoln had built for himself in the Lincoln-Douglas debates. Mass hysteria soon consumed the country: everywhere people crowded the streets of Southern cities with talk of secession and urgent murmuring that a Republican victory meant disunion. Despite Lincoln's best efforts at moderation, the South would read his election in no other way. "The very existence of such a party is an offense to the whole South," explained one Virginia legislative committee. A New Orleans newspaper was just as blunt: every Northern vote cast for Lincoln was "a deliberate cold blooded insult and outrage" to the South. Nor were they alone in their apocalyptic alarums—there were considerable doubters in the North as well. "Free love and free niggers will certainly elect old Abe," warned one Democratic banner in New York. And if it was clear that Lincoln had succeeded in terrifying the South, it was less clear that he had succeeded in convincing the rest of the country of his positions.

Early in 1861, the Republicans in Congress gave their votes to measures organizing the territories in Colorado, Nevada, and Dakota without prohibiting slavery—Douglas's proposed policy, not Abe Lincoln's.

Now the great question would be, was Lincoln equal to the task? Was he equal to the approaching Civil War? Or for that matter, it could well be asked, was he even ready for the presidency? Many thought not. He was widely dismissed as a "gorilla," regarded as a "third rate lawyer," considered a "nullity," and mocked as a "duffer," a "rough farmer," and "a man in the habit of making coarse and clumsy jokes." Members of his own cabinet derided him behind his back: Stanton called him "the original baboon," "a western hick," and that "giraffe"; his first attorney general said he was "unexceptional"; Simon Cameron, his treasury secretary, was "openly discourteous" to him. Lincoln's way of speaking alone made him suspect: he said "kin" for "can," "sot" for "sat," "airth" for "earth," "heered" for "heard," and "Mr. Cheerman," for "Mr. Chairman." His high-pitched twang was an oddity in the genteel salons and artful councils of official Washington. The real Lincoln, a curious amalgam of candor and obfuscation, country boy and learned lawyer, was—and would remain—alien to the city's elite. Yet here he was.

And there remains a larger issue. History should not mask or obscure just how ill-prepared Lincoln really was for the job. Before his stunning victory, consider his résumé. He himself wrote his own campaign autobiography—all 800 words of it—in December 1859. "I was losing interest in politics when the repeal of the Missouri Compromise aroused me again," he cleverly wrote. "What I have done since then is pretty well known." In fact, what was "well known" was not very much. He was a formerly obscure legislator, an equally obscure one-term congressman, and in his first foray into big-time politics, he was a failure in his bid for the U.S. Senate. He was a good party man, first as a Whig and then as a Republican. He was an eloquent orator, had a subtle mind, and his droll ways and dry jokes made him formidable on the stump. He made many speeches and many fine ones. But had he not been elected president, everything about his career thus far would smack of the persistent efforts of a political junkie and an average political hack; a hanger-oner, a man who doesn't know when to quit. Put aside the fact that he had not a single shred of executive experience; he had barely employed a single person in his life. Nor had he ever served in actual combat. Unlike a George Washington or an Andrew Jackson, he had not commanded an army to mighty victories; his sole military experience consisted of a paltry eighty days in the Black Hawk War. (After he was "elected" captain of his volunteer company, the first time he ever gave an order, the soldier snapped back, "Go to Hell." Moreover, foreshadowing later difficulties with aides, he failed to maintain even the minimum discipline among his men, and was subsequently punished by his ranking officers, who ordered him to carry a wooden sword for two days.) Nor was Lincoln cosmopolitan or worldly or schooled in the diplomatic arts. Unlike a Thomas Jefferson, he had not lived abroad, or even been abroad, let alone served as a minister to a foreign country like France. Nor could he claim the benefit of a powerful and thoughtful mentor who had shown him the ropes, or the experience of having apprenticed as secretary of state or vice president, as was the case with a number of his more distinguished predecessors.

And there was an even more troubling question: the simmering matter of his temperament, the fact that he was a man so prone to depressions and a fathomless gloom that he once mourned, "I laugh because I cannot weep." Throughout his life, he had found solace in the incessant activity of politics, but in his depressed moods, we can see him uneasily treading his way through time, hoping for reprieve. Was this the man to guide the country through its greatest crisis? Where, in those darkest moments, would his inner resolve come from? And, as for his election, this in itself said very little; nor was it a guide to how he would perform. Despite calculations by Lincolnographers, or postelection calculations by statisticians, his victory was in many a ways a fluke and nothing more. And while he had a keen and subtle mind, and is judged by history to have bested Douglas in their debates, he was hardly the first brilliant man to occupy the presidency—although as every historian well knows, in the end, it is not brilliance but judgment that separates the great leaders from the routine. As for the passion he brought to the slavery issue, he regarded the institution as ugly and sinister, but even here, his passion was tempered by his innate caution, as well as by his reluctance to get too far ahead of public opinion on this matter. But then, the war entered his life.

He wanted this war the way a felon wants a hangman's noose. Now he was no longer waiting in the wings to stride out onto the stage of history: it had mercilessly arrived at his doorstep—and would provide him with on-the-job training. Like it or not, for this lifelong risk-averse politician, there was no escaping the mayhem to come.

Nothing, then, about his background recommended Lincoln to the daunting task he was about to face. The great question now confronting him, and the country, was ultimately no longer slavery *per se* or freedom in the territories, but the very nation itself. And in answering this, Lincoln turned out to be second to none. Reaching deep down into the wellspring of his soul, no man was more fervent in his belief in the Union; no man loved his country, North as well as South, as much as Lincoln. And no man was more concerned about not simply winning the war, but about keeping the country and the nation together.

Ultimately, it was this belief that would give him the inner strength to go on. In the sobering days and months and years ahead, he would need it. Somehow, at the hour of fate and the crack of doom, he would find himself.

❧   ❧   ❧

As the war ground on, it would become a duel over the soul of America. But not at first, not as Lincoln prowled back and forth in his office, head down, hands clasped behind his back, asking, what now?

What now, indeed. From the start, Lincoln's program was quite clear. His goal was not revolution. Nor was it to destroy the South's social fabric. Nor did he want war. He wanted Union. And he accepted war only when it seemed necessary to keep Union. Everything was subordinate to his mystical attachment to Union, including slavery. In fact, when Congress passed a constitutional amendment (the first and ultimately unratified Thirteenth Amendment) guaranteeing that the Federal government would never interfere with slavery and thus affixing the right of bondage firmly in the constitutional structure of the country, Lincoln supported it: "I have no objection to its being made express and irrevocable." This sentiment would be repeated most poignantly—and for many, quite tragically—when he wrote a reply to Horace Greeley, who had just published a ferocious editorial ("The Prayer of Twenty Millions") that accused Lincoln of being "strangely and disastrously remiss" in not emancipating the slaves. Lincoln ripped back immediately, by letter, for all to see: "My paramount object in this struggle is to save the Union and it is not either to save or destroy slavery. If I could save the Union without freeing any slaves, I would do it; and if I could save it by freeing all the slaves I would do it; and if I could save it by freeing some slaves and leaving others alone I would do that. What I do about slavery and the colored race I do because I believe it helps to save the Union." This, then, was the Lincoln program: save the Union, bring the South back, restore orderly government, establish the principle that force cannot win out—and, he hoped, do it with the least cost of lives.

But did he fully comprehend what war meant? Like just about everyone else, North or South, it is unlikely. He certainly did not expect a long fight—his first call was for a paltry 75,000 volunteers, requiring only a three months' enlistment. These were not the preparations for war, but for a fleeting skirmish. Lincoln had his blind spots; his first was misjudging the mood and the commitment of the South. His second was not initially understanding the dynamics of war that raise passions and harden sides. However, as the war dragged on, and the body count mounted, it became clear that the sacred struggle would be neither brief nor easy, nor, for that matter, necessarily victorious. And herein, too, lay his recalcitrance toward emancipation. Political and strategic considerations had, of necessity, to trump moral considerations. All else was, by definition, secondary. To end slavery he would have to preserve the Union. To preserve the Union he would have to win the war. And to win the war he would have to hold his fragile coalition together. He had four border states, Maryland, Kentucky, Missouri, and Delaware, all of them slave owning (with roughly half a million slaves among them), which were crucial to the war effort. Three of these states, as a simple glance at the map revealed, were vital not only to Union strategy, but to the safety of the Northern capital itself. None would take part in an antislavery campaign. Nor, for that matter, would a majority of the Northern people. While a noisy minority of Radicals insisted that he liberate the slaves, clamoring that it was self-contradictory to fight the war without smashing slavery, Lincoln knew that a far greater section of Northern opinion was willing to fight for the Union, but not for a crusade of emancipation.

In time, as the conflict dragged on, as is always the case, war began to change things. And it would change Lincoln. But Lincoln resisted the forces of social revolution swarming around him; indeed, he resisted the very fate that would make him a living icon of freedom. All was contingent, he believed, upon the survival of the Union. Which meant, of course, the success of the force of arms.

Here, Lincoln also made his share of mistakes, and history should not obscure his patchy record—erased only by adoring hindsight and the brilliant final months of the war. Day in and day out, as he hauled his tired bones to the War Department to read the latest dispatches, as he mulled over his ocean of troubles, his inexperience came back to haunt him. In those early years, he was anything but the picture of the confident, or seasoned, or well-oiled commander in chief. To be sure, he had his work cut out for him. He had generals who wouldn't fight, couldn't fight, failed to press on for the advantage when they did fight, or simply got whipped. What to do? Lincoln's initial response was almost predictable; he checked out books from the Library of Congress on the science and strategy of war and put himself through a rigid crash course on how to command an army. The results of his efforts were less than heartening. A case in point: one evening Lincoln and his secretary of state called upon General in Chief George McClellan at his house. McClellan flatly refused to see them, strolling past the very room where the president sat, and going upstairs to bed. Not anticipating such an insult, Lincoln sat there, in the parlor, for more than an hour. Unthinkable as this was, Lincoln never reprimanded McClellan. And this one incident belies a far deeper irony: we think of Lincoln as a consummate statesman, a humanitarian, a cosmic thinker, all of which is true. But he was unable to inspire or lead some of his own subordinates. He did not routinely dwarf his own aides or generals, as strong presidents must; nor was he invariably feared by his political adversaries and rivals. Too often, they felt that they could defy him.

At times, he seemed downright paralyzed. Later in 1862, when McClellan simply refused to attack the Confederates, Lincoln's response was nothing short of pathetic. While members of the Hill, led by

Benjamin Wade, clamored for McClellan's head, Lincoln asked feebly, "If I remove McClellan, whom shall I put in command?"

"Well, anybody!" Wade said.

"Well *anybody* will do for you," Lincoln said, "but not for me. I must have *somebody*."

But he stuck with McClellan, even as his own cabinet called McClellan's actions "imbecilic," even as he was lectured to "command the commanders," even as his own wife, Mary, sized McClellan up far better than he did. (He's a "humbug," Mary frowned sourly. "But why?" Lincoln asked, almost naively. "Because he talks so much and does so little.") These were clearly the actions of a still tentative man—and a man who was not always a confident judge of people. Only after much wasted time was McClellan finally dismissed. And he was just one of a procession of generals who, in one shape or another, proved woefully unsatisfactory: there were William Rosencrans, Ambrose Burnside, John Pope, and Joseph Hooker (Lincoln fired Burnside and replaced him with Hooker, after Hooker had already called the president "a played out imbecile"), and there was George Meade. But with brooding detachment, Lincoln pressed on, weathering his own mistakes, and equally weathering the brittle highs and deepening lows of the war. If he can best be described during this period, it is with two words: dogged tenacity.

Dogged tenacity. It is a simple explanation for greatness. But, in Lincoln's case, also probably quite true. For one thing, he needed it. One of the great historical questions is, why didn't Lincoln give up or give in? Why, when the opportunity for ending the killing presented itself, did he not grab the easy way out, or the expedient way, as he had so often in the past? Lincoln would hardly have been the first head of state to bend to the rancorous demands of nationalism being pressed upon him in a long and difficult civil war. Had he done so, history might well have deemed it a necessary matter, or even praised him for wisely not subjecting the North to a continuing tornado of blood and wreckage, or for having rescued his shattered, broken country from America's nineteenth-century version, as it were, of Vietnam. He might have been recorded in history books as the man who saved, protected, and preserved the "free" Union. And in any case, he would have been but one member of a long line of kings and monarchs and emperors and other chiefs of state who bowed or compromised to the powerful tide of history, to the irrepressible forces of self-determination and nationalism that were then sweeping the globe, and would continue do so for the next nearly 150 years. Far from being condemned, many of these leaders have been roundly praised.

Consider how tempting it might have been to any other president. At several points during the war, it looked as though the Confederacy could, or even would, win, or at least wouldn't lose, which amounted to much the same thing. Other times, after he finally appointed U. S. Grant ("At last!" Lincoln cried out joyously. "A general who fights!"), it was unclear whether the public would persevere with him. The four-day New York riots of 1863, which left at least 105 dead, the worst *ever* in American history, then or now, was one grim reminder (the city was beset by such turmoil that the *New York Times* on Park Row had three Gatling guns mounted on the roof and in the windows for protection); the storm of protests throughout the Midwest to stop the war was another; the election he feared that he would lose to McClellan in 1864 was still another. As the appalling Union casualties rose still further, the North was indeed in a foul mood; it literally began crying out for peace. One more season of slaughter would likely have been too much; in fact, in four years of war, an estimated 200,000 men deserted from the Federal army. Everywhere Lincoln turned, there were fervent antiwar rallies. As the ever-erratic Horace Greeley wrote in 1864, "Our bleeding, bankrupt, almost dying country longs for peace . . ." And this was not simply the anxious prattle of Copperheads and a few highly visible editors and intellectuals. By now, battalions of peace movements had cropped up across the North and became the basis for the Democratic Party platform of 1864 ("after four years of failure to restore the Union by the experiment of war . . . [we] demand immediate efforts for a cessation of hostilities . . . ").

And for Lincoln himself, the toll on his own psyche, of course, was brutal. During the battle of the Wilderness, Lincoln scarcely slept for four days. As we are reminded in historian Stephen Oates's vivid description, he morosely paced in the War Department, he aimlessly roamed in his office, he wandered about in the White House corridors. "I must have some relief from this terrible anxiety," he moaned, "or it will kill me." And if that didn't kill him, the ongoing avalanche of abuse and criticism might. "There is a cowardly imbecile at the head of the government," warned one newspaper. "I am heartsick," cried one member of Congress, "at the mismanagement of the army." And, "disgust with our government is universal," said another critic. Instead of glory, Lincoln once confessed, he found "only ashes and blood." It is little wonder that the whole experience of the presidency was barren for him. Carl Sandburg would remark that there were thirty-one rooms in the White House—and Lincoln was not at home in any of them.

But even as a deathly weariness settled over him, Lincoln was never mawkishly self-pitying. He did persevere. Consider his dispatches to his generals: "Hold on with a bull-dog grip and chew & choke, as much as possible"; "Stand firm"; "Hold firm, as with a chain of steel"; "watch it every day, and hour, and force it." Once more, dogged tenacity. It was remarkable, and again, the question is why? The answer is complicated. It has often been said that Lincoln was not religious, but there seems to be little doubt that as the war progressed, he became deeply moved by faith. In watching Lincoln evolve, one leaves with the sense that he came to feel that he had somehow been placed on this earth, elected as president, in the eye of this terrible war, for God's own designs. "There is a divinity that shapes our ends," he told one congressman in 1862. "The will of God prevails," he later declared. And perhaps most crucially, he increasingly saw himself as "an instrument of providence," saying, "I am satisfied that when the Almighty wants me to do or not do a particular thing, he finds a way of letting me know it." Amid the scourge of conflict, this provided some of the lubricant for presidential leadership: in waiting for providential guidance at the critical points of the war, for perhaps the first time in his life, he felt not the familiar drumbeat of ambition or of political satisfaction, but of destiny. And when that happened, he was a rock.

And if destiny meant preserving the Union, it also could not shield him forever from slavery. "If slavery is not wrong," he wrote to a friend in Kentucky, "then nothing is wrong." Yet still he waffled. In 1862, when the Radicals were calling for emancipation, he flirted with a fantastic scheme to colonize freed blacks abroad. The first iteration was to resettle blacks in the Chiriqui coal region of Central America. When that fizzled out (the Central Americans would have no part of it), he brazenly suggested to a delegation of blacks that they should lead the way and recruit enough volunteers to "resettle in Liberia." This, too, quickly fizzled. Then he came up with another wild scheme, signing a contract with white promoters to resettle 5,000 Negro volunteers on Haiti's Isle of Vache. By May 1863, only 450 had signed up, and this scheme also collapsed. But by then, it scarcely mattered. In the summer of 1862, Lincoln had experienced a profound change of heart, impelled by a combination of politics and morality. With his generals still floundering, his policies under fierce criticism from the Radicals, the once wavering Lincoln had finally determined to move toward emancipation. He now reached for a formula of his own. Swept up by a sense of high purpose, he would institute a bold war measure while at the same time he would cleanse the lingering sin of the Constitution. By July 22, his mind was made up; it was no longer a question of whether it would be done, but when.

"We mustn't issue it until after a victory," Lincoln told his cabinet. That victory came, at Antietam, on September 17. Five days later, Lincoln made the Emancipation Proclamation public.

The initial reception was decidedly mixed. The Emancipation Proclamation troubled some of Lincoln's critics—then and now. Again came the charge: Lincoln was too timid (one even gibed that he had "no antislavery instincts"). Lincoln was too political. Lincoln was too conservative. The proclamation expressly omitted the loyal slave states from its terms; it contained no indictment of slavery, being based on "military necessity." And it didn't free any slaves, declaring simply that all slaves would be free in "the States and part of the States" where the people were in rebellion: in short, where its effect could not reach. As the *London Spectator* mocked: "The principle is not that a human being cannot justly own another, but that he cannot own him unless he is loyal to the United States." Even Seward was critical, barking, "We show our sympathy with slavery by emancipating the slaves where we cannot reach them and holding them in bondage where we can set them free." In some respects, the Congress was not unfair when it remarked that the proclamation added little to what it had already done with the Confiscation Act. But in the final analysis, these criticisms miss their mark: the Emancipation Proclamation was the most revolutionary document in the country's history since the Declaration of Independence; it truly began the end of slavery, in the North and the South. The psychological impact of the proclamation cannot be underestimated: Lincoln, in a masterful stroke, had become a personal emblem of freedom, and the Emancipation Proclamation was its parchment. As a war act, it was also a stunning measure, imbuing the Northern war effort with a larger moral purpose without overshooting its mark. And for approximately 180,000 blacks—mostly slaves—it was nothing short of a miracle. They would go on to serve valiantly in the Federal army.

To the extent that Lincoln's commitment to eradicating slavery was in doubt, his efforts to pass the second Thirteenth Amendment, codifying the Emancipation Proclamation in the Constitution, put that forever to rest. The year before, in 1864, the amendment had been easily defeated; this time, in January 1865, he again faced an uphill battle. The Democratic Party remained firmly opposed to the measure, having lambasted it as "unwise, impolitic, cruel, and unworthy of the support of civilized people." But for the amendment to pass, Lincoln needed Democrats, at least nineteen; otherwise, the measure would go down in flames, 93–80. The outlook was not good. Interestingly, for a man who often could not control his own generals or his own cabinet, he was invariably at his best in the two-step of party politics. Behind the scenes, Lincoln became a splendid hybrid of the resourceful pol and the voice of a collective conscience—in an unswerving blitzkrieg, he addressed his colleagues quietly, huddled with party chiefs, and met across party lines. And then he began in earnest, rolling up his sleeves, twisting arms, making hard deals, corralling wavering members, and using every measure at his disposal to finagle, garner, or otherwise ensure the necessary two-thirds vote in the House of Representatives. When the roll was finally called, eight Democrats abstained and sixteen went with him; the amendment had been carried by all but the slimmest of margins, three votes—but it was broad enough to end slavery for all time.

But whatever his zeal for ending slavery, there was his even greater zeal for the Union. On November 19, 1863, Lincoln had made a short speech—272 words—at the dedication of a cemetery at Gettysburg. By many lights, this address was a masterful verbal coup, subtly reshaping the Constitution, which permitted slavery, by squaring it with the Declaration of Independence, which was "dedicated to the proposition that all men are created equal." In Garry Wills's phrase, the address corrected the Constitution "without overthrowing it." Making relatively little impact at the time, the words now echo through history and the generations: "Four score and seven years ago, our fathers brought forth on this continent a new nation . . . Now we are engaged in a great civil war, testing whether that nation, or any nation so conceived and so dedicated, can long endure . . . We have come to dedicate a portion of that field as a final resting place for those who gave their lives that that nation might live . . . this nation, under God, shall have a new birth of freedom . . ." But something deeper was taking place in this speech: at stake in this war, Lincoln was contending, was the struggle for the very survival of the nation.

Not once in the speech did he refer to his cherished Union; instead, five times he referred to the "nation." This was no oversight. As a lawyer and careful student of the English language, Lincoln well understood the distinction between "Union" and "nation." Not the greatest orator of his day, he nonetheless had a searing, resonant style, sparkling with nineteenth-century phrases and the soothing rhythmic cadence of classical speech. It is impossible to imagine Lincoln employing a ghostwriter; as Garry Wills has suggested, no one but Lincoln could write Lincolnian prose—the stamp of this man is on everything he uttered. When short, simple words hit hard, he used them; when soaring, rolling, pealing prose served his purpose, then he used it. And his feeling for the English word or turn of phrase was careful, rhythmic, even sensual—and so precise. Thus we are inexorably drawn back to his use of "Union" and "nation." The first was a legal construct of a country; the second referred to the collective and shared identity of a people. Ideally, the two were intertwined, although in the case of Civil War America, they were most certainly not. Clearly, even in those dark days, some seventeen months before April 1865, Lincoln was looking ahead to a time when they would be again.

But looking ahead was one thing, getting there was another. By the end of the war, Lincoln had become a changed man, and most certainly, a changed president. Once, back on the stump, politics had been invigorating sport. Now, operating from his presidential cocoon, he could no longer escape the judgment of his country—or of history. Was he playing to history—or even conscious of its mighty weight? The record suggests he did not overly dwell on his own legacy; but he was deeply conscious of it for the country. Unlike the whole of the rest of his life, his every decision, large and small, now carried grave import, affecting the lives of his soldiers, affecting the outcome of the battles, affecting the outcome of war, affecting the prospects for reconciliation, affecting the life or death of the nation. Presidents may do many things, but they do not have the luxury of complaining, or blaming others, or eluding responsibility, no matter how terrifying it is in all its dimensions. Second-rate presidents may act "great" during routine times, when it is easy to do so, but it is only the truly great ones who act great during the difficult times. And where the second-rate presidents are somehow always shaped, and prodded, and manipulated by the forces of history, great ones find ways to bend those forces of history to their goals. Thus it was for Lincoln. He instinctively understood the moral burdens he had to shoulder; he appreciated the high seriousness of the crisis; he grasped its tragic proportions while never losing sight of the good that could somehow be made out of this awful conflict. And he did all this with a humane detachment that, even now, history has trouble fully sorting out or explaining.

As the Civil War entered its waning months, Lincoln was nevertheless an overwhelmingly melancholy man. Like many great generals who have had to send tens upon tens of thousands to their deaths, he had a corner of remorse lodged deep in his gut, furiously eating away at him. But there was something else, too, which almost seemed to defy explanation: his curious, almost indifferent attitude toward his own death. When he heard rumors of Confederate plots to kidnap or assassinate him, he persistently dismissed them: "Even if true, I do not see what the rebels would gain." In August 1862, while he was riding his horse to the Soldier's Home, a gunshot rang out and a bullet whistled close by. Lincoln laughed it off, calling the incident "ludicrous," "farcical," and an accident. After his reelection in 1864, he began to receive hate mail with frequent regularity, including letters threatening his life. He coolly filed them himself, in an envelope marked "Assassination."

"I know I'm in danger," he once confessed to Seward, "but I am not going to worry about it." So Lincoln walked alone at night, went off to the theater without guards, and repeatedly dismissed the charges made by his security men and Stanton that his life was in danger. "What does anyone want to assassinate me for?" he told Seward. And in Seward's words, "Assassination is not an American practice or habit." Lincoln agreed. "As to crazy folks, I must take my chances," he said. "I long ago made up my mind that if anybody wants to kill me, he will do it . . . There are a thousand ways of getting at a man if it is desired that he should be killed." When Stanton finally provided firm measures for four personal bodyguards as well as a military escort, at least one of whom was to be with Lincoln at any given time, the president snapped back, "It is important that the people know I come among them without fear." But by April 14, as Lincoln readied himself to go to the Ford's Theater, the stage was indeed set. Lincoln had been warned several times that this evening would be a particularly dangerous one, yet he refused to bow out or to take along an extra guard. To some, these are the convictions of a man without hate or malice, or the signs of a cavalier sort of recklessness or of a morbid bit of bravado, or evidence of yet another troubling blind spot, or even of a man who has willingly acceded his control to the larger flow of events. Perhaps all this is true. But with hindsight, we can perhaps see things somewhat differently. They are the actions not of a passive man but of a man hurtling toward his destiny, without fear or hesitation.

And in the end, that destiny, that one issue which most compelled Lincoln, was Union—and the nation. He will always be remembered as freedom's champion when it was called into question, but he must also be judged as the nation's champion in its darkest hour. In no small measure, it explains why he refused to quit, or to compromise, or to take the easy political way out when it presented itself to him. In no small measure, it explains his relentless embrace of total war, and then, even as that war was ticking to a close, it explained his anxieties about unbridled chaos until the very end. And in no small measure, it accounted for his remarkable compassion and charity toward the Confederates that was to be the backbone of his postwar policy—and toward which he would now devote all his energies. All this he felt, and felt most passionately.

But then came the bullet that bore into his brain.

⁂ ⁂ ⁂

"Stop that man! Stop that man!" Clara Harris pleaded at Ford's Theater. But so quickly had it all happened that the images were almost impossible to digest, the reality of the events even less so.

Once John Wilkes Booth, clad in his black felt hat and high boots with spurs, fired that single shot from his derringer, Lincoln's companion, Major Rathbone, sought to wrestle him to the ground. Booth slashed his arm to the bone with a seven-inch dagger and leaped from the box, a difficult two-story jump. Catching his spur in a flag, he crashed onto the stage and broke his left shinbone just above the ankle. There, he delivered his final line: "*Sic semper tyrannis*"—"Thus always to tyrants," the Virginia state motto—and then he hobbled to the backstage door, mounted his mare, and galloped off in the night.

Amid the rush for the exits and shoving in the aisles, the theater was in an uproar. There were wild shrieks from Mary Lincoln: "Help! Help! Help!" There was the call for aid from Clara Harris: "Won't somebody stop that man!" There was the plea to stay calm from Laura Keene: "For God's sake . . . keep your places and all will be well!" There was the rush to assist: "Has anyone any stimulants!" And there was the inevitable, shouted by an unknown member of the audience: "Is there a doctor in the house?" Mary was holding Lincoln in the rocker and sobbing madly when Charles A. Leale, a young army surgeon just two months out of medical school, finally managed to battle his way to the state box. With his eyes closed, Lincoln's head drooped forward to his breast. It immediately looked bad. Leale quickly spread Lincoln on the floor and, cradling his head, could watch the blood slip through his fingers from where the projectile had entered. He could immediately see that Lincoln's breath was shallow, getting weaker by the second. Worse still, his wrist was without a pulse, and he was paralyzed. The bullet had burrowed deep into Lincoln's brain and fixed itself just behind his right eye. Working furiously, Leale dislodged a mass of clotting blood. Then he reached into Lincoln's mouth and, drawing in his own hard breath, began artificial respiration in a desperate attempt to revive the president. Another doctor arrived, and Leale commanded him to raise and lower the president's arms while Leale himself kneaded the left breast with both hands, and then again started with the mouth-to-mouth resuscitation. Finally Lincoln was breathing on his own, his breath irregular, his heart beating feebly. But Leale felt this was only temporary and sadly pronounced, "His wound is mortal. It is impossible for him to recover."

Still, in medicine, as in politics, nothing is ever certain. After some quick deliberation, Leale, joined by two other doctors now, decided not to take him to the White House—it was deemed too far away—but to William Peterson's house across the street, where they would seek to work a miracle. An officer hastily drew his sword to cut a path through the throng anxiously assembled in Tenth Street, and they carried him out into the dark, into the road, and up the curving steps of a modest row house, then along a thin hallway to the back, to the dingy little rented room of a War Department clerk. There, they lay the oversized president diagonally across a seedy Victorian four-poster bed. A hissing gas lamp was lit, emitting a ghastly green light. Thus began the night of April 14–15.

When Mary entered, she fell to her knees, weeping feverishly. Alternately, she whispered pet names and pleaded with him to speak; one word, she implored, anything. But there was only the even, steady sound of his breath, up and down, up and down. By 11 P.M., the Lincolns' family doctor, Robert King Stone, arrived, and he became the physician in charge, assisted by Joseph K. Barnes, the surgeon general of the United States. They immediately sized up the situation as dreadful. Lincoln's right eye was badly swollen and discolored, and despite an army blanket and a colored wool coverlet, his extremities were growing very cold. His pulse was forty-five, and growing weaker.

The doctors all agreed that Lincoln would not survive; they felt the average man would not last more than two hours. But they would try everything: hot water bottles, mustard plasters, blankets, anything to keep him warm and keep his weakened heart beating. In turn, two doctors took it upon themselves to make an extensive record, charting his pulse and respiration. Press bulletins, updating the president's condition, were dispatched every half hour, and quickly coursed over the web of telegraph wires in the North.

When son Robert Lincoln finally arrived, he could see that grief and exhaustion were taking a toll on his mother, and Mary was soon persuaded to retire to the front parlor, where she again broke into convulsive sobbing. The time was 2 A.M.

Now, on its own, Lincoln's body was desperately fighting death; it was not unimpressive. At 11:25, his pulse had dropped to forty-two. But by 12:32, it had climbed eighteen beats to sixty. At 12:45 it scaled another ten beats, reaching seventy. At 12:55, his arms suddenly began to twitch, making a "struggling motion." At 1:30, the pulse had risen more than twofold; it stood at ninety-five, and, as one doctor noted, "appearing easier."

While the night lengthened, a procession of government officials filed into the dim little room, and eventually the entire cabinet—except for Seward—crowded around, while the brigade of doctors continued to try everything at their disposal. All felt despair, disbelief, shock—and prayed for a miracle. When Lincoln's friend and political tormentor, Senator Sumner, came in, his face was paralyzed with grief. He gently fingered Lincoln's limp hand and began speaking to him, but one of the doctors interjected softly, "He can't hear you. He is dead." "No," a trembling Sumner hotly protested, "he isn't dead. Look at his face; he is breathing." As Lincoln lay there on the diagonal, his head propped up by extra pillows, his brain destroyed, his face swollen and discolored, and his blood seeping onto the bedspread and blanket, the doctors assured him that Lincoln would never again regain consciousness. Sumner lowered his head to Lincoln's, clutched his hand even more tightly, and lost all control. Recalled one observer: he wept like "a woman."

After 2 A.M., Lincoln's pulse again began to sink. At 3 A.M., Reverend Phineas Gurley said a prayer. In a hot press room, some 200 miles to the north, the *New York Times* headlined its rush edition: "AWFUL EVENT . . . The President Still Alive at Last Counts. No Hopes Entertained of His Recovery."

With the president dying and the government now at a virtual stand-still, Secretary of War Stanton took charge. Blurry-eyed, and nearly breaking down himself, he set up shop in the back parlor, where a federal judge and two other aides helped him take down testimony from witnesses. It was a frenzy of agitated activity. Soon, he realized that Washington was in the midst of a reign of terror. John Wilkes Booth was quickly identified as the president's assassin. Word also trickled in that another assassin had attempted to murder Seward, who, as it turned out was still alive, but barely; his prognosis was uncertain, though it was thought that he would live. Meanwhile, Stanton feared for Grant's and Sherman's safety as well. He promptly ordered the city to be placed under martial law and dispatched an organized dragnet to hunt down Booth and all other suspects. By morning, accomplices Powell and Atzerodt would be under arrest, but Booth would have escaped. Throughout the night, Stanton became the government, issuing orders, taking testimony, assembling troops, and directing the massive manhunt under way. All major Eastern ports were ordered to be on the lookout for suspicious persons; all traffic was stopped on the Potomac River and the railroads; all bridges and roads out of the capital were closed. Washington's fire brigade was mobilized to stand by for signs of mass arson.

The front parlor now belonged to Mary Lincoln, who, collapsed upon a sofa, seesawed between dreadful spells of high-pitched wailing and disbelieving quiet. At one point, she recalled Lincoln's dream of a dead body in the White House and cried out in a terrible, fearful voice, "His dream was prophetic!" and she asked God to strike her down as well, to let her join her husband. Outside, in the fog and the mist, a crowd gathered, forming a protective sentinel in front of the Peterson house, all the while searching the leaders who came and went for the slightest indication that Lincoln would live.

The minutes drifted by. Dr. Leale cradled the president's hand in his throughout, "so that in the darkness he would know he had a friend." But Lincoln had more than one friend. In all, up to some ninety different people would make their way into the cramped room during the night. Almost hourly, Mary returned, entering the room, looking at her husband, looking at his engorged and swollen eye now turning purple, looking at the man who earlier in the day was "so gay," so "joyous," so "happy," and cried out, "Oh that my little Taddie might see his father before he died!" After some seven hours had passed, Lincoln's ironically calm face suddenly began to twitch. This was too much for the depleted first lady, shattering what residue of calm remained. She fell to the floor and screamed out in horror, prompting Stanton to holler, "Take that woman out and do not let her in again!"

As the night wore on, Lincoln's respiration was increasingly accompanied by a low, guttural sound. Several times, it seemed as though he had ceased breathing altogether, then his lungs would begin to swell again, each breath carrying with it a glimmer of hope. And throughout the room came the continued rise and fall of muffled weeping. Eventually, a heavy rain began to beat against the windowpanes as the first blush of gray dawn seeped through the windows. Lincoln was still alive, but not for much longer. Mary entered, to see her husband one last time; Sumner was still there, now holding Lincoln's hand. Tears in her reddened eyes, she softly pressed her lips to his face and implored, "Love, live but one moment to speak to me once—to speak to our children." As his breathing grew fainter and fainter, she then moaned uncontrollably, "Oh my God, and have I given my husband to die?"

Indeed she had. At 6:00 A.M., the doctor observed, "Pulse failing." At 6:25, he penned, "choking and grunting." At 7:00 A.M., he added: "Symptoms of dissolution."

Now, as the end neared, Lincoln's friends and colleagues huddled tearfully at his bedside. Lincoln's son Robert leaned his head on Sumner's shoulder and dissolved into unmitigated grief. Others, seeing that death was descending, also began to cry. Then the endless nine-hour struggle came to a close. The time was 7:22 A.M., April 15. With finality, the physician wrote: "Death."

"It is all over," the doctors told Mary. "The President is no more."

With this commenced a spontaneous ritual: a doctor laid silver half-dollars on Lincoln's eyelids. The surgeon general slipped a sheet over his face, and the pastor of the New York Presbyterian Church mouthed a soothing prayer. Fighting back his own tears, Stanton, who had in effect become acting president, extended his right arm as in a salute, raised his hat and placed it for an instant on his head, and then in the same precise manner took it away. Gazing deeply at his fallen chief, he pronounced a private epitaph. "Now," he concluded, "he belongs to the angels."*

Moments later, his father left behind, lying on the bed, cool and still, Robert Lincoln led his mother by the hand out into the rain, into the muddy streets, into the uncertain future that Abraham Lincoln had so desperately sought to control.

❧   ❧   ❧

The world now knows well the power and peril of a single gunshot. Europe itself, witness to 500 years of assassinations and attempted assassinations—even Napoleon was almost killed one Christmas Eve by a homemade bomb—would be reminded of its deadly fruits again in June 1914 when a young revolutionary would assassinate the Archduke Francis Ferdinand in the streets of Sarajevo, triggering a chain of events that within little over a month would culminate in a devastating world war. Yet for America, this was a first. Never before had a president been assassinated. Never before had a president died while a war was under way. Never before had an attempt been made to decapitate the very seat of government. All of which raised a host of fateful questions: How would the presidential transition process work in a crisis? Would the Confederate armies still in the field, spent though they might be, seek to take advantage of the chaos gripping Washington? And would Lincoln's legacy of healing devolve into nothing more than an orgy of retribution?

And as sorrow gripped the Union, there remained one more haunting question: would it now all come undone?

---

* Stanton would later revise what he said as, "Now he belongs to the ages," which is the phrase most historians cite. See explanatory note on page 428.

6

Would It All Come Undone?

In retrospect, the air of foreboding about the hours and days that followed in mid-April has dimmed, replaced by the convenient sense that everyone of consequence played his part perfectly, like a well-rehearsed melody. The Constitution did its part; the new president and his cabinet did their part; the people did their part; and, rounded out by the towering might of the Union armies, all tumbled neatly and inevitably into place. But this is, of course, refracted nostalgia and convenient hindsight. Nothing, in fact, could be further from the truth.

What really happened? "It was a night of horrors." So wrote Chief Justice Salmon Chase. And so were the days that followed. As morning broke through the darkened skies on April 15, the North was stunned beyond belief. Lincoln, dead? Seward, attacked? Johnson, a target? A possibly far-reaching Southern plot? But all this was merely a melancholy prelude, for then came the hardest part, sorting it all out. If one were to choose a time when the institutions of American democracy faced perhaps their greatest test, when the country sat at a defining crossroads, ready to veer in one direction, but just as able to choose another, it would not necessarily be the signing of the Declaration of Independence, or the historic closing of the Constitutional Convention, or the Union election of 1864, or even the fateful meeting at Appomattox. It would be this: the nine long hours preceding 7:22 A.M. on April 15 and the three hours hence, until 10 A.M., about twelve hours all told, when the transfer of presidential power was set to take place—and the chaotic, rough, tumultuous days that followed in its uncertain wake.

By 7:30 A.M., a strange light already began to fall and grow upon the Union: vengeance and sorrow and chaos and turmoil threatened not the South, but the North. What could have been more incongruous? This was, after all, just five days after the giddy glow of Appomattox. But as a long wooden coffin was quietly edged down the narrow lodging house steps on Tenth Street, through the mud and onto the roads, carrying Abraham Lincoln's body back to the White House, flags drooped to half-mast everywhere and the muffled ringing of bells could be heard against the rain. Now it was the voices of revenge that could be heard loudest. Citizens poured into the streets, in the downpour, and soon they were nothing more than muttering mobs, a hostile throng angrily congregating from K Street to Lafayette Square: they shook their fists at Ford's Theater, shouting "Burn the theater!"; a cascade of ugly roars and boos spontaneously swelled up, fell, then continued even more loudly; any mention of Confederates brought an equally vociferous reprise: "Shoot them!" "Hang them!" "Hang them again!" "Kill the god damn rebels!" Talk of streets running red with Confederate blood was everywhere. And with the iron hand of martial law imposed upon the Union capital, the city remained edged with fear. In every direction, a phalanx of armed guards sought to keep order, manning stations on all roads to and from the city. Government departments and business houses were abruptly closed; the city was immediately cordoned off; routine market wagons, milk carts, and mail riders were turned around and sent back beyond the outskirts; theaters and music halls hastily canceled their engagements; and concerts and social functions were postponed indefinitely. But if the streets threatened to turn crimson with vengeance, they were just as quickly tinged with the real color of sorrow. Black was ubiquitous. So, too, were the telltale sounds of mourning. The White House columns were draped in black, and somber black folds were looped along all the Federal buildings. The melancholy sound of organs rippled across town, and altar candles were lit. Soldiers fastened shreds of darkened crepe and cut ribbon on their sleeves. Even the poor pinned scraps of black cloth in their windows and on their modest doorposts.

But all did not come to a standstill. It couldn't. For all the grief and rage, it was the tricky business of the war that still most mattered. Tricky because, while the Union armies might be the overseers of the Army of Northern Virginia and the Confederate capital of Richmond, two state capitals still remained in Confederate hands, Austin, Texas, at one end and Tallahassee, Florida, at another; moreover, there were still three separate Confederate Departments spread across the Confederacy to be subdued. Tricky, too, because the Union government was not just temporarily confused, but, for all intents and purposes, headless. Wrote the *New York Times*: "His [Lincoln's] sudden removal from the stage of events naturally excites anxiety and apprehension in the public mind." It added: "If the Emperor NAPOLEON had been assassinated, all France would have been in revolution before 24 hours had passed away." Thus, the most immediate task was actually not military but governmental; this was to be the first ever transfer of power in a crisis. And here again, the path was anything but absolutely clear. For one thing, Andrew Johnson, the new vice president, who had been written off by official Washington as a drunk and widely dismissed by the city's elites as a buffoon, was by most accounts a neophyte: he had never met with the cabinet, had not once been privy to a single decision made by Lincoln, and was not even of the president's political party. In fact, the two men had so little to do with each other that they had met only one time since the inauguration: the day before, for under an hour. Indeed, throughout the evening of April 14–15, it was not Johnson, but the secretary of war, Edwin Stanton, who, from that small sitting room adjacent to a tailor's shop, had assumed the reins of authority. Not elected by a single soul (he actually had tendered his resignation some days earlier, although Lincoln had rejected it), brusque, humorless, authoritarian, at times paranoid, and deeply devoted to Lincoln, Stanton literally became the U.S. government, issuing orders, military and civil, assuming all police control, taking depositions, arresting suspects, and tending to the security of the capital.

And, arguably, he was a questionable man for the job. By his own private admission, weeks earlier Stanton had been so worn out that he had suffered a panic attack while in Savannah; but now, for these crucial twelve hours, he was, as one government subordinate noted, "president, secretary of war, secretary of state, commander in chief, comforter, and dictator." Or as another observer more succinctly put it, "he was the Master, and in reality Acting President of the United States." All quite true—and unprecedented.

But the trickiest part of the transition actually had to do with the Constitution. Today, it is largely assumed that the succession process was neatly and firmly spelled out in the Constitution; that even so cataclysmic an event as a presidential assassination would automatically be followed by the steadying force of vice-presidential succession to the presidency. But in fact, almost uniquely, it is here that the Constitution is riddled with vexing ambiguities at best, fraught with astonishing omissions, and, at times, downright confusing. Seward was fond of saying that assassination was not an American "habit." Perhaps the Founders thought this, too. How else do we explain that of all things, this was one matter that they did not anticipate at any length—or spell out in indisputably clear detail?

Ironically then, on the early morning of April 15, as a badly shaken Andrew Johnson huddled nervously in his hotel room four blocks away at Kirkwood House, the Constitution itself would not be the bulwark to provide a firm guide to presidential succession in the fearful hours to follow. Instead, the actions of an earlier, brash vice president would now become the touchstone for the nation. Looking back, nearly 150 years later, that the Union wound its way through this matter at this moment is perhaps a wonder—and not at all an insignificant one.

❧ ❧ ❧

When the Founders first debated the matter of executive succession upon presidential death, resignation, or disability, the Virginia and New Jersey plans were silent on the matter. It was only Alexander Hamilton, who, on June 18, 1787, first presented a plan for dealing with such a crisis: "On the death[,] resignation or removal of the Governour his authorities to be exercised by the President of the Senate till a Successor be appointed." By August, his suggestions were taken up, and the Committee of Detail reported that "the President of the Senate" was to exercise the duties of the office "until another president of the United States was Chosen." The subject was debated at greater length on August 24 and 25, and then referred to the Committee of Eleven, a body specially created to consider unique problems of state. On September 4, the committee finally issued its report, with a stunning new twist: instead of the president of the Senate, they recommended that a vice president be made the heir apparent. But, they also made clear, the vice president was *not* to become the president; he was only to exercise "the powers and discharge the duties" of the presidential office until "another President was chusen." And for this to occur, it would have to be "supplied by" special election (or be until "the President's inability ceased"). This conclusion was further enshrined in a motion offered by James Madison: "the Legislature may declare by law what officer of the United States shall act as president and Vice president[,] in case of the death, resignation, or disability of the President . . . ; and such officer shall act accordingly, until such disability be removed, or a President shall be elected." After some debate, the Committee of Style reported this "succession clause" out on September 12 with some stylistic changes, including a clause that was widely understood to limit the tenure of an acting president to a shorter period ("until . . . a President shall be elected.") And even after the Committee of Eleven introduced the office of the vice president, nobody ever suggested that he should succeed to the higher office; only that he was to exercise the "presidential powers and duties" in an "acting" capacity. Thus the record was established: from the notes, reports, and debates in the Convention, what clearly comes across is that the Framers did not intend for a vice president (or an officer named by Congress) to be anything other than an interim caretaker, and most certainly, it seems, they did not intend for the vice president to become president.

Unlike a host of other contentious issues roiling the Founders, notably those separating the Federalists and the anti-Federalists, this provision was not terribly controversial. Whenever the matter came up, delegates reflected a unanimous understanding of what the convention called for. At the state ratifying conventions themselves, they were always careful to draw a bright line between "the president" and an "acting

president," or in the words of James Bowdin, the Boston delegate at the
Massachusetts Convention, "the Vice president when acting as President."
The New York Convention almost went a step further, proposing an even
spicier amendment to clarify the matter, which referred to "the person
holding the [president's] place for the time being." As with the Constitutional Convention itself, in not a single state convention did a delegate speak of the vice president "becoming" president. Actually, only
the ratifying Convention of Virginia saw fit to significantly debate the
clause at all. This time, it was George Mason who loudly raised his voice,
decrying the succession clause as deficient because there was no specific
provision for the speedy election in case of a vacancy in both presidential and vice presidential offices. Again, it was Madison who responded, but with this ambiguous riposte: "When the President and Vice
President die," he pointed out, "the election of another President will
immediately take place; and suppose it would not,—what Congress
could do would be to make an appointment between the expiration of
the four years and the last election . . . "

He hastened to add: "This can rarely happen."

There the matter was settled. What settled it even further was *The
Federalist*, No. 68, in which Hamilton buttressed this constitutional
arrangement. "The Vice president," he stated nonchalantly, as if to underscore the lack of discord about the matter, "may occasionally become
a substitute for the President." Many years later, it was perhaps Charles
Warren, the constitutional scholar, who best summed up the intentions
of the Founders, ". . . the delegates probably contemplated that, in such
case [the death of the president], the Vice President would only perform
the duties of the President until a new election should be held; and that
he would not *ipso facto* become President." Noted twentieth-century constitutional scholar Edward S. Corwin was even more emphatic: "It was
clearly the intention of the framers that the Vice President should remain
Vice President, a stop-gap, a *locum tenens*, whatever the occasion of this
succession, and should become President only if and when he was elected as such." Indeed, for the better part of a half century following the
Constitutional Convention, the intention of the Founders was amply
understood and just as amply agreed to: in the event of the death of a

president, a special election would be held; and if both president and vice president were to die, Congress would designate an officer to act as president until that election took place.

But even the Founders were not omniscient; what they didn't anticipate was the raw, naked ambition of a future sitting vice president. Half a century later, and twenty-five years and ten days before Lincoln's assassination, the succession clause was finally put to the test when William Henry Harrison became the first president of the United States to die in office, of pneumonia. The date was April 4, 1841. Harrison had been president only one month. Even now, much of the next sixty hours remain enshrouded in cloak of intrigue, a fog of political manipulation, and considerable mystery, but this much is known. During the weeks that Harrison lay sick and dying, the silver-tongued Daniel Webster, then secretary of state, decided that Vice President John Tyler should become president, largely to serve as a figurehead, whom the cabinet would then control. (In fact, as a sign of the general confusion surrounding the entire issue, evidence suggests that if Tyler were forced "to act" as president, Webster even believed he should be the president for the remainder of the term, whether or not Harrison recovered.) Others, however, were less enthusiastic about Tyler. He had been picked to garner Southern votes, not for what he believed. He was such a secondary figure that he didn't even stay in Washington for Harrison's inaugural celebration, but rather retired unobtrusively to his home, twenty-one hours away in Williamsburg, Virginia. From the desk of his study, the erudite John Quincy Adams, the sixth president of the United States, was even more adamant that Tyler was not suited for the highest office in the land. "This is the first instance," he wrote, "of a Vice President's being called to act as President of the United States, and brings to test the provision of the Constitution which places in the executive chair *a man never thought of for it by anyone.*"

Nevertheless, Washington was alive with fierce speculation about Harrison's succession, and word in the capital salons was that the cabinet felt that Tyler would perform the functions of president while bearing the title of "vice president acting president." In truth, by then the cabinet had already engaged in a steady dose of backroom maneuvering. It had publicly announced Harrison's death and dispatched a carefully crafted message tellingly addressed to "John Tyler, Vice President of the United States." Tyler, a tall, patrician-looking man with a high retreating forehead, returned at once to Washington, where he met with the cabinet at the Brown's Indian Queen Hotel. Behind closed doors, they bargained fiercely, and Tyler proved to be no pushover. The cabinet bluntly explained their proposed arrangement with him: all matters of state would be brought before the entire cabinet and would be decided by majority vote; Tyler would have but one vote. It was a brazen deal. In return for allowing him to become president, the cabinet would run the show. They would become chief executive by fiat. Tyler was just as blunt. He tightened his jaw and demurred, sternly announcing he didn't intend to be a caretaker but to seize the full authority of the presidency. Stunned by Tyler's vehemence, and uncertain of how the complex politics might play out, the cabinet temporarily backed down. For the moment, Tyler had won the showdown.

Tyler quickly took advantage of his opponents' disarray, getting sworn in as president. Interestingly, however, Chief Justice Roger Taney declined the invitation to administer the oath of office to Tyler; it was instead performed by Judge William Cranch, chief of the Circuit Court for the District of Columbia. Tyler himself did not think a second oath was necessary; he had already been sworn in as vice president. And if he were merely acting president, he didn't need to take another oath, but he took it anyway, swearing this time to uphold the presidential duties. Evidently, he was determined to make a show of force to the cabinet—and just as importantly, to the country.

Some confusion reigned, and reaction to Tyler's moves was mixed. Many newspapers questioned whether Tyler was indeed the president. The *Harrisburg Intelligencer* announced that Tyler would act as "President ex officio," while the *Richmond Enquirer* explained that he was only the "acting President." The *New York Post* hastened to add that he possessed all the powers of the presidency but "did not succeed to the title." Other papers, like the *Boston Morning Post*, even continued to refer to Tyler as "Vice President," or "Acting President." On a lighter note, editorials wondered, tongue-in-cheek, whether Tyler should be officially called "His accidental Power," "Under President (acting under Henry Clay's direction)," "Ex

Officio President," or even "His Accidency." On the other hand, Tyler had clearly made some headway: no major newspaper suggested that a special presidential election should be called for. Whatever the case, Tyler boldly asserted his right to the presidential office and to its title, and on April 9, he delivered what he termed his "inaugural address," in which he spoke about the devolution of the presidential office upon him.

His campaign for the presidency had begun in earnest.

Yet others remained unconvinced. Henry Clay privately referred to Tyler's administration as "a regency." Representative John McKeon publicly insisted that Tyler was simply "Vice president now exercising the office of the President." Senators William Allen and Benjamin Tappan were even more vehement in their opposition. After a careful reading of the Constitution, Article II, Section 1, clause 6, Tappan protested, "There was but one mode provided in that instrument . . . of the constitution . . . by which a President could be created . . . The President of the United States, as such, existed and could exist only by an election of the people." Ex-President John Quincy Adams, for his part, felt even more strongly. He anxiously recorded in his private journal that Tyler "styles himself President of the United States, and not Vice President acting as President, which would be correct . . ." He added further that the whole sordid affair "violated" the Constitution.

Nonetheless, recognizing that possession was nine-tenths of the law, Tyler set about waging an energetic two-month crusade to secure for himself, at the very least, de facto recognition as president, including by both houses of Congress. One of Tyler's staunchest supporters, Virginia Representative Henry A. Wise (who would later become a Virginia governor and a high-ranking Confederate official and general) helped set the tone: Tyler could claim the presidency, Wise thundered, "by the Constitution, by election, and by the act of God!" Tyler, who was at heart a renegade Democrat, also set about wooing the one man who could turn the tide: Whig champion Henry Clay. The campaign paid off, and by June 1, Tyler had eased past the final hurdle, securing not only Clay's blessing, but also the recognition of both houses in a special session of Congress. Still, this fight was not without some cost: as late as 1848, a constitutional confusion remained, as did lingering questions about the propriety of Tyler's actions.

Even the State Department, under President James Buchanan, continued to address its correspondence to Tyler as "ex–vice president."

But to a great extent, Tyler's daring political strike had, in the public mind, successfully trumped the constitutional provisions. So much so that within a decade, when Zachary Taylor died in office on July 9, 1850, it was generally assumed Vice President Millard Fillmore would become president. In this case, unlike with John Tyler, the politics inexorably worked in Fillmore's favor: he and Taylor were both loyal Whigs. On the following day, Fillmore was sworn in—and the tentative precedent established by Tyler was now formally carried over to Fillmore (this time, however, the cabinet, eager to secure the position for their new party leader, sent him a letter addressed "To The President"). Implementation then, and not constitutional intent, had won the day. (In both cases, it should be noted, the vice president's office remained stunningly vacant for the balance of the term.) But still, in hindsight, there was a tinge of uncertainty and confusion. For reasons unknown, once again, the oath of office was administered not by Chief Justice Taney, but by Judge Cranch of the District Court.

So by the time Lincoln lay dying, inchoate tradition, not the Constitution, would apparently dictate that Andrew Johnson would accede to the presidency. But at the same time, there were some chronic, lingering, even unsettled questions that still remained about the succession process. And the first among them was not constitutional, but profoundly political, the horror at the fact that it was Andrew Johnson, of all people, who would be the Union's next president.

❧   ❧   ❧

Born in Raleigh, North Carolina, Andrew Johnson was, like Lincoln, from deeply humble origins. Also like Lincoln, he was almost entirely self-educated. The death of his father, a tavern porter, had left his family in grinding poverty, and at the young age of thirteen, Johnson was apprenticed to a tailor. He learned the trade well, but in time, chafing at the cruelties of his master, he ran away, to the mountain country of eastern Tennessee, where he opened a tailor's shop. The foreman taught him to read and write, and he married a shoemaker's daughter; he was twenty-one. From there, Johnson began his scramble up the ladder of success—and it was at this point that the similarities to Lincoln stopped. Unlike Lincoln, he was actually a far more successful politician, rising from local alderman to mayor, then to the state legislature, serving in both bodies, then governor, then congressman, then influential U.S. senator. Where Lincoln was a steady voice of the emerging American middle class, Johnson was an unabashed populist, if not among the earliest forerunners of politicians who would later practice class warfare. As a fierce Jacksonian Democrat and self-proclaimed champion of the common man ("Some day I will show the stuck up aristocrats who are running the country," he once muttered angrily), his hatred of the ruling planter class was matched only by his deep love of the Union. And Johnson was no hypocrite. When the war erupted, he was the only senator from a seceding state who remained loyal to the North, prompting Lincoln to reward him with the military governorship of Tennessee in 1862.

It was in 1864 that Johnson's biggest break came. Fearing he would lose the election, and in an effort to project a broad Union Party image (the Republican Party's new name for itself during the campaign), Lincoln dumped his bland second-in-command, Hannibal Hamlin, for Johnson, the solid war Democrat. With intense dark eyes, an arched skeptical brow, a large nose, and fine silver hair, Johnson looked the part of a healing statesman; a former senator, he could also be a brilliant speaker. But it would not be this simple. For starters, as a Democrat, even a pro-war one, Johnson had no following among Lincoln's Republican cabinet. They distrusted him accordingly. And as a formerly poor Southerner, in a number of ways he remained a crude man, a vulgar renegade, unable or unwilling to shed either his vile temper or the habits of his plebeian upbringing. This, too, set him apart from Lincoln's more refined colleagues. The invidious comparisons with the president didn't help: where Lincoln had been supremely confident of himself, Johnson, despite a long and successful career, was nonetheless a bewildering cauldron of insecurities and resentments; where Lincoln had radiated calm and reasoned eloquence in a crisis, internalizing his anxieties, Johnson was prone to bluster and hyperbole, which was fine in the Senate but not in the executive; and where Lincoln was a marvelous hybrid of intellect and street-savvy politicking, able to woo and charm his opponents, Johnson was overly volatile and melodramatic.

And last but not least, Johnson drank. Not a lot, but enough. At Lincoln's second inaugural, a drunken Johnson, who had had one too many whiskeys that morning, plunged into a long, rambling, incoherent discourse, shouting about his humble origins and lecturing the assembled dignitaries from the Supreme Court and the diplomatic corps ("With all your fine feathers and gew-gaws") that they were merely "creatures of the people." Then, as he took his oath, Johnson visibly and audibly slobbered upon the Bible. The attorney general was so appalled that he muttered in disgust, "This man is deranged." Lincoln was also dismayed, promptly ordering a parade marshal, "Do not let Johnson speak outside!" Johnson didn't. But his prior performance was so devastating that Johnson became the immediate butt of jokes—and was shunned by official Washington. That Mary Lincoln already despised Johnson didn't help. Neither did the fact that now the best Lincoln could say of his vice president was, "Don't worry. Andy ain't a drunkard." And there was a further price to be paid. Aghast and offended, the powerful Senator Charles Sumner quickly assembled the Senate Republican Caucus and demanded that Johnson be forced to resign from the office he had "so dishonored." The forced resignation was ultimately averted, but the disgrace remained. Lincoln and Johnson did not speak again until, of all days, mid-afternoon of April 14.

But there was perhaps no greater testimony to Johnson's diminished stature than this: when he made his way to Peterson House in the middle of the night to gaze upon the dying commander in chief, at one point, Stanton icily informed him that there was no need for Johnson to remain. And the hard headed, stubborn, scowling Andy Johnson, who had once defied the entire Southern establishment and scorned the entire Confederacy, dutifully complied.

❧ ❧ ❧

But to Stanton's credit—and that of the cabinet—neither allowed any personal feelings toward Johnson to get in the way. Unlike with John Tyler, there would be no bargaining, no demands, no negotiations. There was no talk of a regency or temporary cabinet government—tempting though this may have been. Nor any flirtation with limited dictatorship, equally tempting though this may have been. Nor was the fact that Johnson was of the other political party a consideration. The military was not consulted, itself a tribute to the enduring American idiom of civil-military relations, and thus another potentially seductive route was avoided in this fear-filled evening. The peaceful, orderly changing of the guard commenced, without undue holdup, as though it were routine. Yet given the context alone—the assassination of this president as part of this larger murderous plot in the course of this long war—it was anything but routine. Nonetheless, there was a remarkably methodical, even traditional manner to the way the succession was carried out.

It happened like this: after midnight, as word of Lincoln's condition was passed on, with cool dispatch, a detachment of the Washington Provost Guard showed up at the Kirkwood House, for Johnson's protection.

During the night, as the cabinet brooded and wept by the ailing Lincoln's side, the attorney general, himself incredulous and grief-stricken, quietly prepared a note stating to Johnson that he was now the head of government. It was addressed to "The Vice President."

A second letter was quickly sent by Stanton to the chief justice, Salmon Chase, passing on the word for him to stand by: he should now be prepared to administer a new oath to the vice president.

When Lincoln died, a stern message was delivered to Johnson, in person, informing him never to go out except when accompanied "by sufficient guard."

Then, even before the honor guard removed Lincoln's body from the Peterson House, a haggard, sleep-deprived cabinet, suffering from a deadly overdose of frayed nerves, too little sleep, grief, shock, and clouded senses, nonetheless moved quickly, gathering in the back parlor, where the corpse lay. One by one, they carefully affixed their signatures upon the attorney general's letter to Johnson.

After some intense discussion, a procedure was worked out and refined. It was decided that a delegation of two, representing the central government, would carry the letter to the new president: the attorney general and the highest-ranking official among them, the treasury secretary.

They in turn spoke with the chief justice, Salmon Chase, a three-time widower who himself as late as 1864 had coveted the presidency. It was definitively agreed that the chief justice, not a district court judge, would this time administer the oath. It would be done in two hours, leaving just enough time to double-check the precedents for what they were proposing.

Shortly after, Chase raced to the attorney general's office. Tellingly, there was still enough of a residue of doubt and ambiguity about the succession process that he felt compelled to look up the cases involving the two previous presidents, Tyler and Fillmore, to whom the presidency "had devolved." He also read the pertinent clauses in the Constitution. By all accounts, this provided him with sufficient reassurance that the right thing was being done.

As a stunned Washington fell into shock, and hundreds of citizens descended moodily into the streets, a powder keg ready to be ignited, Chase now made his way back to the Kirkwood House, where Johnson was anxiously waiting in the parlor of his suite. Also assembled were a dozen people, members of the cabinet and prominent senators. All showed the strains of their all-night vigil.

It was now ten o'clock. The extemporaneous inaugural began.

Johnson's right hand was raised. Chase slowly read the oath aloud, each word carefully articulated. One hand on the bound Bible, the other still held high, Johnson carefully repeated the words. Then came the chief justice's reply: "You are the President." Chase now instructed, "May God guide, support, and bless you in your arduous labors."

"The duties of the office are mine," Johnson responded. "The consequences are with God." Then he leaned forward to kiss the Bible, and his lips pressed against the twenty-first verse of the eleventh chapter of Ezekiel: *But as for them whose heart walketh after the heart of their detestable things and their abominations, I will recompense their way upon their own heads. Saith the* Lord God.

Less than three hours after Lincoln's death, Andrew Johnson, his face calm yet grave, had become the new president.

❧   ❧   ❧

President Johnson had his own plans for dealing with the rebels, and they gave every appearance of being harsh ones. Twelve days earlier, he had made his way to the steps of the Patent Office, where he cried out in a passionate speech: "Treason is a crime—and crime must be punished." For good measure he added, "Treason must be made infamous, and traitors must be impoverished." And what exactly did that mean? It was as simple as it was stark: "A very good way to disenfranchise the [rebels]," Johnson harshly informed one visitor, "is to break their necks!" That no doubt included Davis, Lee, and the rest of the Confederate leadership. As Mary Chesnut was to write, "Yesterday these poor fellows were heroes. Today, they are only rebels to be hung or shot at the Yankee's pleasure."

Now Johnson had spent the night of April 14 furiously pacing his room, constantly wringing his hands, and mumbling over and over, "they shall suffer for this, they shall suffer for this." Shortly thereafter, his bitter frame of mind was in full view when he met with a delegation of ministers. "I am of the opinion," he said coldly, "the time has come when you and I must understand, must teach that treason is a crime and not a mere difference of political opinion." One reporter, hearing Johnson speak, pointed out that there was no rant or bluster to his threats: they were deep, calm, and conscientious—and, this writer confided, they "made me shiver."

Yet while emotions in the grieving, angry North swung between violent extremes, a small, but highly influential core of Radical Republicans were, in fact, overjoyed by Johnson's ascension to the presidency. Even Senator Sumner, a friend of Lincoln's, saw in his murder the "judgment of the Lord" and believed Providence had ordained Johnson. In an otherwise disconsolate city, the Radicals would be his ardent backers for a brief and tumultuous interim. Calling Lincoln's "known tenderness" toward the rebels "repugnant," Representative George Julian of the Joint Committee on the Conduct of War declared, "the feeling was universal that the accession of Johnson to the Presidency would prove a godsend to the country." Julian also called on the House to hang Davis ("in the name of God"), and Lee, and when that was done, not to "stop there." The next day, on Easter Sunday, the new president met with members of Julian's Joint Committee. Johnson pointedly said or promised little. But the grim and truculent Ohio chairman, Ben Wade, summed up the feeling of most Radical Republicans when he boasted, "Johnson, we have faith in you. By the gods, there will be no trouble *now* in running the government."

And the government would have to run. The situation was now incendiary. At this moment, everyone in Washington was facing enormous pressure: amid the turmoil in the Union capital, and the financial pressure of fighting a war that was still costing the North a staggering $4 million a day, Jefferson Davis and his cabinet remained at large, stubbornly moving southward as fast as the dilapidated railroads and over-taxed horses would carry them. At every stop, Davis exhorted his people to fight on, "operating in the interior" where the enemy's lines of communication would "render our triumph certain." In historian James McPherson's words, to the Union government "it appeared that guerilla warfare might go on for years, turning the South into another Ireland." And once more, the question was raised anew: would Lincoln's sudden death pump new life into the pockets of resistance still alive in the Confederacy?

Of the Confederates still in the field, one notorious rebel in particular would likely have something to say about this: Nathan Bedford Forrest.

❧   ❧   ❧

Of all the men whom one would choose to carry out a prolonged guerrilla campaign against the Union, none was more suited to it than Nathan Bedford Forrest, an incongruous amalgam of the proudest and the darkest sides of the Confederacy, walking not in awkward contradiction, but boldly and comfortably hand in hand.

An expert in the surprise assault and a virtuoso at overcoming impossible odds, Nathan Bedford Forrest was the South's legendary answer to the Union's fighting general, William Tecumseh Sherman: ornery and innately brilliant, an uneducated farmer from the low country and an unabashed racist, a self-made millionaire and a tactical genius, inflammatory, headstrong, imperious, he was the South's most innovative and ruthless fighter. Admirers called him "the wizard of the saddle." Sherman himself once praised Forrest as "the most remarkable man our civil war produced on either side." But he also called him "that devil" or "the very devil" or simply "the devil," and demanded that Forrest be "hunted down and killed if it cost ten thousand lives and bankrupts the Federal Treasury." To friends and foes alike, even before the war was over, Forrest's reputation had become the stuff of folklore legend, and he himself had become almost a living myth.

But behind the myth was a man, a flawed and incorrigible man, and a self-made one at that. Indeed, virtually everything about Forrest was self-made, making him a telling counterpoint to the charge that the South was simply fighting an aristocrat's war. The keystone of his life was his beginnings. Born in the backcountry of Bedford County, Tennessee, Forrest was the son of an illiterate blacksmith, who scraped out a fragile existence before dying when Forrest was sixteen. For the next four years, he became the man of the house, helping his mother raise his siblings—there were ten of them—and run the modest family farm. He had virtually no formal education; he spent just six months in a classroom. And his lack of education showed pitifully. Where countless other Southerners spoke with music and flourish and eloquence, Forrest's mastery of spelling, syntax, and speech remained tenuous throughout his entire life: he never pronounced the final "g" of words, instead saying "ridin" for "riding," "shootin" for "shooting," "killin" for "killing"; he regularly confused his tenses and conjugation, saying "I seen" instead of "I saw," "twicest" for "twice"; he frequently scrambled simple words or common phrases: "help tote" for "help to carry," "but" for "except"; and, in day-to-day speech, he personified the backwoods Southern drawl later glamorized by Hollywood: "jost" for "just," "agin" for "against," "gin'ral" for "general," "git" for "get," and "whup" for "whip." To listen to him was immediately to know that he was not a polished product of West Point or the pupil of private tutors on the South's best plantations, both the traditional breeding grounds for good Southern military leaders and aspiring politicians. Nor was he one to affect the dignified mien of the country squire; he couldn't. The unmistakable conclusion would be that he was, in the pejorative idiom of today, a cracker.

To a point, at least. What he lacked in education he more than made up for with a steely drive and instinctive entrepreneurship. Long before he set foot on a battlefield, and as the two sides of the country watched America draw ever closer to the brink in the 1850s, he was blazing his own audacious trail: making money, a lot of it. By the time the war began, he was thirty-nine years old, meaning he was considerably younger than the patrician Jefferson Davis or the lawyer-politician Abraham Lincoln; but he was also substantially richer, having amassed an astonishing personal fortune that he claimed was worth $1.5 million. Although this was probably an exaggeration, it is undisputed that he was one of the wealthier men in the South, owning over 3,000 acres of land, with real estate holdings at about $200,000, and a personal estate valued at just under $100,000. (Where in a good year Lincoln cleared $5,000, a considerable amount of money in those days, Forrest pulled down almost twenty times that, an impressive $96,000.) And what was his business? In this sense, too, he bore the familiar stamp of his region's culture: he dealt in commodities. Land and livestock and cotton planting—and slave trading, thus making him an acid portrait of the antebellum South.

Here again Forrest defied simple categorization. For all the South's robust support of slavery, most slave agents and small-time speculators were actually social pariahs and outcasts, much like drug dealers today and small-time bootleggers during Prohibition. It was one thing to profit from slavery or to own slaves; it was quite another for a well born gentleman to buy and sell slaves for a living. But nothing quite so succeeds in American life, North or South, as success, and Forrest's immense wealth brought him respectability, and soon, he was counted among Memphis, Tennessee's social elite. He was now welcome in the drawing rooms of the city's finest salons, able to warm his feet by marble Empire fireplaces, or stroll over imported French Aubusson rugs, or sign off on business edicts from a mahogany secretary. By 1858, he had been elected an alderman. But even as he rose in the ranks of Memphis's more refined social strata, Forrest remained an idiosyncrasy, neither fish nor fowl: where prominent Southerners were typically self-deprecating, he was a soft-spoken yet often shameless master of self-promotion; where the newly rich sought to blend into the effete living of the polished upper class, Forrest continued to cuss and gamble; and where much of ante-bellum high society increasingly learned to settle differences amicably over the drawing room table and aged brandy and good conversation, Forrest (who never drank) clung rigidly to the *code duelo*, an elaborate code that brutally mixed honor with violence, and that gave rise to countless duels, feuds, settling of scores, and an unswerving defense of one's name in the face of any affront, real or imagined.

But it was in the war that Forrest most made his mark. In 1861, he enlisted as a private, then assembled and outfitted an entire cavalry battalion out of his own pocket. He began with no battle experience or formal training, but, by the war's end, he had become a lieutenant general, the only man in either army—and the only non–West Pointer—to rise this far. He quickly emerged as the war's most dreaded cavalry commander, known as much for his miraculous escapes as for his fierce exploits: four times, he was wounded in battle (once taking a bullet that penetrated close to his hip and lodged precariously near his spine) and survived; twenty-nine times, he had horses shot out from under him; and thirty times, he killed Federals in personal combat, surely a record for this or most likely any other American war. His temper was sharp, quick, and merciless. Once, in 1863, a lieutenant in his command challenged Forrest in a fit of pique, then drew his gun and fired. Struck at point-blank range, a reeling Forrest reached for a penknife with one hand, grasped his assailant with the other, and proceeded to unclasp the knife with his teeth and stab him. Convinced that his own wound was fatal, Forrest shouted, "No damned man shall kill me and live!" But it was this unlucky soldier who stumbled across the street and later died; Forrest was back in the saddle thirteen days later.

Forrest developed a series of combined mounted and dismounted tactics found nowhere at West Point or in the military textbooks—which, of course, he never read—but which were ideal for warfare in a South marked by heavily wooded terrain and a morass of swamps and winding waterways. His killer instinct was matched only by his aggressiveness and his ability to win against the long odds. Like a musical virtuoso or a child prodigy, he fought, he said, "by ear" and proved able to predict his enemy's every action with unerring accuracy. And he would rather go down fighting than give up. As U. S. Grant prepared to take Fort Donelson in February 1862, the battle that thrust him into the national limelight, Forrest refused to surrender, indignantly telling his superiors, "I did not come here to surrender my command!" He didn't. Leading 700 troops, before daybreak, he escaped across an icy stream judged too deep for infantry to ford and which one of his own Confederate officers warned "would kill the troops." Along the way, they didn't encounter a single Union picket.

His untutored instincts were often uncanny. He didn't know the fine points of drilling or the minutiae of army regulations, but he understood the inherent rhythm of war. After the first day at the battle of Shiloh in 1862, when the Confederates were riding high, he warned his superiors, "We'll be whipped like hell in the morning." He was right. Shiloh was the seesaw battle that doomed any idea that the war could be ended quickly by either side; but for his part, Forrest, who was wounded in a skirmish with Sherman, escaped to fight another day.

And fight he did. A master of the lightning raid, he was invariably one step ahead of the pursuing Federals. Forrest's tactics vividly highlighted the South's advantage in defending its own territory: in July 1862, with a force of only 2,500 men (along with guerrilla John Hunt Morgan), Forrest was able to pin down an invading army of 40,000, almost twenty times its size. Subsisting off the loyal countryside and retreating into the mountains like partisans, Forrest, with his swashbuckling tactics, struck at the times and places of his own choosing. His cavalry captured garrisons, destroyed railroads, and escaped before the Union knew what hit them. After repair crews eventually finished fixing the damage, Forrest would strike again and, just as quickly, escape. Soon, the Union found out the hard way that it was impossible to defend all its bridges, tunnels, and depots along stretches of hundreds of miles of railroad, and this enabled Forrest to carry out hit-and-run raids against remote garrisons and unpatrolled areas on his own terms. In all wars throughout the ages, logistics have always been half the battle; it was no different for the invading Union armies, which, operating on exterior lines over greater distances, depended more on transport than did the Confederates. Sighed Sherman, "Although our armies pass across the land, the war closes in behind and leaves the same enemy behind."

More often than not, in Tennessee, Alabama, and Mississippi, that enemy was Forrest. As a matter of course, he routinely defeated Federal forces twice his size. Time and again, he outfought, outmaneuvered, and outbluffed Union garrisons and cavalry detachments while tearing up tens of miles of railroads and telegraph lines, capturing or destroying great quantities of equipment, and inflicting casualties on the enemy at an often stunning four-to-one ratio. Repeatedly, he forced the Union to suspend important offensive operations or to divert needed resources. In one astonishing raid, in September 1864, Forrest struck at Sherman's supply lines with a vengeance, capturing over 2,300 Union soldiers during two weeks, seizing 800 horses, and wrecking the Tennessee and Alabama Railroad so thoroughly that it took even Sherman's indefatigable crews six weeks to repair it. In an October follow-up raid against Johnsonville, a crucial Union logistics base for Sherman's army, Forrest went a step further, this time capturing two Union gunboats, placing improvised crews aboard them, and using them to terrorize a swath of the Tennessee River for three full days; then came the attack on Johnsonville itself, laying waste to its wharves and its warehouses. In this raid alone, Forrest inflicted more than $6 million in damages to the Union treasury. His casualties for these two combined operations: fewer than 400 men.

The Union managed to surprise him—once—at Parker's Crossroad in Tennessee. It was December 31, 1862; he had just made a daring raid on Grant's lines and was blasting his way through the Federals in front of him when he was unexpectedly struck from behind. A panicked staff aide shouted out for orders. "Split in two," Forrest bellowed, "and charge both ways." The order defied all known military logic, but his men executed it anyway, and they escaped.

But the hot-blooded Forrest wasn't simply unorthodox in war—he was equally unorthodox in dealing with his own Southern high command. Sometimes, his fierce opinions got the better of him. When Confederate General Braxton Bragg won the battle of Chickamauga but refused to push on to destroy Union General William Rosecrans's army, Forrest angrily denounced him: "What does he fight for?" Later, he growled that it was an act of "cowardice." To Forrest, this was a dereliction of duty, pure and simple. Soon thereafter, still fulminating over the reluctance to exploit the Chickamauga victory, Forrest informed Bragg he would no longer serve under him, screaming in his face: "You have played the part of a damned scoundrel . . . If you ever again try to interfere with me or cross my path it will be at the peril of your life." But what Forrest lacked in military manners, he made up for in his fighting, pulverizing the Yankees so often that Sherman said, "There will never be peace in Tennessee until Forrest is dead!" And how the colorful Forrest delighted in his exploits: he bragged about putting "a skeer on the enemy," and he did. He boasted about "hittin' em' on the ee'eend," and he did that, too. He preened about "burst[ing] hell wide open" and having "more fite in our men than you think," which he somehow always managed to do as well. He contributed his own theory to warfare, compacting the art of war in a telling maxim that would come to guide military tacticians well into the twentieth century: "I get there firstest with the mostest." Forrest even looked the part of the daring rebel cavalryman: large, powerful, and fearless, he had swarthy skin, piercing eyes, prominent cheekbones and a high dignified forehead, and a well-cropped black mustache and chin whiskers. Interestingly, in his photos, he looks far more like a refined West Point or University of Virginia graduate than a backwoods boy made good. His vile temper and crude speech were offset by a charming smile and a winning charisma that he could turn on and off, and, along with his personal valor, this, too, helped inspire his men. And, like one of his Union counterparts, Phil Sheridan, he was also a victim of soldierly vanity. He called his horse King Phillip.

But there was a controversy, which in one fashion or another would haunt Forrest for the rest of his life. Whatever his legacy, one has to consider the incident at Fort Pillow, which has been debated by contemporary observers and historians ever since it happened on that fateful day of April 12, 1864. The basic facts are well known. As part of a series of ten separate engagements over several weeks, Forrest came across the Union garrison of Fort Pillow on the Mississippi River. This garrison had little special strategic meaning, although capturing it would be a significant morale booster for the South. But it mattered for other reasons: it was manned by locally recruited Unionists whom Forrest derided as "Tennessee Tories" and some 270 blacks, mostly escaped slaves, whom

Forrest labeled a "damned nigger regiment." Forrest issued his customary demand for surrender, adding, if not, "I cannot be responsible for the fate of your command." Not only did the fort commander refuse, but the cocky Federals openly taunted Forrest, daring him to try to take the garrison. It was the mistake of their lives. The assault came quickly, and within hours, Fort Pillow had devolved into little more than a lurid slaughter pen: many of the blacks, estimated at 100—and a number of whites as well—were not allowed to surrender and were butchered in cold blood instead, even as they fell to their knees and with uplifted hands screamed for mercy. Word of the ghastly slaughter quickly spread throughout the entire North, and soon, the Union was crying out for revenge.

The Union cabinet spent a full two days wrestling with the proper response. (It was Lincoln himself who later sought to dampen the anger, telling his cabinet that "blood can not restore blood" and the government should not "act for revenge.") In the months that followed, some black Union soldiers even sported homemade buttons with the battle cry "avenge Fort Pillow." And questions about Forrest's role lingered: did he order these killings? Or sanction them? Forrest's supporters said no, ascribing the incident to *insanitas belli*, "the fury of battle"; others were vehement in saying that Forrest did not endorse the wanton deaths, but in fact was the one who actually stopped the butchery. Forrest himself said that he "was opposed to the killing of Negro troops; that it was his policy to capture . . . and return them to their owners." It has also been pointed out that he employed forty-five of his own slaves in the war as teamsters and set them all free in 1864. But, in the face of stinging denunciations, it is a fact that Forrest was unapologetic and unyielding. In the tangled farrago of his warrior mind-set, it is just as likely that he fully believed that his victims, "niggers" and "Tories" alike, had it coming, and the truth remains that he never showed the slightest hint of remorse for what had happened, nor did he ever rebuke any of his men. "War," Forrest once roared, "means killing."

Evidence of this cruel sally only further galvanized the North and led it to redouble its efforts to stop Forrest. They failed. At Brice's Cross Roads near Tupelo, Mississippi, Forrest again more than lived up to his name. In late spring of 1864, Sherman had dispatched an 8,000-man Union force, composed of blacks and whites, to hunt Forrest down and prevent him from moving into middle Tennessee. As was often the case, Forrest was outnumbered, this time almost two to one, but he was un-fazed. Using the elements as his ally—the densely wooded terrain and blazing Mississippi heat—he anticipated that the Federal cavalry would arrive well ahead of the infantry, thus allowing him to "whip them" with impunity. When the Union footsoldiers finally caught up, he would then be able to slice them up, too.

It happened just as he said. After a fierce round of fighting, much of it hand-to-hand, the rout was complete: Forrest made short work of 2,400 of his enemies—men either killed, captured, or missing—took much of their artillery, and for good measure, 176 supply wagons. It was, historians note, the most humiliating Union defeat in the Western the-ater, although it at least diverted Forrest from smashing the Tennessee railroad. But for Sherman, this rout was too much. He angrily declared that Forrest could no longer be allowed to roam loose, operating in northern Mississippi and Tennessee; so now he diverted two divisions, nearly 15,000 men, to "follow Forrest to the death."

"These men must all be killed," Sherman icily concluded, "by us before we can hope for peace." Meanwhile, Sherman set off on his march, to Atlanta, and then to the sea.

Forrest's tactical cunning was now on full display. He performed as brilliantly in the following months as at any other time during the war—but any optimism about the long-term effects of his actions were now built on shifting sands. Preoccupied with a repeated series of Federal lunges, he was unable to inflict the kind of direct damage against Sherman's supply lines that many had hoped for. For one thing, Davis had refused to unleash him until it was too late for Forrest's damaging strikes to do any full and sustained harm against Sherman. Nonetheless, Forrest wore on his enemies like an affliction. Quipped one Union gen-eral who had faced off against him earlier: "They removed me from com-mand because I couldn't keep Forrest out of West Tennessee. And now [my replacement] can't keep him out of his own bathroom." A reporter who knew U. S. Grant even claimed that the general in chief, who was seldom rattled by news of enemy cavalry raids, "at once became apprehensive" if Forrest was in command; he was the only cavalryman of whom "Grant stood in much dread." Again, though, it was Sherman who best understood his cold-blooded enemy: in warning Grant about the "Young Bloods of the South," among whom Forrest was the most prominent, Sherman said, "They are the most dangerous set of men that this war has turned loose upon the world . . . War suits them, and the rascals are brave, fine riders . . . and they hate Yankees, per se, and don't bother their brains about the past, present or future."

But even for Forrest, by April 1865, the future was now arriving with a grim vengeance. For one thing, his men were exhausted by months of hard riding and nearly nonstop fighting and skirmishing. For another, his ranks had been thinned; for the first time a motley crew of young boys and elderly men, without adequate training or sufficient discipline, would have to be hastily pressed into his service to augment his veterans. To guard against lethargy or desertion, men were enjoined, under the pain of death, to stay the course. And by this point, fresh Federal forces were swarming down in ever-greater numbers, with some of the finest soldiers that the Union could throw at them. Forrest, who in January 1865 assumed command of the cavalry in the Department of Alabama, Mississippi, and East Louisiana, would now be grossly outnumbered. And this time around, the task of subduing him fell to General James W. Wilson, a youthful Grant protégé and a West Pointer known for his aggressiveness and confidence, who, with the largest cavalry ensemble ever put together in North America—13,000 battle-hardened men—was sent to seize the original capital of the Confederacy, Montgomery, Alabama.

Standing in his way, of course, would be Forrest, willful, bullish, and driven as always. As desperate as the situation may have looked at this late stage of the war, Forrest had lost none of his fight or his spirit. In a meeting with one of Wilson's aides to discuss the status of 7,000 Federal prisoners whom Forrest was holding, he proposed to settle their differences in one fell swoop, with a type of a duel, or something akin to a gladiator event out of Roman times: "Just tell General Wilson," he pointedly told the Federal aide, "I will fight him with any number from 1 to 10,000 cavalry, to abide the issue." It was a brave reply, but it was also calamitous. Wilson didn't abide. Instead, like a mounted panzer division streaming across the plains, he hit Forrest with everything he had, outmanning him by four to one and just as badly outgunning him. This time, it was too much.

After a running series of intense skirmishes over forty-eight straight hours (with a wounded, blood-soaked Forrest shouting, "rally men, rally. For God's sake rally!"), Forrest suffered his first defeat of the war, and it was a considerable one at that. Selma fell on April 2, and within two weeks, after fierce, prolonged sieges of Fort Blakely and Spanish Fort in Alabama, so would Mobile and Montgomery. For the Confederacy, these two losses were nothing short of catastrophic, suggesting that one domino after another was now toppling. Even Forrest acknowledged that this time, he was "beaten badly." He himself was wounded, yet again, and he later commented wryly that had the boy "known enough to give me the point of the saber instead of the edge" he would have been killed. But if luck had spared his own fate, not so with many of his battered soldiers. His face blackened with dirt, his body wet with sweat and matted with caked blood, his sword arm hacked up, he collected his remaining cavalry and drove them through the gathering darkness and the drenching rains to lick their wounds and scramble to safety. For three consecutive days, he pushed his men through pools of mud and more torrents of rain on all-night rides. Along the way, he was aggressive to the bitter end, ambushing a detachment of the Fourth Union cavalry, slaughtering them or taking more prisoners. Even now, Forrest was all hell-for-leather. Then, through more rain and thunder and lightning and mud, he defiantly retreated to the backwoods of Alabama, to Gainesville, safely nestled near the Mississippi state line. It was here he would regroup, catch his breath, hone his men, rest his horses, and plot his next move.

It was around this time that he learned of Lincoln's assassination.

❧   ❧   ❧

What made Forrest so effective on the battlefield—and so suited to a prolonged guerrilla campaign, if he chose it? The short answer is always the same: a gritty, prodigious military aptitude. But there is a longer answer, and as Forrest pondered his next steps, it now mattered.

For one thing, he understood the coarse art of the psychology of war: the role of fear in battle, the role of psychological operations in combat, the role of rattling the opponent and keeping him rattled. Throughout history, from Alexander the Great to Napoleon, the generals who could employ these tactics often won; the generals who couldn't, often didn't. Fear undermines morale; diminished morale breeds low-level panic, and panic fosters poor decisions. But of course, Forrest was a different kind of a general, fighting not with large armies, but commanding and shuffling smaller groups of men to disorient and disable a much larger adversary. Three things enabled him to do this well. He knew how to make his command seem large, and in this case he played upon not just his adversaries' calculations but their battle-frayed emotions as well. He employed deception and skill: so he beat kettledrums constantly to mimic infantry in action; he lit and tended to fires spread over significant areas; he shuttled artillery back and forth, from one distant point to another; and he dressed up his cavalry and paraded them as infantry. With astonishing clarity, he grasped the battle vagaries of space and time: how fast he could realistically move, and how fast his opponent was likely to move, enabling him to turn tactical risks into strategic opportunities. And perhaps most importantly, beyond his own implacable will and leadership ability, with which he relentlessly drove his men, asking them to be better, stronger, tougher, faster, and more fearless than they really were, he understood human nature—in his opponent's men as well as his own. Thus, he could calculate the shape of the enemy for any given battle, and calibrate his actions accordingly; by the same token, he knew not just when to push his troops but, just as importantly, when to let them rest, regroup, and replenish themselves.

And of course, by April 1865, there were the intangibles; as the conflict in this war enlarged and grew, so, it seems, did his courage. He was intuitive; this much was sure, though intuition itself is often volatile, even rash. But he had gotten this far, and now, driven by an inner gyroscope, he was suited to the single-minded pursuit of his raw vision of battle, undiscouraged by rejection, defeat, or even the imminent prospect of death. These ingredients, then, which enabled him to fight the way he did, would have just as handily enabled him to make the adjustment to a prolonged guerrilla campaign for which he was so uniquely suited—should he only so decide.

But would he?

From the field in mid-April, Forrest looked like anything but a man who was ready to quit. In past weeks, he had been a whirlwind of activity, commanding firmly, "spare no time," "be in readiness," "not a moment should be lost," "we have no time to lose." He fought his own war against absenteeism: some days earlier, he had a man and a boy executed for desertion, ordering their bodies to be laid on a well-traveled Confederate road beneath a prominently displayed sign that read: SHOT FOR DESERTION. There was, of course, more strategizing. And he clearly relished more fight, issuing a rousing message on April 25 to his men: "It is the duty of every man to stand firm at his post and true to his colors. Your past services, your gallant and heroic conduct on many victorious fields, forbid the thought that you will ever ground your arms except with honor. Duty to your country, to yourselves, and the gallant dead who have fallen in this great struggle for liberty and independence, demand that every man should continue to do his whole duty . . . be firm and unwavering, discharging promptly and faithfully every duty devolving upon you." These are the words of a man ready and willing to carry on the battle.

But if Forrest was an unconventional rebel, he was not an uncontrollable renegade. Good generals, almost by definition, become political and institutional creatures, even ardent nonconformists like Nathan Bedford Forrest. Whatever their styles, they operate as part of an overall military ethos and a shared warrior structure, and, like careful politicians weighing difficult votes, they look to one another, if not for implicit guidance, then at least to gauge the sentiment of changing events and tough decisions. Much of this communication is tacit, unspoken; but it is no less real. It is a language of order and maneuver. And, as April 1865 progressed, just such an intricate, largely unspoken dialogue was taking place among a handful of men—less between the opposing sides of the Confederacy and the Union, and more among individual Confederate commanders themselves. As such, every bit as much as the formal civil-military chain of command, it was now a handful of military men who were deciding the future actions of the Confederacy—the commanding generals of the Southern forces still at large. And in the weighty calculus of whether to resort to partisan war-fare or to give up the game altogether, the actions of one general would profoundly affect the actions of the others, including of Forrest him-self. Many thousands and tens of thousands of Confederates would then, in turn, follow their lead.

But to a great extent, up to now, Forrest had been operating in a pro-nounced information vacuum, anxiously grabbing for scraps of intelligence any way he could. Unlike the North, where news traveled immediately over an extensive network of telegraph wires and quickly found its way into the next day's newspapers, much of the Confederacy was an isolat-ed wasteland: the war had not only obliterated one-quarter of the Confederacy's white men of military age and almost half of its livestock, destroyed a good 50 percent of the farm machinery and left tens of thou-sands of small farms and sizable plantations alike buried under scraps, weeds, and utter ruin, but it had also mangled thousands of miles of rail-roads and just as many of its telegraph wires. The result was that the Confederacy was awash in gossip and rumor, but little hard fact. Lack of information was one problem; so was the misinformation. Thus, Forrest knew that Lincoln was dead, but he also believed that Grant had lost some 100,000 men through battle and desertion; he had conflicting reports about whether Lee actually had surrendered—some Southern papers denied that he had—and believed he had not, and was now des-perately trying to sort out the truth. He knew there was a flag of truce between his commanding superior, Department Commander General Richard Taylor, the son of U.S. President Zachary Taylor, and Union General Canby, as well as a similar truce between Generals Johnston and Sherman—but in neither case did he read this as a bid to surrender. (Indeed, a number of Taylor's men themselves, even in their diminished condition, wanted to fight "to the last.") He also knew—or believed he knew—that Confederate General E. Kirby Smith was operating with a fairly free hand in the west, in the Trans-Mississippi Department. As to guerrilla warfare and taking to the hills, then, his strategy was now to wait and see—and later decide.

"Resist the sensational rumors and conflicting dispatches," he exhorted his men, instead counseling, "A few days will determine the truth or falsity of the reports now in circulation."

Others, however, were looking to Forrest for just these purposes, alone or in combination with Johnston. After Appomattox, the prominent Baltimore journalist William Wilkins Glenn wrote: "Forrest has genius, popularity, and power. If these two armies [Forrest and Johnston] join and fall back to Texas—they could get 30,000 men, who would be determined men across the Mississippi. An army of 50,000 men in Texas, with plenty of grass for horses and mountain ranges for defense could work miracles." But before Forrest performed any miracles, he was waiting for definitive news of Lee and Grant. And one other man whom he would be watching just as carefully was General Joe Johnston in his discussions with Bill Sherman.

Forrest couldn't have known it then, but in fact Johnston did want to surrender. Nor could he have known that, unlike at Appomattox, Johnston's delicate negotiations with Sherman would take on an astonishing life on their own, then go awry, and then potentially into dangerous disarray.

❧   ❧   ❧

Union General Bill Sherman, volatile, disheveled, irascible, was no ordinary warrior. He is now known for so many colorful exploits, as well as for being the first truly modern strategist in history, that too often we forget this: more than any other single Union figure, he was probably the most prescient man in the war, confounding the predictions of the doubters and nay sayers, the press and the public, and even of his own president. But in mid-April 1865, he had a new set of predictions—and a new set of fears.

While in the halcyon early days of the North-South conflict, most of the Washington establishment expected something akin to a short, jolly little war, riding out to watch the battle of Bull Run in their finest clothes and jauntily dining in the hills above with their good silver and well-stocked picnic baskets, Sherman was suffering a near-breakdown, believing he had too few troops to hold off the enemy. He rightly noted, this war would *not* end in six months, a heretical prediction for which the press labeled him crazy. By 1864, when most of the Union high command was still mired in traditional West Point tactics, it was Sherman who grew exasperated with playing the rebel game of attrition—fixing railroads, holding the roads, getting stung until it finally hurt, and fending off the likes of Nathan Bedford Forrest and his ilk—and he decided to abandon his supply lines in the middle of enemy territory, subsist entirely off hostile country, and begin his relentless march to the sea (Lincoln acceded to this audacious plan, but only reluctantly, and then suffered numerous anxious days and nights worrying about its wisdom). Where many still clung to the gallant notion of army versus army across the well-defined field of battle, Sherman shrewdly understood the deeper, underlying dynamic of war, the critical role of morale ("if we can march a well-appointed army right through [Confederate] territory," he observed, "it is a demonstration to the world . . . that we have a power which Davis cannot resist"). Almost uniquely, he embraced and waged total war ("War is cruelty and you cannot refine it"). And it was, of course, Sherman who knew what would eventually sap the Southern ability to resist, devastating not just the Southern factories, their railroads, their farms, their crown cities, but indeed, their very will to fight. ("We cannot change the hearts of those people of the South, but we can make war so terrible [and] make them so sick of war that generations would pass away before they would again appeal to it.")

Now, on April 10, after Appomattox but before Lincoln's assassination, Sherman had put aside his thoughts about a continuing military campaign in the Carolinas and was concentrating on how best to wrap up this war. On one hand, he believed the battle was all but won, but, as he later recalled, he was unable to shake his latest morbid fear: of anarchy breaking out all over the land.

Far more than the world knew, the Union was broke; in all its glory, the mighty Northern armada was exhausted; bankruptcy was a genuine concern; and the South itself, in no small measure due to his efforts, was a near-wasteland and could be in peril of starving. It was against this troubled backdrop that he was "convinced" that rebel Joe Johnston would take his some 22,000-man force, retreat rapidly to towns far and wide, from Hillsborough to Greensboro, Saulsbury and Charlotte, and take refuge in the mountains of South Carolina and Georgia, "breaking up his army into small bands" and "prolonging the War indefinitely." This, he knew, was what the Spaniards had done to Napoleon, and Sherman had little stomach for it happening here. Indeed, his own men had more than "had enough." They were now exhausted. After nearly four years of hard fighting and marching, and the loss of some 30,000 of their comrades, they, too, were ready for peace, "on any terms." So were all of his officers, who "dreaded" the thought of "chasing" Johnston's army out west and into the Deep South. And, as it turned out, so was Sherman.

It was little wonder then that he could scarcely contain his delight when he received a communiqué from Johnston on April 14, asking to meet with him to discuss terms of "exterminating the existing war."

He answered immediately, planning to meet with Johnston on Monday, April 17: midway between the picket lines of the two armies.

❧ ❧ ❧

At dawn's first light, before Sherman boarded his train, it was already shaping up to be a beautiful day: clear, blustery, very bright, the chirping of birds muffled by the vast open skies. Cherry trees, too, were now in blossom. But the day's beauty was belied by the unexpected word of an urgent message, in code, from the War Department, racing down the coast by steamer; it had already been nearly two days in transit. Sherman delayed his train a half hour to receive it. The cipher message carried, of course, the news of Lincoln's death, word of the grave attack on Seward, and the dire intimations of a larger plot. Sherman immediately surveyed this disorderly scene and realized it could spell disaster. He promptly swore the telegraph operator to secrecy, and told no one else. In his view, this was a calamitous event, less because of Lincoln's death *per se*, and more because of the havoc it could wreak on the country, plunging the North into a vengeful bloodbath against a prostrated and fearful South, which, in turn, would fight back the only way it knew how, with chaos, disorder, and continued violence. Under such circumstances, who knew what would ensue? To Sherman, it made it more, not less imperative, that he reach a prompt accommodation with Johnston.

Sherman met up with Johnston shortly after ten, each man gently riding on horseback, and an instant link developed between them. On the surface, they couldn't have been more different: Sherman was a youngish forty-five; Johnston an older fifty-three; Sherman was brusque, Johnston courtly; Sherman was tall, angular, and fiery; Johnston spare, graying, and methodical. One was an Ohioan; the other a Virginian. But beyond the differences, there were also compelling similarities. Both were West Point graduates; Sherman hated politicians and hated the abuses and calculating escapades of Washington insiders; Johnston feuded endlessly with Jefferson Davis; for all his aggressiveness, Sherman was no Grant or Lee, and contrary to popular belief was actually quite reluctant to commit his men to all-out combat, preferring to "fight" with stealth and maneuver; Johnston, too, was excessively cautious, a defensive strategist unwilling to begin a battle until everything was just right, which was almost never (although he did give Sherman a decent thrashing at Kennesaw Mountain). What most knit these two generals together, however, was the hundred-mile minuet they had danced across the no-man's-land of battle over three brutal months, from early May 1864 to July. Without ever having laid eyes directly on each other, they more than knew one another, feeling the bonds of battle that ineluctably join soldiers' souls. Interestingly enough, there was also affection there—and real respect. And, by now, both men had seen more than their share of war.

As at Appomattox, Sherman let Johnston choose where they would talk; in this case, a small, ramshackle roadside frame house belonging to a local farmer, James Bennett. Unlike at Appomattox, the two retired into the house alone, without aides, notetakers, or the watchful eye of history, closing the doors tightly behind them. This was not yet a formal surrender, but, as it would turn out, a discussion, and then a negotiation, with its own dynamic and its own rhythm. On again, off again, it would end up taking ten and a half days.

It began with some chitchat about mutual acquaintances, but soon enough, Sherman broached the unavoidable subject of Lincoln's death. He thrust the sheet containing the information about Lincoln's assassination into Johnston's hand, commenting that it was bad news, the worst that had happened in a long time.

"Great God!" Johnston said, reading it. "Terrible! The greatest possible calamity to the South!"

Johnston immediately denied that the Confederate government had anything to do with this horrible crime, denouncing it in even stronger language than did Sherman. As Johnston broke out into a sweat—"heavy blots ran down his high, retreating forehead"—Sherman believed him.

Then they got down to business. While both agreed that every life now lost "was murder" and that the resumption of fighting would be the "highest possible crime," they quickly reached an impasse. In hindsight, it was inevitable. Sherman, under orders from Washington, rejected any proposal designed to lead to negotiations between the civil authorities; by contrast, Davis had consented to Johnston's meeting today only on that basis. So when Sherman offered to accept Johnston's surrender on identical terms as those given to Lee at Appomattox, Johnston demurred. Instead, he took an entirely different tack, pointing out that the time was opportune for closing the war across the board.

But that begged the question: Sherman asked, what exactly did this mean?

Johnston led with a stunning suggestion, proposing that he and Sherman "make one job of it," in effect, make the "surrender universal," and thereby settle "the fate of all the armies to the Rio Grande." In short, end the war, once and for all.

Shocked, Sherman inquired if his authority was that broad.

It was, Johnston said, or at any rate, it could be. He suggested that the Confederate secretary of war, John Breckinridge, be brought into the mix. The rest of the Confederate armies would then follow: Taylor, Forrest, even Kirby Smith, each would, to a man, obey his orders. Sherman brightened. This was, of course, attractive to him, and how couldn't it be? Every one of these Confederate generals was keeping his murderous gun barrels hot to the bitter end; if they could be subdued in one fell swoop, it would be a godsend for the country. But desirable as this was, Sherman said no. He couldn't deal with a member of the rebel cabinet. And in any case, Breckinridge was not just any ordinary rebel cabinet member: he was a former vice president of the United States, under James Buchanan. But Johnston had an answer for that, too, reminding Sherman that Breckinridge was also a major general, and could be received on that basis. Intrigued, this time Sherman said yes. Over the course of three hours, they discussed the proposal at greater length. Finally, they were ready to break. Johnston now asked for several days to make all this happen; Sherman smartly gave him one.

Neither yet realized that the following day would take an unexpected, even extraordinary turn, one that soon roiled both the Union capital and the remaining Confederate strongholds.

They met again at the little Bennett House, the same time, on Tuesday.

✴　✴　✴

Rattling around in Sherman's brain was the vivid memory of Lincoln at City Point, just three weeks earlier: he could never forget it. Lincoln's "haggard and careworn look," his concern for avoiding this "last bloody battle," his resolve to get the men of the Confederate armies "back to their homes, at work on their farms and in their shops." As determined and innovative as he had been in war for his commander in chief, Sherman was also determined to honor Lincoln's memory and his departed president's wishes by being equally innovative in peace. Now, meeting with Johnston and Breckinridge, he got his chance. This time, the meeting began with a small ritual, not quite a toast but an important symbol, a small gesture of friendship: Sherman offered them a drink, whiskey, and Breckinridge happily accepted. Then the negotiating started in earnest.

Johnston and Breckinridge both agreed that slavery was dead. This was a good start. To Sherman, Breckinridge, once one of the United States' most talented politicians (at age thirty-six, he was the youngest second-in-command in the country's history), was dazzling, citing every maxim and verse of international and constitutional law. At one point, Sherman pushed his chair back from the table and mumbled lightheartedly, "See here, gentlemen. Who is doing this surrendering anyhow? If this thing goes on, you'll have me sending a letter of apology to Jeff Davis." But in actuality, the real icebreaker that most swayed the Union general was Johnston's heartfelt appeal to Sherman—soldier to soldier, army officer to army officer, man to man—to understand his plight and the plight of the South. The truth was, Sherman had always been a bit of a tender romantic. This day, the moth could not resist the flame. Uncorking his bottle of whiskey again, Sherman sat down, gazed abstractly out the window, and set about composing a draft of terms to be given to the South. Finally, after scratching away for an undetermined time, he pushed the sheet of paper across the table.

"That's the best I can do," he sighed. On the top was written simply "Memorandum, or Basis of Agreement."

It was anything but simple. As Johnston and Breckinridge read it, their jaws practically dropped. From their point of view, it was not just good, but far better than the terms that had been given to Lee. In seven numbered paragraphs, it was in effect a comprehensive peace agreement, calling for all Confederate armies in existence to be "disbanded and conducted to their . . . state capitals, there to deposit their arms and public property in the state arsenals"; for Federal courts to be reestablished throughout the land; for the U.S. president to recognize existing state governments as soon as their officials took loyalty oaths to the Union; and for all citizens to be guaranteed "their political rights and franchises . . . as defined by their constitution." In spirit and specifics, it was generous across the board. The terms were, however, conditional, subject to approval by the superior authorities on both sides. In the meantime, the present truce would be in existence.

Upon reflection, the Bennett House meeting was an astonishing event, astonishing for a number of reasons. Where Appomattox was suffused with a kind of grandeur, this meeting had simplicity; where Appomattox was a controlled, solemn event between two nearly mythical figures, as though scripted to the beat of drums and the blare of horns, and written for the ages, Bennett House was strikingly human in how it gradually folded and unfolded; and where Appomattox will forever be fixed in time, the drama and poignancy of every word and every gesture minutely recorded, much of what happened at Bennett House remains in question for us still; one of the participants did not give an extensive accounting—the other, not a dispassionate one. But what is not in question was its ambition and scope: these two warrior generals had, in effect, sought to finish the work begun by Grant and Lee, and self-convened their own version of a mini–Peace of Westphalia for no less than restoring and reuniting the United States.

As dusk gathered, Sherman returned to Raleigh, North Carolina, convinced he had found a simple, forthright, comprehensive alternative to the beast of chaos and anarchy lurking around the corner; he wrote to the chief of staff of the army: "The point to which I attach most importance is that the dispersement and disbandment of these armies is done in such a manner as to prevent their breaking into guerilla bands." For his part, Johnston's daring gambit, which sought an end run around Jefferson Davis's authority and the smoldering passions of those who wanted to continue this god-awful war, seemed to have worked. Mounting his horse, he retired into the darkening plain, to his battered and weary army, believing that at long last this war would soon be mercifully at an end.

Within five days, both generals would find that they were sorely mistaken. For Sherman, with the best of intentions, it would become one of the most ill-advised days of his life.

Back in Washington, all hell was about to break loose.

❦ ❦ ❦

In the Union capital, Sherman's memorandum was immediately met with a frosty reception. When it crossed his desk, President Johnson was enraged; so was Secretary of War Stanton. And that was just the start.

At Grant's urging, the cabinet hurriedly convened at 8 P.M. on April 21 to consider the Sherman-Johnston peace terms. Grant also attended. The new president had already made post-inaugural statements lumping treason together with rape and murder as a crime that "must be punished." To Johnson, then, this memorandum was heresy; for one thing, no military man had the right to decide political matters, and Sherman had clearly overstepped his authority. For another, there were the terms of the memorandum itself. In strongly suggesting that all Confederates would be exculpated from blame, they all but overrode the executive's authority to decide guilt or innocence of Confederate traitors, including those who had served in the central government. The memorandum was scarcely any better on the matter of the Negro issue: not one of the seven numbered paragraphs made mention of the fate of freed slaves. Worse still, the whole matter reeked, looking as though one of the country's top generals was seeking to end the war by reproducing the conditions that began it. Indeed, the provision that homeward-bound rebels would deposit their arms in state arsenals sounded conspicuously like a plan for keeping them ready and stacked for rebellion, once the Confederates had time to rest themselves and then plot anew.

As furious as Johnson was, the cabinet was even more stunned. Stanton was angriest of all. A whipping boy was demanded, and it would be Sherman. Stanton saw Sherman's memorandum as nothing less than a power grab for the "Copperhead nomination for President" in three years; to the chagrin of the more sober-minded of his colleagues, and hard to fathom today, he even feared that Sherman was preparing to march north and institute a military coup, reminiscent of the European intrigues carried out by both Napoleon and Napoleon III. Remarkably enough, Attorney General James Speed agreed. Actually, Speed was also frantic, expressing fears that at this very moment, Sherman, with "his victorious legions," had immediate "designs upon the government." Speed genuinely believed that Sherman was "plotting to make himself a dictator," and he openly fretted over the recommendation that Grant be sent to talk with Sherman. "Suppose," Speed warned, "he [Sherman] should arrest Grant!" Absent Lincoln's steadying influence, a ludicrous rumor even began that Sherman had been bribed in Confederate gold by Jefferson Davis, thus accounting for the generous treaty he had concluded with Johnston. Notably, this was not dismissed out of hand, not by the cabinet, nor by the Union at large. Rather, the story soon gained in strength and currency, even making its way into Northern newspapers. In a staggering turn of events, the scent of conspiracy surrounding Lincoln's assassination that had ripped through Washington now seemed to have shifted from the Confederacy at large to Sherman himself. Such was the tenor of these late April days.

The cabinet unanimously rejected the terms of the memorandum. As on the night of the assassination, it acted with unusual dispatch and firmness; Grant was ordered to take over Sherman's command and work out a new agreement to replace Sherman's terms. In the meantime, Sherman would be given the following order: the truce between his army and Johnston's would be immediately "terminated" and hostilities would begin "at the earliest possible moment."

Without delay, Grant was dispatched to Raleigh to deal with Sherman in person. At Grant's insistence, the mission was to be conducted in secret. In the wake of Lincoln's murder, passions were already too high all across the board, and Grant also didn't want to embarrass his old friend Bill Sherman.

Still, Grant nursed his own private worries. He knew turmoil was gripping the capital, knew the North was "tired of war," and knew the people were "tired of debt." And most hideous of all for Grant was the prospect of Jefferson Davis safely ensconced in the trans-Mississippi region, from where he could, in Grant's own words, "set up a more contracted Confederacy" and "protract the war another year yet."

That night, Grant left under the cover of darkness, at midnight, steaming away from the Sixth Street wharf.

He would arrive two mornings later, on April 24.

❧　❧　❧

At first, Sherman would not be so easily pacified. When he got wind of his impending rebuke, he began pacing up and down the room of his command post like "a caged lion." He let loose a furious stream of invective against his detractors. He called Stanton a "mean, scheming vindictive politician." He fulminated that his critics were not worth fighting for. And, notwithstanding Grant's efforts, the press had quickly learned of Sherman's actions (they were leaked by Stanton), which did not improve the matter. Indeed, it created such a stir that no other single event in the Civil War itself, outside of Lincoln's assassination, received so much comment in the papers. While his name had once been exalted and aggrandized as the man who had turned the war around, now a blizzard of public criticism was unleashed against him; the *New York Herald* derided Sherman, saying that he had negotiated "under a temporary absence of mind which unfitted him to deal with such shrewd tricksters." The *New York Times* twitted him as "Johnston's outwitted opponent." Others were far more cutting. The *Chicago Tribune* accused him of treason, while the *New Haven Journal* insinuated that Sherman was an accomplice in the plot to assassinate Lincoln and had helped facilitate Davis's escape. And another newspaperman mocked him, saying, "What a contrast between the rashness of Sherman and the steady, never failing equilibrium of Grant."

But of all people, Grant was just the man to handle Sherman. Sherman had once remarked of his old friend, "Grant stood by me when I was crazy, and I stood by him when he was drunk; and now we stand by each other always." Grant did indeed. Smartly acting behind the scenes, he handled the matter with a deft touch, going out of his way to cushion the rebuke and to soften the embarrassment. Handing Sherman a copy of a War Department telegram that Grant had received in March while still in Petersburg ("You are not to decide, discuss, or confer upon any political question. Such questions the President holds in his own hands; and will submit them to no military conference or conventions"), he explained the problem of recognizing "existing local governments." Sherman understood, remarking dryly that he had wished someone had just sent him a copy of the March 3 letter at the time. "It would have saved a whole world of trouble," he morbidly announced. (Although the yeast of anger would continue to work on him. Sometime later, away from Grant, he privately exploded: "Why is it that every bar room loafer in New York . . . [could] read in the morning journals 'official' matter that . . . [was] withheld from a general whose command [extended] from Kentucky to North Carolina!")

But Sherman, while at times irreverent and scornful, was also ever the resolute soldier with a soldier's sense of responsibility. Like his colleagues, he had been well taught at West Point. Grant made his point, and Sherman got the message. Accustomed to adulation as the man who had captured Atlanta and cut a mighty swath to the sea, Sherman now had to endure slights that only weeks before would have been unthinkable. But rather than sulk, he acted, immediately sending a communiqué to Johnston notifying him that Washington had called off their agreement. In its place, he delivered a blunt new ultimatum: hostilities would resume within forty-eight hours unless Johnston surrendered before that time, "on the same terms as were given General Lee at Appomattox on April 9."

Lest there be any mistaken notions about his resolve, he added this stinging phrase, "instant, purely and simply."

✷   ✷   ✷

How much thought was given by the Union cabinet to the Confederate reply? Or to Sherman's concern about the Confederates dissipating into organized guerrilla bands? Were Lincoln's guiding words at City Point recalled or even referenced? The record on this is incomplete, but it is safe to say that the cabinet, like the Union populace at large, was now caught up in the blind fury over Lincoln's death; Lincoln's whole policy of mercy was seemingly unraveling. The record of the Confederate response, however, is unimpeachably clear: at his headquarters, Joe Johnston was dismayed. While Washington had vetoed this agreement, Jefferson Davis had actually approved it—largely because he anticipated, correctly, that the North never would. So this time, cradling Sherman's most recent demand, Johnston asked for further guidance, urgently wiring Breckinridge: "Have you instructions?" And back from the extant Confederate cabinet came the word that Johnston—and Sherman—had dreaded.

The order was to fight on.

The words must have rung in his ears, over and over: *fight on.* Johnston was to take as many of his 22,000–25,000 men as possible and fall back to Georgia with his cavalry, his light guns, and as many infantry as could be mounted on spare horses. In short, what Lee had peremptorily rejected at Appomattox, Davis was now ordering Johnston to make come to pass: a guerrilla campaign.

The order, indeed the present outcome, couldn't have been more disconcerting. Johnston's counterpart, Bill Sherman, perhaps displaying more enthusiasm than judgment, had just been severely rebuked for overstepping his bounds in his attempt to make peace with the remaining South. But had there been some method to his madness? The London *Times* had already warned of "the Armageddon which now seems approaching." Suddenly injected into this volatile mix was now the very specter which Sherman had sought to avoid with his ambitious negotiations: that of Johnston's men taking to the hills. In turn, one must ask: had the Union cabinet potentially—if not unwittingly—played right into Davis's hands? Between them, the battle-hardened Confederates, Nathan Bedford Forrest, Richard Taylor, Kirby Smith, and also Jefferson Davis (along with Johnston), controlled upward of 100,000–175,000 steely soldiers, and each general was still throbbing with patriotic fever, prepared to battle on. Their followers—these filthy, bleeding, bruised, and tired men—were, no less than their superiors, stalwart and hardy Confederates. United by a flickering national spirit, the Confederate colors were the threads still stitching them together. And unlike Lee's Army of Northern Virginia in its final days, while their morale may have been low and their situation may have been desperate—it was—they were not on the verge of starvation. Nor were they surrounded. They had options. Until given the order, they refused to become little more than merely a disorderly or dispirited mob of refugees in their own country. One more thing: many citizens of the Confederate States of America had hardly given up. As one Southern lady enthused defiantly on April 16: "What is it that sustains me? . . . [I]t is faith in the *Country*. Faith in the *Cause*, an earnest belief that eventually we will yet conquer!"

The tinder was there, awaiting a spark. Could the whole process of reconciliation now unravel? It is at this point that a few men would take their places on the historic stage and tip the balance. Sherman's shadow would loom large as ever. From Richmond, Robert E. Lee would again make his voice heard. And for his part, Joe Johnston now had the weightiest decision of his life to make—one that would also prove fateful to the nation at large.

7

Surrender

It is late April of 1865. Across the battered landscape of the Confederacy, there are few poignant reminders of the prewar days. At its best, the Confederacy has the look of a deserted fairground. But for the most part, the sights and colors are ugly, even ungodly. Here and there, dismembered corpses lie scattered about, their stinking, bloated remains eviscerated by rats and scavenger birds, their decaying flesh staring up at the stars at night. Where proud antebellum homes and mansions once stood, there is rotting wood and cracked paint and weed-choked grass; where Southerners once took evening promenade walks down hundred-foot-wide boulevards and through acres of rich green parks, there is the stench of urine and feces and decaying animal carcasses; and where there was once the clamor of commerce and exchange, there are now ghost towns and equally ghostly urban pockets. And of course, there are the ubiquitous chimney stacks, themselves charred and lonely reminders of once thriving cities and bustling plantations. Yet against this backdrop of sorrow, there remains, still, the maddening cacophony of war, as small but deadly skirmishes continue—on April 22 alone, cavalries clashed once again in three separate states: in Munford's Station, Alabama; in Hendersonville, North Carolina; and in Kansas, by Fort Zarah. Even now, from Texas to Florida to the Carolinas, bullets crack and ricochet; shells trill overhead; and gunpowder ignites and burns. And even with the Sherman-Johnston cease-fire, there is more death.

The only way to appreciate the full magnitude of the South's wholesale devastation is to reverse the names: New York, burned to the ground; Boston, burned; Philadelphia, burned; Chicago, burned; Washington, burned. And Lexington and Concord, Massachusetts; and Rye, New York; and New Haven, Connecticut. And also Montclair, New Jersey, and Newport, Rhode Island, and Old Westbury, Long Island. Martha's Vineyard, Massachusetts, a veritable wasteland; Baltimore, Maryland, and Wilmington, Delaware, occupied; Fifth Avenue, barren; West Point ransacked and torched; the *New York Times* and the *Boston Globe* and the *Baltimore Sun*, shut down. And Princeton and Yale, closed; Central Park, Manhattan, a national Confederate graveyard; Tiffany's, a burned-out shell; Niagara Falls, a blackened ruin; the New York City Public Library, trashed; Wall Street, worthless. And the list of those engulfed in the war, dead or wounded, or permanently disfigured by conflict, their careers tragically cut short, is seemingly endless: Walt Whitman and Emily Dickinson and Henry James and Nathaniel Hawthorne; Andrew Carnegie and John D. Rockefeller; J. Pierpont Morgan and Samuel Gompers; Teddy Roosevelt and Thomas Alva Edison; Chester Arthur and Grover Cleveland; Andrew Mellon, Alexander Graham Bell, and Henry Ford; Adolph Ochs, P. T. Barnum, Frank Woolworth, and Albert Bierstadt.

But of course, the names were Southern: Richmond, the Shenandoah, Atlanta, Vicksburg, Columbia, Charleston, Natchez, Nashville, New Orleans, Memphis, Milledgeville, Mobile, Montgomery. And those were only the beginning. So, too, with the people, so many lives destroyed, a whole generation of men dead, dismembered, gone. A generation of women, widowed or forever unwed. A region foundering in confusion.

Ruminating in his camp during these late April days, Joe Johnston knew that civilization in the South would have to be rebuilt, virtually from scratch. But before any rebuilding could begin, there would have to be a decision: to fight on or to give in. For some, Johnston understood, the choice was agonizing. On one hand of the calculus would be honor—honor and a dose of hate; on the other would be these wretched scenes of a ravaged Confederacy. Could it survive more war, more reprisals, more insensate killing? And Johnston wondered if it could survive more Bill Sherman, who as much as any other Union figure cast a prominent and relentless presence over the final days of April 1865. For if he knew one thing, it was this: it was Bill Sherman who was responsible for much of the destruction of the South—and who would be responsible for whatever destruction was to come.

❧ ❧ ❧

Johnston was by no means mistaken.

While it was Grant who initially ordered Sheridan to turn the Shenandoah into a barren wasteland, it was Sherman alone who first glimpsed the true meaning of the maelstrom of total war: that the enemy should be hit, and hit hard, in its ability and its will to fight, meaning that the target was not simply to be opposing armies but the industrial potential and population that lay at the heart of the Confederacy. This entailed no more—and no less—than outright demoralization and devastation, if not the specter of extinction. In its very design and conception, this awesome strategy was, and even today remains, controversial. It meant attacking not just brigades but villages; assaulting not just rebel armies but rebel cities; creating not just outright death but long lines of starving refugees; hitting not just enemy soldiers but enemy livestock, and food, and private homes, and plantations, and shops, and telegraph wires, and railroads. It was terror—organized as well as disorganized—as much as warfare. And, for many Southerners, not since the glory days of the Roman Empire or the subsequent sacking of the Eternal City itself by the Visigoths in the year A.D. 410, which dimmed the lights of civilization for forty generations, had war seemingly been waged by Westerners with such utter ruthlessness and with such a lack of restraint. Critics and ethicists today argue that his scorched-earth policies violated all the strictures of *jus in bello*—justice in warfare, a code carefully built up over a slow and painful 2,000 years of civilization. But Sherman was unapologetic. "War is cruelty," he blasted, "and you cannot refine it."

So who was William Tecumseh Sherman? Actually, his first name was Tecumseh, after the Shawnee chieftain, and it was only years later, when he was baptized, that he was given the name William. For the most part he was "Cump," or "Cumpy," and only in adulthood did he become "William" to associates, "Bill" to his friends. His men affectionately called him "Uncle Billy." But to his Southern victims, he was evil incarnate, truly a latter-day recreation of Attila the Hun, if not Satan himself. In truth, however, Sherman was an exceptionally alert, incisive, and intricate man. Though a graduate of West Point, and the foster son of a prominent United States senator (who was also a cabinet member under two presidents), Sherman cared little for social decorum. Edgy and ill-tempered, he dressed in grubby, soiled uniforms; tall and lanky, he was always thrusting his hands into his pockets or tugging on his mane of rough red hair; his face was furrowed, his hair uncombed, his nose jutting and crimson. More often than not, he looked as though he had just woken up. His manners were even worse than his clothes. But behind the rumpled facade was sheer iron. And he was everything his Union opponents said he was: excitable, incendiary, furious, volatile, and unrelenting. All this, of course, was part of his magic, and also part of his mystique.

The word fits. Rarely does mystique come in one rational, linear package, and it would be futile to look for it in Sherman, who was always a delicate balance of opposing forces and conflicting impulses. He talked rapidly, in a high voice, about almost anything under the sun. But it was no idle rambling. He was at once charismatic but also deliberative; big-hearted and warm, but also cool and gloomy; filled with grand ideas, but also meticulous in detail. And he was an asthmatic. His problem in life was not talent—he had an abundance of that—but temperament. And finding his niche. When President James Polk shook the world with the stunning announcement of a new discovery in California, ushering in the gold rush, Polk quoted, of all things, a memorandum written by Sherman. Sherman had a knack for being on the cutting edge—but he could never sit still or stay in one profession. In varying degrees, he had been successful as a soldier, a banker, an investment broker, and to a much lesser extent, as a lawyer (joining the bar at the late age of thirty-seven). But none of these professions captivated him. He quit the army, he soon tired of banking, and he quickly left the law. He had his share of failures. Then the Civil War began.

There were few cues as to how he would perform. For one thing, unlike most other West Pointers, he saw no action in the Mexican War. In truth, he was untested in battle. For another thing, his personal life was inordinately complicated and filled with incongruities. The last of eleven children, nine-year-old "Cump" was given up by his debt-ridden mother to a neighbor, Thomas Ewing, when his father died. He was not quite an orphan, then, but he was a foster child. Yet he became so much a part of his new family that when he proposed marriage to, of all people, his foster sister, Ellen, one family member gasped: "Why they *can't!*" They did; however, it took eight years for Senator Ewing, his foster father, to approve the marriage. Nor was it just any ordinary wedding: among the guests were President Taylor, his cabinet, and senatorial giants Daniel Webster and Henry Clay. This former foster child had become a child of privilege.

Though he came from Ohio, Sherman loved the South and loved Southerners. While he had a Westerner's indifference to elegance, in clothes, manners, and speech, he nonetheless adored the refinement of the Southern aristocracy. The five years he spent in Charleston were among the best of his life. He was as staunch a Negrophobe as any Southerner, which is to say an inveterate racist by today's standards, and he despised the abolitionists with a fervor that matched that of any plantation owner. But in one crucial respect he was different: what he loved even more than the South was the Union, a sentiment bequeathed to him by his adopted family. Thus, when the new Confederacy offered him a commission, he turned it down.

Sherman almost didn't make it in the war. After seven months of service as commander of the Union forces in Kentucky, he became so panicked by a rebel threat, which he grossly exaggerated, that he was relieved of command and hastily transferred to a backwater post in Missouri. The press labeled him crazy. But he did see combat at the first battle of Bull Run, where he acquitted himself ably, and then at Shiloh, where he distinguished himself by fighting with grit and valor, surviving two minor wounds and three horses being shot out from under him. For the rest of the war, he was, in one manner or another, by U. S. Grant's side. When Grant became general in chief, he promptly made Sherman commander of the Western forces.

Grant and Sherman: their relationship was a complex and ambivalent one. In many respects the two men were alike, creative in war, imaginative, perceptive—both had fought off despair and failure. Sherman was deeply indebted to Grant, and more than that, saw in him a reassuring presence. ("I knew wherever I was that you thought of me," he once wrote Grant, "and if I got in a tight place you would come—if alive.") But in one crucial way theirs was also a tenuous thread. Sherman detested politicians and made no bones about it, and he despised the press even more, whereas Grant submerged his personal feelings and cleverly worked the system. Still, the two fed off each other brilliantly in war. And most brilliant of all was Sherman's bold plan proposed in the early fall of 1864, which Grant approved.

For the Union, these were bleak times. Grant had been pummeled in battle after battle during the Wilderness campaign and had now settled down to a maddening siege; the Northern peace movement was at a feverish high point; and it looked certain that Lincoln would lose the election to McClellan. Even defeat or capitulation seemed possible. Staunch Lincoln Republicans had begun to ask: "Why don't Grant and Sherman do something?" In Grant's case, there was little he could do; he was locked in nine months of grim trench warfare. Sherman, too, looked like he had temporarily stalled.

But while the earlier battles of Vicksburg and Gettysburg were no doubt crucial turning points, no turning point was as crucial as what followed in this decisive election season of 1864, when Sherman proposed one of the boldest gambles in military history. The opposing Confederate army, then under General John Bell Hood, had marched off toward Tennessee in the vain hope that Sherman would feel compelled to abandon Atlanta and come after it. Instead, Sherman basically thumbed his nose at convention and proposed doing the opposite, to ignore the enemy army altogether, head east, and savage the spirit of the South. Taking a page from Grant's Vicksburg campaign, he would abandon his supply line, cut off all communications with the North, and lead his some 62,000 men into the crown jewel of Atlanta and from there, to Savannah and the sea.

"I can make the march, and make Georgia howl!" Sherman boomed to Grant. "I will cut a swath to the sea" and "divide the Confederacy in two." But first, he outfoxed Hood and took Atlanta on September 2, saving Lincoln and quite possibly the Union in the process. "Atlanta is ours," Sherman wired the president cheerfully, "and fairly won." But it was more than won. His soldiers had torched everything of military value, and much that wasn't of any military value as well. By the time his men began their march out of Atlanta, the city was battered beyond recognition. Sherman claimed to try to spare the citizens, but he could not, or would not, or refused to control his high-strung soldiers or the sociopathic bummers, those desperadoes and looters lured to the march for the sheer taste of spoil. They slaughtered all the livestock they couldn't eat, ransacked silver and jewelry, and terrorized old men and helpless women. Next, they laid waste to many of their precious relics and molested slave women. And then they massacred able-bodied males. Even the city library and archives went up in flames, for the sheer naked joy of it. Long lines of innocent civilians fled the city: Sherman had forcefully banned more than 1,500 noncombatants from Atlanta. Trembling, others followed.

When his legions finally embarked toward the seacoast, Atlanta lay behind, a smoldering ruin.

Diarist Mary Chesnut shuddered at what Sherman had wrought. "Since Atlanta I have felt as if all were dead within me, forever," she wrote. "We are going to be wiped off the face of the earth." She was nearly right, for Atlanta was just the start. Sherman himself was unrepentant. "We are not only fighting hostile armies, but a hostile people, and must make old and young, rich and poor, feel the hard hand of war." That's exactly what happened. Sherman then ravaged Georgia, as far south as Savannah, paused, then lunged into South Carolina.

Moving at a relentless pace of a dozen miles per day through the interior of Georgia, he laid waste to a vast corridor stretching 285 miles: warehouses, bridges, barns, machine shops, depots, factories, farms, private homes, livestock, cotton, gin, and even slave cabins and "their niggers" all fell under a cloud of destruction and plunder. Sherman turned a blind eye to the thin line dividing barbaric ruin from the targets vital to winning the war. In December, more of the job was done. He sent another jaunty wire to Lincoln: "I beg to present you, as a Christmas gift, the City of Savannah." And then he commenced his most fearsome efforts yet: a second march through the heart of enemy territory, into South Carolina. "The whole army is burning with an insatiable desire to wreak vengeance upon South Carolina," Sherman rumbled to Washington. "I almost tremble at her fate, but . . . she deserves all that seems in store for her." And what was in store for her was out-and-out destruction, more intense and comprehensive than even in Georgia.

The march, to total 425 miles altogether, began on January 3, 1865.

Little of whatever stood in their way—whether the countryside or villages—remained standing after the army swept through. They burned towns and plantations en route—and magnificent towering live oaks for good measure. The path of ruin made the destruction of Georgia look like child's play. This was no longer war, it was sheer vengeance. Even some of Sherman's own men were shocked. "You have no idea how the women & children suffer here," one private wrote to his wife. But Sherman stopped at nothing to punish the state that had spawned the rebellion. In the rainiest winter in twenty years, his men confronted formidable terrain and weather. They had to cross nine swollen rivers; make their way over scores of tributaries; slog through flat, dense, marshy swamps; evade alligators and snakes; ignore twenty-eight days of cold rain; and skirmish with rebels day in and day out for forty-five days running. A gloomy Joe Johnston stood in awe of Sherman's feat: "When I learned that Sherman's army was marching through the Salk swamps, making its own corduroy roads at the rate of a dozen miles a day, I made up my mind that there had been no such army in existence since the days of Julius Caesar." But even Caesar himself might have wept at the spectacle that soon followed.

Sherman's direct target this time was neither Charleston nor Augusta, as South Carolinians feared, but the capital of Columbia. On February 17, 1865, his units occupied the capital, and by next morning, the city was all rubble and ashes. Even for total war, the destruction was shocking. Sherman later distanced himself from the carnage, considered his greatest atrocity, by claiming that retreating rebels had started the blaze. And some thoughtful historians have agreed with him, partially at least, adding that he in fact did not burn Columbia (although some of his men most likely did, and what attempts were made by his officers to restrain them were too little, too late). But this reasoning is ultimately fragile. However much Sherman and some of his generals may have struggled that evening to put out the fires, some of his soldiers clearly helped inflame them. And when the troops marched into Columbia, there were no orders issued, as had been earlier in 1864, that any man engaging in arson would be shot "on the spot." Like everything else his men touched, in the end, Columbia—but one more stop along the way in his campaign of plunder—was nearly leveled. Sherman himself explained that in his march, he inflicted an astonishing $100 million worth of damage, of which only $20 million was necessary, the rest being "simply waste and destruction."

"This may seem a hard species of warfare," he explained, but it was the only way to bring home "the sad realities of war." That it did.

❧　❧　❧

Two weeks later, flushed with excitement, Sherman's men crossed state lines and marched into North Carolina, en route to Goldsboro. With boyish pride, the general boasted, "There was no place in the Confederacy safe against my army of the West." But this smacked of idle bravado and a touch of bluster. In truth, it was now as if the Westerners were a different army and Sherman a different general. The looting and burning ended; unlike in South Carolina, any soldier caught engaging in such behavior would be executed without trial. "Deal as moderately and fairly by North Carolinians as possible," he ordered. And also: "Leave their families for us to feed and protect." Here in North Carolina, only war property was to be destroyed.

And even that logic did not hold when it came to battlefields and men. In the days that followed, there were a number of little clashes with Johnston's men—actually, they were surprisingly sharp ones—at Averasboro and at Bentonville. Yet while the dilapidated rebels bravely harassed the now assembled Union force of 80,000 men, Sherman, almost inexplicably, went out of his way to limit the conflict. This was more than ironic. In 1864, he had once roared, "I've got Joe Johnston dead!" wildly hammering his supper table until the dishes rattled, convinced he had finally gotten Johnston and gotten him good. But he hadn't. Later that night, in fact, he learned quite the opposite: one of his key lieutenants had failed to take the nearby railroad, Johnston's fortifications had been too strong, and Sherman's own cavalry had arrived too late. Even as Sherman was the artful flanker, he had slowly come to believe that Johnston was a sagacious and cunning defensive strategist. Across a chain of isolated hills, thick forests, and deep, misty ravines, Sherman had been relentless, continually feinting and maneuvering against Johnston; but the Virginian, ever on cat's feet, fell back and back, repeatedly eluding him. In Sherman's words, Johnston turned the whole region into "one vast fortress," and he likened their respective shadowboxing to one "Big Indian War." It so galled him that on most days Sherman would wake up and habitually cry, "Now what is Joe Johnston's game?" But by March 21, two days before he occupied Goldsboro, the game was now surely Sherman's. "I can do no more than annoy him," Johnston told Davis. And Sherman, finally, had Johnston just where he wanted him. His men outnumbered the Confederates by more than three to one, yet somehow, he let Johnston's small and demoralized forces slip away.

Why? One excuse was that he couldn't transport the wounded. But this is mere cant. Another was that Sherman mistakenly believed that Johnston had 40,000 men directly under his command—more than he wanted to fight. This is the more plausible explanation. For one thing, his own soldiers, cocky, hardened, lean men of the West, were themselves thoroughly worn. After seven weeks of continuous, tough campaigning, their greatest of the war, they needed to be replenished and resupplied. And they were themselves sick of war—as Sherman later acknowledged. For another, despite his reputation, Sherman had little taste for direct combat, dismissing it as "glory and all moonshine," even going as far as deriding the greatest battlefield successes as coming at the expense of "dead and mangled bodies." All this naturally suggests the answer to one of the more fascinating questions of the war: how could a man so ruthless in battle suddenly become so generous in peace? And having outwitted and outmaneuvered his rivals, what made this gifted general offer so much to Johnston at Durham Station?

The reality was, Sherman was a bit of a romantic. His feelings in combat were laced with sentimentality for the loser—and respect for a valiant foe. Like Lincoln, his concept of magnanimity was one of his more endearing and important traits. To be sure, defeat had to precede conciliation. There was no way around it. But for Sherman, revenge afterward was unsoldierly, unmanly, and ultimately counterproductive. Particularly after meeting with Lincoln at City Point in late March, he was also thinking ahead: to reunion. "When peace does come," he once said in all sincerity, "You may call on me for anything. Then I will share with you the last cracker." Which is, of course, what ultimately led to his sweeping Bennett House agreement with Johnston on April 19.

But now that agreement had been repudiated by Washington. On April 24, then, for Sherman it was as if everything had changed and nothing had changed. Though confident that the war was nearly over, he remained terrified of guerrilla warfare and of general chaos. After Lincoln's murder, the feisty Ohioan felt "sick" and "powerless"; watching the disorderly events in the capital as well as across the South, he tartly wondered who "was left on this continent to give order and shape to the now disjointed elements of the government"; and as the hours of the ultimatum dwindled, and the uneasy stalemate with Johnston was crumbling, Sherman openly feared that "events are drifting further into another civil and anarchical war."

No matter. Under the strict orders of Johnson and Stanton, and with the watchful eye of U. S. Grant looking over his shoulder, Sherman had little choice but to be poised for one last terrible march of death—if not for weeks and months of lingering pursuit of rebels who had taken to the steep rugged mountains of Georgia and beyond.

Even Grant himself was no longer taking any chances. Before departing for Raleigh—and startlingly enough, without having told Sherman— the commanding general had already issued a single, stern order: "Move Sheridan with his cavalry toward Greensboro as soon as possible. Send one corps of infantry also."

❧　❧　❧

It wouldn't be needed.

One by one the remaining Confederate generals would reciprocate the overtures of their Northern counterparts—call it the Spirit of Appomattox,

The March

Atlantic Ocean

February 18, 1865
Charleston

December 21, 1864
Savannah

Sherman's March to the Sea

GEORGIA

Oconee R.

Macon

Savannah R.

Broad R.

SOUTH CAROLINA

Columbia

SHERMAN

Pee Dee R.

NORTH CAROLINA

Cape Fear R.

Raleigh
Armistice
April 18, 1865   Bentonville

Averasboro
Fayetteville

Union
Confederate retreat

Chattanooga
November 23–25, 1863

TENNESSEE

Chattanooga

SHERMAN

JOHNSTON

Kennesaw Mt.
June 27, 1864

Battles of Atlanta
July 20, 22, 28, 1864

Atlanta

Chattahoochee R.

ALA.

0   40 miles

or Lincoln's *River Queen* Doctrine—and bring calm, dignity, and sobriety to winding down the war. Above all, in peace as in war, it was once again Robert E. Lee's voice that would set the Confederate tone for continuing surrender.

"*Aide-toi et Dien t'aidera*"—"Help yourself and God will help you." That was the inscription on the sword that Lee had worn to the Wilmer McLean House at Appomattox, and those words seemed to guide him now.

It couldn't have been easy. Beyond the heartache of war and the heartbreak of the defeat of his proud army, his own familial possessions had been ransacked by the Union. The cherished family estate at Arlington, belonging to his wife and kept as a shrine to George Washington, had been converted into a national cemetery for Union dead, and was now dotted with little white tombstones; another family estate, known as the White House, had been torched by Federal soldiers; a third, Romancoke, had been so savaged that there was not a single fence post standing. All told, 11,000 acres of prime Virginia land that he had owned now lay in the hands of the Yankees—permanently. So, after Appomattox, his spirit shattered, he mounted his horse and returned to Richmond, to 707 Franklin Street, to the rented red brick row house where an arthritic Mary Custis Lee had lived during the final year of the war.

Lee's revolutionary lineage was as impeccable as any other American, North or South. And his wife was the (step) great-granddaughter of George Washington, making them uniquely descendants of the first family. But now, he was not a citizen of anything. Lee was, to put it bluntly, stateless, a man in limbo, without a country, a paroled prisoner of war living in occupied territory that was no longer the Confederate capital but not yet a Union state, and whose fate had yet to be decided by Northern authorities. Sunken, his white hair thinning, Lee never revealed in any depth what he felt in these days. If there was bitterness, he never showed it. If there was any hardening of the heart, it was difficult to discern. We do know he was depressed, sleeping late and often. We can only surmise that he may have felt like a broken man. But what was most remarkable about Lee was his determination to do his public duty, as he stressed the need for the South to take the painful step of signing the loyalty oath and submitting to the governance of the United States.

And just as significant, and perhaps as fascinating about Lee's actions, is not simply what he did do, but what he chose not to do.

Just hours before Lee made the difficult ride back into Richmond, Lincoln had finally succumbed to the bullet lodged in his head. But this could not have been Lee's greatest concern; Richmond must have been. The sight of the Confederate capital had to have wrenched his soul. He had gone to war for Virginia ("my country"), and its erstwhile capital was now a shambles, overflowing with refugees and beggars, and filled with scorched brick skeletons that hovered madly over rubble-filled streets; nearly a third of central Richmond was so decimated that it would come to be known as "the burnt district." Lee was a passionate man, and an equally fervent nationalist; no sight in the world could have pained him as much as the scene he was witnessing, except for perhaps the actual surrender of his men. But at the news of Lincoln's death, Lee expressed not a single word of hate or bitterness at the fallen enemy commander in chief. Nor did he gloat. Instead, he later called it "a crime that was unexampled," "one of the most deplorable that could have occurred," and one that "must be deprecated by every American."

This was significant. The fact was, the slightest word from Lee, even a small, veiled hint that could be misconstrued, could have done much to reignite Southern passions and breathe new life into the remaining Southern forces still at war. It could have prompted an unearthly guerrilla struggle; it certainly would have ensured organized chaos; and it would most certainly have legitimized ongoing discord. "You have only to blow the bugle," one of his colonels once said to him. So true. All of the Confederacy was looking to him for guidance. "It is the influence of one man which sways the people," noted one journalist. He was referring, of course, to Lee.

Indeed, while the Union armies were masters of the principal cities, there were still holdouts. Across the Confederacy, clashes continued, in Alabama and Tennessee, in North Carolina and Missouri, in Kentucky and Georgia, in Texas and Mississippi, and in Florida and the Indian Territory. They had little names and were little places and were fleeting, but all shared a central ingredient—the shooting, and dying, and the war continued: near Tuskegee, and Mount Pleasant, and Chapel Hill, and Patterson, and Germantown, and Taylorsville, and Barnesville, and

Montpelier Springs, and Buzzard's Roost, and Howard's Gap, and Linn Creek, and Munford's Station, and Hendersonville, and Boonsville, and Fort Adams, and Boggy Depot, and Miami, and elsewhere. But as Lincoln's eyes closed in the early morning of April 15, Robert E. Lee—in a momentous decision—resisted any temptation to call on the Confederacy to take advantage of the Union's disarray and somehow press the chaos of the North to its advantage. He had had enough.

In fact, he decidedly went in the other direction.

❧　❧　❧

One mid-April day, a young cavalry scout from Mosby's rangers, who was considered one of the most daring of the Confederacy's cavalry spies, slipped into the city and made his way to a home where Lee happened to be visiting. He had a message from Mosby: What should the rangers do? Surrender—or fight on?

"Go home," Lee bluntly told the young scout, "all you boys who fought with me." He added, "Help to build up the shattered fortunes of our old state." Like Lincoln, whose embalmed body was now lying on public display, Lee was determined to look ahead, not backward. And that became Lee's tireless message. Later in the month, he consented to an interview with Thomas Cook, a reporter from the *New York Herald*. Interestingly, Lee had been maintaining a public silence, but it is noteworthy that he said yes to this request. The situation across the country was now volatile: since Lincoln's assassination, the North was ablaze with fury at the South; hysteria was widespread; Jefferson Davis was still at large, calling for further resistance; and sporadic fighting was ongoing. The reporter said that the people of the North were interested in what Lee had to say about the current state of affairs. Lee, who throughout the war had assiduously read Northern papers and had always been keenly attuned to Northern opinion, had another idea. He knew that this was a means of talking to the South as well. In more than one way, the interview was extraordinary.

Lee condemned the assassination of Lincoln in the strongest terms ("deplorable," "beyond execration," "A crime," "unexampled"); he celebrated the end of slavery ("I am rejoiced that slavery is abolished," "the

best men of the South have long been anxious to do away with this institution," "slavery [is] forever dead"); and he predictably defended the
Southern view that secession had not been unconstitutional ("It has
remained unsettled until the present time. The war is destined to set it to
rest"). But most astonishing about this interview was this: where just
weeks earlier, even days really, indeed, even at Appomattox, whenever Lee
had said "the country," he had meant the South, and whenever he said
"we," he had meant the Confederacy. But now, the reporter was struck by
the degree to which Lee talked throughout, freely and noticeably, as "a
citizen of the United States." The South, Lee stressed, "was anxious to
get back into the Union and to peace."

And then he promised: "to make any sacrifice or perform any honorable act that would tend to the restoration of peace."

❧   ❧   ❧

At this critical juncture, no words could have said more or meant more
when spoken. One young man, upon taking the loyalty oath, was up-
braided by his patriotic Southern father: "You have disgraced the family!" The son noted that General Lee advised him to do it. "Oh," the
father sighed, "that alters the case. Whatever General Lee says is all right."

Just one week after surrendering his army, Lee reluctantly consented
to being photographed by the famed photographer Mathew Brady
("how can I sit for a photograph with the eyes of the world upon me
as they are today?"). But sit he did. Appearing in simple military dress,
though without his braids or sword, he stepped out onto his herringbone
brick back porch as Brady carefully adjusted the plates. What resulted
was one of the most famous if not intriguing pictures of all the war: Lee
standing erect and proud, his hat in one hand, his other hanging by his
side. Most arresting are his eyes, deep and dark, peering off into the distance. Lee biographer Douglas Southall Freeman sees in this photo "a
stern picture," with Lee's jaw "strongly set" and a "shadow both of
anguish and defiance lingering on his face." Another biographer sees "the
light of battle in his eyes" and "sorrow and determination," and "a man
who has surrendered but is not defeated." But what is most captivating is

the mystery of the photo. Lee is a man in limbo, disenfranchised, without an army, a country, a homeland. Look deeply enough and you see the eyes are staring off into another world, at what might have been.

But the former commander, fatigued and depressed, was now dealing in facts—and the future. He may no longer have had an army, but he had his voice, which could set the tone of reconciliation in the tense days to come. He had seen the fateful picture of a chaotic Richmond all around him, itself a metaphor and disheartening reminder of the desolation spread across the Confederacy. He could scarcely stomach any more. Nor could he have relished another stampede by Sherman, this time through North Carolina. Having already rejected the idea of his army fighting on, in small roving bands, he now sought to forestall Johnston's men—and the rest of the extant armies—from doing so. On April 20, he sat at his desk and penned another communiqué to Jefferson Davis. He had already written a formal report of his final operations, losses, and surrender. Of course, he was now a vanquished general, so there was no compelling reason for him to write to Davis again. Nonetheless, that was exactly what he did.

Interestingly enough, this, his last letter to the Confederate president, though cloaked in the guise of military analysis, was a supremely political act, even if he would have denied it as such. And an act of humanity. Lee took dead aim at Davis's proposed "new phase" of warfare. "A partisan war may be continued," he wrote, and "the hostilities protracted, causing individual suffering and the devastation of the country." But, he continued, "I see no prospect by that means of achieving independence." Knowing that Davis was calling for a guerrilla war if all else failed, he in effect told Davis to think long and hard about his actions: "To save useless effusion of blood, I would recommend measures be taken for the suspension of hostilities and the restoration of peace." Lee could be a shrewd political operator when he so chose; he well knew that word of his letter would seep out into the rest of the Confederacy, for all to see.

In the ensuing days, it did. Meanwhile, on the run, Jefferson Davis would choose to ignore Lee's admonition. But not so with the other men who would matter just as much—the Confederate generals still remaining in the field. Most prominent of these was now, of course, Joe Johnston, who in the early morning of April 25 had just been ominously instructed by Davis to retreat and fight on. Hearing of this, Mary Chesnut wrote: "They say Johnston will not be caught as Lee was. He can retreat. That is his trade . . . thoughts turn to Texas. You remember Davy Crockett's farewell to the democratic party? 'You are going to the devil. I am going to *Texas!*'"

❧   ❧   ❧

But Johnston made his own choice. He wasn't going to Georgia or Texas or anywhere. Instead, he ignored his president's orders—and contacted Sherman for a third time.

To be sure, if Sherman had overstepped his bounds, Johnston would now more than outdo his partner with this out-and-out act of insubordination. Johnston was, in effect, willfully ignoring the edict of the Confederate president. He himself would later acknowledge that he directly "disobey[ed]" his instructions. Quite true. But Johnston, who wired back to Davis that such a plan of retreat was "impracticable," saw no other way. In his view, it would be "the greatest of crimes for us to attempt to continue the war," and making peace was "the only function of [the Confederate] government still [in existence]." Moreover, to fight any further would only "spread ruin all over the south." Nor did he share the notion of the unrepentant fire-eaters that "no suffering which can be inflicted by the passage over our country of the Yankee armies can equal what would fall on us if we return to the Union." There is a vivid paradox to all this. Johnston, then and now, was derided by many as "Retreatin' Joe," a second-rate general, a near-incompetent. Compact and fastidiously dressed, he had a sharp eye, a thin skin, and an inflated sense of honor, and he was known in the antebellum South as a crack shot in duck hunting who, in Mary Chesnut's words, "never pulled the trigger." So, too, in war. Even for those who point to his flashes of tactical cunning—and they were there—and those who see him as a resolute and tactically ingenious army commander, in the larger flow of history what ultimately must stand out is not Johnston's military ability or his daring in battle, but this one decisive act in which he brazenly violated the chain of command—and in doing so, helped heal a country.

It happened rather simply. Johnston immediately contacted Sherman and arranged for a third meeting, again at the Bennett farmhouse, to conclude a surrender on the basis of the revised terms. Sherman himself would later assert that Johnston was "powerless to resist" him; this, of course, was not quite true. But like Lee, Johnston did not see honor in further resistance, only tragedy and sorrow. He followed Lee's lead.

Johnston and Sherman met on April 26, and this time, the two men (who would become lifetime admirers of each other), quickly disposed of the matter. Like Grant before him, Sherman offered concrete assistance to the Confederates, issuing ten days' rations for 25,000 paroled rebels. The intent, as he noted, was "to facilitate what you and I and all good men desire, the return to their homes of the officers and men composing your army." In an unmistakable act of small but touching symbolism, Sherman then graciously allowed Johnston's name to go first in the articles of surrender. (Grant later reversed them so that Sherman's name would come first when they were published in the Northern press.) Moreover, Sherman's field orders went out to "encourage the inhabitants to renew their peaceful pursuits and to restore relations of friendship among our fellow citizens and countrymen."

One good gesture would beget another. Johnston would later note that United States troops, remaining on military duty, treated the Southerners as kindly as they would "those of Ohio or New York." And in turn, he would write to Sherman two days later, "The enlarged patriotism exhibited in your orders reconciles me to what I have previously regarded as the misfortune of my life, that of having to encounter you in the field."

To his own men, Johnston enjoined them to "observe faithfully the terms of pacification agreed upon; and to discharge the obligations of good and peaceful citizens . . . By such a course, you will best secure the comfort of your families and kindred, and restore tranquility to our country."

❧   ❧   ❧

Our country. In bits and pieces, this phrase was again slowly coming to mean North and South, one and the same. By now, the combined impact of Lee's and Johnston's surrenders was profound. As word spread of

Johnston's actions, individual Confederate commanders and their Union adversaries quickly followed suit, making peace on the model established by Grant and Lee, and reiterated by Sherman and Johnston. There was, in the end, no grand, sweeping Congress of Vienna—just military man to military man, forging simple truces with the shake of a hand and the scratch of a pen. Following in their footsteps in the Western theater was General Richard Taylor, commander of the Confederate army, now about 10,000 strong in Alabama, Mississippi, and East Louisiana, hardly enough men to pose a major threat but more than enough to make mischief for years had he so desired. In a small but touching ceremony, Taylor, a short, articulate, dark-complexioned man, educated at Yale, Harvard, and Edinburgh, Scotland, surrendered to Major General Edward Canby in Citronelle, Alabama, on May 4. Two days earlier, these men had themselves bonded, much like Lee and Grant, and Sherman and Johnston, sharing an *al fresco* luncheon topped off with rich pâtés and a number of bottles of champagne ("the first agreeable explosive sounds I had heard in years," Taylor drawled). When the band struck up "Hail Columbia," Canby hastily ordered a quick switch to "Dixie," lest Taylor be offended. He wasn't. Not to be outclassed, in fine Southern style the only son of a U.S. president to fight in the war requested, indeed, no doubt *insisted*, that the original tune continue; evidently, as Shelby Foote notes, the moment had once again come when they could "hail Columbia" together. Taylor, among the most literate of the generals, Union or Confederate, later commended his counterpart for his "intellect" and "candid bearing," which entitled him to "our highest respect and confidence."

And he, too, sounded the call that his brave rebels should now meet "their responsibilities," not simply as "as soldiers" but, just as critically, as good "citizens."

❧   ❧   ❧

So with loose rocks do avalanches begin. The concept of citizens would come to mean much if the country were to become one again. But for the hard-fighting, never-surrendering Nathan Bedford Forrest, now camped out around Gainesville, Alabama, on the surface, no word could have seemed more alien.

Well into late April, nothing rankled this grizzled cavalryman more than the thought of giving up. As he waited for more definitive word about the status of Lee and Johnston, and also Taylor, he toyed with the notion of "going to Mexico." But then the news eventually filtered deep into the backwoods that Lee had in fact surrendered, as had Johnston. When Taylor followed suit on May 4, Forrest saddled up his horse and took off on a night ride with an aide to mull over his options. What should he do? Take to the hills? Mexico? Surrender? At one point, they cantered over to a fork in the road and came to a sudden halt. Their exchange is immortal: "Which way General?" the aide asked. "Either," Forrest growled. "If one road led to Hell and the other to Mexico, I would be indifferent which to take."

In truth, he wasn't. Under the stars, Forrest, the villainous, self-made millionaire who by now had lost everything, talked candidly with his adjutant. Among other things, he considered his responsibilities to his men, and to the South. With the same élan and spirit that he had used to lead his cavalry into death-defying battle, he decided that he could lead them into peace. He agreed to lay down his arms, and to abide by the terms that General Taylor had already agreed to. Thus, in early May, when the Mississippi governor and former governor of Tennessee rode out and urged Forrest to retreat with his cavalry to the Trans-Mississippi theater, Forrest barked back: "Any man who is in favor of further prosecution of this war is a fit subject for a lunatic asylum."

On May 9, Forrest dramatically announced to his riders that they would not take to the woods or the hills. They would not go to Mexico. They would not fight any further. Instead, they should surrender. As always, they followed.

The attempt to establish "a separate and independent confederacy had failed," Forrest noted, and they should meet their responsibilities, "like men." He added, in some ways almost uncharacteristically, "reason dictates and humanity demands that no more blood be shed."

And of the North's demands, he said this: "The [terms] manifest a spirit of magnanimity and liberality on the part of the Federal Authorities which should be met on our part by a faithful compliance with all the stipulations and conditions therein."

He acknowledged rather candidly that "Civil war, such as you have just passed through, naturally engenders feelings of animosity, hatred, and revenge." To which he sharply counseled: "It is our duty to divest ourselves of all such feelings, and . . . to cultivate feelings toward those with whom we have so long contested and . . . so widely but honestly differed."

Then Forrest took one final step that would long surprise many in the North, including his old adversary, Sherman. Echoing the sentiments of Lee before him, in places almost word for word, he added: "I have never on the field of battle sent you where I was unwilling to go myself, nor would I advise you to a course which I felt myself unwilling to pursue. You have been good soldiers, you can be good citizens. Obey the laws, preserve your honor, and the government to which you have surrendered can afford to be and will be magnanimous."

❧　❧　❧

The other principal Confederate forces gave up the fight as well. Learning of Lee's capitulation, partisan hero John Mosby had already disbanded his rangers on April 21, although he personally vowed to fight on. While racing to join Johnston in North Carolina, he received the heart-stopping news of the Bennett House surrender, at which point he finally called it quits. By month's end, in May, the ever-defiant General E. Kirby Smith followed suit, capitulating his ranks, some 36,000 weary troops that composed the Trans-Mississippi Department; Colonel J. Q. Chenowith, commander of the Department of Western Kentucky, similarly surrendered; Major General Sam Jones, commander of the District of Florida, did likewise (his Union counterpart noting that he would "do all in my power . . . to make arrangements such as are honorable to brave enemies and generous foes"). So did the eccentric and brilliant Confederate Brigadier General M. Jeff Thompson, leader of rebel veterans in Missouri and the West. And last but not least, a month later, Brigadier General Stand Watie (a.k.a. "De-ga-ta-ga"), the Cherokee chief, close to sixty years old, weather-beaten and bowlegged, his gray mane of hair fanning out over his shoulders, who had participated in almost two dozen major battles and a hundred smaller skirmishes, became the final Confederate general to lay down his arms. On June 23, 1865, he surrendered his battalion, a diverse amalgam of Confederate Cherokees, Creeks, Seminoles, and Osages, at Doaksville, the Choctaw capital near Fort Towson in Indian Territory.

❧ ❧ ❧

"We are falling to pieces," an aide to Jefferson Davis said ruefully on April 26, when word of Johnston's surrender came in. As an exhausted but still defiant Confederate president fled southward and westward, hoping somehow to rally the Confederacy from a new base in Texas, never were truer words spoken.

Since the fall of Richmond, Davis's skeletal government had been on the run—twelve railroad cars, stuffed to the gills, "a government on wheels" clanking from one makeshift provisional capital to the next: Danville, Virginia; then Charlotte, North Carolina; then Abbeville, South Carolina; then Irwinville, Georgia. At each step of the way, the Confederate president had done everything in his power to ignite the waning Southern heart, but now it was to no avail. One by one, his generals had deserted him, following the example of Robert E. Lee and the inexorable call of military logic, rather than the exhortations of their now quixotic president. In the end, Davis was the last remaining symbol of a dying Confederacy. And that was, to many who knew him, a particular kind of tragedy, even irony.

In 1861, when the delegates of the seceding states had met in Montgomery to cheering crowds and the tune of "Dixie" to elect a new president of the Confederate States of America, the verdict was unanimous: Jefferson Davis. Here was a man brave enough and seasoned enough to lead them to victory. Out came the cry: "The man and the hour have met!" Yet Davis wasn't even there; he was back in Mississippi, with his wife, Varina, pruning rosebushes in the garden of his plantation, Brierfield. In truth, he was dismayed upon learning of the results: he had neither sought the chief office, nor did he want it—he had actually hoped for high command in the Confederate army. Davis was never one to thrive on the eternal round of banquets, rallies, torchlight parades, and wakes that were the province of every politician, North or South. Nor was he a congenital handshaker, a backslapper, or a ready compromiser. "His genius was military" wrote Varina, "but as a party manager he would not succeed. He did not know the arts of the politician and would not practice them if understood . . ." But it was his high sense of duty—and destiny—that moved him reluctantly to accept.

And now, having been there at the birth, he was there at the Confederacy's imminent death, resistant, unswerving, unrepentant, fervent, and unapologetic to the very end.

❧ ❧ ❧

The beginning was quite different. Like Abe Lincoln, Davis was born in a Kentucky log cabin, on June 3, 1808, eight months before the Union president, and less than a hundred miles away. His father soon moved his family to the Mississippi Cotton Kingdom and prospered. Though to an extent Davis bore the familiar stamp of the South—the image of the exacting man ruled by self-control, the picture of the old-fashioned Southern gentleman, the portrait of the florid but uncaring slave owner—in his case this is often misleading. In countless ways, this icon of the South was surprisingly progressive, forward-looking, even cosmopolitan.

His middle name was a whimsical Finis, because he was born when his mother was forty-five, the last of ten. His upbringing was astonishingly modern: his father, though austere, eschewed all forms of corporal punishment, and Davis was fussed over by big sisters (they called him "little Jeffie") and taught riding by doting older brothers. Reared a Baptist, he bore an un-Southern-like recalcitrance toward religion, and only much later, during the Civil War, converted to Episcopalianism. Educated by Roman Catholic Dominican friars, he was raised without prejudice against any sect, and like Lincoln, he violently opposed the anti-Catholic crusade of the Nativists and Know-Nothings during the 1840s and 1850s. His patriotism was unqualified and absolute. It was a lesson he learned at his father's knee, but not the only one: he was also impressively well-educated and well-read, attending the nationally famous Transylvania University in Lexington, Kentucky, at the tender age of fifteen. Transylvania then had a reputation that rivaled Harvard's (Thomas Jefferson would write, "We *must* send our children for education to Kentucky [Transylvania] . . . ") and an enrollment that was even larger. Then, in accord with the wishes of his father, who died a year later, Davis went to West Point, where he graduated twenty-third in a class of thirty-three.

His mediocre standing had less to do with his ability and more to do with the fact that he was a bit of a hell-raiser. Though sturdy discipline was the rule, he often flaunted it: in his first year, as a plebe, he was charged for violating the prohibition against drinking at Benny Haven's tavern, and that was just the beginning. Subsequently, he received demerits for spitting on the floor, for sloppy quarters, for long hair during inspection, for visiting during study hours, for absences during reveille, for absences from class and from the evening parade, for firing his musket out his dormitory window, for disobeying orders and using "spirituous liquors," for refusing to march from mess hall, for cooking in his quarters after 8 P.M., and for "foul clothes not in clothes bag." But his class standing and raucous behavior belied an active mind. He knew both Greek and Latin, and could read them in the original; he had a serviceable command of French; he was a self-styled Spanish scholar; he read Virgil, Burns, and Scott; and he loved poetry, memorizing Moore's *Lalla Rookh* and Byron's *Don Juan*.

As a frontier officer, he fought bravely and well, fighting the Indians and personally transporting the captured Indian warrior Black Hawk. From there, he went on to marry the daughter of General Zachary Taylor; by now, however, his military career had already been checkered by continuing rows, a contentious court-marital, and frustration over slow promotion, and Taylor himself had reservations about his daughter embracing the rough, dull life of a soldier's companion. So Davis left the army. But his beloved wife died three months later of malaria—he almost did, too—and it broke his heart. For eight lonely years, he lived in morbid seclusion as a planter at Brierfield, a modest 800-acre plantation near Vicksburg, Mississippi, lent to him by his older brother, Joseph.

When it came to slaves, Davis was anything but a stereotypical Southerner. He was, to be sure, a firm believer in the Southern slave system, but he genuinely saw it as a benevolent institution; in a sense, this was less an example of self-delusion—though it was also some of that—than of self-indoctrination, born out of parochialism and his own laudable personal experience. For many years, he retained not a cruel white overseer, but a black overseer, Jim Pemberton, a faithful slave left to him by his father. Pemberton had once nursed Davis back to health after a dangerous bout with pneumonia, and Davis never forgot it. He loved him like a brother and treated him largely as an equal, and also as a friend; Davis even shared his cigars with Pemberton. By all accounts, with the rest of his slaves, he was a kind, paternalistic master: reportedly when rules were broken, it was solely by a slave jury that punishments were handed out, and Davis reserved for himself only the right to commute or lessen any sentence he deemed overly harsh, or to pardon the offender altogether. His slaves were never flogged. Families were kept together. The sick and the elderly were cared for. And there was no miscegenation. ("Dem Davises never let nobody touch one of their niggers," said one; "We had good grub and good clothes and nobody worked hard," testified another.) Davis made a point of treating his slaves with extreme courtesy—especially, but not only Pemberton—and equally made a point of returning any salute from a black, giving him an elaborate bow or a friendly shake of the hand. Neighboring plantation owners sniffed that the slaves at Brierfield were "spoiled." But Davis also assumed—wrongly—that the treatment of slaves at Brierfield was commonplace; he refused to believe accounts of cruelty, dismissing them as the meddling handiwork of abolitionist fanatics or simply as Northern malice. It never occurred to Davis that both could be true.

By Southern standards, he was often liberal and astonishingly idealistic: much like Lincoln and Thomas Jefferson, he did not believe slavery was the blacks' permanent condition, although he did insist that it would take several generations before it would be wise and practical to emancipate them. "The slave," he said, must be "made unfit for slavery" and "must be made fit for his freedom by education and discipline." But unlike Lincoln, he could never quite carry his convictions to their inexorable political conclusion (although, of course, there were his con-scription measures in the waning months and days of the war) of call-ing for any kind of an end to the institution; indeed, he embraced it fully and totally. Thus, he believed that the Southern case for slavery and its extension rested on firm constitutional and moral foundations, see-ing the limitations that the North sought to impose on slavery less as a deafening ethical question to be wrestled with and more as a naked grab for influence between the two sections. ("The mask is off: the question is before us," he once memorably thundered. "It is a struggle for political power.")

In 1845, he remarried, choosing the tall, stately brunette Varina Howell of Natchez, who was herself a bit of a rarity in the antebellum South. Though her family had little in the way of wealth or pedigree, she was unusually well educated for a Southern girl of that time, having been thoroughly tutored in the Greek and Latin classics for twelve years. Filled with wit and insight, what she lacked in fine Southern ancestry she made up for in Northern blood: her Whig grandfather had been governor of New Jersey. "Would you believe it," she wrote her mother on first meeting her future husband, "he is refined and cultivated and yet he is a Democrat."

That he was. And he cut quite a figure in Southern political and social circles. Though the Davis family lacked a coat of arms and an aristocratic pedigree, and were only second-generation Southerners, Jefferson Davis had blue-blooded manners and high-minded tastes and values. Tall, slim, dramatically handsome, and often saturnine, he had deep-set gray-blue eyes and a sweet musical Southern voice with great rhetorical power. His political career was soon off and running when he won a spot in the U.S. House of Representatives. But his tenure was punctuated by the Mexican War, during which he was elected to the rank of colonel and served under his former father-in-law. Commanding a volunteer regiment, the Mississippi Rifles, he saw action at Monterrey and then helped win the decisive battle of Buena Vista by drawing his small force into a pin-cer and breaking the exquisitely outfitted Mexican cavalry charge; it was a turning point of the conflict, and a turning point in his life. Davis emerged from the war a national hero, and was labeled "the best volunteer officer in the army." President Polk offered him a general's commission. But because he had been badly wounded in the foot at Buena Vista, he turned it down. Instead, he chose to be nominated to the Senate.

His yin of war had met his yang of politics—but there was little harmony. Politics suited him—yet only to a point, even though he initially earned considerable success. Christened "the gamecock of the south," he took his seat in the Senate, where he was now in the company of such mighty orators and legislative lions as Clay and Webster and his personal hero, John Calhoun. With his erudition and sonorous Southern voice, Davis delivered stem-winding, off-the-cuff speeches that quickly earned him the respect of his colleagues and the attention of the country. And as a fierce proponent of Southern rights and states' rights, he also earned the sobriquet "Calhoun of Mississippi." For a Southerner, of course, there was no greater compliment. When the old Fire-eater died in 1850, it was natural that Davis assumed his mantle, becoming the South's leading spokesman.

But for Davis the politician, there was always a built-in tension that he could never easily reconcile. Austere, able, experienced, incorruptible, he had an abiding dislike of the give-and-take of politics. Privately, he could be warm and cordial; socially, he could be quite pleasant, even charming; but on the floor of the Senate or in committee dealings, he was saddled with an aloof and obstinate streak (Sam Houston, the Texas governor, thought him "cold as a lizard"). Once, when a Senate colleague had simply wondered if he would perhaps vote for an appropriations bill, Davis snapped: "Sir, I make no terms. I accept no compromises." Where Lincoln had the common touch, and even the keen sense of the ridiculous so necessary to the art of politics, Davis was saddled with a dominant streak of self-righteousness. Deep within him lurked a dark, insatiable, stubborn vein. This flaw, and it was a flaw, meant that once he made up his mind and adopted a position, he treated virtually any attempt to argue him out of it as an assault on his integrity. For this reason, he was perhaps temperamentally better suited to senatorial oration or a military career, than to the gritty political necessities of a chief executive—a view that he privately seemed to share. It was understandable, then, that fifteen months after leaving the Senate in a failed gubernatorial bid, he accepted the offer of his good friend, President Franklin Pierce, to be his secretary of war, an office in which Davis became the most powerful voice in the cabinet and a forceful administrator.

As war secretary, he displayed great knowledge, considerable foresight, and an innovative spirit (he introduced the minié ball and experimented with breech-loading rifles; he also introduced the camel corps to the Western frontier—they traveled twice as fast as horses, ate less, and could go for three days without water while carrying heavier loads). But his weaknesses then were self-evident. He got into unnecessary, even trivial, quarrels with his general in chief, Winfield Scott ("he was a regular bulldog when he formed an opinion, for he would never let go," noted one of his clerks). Always a furnace of emotions, his inability to differentiate between passing glances and fatal blows would be an omen of things to come.

Yet like the dog chasing a fly, he returned to politics, back to the Senate. In a number of ways, too often little noted, here again Davis was quite advanced for his time and place. He strongly supported the transcontinental railroad, territorial expansion, and free trade. John Quincy Adams, a staunch abolitionist, even warmly praised him for helping to set up the Smithsonian. And unlike many of his colleagues, Davis was acutely aware of the South's weaknesses, especially its lack of industry. In the 1850s, he also urged the South to build up its railroads, to foster greater immigration, and to provide greater state support for higher education. But in each of these cases, he acted as he did because he was an unswerving Southern nationalist. Herein, too, lay the dilemma of Jefferson Davis. He took a progressive line on just about everything— that is, everything except the intertwining issues of Southern rights, states' rights, and slavery, and in this sense, he was bound by the procrustean chains of his Southern environs. As his career advanced, so, too, did his unwavering devotion to the unlimited expansion of slavery, and an equally unwavering devotion to Southern heritage. For this reason, he was ultimately a tragic, even confused creature of historical circumstance: progressive on a host of issues, he was inflexible and dogmatic on one of the greatest issues of his time, slavery; no great believer in the racist theories undergirding slavery, he stoutly defended the institution; a fervent lover of his country, he loved his region even more; a believer in education, he was determined to wall off Northern ideas; he opposed secession, working tirelessly to find common ground between radicals on both sides of the Mason-Dixon line, yet he battled for the extreme claims of the South; a man with a deep humanitarian nature who treated slaves like family, he was woefully blind to the evils of the institution; and immensely talented in the craft of war, he repeatedly gravitated to, or was thrust or drafted into, politics.

Which meant, of course, the presidency of the Confederate States of America.

❧   ❧   ❧

By 1861, he was a sickly man, having suffered from malaria; pneumonia; habitual facial pains; stinging, chronic pain from his war wound; severe earaches; an inflamed red eye; and eyesight that was permanently impaired by prolonged exposure to the blinding snows of the Western frontier. Throughout the war, these conditions only dangerously worsened: to the very end, he was frail, gaunt, agitated, and dyspeptic, with a recurring facial tic, a legacy of the neuralgia that would eventually render him blind in one eye. His physical condition was of course one matter; his leadership the other. Was he equal to the challenge? While many scholars think not, in truth, the picture is often more mixed.

Photographs of Davis at the time neatly capture him: thin-lipped, long-nosed, eyes hooded, the expression forbidding. When he should have been leading, Davis was instead engaged in too many endless quarrels, feuding heedlessly with Joe Johnston and Robert Toombs and Vice President Alexander Stephens and Texas Senator Wigfall and Governor Joseph Brown. His executive management was poor: he never really could decide whether he wanted to be president or secretary of war, and in often seeking to do both, it could be argued he did neither well. He lacked the necessary art of persuasion: Lincoln had to use the veto only three times, and in each case it stuck, while Davis vetoed thirty-eight bills, and all but one was later passed by the Confederate Congress. He was frequently ill, or short-tempered, or autocratic. Some thought him a dictator. And for all his expertise in military affairs, he couldn't make up his mind on what strategy the South should pursue. Should it be offensive? Or defensive? On the one hand, he generally embraced a strategy like that of George Washington in the Revolution, who defended the nation from conquest—and who won by not losing. This meant repeatedly trading space for time, retreating when attacked, avoiding full-scale battles that imperiled his own forces, and counterattacking only when such assaults heralded success. In short, a strategy of attrition, wearing out a better-equipped and far more numerous adversary by compelling him to give up simply by making the war too costly. Yet Davis undercut his own instincts, taking much too seriously his pledge to protect every inch of Confederate soil, thus unwisely dispersing his forces instead of concentrating his smaller numbers of men in more discretely defined areas. Nor did he successfully subdue the hue and cry of Confederate politicians to go on the offensive, to aggressively bring the war to the Yankees, even though it often meant that such bloody victories would ultimately be Pyrrhic ones. In the end, this was one matter where his dogmatism might have served him well, had he stubbornly clung to his own ideas about war-fighting. Instead, here he acted too much like a politician, splitting the difference, with his "offensive-defensive strategy." The strategy in itself was a sensible one, or at least could have been. But because it was never comprehensively or fully thought out, it was applied piecemeal. As a result, the South paid dearly.

Without doubt, his task was an immense one. Born out of conflict, the Confederate nation was riven by rancorous factions, endless bitter disputes, and savage feuding. The striking lack of political parties meant that Davis had no organized structure with which to cultivate discipline or institutionalized loyalty, which, by comparison, had served Lincoln so well. It cost Davis. A martyr to its own ideology of states' rights, the Confederacy was also saddled with a political system wholly unsuited to the grim challenge of total war. A case in point: each state at first raised its own forces and decided when and where they were to be used and who commanded them. For far too many of the South's leaders, the rights of their states were more important than the Confederacy itself; in this regard, the Confederacy went on to repeat many of the mistakes of the early American republic, to which it looked for inspiration. Men from one state at times resisted serving under a general from another—some even disliked leaving their own states to fight; commanders with troops from various states had to negotiate with the states themselves to get more men; the general government repeatedly wrangled with the state governments; and so on, with melancholy regularity. Davis accordingly had to contend with many of the struggles—over men, over money, over supplies—that nearly ruined George Washington in the 1770s. Significantly, like the Founders before him, he only slowly understood the need for a serious federal element to work hand in hand with states' rights in waging a war. As the conflict progressed, Davis increasingly came to embrace the basic tenets of a centralized national state that had been such an anathema to Confederate ideology: national draft laws, impressment, habeas corpus suspension, centralized economic management, and confiscatory taxation. But by then, it would be too late.

Yet for all his considerable weaknesses, Davis was not as totally guileless or ill-suited to the task as his critics may contend.

He grasped the central matter before the Confederacy: battle. "We are," he cried out, "fighting for our existence, and by fighting alone can independence be gained." He did show a surprising capacity for growth, as evidenced by his dispensing with one brick after another of states' rights if they impeded the war effort, right up to his eventual willingness to grant emancipation to slaves who fought for the Confederacy, thereby dooming the institution itself. And he insisted, rightly so, that secession was not a revolution: such logic, Davis averred, was "an abuse of language." We left the Union, he thundered, "to save ourselves from a revolution." Indeed, almost a hundred years of history had made the Confederacy anything but a complete aberration. The Constitution appeared to be largely on his side, as was tradition, and, some could argue, the larger and much longer historical trend of self-determination that would more fully flower in the century to come.

Perhaps most importantly, Davis had guts—and a kind of religious, even mystical belief in his country. But was he now acting like a dreamy madman? as some have said. Or a crazy zealot? Did he not sense what was to come? To be sure, he was thin-skinned, humorless, narrow-minded, and, at times, fatally unimaginative. Yet somebody had to believe in the Confederacy throughout its darkest hours. In history, nearly all leaders who have given birth to new nations or religious movements or empires or great discoveries were, to one extent or another, fanatical. They had to be. From Julius Caesar to Martin Luther, from Magellan to Napoleon, from Bolívar to Galileo, all these men shared common traits: stubborn, steel-willed, driven, secretive, fastidious, zealous, short-tempered. Each, in his own way, was a profound dreamer. To a man, each was ultimately pre-pared to act alone, without encouragement, relying solely on his own inner resolve. Indifferent to approval, reputation, wealth, or even love, they cherished their personal sense of honor, which they allowed no one else to judge. What went wrong, then—and what is perhaps most tragic for Davis personally (though not, of course, for the United States)—was that he was on the losing side. We view him accordingly.

In his final flight, he never gave up, not until the bitter end. Those last April and then early May days of 1865 were frenetic, tense, harrowing. The pace was excruciating. Throughout, he was often agitated or anx-ious. But he never complained or lost his composure. He was always dig-nified. And, as the chase for him grew, so, it seems, did his courage.

The biggest blow—for which he was wholly unprepared—was Lee's surrender. When he first learned of it, he was in Danville, Virginia, with his cabinet. The message was received like a sharp cuff to the stomach; he and his aides fell deathly silent, as the folded note bearing the news passed quietly from hand to hand to hand. In private, Davis later wept. Nonetheless, he was only momentarily fazed by the setback, stubbornly refusing to concede defeat, and resolving to fight all the way to the Mississippi.

He rapped out the order to keep on moving.

Yet after April 15, that task became all the more difficult. He no longer went by train but was escorted by a small band of Tennessee cavalry. Over the course of thirty days, in great heat and through driving rains, with too little sleep and too little nourishment, this fifty-seven-year-old man and his shrinking cabinet would cover a startling 400 miles, 320 of them on horseback: 163 miles more than the distance from Washington, D.C., to New York City, 350 more than a trip from Boston, Massachusetts, to Providence, Rhode Island, 296 more than from Philadelphia to Baltimore.

Davis could withstand the exhaustion. But not so the loss of his generals, or the echoing words of Lee calling on him to give up any thought of partisan warfare.

On April 19, he learned about Lincoln's assassination. "Certainly I have no special regard for Mr. Lincoln," he said. "But there are a great many men of whose end I would rather hear than his. I fear it will be disastrous for our people and I regret it." What he feared even more was Andrew Johnson, whom he regarded as a bitter and vindictive man, who, unlike Lincoln, would grossly punish the South. The retreat continued.

Then to Davis's horror came Johnston's insubordination and surrender on April 26. "I fear the spirit of the people is broken," one Davis aide noted. A disbelieving Davis himself gloomily wrote to his wife, "Panic has seized the country." Actually, by now, the prospects were far bleaker. But despite the harsh judgments of some contemporaries, including Southerners, and by scholars, Davis at least deserves his due for this: he was anything but a coward. Now, with a heightened sense of urgency, he and his entourage kept moving. On to Yorkville, South Carolina, then across the Broad River, then over to the Saludin River, then to Cokesbury. Astonishingly enough, as he moved through a war-torn South Carolina, here, in the lengthy shadow of John Calhoun, the public affection for him was as deep as ever, with buoyant crowds turning out at every stop to cheer him on and to wish him well.

He pledged not to leave Confederate soil as long as there were men in uniform willing to fight for the cause. But in now rejecting surrender, he had assured his own isolation and condemnation. He pressed on.

By May 2, there were far fewer men in his caravan, although there were still 3,000 troops providing him protection. Now came another Rubicon: he huddled privately with his military aides to make one last appeal to those loyal cabinet assistants and military men remaining by his side. It was his last council of war. Remarkably, Davis's passion had not been dimmed by the events of the last thirty days. He believed that if they could somehow weather the temporary panic, the people would once again rally. One more time—and with a straight face—he gave it everything he had, and, on one level, he was not unpersuasive.

"He appealed eloquently to every sentiment and reminiscences that might . . . move a southern soldier," noted one of his aides. But at this stage, he displayed more fervor than judgment. And at this point, it was too late.

The aides shook their heads sadly. Their rejection, though couched in soft terms—they were loyal still—was blunt. They agreed with Lee. The country was exhausted. Any attempt to prolong the war with partisan conflict would be a "cruel injustice." It was time.

Davis rose unsteadily to his feet, curiously feeble, almost tottering. For the first time in the war, he was a thoroughly shaken man.

"Then all is lost," he muttered.

❧   ❧   ❧

Yet Davis, his face lined and lean and intent, refused to quit. In his final flight, he remained dignified, although these were high-strung moments. He bravely sought to put the best face on it. "Dear wife," he wrote to Varina, "This is not the fate to which I invited [you] when the future was rose colored to us both; but I know you will bear it even better than myself, and that, for the two of us, I alone will ever look back reproachfully on my past career." On May 3, Davis's dwindling procession of horses and carriages crossed the Savannah River, into Georgia. Accusing him, falsely, of complicity in Lincoln's assassination, the Union had put a $100,000 price tag on his head. The search for Davis intensified.

Through yet another downpour, he continued to flee.

On May 10, it happened, the very thing Lincoln wanted never to occur. In Georgia, amid talk of hanging and treason, Jefferson Davis was captured by Union cavalry, who taunted him mercilessly. In the wake of Lincoln's death, one of the now departed president's greatest fears had come to pass: the last thin membrane of civility, instead of being strengthened, had seemingly evaporated. To Davis's face, the troops mocked him, like a common criminal, or a babbling, vulgar demagogue. If this was a harbinger of things to come, it was an ominous sign. But there was little doubting that the last vestige of the Confederate government had now ceased to exist.

That very same day, United States President Andrew Johnson issued a formal proclamation. The "armed resistance to the authority of this Government," he declared, ". . . may be regarded as virtually at an end."

✻ ✻ ✻

But for all to be at an end, there was one more boil to be lanced: the capture of the assassin, John Wilkes Booth.

Since Easter Sunday, April 16, an unprecedented manhunt had been under way for Booth and his accomplices. In Washington, Stanton and Gideon Welles worked furiously, pressing every bit of the War and Navy Departments' resources and personnel into a round-the-clock search: soldiers, sailors, cavalry troops, civilians, marshals, the police, detectives, and secret service agents all joined the fray. "Let the stain of innocent blood be removed from the land by the arrest and punishment of the murderers," one War Department poster declared. "Rest neither night nor day until it be accomplished." Now every vessel in the Chesapeake Bay, the Potomac River, and the Virginia shores was scoured. Anyone remotely suspicious was picked up. Even Booth's relatives and his brother, Junius, were fair game. In the days that followed, a reward of $50,000 was placed on Booth's head; lesser amounts for his accomplices. It was an impressive display of force, and mass arrests were soon widespread.

In short order, the prisons were overflowing with hundreds of suspects, an erratic array of potential witnesses and possible conspirators. Most were held for several weeks, usually without any charges. Literally anyone who had the slightest contact with Booth was tossed in jail either as a witness or a coconspirator, including friends, employees at Ford's Theater, and dozens of hapless souls vaguely matching Booth's description, who were randomly picked up in cities across the Union. The belief, widely held, was that the South was responsible. "All circumstances signify," Stanton wrote in one telegram, "a plot laid in Richmond before the capture of that city."

The chase mounted.

By week's end, the extensive search had borne some initial results: Lewis Powell, George Atzerodt, and a host of other more tangential Booth accomplices—Samuel B. Arnold, Michael O'Laughlen, and Edman

Spangler—were all seized and locked in double irons in the hold of an ironclad ship anchored in the Potomac. But, for all the manpower being dedicated to their capture, the dart had not yet quite hit its target.

Booth, and another erstwhile accomplice, Davy Herold, remained at large.

❧   ❧   ❧

From the perspective of today's world, an era of instantaneous communication—modems, faxes, telephones, and e-mail shuffling information from one corner of the globe to another in a matter of nanoseconds, Booth's escape is almost impossible to fathom. But in the beginning, it was almost astonishingly simple. After shooting Lincoln, Booth raced off from the back alley of Ford's Theater, galloping at a full clip toward the Navy Yard Bridge, twenty minutes away. His destination was the backcountry of southern Maryland. At the Navy Yard Bridge, a sentry questioned him closely; remarkably, Booth was able to move considerably faster than the actual news of Lincoln's shooting. Cleverly, Booth provided the sentry with his real name—he was, after all, one of the best-known actors in the world. This did the trick. He was allowed to cross the Anacostia River, the eastern branch of the Potomac. In darkness, he thundered off.

Davy Herold also escaped across the bridge, soon catching up to Booth. The pair pressed on at high speed.

Eight miles south of Washington, they paused at Mary Surratt's tavern in Surrattsville, where they picked up two Spencer carbines, ammunition, and field glasses that had earlier been squirreled away. Booth told the innkeeper, a Confederate sympathizer, "I am pretty certain that we have assassinated the President and Secretary Seward." Again into the night they went. It began to rain.

At four o'clock in the morning, Booth and Herold arrived at the farm of Dr. Samuel Mudd in Charles County, Maryland. Mudd was another sympathizer to the rebellion. Booth was tired, wet, and in pain, his leg having been broken by his twelve-foot jump from the presidential box. Mudd set Booth's injured leg, fashioned a pair of crude crutches for him, and gave him shelter. The actor then slept for most of the day, in an upstairs bedroom, his face buried in his pillow, against the wall. This time, he apparently said nothing about the assassination. Dr. Mudd was totally in the dark.

But as Booth slept, thousands of Union troops were now crawling over the countryside. A detachment of cavalry came close enough that an unnerved Mudd insisted the fugitives leave his property. They raced off, still out of the reach of Union authorities. Mudd would not be so lucky. Within six days, detectives would discover Booth's slit riding boot at his house; Mudd was summarily arrested. But his bad luck would also be Booth's. It was from Mudd that they would learn that Booth was injured. For Stanton's pursuers, this little piece of information was a godsend.

They now concentrated their search on "lame-man" sightings.

But the lame man was nowhere to be found. The fugitives were hiding out amid the dreary thickets and insects of the Zekiah swamp, hoping to cross the Potomac River into Virginia. Normally, this would have been an easy matter; the area was a stronghold of a notoriously pro-Southern population, which in past days would have readily ferried them across. But an ever-growing number of Union troops was combing the countryside and manhandling local residents in the search for information. Frenetic ("I have too great a soul to die like a criminal," Booth explained), he and Herold finally hooked up with a Confederate agent, Thomas Jones, who took care of them for several days. Booth was "exceedingly pale" and his face bore "evident traces of suffering." The agent fed them ham and bread and butter.

Now, listening to the scratch of his own breath, his mouth tightened and eyes pinched, and dreadfully cold, Booth could hear the swishing of feet through the marsh and the rattling of soldiers' sabers, looking for them. On April 21, as ribbons of smoky light filtered off the river and birds beat their wings against the water, there was a break; on a narrow beach where a stream flowed into the Potomac, Booth and Herold boarded a little twelve-foot rowboat. Taking advantage of the momentary lull, they slipped the boat into the water. On their first attempt, however, they failed to catch the right tide and were swept upriver, landing back on the Maryland shore. "I am here in despair," Booth exclaimed. Again they hid. The next evening, they tried again; "Tonight," he noted, "I try to escape these bloodhounds once more." This time the current held. It took them several hours to cross the Potomac in darkness.

Finally, they were in the friendlier territory of Virginia. But even here, help was scarce; otherwise loyal Confederates were worried about the consequences of housing such a prominent fugitive.

Filthy and unshaven, Booth had nowhere to go. The actor resorted to brute force and intimidation. On April 23, he and Herold bullied their way into the one-room cabin of a freeborn black, brutally kicking him and his sick wife out at knifepoint. From there, the next day, they arranged to be ferried on the Rappahannock River, over to Port Royal on the opposite shore. Exhausted, their nerves frayed, they sought refuge at Richard Garrett's tobacco farm. This time, Booth used the alias of James W. Boyd, to match the initials visibly tattooed on his hand. The farm was so isolated that news of the assassination had not yet reached it. Once more, this proved to be Booth's good luck. He began to plot his final escape, to Mexico.

But the luck soon ran out. On Tuesday, April 25, to be precise. Late that afternoon, a detachment of Union cavalry passed right by the Garrett farm; Booth and Herold quickly hid in the woods, weapons at the ready. They successfully eluded the Unionists but in doing so fatally alarmed their hosts. The strange reaction of their guests deeply rattled the Garrett family. "I'm afraid these men will get us into trouble," the father whispered to his two sons. "You had better watch them tonight." He angrily told Booth and Herold that they were no longer welcome. The two anxiously pleaded with him. Could they at least buy his horses? No, Garrett said. Well, one more night, they asked. Eventually, Garrett relented. They could spend the evening, but it would have to be in the tobacco barn.

Around midnight Union troops nearby got a tip as to where Booth was staying. The dragnet quickly closed in. In darkness, by 2 A.M. Wednesday morning, a heavily armed search party had dismounted and was quietly deployed around the Garrett farm. Garrett's dogs suddenly began to bark. When a stunned Richard Garrett opened the front door, in his nightshirt, he found a pistol shoved in his face. "Where are they!" the Union officer demanded.

Garrett stammered, unsure of what to do but refusing to give them up. Eventually the son mutely pointed. Then he blurted out, "They're in there."

"There," of course, was the barn, about fifty yards from the house. Within moments, it was surrounded.

"You men better come out here!" the Union officer shouted, pounding on the double door with the butt of his revolver. Herold came out with his hands up, but Booth refused. Cradling his three pistols and a carbine, he asked for a sporting chance to shoot it out; the Union officer denied his request.

"Well, my brave boys," Booth then shouted defiantly, "then you can prepare a stretcher for me!"

It was at that point that one of the Union officers twisted some hay into a rope, lit it, and threw it through a slat in the back of the barn. It began to burn, exploding into flames.

❧   ❧   ❧

It is a paradox that during the tumult of the Civil War, the theater flourished. The deplorable circumstances of the time, the ferment, the controversy and death, all seemed to create a yearning for entertainment. Consider Lincoln's theatergoing schedule in February and March of 1864 alone. In wartime, he had already seen such second-rate productions as *Leah*, featuring Avonia Jones; the performance of Barney Williams, the Irish comedian; the middlebrow *The Marble Heart*, starring John Wilkes Booth; and James Hackett in the far better *Henry IV*. Even while the war raged, during this, one of its most precarious periods, he somehow squeezed in time to watch a rash of Shakespeare's plays: *Richard III, Julius Caesar, The Merchant of Venice*, and *Hamlet*. Such widespread interest in the theater was, of course, good news for the Booth family, considered the first family of American entertainment. And the widespread interest of the first citizen of the Union would prove to be something else entirely for the youngest Booth son, John Wilkes.

Even for the times, the affinity between John Wilkes Booth and Abraham Lincoln stands as one of the most curious relationships imaginable. For one thing, too often forgotten in the wake of later events is that Lincoln, the war president, was as loathed in his day as he was loved; he may well have been the most reviled president of all. Ironically, Booth the entertainer was far more universally popular among those who knew him, enjoying enthusiastic plaudits and widespread fame, in the North as well as the South. One of his admirers, of course, was President Lincoln. And it is here that the tale darkens.

John Wilkes Booth was born in 1838 in Bel Air, Maryland, the ninth son of ten children, and a bastard at that (his father, Junius Brutus Booth, an alcoholic and mentally unstable rogue, had two wives, one back in England, and one in America). But the Booth family had few peers when it came to the theater. Talented and quirky, Booth's father was considered the greatest Shakespearean performer of his generation; John Wilkes's brother Edwin was even better, and is regarded by many to be among the finest actors in America of all time—Lincoln saw him in four plays during a mere eight weeks in 1864; his brother Junius Booth, Jr., was a successful producer; and his brother-in-law was a noted comedian. A striking, self-centered young man, Booth was his mother's darling. He studied in several private academies around Baltimore, where he made his stage debut at the age of seventeen. By then, he was a serious athlete, too: an expert horseman, a fencer, and a crack pistol shot. His earliest performances were coarse and, some said less charitably, even comical. But he quickly improved, taking on a slew of demanding roles. Soon, he established himself as a rising young Shakespearean star, especially in the South.

He had just the right appearance. A devastatingly handsome man, with dark wavy hair, enticing hazel eyes, and a neatly cropped full mustache, he had an unmistakably alluring look about him, what the Italians might call a *dolce cera* (sweet face), and even a touch of Oriental mystery. Women found him irresistible, and so did his audiences, who were drawn to his exotic demeanor, his flamboyant gestures, and his ranting eloquence. They also took to his impassioned, athletic style of acting. Though he was only five-eight, his bearing was impressively erect and his chest broad, giving the impression of virility and masculinity—which was no doubt helped by the difficult leaps that he used to announce his first appearance on stage, the dashing duels so true-to-life that real blood was drawn, and the torrid love scenes with his stage paramours. The true challenge for an actor in the 1850s was then, as now, Shakespearean roles, and enchanted Dixie audiences flocked to his captivating portrayals of Hamlet as the eccentrically tortured prince and Richard III as the sinister fiend. Theater critics were rare back then, but Booth was subjected to some harsh criticism (while one termed him an actor of "genius and talent," another lashed into him as "crude," "raw," "given to boisterous declamation"). The criticism stung deeply. Still, as is often the case, popular acclaim ruled, and audiences packed his performances, making him one of the most prized actors in the country. By 1864, he was earning $20,000 a year, double what Robert E. Lee was making as general in chief of the Confederate armies, infinitely more than the rebel privates, who had just been given a raise to $18 a month, and considerably more than the average annual earnings for a working family in the North, which was $297.

He was also one of history's great scamps. Southerners loved his vivacity, his passion, his talent as a raconteur, his ability to hold a good stiff drink. More often than not, he was irritable, moody, prone to depressions, and just as prone to getting drunk ("anything," he once said, "to drive away the blues"). And his erotic exploits were the stuff of Hollywood legend: he was notoriously available to assorted mistresses, lovers, adoring young virgins, actresses, prostitutes, and theater groupies all over. One young lover, scorned in Albany, stabbed herself in a fit of distress. At another point, while betrothed to the daughter of a prominent senator, the ever-faithful Lucy Hale of New Hampshire, he was regularly slipping naked into the bed of his mistress, Ella Turner, a lusty diminutive redhead. At the same time, there were at least four other women whose skirts he evidently sought. Upon his death, photographs of each of them would be found on his person. Yet all this was not out of pure lasciviousness; he also used his good looks and sexual appetite as pawns in a much larger stage on which he was determined to play the leading role. That, of course, came later.

While he was from Maryland, technically the dividing line between North and South, like many other Marylanders, he fancied himself a member of the Southern gentry. And where his older brother Edwin harbored deep and abiding Union tendencies, voting for Lincoln *twice*, Booth held militant Confederate sympathies. "If the North conquers us," he grumbled to his sister Asia, "it will be by numbers only." "If the

North conquer *us?*" his sister replied, astonished. But "we are *of* the North." "Not I!" Booth scornfully responded. "So help me God! My soul, life, and possessions are for the South."

Apparently so. When the war broke out, he did little to conceal his sympathies for the Confederacy. He was a staunch supporter of slavery (in his words, "one of the greatest blessings [both for themselves and us . . .]"), and his contempt for Lincoln was rabid and untamed. He was offended by Lincoln's "appearance," "his pedigree," "his coarse low jokes and anecdotes," "his vulgar similes," and "his frivolity." He was also offended by Lincoln's war efforts, seeing him as the vilest of tyrants. Soon, hate became preoccupation, preoccupation became fixation, then fixation became fanaticism. He worried that the Northern president would overthrow the "constitution," and that he would be "made a King in America," as he once told his brother. And that was what he eventually would become determined to prevent.

Lincoln's reelection in 1864 drove Booth to the breaking point, until he hatched a plan to kidnap the tyrant in the White House and take him to Richmond, to be held for the ransom of the thousands of rebel prisoners now withering away in Union jails. To carry out his plan, he recruited a band of misfits, dregs, and old friends drawn from Washington and Baltimore. Nonetheless, given the circumstances, there was a sort of crude logic to his scheme—and to the men he chose. There were his boyhood chums Samuel Arnold and Michael O'Laughlen; there was baby-faced John Surratt, who had once studied to be a Catholic priest and who had firsthand knowledge of the Confederate underground active in southern Maryland; there was George Atzerodt, the German immigrant, who ferried Confederate spies across the Potomac and knew all the creeks and inlets; there was the hulking Lewis Powell, who had once ridden with Mosby (or so he said) and could provide brawn and violence; and there was young Davy Herold, dim-witted and immature, whose principal value oddly seemed to be that he clerked in the drugstore where Lincoln bought his medicines, but who also knew the poorly mapped roads below Washington well.

The circumstances surrounding Booth's exploits are among the murkiest of the war, and impossible to confirm or explain with total certitude.

Almost unique in Civil War America, he moved with unfettered freedom across Confederate and Union lines alike—his traveling pass was, he boasted, signed by General Grant—shuttling from Montgomery, Columbus, and Richmond in the South, to Albany, Cincinnati, Philadelphia, and New York in the North. At various points, he conferred with rebel agents in Maryland, then Boston, then Canada, out of which he eventually came up with the scheme to abduct Lincoln and spirit him behind Confederate lines in Virginia. Did the Confederate government know about any of this? Or authorize, or approve of any of Booth's plans? Like all great mysteries, this one appears destined to remain unsolved. But it is certainly tinged with conspiracy, the only question being, conspiracy with whom? Most historians dismiss any involvement of the Confederate leadership, including Jefferson Davis, although newer scholarship has reopened the debate. But whatever Davis's role, which does seem unlikely, it is clear that at the lower levels of the Confederate secret service, the abduction of the Union president was under consideration: in fact, Booth's scheme was very much like one which Confederate authorities permitted Thomas Conrad to attempt in the fall of 1864. (And it wouldn't have been the first time that a secret service had carried out plans of which its higher-ups would never have approved.)

Whatever the case, throughout these dismal months of fall 1864, Booth and his fellow conspirators hunched over maps, explored roads, and examined drawings of the White House. They trailed the president on his carriage and horseback rides, as well as on his frequent theater visits, invariably kept at an annoying distance by the heavy cavalry guard or private detail watching the chief executive. The plotting continued. Booth had special riding boots made, complete with pockets sewn into them that enabled him to carry letters and illicit communiqués. That winter, he went a step further, giving up acting altogether so that he could devote his energies full-time to his plans. His meetings often took place at the Surratt tavern, owned by Surratt's mother, Mary, or at her Washington boardinghouse on H Street. Over the ensuing months, he shelled out more than a hefty $10,000 to pay for supplies: weapons, chloroform, ropes, a boat, horses, a wagon, a stable behind Ford's; and meals, drink, and lodging for the plotters. He feted the assassins with oysters and champagne. Finally, he booked a room at the National Hotel near Ford's Theater. This was to be his personal base of operations. All was now ready.

His first plan, to capture Lincoln while he was attending Ford's, and bind and lower him from the box, fizzled as a result of its own tenuousness; it was almost laughable in its conception. A second, far more practical plan, also went awry: on March 17, 1865, he had planned to capture Lincoln while he was riding his carriage on the outskirts of the city. At the last moment, Lincoln changed itineraries, electing to remain in the city and review a regiment of returning Indiana volunteers. Ironically, that day Lincoln himself was at the National Hotel, accepting a captured Confederate flag.

For Booth, it was a debacle—and mortifying. But more chances would present themselves. He persevered. His first real opportunity for action had actually come on March 4, Inauguration Day, which he had attended with Senator Hale's daughter, Lucy. It was around this time when the thought struck him that rather than abduct the president, he could simply assassinate him. Standing there outside the Capitol rotunda, in plain sight of Lincoln, he told himself, "What an excellent chance I had to kill the president."

After these lost opportunities, O'Laughlen, Surratt, and Arnold broke away, but the other three remained. That was more than enough for Booth, as his new plan metastasized and slowly evolved. For Booth, these were difficult days. The waning of the fortunes of the Confederacy drove him into deep depression. So did some questionable investments that lost him money. He began drinking heavily. And, having always had trouble sifting illusion from reality, he now began concocting a fervid new role for himself: not as Confederate agent but as something much grander, a kind of messianic reincarnation, a second coming of the larger-than-life characters whose lines he had so passionately uttered, William Tell and, more often than not, the family hero, Brutus, who brought down the tyrannical Caesar. Just as he had stood there in 1859 at the hanging of John Brown, the madman who helped instigate the war, he was also there at Lincoln's White House address on the rainy evening of April 11, as the war was coming to a close. When the president recommended suffrage for educated blacks, Booth now snarled, "By God I'll put him through." He even urged

Lewis Powell to shoot Lincoln on the spot. Powell refused. At this point, in disgust, he muttered, "that is the last speech he will ever make." No more accurate prediction had ever been delivered.

The time had finally come. After April 11, he concluded, "Our cause being almost lost, something decisive and great must be done." Three days later, on April 14, he learned that Lincoln would be attending Ford's; it was then that he decided to implement his plan. Was he now dwelling solely in hate-filled fantasy? Consider this: for all the harebrained scheming, and despite his decidedly amateur coconspirators, what is so remarkable is how close he actually came not simply to killing Lincoln but to decapitating the executive trio of the United States. The weakest link in his plan turned out to be George Atzerodt, who *only* at the last second begged off (as would later be revealed, he had said, "I enlisted to abduct the President of the United States, not to kill him"). Only history can contemplate the enormous consequences had Andrew Johnson been successfully murdered as well—or if the still largely untested presidential transition process had gone awry.

But that is small consolation. For on April 14, at 10:14 that night, when Booth pulled the trigger of his derringer, he forever mingled his fate with Abraham Lincoln's—and with the history of the nation. And like many a fanatic, he jeopardized what he had hoped to save: placing the enormous stock of the Union government's goodwill, engendered toward the South by the touching surrender at Appomattox, at total risk.

Notably, that seemed as true on April 26, when the barn he was hiding in at the Garrett farm went up in flames and lit the darkness, as it does now.

❧　❧　❧

"Let me die bravely," Booth had written just days earlier.

It was now around 4:30 A.M. Union troopers, peering through the gaps between the barn boards, could see Booth hobbling about with a carbine in one hand and a revolver in another. "He was as beautiful as the statue of a Greek god," recalled the young Richard Garrett, "and as calm in that awful hour." As Booth made his move toward the barn door, a shot rang out. Booth fell to the ground, face first, then pitched over.

He was still breathing. But barely. The bullet had cut through the right side of the assassin's neck, severing his spinal cord. He was paralyzed. And dying.

In the half-light that precedes dawn, Union solders dragged him away from the burning barn and placed him on the porch of the Garrett farmhouse. Bleeding, dirty, and sweaty, his breath shallow, he hovered in and out of consciousness, at one point begging his captors to kill him. They refused. They wanted the reward—and vengeance. A doctor arrived from nearby Port Royal, but announced there was nothing he could do. The wound was mortal. Slowly, the sun began to climb into the sky, signaling a new day. By happenstance, it was Booth's birthday. He was twenty-seven.

It was all morbid and melodramatic, and quite real. And in a last bit of telling symbolism, while Lincoln lasted a full nine hours and seven minutes with a bullet in his head, Booth survived only two and a half hours. Just before he died, he asked to see his hands.

"Useless," his purple lips muttered, "useless."

Whatever he meant by this—his paralyzed hands? the assassination? the rebellion?—we will never know. At another point he had moaned, "Tell my mother that I did it for my country—that I die for my country." This final statement contained perhaps the most pungent note. Booth had always clamored for fame. As he once said to a friend, he would "make his name remembered by succeeding generations." In all his infamy, that was certainly proven true. But there was another, far more profound truth that, in his growing rage and madness, Booth had somehow gleaned. About a week earlier, while on the run, Booth had ripped out several pages from his pocket diary and written a long, rambling explanation of his actions. Much of what he said was labored, contrived, dissembling, or inflated.

But not this one observation: "The country is not—April 1865 what it was."

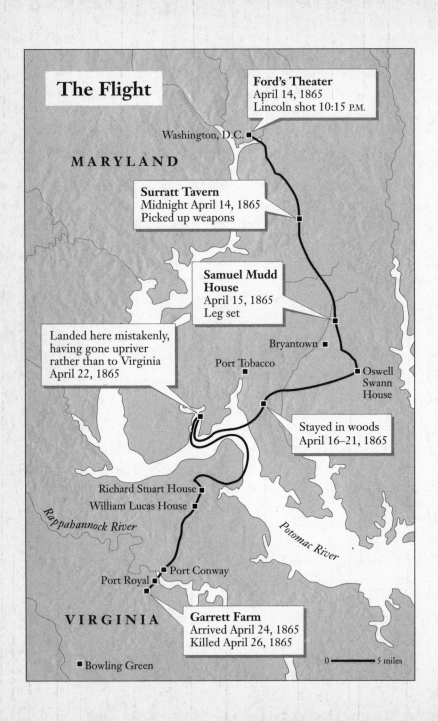

The Flight

Ford's Theater
April 14, 1865
Lincoln shot 10:15 P.M.

Washington, D.C.

MARYLAND

Surratt Tavern
Midnight April 14, 1865
Picked up weapons

Samuel Mudd House
April 15, 1865
Leg set

Landed here mistakenly, having gone upriver rather than to Virginia
April 22, 1865

Bryantown

Port Tobacco

Oswell Swann House

Stayed in woods
April 16–21, 1865

Richard Stuart House

William Lucas House

Rappahannock River

Potomac River

Port Conway

Port Royal

VIRGINIA

Garrett Farm
Arrived April 24, 1865
Killed April 26, 1865

Bowling Green

0 —— 5 miles

PART 4

Late Spring, 1865

8

Reconciliation

As long lines of refugees crept home, news of the war's end spread rapidly across the Northern capital, across the Union, across America. In the North, it raced instantaneously, over the vast web of telegraph wires, from city to city. In the South, it moved far more slowly, often crawling from town to town, from mouth to mouth. But move it did.

And what now? These final days turned not on the issues of battle or the fibers of war, but on the sinews of politics and justice. But foremost was the question of healing. The North had gambled with total war and won; the South had wagered all and lost; the Confederacy was no more. Could these two distant sides now reconcile themselves to each other?

Even as the guns of war grew still, emotions seethed. The hate, of course, was the most perilous. In the South, it was perhaps understandable—but it did not augur well for the future. One Southern innkeeper told a journalist that Yankees had murdered his soldier sons, torched his house, and taken his slaves. "They left me one inestimable privilege—to hate 'em," he drawled. "I git up at half past four in the morning, and sit up till twelve at night, to hate 'em." Swore another Southerner, a young planter: "I have vowed that if I should have children—the first ingredient of the first principle of their education shall be uncompromising hatred and contempt of the Yankee." To which he added: "Day by day and hour by hour does the deep seated enmity I have always had . . . for the accursed Yankee nation increase & burn higher." A Confederate matron, Henrietta Lee, whose house and seven outbuildings had been set aflame by the Union, made her venomous feelings known directly to the Federal commander: "Hyena-like, you have torn my heart to pieces! . . . Demon-like, you have done it without pretext of revenge . . . Your name will stand on history's pages as the Hunter of weak women, and innocent children: the Hunter to destroy defenseless villages and . . . torture afresh the agonized hearts of widows."

Said another woman quite simply: "Oh how I hate the Yankees! I could trample on their dead bodies and spit on them!"

The hatred, the bitterness, the vehemence would not dissipate overnight. Nor would the despondency. Whatever the grievous moral sins of the South, the economic damage and annihilation of Southern property was largely without parallel. At least two-thirds of assessed Southern wealth had vanished during the war. Neither the nobility in the French revolution, nor the Russian serf owners in 1861, nor the slave owners of the West Indies in the nineteenth century (nor, for that matter, the owners of businesses nationalized by twentieth-century socialists in Western Europe) had to face such an overwhelming loss of property as did the slave owners of the South. To many Southerners, it seemed that not since Roman times had an entire people lost so much.

Most daunting of all was perhaps not the physical or economic damage but the emotional wreckage. Mary Chesnut, the astute, articulate Southern hostess and socialite, her home ransacked and she reduced to selling butter and eggs with her faithful maid to earn a little money ($12 a month), expressed this cascade of sentiments eloquently in her diary. "The deep waters are closing over us," she wrote. "We are scattered—stunned—the remnant of heart left alive with us." Elsewhere she penned, "A feeling of sadness hovers over me now, day and night, that no words can express . . . They are everywhere these Yankees—like red ants—like the locusts and frogs which were the plagues of Egypt." She later continued, "I do not think I ever did as much weeping—or as bitter—in the same space of time. I let myself go." And again, "I cried with a will . . . I thought I was very ill. They thought I was dying." And finally, she added, "I wish I had died." Nor was she alone. Listen to the suicidal words of the widow Mary Vaughn— her father, her infant son, and her husband now all dead. Writing from her plantation home, ironically named Sunny Side, she said, "I have but one wish and that is to die." "Why," she asked, "will not God smite me . . . too?" "I have not read my bible since Charlie [my husband] died," she confided. "My tears and feelings seem frozen. I feel but one thing, I am alone, utterly desolate."

By late April 1865, then, the Confederate world heard only faint echoes of the lively, hotheaded, hot-blooded, vivacious, bustling antebellum era: the streets were filled with barefoot survivors ambling despondently, women sorting through piles of rubble, pale men gathering to exchange meager goods. The enormity of the Reconstruction challenge was staggering: powerful plantation owners were now without homes; prosperous bankers were now beggars; hordes of hungry young children, roaming the alleyways, were now dirt-smudged orphans; robust generals, hobbling on homemade crutches, were now cripples; rigidly proud Southern ladies now humbly lined up for Federal rations. For far too many, the faculty of wonder had been dulled; enthusiasm had given way to endurance, excitement to bankruptcy; death was glumly familiar, and sorrow all too tragically numbed. It was there to see, in every direction: railroad service had largely come to a halt; commerce was virtually nonexistent ("our people haven't any money, Sir!"); civil authority was scant. Refugees packed the roads, the saddest sight of all. Psychologists who have studied the impact of natural disasters on society—earthquakes, hurricanes, fires, floods—speak bleakly of a broad and terrible social numbing that occurs, afflicting not simply those directly affected but whole generations living in a disaster's merciless wake. It is impossible to measure the full-fledged effect of the war on the Southern psyche. But this much can be said: in these waning days, Southerners were incoherent with grief, their land diseased and without a cure.

So great was the sense of gloom across the battle-scarred South that a Northern journalist, eyeing the defeated Southerners, penned the following glum observation: "They expected nothing, were prepared for the worst; would have been thankful for anything . . . They asked no terms, made no conditions. They were defeated and helpless—they submitted."

By contrast, in the North, the picture was mixed. For many, they or their loved ones had cheated death and survived. The war had been fought; a great victory had been won; the Union had been preserved; and they were rejoicing high on a cloud of euphoria, which was both understandable and ominous—ominous because their celebration was the South's heartbreak, and the two were largely irreconcilable. And across much of the North, too, anger and rage also ruled. "All over the Union," wrote Margaret Leech, the noted historian, "a hoarse cry of vengeance sounded a discordant requiem for Lincoln." Discordant it was. It was one thing to keep the country together by the force of arms, quite another, as Lincoln had so fervently recognized, to bind up its wounds. Was this to be, then, only a temporary reconciliation—with Lincoln's vision ready to become unglued and undone at the next opportunity?

Hate, despondency, and vengeance now loomed like a hydra for America: they could have steeped the country in rancor and chaos, and destroyed any possibility of true union.

*   *   *

But they did not. Over 620,000 lay dead, one-twelfth of the North and an astonishing one-fifth of the South; all told, it was the most battle deaths in the country's history, as great as in all of the nation's other wars combined. Yet, remarkably, as the North and South, leaders and citizens alike, struggled to adjust to the new order, they rose to the occasion. Somehow, through the blurry, snarling mists of war, and for a brief shining moment before the bitter taste of Reconstruction, civility and restraint ruled long enough to avert disarray and turmoil.

For Unionists and Confederates both, there was everywhere a notion that somehow they had lived through history—and everyone wanted a piece of it, literally. The apple tree under whose shade Lee had rested before surrendering at Appomattox, was quickly sliced up, hacked away at, and peeled off by enterprising soldiers and, within hours, had been stripped clean, until all that was left was a gigantic hole, every little piece of bark and wood taken to be enshrined as an heirloom, passing from one generation to the next. As soon as Lee and Grant had left the Wilmer McLean house, that, too, was stripped—Lee's table, Grant's table, the brass candlesticks, a stone inkstand, a child's doll, the upholstery from the chairs and sofas cut to ribbons and the cane-bottom seats sliced into strips—each item taken for posterity. At the passing of the armies, bits of the Confederate battle flags were ripped, lovingly folded, and carefully stowed away in pants pockets, to become treasured reminders for the ages; and so, too, the Peterson House, where Lincoln died, again stripped clean, the very wallpaper peeled off the walls. Even the scaffold on which the Confederate assassination conspirators were later hanged was cut up for souvenirs. And in countless parlors and porches, battle stories would be told and retold, to the merry rumble of children's and grandchildren's voices, or amid the scent of pine and wax candles and steaming hot cider on a cold winter's day, until the feeling prevailed that everyone of consequence had been there, had valiantly climbed those hills, dodged those bullets, survived those wounds.

Indeed, everywhere across America there was an awareness of endings and beginnings. The South had to struggle with its destitution; the North had to wrestle with its grief; the country as a whole had to ponder: what next?

❧   ❧   ❧

In the North, it began with mourning.

In New York, on 550 Broadway, precisely at 7:22 A.M. on April 15, the clock at Tiffany's & Co., held aloft by a huge wooden Atlas, had come to a halt. This was no doubt fitting, for, as was well known, Charles Lewis Tiffany greatly esteemed Lincoln.

Across town, in Brooklyn, Walt Whitman was at home when he heard the news. His mother prepared their breakfast, as usual, but it was left untouched and unnoticed, as were the rest of the day's meals. He sipped a half cup of coffee, and after pushing his plate of food away, he scoured every newspaper, silently passing them back and forth with his mother. Then he crossed over to Manhattan and, to darkening skies and driving rain, trudged up Broadway, past shuttered stores hung with black.

"Lincoln's death," he wrote in his notebook, "—black, black, black—as you look toward the sky—long broad black, like great serpents."

Four days later, farther north, in Concord, Massachusetts, all business and labor was suspended between eleven and two o'clock, as the townspeople moodily gathered in the local Unitarian church. Music was played and selections from the Scriptures and prayers were read. Then Ralph Waldo Emerson gave a somber address: "Rarely was [a] man so fitted to events," he said of Lincoln, about whom he had often had severe reservations. "Only Washington can compare with him in the future."

To the south, it would take a full seven days for Mary Chesnut to receive the news of the assassination, which arrived for her husband on April 22 in a sealed envelope, by secret dispatch. She opened it. "It is simply maddening, all this," she wrote. A friend of hers saw it differently: "See if they don't take vengeance on us," she warned, "now that we are ruined and cannot repel them any longer." Another friend quipped defiantly: "I call that a warning to tyrants!"

By then, though, Lincoln had been eulogized, his funeral had been held, and his remains had begun the long journey home to Springfield. On Wednesday, April 19, Lincoln's casket spent its final hours lying in state in the East Room of the White House. Outside, the sun beamed, and a gentle breeze caressed the sky. Inside, black was everywhere: on the chandeliers, on the ornate gilt frames of the mirrors, in the adjoining rooms, even on the steps. The East Room itself was hushed, dim, somber. Lincoln's coffin rested on a flower-covered catafalque, a bed of roses at his feet. Even in death, his gangly frame filled the open casket; his head rested on a white pillow, a queer smile fixed on his lips. At eleven that morning, the services began.

Six hundred people crowded into the room. All of official Washington was here: President Johnson and his cabinet, Senator Sumner and his congressional colleagues, Justice Chase and the Supreme Court, generals and the diplomatic corps, Lincoln's personal cavalry and bodyguards, his personal aides and his sons, Robert and Tad, standing at the foot of the coffin, grief-stricken. At the other end, General Grant sat, alone, his numbed gaze fixed on a cross of lilies, a black mourning crepe wound around his arm. In full view, he wept, later maintaining that this was the saddest day of his life. For his part, President Johnson stood erect and quiet, facing the middle, his hands crossed on his breast. Four ministers spoke and delivered their prayers. Then the casket was closed.

With machinelike efficiency, twelve veteran corps sergeants lifted the coffin, carrying it out into the funeral car, into the sunlit day, into the dirge of bells tolling and bands playing for the dead. In slow time, the funeral procession started up Pennsylvania Avenue. With a detachment of black troops in the lead, it moved, in careful, measured, rhythmic steps. Lincoln's empty boots sat eerily in the stirrups of his riderless horse, which followed behind, as though ready to join his master in the afterlife, while columns of mourners trudged to the steady, muffled roll of drums. Arms reversed, battalions and regiments were next. Soon the lines curved and swelled, like the great blue sky, with wounded soldiers, torn and bandaged men, marching along. Behind them came a cortege of black citizens, stretching from curb to curb in neatly ordered lines of forty—4,000 of them all told, in dark coats and shiny white gloves, clasping hands, and quiet, as they strode along. In their wake, heavy artillery rumbled.

When the procession reached the Capitol, the sergeants gently lifted Lincoln into the rotunda, where he lay in state on another catafalque. All the oil paintings and bright white statues were covered, except for the figure of George Washington, on which a simple black sash was tied. During that day, and the next, thousands of people filed through, to get one last glimpse and pay their last respects. Noah Brooks recorded: "Like black atoms moving over a sheet of gray, the slow moving mourners . . . crept silently in two dark lines across the pavement of the rotunda . . . "

The next day, April 21, a nine-car funeral train bore Lincoln from the capital. It would make a journey of fourteen days and 1,662 miles, back to Illinois, retracing the route that a freshly elected United States president had taken to Washington four years earlier.

The train crept forward, to ringing bells and through the soft, spring landscape. All along the route, people gathered, watching in stunned silence as the train rolled by under the velvety sky. In Philadelphia, Lincoln's coffin was placed in Independence Hall, where a double line of mourners stretched three miles deep. Among them was former President Buchanan, just one day shy of his seventieth birthday; ignoring his advancing age, he had driven his buggy all the way from Lancaster, Pennsylvania, to see the fallen president. In New York City, the procession continued for four hours. Eighty-five thousand mourners accompanied the funeral hearse through the streets beneath a thicket of signs. "Mankind has lost a friend and we a President," one sign said. Another read: "In sorrowing tears the nation's grief is spent." A tearful Walt Whitman would never forget this moment: from that time on, every spring, with its lilacs blooming and the season blossoming, would remind him of the coffin passing in the street. Six-year-old Theodore Roosevelt was there, too, leaning out of the second-floor window, watching the spectacle from his grandfather's town house on Broadway. In Albany, Lincoln rested in the statehouse, and people came all though the night to lay their eyes on his open coffin. Two presidents, one former and one future, would rush to Buffalo to join the long lines of mourners: Millard Fillmore and Grover Cleveland. Then the train steamed west, past farmers kneeling in their planting fields, to Cleveland, where a special outdoor pavilion was set up—for no outdoor public building was large enough to accommodate the expected crowds—through which 10,000 mourners passed each hour, braving a cold, steady rain. In all, 150,000 came. Indianapolis followed, on the night run. It was lit up by bonfires, with attentive crowds standing in the rain, mute and still, as the train slowly glided by, like a ghost. In Chicago, the hearse was shepherded by thirty-six young women, dressed in white, representing each state in the restored Union. There, too, were Lincoln's fellow Illinoisians, silent columns of heartbroken colleagues and friends marching lockstep by his side in one subdued, final tribute.

On May 4, the procession came to an end, across the prairies to Springfield, Lincoln's home. Carried in a magnificent black and silver hearse, Lincoln was then gently lifted into the chamber of the Illinois house of representatives, where an unknown but ambitious lawyer had gotten his political start and would later warn, "A house divided against itself cannot stand . . ." The official Illinois delegation of mourners, swathed in black, gathered before his home like a Union brigade, preparing its gallant charge for the final funeral run to Oak Ridge Cemetery. In fact, the procession was led by a general, Joseph Hooker. Here, a vault had been cut deep into the green hillside, amid evergreens and sprays of hundreds of spring flowers. Through another rain, this one soft, the slow march began, as thousands more followed to watch as Lincoln's casket was laid to rest.

The final tribute for "Father Abraham" was more symbolic, but no less appropriate. Searching for some way to express their grief, countless Americans gravitated to bouquets of flowers: lilies, lilacs, roses, and orange blossoms, anything which was in bloom across the land. Thus was born a new American tradition: laying flowers at a funeral.

❧　❧　❧

After the mourning came pageantry, two days of mighty national catharsis and unity.

On May 22, the emblems of mourning were taken down, as Washington prepared itself for the Grand Review of the Armies of the Republic. For four war-filled years, the city had been crowded, but never quite like this. All across town, throngs collected in anticipation, by Willard's and Lafayette Square, the Capitol and the Patent Office, the Treasury and the Canal. In Georgetown, a group of Boston girls, glowing, proud, tearful, excited, and jubilant, assembled. In the nostalgic chamber of the country's mind, their chant upon seeing the gathering troops that day would never be forgotten: "What regiment are you?" they cried, and the roar would come back: "Michigan!" Then once more: "What regiment are you?" And this time came: "Wisconsin!" Again a thundering: *"What regiment are you?"* And back came the shout: "IOWA!" And on it went.

At dawn the next morning, as a soft breeze blew, the American flag was run up the pole of the White House, now at full staff for the first time since Lincoln's death. Miles upon miles of Stars and Stripes were everywhere, as U. S. Grant took his place, side by side with President Johnson, to watch the march of the triumphant Union armies down Pennsylvania Avenue from the Capitol. This great procession of 150,000 men would take two full days, while thousands of schoolchildren on holiday lined the avenue, hoisting flags, humming patriotic songs, raining the soldiers' path with a bountiful shower of flowers. Here was the titanic armada of the United States, the mightiest concentration of power in history. The first day was dominated by the Army of the Potomac, Washington's own army. This was the machine that had halted Robert E. Lee at Antietam, stymied him on the third day at Gettysburg, chased him down along the horrible and bloodstained path to Appomattox, and subdued him at the McLean House. Brilliantly uniformed, it moved with the clean, disciplined strides mastered on a thousand marches between the bloodshed of Bull Run and Sayler's Creek. The mechanical precision of the day was interrupted only when General George Custer's horse was startled by a wreath thrown in the road. With his buckskin breeches, trademark red scarf, and mane of long yellow hair flapping in the wind, Custer galloped madly past the reviewing stand—as the crowd gasped—and then with a kick, he wheeled his horse gracefully around and returned to the head of his column. On this day, all was well with the Union.

And so, too, the next. At nine sharp, Sherman's great army took its turn. Their contrast with the troops the day before couldn't have been greater: where the men of the East were crisp and well kept, they were sunburned and shaggy and wore loose shirts; and where the Easterners were stocky, sophisticated, mesomorphic, Sherman's men of the West were taller, bonier, with the rough, gaunt look of the frontier. The crowd loved them just the same. They erupted in shouts of "Hurrah!" Weren't these the men who had rescued Lincoln before the fateful, decisive election of 1864? Weren't these the men who had taken Atlanta and burned Columbia? And the cheers grew even louder at the sight of Sherman himself, with his battered slouch hat in hand, his auburn beard grizzled, his face wrinkled, his popularity now greater than ever.

By day's end, at long last, it had come time for closure and moving on—at least, for the Union.

❧ ❧ ❧

George Bancroft, the eminent nineteenth-century American historian, told a Massachusetts regiment in 1861: "We have heard much talk about the power of the people; it is left to you to demonstrate that there is in existence a people of the United States." Lincoln was now buried; the North had witnessed an astonishing display of pomp in the grand review; and now, in the South, however much it may have chafed at the Union festivities—and it did—there remained the task of becoming part of the country again. There was, however, an ironic interlude. After driving rains, on May 12 and 13, 1865, one more sizable battle was waged, this time on the banks of the Rio Grande at Palmito Ranch in Texas. Here, where the air is sweet with oranges and lemons, and lush green fields run with the river, squared off by towering palms, the two armies battled once more and the last one killed was a Union man: Private John J. Williams of the Thirty-fourth Indiana. This final skirmish was a resounding Confederate victory.

It was of little solace. For the South, theirs would not be an overnight chameleonlike adaptation to the changing world; good Southerners, then or now, would not as likely make it on Madison Avenue. They were too proud of their eccentricities, of their fanciful customs and ingrained sense of tradition, of their antique etiquette and equally antique honor, of their syrupy voices and refusal to be seduced by the latest fashion and swept away by the latest tide of changing sentiment. But tradition was one thing, the future was another. Now the Stars and Stripes flew indisputably across the South, not everywhere, but enough places: Richmond and Montgomery, Atlanta and Charleston, Mobile and Tallahassee. And once proud Confederates struggled to reintegrate themselves into the United States, and to once again become, as Robert E. Lee had urged, "loyal citizens." Too often uncelebrated by history and at the time little noticed, it happened—in fits and starts but it did happen—in a thousand little ways and in a thousand places, all across the South.

"I am a pauper," noted one now destitute Southerner, a friend of Mary Chesnut's. But, she added stoically, putting her best face on things: "I am smiling and as comfortable as ever." Another, Sam Watkins, a Confederate private who had quietly returned to the family farm in Columbia, Tennessee, when the war was all over, to work the fields by day and write his memoirs by night, concluded, "the sun rises over the hills and sets over the mountains, the compass just points up and down, and we can laugh now at the absurd notion of there being a north and a south . . . We are one and undivided."

Not completely, for the hate was still too strong, but it was a start. And people looked for signs of healing. One of the more poignant moments occurred in Richmond late that spring. It was a warm Sunday at St. Paul's Episcopal Church, and an older man, one of the church's many distinguished communicants, who had spent the last four years in war, was sitting in his customary pew. With his shoulders rounded, his middle thickened, his hair snow-white and beard gray, as usual, he attracted the attention of the rest of the church. But then so did another parishioner.

As the minister, Dr. Charles Minnergerode, was about to administer Holy Communion, a tall, well-dressed black man sitting at the western gallery (which was reserved for Negroes) unexpectedly advanced to the communion table—unexpectedly because this had never happened here before. Suddenly, the image of Richmond redux was conjured up—a flashback to prewar years. Usually whites received communion first, then blacks—a small but strictly adhered to ritual, repeated so often that to alter it was unthinkable. This one small act, then, was like a large frontier separating two worlds: the first being that of the antebellum South, the second being that of post–Civil War America. The congregation froze; those who had been ready to go forward and kneel at the altar rail remained fixed in their pews. Momentarily stunned, Minnergerode himself was clearly embarrassed. The horror—and surprise—of the congregation were no doubt largely visceral, but Minnergerode's silent retreat was evident. It was one thing for the white South to endure defeat and poverty, or to accept the fact that slaves were now free; it was quite another for a black man to stride up to the front of the church as though an equal. And not just at any church, but here, at the sanctuary for Richmond's elite, the wealthy, the well-bred, the high-cultured.

The black man slowly lowered his body, kneeling, while the rest of the congregation tensed in their pews. For his part, the minister stood, clearly uncomfortable and still dumbfounded. After what seemed to be an interminable amount of time—although it was probably only seconds—the white man arose, his gait erect, head up and eyes proud, and walked quietly up the aisle to the chancel rail. His face was a portrait of exhaustion, and he looked far older than most people had remembered from when the war had just begun. These days had been hard on him. Recently, in a rare, unguarded moment he had uncharacteristically blurted out, "I'm homeless—I have nothing on earth."

Yet these Richmonders, like all of the South, still looked to him for a sense of purpose and guidance. No less so now as, with quiet dignity and self-possession, he knelt down to partake of the communion, along the same rail with the black man.

Watching Robert E. Lee, the other communicants slowly followed in his path, going forward to the altar, and, with a mixture of reluctance and fear, hope and awkward expectation, into the future.

EPILOGUE

To Make a Nation

L ate spring, 1865.

Eighteen-year-old guerrilla Jesse James returned from a stay in Texas, and, though he never formally surrendered, he was wounded by a Union man apparently under a flag of truce. His family had been banished from Clay County, Missouri, and fled to Nebraska, where they felt displaced. In the weeks that followed, with a bullet lodged in his chest and a terrible hacking cough, James stayed with his mother. The convalescence went poorly. Making so little progress, and convinced that the end was near, he begged his mother that he might somehow return to Missouri so he might "die in a Southern state."

On the other side of the country, in California, Sam Clemens, the far-Western correspondent and journalist, was using his "nom de guerre," Mark Twain. His ill-fated fling as a Confederate soldier had been short-lived, and, though his sympathies were with the South, he was now focusing his energies on his writing career. It was going badly. Recently fired from his job at the *Call* and practically penniless, he was studying French grammar to improve himself and hanging around the Olympic Club gymnasium in San Francisco to keep up appearances. He had gotten one minor break. A little essay he contributed to the *Saturday Press* in New York ("Jim Smiley and His Jumping Frog") made him the roar of the town; but after all he had written, he was thoroughly incensed "that those New York people should single out a villainous backwoods sketch on which to compliment me." One critic, however, had called him "all played out." Clemens seemed to agree. "I don't know what to write," he penned to his mother, "—my life is so uneventful." After Appomattox, depressed and at wit's end, he planned to go to Hawaii. "Who knows?" he noted. "I may be an old man before I finish [my book.]"

The Great Atlantic and Pacific Tea Company (later known as the A&P) was now in its sixth tentative year. Originally founded to bring down the price of tea and coffee, it had been operating solely through mail order and clubs. Hampered by the war, it faced an uncertain future.

On a quiet farm in Dearborn, Michigan, William Ford, who had avoided the war, was indulging his pride and joy, his two-year-old son, Henry. With ninety acres, a handsome two-story house surrounded by evergreens, a pear tree, an apple orchard, and a large willow, the father felt the life of the prosperous, self-sufficient farmer was the American dream. But William would soon become deeply disappointed with his son, as young Henry's attention span repeatedly wandered. To the father's even greater disappointment, Henry would, at the first opportunity, desert the family farm. William became convinced that Henry, a bit of a "queer duck," was incapable of settling down. "Henry [Ford] is not much of a farmer," his father sadly concluded. "He's a tinkerer."

In Rodham, New York, thirteen-year-old Frank Woolworth was also dreaming of escaping from the drudgery of the remote family farm. When he was not sweating in the fields, his favorite game was setting up household items on the dining room table and, with his brother, pretending to sell them to imaginary customers. Even now, he yearned to fulfill his burning ambition: becoming a store clerk.

Another dreamer, on the East Coast, was John Roebling. At fifty-nine, he had only four more years to live. He was finalizing a design for what he hoped would become the longest suspension bridge in the world. Unfinished in his day, it would be completed by his son. It would not bear his name, however, but would be named after the borough it touched, as the Brooklyn Bridge.

Meanwhile, in Stewartsville, Minnesota, two-year-old Richard Warren Sears was enjoying a toddler's life in a wealthy family. But unknown to the infant, his father had invested poorly, and would soon leave the family destitute and penniless. It would forever change his life.

In Camden, New Jersey, forty-eight-year-old Joseph Campbell, filled with ideas and business zeal, was rapidly forging a close friendship with Abraham Anderson; within three years, the two would go into business together, "canning" foods.

The son of an unsuccessful lumbermill jack, eighteen-year-old Thomas Alva Edison was a long way from his home in Port Huron, Michigan. The war had touched him, but only remotely. Living in cheap boarding-houses, he slept on any available floor while moving around the country and struggling to keep a job. His grade school teacher had been convinced that he was retarded; his parents noticed he was a weak and somber boy; and other youngsters had teased him so mercilessly that he ran away from school and refused to return. With only three months of formal education (although he was an avid devotee of Thomas Jefferson), and looking like a tramp, he seemed destined to drift for his whole life. Moody and cranky, in 1865, he was working as a "plug," a second-class night shift operation in the Western Union office in Cincinnati. At long last, he seemed to find his stride, getting promoted to a first-class operator, for which his salary was boosted to $125 a month. But from there, he abruptly moved to a ramshackle telegraph office in, of all places, war-torn Mississippi, where he was again fired.

Eighteen-year-old Alexander Graham Bell had not yet emigrated from Edinburgh, Scotland, to America. A shy young man, with poor grades, his favorite subject was phonetics: the study of speech.

Plans were being made by a group of forty sponsors to publish the first edition, in July 1865, of *The Nation*—"a weekly journal devoted to Politics, Literature, Science, and Art." Frederick Law Olmsted, the architect and writer; Charles Eliot Norton, the Harvard scholar; and abolitionist spokesman William Lloyd Garrison and his son, Wendell Phillips Garrison, were among the founders. Expressing concern with the South and the problems faced by the American Negro, the prospectus eagerly promised that "a special correspondent" would travel through the former

Confederacy and dispatch a series of weekly articles covering "The South As It Is."

Fifteen-year-old Samuel Gompers, upon learning about Lincoln's assassination, was depressed for days. In New York, the youngster waited in line for hours "for the privilege of looking at his face." Immigrants from East London just two years before, his family lived east of the lower Bowery in dire poverty, a stone's throw away from the squalid, crime-infested Five Points district, where tens of thousands of immigrants were crowded in foul, dark, underground lodging houses overrun by vermin. The garbage-strewn tenement that the Gompers family lived in, without sunlight or air, and squeezed between a brewery and a slaughterhouse, was only marginally better. Every day, Gompers and his father, Solomon, sat in their cramped, dirty combination kitchen, dining room, and living room, where the two rolled cigars, the family trade. If his father had his way, this would be the young immigrant's livelihood. Soon after April, Sam managed to get a proper job in a real cigar factory. "This is Mr. Gompers," his employer bellowed to a visitor one day that spring of 1865. "He is an agitator, but I don't give a damn. He makes me good cigars!"

In Cleveland, Ohio, an already deeply ambitious twenty-six-year-old John D. Rockefeller had become convinced that oil refining would become one of the most prosperous industries in the country. Despite his claims that he wanted to "go in the army," he never did, although he paid for seven substitutes in the war and gave freely of his limited money to such charities as a Catholic orphanage, a colored mute and blind society, a Jewish missionary, and an industrial school. Every day throughout the late stages of the war, he talked "oil, oil, oil." Weeks before April 1865, he had bought at auction the partnership of Andrews, Clark & Company. To his doubting critics at the time, this young man promised that this investment would be "something big."

In Pittsburgh, Andrew Carnegie, a Scottish immigrant, had just resigned from the Pennsylvania railroad, where he was a superintendent. Vain, boastful, cocksure, driven, a touch ruthless, he had known more than his share of hardship as a boy. Living in an Allegheny slum in Pennsylvania, he had worked as a bobbin boy at $1.50 a week. Since then, he had been a telegraph messenger, a telegraph operator, a War Department assistant (and a fierce Union patriot), and a railroad superintendent. Already, he had proved himself a shrewd investor, including in oil. Curiously, at the age of thirty, he was now preparing to abandon railroads at just the time when they seemed poised to make a fortune for other entrepreneurs: the Vanderbilts, the Garretts, the Goulds, the Huntingtons. Having made the decision that working for other people was unprofitable, he now had decided to manage his own investments full-time—and to scout around for a line of enterprise in which to be his own boss.

As he finished his second term at the Western Pennsylvania Classical and Scientific Institute, teachers declared sixteen-year-old Henry Clay Frick an "average scholar," though they noted he was "splendid in arithmetic." Frick did seem to have a love of drawing; his family living room was covered with "prints and sketches."

Far across the country, thirty-five-year-old Albert Bierstadt, on his way to becoming General Custer's favorite artist, began painting *Looking Up the Yosemite Valley*. Captivated by the majesty and savagery of the Rockies, he was the first artist to bring the High West to the sophisticated East Coast. That year alone, in the depressed Civil War market of 1865, he sold his great canvas *Lander's Peak* to the railroad financier James McHenry, for a stunning $25,000.

Frederic Remington was four years old.

Amid buoyant talk and much hard work, progress was fervently proceeding apace by a combination of New York women's rights advocates and abolitionists, who, one year later at the Church of the Puritans, on May 10, 1866, would launch the American Equal Rights Association. Elizabeth Cady Stanton would declare, "Our time is now!" Lucretia Mott took a more measured stance, telling her audience, "all great achievements in the progress of the human race must be slow, and are ever wrought out by the few in isolation and ridicule." Within three years, the group would splinter, rent asunder by infighting and ideological differences.

Forty-two-year-old Hiram Revels, born in North Carolina, now an educator and minister, would soon be on his way to Kansas as a Christian missionary crusading for temperance. His work would unexpectedly lead him to Natchez, Mississippi, where he would embark on a political career. A stunning orator, he would rise through the ranks, from alderman to state senator. And the former clergyman and school principal never dreamed what would happen next: he would be elected to the U.S. Senate in 1870, filling Jefferson Davis's seat and becoming the first black man to serve in that institution.

Patrick Cleburne had lain long in his grave by April 1865, killed the previous fall in the battle of Franklin, Tennessee. Among those who attended his funeral, "a sad and silent sermon," was Jefferson Davis, who quietly lowered his head and kissed Cleburne's coffin. Cleburne's fiancée, Sue Tarleton, was there, too, prostrate with grief. In April 1865, she was still dressed in black, wearing her mourning clothes, and would do so whenever in public every day for another seven months—a full year. Cleburne's body was briefly interred in the paupers' section in Columbia, but was then moved to a small churchyard at Ash Hill, which Cleburne had once thought "beautiful." He was both missed and remembered. Robert E. Lee called him "A meteor shining from a clouded sky." General John Bell Hood wrote, "He possessed the boldness and wisdom to earnestly advocate at an early period of the war the freedom of the negro and the enrollment of the young and able bodied men of that race. This stroke . . . would have given us independence." At thirty-seven, Cleburne had lived in America for only fifteen years. Four of them were under arms.

Spurred on by the Civil War, baseball was now the rage.

At fifty-five, P. T. Barnum, having already made and lost a fortune, was embarking upon a new career: in politics. Thirty years earlier, the Connecticut resident had captivated the public's attention with a most unusual show, featuring a rented theater and his black slave, Joyce Heth. Claiming she was 161 years old (she was really 80), Barnum charged admission to catch a glimpse of her. But with those days now behind him, he was seeking a seat in the Connecticut legislature and contemplating a run for mayor of Bridgeport. Six years later, he will tire of politics and begin yet another career. It would prove to be his most prosperous.

Seven-year-old Adolph Ochs, the son of a German-Jewish immigrant, would, to his father's horror, quit school at the age of thirteen to become a printer's apprentice.

New York Times founder and publisher, staunch Republican Henry J. Raymond, had inadvertently jeopardized the well-being and integrity of his young newspaper, taking a seat in Congress in a special session called in March 1865. Though prosperous (the paper was now up to eight pages and cost a hefty four cents a copy), the *Times* now began a slow, downward slide. Eventually, it would be floundering, some $300,000 in debt, and losing more than $2,000 a week. Finally, in 1896, it would be sold for $75,000 to a former printer's apprentice. With its once bright future uncertain, the new owner began by sponsoring a contest for the paper's slogan. The winning one was: "All the World News, but Not a School for Scandal."

In one way or another, the paths of these people would cross and intermingle in a united America—but that was in the future.

❧　❧　❧

The future. Like the stars high above, dangling in the overarching vault of history, the question was there, indeed, it had always been there, and never more so than at April 1865's end: would the United States prosper and endure, or disintegrate and decline? Throughout history's long, checkered span, for republics, particularly those that undergo civil wars, the odds were not good, and, in fact, never had been.

The Greek example, to recall Alexander Hamilton's immortal words, was "disgust[ing]." After a reign of splendor, the Roman Republic fell ignominiously. There were a few republics in Europe, but none of them was large—and most had not acquitted themselves particularly well, either. The United Netherlands had collapsed in 1787; Santo Domingo disintegrated in 1791; the monarchical British were unable to adapt their version of representative government to include the far-off colonies; and France, after undergoing nine civil wars in the final four decades of the sixteenth century, would take up arms again in the seventeenth and eighteenth centuries, before descending into its own long, terrible nightmare of a failed republic and the Revolution. The Founding Fathers were, of course, aware of all this, and, more than that, were haunted by it. Today, it is hard for us to imagine, but in their world—and it was the only world they really knew—the sense of time and space was dramatically different; they felt as close, perhaps even closer, to the Romans and Greeks of 2,000 years ago, or to Europe over the last millennium, as Americans today do to the most recent generation before their own. They, however, lacked our perspective. They could not hold up a mirror to the future. They could only be guided by the past. And, as it turned out, that past spoke of fragility.

Among other things, the Founders were convinced by historical example that for a republican government to last, it could not function over a large area. As the dominant political philosopher of his time, Montesquieu wrote in 1748, "it is natural for a republic to have only a small territory." This notion became as axiomatic in American popular thought as in its doctrine. Both John Adams and Alexander Hamilton drew the lesson that the vast expanse of the United States—not as it is today, but as they knew it *then*—made it likely that a durable central government would have to verge on monarchy. For his part, Patrick Henry was hardly alone when, in 1788, he warned, "Our government cannot reign over so extensive a country as this, without absolute despotism."

But the question was hardly one of geography alone. For the Founders, the destiny of republics was their very nature, that they inevitably rise and fall, withering through fragmentation, failing through conquest, dying through despotism. Republics had always been not just vulnerable but precarious and contingent, and always would be. So ingrained was this view that nowhere did the Constitution promise perpetuity for the United States as a country. It still does not today. George Washington, as fervent a patriot as ever lived, and a good Federalist, agreed. In his first inaugural, he spoke of the "Republican model of government" as an "experiment." In his Farewell Address, he was equally fatalistic. "I dare not hope they will make the strong and lasting impression I could wish," he advised, "that they will control the usual current of the passions or prevent our nation from running the course which has hitherto marked the destiny of nations." Washington, like most of the other Founding Fathers, like most of the country, and like most of the world, was not sure that the United States would work.

At the core of the problem, of course, was the remarkable yet perplexing birth of America. Virtually unique to all of human history,

Americans had a Constitution and a country before they had a nation. And until the Civil War, America remained just that, an artificial state, or, to be more exact, a series of states, and even several inchoate nations, bound together not by a thousand years of kinship and shared memory, but by loosely negotiated agreements and compacts, neither wholly federal nor national. This was not accidental. When the men of 1787 spoke of forming a federal Union, they had in mind a drawing together of sovereign states. Federal, of course, was used in a sense close to its Latin origin to describe a relationship resting on good faith—*foedus* being the cognate of *fides*, or faith. In the end, while the Founders made something different from a "foederal" compact in the old sense, they were devising a republic but not yet a nation. Indeed, by design, it is no accident that the word "nation" appears nowhere in the Constitution or in the Declaration of Independence. So the question remained, was America a nation? And would it last?

The price of such ingenuity—some have said hubris—in the country's formation was one episode of secession after another, and all of them, to varying degrees, endangering America: the Western frontiersman threatened it in the Whiskey Rebellion; then it was New England's turn, as the Federalists flirted with secession and openly cavorted with the enemy during the war of 1812, until they finally tempered their actions at the Hartford Convention of 1814. Right up to the Civil War itself, New York City repeatedly threatened to secede. So did New Jersey. So did Oregon and California. The Mormons of Utah wanted to stay independent, and fought a bloody war against the Union. The Cherokees tried to establish an independent republic in Georgia; they, too, were forcibly denied. For years, well into the nineteenth century, there was talk of an independent Pacific republic being one day established, a vision shared by no less than Thomas Jefferson, first and foremost, but also by Albert Gallatin, James Monroe, Henry Clay, Thomas Hart Benton, and probably James Madison. In Senator Benton's richly descriptive words (and Benton himself was one of manifest destiny's most fervid proponents), ". . . the new Government should separate from the mother Empire as the child separates from the parent in the age of manhood." For nine years, Texas was an independent republic, and when it was finally incorporated into the Union in 1845, opposition was violent—in Texas as well as the United States. And Kansas had already undergone its own civil war. In the spirit of this age, then, and when viewed through the larger prism of the United States experience, the effort by the South to set itself up as an independent Confederate country was hardly a mad enterprise or some great break with the past. Instead, it was but one more thread of a very long, even honorable rope in American—and, for that matter, world—history.

The task of forging an American nation was always a daunting one. The glibness and comfort of the late twentieth century and the new millennium should not obscure the following: the Civil War could have ended in many ways. As R. R. Palmer and Joel Colton have pointed out in their classic work, *A History of the Modern World*, it could have reduced English-speaking America to a scramble of jealously competing minor republics. But there were other, equally worrisome outcomes.

To start, wars are transforming dramas. And of all the kinds of wars, civil wars are the most scarring—some countries never heal from them. Atavistic hatreds simmer, persist, and steadily mount for years, sometimes centuries, only to be rekindled by more civil war and even more intense civil strife: witness the renewed bloodshed in Bosnia and Serbia and Croatia, smack in the heart of Europe today. Yet just over a decade ago, the former Yugoslavia was widely hailed as a pillar of stability and even a second Riviera in an otherwise fragile Eastern European zone. Or Afghanistan, where any promise of democracy was first aborted by civil war in 1863, and which in recent years has once again descended into more bloody internal conflict, occurring on and off with ferocity for the last two decades. Or Northern Ireland, which, year after year—some 200 all told—eludes easy answer.

By April 1865, even as it became apparent that the Union was in one manner or another going to win the war, the fate of the country still remained very much in doubt. The conclusions of wars are every bit as crucial as how and why they begin and how and why they are fought. History is littered with the wreckage of bad endings. This was complicated, of course, by the fact that at that moment, the South had also changed. Lincoln had always contended that the South had never left the Union: he spoke of the "so-called Confederacy," insisting that the states had not really seceded from the Union because they could not; he even went as far as to maintain that "the whole country is our soil" and the South still remained in the Union. And further, he said that it was not a war between states but an insurrection, in effect, warranting a large police action. But at best, this logic was little more than a legal technicality (and a debatable one at that), at odds with the reality on the ground, if not wishful thinking on the part of Lincoln. Through its darkest days, from first Manassas to Sayler's Creek, from Fort Sumter to Appomattox and Durham Station, the Confederacy had become something that even the United States itself at its founding was truly not: a separate nation, sharing not simply a common language but a common culture, heritage, identity; common heroes; and, perhaps most importantly, a common sense of destiny. In British statesman William Gladstone's memorable words in 1863: "Jefferson Davis and the other leaders of the South have made an army; they are making, it appears, a navy; and they have made what is more than either, they have made a nation." The unanimity of Confederate nationality may be overstated, but the Union's task of reabsorbing an essentially hostile entity, to which it had just laid siege, can not be. Susan Emiline Jeffords Caldwell, of Virginia, neatly summed up this problem in March 1865: "I want peace but I don't want to go back into the Union. I want *Independence* and nothing else.—I could not consent to go back with a people that has been bent on exterminating us." Nor can the challenge of overcoming deep and abiding enmity be overestimated. Lincoln knew this—it was one of his wisest, greatest insights. That is why he refused to gloat, or smugly indulge in celebration, or demonize his foe. Remarkably, and importantly, on this last point, neither did the leaders of the Confederacy, Robert E. Lee most notably among them.

These men of battle knew that war most often engenders hatred. But by their collective actions in ending the war, they, along with Lincoln, helped to constitute a country. In mid-April, as the cataclysmic events rushed together, when Lee surrendered at Appomattox—"as much to Lincoln's goodness as to Grant's armies," he would say—then Johnston at Durham Station, and then Taylor and Forrest and all the rest followed, they were asking something quite remarkable of the people whom they had just led through four years of bloody battle: to become good citizens of a United States that had thwarted their bid for independence and stymied their urge for self-determination. And above all, Lincoln, and men like Grant and Sherman, would call on the North to be equally remarkable, appealing to reconciliation, not vengeance, to common ground, not revenge, to mutual citizenship, not differences.

Would it work? Could it work? The United States was like an enormous jigsaw puzzle whose many pieces could be slowly pulled into place, or irrevocably fall apart. For a while, in fact, a very long while, it had been touch and go. The Civil War was not just a war between states, or an insurrection, but by the end, with the entire institution of slavery overthrown, the South laid waste, setting it back generations, it was also a revolution. And revolutions rarely go quietly. Was this revolution, like Saturn, like so many revolutions, destined to eat its own children, which Lincoln himself had warned against early on? In the fateful days of April 1865, this haunting question would turn on a handful of choices and decisions: what if Lee had found an abundance of food at Amelia Court House—and safely made his way south to link up with Joe Johnston? Or if he had decided that honor lay not in surrendering but in fighting on and on for the mother South—with organized guerrilla warfare? Or if Lee had responded to surrender not with dignity and honor, but with rage? Or if Grant and Sherman had neglected Lincoln's admonitions at City Point and responded not with generosity of spirit, but with unbridled anger? Or if there had not been an honorable stacking of the arms and mutual salute to set the tone for the end of the war, but hangings and humiliation? Or if Andrew Johnson had been assassinated after all—and the blade hadn't missed its mark of Seward's jugular? Or if after the assassination of Lincoln, all went to pieces and the presidential transition process fell prey to momentary passions and fears? Or if Joe Johnston had not decided to disobey Jefferson Davis's orders?

To ask these questions, just a number of those faced by North and South at critical turning points in April, is to contemplate the answers— and in each case, the answers are terrible; the ugly consequences indeed incalculable. In Europe, by way of analogy, when the revolution in France finally quieted down, it could not be forgotten. Instead, it became lodged in the collective memory, a frightful, defining event with which each succeeding generation had to come to terms. Some lived in fear, others in hope that the giant was only sleeping and might be aroused. And aroused it was, as Europe felt the aftershocks of upheaval for the better part of a century to follow, a contagion of strife and conflict that swept across an entire continent, leaving a trail of tears and disorder.

Closer to home, other examples were even less heartening. At the turn of the nineteenth century, civil war in South and Central America, the other America, had slid into guerrilla war, the two becoming so intermingled that the wars between the rebels and Spain and between pro- and anti-royalist elements literally dragged on for decades. The effect was terrible: it hindered the rule of law and the development of stable democracy, and it devolved into Caesarism, military rule, army mutinies and revolts, and, as scholars ruefully note, every kind of barbaric cruelty. The suffering and bitterness that it engendered led to ongoing revolutionary struggles and profound weaknesses and instability in the independent civil and political societies that arose from it, lasting in one shape or form to this very day.

So, after April 1865, when the blood had clotted and dried, when the cadavers had been removed and the graves filled in, what America was asking for, at the war's end, was in fact something quite unique: a special exemption from the cruel edicts of history.

❧   ❧   ❧

But that is largely what happened. By April's end, the country had been changed. Amid the wreckage of war, a kind of universal joint had been shifted, creating one of those rare seismic jolts that history rarely notes more than once a century or even once a millennium. Slowly across the land, in the North as well as the South, a powerful new mood was rising, which would alter the great stream of American—and hence, world—events. In no small measure, this was due, as we have seen, to the actions of a handful of leaders, Union as well as Confederate. And in a way, it calls to mind another pivotal era. Inspired by fifteenth-century Florence, the French sought to capture the awakening of the human spirit and combined the verb *renaître*, "revive," with the feminine noun *naissance*, "birth," to form Renaissance—rebirth. This, too, was a kind of rebirth and was equally compelling; but this new beginning was also something quite different. One ingredient that had heretofore been missing in American life would now emerge, phoenixlike, out of the war's ashes.

"It seems as if we were never alive until now," one New York woman had exulted after Fort Sumter, "never had a country till now." But never was this more true than, paradoxically, in the latticed gloom of the war's end. Walt Whitman said it well: "Strange, (is it not?) that battle, martyrs, blood, even assassination should so condense—perhaps only really, lastingly condense—a Nationality." So did the newly constituted periodical *The Nation*, which wrote, "The measure of the nation is now ratified by the blood of thousands of her sons." And now, remarkably, perhaps bafflingly, that nation at long last included the South—the South, which was unique and separate *before* the war began; the South, which had been literally turned upside down by its Northern enemies; the South, which had seen almost all that it loved and cherished wrecked and ruined. But there it was. "Strange as it may seem," observed T. Morris Chester, the black correspondent filing his vivid April and May 1865 dispatches from Richmond, "the better class of Southern People generally are of the opinion, and I think they are sincere, that the government and the union are now stronger today than ever before . . . [and] with great unanimity agree that slavery and rebellion are both consigned to one grave." And he added this stunning note: "All classes of persons . . ." he wrote, "have announced with a great deal of unanimity, that they were heartily rejoiced to be back in the old Union again of a grand and great country; many of them rebels from the beginning."

In truth, more than the Confederacy was vanquished by war's end. This is a subtle point but crucial to understand. In a profound but real sense, the chain of history had been irrevocably broken, for also destroyed was the Union, which would soon become little more than a distant, quaint, outdated concept. Regionalism would always be a factor in American life. But obliterated was any serious thought of future secession, by any side, any state, any section. Before the war, Americans often spoke of the United States in the plural—"The United States are . . ." For example, in his classic work on the history of America, noted historian John H. Hinton wrote in 1834: "By some, the United States are highly eulogized; by others, they are eagerly depreciated." Sometime after the war, however, so changed was America that this was now modified to a singular noun. Thus, Hinton's words would become, "The United States is . . ." The war's end—and how it ended, both manner and means—had, in fact, marked a decisive break with the past, the great chasm between the era of contingent republics and permanent nations, which until then was all of human doings. No less than the Founders who assembled in 1776, it made America.

Of course, this was not sudden. The process had, in one form or another, been under way before the war began. In a sense, the concept of secession had already been heatedly contested. Centrifugal change had been moving fervently apace for decades, hastened by the fervent push-pull of European emigration and American migration; by the stunning emergence of industrial capitalism and by a bountiful economy; by new horizons created by the rising expansion of education and literacy and by the dazzling information and transportation revolutions that knit together a growing landmass; and by the astonishing growth of a nascent phenomenon that would come to be known as the "middle class." All these forces suggested unity, discredited disharmony, loosened the allure of sectionalism and secession, and strengthened the appeal of nationalism. Yet in the end, they would have been largely moot had the war—and had the days of April—gone differently. In the midst of all this ferment, anything could still have happened. Instead, April was that magic moment when these ideas joined together. Amid the long lists of heroic and historic actions for this country, April 1865 was incontestably one of America's finest hours: for it was not the deranged spirit of an assassin that defined the country at war's end, but the conciliatory spirit of leaders who led as much in peace as in war, warriors and politicians who, by their example, their exhortation, and their deeds, overcame their personal rancor, their heartache, and spoke as citizens of not two lands, but one, thereby bringing the country together. True, much hard work remained. But much, too, had already been accomplished.

And thus, by the war's end, this, too, was surely the case: the states alone were no longer America, and America was no longer simply states.

Gone forever was the talk of replicating other civilizations—a new Rome or a new Athens, even a new London.

That was the meaning of April 1865.

❧ ❧ ❧

One task, however, that would challenge this new nation was making flesh of emancipation. For the freed slaves, a complicated chapter in America was just beginning. "Verily," Frederick Douglass had said, "the work does not end with the abolition of slavery, it only begins." He was more than right. During the war, these men and women faced a situation fraught with ambiguity, tragedy, and complexity. Some felt deep kinship with their former masters, and just as deep a sense of loyalty and duty to the South—yet at the same time, every moment that prolonged the Confederacy only prolonged, as historian Leon Litwack points out, their own enslavement, debasement, or lack of freedom. It was for the slave children, however, that the war was often the most cruel and confusing. As slave fathers fled the plantations—or were recruited to join the Confederate war effort—many of the wives and children were left behind, forced to shoulder the additional burden. It was often a crushing experience. Fifteen-year-old Eliza Scantling remembered it well: "[I] plowed a mule an' a wild un at dat. Sometimes me hands get so cold I jes cry." Little ten-year-old Mittie Freeman found the invading bluecoats so terrifying and bewildering that she hid in a tree when the first Union troops arrived. And of course, there was the heartbreak of being orphaned. "My daddy go 'way to de war 'bout dis time, and my mammy and me stay in our cabin alone," Amy Lumpkin of South Carolina recalled. "She cry and wonder where he be, if he is well or be killed, and one day, we hear he is dead. My mammy, too, pass in a short time."

But as April 1865 rolled around, in the former slave quarters and plantation houses, in the hot fields and in the steaming kitchens, there arose excited talk of a changing world: the ability to choose where one lived and worked; how one educated his children—or himself; where and whom one married—and when; and instead of being property, owning property. By all accounts, it was at once a moment fervent with hope and paralyzing with possibilities, as African Americans caught sight of the edges of the new reality that now existed, a life with freedom. Houston Holloway, who had been sold three times before the age of twenty, in 1865 recalled his emancipation: "I felt like a bird out of a cage. Amen. Amen. Amen." Booker T. Washington, then a nine-year-old-child, would remember the dizzying moments after Appomattox at Hales Ford, in the quiet foothills of the Virginia Blue Ridge mountains. On one hand, he would later note that to defend the white women and children, "the slaves would have laid down their lives." Yet freedom had its own allure. Washington's masters, who were themselves largely poor, living in the rough comfort and self-sufficiency of small, backwoods farmers, gathered Booker and the five other slaves at the front door of their small log cabin home. With "deep interest" and "sadness" on their faces—and not a hint of bitterness—they listened intently as a Federal officer told the slaves that they were all free, that they could go when and where they pleased. As Booker and his brother and sisters huddled by their mother's side, the scene dissolved into "great rejoicing, and thanksgiving, and wild scenes of ecstasy." She then leaned over and kissed her children, "tears of joy [running] down her cheeks."

In time, though, the path to freedom would be littered with the dismembered dreams of many black Americans and others. The story is a difficult one. Suffice to say, postwar Reconstruction would prove to be a painful, slow, and flawed nightmare. In April 1865, where a broad-minded Abraham Lincoln saw that the burden of Reconstruction was not just the South's alone—that the North was also culpable in the shame of slavery—and thus, in some measure, that it was not one but both sides that were in need of repair, a jaundiced Andrew Johnson proved wholly ill-suited to the immediate task ahead. Whether on the matters of pardons, black suffrage and black civil rights, Northern racism and Southern terror, Southern debt and Northern carpetbaggers, or reconciliation between Union and Confederacy, Johnson, narrow, bigoted, and inflexible, repeatedly fumbled, and no one was satisfied. As a result, the healing was at first halting and tortured. By March 1867, with an act of Congress, the South would devolve once more into military rule. Violence quickly followed. So did fear. The Ku Klux Klan, which began in 1866 as little more than bullying pranksters, soon turned brutal, tainting each state with terror, hangings, and voter fraud that stifled political dissent. For their part, frustrated Southern governors repeatedly relied on Federal troops to keep the peace, and, almost as if the war had started all over again, habeas corpus was suspended to cope with the attacks and intimidation that seemed to flourish every election season. All this was, of course, everything that Lincoln would have deplored. So, too, the fact that it would not be until 1870 that Virginia, Georgia, Mississippi, and Texas rejoined the Union—five long years after Appomattox, Durham Station, and the Grand Review of the Armies.

But where Lincoln's absent hand was felt most keenly was in race relations. Black codes were passed in state after state across the South— as restrictive as the antebellum laws governing free blacks (Richmond's old laws had even regulated the carrying of canes). These codes propounded segregation, banned intermarriage, provided for special punishments for blacks, and, in one state, Mississippi, also prevented the ownership of land. Not even a congressional civil rights bill, passed over Johnson's veto, could undo them. For their part, the Northern states were little better. During Reconstruction, employing a deadly brew of poll taxes, literacy requirements, and property qualifications, they abridged the right to vote more extensively than did their Southern counterparts. California went a step further, expressly forbidding the Chinese to vote altogether. Nor would such biting strictures be limited to the democratic process; the atrocious treatment of Native Americans during the coming westward expansion would also prove to be a tragic and grievous national stain. And as the nineteenth century lumbered forward, there remained an old and deep Know-Nothing streak of nativism that would not wither overnight: a virulent mix of black haters, Catholic haters, Jew haters, immigrant haters, Northern haters, and just plain haters.

Sadly, though, it was black Americans who would find that their own struggle for true freedom, one fundamental goal and one principal legacy of this war, would haunt the country for over a century to come. Indeed, a lamentable conclusion is that much of the battle of postwar America would center around the unfulfilled promise of emancipation—

and would be marred by terrible brutality, horrific violence, and often unspeakable racial repression on which, paradoxically, the strands of reconciliation frequently rested.

❧   ❧   ❧

But that would come later—and it would not ultimately vitiate this central fact, a fact that Lincoln foremost would have appreciated: America would now be something different, not simply a clever political arrangement but a transcendent and pervading idea; it would be a new America, reunited, yes, scarred, certainly, but for the first time, largely whole, looking as much to the future as to the past. For some 135 years afterward, it would remain a diverse and democratic country, inspiring quests for freedom around the globe. And that same global stage, all too often riddled with malignant hatreds and civil strife, would remind us that it did not have to be this way. However successful or pervasive, an idea can be replaced, altered, modified, ignored. It could still be today; complacency should never allow one to think otherwise. As Lincoln understood most poignantly, it is not merely how arms are taken up, and why, but equally how they are laid back down, and why. And what then follows.

❧   ❧   ❧

In the fading light of dusk after the grand review, more than the Confederacy and Union had vanished; so, too, had the pleasant, provincial society that had been the nation's capital.

Before the war, Washington was a distinctly Southern town: small, tightly knit, and socially cozy, where a handful of hostesses determined who was in and who was out, and where flocks of geese waddled down the avenues and hogs of all shapes wandered across Capitol Hill and Judiciary Square. Frogs kept up a constant din. Accustomed to the culture and refinement of London and Paris, Vienna and Rome, sophisticated European diplomats thus viewed Washington with a mixture of dread and condescension. For among all the capitals of the Western world, Washington was singularly perplexing and unique: it was devoted to politics and politics alone, with the nation's cultural and commercial center woefully situated in far-off New York. Little wonder, then, that for Europeans, hankering for the splendor of a Buckingham Palace or the Tuileries, for the dramatic vistas and grand boulevards of Haussmann's Paris or the intimate squares of London, a tour in Washington was regarded as "a season in purgatory."

For all its lofty intentions, the city was an infant capital. Built to order at the century's dawn, in 1860 it still gave the impression of having just begun. Rain regularly turned the roadbeds into vexing channels of mud; erected on a swamp and surrounded by noxious flats and a stinking canal, the city emitted suffocating odors everywhere, which even drifted into the presidential quarters; and the very political rhythm of the capital was dominated by a peculiar, lumbering seasonal character. All said and done, it was a winter resort, awakening only after the long slumber of summer and the slow opening of Congress in the late autumn. To be sure, by the standards of the day, vast sums had been spent to create the city. There was the Capitol, the most splendid building of them all, the General Post Office, the Patent Office, the Treasury, the Executive Mansion, and the Smithsonian—each an imposing structure. But in truth, however grand in conception, everywhere one looked, the city evoked unfulfilled promise. After sixty years, the inescapable conclusion was that much of the city remained unclear in principle, inchoate in design, unfinished in actuality.

It was a correct conclusion. The main buildings themselves were widely spaced, maddeningly unrelated, and, for the most part, incomplete. (Thus the sarcastic swipe that Washington was a "city of magnificent distances.") Consider the Capitol, the proudest glory of Washingtonians. Topped by scaffolding and a towering crane, surrounded by blocks of marble, lumber, and iron plates strewn erratically about the grounds, the Capitol dome was being refurbished—but painfully slowly. So, too, were the new wings of the Capitol, one at both ends, where glittering marble structures lay maddeningly unfinished; of the hundred Corinthian columns needed for completion of the porticoes, only three had been set in place. The magnificent Post Office at Seventh and F, and the huge brick Patent Office across the street, stood facing each other like grand marble palaces, but they were not yet completed. (Henry Adams quipped that they were "like White Greek temples in the abandoned gravel pits of a deserted Syrian city.") The main thoroughfare, Pennsylvania Avenue, "*the* avenue," as it was called, did have some cobblestone, but it was thin and broken up by faulty drainage. The cramped quarters of the State Department were relegated to a little brick building, as was the War Department, both attracting no more interest than the Navy Department housed inconspicuously in an old-fashioned home on the western side of the Executive Mansion. And for its part, the Executive Mansion, though growing in elegance, tradition, and the affection of the American people, was nonetheless compared to a rundown Southern plantation.

Solemnly conceived, Washington was, in fact, often a joke. For many visitors, it was likened to a Southern town but without being picturesque. The city was saddled with sloth, clutter, and the pronounced lack of sanitation. Instead of high culture, there were profusions of saloons; instead of the drumbeat of commerce, there was the eyesore of brothels; instead of the trappings of a great capital, the vista down the Potomac appeared to be that of one unbroken line of swamp. In all directions lay remnants of once great trees and piles of discarded brick and stone. And while there were several large, genteel hotels, notably the Willard on Fourteenth Street, an elegant, fortresslike structure that boasted running tap water in every room, and the Kirkwood on Twelfth, for the most part, the city was littered with unpaved streets, odd concrete slabs scattered here and there, and unsightly groups of shacks and backyard privies cluttered about. "To make a Washington street," one Brit derided, "take one marble temple, or public office, a dozen good houses of brick and a dozen of wood and fill in with sheds and fields." Quite true. For all the improvements, the roads themselves were so awful that Anthony Trollope warned that even with the most accurate of maps, a visitor still would find the city a disconcerting maze. One was sure to "lose himself," he noted, not pleasantly, as one is lost in London "between Shoreditch and Russell Square," but "as one does in the deserts of the holy land, between Emmaus and Arimathea."

While a work in progress, Washington was not, however, without some splendor or charm. The Capitol, though domeless, was indeed commanding, and the actual chambers of the Senate and House, with their forty-one-foot ceilings and ornate gilt mirrors, their fine Empire fire-places and their red-and-gold inlaid marble floors, their flowered carpets and chairs upholstered in morocco leather, were both magnificent. In its own way, so was the congressional privy, built for $234. Farther down the road, the Smithsonian, with its lush, colorful gardens, was a soothing balm to the burning eye. And the salons of Washington, fresh with talk of democracy and republics and progress, were stirring with a new rhythm and pulse that suggested a city of far greater magnitude than did its otherwise rough facade. But at the start of the war, it was nonetheless inescapable that the presence of the Federal government was symbolized by little more than ten build-ings, a few statues, and the truncated, incomplete obelisk of the Washington Monument, which resembled a large, white stump.

Likened to "the ruins of Carthage," then, it was, in one observer's words, a child capital, an ambitious beginner. And as a place merely for the government, it was ultimately an idea set in the wilderness, a capital that rarely touched the average American citizen except through the mail.

❧   ❧   ❧

But during the war this wilderness became a city transformed. Extensive earthworks were dug around the city's perimeter, forts were erected and manned, armed guards were placed at all the main bridges coming into and out of the city, and soldiers poured daily into the capital. And before their very eyes, Washingtonians watched their city change overnight, from an unruly country town to a bustling, modern metropolitan center. A huge civil service mushroomed, as did new housing. Where foreign ministers once had to consult a map of America in making up seating arrangements for dinner parties, or where a United States representative once suggested— in full earnestness—that the city might become the capital of the Southern Confederacy, Washington now took on all the trappings of a national state. Men were drafted into a Federal army; people were taxed directly; the power and reach of the Federal courts were expanded; the first national cur-rency was unveiled; public education was promoted; Western territories were settled; and centralized assistance was promulgated through the Freedman's Bureau.

All throughout the war, one could hear the banging of nails and the squeal of saws vying with the echo of cannons on far-off battlefields, and, almost daily, one could watch the carpenters and masons compete with the soldiers and bureaucrats. By the end of April 1865, stunning progress on both scores had indeed been made. Among other things, the Capitol dome was finally complete, with the statue of armed Freedom standing proudly at rest; like George Washington in retirement, her sword now sheathed. And Washington itself was a world transformed: never again would it regain its "old jog trot way of life." No one would doubt that it had been definitively established as the powerful seat of a federal authority. But in the end, most grand of all was not the city's architecture nearing completion, or the mighty reach of its representative government, or the expanded authority of its chief magistrate, or any of its specific programs, but its very idea: the nation it had been tasked to represent.

❧   ❧   ❧

The nation. For all the changes, the nation was now a powerful, compelling, enthralling idea, a symbol of a sturdy country, an embodiment of an enduring people, an arena for the peaceful resolution of differences, the stitch in the fabric that even the Founders missed. Political tastes would come and go; political fashions and exigencies would change; affairs of state would shift this way and that; and over the years and the ages, arguments would be feverishly waged—about political candidates, about political policies, about political parties, and, just as certainly, about government itself. But on one fact, and one fact alone, would there continue to be unity: the idea of the nation. And in the late spring days of 1865 following the grand review, after the cheering troops in blue had departed, you could glimpse it even then.

Across the Potomac, the guns had fallen silent. The watch guards had departed from the Washington bridges. And the sound of bugles piercing the raw air or the chilling yip-yip of the rebel yell would never again be heard. In this one fleeting moment, this one shining point in time, a bittersweet process of rebuilding began. T. S. Eliot, in part recalling Chaucer's pilgrims, would one day write: "April is the cruelest month . . ."

And he would also write: "I had not thought death had undone so many." Therein lay the terrible grandeur to the war. As flag-draped, homemade coffins were lowered slowly into the ground; as tearful widows combed the remains of battlefields, lamps held aloft in one hand, turning over corpses to search for their husbands with the other; as bareheaded Americans everywhere trembled in the evening's chill; as young wives hesitantly watched the road through their windows; and as exhausted, hungry, maimed, and brooding ex-soldiers limped their way to their homes, the nation collectively strode into a new era. It continues still.

NOTES

To avoid an extremely cumbersome and unwieldy endnotes section, I have adopted the widespread practice of a collective reference, rather than numerical citations. This section also does not list every book, journal article, and published document that I consulted in constructing this book, because, again, to do so would have been extremely unwieldy. Instead, to the maximum extent possible, I have sought to list, generally in the order in which they were used, those books, monographs, diaries, newspapers, and journal articles that have been most influential in shaping my thinking and writing, including quotations and interpretations. Similarly, in the interest of readability, I have not referenced every quotation, particularly those that are drawn from the common "text" or "body" of Civil War literature. Moreover, I have also extensively listed works that provided useful background for me and that interested readers may consult for further reference; these are sometimes accompanied by a brief discussion of the sources. And in a number of places, I have taken the opportunity to comment on scholarly controversies and debates that would otherwise be cumbersome in the actual body of the text, or added other useful bits of information and discussion.

An additional word about my approach. The literature on the Civil War, primary and secondary, is vast, varied, fascinating, and often distinguished. For *April 1865*, a book principally of interpretation and analysis, woven into a narrative of the month of April 1865 and surrounded by a shell of larger history, I have sought to reference for interested readers the best of Civil War works, both scholarly and commercial, books and articles. In addition, I have combed relevant newspapers of the time, Northern and Southern alike. A number of the most useful are mentioned. The same can be said of the many trips I have taken to battlefields themselves, as well as to different Southern cities, particularly Richmond; there is no substitute for actually walking, feeling, and trying to relive what really happened. The many days I spent on Lee's retreat—

by car and on foot, on those same hot April days—is but one example of this; so, too, in trying to recreate Booth's escape, or walking the streets of Richmond, seeking to understand how its fall unfolded, in all its agony and splendor; or leaving Ford's Theater, trying to understand the chaos that gripped Washington in the wake of Lincoln's assassination.

Finally, given that my initial training was in international affairs and political science, and that I have spent many years in the foreign policy and defense worlds advising politicians and senior administration officials, including two secretaries of defense, I have not hesitated to rely upon or use non–Civil War studies that I have felt shed valuable light on the subject or that have provided otherwise invaluable insights. Such an approach has assisted me in a number of places, for example, understanding the complex dynamics of how the Confederacy ultimately surrendered across-the-board or the intricate and tense discussions within the Lincoln cabinet after the assassination. Also, in the broader applications of this project, I have, of course, been somewhat shaped by the number of years I had spent actually dealing with the question of contemporary civil wars, like those in El Salvador; Cambodia, where I was on the first American plane to touch down in Phnom Penh since the United States broke off relations after the Vietnam War; Yugoslavia; and even the dissolution of the Soviet empire, when from the docks of Poland I had the privilege of spending time with Lech Walesa, then a "dissident-rebel," and when on a soft couch in the salons of Czechoslovakia, I met with Vaclav Havel, then an obscure, dissenting intellectual. Ultimately, of course, our Civil War was a very different affair. Nonetheless, it should not be surprising that my frame of reference is at times somewhat different from that of recent or dominant trends in Civil War historiography.

As much as possible, I have sought to bring my subject alive with vivid writing, something a vast array of historians from Doris Kearns Goodwin to Stephen Ambrose, James McPherson to Daniel Boorstin, David McCullough and Paul Johnson and William Manchester, all recognize as crucial to the craft. And throughout the course of writing this book, I have been keenly mindful of Daniel Boorstin's exhortation that the historian and author is both "discoverer and creator" (*Hidden History: Exploring Our Secret Past*, Harper and Row, 1987, 3–23). At the same time, Boorstin reminds us that the historian, in search of an original vision, is always dealing with a difficult, even impossible task. Quoting the great Dutch historian J. H. Huizinga, such a task is, and I paraphrase slightly, a matter of always "wrestling with the Angels." This is no less true here.

A number of distinguished works have been employed throughout this study. Their abbreviations are:

Boorstin	Daniel J. Boorstin, *The Americans: The National Experience* (Vintage, 1965).
BC	James McPherson, *Battle Cry of Freedom* (Oxford University Press, 1988).
CWH	*Civil War History*.
Donald	David Herbert Donald, *Lincoln* (Simon and Schuster, 1995).
Foote	Shelby Foote, *The Civil War: A Narrative*, 3 vols. (Random House, 1986); vol. 3 unless otherwise noted.

Freeman	Douglas Southall Freeman, *R. E. Lee: A Biography*, 4 vols. (Scribner's, 1934–35); vol. 4 unless otherwise noted.
Gallagher	Gary Gallagher, *The Confederate War* (Harvard University Press, 1997).
Glenn	Bayly E. Marks and Mark N. Schatz, eds., *Between North and South, a Maryland Journalist Views the Civil War: The Narrative of William Wilkins Glenn 1861–1869* (Associated University Presses, 1976).
Grant	U. S. Grant, *Personal Memoirs of U. S. Grant* (Smithmark, 1994).
Johnson	Paul Johnson, *A History of the American People* (HarperCollins, 1997).
Leech	Margaret Leech, *Reveille in Washington 1860–1865* (Carroll and Graf, 1991).
Oates	Stephen B. Oates, *With Malice Toward None: A Life of Abraham Lincoln* (HarperCollins, 1994).
OR	*War of the Rebellion . . . Official Records of the Union and Confederate Armies*, 128 vols. (Washington, D.C., 1880–1901).
Palmer and Colton	R. R. Palmer and Joel Colton, *A History of the Modern World* (Knopf, 1978).
MC	C. Vann Woodward, ed., *Mary Chesnut's Civil War* (Yale University Press, 1981).

Other abbreviated titles are listed in the body of the notes. While broken down by chapter, to save space the notes are done in a running order, starting from the beginning.

INTRODUCTION

story of the Civil War stops: For example, see *BC*. One of the very best accounts of the war in a single volume, James McPherson's 862-page book on the Civil War addresses the month of April 1865 in a mere nine pages, the events after Appomattox in just four pages. Similarly, Burke Davis's classic, *To Appomattox: Nine April Days* (Eastern Acorn Press, 1992), ends promptly with Lee's surrender, as does Bruce Catton's marvelous *A Stillness at Appomattox* (Anchor Books, 1990). **the whole of April 1865:** A number of very good books deal with this time period. One of the most recent, and quite excellent, which incorporates much new scholarship, is Noah Andre Trudeau, *Out of the Storm: The End of the Civil War* (Little, Brown, 1994). Other older but very important studies are Davis, *To Appomattox*, and Philip Van Doren Stern, *An End to Valor: The Last Days of the Civil War* (Houghton Mifflin, 1958), as well as Christopher M. Calkins, *The Appomattox Campaign* (Combined Books, 1997). Also useful is Robert Hendrickson, *The Road to Appomattox* (Wiley, 1988), and Richard Wheeler, *Witness to Appomattox* (Harper and Row, 1989). **the story of the making of our nation:** In Daniel Boostin's rich phrase, this book seeks to explore what would constitute a "Fertile verge" in history, separating one era from another; see his marvelous *Hidden History*, xiii.

For historians, it is axiomatic: See R. R. Palmer, *The World of the French Revolution* (Harper and Row, 1971), 1–47, esp. 3–5. **historians often call "contingency":** See discussion in *BC*, 853–62, esp. 857–58. In effect, the reader will see that I have applied the notion of contingency to the period of April 1865. Also see James McPherson in "American Victory, American Defeat" in

Gabor S. Boritt's important edited work, *Why the Confederacy Lost* (Oxford University Press, 1992), esp. 40–41, and Boritt's "Introduction" in that same work, 14, as well as E. H. Carr, *What Is History?* (Penguin, 1980). In this little gem of a book, Carr refers to "an unending dialogue between the present and past." For other viewpoints, see Geoffrey Barraclough, *An Introduction to Contemporary History* (Penguin, 1977), 9–42, and *History in a Changing World* (Penguin, 1955), 14; and Hugh Trevor-Roper, *The Rise of Christian Europe* (Harcourt Brace Jovanovich, 1975), 7–33. Also see Gary Gallagher's review essay "Civil War Military Leaders Reassessed," *Reviews in American History* 23 (1995), where he asserts that new studies should "ask different questions," 226. Daniel Boorstin sums up this task of historical inquiry nicely: while seeking to create "an original vision," "the successful historian at his best demands and secures a willing suspension of knowledge. He asks the reader to pretend that he does not already know . . . and adds new drama to everything we thought we already knew," *Hidden History*, 22. **of decisions made, but also one of decisions rejected:** On this point, see discussion in "Introduction" in Stephen E. Ambrose, *Americans at War* (Berkley, 1998), ix–xvi. Ambrose makes the point that "history is about people, leaders and led." He further notes that in history, "nothing is inevitable." Author-columnist William Safire once offered me this spirited question: "What if Lincoln had lost the 1864 election? Which almost happened . . ." Gabor S. Boritt, invoking French thinker Raymond Aron, warns that "overlooking the 'might have beens' may prevent the full understanding of 'the have-beens' that make up history," Boritt, "Introduction," esp. 5. The spirit of these points by Ambrose, Safire, Boorstin and Boritt, and McPherson on "contingency" or "turning points," suffuse this study. For further discussion, see the essay "The Fool Who Saved the Nation, and Other Historical What-If's," *New York Times*, July 17, 1999, and Robert Cowley's excellent essay "The Road Not Taken," *MHQ: The Quarterly Journal of Military History* 10, no. 3 (Spring 1998): 64–89. Cowley writes, "Might-have-beens lead us to question long-held assumptions" and they "define true turning points." He adds that "small changes are likely . . . to have major repercussions," 65; also George M. Frederickson, *Why the Confederacy Did Not Fight a Guerilla War After the Fall of Richmond: A Comparative View* (Gettysburg College, 35th Annual Fortenbaugh Memorial Lecture), another outstanding discussion; and Howard Mean's novelistic treatment, *CSA—The Confederate States of America* (Morrow, 1998). **"hoarse cry of vengeance":** Quote in Leech, 400. **How this came about:** See Trevor-Roper, *Rise of Christian Europe*. Roper stresses that history should not remove "the sense of wonder," "the unpredictability," and "therefore the freshness [events] ought to have," 24. Restoring the sense of contingency, and the freshness, to the events of April 1865 is precisely in this vein. Trevor-Roper also encourages historians to "occasionally trespass into less familiar circumstances," 7. This, too, I have done.

how to bring peace . . . in the wake of a civil war's bloody aftermath: There is, of course, a huge body of literature dealing precisely with this question that has arisen in the last decade, particularly in the fields of political science and international affairs, and among policy makers. The United States Institute of Peace in Washington, D.C., to take another example, has also been quite vigorous in pursuing this question. **Far too many civil wars end quite badly:** For instance, see William Shawcross, *Deliver Us from Evil: Peacekeepers, Warlords and a World of Endless Conflict* (Simon and Schuster, 2000), and Fred Ikle, *Every War Must End* (Columbia University Press, 1971);

also Fen Osler Hampson, *Why Peace Settlements Succeed or Fail* (USIP Press, 1996); John Paul Lederach, *Building Sustainable Reconciliation in Divided Societies* (USIP Press, 1997); and Michael Howard, "When Are Wars Decisive?" in *Survival* 41, no. 1 (Spring 1999): 126–35. My thanks to the Honorable Andrew Marshall, director of the Pentagon Office of Net Assessment and adviser to seven secretaries of defense, for bringing this to my attention.

Prelude : "A Nation Delayed"

Thomas Jefferson decided to call it Monticello: For the following section, the principal sources I have relied upon heavily for the intertwined stories of Jefferson and Monticello are: Jack McLaughlin, *Jefferson and Monticello: The Biography of a Builder* (Henry Holt, 1988), which is the best book on Monticello, and David McCullough, "House as Autobiography," in *House Beautiful* 139, no. 2 (February 1997): 78–85, a wonderful essay. Also "Journal of Anna Maria Brodeau, Wife of Dr. William Thorton of Washington, D.C.," in Manuscript Division, Library of Congress, Washington, D.C.; Mary Cable and Annabelle Prager, "The Levys of Monticello," in *American Heritage* 29, no. 2 (February/March 1978): 32–39; Thomas Rhodes (as told by) and Frank B. Lord, *The Story of Monticello* (American Publishing, 1928), esp. 79–93; and Henry N. Ferguson, "The Man Who Saved Monticello," in *American History Illustrated* 14, no. 10 (1980): 20–28; Thomas Fleming, "Monticello's Long Career—From Riches to Rags to Riches," *Smithsonian* 4, no. 3 (1973): 62–69. **"I view cities as pestilent to the morals":** Richard Hofstadter, "Thomas Jefferson: The Aristocrat as Democrat," *The American Political Tradition and the Men Who Made It* (Vintage, 1955), 32. **"the ink freezes":** Quote from McCullough, "House as Autobiography," p. 80. **"it is falling around their ears":** Quote from McLaughlin, *Jefferson and Monticello*, 15. **dinners reverberated . . . like Greek colloquia:** McLaughlin, *Jefferson and Monticello*, 43. **lay the seeds of a second Athens:** Stephen Ambrose, *Undaunted Courage* (Simon and Schuster, 1996) 33–34, hereafter *UC*. **preferably, a new Rome:** See Garry Wills, *Lincoln at Gettysburg: The Words That Remade America* (Simon and Schuster, 1992), who points out that America's Greek revival was, even more than the American love affair with Rome, an idea whose moment had come in the nineteenth century, esp. 41–44; for more on Roman symbolism in eighteenth-century America, see Wills's *Cincinnatus: George Washington and the Enlightenment* (Doubleday, 1984); the standard text on the Republican tradition of Rome in the modern world remains J. G. A. Pocock, *The Machiavellian Moment* (Princeton University Press, 1975). **"It fell to the lot of one Virginian to define America":** C. Vann Woodward quote in C. Vann Woodward, *The Guardian of Southern History* (Vintage, 1961), 25.

Few men, even among the Founding Fathers: The principal sources I have used for Jefferson in this section, in addition to those cites named for Monticello, are: Ambrose, *UC*; Hofstadter, *American Political Tradition*, 18–44; Fawn Brodie, *Thomas Jefferson: An Intimate History* (Norton, 1974); and Albert Jay Nock, *Jefferson* (Harcourt Brace, 1926). Quotes used are from these sources, unless otherwise noted. Also J. C. Miller, *The Wolf by the Ears: Jefferson and Slavery* (Free Press, 1977); Joseph Ellis, *American Sphinx* (Vintage, 1998) Dumas Malone, *Jefferson, the Virginian* (Little, Brown, 1948); Connor Cruise O'Brien, *The Long Affair: Thomas Jefferson and the French Revolution* (1996) and O'Brien, "Thomas

Jefferson: Radical and Racist," *Atlantic Monthly* (October 1996): 53–68; Merrill Peterson, *The Jefferson Image in the American Mind* (Oxford University Press, 1960); Henry Adams, *History of the United States During the Administrations of Jefferson and Madison*, 9 vols. (Viking Press, 1891–93); Bernard Bailyn, "Boyd's Jefferson: Notes for a Sketch," *New England Quarterly* 33 (1960), 380–401; and Paul Johnson's richly textured *History of the American People*, esp. 241–56. **He quickly rose to the task:** O'Brien, one of Jefferson's critics, refers to him less in the exalted role as the Declaration's author and more as a "draughtsman." He also quotes William Cohen's 1969 contention that Jefferson was "able to discuss the matter of slave breeding in much the same terms that one would use when speaking of the propagation of dogs and horses," "Thomas Jefferson," 67. **"kissing his hands and feet, some crying":** Also from McLaughlin, *Jefferson and Monticello*, see 240 and chapter 4, "To Possess Living Souls," 94–145. **The daily routine:** See McLaughlin on this point. **the greatest empire builder:** At one point, for instance, he frankly discussed acquiring Cuba from Napoleon and Canada through a war with Britain, see Brodie, *Thomas Jefferson*, 417. **his mind encompassed:** Ambrose, *UC*, 56. **what kind of civilization?:** See Ambrose, *UC*, 51–54. **Jefferson was torn:** Nock, *Jefferson*, 198–99.

The fragility of America as a nation: For the following discussion, see John H. Murrin, "A Roof Without Walls: The Dilemma of American National Identity" in *Beyond Confederation: Origins of the Constitution and American National Identity*, Richard Beeman, Stephen Botein, and Edward Carter II, eds. (University of North Carolina Press, 1987), 333–48, and also Boorstin, esp. 327–430. (Boorstin's terrific book is a must read for anyone wanting to understand the period of American history from its earliest days to the Civil War itself.) The following draws extensively upon these two outstanding works, from which quotes are taken unless indicated otherwise. Also see Boorstin's lengthy bibliographic note on 489–95. For further in-depth works, I would strongly encourage readers to consult this note. Further see Carl N. Dengler's excellent essay "One Among Many: The United States and National Unification," in *Lincoln, the War President: The Gettysburg Lectures*, 89–119; Boritt, ed., *Why the Confederacy Lost;* Johnson, 123–210, for a good overview; and David M. Potter, *The Impending Crisis 1848–1861* (Harper and Row, 1976); for basic but helpful discussion of what constitutes a nation, the rise of the nation-state, and nationalism, see Palmer and Colton, 400, 433, 503–4. The literature on this subject is vast, especially in political science; a few other readings are L. L. Snyder, *Varieties of Nationalism: A Comparative Study* (Hinsdale, 1970); P. C. Jessup, *The Birth of Nations* (Columbia Univeristy Press, 1974); and O. Dann and J. R. Dinwiddy, eds., *Nationalism in the Age of the French Revolution* (London and Ronceverte, 1988). **they were for more than a century and a half British:** In fact, vestiges of a British identity and sympathy lasted for many years after independence. Consider this from John Howard Hinton's introduction to his history of the United States, *The History and Topography of the United States* (Samuel Walker), published in 1834: "We are aware that the circumstances by which the last of nations came to birth, and the republican character of its institutions, are apt to produce soreness in the minds of a large portion of influential persons among us," 9; "The history of the United States is in many respects humiliating and painful to the feelings of Englishmen," 11; also see Murrin, "Roof Without Walls," on this general point, esp. 338. **Thus, the very heading:** See Boorstin, 402–3 and 405 on this point, including quotes. **not created one nation but thirteen:** "Yes," quipped one British diplomat at the time, "and they will all speak English," Hinton, *History and*

Topography of the United States, fifty years later pointed out: "the peculiarity of the republic, in its consisting of many different *sovereign* states, has tended very considerably to multiply the number of publications, each author naturally desirous to detail most minutely the circumstances which occurred in his own *states* . . . ," 8, emphasis added; see also Boorstin on 405 for this general point, and Dengler, "One Among Many," who refers to "the incomplete character of American nationalism," 101. **new states were as dramatically different:** Boorstin, 413. **constitutions were not national codes:** Boorstin, 428. **Even the very use:** Boorstin, 415. **Washington's parting speech:** See Richard Norton Smith's outstanding biography, *Patriarch: George Washington and the New American Nation* (Houghton Mifflin, 1993), 280. Smith points out that the early America was like "ancient Gaul," "divided into three parts, each with its own climate, social system and economic requirement," 31. **"Americans erected their constitutional roof":** Murrin, "Roof Without Walls," 347. Also see Daniel J. Boorstin, *The Genius of American Politics* (University of Chicago Press, 1953). Boorstin reminds us that the American Revolution "was not the product of a nationalistic spirit," and that it lacked an "enthusiasm for the birth of a new nation"; and adds that it was "notably lacking in cultural self-consciousness and . . . any passion for national unity," 70, 72–73. **Wills has stated:** Wills, *Lincoln at Gettysburg*, 86.

    across a vast domain: Boorstin, 417. **Tradition was against them:** Theodore Draper, "The Constitution Was Made, Not Born," in *New York Times Book Review*, October 10, 1993, review of Bernard Bailyn, ed., *Federalist and Antifederalist Speeches, Articles and Letters During the Struggle over Ratification* (Library of America, 1993) 2 vols.; see Bailyn books as well. **What did not change:** See 407–30 for this paragraph in Boorstin, esp. 417–18; also see Kenneth Stampp, *The Imperiled Union, Essays on the Background of the Civil War* (Oxford University Press, 1980), esp. Stampp chapter on "The Concept of a Perpetual Union," 3–36, a superb essay and overview on this subject; I draw heavily upon this chapter for the ensuing discussion on union and disunion. **The first spark assaulting national unity:** See Thomas P. Slaughter, *The Whiskey Rebellion: Frontier Epilogue to the American Revolution* (Oxford University Press, 1986). This is the best discussion on the matter, a fine scholarly work that is wonderfully narrated. Also see Ambrose, *UC*, 38–43. He calls the rebellion "the greatest threat to national unity" between the Revolutionary War and the Civil War, 38, adding "this threat of secession was quite real," 52; actually, it could be added that as early as 1779–80, with the war going badly, discontented farmers in Berkshire County held a convention and threatened to secede from Massachusetts. Washington biographer Smith, *Patriarch*, 210–26, adds that for George Washington "nothing less was at stake than the survival of the central government," esp. 226. For further study, see Jeffrey Crow, "The Whiskey Rebellion in North Carolina," *North Carolina Historical Review* 66, no. 1 (1989): 1–28; Mary Bonsteel Tachau, "The Whiskey Rebellion in Kentucky: A Forgotten Episode of Civil Disobedience," *Journal of the Early American Republic* 2, no. 3 (1982): 239–59; and George Connor, "The Politics of Insurrection: A Comparative Analysis of the Shays', Whiskey, and Fries' Rebellion, *Social Science Journal* 29, no. 3 (1992): 259–81. **the next alarum came:** For discussion of Virginia and Kentucky resolutions, see Dumas Malone, *Jefferson and the Ordeal of Liberty* (Little, Brown, 1962), vol. 3, 395–409; also Ethelbert Dudley Warfield, *The Kentucky Resolutions of 1798: An Historical Study* (Putnam's, 1887); Stampp, *Imperiled Union*, 22–24. **fatal to the ten-year-old Constitution:** Among others, Palmer, *World of the French Revolution*, 230–31;

on the threat of secession, for further reading, see Kenneth Stampp, ed., *The Causes of the Civil War* (Touchstone, 1991). **affirmed a basis:** Brodie makes this point, too, *Thomas Jefferson*, 311. **during the War of 1812:** See James Banner Jr., "A Shadow of Secession? The Hartford Convention, 1814," *History Today* 38 (September 1988): 34–41, for excellent overview; quotes from Banner and Stampp, *Imperiled Union*, unless otherwise noted; also see Banner, *To the Hartford Convention: The Federalists and the Origins of Party Politics in Massachusetts, 1789–1815* (Knopf, 1970); Reginald Horseman, *The War of 1812* (Knopf, 1969); J. C. A. Stagg, *Mr. Madison's War: Politics, Diplomacy, and Warfare in the Early American Republic, 1783–1830* (Princeton University Press, 1983). Robert Leckie, in *The Wars of America* (Harper and Row, 1968), states firmly: "the Hartford Convention pointed a pistol at the heart of the Union. In simplest terms, New England proposed to defend herself with her own forces financed by tax monies collected within her own borders. As the Federalists well knew, what New England could do the other sections might also do . . . ," 302. **To the horror and disgust of Southerners:** Southerners deeply resented the actions of New England, creating profound friction between the two sections. Consider the words of one Southern senator, dripping with sarcasm and disgust: "whatever differences of opinion might have existed to the cause of the war, the country has a right to expect that when once invoked on the contest, all Americans would cordially unite . . . as in the South . . . But not so in New England; there great efforts were made to stir up the minds of the people to oppose it. Nothing was left undone to embarrass the financial operations of the government, to prevent the enlistment of troops, to keep back the men and money of New England from service to the Union, to force the president from his Senate. 'Yes sir,' the Island of Elbe! Or a halter! were the alternatives they presented to Madison!" Hinton, *History and Topography of the United States*, 393–94. **Ultimately, cooler heads prevailed:** According to Lawrence Cress, Federalist calls for secession provoked fears of civil war, military despotism, and the kind of demagoguery that had doomed the French Revolution to tyranny, see "'Cool and Serious Reflection': Federalist Attitudes Toward War in 1812," *Journal of the Early Republic* (Summer 1987): 123–45, esp. 134–37. **Nullification and secession:** Many Southerners, interestingly enough, saw the North as initiating secession. That the mood was raw and bitter long before the Civil War was without doubt. Listen to Southerner Mathew Carey in 1834: "demagogues from the eastern states, and regardless of their vital interests, were courting their own destruction by allowing a few restless, turbulent men, to lead them blindfolded to a separation pregnant with their own ruin." And also: ". . . if a separation to the latter who have so long been harassed with complaints, the ingratitude, the restlessness, the turbulence, that their patience has been tried almost to endurance." Both quotes in Hinton, *History and Topography of the United States*, at note, 389. **Nor did the studied ambiguities:** For following discussion, see Stampp, *Imperiled Union*; for divergent views, the interested reader may also refer to *The Writings and Speeches of Daniel Webster: Speeches in Congress* (Little, Brown, 1903), vol. 6; and Richard K. Cralle, ed., *Speeches of John C. Calhoun, Delivered in the House of Representatives and in the Senate* (Appleton, 1851). **Union's perpetuity:** See Charles Royster's discussion of how Americans saw their republic as a "vulnerable" and "short-lived" one, with no promise of "perpetuity." Royster even contends that George Washington thought "failure inevitable," *The Destructive War: William Tecumseh Sherman, Stonewall Jackson, and the Americans* (Vintage, 1993), esp. 146.

By mid-century: On this matter, see, for instance, McPherson's sweeping overview, 6–46, and Johnson, 283–419. **"I, for one"** and **"I love the Union as I love my wife":** Quotes in Stampp, *Imperiled Union*, 27, 25. **But it was by no means:** See Paul Nagel, *One Nation Indivisible: The Union in American Thought, 1776–1861* (Oxford University Press, 1964), for analysis of the Union as an experiment; also see Peter Onuf, "'It Is Not a Union,'" *Wilson Quarterly* 11, no. 2 (Spring 1987): 97–104. **as did California:** See Boorstin, 264–74, esp. 270–72; he reminds us, for instance, that Jefferson admired John Jacob Astor's Pacific Northwest outpost, Astoria, as "the germ of a great, free and independent empire on that side of the continent," 270. Also see Richard D. Poll and William MacKinnon, "Causes of the Utah War Reconsidered," *Journal of Mormon History* 20, no. 2 (1994): 16–44; Robert Chandler, "The Velvet Glove: The Army During the Secession Crisis in California, 1860–1861," *Journal of the West* 20, no. 4 (1981): 35–42, esp. 42, on Californian secession and the Pacific republic; as the *California Herald* put it in 1861: "Long Live the Pacific Republic!," 36; also Ronald Woolsey, "The Politics of a Lost Cause: 'Seceshers' and Democrats in Southern California During the Civil War," *California History* 69, no. 4 (1990–91): 372–83. For more detail, also see Alvin M. Josephy Jr., *The Civil War in the American West* (Knopf, 1991), 233–34; one could also add the example of Vice President Aaron Burr, who after 1804 entered into a conspiracy with some New England Federalists who hoped to secede from the Union and form a Northern Confederacy, of which New York State was to be the keystone. He later went west after March 1805, where his machinations included setting up an independent republic in Louisiana. See Thomas P. Slaughter's review essay "Conspiratorial Politics: The Public Life of Aaron Burr," *New Jersey History* 103 (1985): 68–81, and Leckie, *Wars of America*, 228. **New York City:** See Tyler Anbinder, "Fernando Wood and New York City's Secession from the Union: A Political Appraisal," *New York History* 68, no. 1 (January 1987): 66–92. For a host of fascinating reasons, Wood openly advocated New York City secession. Anbinder suggests that his sympathy for the South arose from a plight that he saw as similar to New York City's, see esp. 92; Mayor Wood thought of renaming a transformed New York "Tri–Insula," Roy Morris, *The Better Angel* (Oxford University Press, 2000), 10. **three or four "confederacies":** *BC*, 247.

To the south: Murrin, "Roof Without Walls," 334. **the Terror:** For overview, see Palmer and Colton, 341–416. *ronds-points:* Nock, *Jefferson*, 288–89. **fragmented, ever ready to disintegrate:** See, for instance, Peter N. Stearns, *1848: The Revolutionary Tide in Europe* (Norton, 1974); for American fears of suffering Europe's fate, see Palmer, *World of the French Revolution*, esp. 218–32, and Palmer and Colton, 416–61, for description of ongoing turmoil that gripped Europe like a "contagion." Further, see Boorstin, *Genius of American Politics*, 72–75; interestingly enough, it can be noted that those like the abolitionist Wendell Philips worried that "homogenous nations like France tend toward centralization; Confederations like ours tend inevitably to dismemberment," quoted in Dengler, "One Among Many," 111. **it was a larger fight . . . to construct a nation:** To underscore the magnitude of the task, consider Dengler's point that the Civil War, as a war for Southern independence, was actually "in the same league as Poland's and Hungary's wars of national liberation," taking place around the same time, "One Among Many," 101. **It was in April 1865:** Dengler refers to America as "an unfinished nation," much like Italy and Germany at the time, "One Among Many," 101.

As spring crept north: The following section on Monticello, and the beginning of this chapter, owes many thanks to "Monticello During the Civil War," a Research Memorandum prepared by the Monticello Research Department of the Thomas Jefferson Memorial Foundation. Special thanks to Cinder Stanton and Camile Wells for their assistance.

CHAPTER ONE: THE DILEMMA

Inauguration Day in the Union: The principal sources that I have drawn extensively upon for descriptions of Lincoln and the Lincoln inauguration are: Donald, esp. 565–68; Oates, esp. 409–12; Foote, esp. 810–17; Roy Basler, ed., *Abraham Lincoln: His Speeches and Writings* (Da Capo, 1946), esp. 792–94; also Leech, esp. 365–73; and editions of the *New York Times*, March 3, 4, 5, 1865, in Library of Congress. Quotes from these sources unless otherwise noted. See also Frederick Douglass, *Life and Times* (Park Publishing, 1881), 365–66, and William Lee Miller, "Lincoln's Second Inaugural: The Zenith of Statecraft," *Center Magazine* 13 (July/August 1980): 53–64, for thoughtful analysis. The relevance of bells as a great tradition owes a debt to Robert Massie, *Peter the Great* (Knopf, 1980), 7–8, and Boorstin, *Hidden History*, 28.

As he rode into Richmond, Virginia: The principal source used for Lee's meetings here are Freeman, esp. 1–22, and John B. Gordon, *Reminiscences of the Civil War* (Scribner's Sons, 1903), 385–94, which my section here tracks. Also Emory Thomas, *Robert E. Lee: A Biography* (Norton, 1995); Noah Andre Trudeau, "'A Mere Question of Time': Robert E. Lee from the Wilderness to Appomattox Court House," in Gary W. Gallagher, ed., *Lee: The Soldier* (University of Nebraska Press, 1996), 523–58; Ernest B. Furgurson, *Ashes of Glory: Richmond at War* (Knopf, 1996), 306–7; Foote, 839–40. **fewer than 35,000 were present for duty:** There is considerable—and unsettled— debate about the actual numbers in Lee's army at this time. Most accounts, especially Southern, place the total in the final days of surrender at around 35,000 men; Christopher M. Calkins, fac- toring backward from the number surrendered at Appomattox, adding those captured in the Appomattox campaign with those killed or wounded, and factoring desertions at 100 per day, arrives at a figure of 58,000 men. See *The Final Bivouac: The Surrender Parade at Appomattox and the Disbanding of the Armies, April 10–May 20, 1865* (H. E. Howard, 1998), 193. **River Queen, anchored off Hampton Roads:** For further reading, see Alexander H. Stephens, *A Constitutional View of the War Between the States*, 2 vols. (National Pub. Co., 1868–70), vol. 2, 611–12, which is the fullest account by a participant. Detailed secondary accounts include John G. Nicolay and John Hay, *Abraham Lincoln: A History*, 10 vols. (Century, 1890), vol. 10, 91–129, and Edward Chase Kirkland, *The Peacemakers of 1864* (Macmillan, 1927), 197–251; because there was no agenda and no notes taken, it is not possible to recreate the precise sequence of events. **a meeting of generals, led by Grant and Lee:** Donald, 573.

as compensation for their lost slaves: When he returned to Washington, Lincoln actually drafted a message to Congress asking for this appropriation to compensate slave owners once the Confederacy surrendered and the Thirteenth Amendment was ratified. There is also some debate as to whether Lincoln was willing to consider a peace settlement that did not include uni- versal emancipation. For discussion, see *BC*, 823 and footnote 30; for further, see Roy C. Basler, ed., *The Collected Works of Abraham Lincoln*, 9 vols. (Rutgers University Press, 1952–55), vol. 8, 260–61; Richard N. Current, *The Lincoln Nobody Knows* (Hill and Wang, 1958), 243–47. **Strangely lack- ing:** For this section, see Donald; also Oates and Foote.

Lee had secretly told congressional questioners: This was according to Confederate Senator Benjamin Hill, quoted in Furgurson, *Ashes of Glory* (hereafter *Ashes*) 306–7; Senator Williamson S. Oldham of Texas later said that a joint congressional committee that winter came to a "unanimous conclusion" that the South had "sufficient resources to . . . carry out the war for an indefinite period." See also Richard E. Beringer, Herman Hattaway, Archer Jones, and William Still Jr., *Why the South Lost the Civil War* (University of Georgia Press, 1986) 32–33.

what about Richmond?: The major sources that I have used on Richmond are a number of excellent accounts, primarily Emory M. Thomas, *The Confederate State of Richmond* (University of Texas Press, 1971); Emory M. Thomas, *The Confederate Nation: 1861–1865* (Harper Torchbooks, 1979), hereafter *CN*; and Furgurson, *Ashes of Glory*; all are outstanding accounts, which I extensively draw upon; also Johnson, 22–28, for Virginia history and settlers and K. M. Kostyal, *Virginia* (Compass American Guides, 1994), 17–31. Other sources consulted are Alfred Hoyt Bill, *The Beleaguered City* (Knopf, 1946); Virginius Dabney, *Richmond: The Story of a City* (Doubleday, 1976); firsthand accounts, including Warren Akin, *Letters of Warren Akin, Confederate Congressman*, Bell Irvin Wiley, ed. (University of Georgia Press, 1959); Robert G. H. Kean, *Inside the Confederate Government: The Diary of Robert Garlick Hill Kean*, Edward Younger, ed. (LSU Press, 1985); J. B. Jones, *A Rebel War Clerk's Diary*, Earl Schenck Miers, ed. (Sagamore Press, 1958); T. C. DeLeon, *Four Years in Rebel Capitals* (Gossip Printing, 1890); William J. Kimball, *Richmond in Time of War* (Houghton Mifflin, 1960); Katherine Jones, *Ladies of Richmond: Confederate Capital* (Bobbs-Merrill, 1962); Judith McQuire, *Diary of a Southern Refugee* (E. J. Hale and Son, 1867); Josiah Gorgas, *The Civil War Diary of General Josiah Gorgas*, Frank Vandiver, ed. (University of Alabama Press, 1947); also Douglas Southall Freeman, "The Confederate Tradition of Richmond," *Richmond Magazine* (June 1932): 42; Stephen W. Sears, *To the Gates of Richmond* (Ticknor and Fields, 1992); and Mary Wingfield Scott, *Houses of Old Richmond* (Whittet and Shepperson, 1950). **earliest years:** Thomas, *Confederate State of Richmond*, 3. **Patrick Henry . . . as Thomas Jefferson:** Brodie, *Thomas Jefferson*, 104. **Gabriel Prosser:** For more detail, see David Robertson, *Denmark Vessey: The Buried History of America's Largest Slave Rebellion and the Man Who Led It* (Knopf, 1999). **"the Dale's Code" . . . New World:** Johnson, 25–26. **As the capital** to **intricate landscaping of Capitol Square:** See Thomas, *Confederate State of Richmond*, 5–31, and Furgurson, *Ashes*, 3–30. **Thomas Ritchie of the Richmond Enquirer:** See Stampp, "Concept of a Perpetual Union," 25. Ritchie also accused delegates to the Hartford Convention of "plotting secession" and of "treason." **By 1859** to **young American republic:** Thomas, *Confederate State* and *CN*, and Furgurson, *Ashes*. To visit Richmond even now is to get a sense of the vast history surrounding the city. One gets a feeling that in many ways it, as much as Washington, D.C., has a deep attachment and roots to the country's beginnings. The statue of Washington and the Houdon busts in the capitol are especially a treat to see. **Jewish synagogues:** For further, see Bertram W. Korn, "The Jews of the Confederacy," *American Jewish Archives* 13 (1961), 3–90. **With its four newspapers:** On the Confederate press, see J. Cutler Andrews, *The South Reports the Civil War* (Princeton University Press, 1970). **"flushed faces" . . . "jubilant demonstrations,"** Quotes in *BC*, 278. **Amid the ever-increasing stress** to **"we will not surrender!":** See esp. Thomas, *The Confederate State*, 179–91; also Furgurson, *Ashes*, 287–302. **Spring meant a renewed campaign:** Dallas Tucker, "Fall of Richmond," *Richmond Dispatch*, 3 Feb. 1902, 153. **Richmonders had endured . . . littered the hillsides:** Thomas, *The Confederate State*, 190, 175. **"a dog bark or a cat**

meow": Furgurson, *Ashes*, 301. **amazing sight:** On gaiety and parties, see DeLeon, *Four Years in Rebel Capitols*, 351; McQuire, *Diary of a Southern Refugee*, 359. McQuire observed, "there seems to be a perfect mania on the subject of matrimony." Also Davis, *To Appomattox*, 11–13. **Confederate national identity:** Murrin, "Roof Without Walls," 344–45. For more extensive discussion, see John H. Murrin, "War, Revolution, and Nation-Making: The American Revolution versus the Civil War," John H. Murrin (unpublished paper furnished by Murrin to author). By way of comparison, Murrin notes further that by 1786, after Congress was on the run, New England delegates and others were openly talking of disunion and of partial confederacies; on this see *Boston Independent Chronicle*, February 15, 1787. **united by a sense of common culture . . . spring of 1865:** For a different wrinkle on this point, see Thomas, *CN*, who says that at this juncture the Southern nation was "coming apart," 277, and 278–306. **very different conception of itself:** The debate over Confederate nationalism is a considerable one, worthy of a set of essays unto itself: for starters, see Gary W. Gallagher's outstanding essay "Nationalism" in *The Confederate War* (Harvard University Press, 1996), 61–113; among critics of the strength of Confederate nationalism, see Paul D. Escott, "The Failure of Confederate Nationalism: The Old South's Class System in the Crucible of War," Harry P. Owens and James Cooke, *The Old South in the Crucible of War* (University Press of Mississippi, 1983), esp. 9–10, 12, and Paul D. Escott, *After Secession: Jefferson Davis and the Failure of Confederate Nationalism* (LSU Press, 1978); Drew Gilpin Faust, *The Creation of Confederate Nationalism: Ideology and Identity in the Civil War South* (LSU Press, 1988), esp. 6–7, 22, 42, 60, 84; Stampp, "The Southern Road to Appomattox," *Imperiled Union*, also speaks of the fragility of Confederate national sentiment, esp. 255–56, 259–60; Beringer, Hattaway, Jones, and Still, *Why the South Lost the Civil War*, talk of Southern nationalism, but then allude to the lack of "widely accepted mystical sense of distinct nationality." See esp. 66, 425–26; Reid Mitchell, "The Perseverance of the Soldiers," in Gabor S. Boritt, ed., *Why the Confederacy Lost* (Oxford University Press, 1992), 124; for a good detached essay, see David M. Potter, "The Historian's Use of Nationalism and Vice Versa," in David Potter, *The South and Sectional Conflict* (LSU Press, 1968), esp. 43, 45, and 63. This essay is a thorough work on the pitfalls accrued in examining the subject of Confederate nationalism. Potter notes that historians often deny nationality to groups of which it "morally disapproves," 9; Faust buttresses this point, saying that scholars have feared accepting the reality of Confederate nationalism, as if this would imply "legitimacy," *Creation of Confederate Nationalism*, 3.

"**About the last of August**": Johnson, 26–27. **Southerners clung . . . Constitution:** BC, 40. **In ensuing years** to "**freemen out of it**": For concise summaries of the slavery issue, see BC, esp. 37–46; Johnson, 72–79, 307–20; 399–401; Robert Leckie, *None Died in Vain*, 7–27 (HarperCollins, 1990); and for more detailed reading, see Edgar Toppin, *The Black American in United States History* (Allyn and Bacon, 1973); Eugene Genovese, ed., *The Political Economy of Slavery: Studies in the Economy and Society of the Slave South* (Vintage, 1965); Louis Filler, *The Crusade Against Slavery* (Harper and Row, 1960); Kenneth Stampp, *The Peculiar Institution: Slavery in the Ante-Bellum South* (Knopf, 1956); Leon Litwack, *North of Slavery: The Negro in the Free States 1790–1860* (University of Chicago Press, 1961), which addresses racial tensions and discrimination in the North; James Oakes, *The Ruling Race: A History of American Slaveholders* (Knopf, 1982); John Blassingame, *The Slave Community: Plantation Life in the Antebellum South* (Oxford University Press, 1979); Ira Berlin, *Slaves Without Masters: The Free Negro in the Antebellum South*

(Pantheon, 1974); and Paul David et al., *Reckoning with Slavery* (Oxford University Press, 1976). **Confederate Constitution:** See Thomas, *CN*, 307–22. **arming of any of the 4 million slaves** to **beginning of the end of slavery:** This is one of the least studied but most fascinating aspects of both the black experience in slavery and the changing nature of the Confederacy during the war, one that cries out for more extensive research. The classic work, which I have drawn upon, remains Robert F. Durden, *The Gray and the Black: The Confederate Debate on Emancipation* (LSU Press, 1979); quotes from Durden unless otherwise noted. Also see compact discussions in *BC*, 831–38; Furgurson, *Ashes*, 280–83, 293–94, 299, 307–09, 313; Thomas, *CN*, 290–99; also see the thorough and balanced treatment in Ervin Jordan Jr.'s excellent "Uncommon Defenders: Confederate States Colored Troops as the Great White Hope," in *Black Confederates and Afro Yankees in Civil War Virginia* (University of Virginia Press, 1995), 232–63; the following section draws extensively from Durden and is informed by these other works. Durden's study replaces older, more dated and limited, albeit still useful studies; Nathaniel W. Stephenson, "The Question of Arming the Slaves," *American Historical Review* 18 (1913), 295–308; Charles H. Wesley, "The Employment of Negroes as Soldiers in the Confederate Army," *Journal of Negro History* 4 (July 1919): 239–53; and Thomas R. Hay, "The South and the Arming of the Slaves," *Mississippi Valley Historical Review* 6 (1919): 34–73; recent work by J. Tracy Power, *Lee's Miserables: Life in the Army of Northern Virginia from the Wilderness to Appomattox* (University of North Carolina Press, 1998), has some important material on this debate, 263–70; one of the better commentaries is still Clarence L. Mohr, "Southern Blacks in the Civil War," *Journal of Negro History* 49 (1974): 177–95. One of the better works on black Confederates remains Bell Irwin Wiley, *Southern Negroes, 1861–1865* (LSU Press, 1974); Thomas M. Preisser, "The Virginia Decision to Use Negro Soldiers in the Civil War, 1864–1865," *VMHB* 83 (January 1975): 99–111; also see Beringer, Hattaway, Jones, and Still, *Why the South Lost the Civil War*, 365–97. For a counterpoint on blacks in the Union army, see the authoritative Dudley T. Cornish, *The Sable Arm: Negro Troops in the Union Army, 1861–1865* (Longmans, Green, 1956); for a broader view of the Union at large, including racist resistance to emancipation in the North, see Forrest Wood, *Black Scare: The Racist Response to Emancipation and Reconstruction* (University of California Press, 1968); and see James McPherson, *The Negro's Civil War: How American Blacks Felt and Acted During the War for the Union* (Pantheon, 1965); Joseph T. Glatthaar, *Forged in Battle: The Civil War Alliance of Black Soldiers and White Officers* (Free Press, 1990); Noah Andre Trudeau, *Like Men of War: Black Troops in the Civil War* (Little, Brown, 1998); and Benjamin Quarles, *The Negro in the Civil War* (Little, Brown, 1953). Interest is being heightened in the controversial but important topic of blacks and slaves fighting for the Confederacy. See two fascinating pieces, one by Tony Horowitz, "Shades of Gray: Did Blacks Fight Freely for the Confederacy?" *Wall Street Journal*, May 8, 1997, A1, and Linda Wheeler, "Honoring a Son of the South: Descendants of White Confederates Salute Black Man's Service," *Washington Post*, December 4, 1999, B1; for more on the blacks in the Civil War, see McPherson, *Negro's Civil War*, an important study; James H. Brewer, *The Confederate Negro: Virginia's Craftsman and Military Laborers, 1861–1865* (Duke University Press, 1969); Robertson, *Denmark Vessey;* and Vincent Harding, *There Is a River: The Black Struggle for Freedom in America* (Harcourt Brace Jovanovich, 1981). **"Our only chance":** Quote from *MC.* **We are forced"** . . . **"THE COST":** Quotes from Durden, *Gray and the Black*, 24, 30–35, 42–44; also *BC*, 831–32. **Southern blacks . . . only to be turned down**, see Edgar Toppin, *Encyclopedia of the Confederacy*, vol.

1, "African-Americans in the Confederacy" (Simon and Schuster, 1993), 4–7, for a good overview ,and his *Black American in United States History*; also Mary F. Berry, "Negro Troops in Blue and Gray, the Louisiana Native Guards, 1861–1863," *Louisiana History* 8 (Spring 1967): 165–90. **"One man cannot do it"**: *MC*, 313. **"I was never much for niggers"**: Quote from Dudley T. Cornish, "African American Troops in the Union Army," *Encyclopedia of the Confederacy*, Richard N. Current, ed. (Simon and Schuster, 1993), 12, and Cornish's overview, 9–12, and also his *Sable Arm* for excellent treatment of this matter; for further, James McPherson, *Abraham Lincoln and the Second American Revolution* (Oxford University Press, 1990) and Glatthaar, *Forged in Battle*. **Patrick Cleburne:** Cleburne is one of the more understudied but truly fascinating—and actually historic—figures in the war. For more on this former druggist, see Craig L. Symonds, *Stonewall of the West: Patrick Cleburne and the Civil War* (University Press of Kansas, 1997), and Irving A. Buck, *Cleburne and His Command*, Thomas Robson Hay, ed. (McCowat Mercer, 1959). **"memorial" presentation . . . to the South**, and quotes: See Durden, *Gray and the Black*, 53–63; see also Irving A. Buck, "Negroes in Our Army," *Southern Historical Society Papers* 31 (1903): 215. **"monstrous . . . whipped"**: *BC*, 833. **"discouragements"**: *OR*, series 4, vol. 52, part 2, 608. **Ralph Waldo Emerson:** See Ralph L. Rusk, *The Life of Ralph Waldo Emerson* (Columbia University Press, 1949), 416. **"It is a question"**: Warren Akin to Mary Akin, November 14, 1862, *Letters of Warren Akin*, 32–33, reprinted in Furgurson, *Ashes*, 383; Akin, a member of the House Committee on Claims and an ordained Methodist minister, was known for his sympathy for the common people. **Davis cautiously moved:** On this point, see also *MC*, 696, 678–79, 586. **"The slave . . . a person"**: Davis to Congress, November 7, 1864, James D. Richardson, ed., *A Compilation of Messages and Papers of the Confederacy*, 2 vols. (United States Publishing Co., 1906), 482–98; also Thomas, *CN*, 290. **too much for the Confederate Congress:** For more on the Confederate Congress, see two crucial works, Wilfred Buck Yearns, *The Confederate Congress* (University of Georgia Press, 1960), and Thomas B. Alexander and Richard Beringer, *The Anatomy of the Confederate Congress: A Study of the Influence of Member Characteristics on Legislative Voting Behavior, 1861–1865* (Vanderbilt University Press, 1972); also David M. Potter's essay "Jefferson Davis and the Political Factors in Confederate Defeat," David Donald, ed., *Why the North Won the Civil War* (Touchstone, 1996), 93–114; and Merton E. Coulter, *The Confederate States of America 1861–1865* (LSU Press, 1950). **"We are reduced"**: Preisser, "Virginia Decision to Use Negro Soldiers in the Civil War," 99. **Robert Tooms:** Foote, 860. **Howell Cobb:** *OR*, series 4, vol. 3, 1009–10. **Every seat to "make up your mind!"**: Durden, *Gray and the Black*, 187–95; *Richmond Examiner*, February 19, 1865; Furgurson, *Ashes*, 293. **Secretary of State Judah P. Benjamin:** For more on Benjamin, see Eli N. Evans, *Judah P. Benjamin, The Jewish Confederate* (Free Press, 1988), especially pp. 249 and 259–291 for more on debate about "The Confederate Emancipation Proclamation." **"Freeing negroes"**: *MC*, 696. **"Victory itself"**: Durden, *Gray and the Black*, 140. **"poor man . . . reduced"**: Wiley, *Southern Negroes*, 156–57. **"terrible calamity"**: Durden, *Gray and the Black*, 99; also *BC*, 836. **Nathan Bedford Forrest:** See Jack Hurst, *Nathan Bedford Forrest: A Life* (Knopf, 1993), 246–47. **"If the public exigencies . . . any other regiment"**: Quotes from Durden, *Gray and the Black*, 222–23; Allen to James Seddon, September 26, 1864, reprinted in Durden, *Gray and the Black*, 74. **"color of the arm . . . independence"**: Quote from Power, *Lee's Miserables*, 251. **"tender-footed"**: Durden, *Gray and the Black*, 220–23, and 216. **Francis Lawley:** The date was February 16, 1865, Ian F. W. Beckett, ed., *The War Correspondents: The Civil War* (Grange, 1997), 166–67. **As early as 1863:** See, among others, Chesnut on this point, *MC*, 464; also Jones, 500–501. **far more blunt:** *Glenn*, 202. William Allan notes that Lee told Davis, "often and early," that slaves should be emancipated, see William Allan, "Memorandum of Conversations with General Robert Lee," in *Lee: The Soldier*, Gary Gallagher, ed. (University of Nebraska Press, 1996), 12. **"we should employ":** *Richmond Whig*, February 23, 1865. **"This measure . . . as slaves":** Durden, *Gray and the Black*, 206, 204–9; also see Barksdale's impassioned speech in defense of enlisting slaves, Durden, *Gray and the Black*, 242–49. **"author of this scheme" . . . "anything he may ask for":** *Mercury* and *Examiner*, February 16, 1865, in Durden, *Gray and the Black*, 206, and 204–24. **urgings of the governor, William Smith:** Durden, *Gray and the Black*, 202–3. **"rights of freedman":** On this, see Durden, *Gray and the Black*, 199–202, 215–24, 249–50, 268–69; there were still troubling obstacles: for one, slaves had to be volunteers, "patriotically rented by their masters." **Congressman Akin's wife was even more emphatic:** Beringer, Hattaway, Jones, and Still, *Why the South Lost the Civil War*, 382. **"If we had only freed":** *MC*, 678. **Sixteenth Georgia . . . Third Corps . . . Colonel Willy Pegram:** Gallagher, *Confederate War*, 83;, Power, *Lee's Miserables*, 267–68; also see recruitment appeal by Pegram in *Richmond Dispatch*, March 21, 1865. **volunteered to form a company of blacks:** In one novel idea, a surgeon of the Fifty-seventh Virginia Infantry proposed the creation of a black corps as a retaliatory mobile force to ravage the North with the sort of warfare done to Georgia by Sherman's army, see Jordan, *Black Confederates and Afro Yankees in Civil War Virginia*, 242. **Lee proposed to integrate:** Power, *Lee's Miserables*, 267. Orders from the adjutant general's office established guidelines for black Confederate recruitment. Officers were directed to treat blacks humanely and protect them from "injustice and oppression." Jordan, *Black Confederates and Afro Yankees in Civil War Virginia*, 247. **"I hope we will be able":** Letter of John W. Pilcher, March 22, 1865, exhibit in the Museum of the Confederacy, Richmond, Virginia; April 1998. **Early in the war . . . "fire on our side?":** The year was 1862, *MC*, 340; concerning this question of would they, consider the following example. F. W. Hancock, chief surgeon at Richmond's Jackson Hospital, polled his facility's hired black male slaves on Valentine's Day, 1865, to assess "if they would be willing to take up arms to protect their masters' families, homes and their own . . ." Of the seventy-two polled, sixty volunteered to fight the Yankees, "to the bitter end," Jordan, *Black Confederates and Afro Yankees in Civil War Virginia*, 245. **Horace Greeley's:** Durden, *Gray and the Black*, 228–29. **rarest sights in all the South:** Furgurson, *Ashes*, 313; Jordan, *Black Confederates and Afro Yankees in Civil War Virginia*, 247; *Richmond Examiner*, March 15, 18, 20, 1865, Library of Congress. Actually, there were other rare sights. For instance, a Virginia Military Institute cadet on picket duty at the Richmond front was amazed to be relieved by black soldiers who "politely intimated with the character of their orders, and took their position . . . with all the precision and alacrity of old soldiers," see Jordan, *Black Confederates and Afro Yankees in Civil War Virginia*, 246. **"with themselves."** *Richmond Examiner*, March 15, 18, 20, 1865, also Durden, *Gray and the Black*, 274–75 and Thomas, *Confederate State of Richmond*, 189–90. **beloved Army of Northern Virginia:** On blacks in Army of Northern Virginia during Lee's retreat, see important work by Trudeau, *Like Men of War*, 409–14; also see Calkins, *Appomattox Campaign*, 183–84. For instance, a Union chaplain observed, "a squad [of] many negroes recently armed by Jeff. Davis." According to Jordan, sixty blacks at Jackson Hospital already saw limited combat on March 11, 1865, two days before the Confederate Congress approved the enlistment of blacks; two companies of blacks, at the Petersburg front, saw combat under the command of Colonel Scott Shipp, commandant of the VMI Cadet Corps. Of their service, Major Henry Scott reported proudly, "I have the great pleasure in stating that my men acted with the utmost promptness and good will . . . Allow me to state Sir that they [the portion of his black company] behaved in an extraordinary acceptable manner," Jordan, *Black Confederates and Afro Yankees in Civil War Virginia*, 246. **James Longstreet:** Longstreet to W. H. Taylor correspondence, *OR*, series 1, vol. 46, part 3, 1367. He begins, "I have the honor respectfully to recommend the appointment . . . " **number of opponents:** For instance, South Carolina legislators were hotly holding out approval. By contrast, on April 2, Lee sent a hurried letter to President Davis on the organization and deployment of the black Confederate soldiers, reaffirming his willingness to detach whatever officers could be spared from the Petersburg front to lead black troops and promising to send their names to the War Department; he spoke of "the numerous applications which are present" and that "it is difficult for me to decide who are suitable for duty." He sent forth a list of twenty potential commanders of black confederates, Jordan, *Black Confederates and Afro Yankees in Civil War Virginia*, 249–50; 332–33. **done more for utilitarian reasons:** Ervin Jordan believes that a full-scale mobilization of Confederate blacks "might have tipped the scale in favor of the Confederacy," Jordan, *Black Confederates and Afro Yankees in Civil War Virginia*, 247. **"next summer's campaign":** Reprinted in *Richmond Examiner*, March 4, 1865. **end of slavery:** As Confederate soldier John Speer put it, "slavery is doomed," letter in Museum of Confederacy Exhibition, April 9, 1998. **"such a measure . . . abolishing slavery *entirely*":** Osmun Latrobe circular to division commanders, February 16, 1865, *OR*, series 4, vol. 12, 1263; Power, *Lee's Miserables*, 252–53; Durden, *Gray and the Black*, 217. **its independence:** On this see Gallagher's excellent essay "Nationalism," 63–111, esp. 81–82. He refers to the firestorm of controversy in the North over emancipation of slaves even though slave property was not at risk; also see Raimundo Luraghi, *The Rise and Fall of the Plantation South* (New Viewpoints, 1978), esp. 142–43.

"Mr. Custis . . . repent," "I do not think" . . . "stuff we are made": Walter H. Taylor, *Four Years with General Lee* (Appleton, 1877), 236–37, 144–46. **Under a moonlit night . . . solid tenth of his command:** For example, see Gordon, *Reminiscences of the Civil War*, 408–9; Foote, 841–44. There are serious critiques to be made of Lee's Fort Stedman raid. For instance, one eloquent Lee supporter, Clifford Dowdey, calls the raid "cloudy minded"; Trudeau says it smacked of "desperation" and "delusion." Quotes in Gary Gallagher, ed., *Lee: The Soldier* (University of Nebraska Press, 1996), 544, 548.

City Point: See Grant, 596–97; Oates, 417–18; Bruce Catton, *Stillness at Appomattox*, 321–23, and Bruce Catton, *Grant Takes Command* (Little, Brown, 1968), 434–36. **mementos of war:** See also, for instance, Davis, *To Appomattox*, 429–30, and also John S. Barnes, "With Lincoln from Washington to Richmond in 1865," *Appleton's Magazine* (May 1907): 520–22. **River Queen** (and meeting): See Donald, 571–74, which I draw heavily upon; also Foote, 854–57; Davis, *To Appomattox*, 24–28. **Grant would later describe:** On his anxieties, see Grant, esp. 592.

president nervously roamed: Oates, 419–20. **Grant triumphantly telegraphed:** Foote, 863–65.

Chapter Two: The Fall

plans of retreat . . . fight and fight valiantly: In addition to references already cited, there are a number of excellent treatments of Lee's retreat that I have drawn upon, including: Noah Andre

Trudeau, *The Campaign to Appomattox* (Eastern National Park and Monument Association, 1995); Trudeau, "'A Mere Question of Time,'" 523–58; Jerry Korn, *Pursuit to Appomattox* (Time-Life, 1987); Burleigh Rodick, *Appomattox: The Last Campaign* (Philosophical Library, 1965); Calkins, *Appomattox Campaign* and *Final Bivouac*; Hendrickson, *Road to Appomattox*; Wheeler, *Witness to Appomattox*; Stern, *End to Valor* (an older rendition, yet still very good); Foote, 864–956; and Freeman, esp. 22–164; Power, *Lee's Miserables*; also, the Virginia Park Service has recreated Lee's withdrawal, the route that interested readers should take, preferably coupled with a tour of Richmond, the Wilderness, and Petersburg; on this see, Christopher M. Calkins's accompanying monograph, *From Petersburg to Appomattox: A Tour Guide to the Routes of Lee's Withdrawal and Grant's Pursuit* (Farmville Herald, 1995). **their resolve—and even their sanity:** For instance, see Power, *Lee's Miserables*, 286–321. **reverence in which they hold Robert E. Lee,** and for the Lee extended profile (**At long last to let destiny slip through his fingers**): I have used the following: Freeman's *R. E. Lee: A Biography*, the classic text on Lee, vols. 1–4; while Freeman is reluctant to discuss Lee's flaws, his work remains the most thorough and most complete treatment, and much of his analysis is first-rate; Thomas, *Robert E. Lee*, up-to-date and a very balanced treatment, and along with Freeman, probably the best of the Lee biographies, steering its way through hagiography and wanton idol-smashing; Charles Flood, *Lee: The Final Years* (Houghton Mifflin, 1981), a book often overshadowed by other more popular treatments, but very useful; I am heavily indebted to these three. For more critical treatments, also Thomas Connelly, *The Marble Man: Robert E. Lee and His Image in American Society* (Knopf, 1977), and Alan T. Knoll, *Lee Considered: General Robert E. Lee and Civil War History* (University of North Carolina Press, 1991); John Keegan, the respected military historian, also takes a harsh view of Lee, see his *The Mask of Command* (Viking, 1987), calling him a man of "limited imagination" with a "conventional outlook," 197. The entire volume of Gallagher, ed., *Lee*, is an excellent reference, with some outstanding essays, a number reprinted, including: Gallagher, "Another Look at the Generalship of R. E. Lee," 275–91; Albert Castel, "The Historians and the General: Thomas L. Connelly versus Robert E. Lee," 209–25; Alan T. Knoll, "General Lee," 225–74; Gallagher, "If the Enemy Is There, We Must Attack Him," 497–522; also Clifford Dowdey, *Lee* (Gettysburg, 1991); finally, the Lee biographies in Geoffrey Ward, *The Civil War* (Knopf, 1990), 282–85; and Leckie, *None Died in Vain*, 332–40; Nancy S. Anderson and Dawn Anderson, *The Generals: Ulysses S. Grant and Robert E. Lee* (Knopf, 1988), a highly readable and thought-provoking account of both men; all quotes from these sources unless otherwise noted. **grazed his cheek . . . does not fear death:** Lee calmly showed his aides his cheek and nonchalantly announced that he had almost just been killed, Thomas, *Robert E. Lee*, 253. **King Arthur, the mighty English Dux Bellorum . . . the coda of the courtly knight:** For this historical background, see Edward Peters, *Europe and the Middle Ages* (Prentice-Hall, 1983), esp. 148–49, 230–31, 233; and Trevor-Roper, *Rise of Christian Europe*, 114–22. **general's intensity never wanes:** His aide Armistead Long commented that Lee "seemed able to bear any amount of fatigue" around the clock, even as he aged visibly, Thomas, *Robert E. Lee*, 352. **On March 29 to Hope against hope:** For brief overviews, also see *BC*, 844–46; and E. B. Long, *The Civil War Day by Day: An Almanac 1861–1865* (Da Capo, 1971), 658–62, an excellent resource for the Civil War student. **one prominent Federal general as "confused and conflicting":** This general was Joshua Lawrence Chamberlain, Gettysburg hero and author of *The Passing of the Armies* (1915; reprint, Stan Clark Press, 1994).

Lighthorse Harry Lee to **"first in war"**: See Smith, *Patriarch*; also Richard Brookheiser, *George Washington: Founding Father* (Free Press, 1996). **"Shake off these gloomy feelings"** . . . **"act right whatever the consequences"**: These quotes from Thomas, *Robert E. Lee*, 149–52. **He brooded:** Some general historians, like William Manchester and Paul Johnson, speak of Lee as potentially being a depressive, which, if true, would make his exploits all the more remarkable given how he withstood the enormous physical and emotional strains of battle, month after month; my sense is that he was not clinically depressive but deeply emotional. **"I foresee that the country"**: In this regard, of course, Lee was prescient; on the Union side, William Sherman showed equal prescience. **queer old genius:** This was Walter Taylor, one of his closest aides, A. B. Long, *Memoirs of Robert E. Lee* (Blue and Gray Press, 1983), 399–400. **Chancellorsville:** For more, see overviews in *BC*, 639–45; Thomas, *Robert E. Lee*, 275–86; and Ernest B. Furguson, *Chancellorsville, 1863: The Souls of the Brave* (Knopf, 1992); **war as a profession . . . not clear he loved war itself:** Thomas, *Robert E. Lee*, 250, 271–73. **spoke fervently about a "battle of annihilation":** Over time, one can see Lee becoming ever more aggressive, even as resources dwindled and he was forced on the defensive. Emory Thomas calls his Chancellorsville campaign "audacity to the point of madness," *Robert E. Lee*, 283. **Lee . . . had his flaws:** See Gallagher, ed., *Lee*, on this, esp. debate over Gettysburg, when he went forward without use of Jeb Stuart, who otherwise provided him critical intelligence as his "eyes," 381–522. **"those people":** It is not true, as some have contended or myth often has it, that he never referred to the Union as "the enemy"; he often did; but never did he refer to them with hate or spite, which is the larger point.

Grant had worked out a coordinated plan: For Grant's plans, see Catton, *Grant Takes Command*, esp. 104–78; for more on the Wilderness and Overland campaign, see, for example, *BC*, 725–42; Edward Steere, *The Wilderness Campaign* (Stackpole Books, 1960); Clifford Dowdey, *Lee's Last Campaign* (University of Nebraska Press, 1988); Freeman, vol. 3, esp. 342–410, also 551–56; also Noah Andre Trudeau, *Bloody Roads South: The Wilderness to Cold Harbor, May–June 1864* (Little, Brown, 1989), and his essay "'A Mere Question of Time,'" 523–60; Catton, *Stillness at Appomattox*, esp. 42–130, a marvelous book that is every bit as good today as when it first came out in 1953; too late for me to specifically use, but also quite good, Ernest Furguson, *Not War But Murder: Cold Harbor 1864* (Knopf, 2000), galley edition; for impact of campaign on Lee's men, see Herman Hattaway and Archer Jones, *How the North Won* (University of Illinois Press, 1991), 561–62; 570–71, 590–93; and Power, *Lee's Miserables*, 293–306; I have drawn extensively from these sources, from which the quotes are also derived, unless otherwise noted; also Gordon Rhea's important *The Battle of the Wilderness, May 5–6, 1864* (LSU Press, 1994). **Grant enjoyed a two-to-one advantage:** On the Confederacy's circumstances and prospects in spring of 1864, see Allan Nevins, *The War for Union*, vol. 4, *The Organized War to Victory, 1864–1865*, 4 vols. (New York, 1959–71), 1–18. **Lee was oblivious:** Indeed, his blood was so up that he shouted to a group of retreating rebels and their commander, "My God, General McGowan, is that splendid brigade of yours running like a flock of geese!" Thomas, *Robert E. Lee*, 321. **Grant kept coming:** General Longstreet prophetically remarked, "That man will fight us every day and every hour till the end of the war," Catton, *Stillness at Appomattox*, 139; for example of Spotsylvania, see Catton, *A Stillness*, 122–27, for the savagery of the fighting. **James McPherson's words:** *BC*, 729–31. **Cold Harbor:** See Catton, *A Stillness*, for example, 149–66. **Grant's critics:** Of course, the counterpoint, seen in hindsight, was the difference between strategic and tactical victories; Grant had the resources, men, and material, to spare, as long as the Union was willing to continue fighting; Lee did not have that luxury, and among other things, this campaign practically obliterated his command structure, see Power, *Lee's Miserables*, 297, and Gallagher, "The Army of Northern Virginia in May 1864," 108.

a dreadful siege: Freeman, vol. 3, 434–514, 528–38: technically, it can be pointed out, it wasn't a siege—the Confederates were never wholly surrounded; on the siege, see Richard Sommers, *Richmond Redeemed: The Siege of Petersburg* (Doubleday, 1981). Sommers concludes that Lee was "reduced" to "counterpunching, striking back, looking—hoping—for an opening and all the while trying to fend off the Northerners' blows," 207.

Five Forks to **Lee's new destination . . . hard forty-mile march:** See, for instance, Foote, 864–85. **"sufficient notice":** Five days earlier, Lee had told Secretary of War Breckinridge that he would give ten to twelve days' notice, Foote, 884. This incident surely shows the sign of mounting strain upon Lee; for more, including Forts Baldwin and Gregg, see Korn, *Pursuit to Appomattox*, 87–100; Trudeau, *Campaign to Appomattox*, 2–5; Stern, *End to Valor*, 129–52, 160–64; Freeman, 41–52.

Aboard the *River Queen*: Davis, *To Appomattox*, 60.

April 2, 1865, began to **Richmond would be occupied territory:** For the fall of Richmond, in addition to Stern, *End to Valor*, 171–92; Furgurson, *Ashes*, 316–40; Thomas, *The Confederate State*, 194–98; Foote 885–93; Davis, *To Appomattox*, 63–174, all excellent accounts that complement one another; I have also extensively used Rembert W. Patrick, *The Fall of Richmond* (LSU Press, 1960), an excellent and thorough work, even if older; A. A. Hoehling and Mary Hoehling, *The Day Richmond Died* (Madison, 1981); also Warren Spencer, "A French View of the Fall of Richmond: Alfred Paul's Report to Drouyn de Llys, April 11, 1865," *Virginia Magazine of History and Biography* 73 (April 1965): 177–88; John Leyburn, "The Fall of Richmond," *Harper's New Monthly Magazine* 33 (1866): 92–96; Edward M. Boykin, *The Falling Flag: Evacuation of Richmond, Retreat, and Surrender at Appomattox* (E. Hale and Son, 1874); and William J. Kimball, "Richmond 1865: The Final Three Months," *Virginia Cavalcade* (Spring 1962): 33–40; all quotes from these works unless otherwise noted. **St. Paul's Episcopal:** This beautiful church is still open today and, with a few modifications, is largely similar to what stood in April 1865; for further information, there is a church historian, Calder Loth, who can be consulted. **Minnigerode:** Saint Paul's Church, *Rev. Charles F. E. Minnergerode, D.D., Presbyter of the Diocese of Virginia* (James Pott, 1895); Minnigerode often hosted elegant dinner parties that included Lee and President Davis. **Hoge:** For more on Hoge, see Peyton Harrison Hoge, *Moses Drury Hoge: Life and Letters* (Presbyterian Committee of Publication, 1899).

Pistols were placed at the ready: Including by women. Phoebe Pember held off a gang of hooligans and then slept with her pistol "cocked," just within reach, Davis, *To Appomattox*, 138–39. **each car poignantly labeled:** Foote, 890; Stern, *End to Valor*, 191; Davis, *To Appomattox*, 161; **a new terror now struck: fire:** Among the historians, there is not agreement on the chronology of how the fire spread, or, for that matter, on a number of events that evening. I have sought to recreate it as best as I could. Where there were disputes between historians, I have often used Shelby Foote's account, 885–89; but his is very much an attenuated version, and in the end, all final judgments were mine. In recreating and visualizing this, I have also been invaluably helped by accounts of two other disasters: Kai Erickson, *Everything in Its Path* (Simon and Schuster, 1976), and David McCullough, *The Johnstown Flood* (Simon and Schuster, 1987); **An elderly black man . . . small black girl:** Patrick, *Fall of Richmond*, 45, 47.

"A single blue jacket": Foote, 889–90. **covered by enemy land mines:** Patrick, *Fall of Richmond*, 65. One soldier, a Vermonter, was killed by the explosion of a Confederate "torpedo" when he veered off the path by mistake, see Davis, *To Appomattox*, 142.

"We tried to comfort ourselves . . . Alas, alas": The resident was Josiah Gorgas's wife, Amelia, Davis, *To Appomattox*, 134, see also Gorgas, *Civil War Diary of General Josiah Gorgas*. **New York Times:** New *York Times*, April 4, 1865, Library of Congress. **New York World:** Quote from Ward, *Civil War*, 374.

black Richmond spontaneously and **President Abraham Lincoln** (visit to Richmond): for this section, Stern, *End to Valor*, 193–206; Patrick, *Fall of Richmond*, 66–70; 80–81; 119–22; Davis, *To Appomattox*, 181–87; Donald, 576–78; a full account of Lincoln's visit to Richmond can also be found in Donald C. Pfanz, *The Petersburg Campaign: Abraham Lincoln at City Point* (H. E. Howard, 1989). **"Richmond at last!":** Davis, *To Appomattox*, 132. **had long eavesdropped on parlor conversations:** See Louis R. Harlan, *Booker T. Washington: The Making of a Black Leader, 1856–1901* (Oxford University Press, 1972), 23–24. **"Bress God . . . "** and **"I'd risk my life":** Quotes from Patrick, *Fall of Richmond*, 61–63. **T. Morris Chester:** *Philadelphia Press*, April 11, 12, 1865; Patrick, *Fall of Richmond*, 119–20, and BC, 846–47; also see Thomas Morris Chester, *Black Civil War Correspondent—His Dispatches from the Virginia Front*, R. J. M. Blackett, ed. (Da Capo, 1989). Chester's insights make for fascinating, compelling, and important reading. He was, by all accounts, an astute observer of the war and its effects on the South, as his dispatches reveal.

April 4, brought an equally stunning sight: For the following section, see also Foote, 896–99; Patrick, *Fall of Richmond*, 127–35; Oates, 420–21; and Donald, 576–80. **meals on a tray:** Davis, *To Appomattox*, 207.

"I have got my army safely": Davis, *To Appomattox*, 162; Freeman, 59, qualifies this statement, noting that Lee "himself is credited, though not on specific authority, with saying . . ." Most historians do accept it, however. **April 3 to the "if" . . . Confederate ranks . . . general exuded good humor:** See Freeman, 58–59; Stern, *End to Valor*, 191; Davis, *To Appomattox*, 162.

Chapter Three: The Chase—and the Decision

hadn't he bested them before?: Douglas Southall Freeman points out that this retreat, however, was far more difficult than his 1862 Maryland withdrawal and his retreat after Gettysburg, 53. **the signs of progress were still promising:** Much has been made, rightly, by historians about the loss of will and ebbing morale of Confederate soldiers in the face of repeated deprivations and a now ten-month siege. But as Gary Gallagher points out, perhaps too much. Evidence strongly suggests Confederate soldiers' morale held to the very end of the war. Moreover, consider a few facts that stand, he notes, as an index of commitment. The Confederates mobilized 75–85 percent of available draft age white males, an astonishing number; one of every three men in uniform died, with 37–39 percent killed or wounded in action, a far higher rate of casualties than the Union sustained. By contrast, consider other American wars: 4.2–5.7 percent died in the American Revolution; in the War of 1812, 2.4 percent; the War with Mexico, 5.1 percent; World War I, 5.4 percent; World War II,

5.8 percent; the Korean War, 2.4 percent; and Vietnam, 7.7 percent. In concrete numbers, it would be as though there were 6 million casualties in WWI—or nearly half a million in Vietnam. In the North, Union fatalities were 17.5 percent, but if the rate were comparable to that in the South, the deaths would have been around 385,000. Gallagher asks, "how would northern society have stood up to [such] battlefield losses?," 30. The desertion numbers reveal a pattern of shaky support: 200,000 Northern soldiers deserted; another 120,000 evaded conscription; and some 90,000 fled to Canada to avoid the draft, while thousands more congregated in the mountainous counties of Pennsylvania to be out of reach of enrolling officers. Evidence mustered by Gallagher suggests that the North could not have withstood further privations—which is to say the war ended in the nick of time; see Gallagher, *Confederate War*, 31. Also see Elle Lonn's pioneering work on desertion, *Desertion During the Civil War* (Century, 1928), 205–6; Lonn notes, for instance, that some Confederates deserted Lee's army in Virginia, going home to check on their families, but then rejoined the army in North Carolina. Also see Gallagher on this point, 28–33. **It was happening like this:** The following sources have been used extensively for Lee's retreat and Grant's pursuit in this chapter, from which quotes are taken, unless otherwise indicated: Freeman, 58–133, which remains an outstanding source; Foote, 907–43; Stern, *End to Valor*, 210–57; Catton, *A Stillness*, 342–75 (for Union soldier point of view); Korn, *Pursuit to Appomattox*, 108–45; Davis, *To Appomattox*, 166–70, 189–99 (Confederate), 200–6 (Union), 213–31(Confederate), 231–35 (Union), 242–66 (Confederate), 266–71 (Union), 278–328 (Confederate), 329–35 (Union), 341–67 (Confederate), 367–73 (Union); Calkins, *Appomattox Campaign*, 63–184; Trudeau, *Campaign to Appomattox*, 3–40 (a wonderfully concise and readable overview); Trudeau, *Out of the Storm*, 89–142; Hendrickson, *Road to Appomattox*, 159–86; **packed roads and stubby rural cut-throughs:** There was variation. The roads themselves often were reasonably straight, at least in spurts; for instance, they were relatively good between Amelia Springs and Farmville, except between Old Genito Road and Deatonsville, Davis, *To Appomattox*, 244. **once replenished, their lead over Grant solidified:** It is worth pointing out that the Union men had this ongoing, almost existential fear that Lee would "strike a blow" before being crippled by desertions, and when the blow came, it would "fall with savage force," Catton, *A Stillness*, 331. **But U. S. Grant was not so forgiving:** In fact, Grant thought he would ensnare Lee by April 5. This, of course, did not happen. See for example, Davis, *To Appomattox*, 173. **at his house, Clover Hill:** At Clover Hill, over iced tea, Judge Cox's daughter Kate quipped to Lee: "General, we will still win. You will join General Johnston in North Carolina, and together you will win!" Lee replied: "Know this, whatever happens, no men fought better than mine," Davis, *To Appomattox*, 166–70; Trudeau, *Campaign to Appomattox*, 9. **But now, a mere administrative mix-up:** To this day, it is not clear just what happened and how; it remains one of the great historical mysteries of this war; Trudeau does say that "Lee himself doomed this plan when, on April 4, he decided to stop at Amelia . . . to reprovision his army. The stop accomplished none of Lee's intended objectives," "'A Mere Question of Time,'" 549; of course, it would have been different had there been food; Trudeau further counters that there was "something irrational about the whole enterprise . . . Lee made no *effective* attempt to provide rations in anticipation of the move," 548–49. For his part, Calkins says that the heart of the Confederate cause had stopped beating long before its military and political leaders acknowledged the fact, *Final Bivouac*, 201, 208. I would put it differently. The heart was there, but in light of the

Amelia disaster, the food wasn't—and now the Confederate limbs began inexorably to fail. **fate and luck . . . smoke of a skirmish:** Indeed, on the morning of April 9, Phil Sheridan, on the way to meet with Gordon, narrowly missed getting killed by a Confederate sharpshooter's bullet, Stern, *End to Valor*, 253.

veterans were hardly giving up: Rebel soldier John E. Cooke observed that "men and officers were tired and hungry but laughing; and nowhere could be seen [yet] a particle of gloom [or] shrinking . . . ," John E. Cooke, *Wearing of the Gray: Scenes and Adventures of the War* (E. B. Treat & Co., 1867), 558, quoted in Freeman, 68.

Lee, however, would not be denied . . . final assault: Freeman likens it to throwing the "old guard" at Waterloo. For more detail, see Freeman, 74–75. Interestingly enough, since Five Forks, Grant himself worried that Lee would "risk everything upon the cast of a single die," *Memoirs*, 605.

"tax their strength": See Korn, *Pursuit to Appomattox*, 113. **dreadful consequences were inevitable to up a mountain:** Thanks to Dr. Ronald Kurstin for outlining these effects. **So does thirst:** In truth, it was not simply lack of food, but also water, which is even more deleterious. Listen to the words of Georgia soldier William Graham: he wrote of being "utterly worn out" under the blazing sun, and "of the great demand for water." There were "few canteens," and when there were, men were "too tired to carry water for others," see William Graham, *A Confederate Diary of the Retreat from Petersburg*, R. B. Harwell, ed. (Emory University Library, 1953), also quoted in Davis, *To Appomattox*, 216. **in their cause:** Of historic note, on April 5, according to M. Doswell, a Confederate courier, a wagon train under guard by Confederate black troops raised in the wake of the heated debate over conscription of slaves (although there is some evidence that black units may have been raised even earlier, Trudeau, *Like Men of War*, 410), traveling with General Custis Lee, drove off an attacking Federal cavalry regiment. They were later captured the same day by another charge of the cavalry. This may be the one recorded instance of black Confederates directly engaging in battle. On that same day, according to a *New York Times* correspondent, "several hundred negroes were brought in" around Jetersville. On April 6, near Farmville, and again on April 10, there were more sightings of "colored troops in the Confederate service" and "negroes recently armed by Jeff. Davis," all belonging, it appears, to Major Thomas Turner's company, see Davis, *To Appomattox*, 196; Trudeau, *Like Men of War*, 412–14; Calkins, *Appomattox Campaign*, 182–84. **not even a full 100:** Davis, *To Appomattox*, 174. **tore branches off . . . ate the bark itself:** Consider the words of one retreating soldier on April 4, fortunate enough to get some food: "Had pretty good luck today—got biscuits and a piece of raw bacon . . . this I thought at the time a princely meal," Davis, *To Appomattox*, 145. And what else did they eat? Another soldier remarked that he "thought cow hooves a delicacy." Other troops resorted to downing boiled shucks and corn and turnips used for cattle and hog feed, which they deemed a "savory meal." Among other things soldiers managed to eat were sheep, when they could catch them; Nassau bacon, a scaly, rancid, odorous meat that was probably discarded "ship's pork" (of this prospect, one soldier commented, "by a desperate effort you would gulp it down . . . out of sight, out of mind"); and for the more fortunate, corn bread, ashcakes, molasses, in a few instances fried chicken; there is some speculation that they also may have eaten horse or mule meat, Stern, *End to Valor*, 238–39. **"race for life or death":** The soldier was William Owen, an artillerist, Davis, *To Appomattox*, 229. **the Union was gaining ground:** Grant put it thus: "I did not want to follow him; I wanted to get ahead of him," Grant, 610.

"setting for a military tragedy": The words are Douglas Southall Freeman's, 83.

Union men . . . seemed incapable of straggling: This was Grant's observation, that after four years, and with victory now finally within sight, men found new-gained stamina ("Nothing," he later wrote, "seemed to fatigue them"), see Grant, 624.

"Over sir? Over? . . . it's just begun": The words are Robert Stiles's, Yale 1859 and winner of the Deforest Gold Medal, see Robert Stiles, *Four Years Under Marse Robert* (Morningside Bookshop, 1903), quoted in Davis, *To Appomattox*, 227. **Sayler's Creek:** In a wonderful little essay, Christopher M. Calkins says the proper name for this battle should actually be "Little Sailor's creek," *Appomattox Campaign*, 118; I am following the more recent, postwar usage, however. **passed out ash-cakes:** This is oral history of Hilsman House, April 1999. **"The bullets began . . . I was shot":** Quotes from Calkins, *Appomattox Campaign*, 120–22. **forever known as "Black Thursday":** Lee is reported to have said, according to eighteen-year-old John Wise, "A few more Sayler's Creeks and it will all be over—ended just as I expected it would end from the first," suggesting his belief in the inevitability of the Southern failure; many historians seem to accept that Lee did say this. Walter Taylor, one of Lee's closest aides, however, took sharp issue with this. See expansive discussion in Freeman, footnote on 94–95.

controversial, if not flawed, decision: Clearly the lack of sleep, the growing odds against him, and the strain of defeat staring him in the face were showing upon Lee at this juncture and deeply coloring his judgment. Consider this contentious exchange between Lee and his trusted aide General E. P. Alexander. Alexander showed Lee a map and pointed out "the most direct and shortest road to Lynchburg from Farmville did not cross the river," as Lee proposed, and that "there we might have [the] most trouble." Lee shot back, "Well there is time enough to think about that. Go now and attend to these matters." Edward Porter Alexander, *Fighting for the Confederacy: The Personal Recollections of General Edward Porter Alexander*, Gary Gallagher, ed. (University of North Carolina Press, 1989), 525. **The priceless supply train quickly rolled away:** The four trains were sent farther up the railroad, and were later captured, after sharp fighting, by Sheridan and Custer on April 8 at Appomattox Station, see, for example, Stern, *End to Valor*, 236–38.

morning of April 8 . . . frantic retreat continued: This, of course, was the day the supply trains were captured, Korn, *Pursuit to Appomattox*, 135. **despite three consecutive all-night marches:** No one was immune to the effects of exhaustion and sleeplessness at this point. Even twenty-nine-year-old General Alexander noted: "it was the third consecutive night of marching, and I was . . . scarcely able to keep from falling off my horse," Davis, *To Appomattox*, 307. **"They still fight with great spirit":** Lee may also have said on this day, "We [have] sacred principles and rights to defend . . . even if we peris[h] in the endeavor . . . ," Freeman, note on 110.

"Lee still means to fight": Foote, 936.

fires were of cavalry, not infantrymen: By this point, Lee's intelligence service had almost totally broken down, meaning that he had no way of knowing there were two Union corps ahead of him. See, for example, Freeman, 108–9. **Neither the day nor its significance . . . Lee or his**

men: Of this moment, Catton writes, the "men were marching up in the moment of apotheosis and glory," *A Stillness*, 380.

"I can do nothing": Catton writes that "the Battle of Appomattox Station was the last battle of the war," *A Stillness*, 377. In myth and imagination yes, but this, actually, is incorrect. See Long, *Civil War Day by Day*, 673–88. Note, of course, skirmishes on April 22, April 27, May 4, and May 12, 377. More accurate, perhaps, would be to say that Appomattox Station was the last "full-scale battle." **E. Porter Alexander:** For further reading, see Maury Klein, *Edward Porter Alexander* (University of Georgia Press, 1971). **"one of a very few whom":** Quote from Peter S. Carmichael, "Edward Porter Alexander," *Encyclopedia of the Confederacy*, vol. 1, 25.

Throughout the years . . . as "guerrillaism" to Robert E. Lee himself had come to harbor considerable doubts about the bushwhackers: The following section draws extensively upon the following sources, and quotes from these references unless otherwise noted: Walter Laqueur, "The Origins of Guerrilla Doctrine," *Journal of Contemporary History* (Great Britain) 10, no. 3 (1975): 341–82; also Laqueur, *The Guerrilla Reader: A Historical Anthology* (New American Library, 1977), and Laqueur, *Terrorism* (Little, Brown, 1977); Robert B. Asprey, *War in the Shadows: The History, Two Thousand Years of the Guerrilla at War from Ancient Persia to the Present* (Morrow, 1994), one of the very best anthologies on guerrilla history; Albert Castel, The Guerrilla War, 1861–1865, *A Special Issue from Civil War Times Illustrated* 13, no. 6 (1974): 1–50, an outstanding compilation of guerrilla activities across the spectrum during the war, hereafter *CWT*; Anthony James Joes, *Guerrilla Warfare, a Historical, Biographical, and Bibliographical Sourcebook* (Greenwood, 1996), also very good; Frederickson, *Why the Confederacy Did Not Fight a Guerrilla War*, is another outstanding discussion. The extensive and authoritative discussion by four prominent military historians in Beringer, Hattaway, Jones, and Still, *Why the South Lost the Civil War* (deals further with the Confederacy's "lack of will"); also Robert L. Kerby, "Why the Confederacy Lost," *Review of Politics* 35 (July 1973): 326–45, written in the wake of the Vietnam turmoil, and shaped by events in Southeast Asia; Charles Francis Adams, *Lee at Appomattox and Other Papers* (Houghton Mifflin, 1902), 1–19; Brian Holden Reid, "Why the Confederacy Lost," *History Today* (Great Britain) 38 (November 1988): 32–41; Thomas Goodrich, "Guerrilla Warfare" section in *Encyclopedia of the Confederacy* (Simon and Schuster, 1993), vol. 2. For other good general sources, Chaliand Gerard, *Guerrilla Strategies: A Historical Anthology from the Long March to Afghanistan* (University of California Press, 1982), and Irwin Blacker, *Irregulars, Partisans, Guerrillas: Great Stories from Roger's Rangers to the Haganah* (Simon and Schuster, 1954); for further case studies of guerrilla warfare in specific areas, see also: Gary Cheatham, "Desperate Characters: The Development of the Confederate Guerrillas in Kansas," *Kansas History* 14, no. 3 (1991): 144–61.

"Guerrillaism" . . . "bushwhackers": Quotes from Laqueur, "Origins of Guerrilla Doctrine," 350, 371, 381. **They move quickly** to **maximize impact:** See, for instance, Joes, *Guerrilla Warfare*, 3–4. **success in Vietnam:** Kerby, a political scientist, wrote this work in the course of the ongoing Vietnam War tragedy. He attributed the Confederate defeat to its failure to wage a "war of national liberation." He believes, however, that by the fall of Richmond the will of Southerners was too sapped. **Boers in South Africa:** See Frederickson, *Why the Confederacy Did Not Fight a Guerrilla War*. **The Algerians:** On this, see Stampp, "The Southern Road to Appomattox," *Imperiled Union*, 265. Stampp vividly highlights the unrelenting nationalism of Algerian revolutionaries. He concludes,

"In spite of its great physical superiority [France] had to withdraw." One important point, how-ever, to be added, was Algeria's spectacular willingness not simply to wage guerrilla war, but to resort to what experts in terrorism such as Brian Jenkins of the Rand Corporation and Algerian expert Lisa Anderson call "spectacular terrorism" against all targets, civilian and otherwise, vir-tually without limits (oral briefings with staff of the House U.S. Armed Services Committee, 1986, and at Rand Corporation, 1981). **in Cambodia:** See Elizabeth Becker, *When the War Was Over: The Voices of Cambodia's Revolution* (Simon and Schuster, 1986), and Jay Winik, *U.S. Policy Toward Cambodia in the 101st Congress: A Case Study of Congressional Initiation and Influence in Foreign Policy,* doctoral dissertation, Yale University, December 1993. **The list of effective guerrilla wars** to **ensuing cen-turies:** See Joes, *Guerrilla Warfare,* 4–5. **"the small war"** and **"for this is a war":** Quotes from Laqueur, "The Origins of Guerrilla Doctrine," 377, 354; the Prussian general was Berenhorst. *Précis de l'art de la guerre:* Asprey, *War in the Shadows,* 94; on Jomini, see Beringer, Hattaway, Jones, and Still, *Why the South Lost the Civil War,* including 340–41. **"bellum omnium contra omnes":** Palmer and Colton, 470. **In 1807, while Napoleon's mighty legions ... Napoleon's armies ... known to Lee and Davis:** See Asprey, *War in the Shadows,* 76–83, and 70–73; also Palmer and Colton, 385–88. For more on the Spanish and Greek struggles, see John Ellis, *A Short History of Guerrilla Warfare* (Allan, 1975), 59–61, 73–75; Gallagher, 140–53. **tiny country of Paraguay:** See the important study of Beringer, Hattaway, Jones, and Still, *Why the South Lost the Civil War,* for extensive discussion of this exam-ple, including, for instance, 440–41. It could be pointed out that many Confederates were actu-ally taking careful note of this conflict that was just beginning. E. P. Alexander quipped that he was considering going to Brazil and joining the fight against Paraguay, adding this lighthearted note: "And, judging from the map ... for once I would be on the winning side," see Alexander, *Fighting for the Confederacy,* 531. In truth, he misjudged how difficult *that* war would be. Another intriguing example of the lack of inevitablity in unequal conflicts could be found—by analogy—in Michael Howard, *War in European History* (Oxford University Press, 1976). "European artillery, breech loading rifles and machine guns made the outcome of any fighting almost a foregone con-clusion," Howard writes—"but not quite ... as the British survivors of the Zulu victory at Isandhlwana in 1897 and the Italian survivors of the Ethiopian victory in 1896 would have been able to testify." Howard concludes that success "still owed at least as much to the superior cohe-sion, organization, and above all self-confidence of the Europeans as it did to their weapons," 122–23. Therefore, he generally agrees with Beringer, Hattaway, Jones, and Still, *Why the South Lost the Civil War,* about the need for "will." **And then, of course, there was the most honorable exam-ple** to **"sort of victory which ruins an army":** See Asprey, *War in the Shadows,* 63–71; B. Reid, "Why the Confederacy Lost," 36; also see Don Higginbotham, "Daniel Morgan: Guerilla Fighter," in *George Washington's Generals,* George Billias, ed. (Morrow, 1964), 291–313, and John Shy, *A People Numerous and Armed: Reflection on the Military Struggle for American Independence* (Oxford University Press, 1976), esp. 200–201. For overview of Revolutionary War and guerrilla activities, see Leckie, *Wars of America,* 121–216. **For his part, West Point graduate:** On the education of most Civil War gen-erals, see John C. Waugh's terrific *The Class of 1846* (Warner, 1994) and James Morrison, "Educating the Civil War Generals: West Point, 1833–1861, *Military Affairs* 38 (September 1974): 108–11; also Thomas, *Robert E. Lee,* 153–60. **"We have now entered ... Let us but will it, and we**

are free": Jefferson Davis, *Jefferson Davis Constitutionalist: His Letters, Papers and Speeches*, Dunbar Rowland, ed., 10 vols. (Jackson, 1923), vol. 6, 530; also Emory Thomas, *CN*, 300–304. Gallagher has suggested that this did not mean partisan warfare outside of Lee's army, but that it meant the "'unleashing' of an offensive against whatever pieces of the federal army it could find," *Confederate War*, 141–42. One Davis biographer, Michael Ballard, puts it somewhat differently: Davis did not advocate guerrilla war *"per se,"* he suggests. See *A Long Shadow: Jefferson Davis and the Final Days of the Confederacy* (University of Mississippi Press, 1992). **Charles Adams:** Of note, Adams's tribute to Lee on this and other times greatly fostered sectional reconciliation around the turn of the century; for more on the North's glorification of Lee and Adams's contribution to it, see Paul Buck, *The Road to Reunion, 1865–1900* (Little, Brown, 1937), esp. 260–63. **in early April 1865 . . . relatively small part of the physical South:** See, for instance, Beringer, Hattaway, Jones, and Still, *Why the South Lost the Civil War*. The authors also conclude "the Confederate refusal to consider the guerilla alternative may be a major reason why the South lost the Civil War," 338–39. **ancient commanders . . . called *"impedimenta"*:** Joes, *Guerrilla Warfare*, 4. **Even the North would not be safe . . . likely harbinger of things to come:** See Hendrickson, *Road to Appomattox*, 110–15; *BC*, 764. **up to 175,000 men under arms who could be called upon:** See also Gallagher's general point on this, *Confederate War*, 95. **As Marx would later comment . . . "by a gnat":** Laqueur, "The Origins of Guerrilla Doctrine," 371. **Where would the stamina come from?:** See B. Reid, "Why the Confederacy Lost," on weak Northern morale in face of even the most limited Confederate advances," 40; see also Beringer, Hattaway, Jones, and Still, *Why the South Lost the Civil War*, who conclude, "Through most of the war, the possibility of a collapse of the Union home front had every bit as much likelihood as disintegration of the Confederate home front," 421. **"We have surpassed in barbarity":** Quote from Asprey, *War in the Shadows*, 97. **Grant himself ruminated:** See Joes, *Guerrilla Warfare*, 39. **John Brown and five other abolitionists:** For more on John Brown, see Stephen Oates, *To Purge This Land with Blood: A Biography of John Brown* (University of Massachusetts Press, 1984), esp. 243–47. **One partisan recruiter** and quote: This was Virginia Colonel John Imboden; Castel, "The Guerrilla War," *CWT*, 9. **found their men in abundance:** See Castel, *CWT*, 34–38. **Champ Ferguson:** Castel, *CWT*, 31–33; Goodrich, "Guerrilla Warfare," 724. For further, see Thurman Sensing, *Champ Ferguson: Confederate Guerrilla* (Vanderbilt Press, 1942). **In the swamps of Florida:** Castel, *CWT*, 31–32, 47. **Marcellus Clark . . . Jesse McNeil:** Goodrich, "Guerrilla Warfare," 725. **captured two Union generals . . . Stand Watie:** See Wilfred Knight, *Red Fox: Stand Watie and the Confederate Indian Nations During the Civil War Years in Indian Territory* (Arthur Clark, 1988); Kenny Franks, *Stand Watie and the Agony of the Cherokee Nation* (Memphis State University Press, 1979); and Josephy, *Civil War in the American West*, an important study of the war out west that has much on Watie, all of it vividly written, esp. 350–85. Senator Ben Wade of Ohio called one of the Indian massacres, at Sand Creek, "The scene of murder and barbarity . . . of the most revolting character," 302. See further, 377, for attack on the Federal steamboat *J. R. Williams*, which earned Watie a promotion to brigadier general. **Of these, John Mosby:** For John Mosby profile here, see Jeffrey D. Wert, *Mosby's Rangers* (Simon and Schuster, 1990); Kevin H. Siepel, *Rebel: The Life and Times of John Singleton Mosby* (Da Capo, 1981), a very nicely done account; and Richard S. Brownlee, *Gray Ghosts of the Confederacy: Guerrilla Warfare in the West* (LSU Press, 1990); also used, Castel, "The Guerrilla War," *CWT*, 16–19, 39–42; Asprey, *War in the Shadows*,

106–7. I am heavily indebted to these works. **Another dreaded guerrilla . . . John Hunt Morgan:** Asprey, *War in the Shadows*, 105–6; B. Reid, "Why the Confederacy Lost," who notes Morgan was a vocal proponent of guerrilla warfare, 36; *BC*, 513–16; 579; 763.

   Throughout the Civil War, Missouri was labeled: In addition to other reference sources cited above for this chapter, this section on Missouri draws extensively upon Michael Fellman, *Inside War: The Guerrilla Conflict in Missouri During the American Civil War* (Oxford University Press 1989), the most authoritative study on this important subject and a crucial study to read. **William Clarke Quantrill:** See Castel, *CWT*, 11–15, 28–29, and for more, see Albert Castel, *William Clarke Quantrill: His Life and Times* (F. Fell, 1962), and also his "Quantrill's Bushwhackers: A Case Study in Partisan Warfare," *CWH* 13, no. 1 (1967): 40–50, for a good overview. **Lawrence, Kansas:** On this episode and aftermath, see Castel, *CWT*, 19–22; Josephy, *Civil War in the American West*, 373–74; and for more detail, see Thomas Goodrich, *Bloody Dawn: The Story of the Lawrence Massacre* (Kent State University Press, 1991). On Jesse and Frank James, see Robert Barr Smith, "The James Boys Go to War," *Civil War Times Illustrated* (Jan./Feb. 1994): 29–58. **captured the attention of the world:** Even the London *Times* carried a story on the massacre, see Cheatham, "Desperate Characters," 158; Castel, *CWT*, 22–23. At Gettysburg, Edward C. Everett called Quantrill a "wretch." He also spoke of "lawless guerrillas" throughout the land, see Wills, *Lincoln at Gettysburg*, 241, 239. For other incidents similar to Lawrence, Jonathan Sarris, "Anatomy of an Atrocity: The Madden Branch Massacre and Guerrilla Warfare in North Georgia, 1861–1865," *Georgia Historical Quarterly* 77, no. 4 (Winter 1993): 679–710. **known as General Order Number Eleven:** For more on this controversial order, see Paul B. Hatley and Noor Ampssler, "General Orders Number 11: Final Valid Option or Wanton Act of Brutality?," *Journal of the West* 33, no. 3 (1994): 77–87. They also present a good overview of the guerrilla conflict and the inability of authorities to bring it under control—and the anarchy that reigned, see 82–86. They deem it "perhaps the harshest set of instructions aimed at civilians during the Civil War," 77. **Francis Lieber:** Francis Leiber, *Guerrilla Parties Considered with Reference to the Laws and Usages of War* (Van Nostrand, 1862); in an attempt to understand the war the rebel guerrillas were waging, the Union published Leiber's findings in this small book. **just as often, scalped:** On one body a note was left: "You come to hunt bush whackers. Now you are skelpt. Wm. Anderson." See Castel, *CWT*, 45. **dead were stripped:** Castel, ibid., 44–46. **stepped on 124 corpses:** Jesse James was part of this massacre. **"heartless and merciless fiends":** Castel, ibid., 44–46. **Nor did it end there** to **"The very air seems charged with blood and death":** For example, see Castel, ibid., 45, 42 and Goodrich, "Guerrilla Warfare," 725; for further scholarly case studies beyond Missouri, see James B. Martin, "Blue Flag Over the Bluegrass: Guerrilla Warfare in Kentucky, 1863–1865," *Register of the Kentucky Historical Society* 86, no. 4 (1988): 352–75; Samuel Hyde Jr., "Bushwhacking and Barn Burning: Civil War Operations and the Florida Parishes' Tradition of Violence," *Louisiana History* 36, no. 2 (1995): 171–86. He notes that "the tendency of many historians to overlook or give only casual mention to smaller regional theatres of the war has created a gap in our efforts to determine . . . the outcome of the war," 172. While one has to be careful about overgeneralizing from these smaller conflicts, this point is well taken. See further, Wayne K. Durrill, *War of Another Kind: A Southern Community in the Great Rebellion* (Oxford University Press, 1990); and Steven V. Ash, *Middle Tennessee Transformed, 1860–1870: War and Peace in the Upper South* (LSU Press, 1988), both attempts to correct this imbalance; Daniel Sutherland, "Guerrilla: The Real War in Arkansas," *Arkansas Historical Quarterly* 7, no. 3 (Autumn 1993): 257–85, which highlights the considerable effectiveness of bushwhackers in frustrating Union troops; Zack Waters, "Florida's Confederate Guerrillas: John W. Pearson and the Oklawaha Rangers, *Florida Historical Quarterly* 70, no. 2 (1991): 133–49; and Sarris, "Anatomy of an Atrocity"; and also the multidisciplinary approach in Phillip S. Paludan, *Victims, a True Story of the Civil War* (University of Tennessee Press, 1991). **Missouri was something that had never been witnessed before** to **all civilians were seen as enemies:** This section relies heavily upon Fellman, *Inside War,* including quotes. I am heavily indebted to this study. Also used was Donald Gilmore, "Total War on the Missouri Border," *Journal of the West* 35 (July 1996), 370–80; Don Bowen, "Guerrilla War in Western Missouri, 1862–65: Historical Extensions of the Relative Deprivation Hypothesis," *Comparative Studies in Society and History* (Jan. 1977): 46–49, for an account with problems of biased data, but still worth perusing; John Newman Edwards, *Noted Guerrillas, or the Warfare on the Border* (Bryan Brand, 1877). **Wrote the *Kansas City Journal of Commerce*:** Quote from Castel, *CWT,* 42.

To the chivalric Southerners, war was about noble sacrifice . . . aristocratic code of honor: For more on the South's commitment to a code of honor, see Bertram Watt-Brown, *Southern Honor: Ethics and Behavior in the Old South* (Oxford University Press, 1982); also Frederickson, *Why the Confederacy Did Not Fight a Guerrilla War,* 24–25, and his comparison with the South Africa war. For more on the Boer War, see one of the best military histories of the South Africa war, Thomas Pakenham, *The Boer War* (Random House, 1979); also G. H. L. Le May, *British Supremacy in South Africa, 1989–1907* (Oxford University Press, 1965), and Leonard Thompson, *A History of South Africa* (Yale University Press, 1990), esp. 140–44. **Richmond's official policy was of two minds . . . Robert E. Lee himself had come to harbor considerable doubts:** There is much on this point. See, in brief, Castel, *CWT* 26–28.

"Richmond *must* not be given up": See Thomas, *Robert E. Lee,* 223; indeed, it is too often forgotten that Lee was not a monolith in his views. **against the advice of Jefferson Davis:** For contrasting Lee and Davis views, see Beringer, Hattaway, Jones, and Still, *Why the South Lost the Civil War,* 339–45, and then Gallagher, *Confederate War,* 142–43, and Davis, *Jefferson Davis Constitutionalist,* vol. 6, 530.

Thus did Robert E. Lee . . . make his most historic contribution: The argument has been made that the aversion to partisan conflict was deeply rooted in the Southern psyche, and that the decision over guerrilla warfare wasn't Lee's alone to make. This is true; see Beringer, Hattaway, Jones, and Still, *Why the South Lost the Civil War,* for extensive discussion of this point; for example, 343–45. But just as Lee was a critical voice in swaying the entire Confederacy over to the momentous decision to induct slaves into the army, itself once unthinkable, so he could have been—and indeed, surely was—the dominant voice on this matter. **"Vietnamization of America":** On these points, see Tom Wicker's penetrating and important essay "Vietnam in America, 1865," *MHQ: The Quarterly Journal of Military History* 10, no. 3 (Spring 1998): 79; Also see the other fascinating essays in the same issue; in "The Road Not Taken," 65–89, Robert Cowley writes, "What ifs . . . reveal in startling outlines the essential stakes of a confrontation, as well as its potentially abiding consequences . . . Might-have-beens can lead us to question long-held assumptions. They can define true turning points, just as this momentous decision surely did. They can show that small changes are likely—more likely, perhaps—to have major repercussions than large ones," 65. On this issue, also see Noah Andre Trudeau, "What Might Have Been," *Civil War Times Illustrated* 33, no. 4 (September/October 1994): 56–58; Nelson W. Polsby, ed., *"What If . . . ?"* a collection of historical fictions, (Lewis Pub. Co., 1982). **cleave North from South:** Castel, *CWT*, and other historians point out that the guerrilla war did not actually prolong the conflict all that much, about which they are probably right, although this is not something that can easily be quantifiable. With his usual rigorous logic, Gary Gallagher, for his part, in *Confederate War*, finds the concept of a massive guerrilla war as a " Confederate national strategy . . . " "even more far-fetched than a determinedly defensive one . . ." For the better part of the war, on this point I agree. He also notes that this view is of "scant relevance to the Confederacy" and a "twentieth-century example appl[ied] to a nineteenth-century example," 140–41. Here there is room for discussion. There were plenty of rich examples of guerrilla efforts throughout history pre-1865, and more importantly, what is being discussed here is not a massive strategy from the outset, but something quite different: the consideration of an organized—or at least *sanctioned*—guerrilla effort at the war's end, feeding off the South's hatred of the North and a continuing desire for independence. Why should this be any more heretical than inducting slaves, or Lee changing his mind about the defense of Richmond? All of which makes this—and Lee's actions—such a rich topic to explore. Further, in this discussion, it is important to remember that it is not the case that the Confederacy didn't employ guerrilla tactics—it did, for several years, as an adjunct to its strategy. On these points, also see Beringer, Hattaway, Jones, and Still, *Why the South Lost the Civil War*, esp. 343, for their discussion of the Confederates' ample familiarity with other guerrilla campaigns.

half sentences and fragments: This is from Freeman, 131. It is surprising how most of the popular imagination and even the consensus among much scholarship seems to take it in stride that Appomattox would have the smooth outcome it did—the result of generations of myth and hindsight—and that Lee was not filled with anxieties. Lee biographer Emory Thomas does note, "As Lee should have known, civil wars often end in acrimony and executions," *Robert E. Lee*, 369. It's a safe bet that Lee surely did know all this, as evidenced by his growing anxiety that morning. **"good terms":** Lee told E. Porter Alexander earlier that morning that Grant would give them "honorable terms," Alexander, *Fighting for the Confederacy*, 533. **clearly growing anxious:** Lee actually thought that Grant's terms might now be stiffer, given the Union general's declination of those offered the previous days. Longstreet thought otherwise, Freeman, 131. For historical inquiry, this may be an example of the tendency to work backward from what happened, as opposed to capturing the actual moments as they happened. On this phenomenon, see Trevor-Roper, *Rise of Christian Europe*, 7–11, and especially Daniel Boorstin's thoughtful chapter in *Hidden History*, 3–23. **banished to the distant Atlantic island:** It is worth recalling that just some years earlier, in the War of 1812, a popular New England chant—used at the time for President James Madison—was to banish him "to the Isle of Elbe!," Hinton, *History and Topography of the United States*, 393–94. **Porter Alexander later confessed:** He also added, "to me, either capture or surrender meant going to prison for an indefinite period, maybe for years, & with all sorts of hardships & persecutions," Alexander, *Fighting for the Confederacy*, 530, 539; also Alexander, "With Lee at Appomattox," in "Voices from the Past," *American History Illustrated* 22, no. 5 (1987): 40–45, 50–54. "I was never so wrought up upon any subject as this," Alexander later wrote, "For no one could deny the importance of terms to prevent vindictive trials and punishments, and there seemed to be no chance to secure them," 50. **Bill Anderson, the rebel bushwhacker:** Castel, *CWT*, 46. " *LET HER BURN!*": This was the crowd reply to a Seward speech. **"Treason is the highest crime"** . . . **"*HANG* him twenty times!"** . . . **"stretch the first rope!"** . . . **"I would try them . . . and I would hang them":** These four quotes are from no less than Vice President Johnson, the first two made from the steps of the U.S. Patent Office. Throughout the ranting speech, he was repeatedly met with loud and prolonged cheers. On the night of April 11, after Lincoln's speech, Senator James Harlan of Iowa was also met with the refrain "hang em!," see Foote, 900–901; Patrick, *Fall of Richmond*, 83–86; Leech, 382–83. *"Hang Lee!":* See Flood, *Lee*, 58. Many Southerners feared harsh punishment and/or confinement for Lee. For example, Catherine Edmondston, upon hearing of Lee's surrender, poignantly wrote: "How to find words to tell what has befallen us? *Gen Lee has surrendered!* . . . We stand appalled at our disaster! . . . *Lee*, Lee upon whom hung the hopes of the whole country, should be a *prisoner* seems almost too dreadful to be realized!," in Beth Gilbert Crabtree and James W. Patton, eds., *"Journal of a Secesh Lady": The Diary of Catherine Ann Devereux Edmondston, 1860–1866* (North Carolina Division of Archives and History, 1979), 694–95.

CHAPTER FOUR: THE MEETING

For this chapter, I have drawn upon the following sources, from which quotes are taken, unless otherwise noted. For Grant profile and background (**Now, at last . . . the hour has struck** to **But to his everlasting credit . . . Grant never considered that it could be otherwise**): Grant; Catton's superb *Stillness at Appomattox*, esp. 36–50, and his two-volume *Grant Moves South* (Little, Brown, 1969), and *Grant Takes Command* (1968); British military expert and historian who provides insights into Grant's strategic and military gifts, Major General J. F. C. Fuller, *The Generalship of Ulysses S. Grant* (J. Murray, 1929), and his *Grant and Lee: A Study in Personality and Generalship* (Scribner's Sons, 1923); William McFeely's, *Grant: A Biography* (Norton, 1981), and John Keegan's important book, *Mask of Command*; Richard Goldhurst, *Many Are the Hearts: The Agony and the Triumph of Ulysses S. Grant* (Reader's Digest Press, 1975), esp. 29–91; Grant biographies in Ward, *Civil War*, 276–82; and Leckie, *None Died in Vain*, 219–30; Anderson and Anderson, *Generals*, is also very good; *BC*, esp. 395–96, 419, 423, 457, 588–90, 622–23, 742–43, 759. Published too late for me to use but worth reading is the recent biography, Brooks D. Simpson, *Ulysses S. Grant: Triumph over Adversity 1822–1865* (Houghton Mifflin, 2000); also very useful, Sylvanus Cadwallader, *Three Years with Grant*, Benjamin Thomas, ed. (Knopf, 1955), and Charles A. Dana and J. G. Wilson, *The Life of Ulysses S. Grant* (Gordon Bill & Co., 1868). **he married Julia Dent:** For more, see Julia A. Dent, *The Personal Memoirs of Julia Dent Grant (Mrs. Ulysses S. Grant)*, John Y. Simon, ed. (Putnam, 1975). **innate genius for reading maps:** Which, of course, invaluably served him in moving out of the Overland campaign against Lee, and then again during Lee's retreat. **And that goal was always to crush the enemy:** Military strategist Russell Weigley says Grant "developed a highly uncommon ability to rise above the fortunes of a single battle and to master the flow of a long series of events," *The American Way of War* (Macmillan, 1973), 139; also see James R. Arnold, *Grant Wins the War: Decision at Vicksburg* (Wiley, 1997), who compares Grant at Vicksburg to Napoleon, 3–4. **In**

March 1864 . . . charmed official and social Washington: On this, see Leech, 311–28, esp. 311–13. "The Union had some queer heroes," she wrote, "but none as unlikely as the one on whom, after three years of war, its ardent hopes were fixed." **It wasn't just the episodic binge drinking:** On this point, there continues to be much debate; for instance, see Catton, *Stillness at Appomattox*, where he reminds us that as Congress passed an act creating the post of lieutenant general, held previously only by George Washington and Winfield Scott, a worry now consumed many in the Union capital: "If we turn the country's armies over to this man," it was asked, "will he stay sober?" Catton adds that while Grant surely did drink, he "was no drunkard," 40–41. For more, see Catton, *Grant Moves South*, 96–97, 396–97, 462–65. By way of comparison, Lincoln also once said of Andrew Johnson, "he ain't no drunkard." Yet the two men obviously couldn't have been more different.

On Appomattox surrender (**As the blazing yellow sun climbed high overhead** to "**Such a scene only happens once in centuries**") and exchange of arms (**Euphoria quickly spread** to "**praying God to pity and forgive us all!**"): Korn, *Pursuit to Appomattox*, 141–51, 151–55; Stern, *End to Valor* 271–83, 283–88; Foote, 943–50, 951–56; Freeman, 124–48, 149–58; Davis and Davis, *Generals*, 448–60; Foote 841–44; Trudeau, *Out of the Storm*, 138–44, 145–52; Calkins, *Appomattox Campaign*, 68–179, 185–95; Hendrickson, *Road to Appomattox*, 181–200, 205–17; Wheeler, *Witness to Appomattox*, 215–23, 224–38; Chamberlain, *Passing of the Armies*, 230–72, esp. 258–70; Grant, 627–34, and Taylor, *Four Years with General Lee;* and Gordon, *Reminiscences of the Civil War*, 408–9. **Wilmer McLean:** A further little touch of poignancy is that he was married to an aunt of Edward Porter Alexander's wife. **If this account is to be believed, Parker responded:** Though it has taken on mythic proportions, there is some debate as to whether this exchange ever actually happened. It has also been speculated that Lee at first may have thought Parker was a black man, see Freeman, 140.

And there were still some 175,000 other Confederates under arms elsewhere: Korn, *Pursuit to Appomattox*, 155. For instance, though winding down, see Trudeau's *Out of the Storm* for accounts of other battles raging simultaneously. It is for this reason that Beringer, Hattaway, Jones, and Still assert flatly, "When Lee met Grant at Appomattox Court House, surrender was not the only choice open to him," *Why the South Lost the Civil War*, 20.

so, too, were they Grant's greatest moments: For example, Alexander, who wanted to continue guerrilla warfare, had this to say about Grant: "Grant's conduct toward us in the whole matter is worthy of the very highest praise & indicates a great & broad & generous mind. *For all of time it will be a good thing for the whole United States, that of all the Federal generals it fell to Grant to receive the surrender of Lee.*" Alexander, *Fighting for the Confederacy*, 540, emphasis in original; see also Alexander, "With Lee at Appomattox," 40–45, 50–54.

Lee pointedly struck out a draft paragraph: Flood, *Lee*, 23. **Once again, Grant sought to use Lee's influence:** On this meeting, see Alexander, *Fighting for the Confederacy*, 541, and Flood, *Lee*, 21–23; also Grant, 634.

As Henry Steele Commager: See Samuel Eliot Morison and Henry Steele Commager, *The Growth of the American Republic* (Oxford University Press, 1962), 23. **Joshua L. Chamberlain:** It is almost futile to try to improve upon Chamberlain's richly moving words in describing the events of April 12. Rightly so, few try.

Would Lee's rejection of guerrilla warfare prevail over Davis's embrace?: Beringer, Hattaway, Jones, and Still conclude, "by April of 1865 . . . an unconventional military strategy still presented a viable alternative to the Confederates," *Why the South Lost the Civil War*, 421. The failure to do so, they ultimately attribute to a "lack of will" and "tenuous nationalism." Also see, on this point, the review essay of Beringer, Hattaway, Jones, and Still's *Why the South Lost the Civil War* by Brooks D. Simpson, "Why the Cause Lost," *Reviews in American History* 22 (1994): 73–81. **"apocalyptic engagement":** The phrase is Oates's, 386. **Even Mary Custis Lee:** Judtith W. McGuire, *Diary of a Southern Refugee* (University of Nebraska Press, 1995), 356. **daunting obstacles remained:** See Ronald A. Mosocco, *The Chronological Tracking of the American Civil War, Per the Official Records of the War of Rebellion* (James River, 1994), 322–33; also see Grant on Northern war-weariness, 599.

Chapter Five: The Unraveling

The principal sources that I have used extensively for this chapter on Lincoln, his biographical sketch, and the week after Appomattox are two outstanding relatively new biographies, which have greatly affected my thinking and which I have drawn upon equally greatly: Oates, which stands as a model of outstanding historical writing; and Donald's *Lincoln*, which may well become a modern classic; as well as Richard Hofstadter's profile "Abraham Lincoln and the Self-Made Myth," in *American Political Tradition*, 93–136; taken together, these three works nicely complement one another. One cannot ignore the invaluable Roy Basler's (and Marion Pratt and Lloyd Dunlop), *The Collected Works of Abraham Lincoln*, 8 vols. (Rutgers University Press, 1953), and his *Abraham Lincoln*, which I also have used extensively. All quotes are readily found in these sources, unless otherwise noted. I have also benefited much from reading Mark E. Neely Jr.'s wonderful *The Last Best Hope of Earth: Abraham Lincoln and the Promise of America* (Harvard University Press, 1993); Phillip S. Paludan, *The Presidency of Abraham Lincoln* (University Press of Kansas, 1994), which emphasizes the war years; Reinhard H. Luthin, *The Real Abraham Lincoln* (Prentice-Hall, 1960), and Benjamin P. Thomas, *Portrait for Posterity: Lincoln and His Biographers* (Rutgers University Press, 1947). Also helpful as a research source was the important Nicolay and Hay, *Abraham Lincoln*, and Alfred J. Beveridge, *Abraham Lincoln, 1809–1858*, 2 vols. (Houghton Mifflin, 1928), for prewar years. Further, Oates's *Abraham Lincoln: The Man Behind the Myths* (Harper and Row, 1994) is littered with keen insights, as is the recent work by Allen Guelzo, *Abraham Lincoln: Redeemer President* (Eerdman's, 1999). Though they are not Lincoln scholars *per se*, both have much to offer, and therefore I have paid careful attention to the interpretations in *BC* and McPherson's essay "Lincoln and the Strategy of Unconditional Surrender" in *Lincoln: The War President; The Gettysburg Lectures*, Gabor S. Boritt, ed. (Oxford University Press, 1992), 29–62 (and this entire important book as well); Foote's assessments in *Civil War;* and Paul Johnson's profile of Lincoln in *A History of the American People*, 435–50, 485–90. Indispensible, too, is *Lincoln Day by Day, A Chronology*, 3 vols. (Sesquicentennial Commission, 1960), Earl Schenk Miers, ed., and for my purposes, vol. 3, 1861–65, as well as W. Emerson Reck, *A. Lincoln, His Last 24 Hours* (McFarland, 1987), among the most thorough accounts of the last day; I have used these two works heavily. Two other excellent books are Richard Bak's *The Day Lincoln Was Shot* (Taylor, 1998), and Dorothy Kunhardt and Philip

Kunhardt Jr., *Twenty Days* (Harper and Row, 1965). Finally, Ruth Painter Randall, *Mary Lincoln: Biography of a Marriage* (Little, Brown, 1953), the standard work on the Lincoln marriage, is filled with information on this period, and is elegantly—and carefully—written as well. Other works I have used are listed in the notes, as necessary. For more on Lincoln historiography, see Merrill D. Peterson, *Lincoln in American Memory* (Oxford University Press, 1994), and David M. Potter, *The South and the Sectional Conflict* (LSU Press, 1968).

"I think we are near" to **"some quiet place like this":** Oates, 422–23; Donald, 581; Foote, 956–57; Reck, *A. Lincoln*, 7, 9; Gideon Welles, *Diary*, vol. 2 (Norton, 1960), 280–83; Frederick W. Seward, *Reminiscences of a War-Time Statesman and Diplomat* (G. P. Putnam's Sons, 1916), 254–57; Leech, 377–78. **"You will survive me":** Quote in Randall, *Mary Lincoln*, 378. **"Ironically, though, it is one of his own dreams"** to **"Well, let it go":** Oates, 425–26; Randall, *Mary Lincoln*, 378–80; Bak, *Day Lincoln Was Shot*, 71–73.

But in the chill, early morning to **At Ford's:** Oates, 426–27; Foote, 973–75; Randall, *Mary Lincoln*, 380.

In the meantime, a far more powerful to **Friday, April 14:** Donald, 586–90; Oates, 426–27; Foote, 899 ("Let em up easy"). **And thus his choice to make** to **"your good manners":** There is some scholarly discussion and debate about Lincoln visiting Pickett's home, centering around the veracity of the assertions of Mrs. Pickett. See, for instance, Lesley J. Cordon, *General George E. Pickett in Life and Legend* (U. of North Carolina Press, 1998), note 91 for pages 151–156, page 232, who casts doubt on the visit. For the alternative view, see, for example, Charles Flood, *Lee: The Final Years* (Houghton-Mifflin, 1981).

Yet Reconstruction is complex to **on April 12, he revoked the order:** Donald, 561–65, 583–84. **In fact, more often . . . Lincoln and his Republican colleagues** (and similar points in this section): On Lincoln's growing conflict with Congress concerning Reconstruction, see Belz, *Reconstructing the Union: Theory and Practice During the Civil War* (Cornell University Press, 1969), and on congressional opposition, see David Herbert Donald, *Sumner and the Rights of Man* (Knopf, 1970), 179–80, and Nevins, *War for Union*, vol. 3, 417–44. **The Radicals wanted to recast:** Oates, 367–72, 377–79, 391–93, 406–7; Garry Wills, "Lincoln's Greatest Speech," *Atlantic Monthly* (September 1999): 60–70; Morison and Commager, *Growth of the American Republic*, 19–51, esp. 19–23; Eric Foner, *A Short History of Reconstruction 1863–1867* (Harper and Row, 1990), 28–34; on Sumner and Lincoln, see Donald, *Sumner and the Rights of Man*, 196–207. **So, time and again, Lincoln straddled:** For more on congressional criticisms and radicals, see T. Harry Williams, *Lincoln and the Radicals* (University of Wisconsin Press, 1941); for more on the Congresses he had to deal with, see Allan Bogue, *The Congressman's Civil War* (Cambridge University Press, 1989), and Allan Bogue, *The Earnest Men: Republicans of the Civil War Senate* (Cornell University Press, 1981); for more on the Joint Committee on Conduct of War, see Brian Holden Reid, "Historians and the Joint Committee on the Conduct of the War 1861–1865," *CWH* 38 (December 1992): 319–41. **when Lincoln met with the three Confederate commissioners at Hampton Roads:** See Donald, 557–61; also see Kirkland, *Peacemakers of 1864*, and *BC*, 822–24. There is also some contention that Lincoln would have considered a peace settlement that did not include universal emancipation. See Current, *Lincoln Nobody Knows*, 243–347. McPherson thinks this highly improbable. **When he visited Richmond** (and cabinet rebuff): Donald, 589–90; Oates, 525; Foote, 901–2, 962–64; Reck, *A. Lincoln*, 22–23. **But with his entire cabinet again arrayed against him:** For more on Lincoln's dilemmas with his cabinet, including selecting it, see William Baringer, *A House Dividing: Lincoln as President Elect* (Abraham Lincoln Association, 1945).

the evening of April 11: Oates, 423–26; Donald, 581–84; Foote, 959–61; Lincoln speech in Basler, *Abraham Lincoln, His Speeches and Writings*, 796–801. **"knotty problems" of Reconstruction:** For further on Reconstruction, see Eric Foner's excellent *Short History of Reconstruction*, esp. 28–34, and his *Reconstruction: America's Unfinished Revolution* (Harper and Row, 1988); also excellent, Belz, *Reconstructing the Union*, one of the best accounts. **interim state government . . . in Louisiana** (and Reconstruction): See Peyton McCrary, *Abraham Lincoln and Reconstruction: The Louisiana Experiment* (Princeton University Press, 1978); for a discussion of trends in Reconstruction historiography, see Eric Foner, "Reconstruction Revisited," *Reviews in American History* 10 (December 1982): 82–100. **This final cryptic message again befuddles the crowd:** There is not universal agreement on the meaning of the speech. See, for instance, two of Lincoln's recent biographers, Oates and Donald, who offer versions at some considerable odds. Donald believes Lincoln had a plan that was an extension of his Virginia plan with the rebel legislature, which would contemplate *limited* recognition to *interim* governments for the purpose of withdrawing troops from the Confederate armies, 583–84 (emphasis mine); by contrast, Oates suggests Lincoln had in mind not "tender magnanimity" but a "new and tougher program" (including Negro suffrage in some form, and an army of occupation for the postwar South), similar to what Congress would "later adopt in the days of Radical Reconstruction." See Oates, *Abraham Lincoln*, 143–46, esp. 145–46. For his part, Grant said in his *Memoirs* that "Lincoln would have proved the best friend the South could ever have," 648.

However, Lincoln is in no mood to **"My thoughts are in that direction":** Foote, 974–80; Oates, 427–28; Donald, 590–94; Reck, *A. Lincoln*, 42–61.

Though he does not know it yet to **"the President is shot!":** Among others, Oates, 428–30, 430–33; Donald, 592–94, 595–96; Kunhardt and Kunhardt, *Twenty Days*, 22–29; and Randall, *Mary Lincoln*, 380–84. **Crook, his bodyguard:** Bak, *Day Lincoln Was Shot*, 74; Reck, *A. Lincoln*, 54; and William H. Crook, "Lincoln's Last Day," *Harper's* (September 1907) 525–30; Crook described this as "a hurried visit" and found Lincoln "more depressed than he had ever seen him." This, of course, is greatly at odds with his mood with Mary earlier in the day. **Grant begged off:** Tensions were great between Julia Grant and Mary, exacerbated by an altercation at City Point in which Julia watched Mary fly into a jealous rage of Mrs. Ord; see Oates, 419. **Remarkably, Grant and his wife:** It would, for instance, be almost unthinkable that this many people would turn down FDR in the midst of WWII's imminent end, or JFK after the Bay of Pigs, or George Bush after the Gulf War, all conflicts that were of far less significance in terms of the survival of the country and not nearly as traumatic as the Civil War. **Colfax, the House speaker:** Colfax, who was one of the most effective speakers in history, would become Grant's vice president. **even the Lincolns' son:** Leech, 392. **John F. Parker:** For more on this infamous character, see Reck, *A. Lincoln*, 162–65; also see Champ Clark, *The Assassination: The Death of the*

President (Time-Life, 1987), 82–83, for one clear statement of his whereabouts later on. **Henry J. Raymond:** Raymond was also almost designated a peace commission representative for Lincoln; see *BC*, 770. **At roughly 10:07 . . . S. P. Hanscom:** Reck, *A. Lincoln*, 92. I am grateful to Michael Maione of Ford's Theater for underscoring the fact that people routinely went in and out of the presidential box. **now about five minutes later:** After much research, the time of the shooting was pegged at 10:13, according to Otto Eisenschiml, *The Case of A. L., Aged 56* (Abraham Lincoln Book Shop, 1943), 13.

If both the president and vice president are incapacitated: Donald, 596; Bak, *Day Lincoln Was Shot*, 68; Ruth C. Silva, *Presidential Succession* (University of Michigan Press, 1951). **the second attack does take place:** About the Seward attack, see, for instance, Bak, *Day Lincoln Was Shot*, 93–96; Reck, *A. Lincoln*, 132–35; Kunhardt and Kunhardt, *Twenty Days*, 50–53; Leech, 393–95. For more, see also the lively account of Patricia Carley Johnson, ed., *Sensitivity and the Civil War: The Selected Diaries and Papers, 1858–1866, of Francis Adeline [Fanny] Seward*, unpublished doctoral dissertation, University of Rochester, 1963), 875–92; also see *New York Times* for account that is remarkably accurate given the shortness of time and panic ("inflicted three stabs in the neck, but severing, it is thought and hoped, no arteries, though [Seward] bled profusely"), April 15, 1865, in Library of Congress.

"Lewis Powell," or the alias "Lewis Paine": For further, see Betty Ownsbey, *Alias "Paine": Lewis Thorton Powell, The Mystery Man of the Lincoln Conspiracy* (MacFarland, 1993).

A few blocks away: For more on Johnson and Atzerodt, see Gene Smith, *High Crimes and Misdemeanors: The Impeachment and Trial of Andrew Johnson* (Morrow, 1977), 74–76.

In the next terror-stricken half hour: One black servant burst into the room of three senators on Thirteenth Street and shouted, "Mr. Lincoln is assassinated in the theatre. Mr. Seward is murdered in his bed. There's murder in the streets!" Also see *New York Times*, April 15, 1865, for description of widespread fear and panic. **"They have murdered my husband!":** Quote from Donald, *Sumner and the Rights of Man*, 216. Seward, in fact, was saved only by the dumbest of dumb luck. He had earlier been severely injured in a carriage accident, suffering from facial lacerations, a fractured jaw, and a broken arm, and was covered with bandages, with his neck in a steel brace. The steel brace surely saved his life, protecting his otherwise exposed neck—somewhat at least.

Abraham Lincoln was an American original to **bullet that bore into his brain:** In addition to sources already cited for this chapter, I have also used Bak, *Day Lincoln Was Shot*, 1–27, for this section and consulted Robert Leckie's profile of Lincoln, 35–54. **called him "peculiar":** *New York Times*, April 17, 1865, in Library of Congress. The same *Times* article added: "Without anything like brilliancy of genius or literary accomplishment, he still had that perfect balance of thoroughly sound faculties . . . " **Yet from those earliest years, it seemed:** I am particularly indebted to Hofstadter's insights on this theme, *American Political Tradition*, 95.

the elder Lincoln, Thomas: It is quite possible that Lincoln doubted that Thomas Lincoln was his real father, even though scholarship has debunked myths to the contrary. See William Barton, *The Paternity of Abraham Lincoln: Was He the Son of Thomas Lincoln?* (George Doran, 1920). As a sign of the persistence of this myth, Donald, note, 605, reminds us of the following correspondence by John Joel to William Seward on July 22, 1863, that "the President's real name is Abraham

Hanks.—He is the illegitimate son by a man named Inlow—from a Negress named Hanna Hanks." **history or biography:** Indeed, and perhaps surprisingly, biography in general "bored" him. See William Herndon and Jesse Weik, *Herndon's Lincoln: The True Story of a Great Life* (1889; Da Capo reprint, 1942), 353. **even a smutty story:** This is not to say they were sexual stories; more likely, given the culture and mores of the day, they related to bodily functions, like passing gas or "farting," which his Victorian generation would have considered dirty. See Donald, 639, and also P. M. Zall, *Abe Lincoln Laughing: Humorous Anecdotes from Original Sources by and About Abraham Lincoln* (University of California Press, 1982). **The marriage was a curious one:** For more, see Randall, *Mary Lincoln,* which is a standard work, as well as her *The Courtship of Mr. Lincoln* (Little, Brown, 1957). **lower Illinois House:** For more on his life there, see William Baringer, *Lincoln's Vandalia: A Pioneer Portrait* (Rutgers, 1949). **he was either campaigning, serving in office, or out on the stump:** For a full account of his continuing quest for office, see Donald Riddle, *Lincoln Runs for Congress* (Rutgers, 1948).

The **authenticity of this tale is suspect:** Hofstadter, *American Political Tradition,* 107; on his two flatboat trips, Lincoln at the time was far less concerned with matters of state or social institutions than "river currents" (Donald's phrase, 625). Benjamin Quarles in *Lincoln and the Negro* (Oxford University Press, 1962) asserts that Lincoln "could scarcely have missed seeing one or more" of the whipping posts, the slave pens, and the slave auctions in Lexington, 18. But neither does he give evidence that Lincoln did see it—or that it made any marked impression upon him, and he takes as fact that Lincoln did say that he would hit "slavery [that thing] and hit it hard," see 17–19. **Lincoln the politician, versus Lincoln the principled leader:** See the varying interpretations of Oates and Donald on this point. For more on Lincoln and what he would call "gradual, and not sudden emancipation," see J. G. Randall, *Lincoln the President: Springfield to Gettysburg* (Dodd, Mead, 1945), vol. 2 , chapter 21. **intellectual idol, Thomas Jefferson:** The two shared, for example, quite similar views on colonizing blacks, and relatively enlightened views of blacks, while having a distaste for the institution of slavery; Lincoln, of course, did far more to end slavery. **As a lame-duck congressman:** For greater detail, see Donald Riddle, *Congressman Abraham Lincoln* (Greenwood, 1979). **Stephen Douglas:** For further, see Robert Johannsen, *Stephen Douglas* (Oxford University Press, 1973). **From August to October, the verbal jousting began:** For more on the Lincoln-Douglas debates, see Don E. Fehrenbacher's *Prelude to Greatness: Lincoln in the 1850's* (Stanford University Press, 1962), among the best analyses of the debates; also Allan Nevins, *The Emergence of Lincoln: Douglas, Buchanan, and Party Chaos, 1857–1859* (Scribner's, 1950), and Kenneth Stampp, *America in 1857: A Nation on the Brink* (Oxford University Press, 1990), for analysis of events leading up to the debates; also David Zarefsky, *Lincoln, Douglas and Slavery: In the Crucible of Public Debate* (Chicago Press, 1990), and Harry Jaffa's very important *Crisis of the House Divided: An Interpretation of the Issues in the Lincoln-Douglas Debates* (Doubleday, 1959); Jaffa's work was critical in underscoring the debates as both significant and emblematic of basic American beliefs, thus reversing a long-term trend, one that "the debates themselves deserve little notice." See, for instance, Randall, *Lincoln the President,* vol. 1, 127. My thanks to Michael Uhlmann for first bringing Jaffa's work to my attention. For the actual debates, see Richard Allen Heckman, *Lincoln Versus Douglas: The Great Debates Campaign* (Public Affairs Press, 1967). For concise version, see *BC,* 181–89, which reminds us that "technically," neither Lincoln nor

Douglas was a candidate, as the state legislature chose senators, 181. **he was often caught in embarrassing contradictions:** See Hofstadter, *American Political Tradition*, 116. For alternative view, see Wills, *Lincoln at Gettysburg*, who counters that it was actually not a contradiction at all. My view leans more toward the Hofstadter interpretation. **he was told . . . "awoke to find himself famous":** For more detail on Lincoln's emergence as a political leader, see Fehrenbacher, *Prelude to Greatness*. **The dynamic of the election:** For an excellent interpretation of the election returns, see William E. Gienapp, "Who Voted for Lincoln?," John Thomas, ed., *Abraham Lincoln and the American Political Tradition* (University of Massachusetts Press, 1986), 50–97. **"The very existence" . . . "a deliberate cold blooded insult . . . "Free love and free niggers":** Quotes from *BC*, 230–31; also see 244–45, for more of the same. **Early in 1861:** See *BC*, for example, 256. **Members of his own cabinet:** For more on Lincoln's dilemmas with his cabinet, including selecting it, see William Baringer, *House Dividing*. **History should not mask . . . how ill-prepared Lincoln really was for the job:** Lincoln biographers would agree with this point. See Donald, 645, note for 292. Concerning Lincoln's objectives at the war's start, Donald points out, rightly in my view, the pitfalls of Lincoln's newness to Washington, his inexperience as an administrator, and his preference to react to events. **Black Hawk War:** For more, see Harry Pratt, *Lincoln in the Black Hawk War* (Bulletin of the Abraham Lincoln Association, December 1938), 3–13. **Where, in those darkest moments . . . inner resolve:** From Sandburg to Hofstadter and Oates and Donald, all wonderfully capture the depths of Lincoln's depressions and moroseness. Iowa Senator James Harlan, for one, observed Lincoln's moods, Donald, 593. On the very last day of his life, when he was jubilant over Lee's surrender and after he had had his carriage ride with Mary, it is worth recalling that he was suffering from a fierce headache, Leech, 386. That Lincoln could summon the energy, clarity of thought, and measure of strength in a crisis such as this is all the more remarkable—not to mention unusual for someone prone to such depressions over a long period of crises, as clinicians point out. By way of comparison, consider Lincoln's secretary of war. Oates reminds us that after one typically hectic day, Stanton nearly broke under the strain—and this was early on—and an assistant found him alone in his office, sobbing, with his head on his desk, 279. Rather than being worn down, over time, Lincoln became a "tough wartime president," Oates, *The Man Nobody Knows*, 120.

mystical attachment to Union: Ironically, the first person to make this point was Confederate Vice President Alexander H. Stephens, after the war; it was not meant, however, as a compliment, but as a criticism for being unrealistic. **Lincoln had his blind spots:** This point again recalls his gross inexperience upon entering the presidency. Concerning Lincoln's objectives at the war's start, Donald also points out, rightly in my view, the pitfalls of Lincoln's newness to Washington, his inexperience, and his fatigue. I find the fatigue element least compelling; Lincoln was far more fatigued during the war, and at its last stages, when he arguably made some of his wisest decisions. **his recalcitrance toward emancipation:** This, along with his colonization schemes, raises for some the ultimate question of whether Lincoln was a racist. In fact, Lerone Bennett Jr., for one, has labeled Lincoln a racist; see "Was Abe Lincoln a White Supremacist?," *Ebony* 23 (February 1968), 35–42. For further on this extremely complex subject, including whether Lincoln was or wasn't a racist, see Fehrenbacher, "Only His Stepchildren," in *Lincoln in Text and Context* (Stanford University, 1987), 95–112, and George M. Fredrickson, "A Man but Not a Brother: Abraham Lincoln and

Racial Equality," *Journal of Southern History* 41 (February 1975): 39–58; Lincoln's views fit racist confines of his day and time, and were at times bold, at other times timid, but on the whole, cautiously progressive. This is no small feat, given, as Oates says, "slavery was the most inflammable issue of the generation," *Abraham Lincoln, The Man Behind the Myth*, 61. Unlike many others, Lincoln did not speak of the physical or innate inferiority of blacks, or of their inability for intellectual development. Donald thus suggests that Lincoln escaped "the more virulent strains of racism." This is probably the right way to put it. See his note, 633. But understanding the age in which Lincoln lived is crucial. For instance, in April 1865 it had been only thirty-seven years since the Vatican's ban on Copernicus's *De revolutionibus orbium coelestium* had been lifted. **war began to change things:** See, for example, Oates, *Man Behind the Myth*, 92. **anything but the picture of the confident . . . commander in chief:** For further on Lincoln's constant search for effective generals, see T. Harry Williams, *Lincoln and His Generals* (Knopf, 1952). **George McClellan:** See Kenneth Williams, *Lincoln Finds a General: A Military Study of the Civil War* (Macmillan, 1949); and Stephen Sear's *George B. McClellan: The Young Napoleon* (Ticknor and Fields, 1988), an outstanding biography. **the actions of a still tentative man:** Stephen Ambrose points out another stunning example of Lincoln's early lack of experience and judgment concerning wartime operations. In August 1862, John A. McClernand, an Illinois Democrat wearing a major general's uniform, came to Lincoln and cursed Grant for being too cautious, and said he could take Vicksburg by Christmas. Lincoln and Stanton arranged for McClernand to raise a private "army" in the Northwest, and he would operate independently of Grant. At first they didn't even tell their general in chief Henry Hallek, and when they did, they ordered him, even more remarkably, to keep it secret from Grant. Eventually, Hallek spoiled McClernand's machinations—and inadvertently helped Lincoln—by telling Grant the "secret," and foiling McClernand's ability to raise an army. See Ambrose, *Americans at War*, 4–5. **looked as though the Confederacy could . . . win:** "The army is tired with its hard and terrible experience," Captain Oliver Wendell Holmes said in the winter of 1862–63. "I've pretty much made up my mind that the South have achieved their independence." Or there is the example, of course, of Lincoln's famous "blind memorandum" asking for the resignation of his entire cabinet on August 23, 1864. Before Atlanta, he was convinced he would lose the election—with all the fateful consequences. As author-columnist William Safire reminds me, anything could then have happened in the war. **three Gatling guns:** Account in Elmer Davis, *History of the New York Times 1851–1921* (New York Times, 1921), 60. **crying out for peace:** For more on Northern antiwar movements, see two older studies that have conflicting interpretations: Wood Gray, *The Hidden Civil War: The Story of the Copperheads* (Viking, 1942), and Frank Klement, *The Copperheads in the Middle West* (University of Chicago Press, 1960), and also *BC*, 760–72. **the Democratic Party platform:** On the Democratic Party and Lincoln's opponents in 1864, see Joel Silby, *A Respectable Minority: The Democratic Party in the Civil War Era, 1860–1868* (Norton, 1977), and conversely, T. Harry Williams, *Lincoln and the Radicals*, on the Radicals' plan to unseat Lincoln. **Lincoln was not religious:** For more on Lincoln and religion, see William Wolf, *The Almost Chosen People: A Study of the Religion of Abraham Lincoln* (Doubleday, 1959). **scheme to colonize freed blacks:** It is worth noting that Lincoln's ideas were in many respects similar to Jefferson's. For further on this subject, one of the best works is Michael Vorenberg, "Abraham Lincoln and the Politics of Black Colonization," *Journal of the Abraham Lincoln*

Association 14 (Summer 1993): 23–45. Also see McPherson, *Negro's Civil War*, 96–97; and Gabor S. Boritt's insightful "The Voyage the Colony of Linconia: The Sixteenth President, Black Colonization, and the Defense Mechanism of Avoidance," *Historian* 37 (August 1975): 619–32. **the Emancipation Proclamation:** For further on emancipation, see Randall, *Lincoln the President*, vol 2. Also see William Safire, *Freedom* (Doubleday, 1987). Though fictional, this account is documented in his "Underbook" of notes and helpful. **approximately 180,000 blacks:** For further on Lincoln and recruitment of blacks, see the authoritative Cornish, *Sable Arm*, 94–131, and McPherson, *Negro's Civil War*, 173–87. **Thirteenth Amendment:** For more on the Congresses he had to deal with, his own Republican Party, and factionalism, see Bogue, *Earnest Men*, esp. chapter 3; T. Harry Williams's *Lincoln and the Radicals* has much on the extreme criticism to which Lincoln was subjected; Oates notes that as the "debacles mounted up," there were "deepening schisms in Lincoln's official family, too," i.e., his own cabinet, 327; for success of Thirteenth Amendment, see *BC*, 838–50; Oates, 404–6. **Gettysburg:** See Wills, *Lincoln at Gettysburg*. **refer to his cherished Union:** See Carl M. Dengler, "The United States and National Unification," 107; also James McPherson, "The Art of Abraham Lincoln," Review of Wills's *Lincoln at Gettysburg*, *New York Review of Books* (July 16, 1992), 3–5, esp. 5. **Like many great generals:** For more about Lincoln's expanded views of his war powers as the war ground on, see Mark Neely Jr., *The Fate of Liberty: Abraham Lincoln and Civil Liberties* (Oxford University Press, 1991). **envelope marked "Assassination":** For fears about Lincoln's safety, see Oates, 415–17; gunshot story and Lamon's fears, Ward Lamon, *Recollections of Abraham Lincoln* (A. L. McClurg, 1895), 263–81. **"not an American practice":** Frederick Bancroft, *Life of Seward* (Harper and Brothers, 1900), vol. 2, 418. **"made up my mind":** Noah Brooks, *Washington, D.C., in Lincoln's Time* (Quadrangle Books, 1971), 43–44. **To some, these are the convictions:** For example, see on this point, Hofstadter, *American Political Tradition*, 129.

"**Stop that man!** to sought to control: Oates, 431–34; Bak, *Day Lincoln Was Shot*, 96–98; Donald, 596–99; Randall, *Mary Lincoln*, 382–84; Foote, 980–86; Reck, *A. Lincoln*, 81–112, 113–32, 136–68; Kunhardt and Kunhardt, *Twenty Days*, 40–49, 78–79; also see Lloyd Lewis, *The Assassination of Lincoln: History and Myth* (Nebraska University Press, 1929). This book has some errors and outdated interpretations of Reconstruction, yet Lewis was a keen and shrewd historian of the Civil War. "**Help!**" ... "**Won't somebody**" ... "**For God's sake . . .**" and other cries for help: Also see *New York Herald*, April 17, 1865, and *New York Times*, April 15, 16, 17, 1865, in Library of Congress; Charles Sabin Taft, M.D., "A. L.'s Last hours," *Century Magazine* (February 1893) 634; Welles, *Diary*, 286–88; Thomas and Hyman, *Stanton*, 396–410. **Charles A. Leale:** See Ralph Borreson, *When Lincoln Died* (Appleton-Century, 1965), 15–31, including excerpts from Leale. **"His wound is mortal":** There is a general consensus that the shot was fatal, but at least one doctor, Richard A. Fraser of New York Hospital–Cornell Medical Center, has suggested that the bullet wound was not necessarily fatal, and that the probing by Leale and Dr. Stone in fact did irreversible damage, UPI dispatch, January 25, 1995; given the medicine of the day, and the risk of infection, Dr. Ronald Kurstin of Sibley Hospital tells me that in either case, Lincoln would almost certainly have died. **His pulse was forty-five:** See *New York Times*, April 16, 1865, for detailed list of his pulse readings and times, including when "Mrs. Lincoln was present." Starting at 10:55, Dr. Ezra Abbott and Dr. Albert King recorded the first of fifty readings of Lincoln's pulse and twenty of his respiration, Reck, *A. Lincoln*,

147. Of Lincoln's medical condition and pulse rates, details taken from Reck, *A. Lincoln*, and *New York Times*, and also Dr. John Lattimer's study, *Kennedy and Lincoln: Medical and Ballistic Comparisons of Their Assassinations* (Harcourt Brace, 1980), esp. Dr. Leale's report, 28–32. **"No . . . he isn't dead"**: Sumner quote in Donald, *Sumner and the Rights of Man*, 216. **"AWFUL EVENT"**: Headline from *New York Times*, April 15, 1865. **Throughout the night, Stanton**: Leech, 400–401; George S. Bryan, in *The Great American Myth* (Carrick and Evans, 1940), has thoroughly destroyed the myth that Stanton was at all involved in the assassination. **"Oh my God, and have I given my husband"**: There are variations of what Mary Lincoln actually said. I have used Randall's *Mary Lincoln*, 384, which strikes me as the most accurate. **Sumner's shoulder**: Donald, *Sumner and the Rights of Man*, 216–17. **"he belongs to the angels"**: There are a number of variations of what Stanton actually said. ("He belongs to the ages now," "he is a man for the ages," "he now belongs to the ages.") The most widely used by historians is the one that Stanton himself amended later that evening to give it more dramatic impact: "Now he belongs to the ages." That Stanton did revise his words for history—something that in his time Lincoln did not do—is fascinating in itself. The quote I use is from the attending stenographer, James Tanner (see Bak, *Day Lincoln Was Shot*, 98), which strikes me as most accurate. See also Eisenschiml, *Why Was Lincoln Murdered?*, 482–85; and Bryan, *Great American Myth*, 189.

CHAPTER SIX: WOULD IT ALL COME UNDONE?

"a night of horrors": Chase also added, "the guard came . . . and their heavy tramp was heard under my window all night . . . ," Salmon P. Chase, *Inside Lincoln's Cabinet: The Civil War Diaries of Salmon P. Chase*, David Donald, ed. (Longmans, Green, 1954), 267. **By 7:30 A.M., a strange light to not at all an insignificant one**: See, for instance, *New York Times* and *New York Tribune*, April 15, 16, 17, 1865. Considering the chaos, and some glaring inaccuracies due to lack of adequate sources, some of the early reporting of Lincoln's death and the aftermath was quite accurate. Also see Leech, 395–400; Bak, *Day Lincoln Was Shot*, 110; Thomas Reed Turner, *Beware the People Weeping: Public Opinion and the Assassination of Abraham Lincoln* (LSU Press, 1982), 25–52; Lewis, *Assassination of Lincoln*, 48–49, 56, 58–59; from which quotes are taken, unless otherwise noted. **Talk of streets running red**: Across the Union, those who professed the slightest sympathy for the killing of Lincoln put their life in danger—literally. Thirty-five-year-old Joseph Shaw, the editor of the *Westminster* (Maryland) *Democrat*, was killed in Zachariah's Hotel while defending himself from a hostile mob, who physically broke into his hotel room. They brutally fell upon him and killed him because of "disrespectful language" about Lincoln in his paper, Turner, *Beware the People Weeping*, 50–51; his press was also destroyed by mob action. In another instance, at the Mission Church in the First Ward, a preacher made some insulting comments about Lincoln in the course of a Sunday sermon; he was dragged from the pulpit, assaulted, then arrested, Leech, 369. Instances like this, of assault, mob rule, or murder, were commonplace in the days that followed. On this also see *Glenn*, 206–9. **Wrote the New York Times**: Quotes are from April 17, 1865. **for under an hour**: Remarkably, outside of speculation, it is not known what the two men even talked about. **Edwin Stanton . . . tendered his resignation**: Oates describes him "as looking exhausted and utterly worn down from illness" and strain. He stayed on only because Lincoln prevailed upon him to remain. "Reluctantly," Stanton said, he would (Oates's words), "stay with Lincoln a little longer," 423. By any measure, Stanton would become one of the most controversial characters of this time period, and then again of the Johnson administration. Ironically, the flap over Johnson's impeachment was about Stanton's refusal to be fired, which sheds some light on his actions during these April days. **"Acting President"**: Foote, 983; Grant wrote in his *Memoirs* that "Stanton felt little hesitation in assuming the function of the executive," 656. By comparison—and this underscores how ill-formed the succession mechanism still was—consider the enormous criticism that Ronald Reagan's secretary of state, Alexander Haig, received for asserting temporarily, "I'm in charge here," after the failed attempt on Reagan's life.

When the Founders first debated to who would be the Union's next president (entire section on succession): For the best treatment of this too little studied but crucial subject, see Silva, *Presidential Succession*, which has the most precise statement of what the Framers intended, and Stephen W. Stathis's excellent "John Tyler's Presidential Succession: A Reappraisal," in *Prologue* 8, no. 4 (1976): 223–36. Also Stephen Wilhelm, "The Origins of the Office of the Vice Presidency," *Presidential Studies Quarterly* 7, no. 4 (1977): 206–14. This section draws extensively upon these three fine works, from which all quotes are taken, unless otherwise noted, and which have influenced my thinking and argumentation heavily. I am much indebted to these studies. Other very useful studies that I have used are: Michael DiSalle, *Second Choice* (Hawthorne, 1966); Merrill Jensen, *The Making of the American Constitution* (Van Nostrand, 1964); Jonathan Elliot, ed., *The Debates on the Adoption of the Federal Constitution*, vols. 1–5 (William S. Hein, 1888); and Edward S. Corwin, *The President: Office and Powers 1787–1957* (New York University Press, 1991). **When the Founders to until that election took place**: For this section, see esp. Silva, *Presidential Succession*, 1–13, and Wilhelm, "Origins of the Office of the Vice Presidency," 36–51; also Michael Dorman, *The Second Man: The Changing Role of the Vice Presidency* (Delacorte, 1968), 45–46. **they did not intend for the vice president to become president**: Wilhelm agrees with this. He also notes that the delegates at the convention did not consider the matter "a major topic." And further, that historical documents still "leave the question of why the office was even created a mystery," "Origins of the Office of the Vice Presidency," 214; Jefferson ally William Rives referred to the whole matter of succession as a "remote and shadowy inheritance," Silva, *Presidential Succession*, 114–15. **Edward S. Corwin**: See Corwin, *President*, esp. 54. For similar commentaries to Corwin, see also Donald B. Chidsey, *And Tyler Too* (Nelson, 1978), 44–46; Herbert Horwill, *The Usages of the American Constitution* (Oxford University Press, 1969), 268–69; Wilfred Binkley, *The Man in the White House* (Johns Hopkins University Press, 1968), 268–69; Richard H. Hansen, *The Year We Had No President* (Lincoln, 1962), 13–20; James Kent, *Commentaries on American Law*, 4 vols. (W. Kent, 1854), vol. 1, 298; Charles Warren, *The Making of the Constitution* (Little, Brown, 1937), note at 637; and Charles K. Burdick, *The Law of the American Constitution: Its Origin and Development* (F. B. Rothman, 1922), 59–60; for earlier opinions, see John W. Burgess, *Political Science and Comparative Constitutional Law* (Ginn & Company, 1891), 239; William Rawle, *A View of the Constitution of the United States* (H. C. Carey & I. Lea, 1825), vol. 1, 711; David Watson, *The Constitution of the United States: Its History, Application, and Construction*, 2 vols. (University of Chicago Press, 1910), vol. 1, 891–902. **Indeed, for the better part of a half century**: On March 1, 1792, Congress did pass a presidential succession law, which provided that a vice president can resign or refuse election in one way only, with a written refusal signed and dated and delivered to the secretary of state, Wilhelm, "Origins of the Office of the Vice Presidency," 213. The law also provided that the president pro tempore of the Senate or speaker of the house would be in line to act as president, until presidential electors were chosen or elected and a special election held. One may ask, why was the secretary of state not put in line? The reason was politics, having to do with Alexander Hamilton's hatred of Thomas Jefferson. On this point, the choleric Fisher Ames, Federalist leader in Massachusetts, gleefully reported to Thomas Dwight: "The Secretary of State is struck out of the bill for the future presidency, in case of the first two offices becoming vacant. His friends think it important to hold him up as King of the Romans. The firmness of the Senate kept him out." See Silva, *Presidential Succession*, 113–14; for a larger discussion of congressional actions on this matter, occurring in 1792, 1820–21, and 1842, see Silva, *Presidential Succession*, 112–16, 166–68. Interestingly, when President Johnson was later impeached, many in Congress asserted that he was still "vice president," and for the time, only "acting president." Others noted simply that he was serving out "Lincoln's term." Indeed, the three original impeachment resolutions introduced by Benjamin F. Loan and John Kelso spoke of "the officer now exercising the function pertaining to the office of President of the United States"; James Ashley's resolution referred to "Andrew Johnson, Vice President and acting President of the United States"; and another resolution put it this way: "Vice President of the United States, discharging the powers and duties of the office of the President." The Final Judiciary Committee resolutions that impeached him, however, did so as the "president." See Silva, *Presidential Succession*, note on 26 and 27. **But even the Founders were not omniscient** to **So by the time Lincoln lay dying:** Silva, *Presidential Succession*, 14–31, and conclusions, esp. 166–69; Stathis, "John Tyler's Presidential Succession"; also Chidsey, *And Tyler Too*, esp. 41–53; and Dorman, *Second Man*, esp. 45–55. **hours away in Williamsburg:** Some 230 miles and at least twenty-one hours, to be exact. This in itself was a telling fact about the lack of importance of the vice presidency. **Washington was alive with fierce speculation:** Chidsey writes that the capital was in a "state of pitiful bewilderment" over the succession issue. "Learned statesman everywhere were asking themselves the question" of succession, which had been left "in the air." **the cabinet would run the show:** As Chidsey puts it: "That this amiable Virginian might become . . . the full time, undisputed president, Webster did not for a moment believe"; moreover, the secretaries assembled "were to rule the nation in Tyler's name," *And Tyler Too*, 44–45. Before relatively newer scholarship, Tyler's succession had been blandly portrayed by some as almost devoid of political intrigue. See Oliver Chitwood, *John Tyler: Champion of the Old South* (D. Appleton, 1939), 202–6; Leonard Dinnerstein, "The Accession of John Tyler to the Presidency," *Virginia Magazine of History and Biography* 70 (October 1952): 447–58; Robert Seager, *And Tyler Too* (Easton Press, 1963). **Tyler had won the showdown:** Claude Fuess says that Tyler "made it entirely clear that he intended to seize full authority," Claude M. Fuess, *Daniel Webster*, 2 vols. (Little, Brown, 1930), vol. 1, 95. Similarly, of the ambitious Tyler, Morgan argues, "Tyler's whole course of action after he arrived in the capital demonstrated [his] serious deliberation to establish himself as President in his own right and not as a mere caretaker for the departed Harrison," Robert J. Morgan, *A Whig Embattled: The Presidency Under John Tyler* (Lincoln, 1954), 9. **special presidential election should be called for:** Chidsey points out, however, "Could a man in truth be

President who had never been elected President? This was the question that perplexed even the most expert hairsplitters in Washington," *And Tyler Too*, 50. **administered not by Chief Justice Taney:** One unsatisfactory reason could be that Taney was a resident of Baltimore, while Cranch lived in Washington. But this still does not explain his essential refusal to administer the oath to Tyler. See Bernard Steiner, *Life of Brooke Taney: Chief Justice of the United States Supreme Court* (Williams & Wilkins, 1922), 257–58.

Andrew Johnson: Historians have long been puzzled about how exactly to assess Johnson, and exactly what made "him tick" (Brooks Simpson's phrase). Biographies and in-depth studies have appeared in waves, coinciding with sharply divergent assessments of Reconstruction over the years. Books written in the 1920s and 1930s lauded him for his conciliatory stances toward a prostrate South, while accounts after 1960 excoriated him for incompetence and wrongheaded obstinacy. Moralizing, of either stripe, aside, the question of understanding Johnson remains. For further readings, which I have consulted, used, or perused, see Paul H. Bergeron, ed., *The Papers of Andrew Johnson*, vol. 8: May–August 1865 (University of Tennessee Press, 1989), which helps us understand the context in which he operated, crucial because the new president was immediately bombarded with advice and suggestions from across the entire political spectrum; David Bowen's perceptive *Andrew Johnson and the Negro* (University of Tennessee Press, 1989), which nicely explores Johnson's racial attitudes and his political and social philosophy; Albert Castel's *The Presidency of Andrew Johnson* (University Press of Kansas, 1979), a solid evaluation of Johnson's effectiveness as a politician and a policy maker, which lays out the pitfalls created by his stubbornness; James E. Sefton, *Andrew Johnson and the Uses of Constitutional Power* (Little, Brown, 1990), a short but lively biography that offers the reader the challenge of "coping with Johnson on his terms"; Hans Trefousse's biography, *Andrew Johnson: A Biography* (Norton, 1989), which clarifies a number of details about Johnson's life, written by a professional historian. It also is fairly balanced (the author does not like Johnson, but has begrudging admiration for him), albeit short on the actual inner life of Johnson himself. Also see Brooks D. Simpson's review essay "Reconstructing Andrew Johnson," *Congress and the Presidency* 7, no. 2 (Autumn 1990): 167–73, and Michael Perman, "Solving the Riddle of Andrew Johnson," *Journal of East Tennessee History* 62 (1990): 105–14. For an example of a particularly harsh critique of Johnson, see Eric McKitrick, *Andrew Johnson: A Profile* (Hill and Wang, 1969). Also used for this section on Johnson, from which quotes are further taken, see Foote, 986–89; Dorman, *Second Man*, 66–87; Gene Smith, *High Crimes and Misdemeanors: The Impeachment and Trial of Andrew Johnson* (Morrow, 1976), esp. 7–126; also Donald, *Sumner and the Rights of Man*, 218–30, and James McPherson, *Ordeal by Fire: The Civil War and Reconstruction* (Knopf, 1982), 495–96. **taught him how to read and write:** Trefousse presents convincing evidence that it was not his wife but probably the foreman at Selby's tailor shop in Raleigh who taught him literacy. **Lincoln's second inaugural:** See, for instance, Foote, 810–12; Smith, *High Crimes*, 60–65. **Johnson be forced to resign . . . "so dishonored":** Donald, *Sumner and the Rights of Man*, 218. **no greater testimony to Johnson's diminished stature . . . dutifully complied:** The reader may note here that the succession process was still so relatively new that that it didn't occur to anyone, including Johnson, that the "acting presidency" or the "presidency itself" should have already devolved upon Johnson. Instead, he waited to take the oath of office. By comparison, John Tyler, with no precedent to back him up, did not think the oath of office was even needed.

But to Stanton's credit to **running the government:** Taken, in part, from *New York Times*, April 15, 16 (succession on this day), 17, 1865; the *Times* noted on April 17, of Johnson, "his sympathies are with the people and all his actions will be for their good." Also Smith, *High Crimes*, 74–83; Foote, 986–87; Dorman, *Second Man*, 64–66; Chase, *Inside Lincoln's Cabinet*, 260–71, esp. 267–69.

Mary Chesnut: *MC*, 796. **One reporter, hearing Johnson speak:** Smith, *High Crimes*, 66. **Even Senator Sumner . . . believed Providence had ordained:** Donald, *Sumner and the Rights of Man*, 220. Actually, this was not a new phenomenon. When President Harrison died, it was widely believed that he was sacrificed for the sins of the American people throughout the 1830s, and for many, Tyler's succession was "an act of god," Stathis, "John Tyler's Presidential Succession," 230. **in historian James McPherson's words:** See *Ordeal by Fire*, 485.

Of all the men who would choose to **Forrest couldn't have known it then, but in fact Johnston did want to surrender:** For Forrest biographical sketch and role of Forrest, I have relied heavily upon the following sources, from which all quotes are taken unless otherwise noted: On Forrest, see two recent biographies, each written in a lively, readable style, Jack Hurst, *Nathan Bedford Forrest*, and Brian Steel Wills, *A Battle from the Start: The Life of Nathan Bedford Forrest* (HarperCollins, 1992), both of which offer full coverage of Forrest's prewar and postwar life, but are sometimes short of description of his wartime activities; John A. Wyeth, *Life of General Nathan Bedford Forrest* (Harper and Bros., 1899), one of the better turn-of-the-century studies; Andrew N. Lytle, *Bedford Forrest and His Critter Company* (J. S. Sanders, 1992), esp. 355–77 for final months of war, but which suffers in some respects from lack of scholarship; for a more outdated work, see Thomas Jordan and J. P. Pryor, *The Campaigns of Lieut.-Gen. N. B. Forrest* (1868, Da Capo reprint 1996) (marred, however, by unfortunate errors); also Robert Selph Henry, *"First with the Most" Forrest* (Bobbs-Merrill, 1944), which for many is still the best text. It is extremely useful and provides a great chronological narrative of Forrest's battles, and in many ways the best accounts of his campaigns. At times, however, it is short on critical analysis of Forrest himself; also R. S. Henry, ed., *As They Saw Forrest: Some Recollections and Comments of Contemporaries* (McCowat Mercer, 1956), perhaps overwrought in some areas, but still very useful; also outstanding and extremely helpful to me was a three-part condensed biography of the life of Nathan Bedford Forrest by Mark Grimsley in *Civil War Times Illustrated*, "Millionaire Rebel Raider, Part I" (September/October 1993), 59–73; "The Great Deceiver, Part II" (November/December 1993), 33–96; and "Leader of the Klan," Part III (January/February 1994), 35–73; I am heavily indebted to this concise sketch for helping make sense of this complex man, and have drawn upon it extensively. See further, sketch of Forrest in Ward, *Civil War*, 346, and comments by Foote, 245–46, and discussion in *BC*, esp. 513–15, 723, 807–8. **none was more suited:** Emory Thomas, *CN*, points out that during the Confederacy's darkest hours in these waning months, Forrest won some of his "greatest victories," 288. **But nothing quite so succeeds in American life, North or South, as success:** I am indebted to the author Tom Wolfe for this insight. Wolfe points out that in the South, much of the old money was in fact new money, and that the nouveaux riches were always prevalent while affecting the status of old South. **pin down an invading army of 40,000:** See *BC*, on this point, 514. **logistics have always been half the battle:** Jay Winik briefing to Defense Secretary Les Aspin, 1992. **"I get there firstest with the mostest":** Did Forrest ever actually say this? Or is it folklore? Most likely, he said something like it, although in Henry's terms, not so self-consciously a piece of literary description. The phrase, in whatever form it occurred, originated from a discussion between Forrest and John Hunt Morgan while the two were comparing notes at Murfreesboro, Tennessee, after operations in Kentucky and middle Tennessee. Forrest explained his success this way: "I just got there first with the most men." (Actually, he probably pronounced this "git tar fuss"). But in truth, while he often got there first, rarely did he have the most men. See Henry, *"First with the Most" Forrest*, 18–20; later in the war, he met with Union representatives Colonel John G. Parkenhurst and Captain Lewis Hosea on February 23–24. Here again he spoke of his unorthodox philosophy of war, and reiterated his maxim of getting there first. He also said he preferred "pistols to sidearms." In this same meeting, he spoke openly, without recrimination, of the rebel effort in Mississippi to enroll Negroes in the army, suggesting he was a convert to this view, see, for example, Hurst, *Nathan Bedford Forrest*, 246–47. **Fort Pillow:** The truth of the killing of several dozen black prisoners and some whites—including Major William Bradford, the commander, who was captured and subsequently killed, is now generally accepted. For more on Fort Pillow, see Ronald K. Hugh, "Fort Pillow Massacre: Aftermath of Paducah," *Illinois State Historical Society Journal* 66 (1973): 62–70, and George Bodnia, ed., "Fort Pillow 'Massacre,' Observations of a Minnesotan," *Minnesota History* 4 (1973): 186–90; Albert Castel, "The Fort Pillow Massacre: A Fresh Examination of the Evidence," *CWH* 4, no. 1 (March 1958): 48; and John Cimprich and Robert Mainfort Jr., "Fort Pillow Revisited: New Evidence About an Old Controversy" *CWH* 28 (1982): 293–306. It could be added that General Bill Sherman, who faced accusations of brutality as well, after examining the evidence, was satisfied that Forrest had done what he could to halt excesses, and that the slaughter of "negro troops" was not, "properly speaking, a 'massacre' so much as the rather unnecessary killing of blacks due to their panic," see Lewis, *Sherman*, 370. Qualifying a wholesale acceptance of Sherman's assessments are his own questionable racial biases and the accusations he had to face. **significant morale booster for the South:** See Gallagher, *Confederate War*, 36–37. **"blood can not restore blood":** See *BC*, 794. **"niggers" and "Tories" alike, had it coming:** See Albert Castel's introduction on this point in Jordan and Pryor, *Campaigns of Lieut.-Gen. N. B. Forrest*, esp. viii. He asserts that Forrest "was no more to blame for what happened than Lee was for the similar mass killing of black troops in the Battle of the Crater in Virginia on July 30, 1864." By contrast, Grimsley notes that what occurred was clearly an "atrocity," but that Forrest's role is "controversial" and that it is one thing to say Forrest did not order the killings—evidence suggests he didn't—and another to "absolve him of responsibility," Grimsley, "Great Deceiver," 38; that both blacks and whites were killed does dampen the notion that it was wholly racially motivated. James Webb, much-decorated Vietnam War hero, former navy secretary, and best-selling novelist, tells me that it is his view that Forrest and his men did not do anything in the heat of the battle that other armies throughout history haven't done, and warns of the peril of applying contemporary standards to Forrest at Fort Pillow. In short, from his experience, he would subscribe to the *insanitas belli* thesis. That Lincoln was less bothered by this issue than many others may lend some credence to this view. **"War . . . means killing":** See Hurst, *Nathan Bedford Forrest*, 263. **the most humiliating Union defeat:** McPherson, for example, makes this point, *BC*, 748. **James W. Wilson:** See, for example, Foote, 847–50, 904–5. **Wilson's aides:** This famous meeting, of course, was with Colonel John G. Parkenhurst and Captain Lewis Hosea on February 23–24,

1865. **sieges of Fort Blakely and Spanish Fort:** For more on these two battles, which don't receive nearly enough attention, see Trudeau, *Out of the Storm*, 153–87. **"point of the saber instead of the edge":** In fact, this was no mere bluster. The running battle continued over a full 200 yards. See Hurst, *Nathan Bedford Forrest*, 256.

What made Forrest so effective on the battlefield: I am especially indebted for the next two paragraphs to Grimsley's thoughtful and compact discussion ("Great Deceiver"), 37, 39, 94. **Confederacy was an isolated wasteland:** *BC*, 818. **As to guerrilla warfare:** It is important to note that Forrest did not see himself as a "guerrilla" or "partisan" as the term was used, which usually meant those like William Quantrill in Missouri. Indeed, Forrest himself wanted to rid the land of such lawless guerrillas, as he told Wilson's aides, Parkenhurst and Hosea, in February 1865 (see Hurst, *Nathan Bedford Forrest*, 247). But as a cavalryman taking to the hills, under direction from Davis or Lee, that would surely be a different matter. **"Resist the sensational rumors":** See Forrest letter from the field in *OR*, series 1, vol. 49, 1263–64; at this point, Forrest resisted all notion of a final surrender. See T. Michael Parrish, *Richard Taylor, Soldier Prince of Dixie* (University of North Carolina Press, 1991), 438. **"Forrest has genius, popularity, and power":** Quote in *Glenn*, 191.

Now, on April 10, after Appomattox to he added this stinging phrase, "instant, purely, and simply": For this section, I have relied heavily upon the following, from which quotes are taken unless otherwise indicated: William T. Sherman, "'To Execute the Terms of Surrender,' Sherman's Own Version of Johnston's Acceptance—and Washington's Reaction," letter to Dr. John W. Draper, June 30, 1867, reprinted in *Civil War Times Illustrated* 15, no. 9 (1977): 34–42; John F. Marszalek Jr., "The Stanton-Sherman Controversy," *Civil War Times Illustrated* 9, no. 6 (October 1970): 4–13; and Beverly Bone, "Edwin Stanton in the Wake of the Lincoln Assassination," *Lincoln Herald* 82, no. 4 (1980): 508–21; Foote, 998–969; William M. Vatavuk, *Dawn of Peace: The Bennett Place State Historic Site* (Bennett Place Support Fund, 1989); Lloyd Lewis, *Sherman: Fighting Prophet* (1932; reprint, University of Nebraska, 1993), esp. 526–55. Also see William T. Sherman, *Memoirs of General William T. Sherman*, 2 vols. (Appleton, 1886); Joseph E. Johnston, *Narrative of Military Operations*, Frank E. Vandiver, ed. (1874; reprint, Da Capo, 1959), 399–420; Grant, esp. 568–70; also Trudeau, *Out of the Storm*, 237–44. **Far more than the world knew** and quotes: See also Sherman letter to Draper.

James Bennett: The spelling of the family name was actually Bennitt; it was changed in the late 1800s, Vatavuk, *Dawn of Peace*, 5. **Johnston, too, was excessively cautious:** I have taken McPherson's assessment here, *BC*, 857, similar to Mary Chestnut's. Of Johnston, she wrote: "He was too fussy, too hard to please, too cautious, too much afraid to miss and risk his fine reputation . . . ," 268, *MC*.

Sherman had always been a bit of a tender romantic: Indeed, he wrote to Grant, "The South is broken and ruined, and appeals to our pity. To ride the people down with persecution and military exactions would be like slashing away at the crew of a sinking ship," Michael Fellman, *Citizen Sherman* (Random House, 1995), 240–41; for a modern profile of Sherman and his "inner" motives, see Fellman's account of this time period, 238–56. **"Memorandum, or Basis of Agreement":** See Johnston, *Narrative of Military Operations*, 405–7; Lewis, *Sherman*, 540–41. **anything but simple:** See John F. Marszalek, *Sherman: A Soldier's Passion for Order* (Free Press, 1993), 5–6.

Secretary of War Stanton: For more on this fascinating figure, see Benjamin Thomas and Harold Hyman, *Stanton: Life and Times of Lincoln's Secretary of War* (Knopf, 1962); for discussion of his role on evening of assassination and aftermath, see Turner, *Beware the People Weeping*, 53–64. **Sherman had clearly overstepped his authority:** For further on Sherman and Bennett House agreement, see Raoul S. Naroll, "Lincoln and the Sherman Peace Fiasco—Another Fable?," *Journal of Southern History* 20 (November 1954), 459–83. He contends that Sherman clearly exceeded his instructions, yet it is apparent that Lincoln surely discussed—though it is not absolutely clear if he endorsed—recognition of Confederate state authorities at this City Point meeting. Sherman defended himself, contending the president said "That to avoid anarchy the State governments then in existence, with their civil functionaries, would be recognized by him as the government de facto till Congress would provide others," see Sherman, *Memoirs*, vol. 2, 327. **The memorandum was scarcely any better:** See Marszalek, *Sherman*, 6; Foote, 994; Fellman, *Citizen Sherman*, 246. **European intrigues:** It's worth recalling that not even fifty years had passed since Napoleon; indeed, until April 1865 of the Civil War—which marked a major historical break with the past—history since Roman times had been full of professional armies marching home from victorious campaigns of pillage and conquest to overthrow civilian rulers and put idolized generals on the throne. On this point, also see Palmer and Colton, 5–15, and Lewis, *Sherman*, 553. **"victorious legions" . . . "dictator" . . . "arrest Grant!":** Quotes from Lewis, ibid., 550, 555.

like "a caged lion": See Marszalek, *Sherman*, 6, and Trudeau, *Out of the Storm*, 244. **Chicago Tribune:** *Chicago Tribune*, April 24, 1865; *New Haven Journal*, April 27, 1865; *Herald* and *Times* in Marszalek, *Sherman*, 8.

fight on: Johnston, *Narrative of Military Operations*, 411–12; Foote, 996. **The London Times:** See Lewis, *Sherman*, 553. **"What is it that sustains me?":** Quote in Gallagher, *Confederate War*, 84–85. Around this time, one Confederate woman, Emma LeConte, insisted that Davis should call out the women of the South to fight. All measures should be taken, she insisted, "that will give us freedom and not force us to live with such people—to be ruled by such horrible and contemptible creatures—to submit to them when we hate them so bitterly." Emma LeConte, *When the World Ended: The Diary of Emma LeConte*, Earl Schenck Miers, ed. (Oxford University Press, 1957), 9.

CHAPTER SEVEN: SURRENDER

Across the battered landscape: "*All, all* was lost, except for my debts!" Confederate General Braxton Bragg cried out, upon returning to his once prosperous home. For descriptions and information on the devastation, see Ralph Anderson, ed., *The Economic Impact of the American Civil War* (Cambridge University Press, 1962); Foner, *Short History of Reconstruction*, 55–56; *BC*, 818, and McPherson, *Ordeal by Fire*, 493; Morison and Commager, *Growth of the American Republic* ("The Prostrate South"), 11–14; Lewis, *Sherman*, 365. **Yet against this backdrop of sorrow:** Morison and Commager assert that the physical devastation "was without parallel," *Growth of the American Republic*, 11. **small but deadly skirmishes:** See Long, *Civil War Day by Day*, 677–81. **reverse the names:** Brian Holden Reid would add other things to this list: an effective Confederate blockade of Atlanta and all seaboard ports; control of a belt of land cutting off everything west of Indiana from the rest of the North; and pro-Confederate governments in southern Pennsylvania, southern Ohio, and southern Indiana, see "Why the Confederacy Lost," 32–41. **honor and a dose of hate:** As an antidote to the view that overly romanticizes the war's end, Gallagher rightly reminds us that the Civil War wasn't simply a brothers' war, itself often a romantic description that obscures the true bitterness, but that the hate was still palpably strong, and by implication thus complicating any attempts at reconciliation, *Confederate War*, 105. This is a crucial point to bear in mind in understanding the actions and achievements of this period.

   maelstrom of total war: See Liddell Hart's excellent essay on Sherman, in his *Strategy* (Meridian, 1991), 124–37; also John Keegan's excellent *Face of War*. **Critics and ethicists:** See, for example, Michael Walzer, *Just and Unjust Wars: A Moral Argument with Historical Illustrations* (Basic Books, 1977). **"War is cruelty":** There is considerable debate about whether Sherman actually waged total war, and if so, to what degree. Michael Walzer, a leading political scientist and ethicist, resoundingly says he did wage total war, and an unjustified one at that—one that cruelly broke down the barriers between combatants and noncombatants. In Walzer's words, Sherman is on the "extreme form" of "a one-sided and partial way of thinking," and what Walzer calls "the sliding scale argument" in which "no limits [are] left except force itself." This, in Walzer's view, is unacceptable, see *Just and Unjust Wars*, 32–33, 37, 230; James Reston Jr., *Sherman's March and Vietnam* (Macmillan, 1984), further portrays Sherman as the progenitor of modern "total war," which reached its conclusion in World War II. See also Bruce Russett and Harvey Starr, "Ethics and War," *World Politics* (Freeman, 1996), 316–22; Malham M. Wakin, *War, Morality, and the Military Profession* (Westview, 1986), esp. 284–16, 341–65; Paul Ramsey, *The Just War* (Scribner's, 1968); by contrast, see Mark Neely Jr., "Was the Civil War a Total War?," *CWH* 37 (1991): 14-15, 27, who maintains that true total war is "without scruples or limitations" and that it must "break down the distinction between soldiers and civilians, combatants and noncombatants," which sounds like Walzer. Neely, however, doe not feel that this happened, see 14–16, 27. Mark Grimsley, in *The Hard Hand of War: Union Military Policy Toward Southern Civilians, 1861–1865* (Cambridge University Press, 1995), largely agrees. Where Walzer sees the perils of the "sliding scale" of the "war is hell doctrine," Grimsley maintains that the actions of Sherman were "seldom the wanton wholesale fury of legend," but instead, a "balance between severity and restraint," and were "roughly proportional to legitimate needs." He labels Sherman's efforts "hard war," characterized by "direct severity." James McPherson comes down in their support, adding that compared with ethnic cleansing by Serbian armies in Bosnia or Allied bombing in WWII, Sherman's soldiers were a "model of decorum," see review essay "Götterdämmerung," *New York Review of Books*, December 21, 1995, 10–16. Michael Fellman, often a critic of Sherman, also says that the army "placed limits on itself," *Citizen Sherman*, 225. However, that Sherman did wage at least something approaching total war in South Carolina, all agree. Does that then absolve Sherman of the change? That he was perhaps less severe than, say, the British in Ireland or Philip II of Spain against the Dutch does not completely vitiate the severity of his total war policies against *part* of the South. Also, some of the comparisons may not tell the full story. It is quite clear that in the American context, and as practiced by American soldiers, Sherman introduced a whole new brand of warfare. This is not a judgment, merely a historical observation. One may further take note that Robert E. Lee rejected precisely this sort of warfare—and the Confederacy surely paid a price for it. For broader historical perspective on the growth of war and changing norms of conflict, see Michael Howard, *War in European History* (Oxford University Press, 1976), esp. 1–115; and Liddell Hart, *Strategy*, 1–147. **So who was William Tecumseh Sherman to "Send one corps of infantry also":** For the following biographical sketch and section on Sherman's march through the South, I have drawn heavily upon the following, from which all quotes are taken unless otherwise noted: Marszalek, *Sherman*; Lewis, *Sherman*; B. H. Liddell Hart, *Sherman* (New York, 1958)— perhaps the three best works on Sherman. Also excellent, and supplementary to the above, Fellman, *Citizen Sherman*; Royster, *Destructive War*, esp. 3–34; 79–143; Charles E. Vetter, *Sherman: Merchant of Terror, Advocate of Peace* (Pelican, 1992); John B. Walters, *Merchant of Terror: General Sherman and the Total War* (Bobbs-Merrill, 1973); James M. Merrill, *William Tecumseh Sherman* (Rand McNally, 1971); Sherman, *Memoirs*; and short biographical sketches in Ward, *Civil War*, 321–22; Leckie, *None Died in Vain*, 268–76; and observations of McPherson, throughout *BC*.

"I knew wherever I was that you thought of me": Quote in Gary Gallagher, "How Familiarity Bred Success: Military Campaigns and Leaders in Ken Burns's Civil War," *Ken Burns's The Civil War: Historians Respond*, Robert B. Toplin, ed. (Oxford University Press, 1996), 53. **no turning point was as crucial:** Ralph Waldo Emerson had this to say: "Seldom in history was so much staked on a popular vote—I suppose never in history," Rusk, *Life of Ralph Waldo Emerson*, 46; also see Liddell Hart, *Strategy*, 133. **Taking a page from Grant's:** Lincoln acceded to this plan, but only reluctantly, and spent countless days and nights of anxiety over its wisdom. He worried that the rebels might somehow trap Sherman in the interior. See Oates, 403. **torched everything of military value:** For alternative view, see Reston, *Sherman's March*, chapter 4, who retraced Sherman's route through Georgia and maintains that far fewer houses were actually burned than claimed. **the city was battered:** Ironically, early in the war, in 1861, Sherman deeply deplored the marauding tendencies of Union soldiers in Virginia. "No Goths or vandals," he said, "ever had less respect for the lives and property of friends and foes . . . ," see McPherson, "Götterdämmerung," 10. Like countless others, North and South, over time Sherman, too, was changed by this war. Later, when he did resort to total war, Sherman still grieved. "Even yet my heart bleeds when I see the carnage of battle . . ." he wrote in 1864. See Lewis, *Sherman*, 421. **Moving at a relentless pace:** Liddell Hart says that Sherman was developing a whole new strategic practice and likens his efforts to the panzer troops that swept through France in 1940, *Strategy*, 134. **"You have no idea how the women & children suffer:** Quote in Fellman, *Citizen Sherman*, 215. **Sherman later distanced himself:** In his own defense, he referred to Article 19 of *Instructions for the Government of Armies of the United States*, see Lewis, *Sherman*, 418–19. **thoughtful historians have agreed:** See Marion Brunson Lucas, *Sherman and the Burning of Columbia* (College Station, 1976), for what is considered one of the most thorough studies of the controversy. It can be noted, however, that unlike in North Carolina, there was no edict by Sherman that any soldier caught robbing or burning would be shot (see Leckie, *None Died in Vain*, 627). In other words, the license for destruction was de facto handed out. **"sad realities of war":** Others agreed, including intellectual Harriet Beecher Stowe, who glowingly called Sherman "a War Prophet." See Royster, *Destructive War*, 364.

Bentonville: Emory Thomas notes that at the battle of Bentonville, the Army of Tennessee under Johnston stopped Sherman dead in his tracks for a good three days and then broke Sherman's line, a "final victory," see *CN*, 288. **In 1864, he had once roared . . . "what is Joe Johnston's game?":** For this paragraph and quotes, see Lewis, *Sherman*, for example, 357–58, 568, 362. **his own soldiers . . . thoroughly worn:** Sherman was, too. Throughout the later stages of the war, he was sleeping only four hours a night, and suffering from asthma. **the feisty Ohioan felt "sick" and "events are drifting":** For quotes, consult Lewis, *Sherman*, 561–62. **It wouldn't be needed . . . "restoration of peace":** Freeman, 188–214; Flood, *Lee*, 41–65; this section tracks these two works, from which quotes are taken, unless otherwise noted; also see Anderson and Anderson, *Generals*, 463–70. **Lee's voice . . . set the Confederate tone:** See, for example, Thomas, *Robert E. Lee*, 370. **Lee was . . . stateless:** And with Arlington now gone, it could be added, he was also homeless. Thus he wrote that he wanted "some quiet home in the woods, where I can procure shelter and daily bread, if permitted by the victor," Thomas, ibid., 369. **broken man:** He was also sick, suffering from angina pectoris and the uncommonly rapid onset of arteriosclerosis. **signing the loyalty oath:** See Thomas, *Robert E. Lee*, 371. **"a crime that was unexampled" . . . "deplorable":** Quotes from *New York Herald*, April 29, Library of Congress, and reprinted in Freeman, 190. **"It is the influence":** Quote in *Glenn*, 191. **Tuskegee to Miami:** See Long, *Civil War Day by Day*, 666–85.

"Go home": See Freeman, 191–92; Flood, *Lee*, 65. **"deplorable" . . . "slavery [is] forever dead":** All quotes from Flood, *Lee*, 50–52.

Lee biographer: Freeman, 193. **So on April 20** (Lee communiqué): Lee to Davis, Richmond, *Wartime Papers*, April 20, 1865, 938–39. **Another biographer:** Flood, *Lee*, 44; ironically, not long after that, on June 7, 1865, Lee was indicted for treason by a federal grand jury in Norfolk, saved only by Grant, who personally interceded, insisting that the terms of surrender precluded trials for treason. Grant, believing that his terms at Appomattox were forestalling guerrilla war/threatened to resign if Johnson abrogated the agreement. See Thomas, *Robert E. Lee*, 370–71. **"They say Johnston will not be caught":** Quote in *MC*, 790.

But Johnston made his own choice to "restore tranquility to our country": Lewis, *Sherman*, 555–56; Johnston, *Narrative of Military Operations*, 411–20; Foote, 996. **"never pulled the trigger":** *MC*, 268. For further on Johnston, see James W. Livingood, *A Different Valor: The Story of General Joseph E. Johnston, C.S.A.* (Bobbs-Merrill, 1956), esp. 235–39. For his campaign against Sherman, Thomas L. Connelly, *Autumn of Glory*, 1862–1865 (LSU Press, 1971), esp. 141–43, 261–95; and of course Johnston's *Narrative of Military Operations*, esp. 262–344. Johnston does have his supporters. For example, Emory Thomas calls his withdrawal and delaying actions "brilliant," see *CN*, 271. Historian Paul Johnson calls him "a resolute and ingenious army commander," 475; Grant, in his *Memoirs*, calls Johnston's tactics "sensible."

Our country to good "citizens": See Parrish, *Richard Taylor*, 439–46; Foote, 1018–19; Trudeau, *Out of the Storm*, 259–60, 335–41. **Taylor, among the most literate:** See Richard Taylor, *Destruction and Reconstruction; Reminiscences of the Late War* (D. Appleton and Co., 1879).

So with loose rocks to "will be magnanimous": On the Forrest surrender, see Jack Hurst, *Nathan Bedford Forrest*, 255–58; Henry, *"First with the Most" Forrest*, 435–38; Wills, *Battle from* *the Start*; Andrew N. Lytle, *Bedford Forrest and His Critter Company* (J. S. Sanders, 1992), 375–77; see Jordan and Pryor, *Campaigns of Lieut.-Gen. N. B. Forrest*, 679–82; Foote, 1000–02; Trudeau, *Out of the Storm*, 261–62.

John Mosby: Though he was a diehard to the bitter end, Mosby later embraced U. S. Grant, spoke out fervently for Union, became a frequent visitor at the White House, and was made U.S. consul at Hong Kong, see Kevin Siepel, *Rebel: The Life and Times of John Singleton Mosby* (Da Capo, 1997). **some 36,000 weary troops:** This estimate is from a March headcount, see Trudeau, *Out of the Storm*, 335. **Stand Watie:** Alvin Josephy, *Civil War in the American West*, writes that his mixed forces of pro-Confederate Cherokees "were a menacing reality," 328. **a diverse amalgam:** These were dubbed the powerful "Five Civilized Tribes," Josephy, *Civil War in the American West*, 324.

"We are falling to pieces" to **"may be regarded as virtually at an end":** For the following sketch of Davis and his final flight, I have relied heavily upon the following sources, from which all quotes are taken unless otherwise noted: Clement Eaton, *Jefferson Davis* (Free Press, 1977), much better than older sources, which are either dated, prejudiced, or too adulatory, and also William C. Davis, *Jefferson Davis: The Man and His Hour* (HarperCollins, 1991); Ballard, *Long Shadow*, which is quite good; Bell Irvin Wiley, *The Road to Appomattox* (Atheneum, 1983), esp. 1–42 for analysis of Davis, and 77–121; McPherson, "American Victory, American Defeat," esp. 38–40; Potter, "Jefferson Davis and the Political Factors in Confederate Defeat," 91–114; Allan Nevins, *The Statesmanship of the Civil War* (New York, 1953), chapter 3; Bell Irvin Wiley, ed., *The Rise and Fall of the Confederate Government by Jefferson Davis* (T. Yoseloff, 1958), i, foreword. For his flight, also Foote, 965–69, 1001–13 (and for imprisonment, 1034–39), and Trudeau, *Out of the Storm*, 283–98; also see more compact assessments in *BC* (throughout) and McPherson, "American Victory, American Defeat," 36–37; Ward, *Civil War*, 27–28, 193–96, and 271–72; Leckie, *None Died in Vain*, 93–107; Long, *Civil War Day by Day*; and Johnson, 450–59, 464–67. For further on Davis, Frank Vandiver, "Jefferson Davis and Confederate Strategy," in Frank E. Vandiver and Avery Craven, eds., *The American Tragedy: The Civil War in Retrospect* (Hampden Sydney, 1959), 52–69, and Grady McWhiney, "Jefferson Davis and the Art of War," *CWH* 21 (1975), 101–12. For more on Confederate strategy, see Frank E. Vandiver, *Rebel Brass* (LSU Press, 1975), and T. Harry Williams, "The Military Leadership of North and South," in David Donald, ed., *Why the North Won the Civil War* (LSU Press, 1960), and Russell Weigley, *The American Way of War* (Macmillan, 1973). While not about the Civil War, John Keegan's important *The Face of Battle* (Viking, 1976) is crucial in order to grasp how armies and strategy work, which bears on the question of Davis's stewardship of military policies.

Thomas Jefferson would write: As a sign of Southern thinking long before the Civil War, it is worth examining the rest of Jefferson's quote. It continues, ". . . or Cambridge [Harvard]" but adds ominously, "the latter will return them to us as fanatics and tories . . . ," see Jefferson to Joseph Cabell, January 22, 1820, in P. L. Ford, ed., *The Works of Thomas Jefferson* (Macmillan, 1912), vol. 12. **When it came to slaves:** On this matter, see, for instance, Eaton, *Jefferson Davis*, 33–46. **Varina Howell:** For further, see Eron Rowland, *Varina Howell, Wife of Jefferson Davis* (Macmillan, 1931). **Politics suited him—yet only to a point:** This is a view shared not only by scholars, but by Varina and Davis himself. Still, it is not to say he was not suited to life in politics outside of the presidency. There is a rich and long tradition of some of the finest members of the Senate being either mavericks, regional voices, or just outright quirky; their principled stances stand as accomplishments that enrich both the Senate and the nation although they are without a significant legislative record. In our own time, Senator Daniel Patrick Moynihan of New York, who actually has quite a modest record, stands as one of the modern giants in that institution in the last half of the twentieth century. He has long been a joy to watch. The same could arguably said for Robert Byrd, the former Democratic majority leader, who is known as much for fighting tenaciously for "pork" for his home state—and the institutional prerogatives of the Senate—as for for any piece of legislation, and who shares a number of the same personality traits as Davis (derived from author's personal observations while working in the Senate and with Byrd). For more on this, see William S. White's classic study of the Senate, *Citadel: The Story of the United States Senate* (Harper and Brothers, 1971). **Sam Houston . . . "cold as a lizard":** This is the standard quote. Houston even sarcastically derided Davis behind his back, calling him "Jeffie." But worth remembering, the two were fierce political rivals, with a sharp distaste for each other. Davis was no less scathing or sarcastic in his treatment of Houston, once accusing him of "rank ignorance" and a "lack of industry." See Donald Day and Harry Ullom, eds., *The Autobiography of Sam Houston* (University of Oklahoma Press, 1954), esp. 252, 266.

While many scholars think not: For example, Wiley speaks of Davis's lack of administrative capacity, his inability to get along with people, his aloofness, and the fact that he was out of his depth as president; David Potter dissects him thoroughly, among other things, criticizing him for his conservative mind; Allan Nevins, in his study of statesmanship of the Civil War, accuses Davis of a lack of passion and inability to rouse his people as did a Lincoln or a Churchill. **Some thought him a dictator:** Of his many flaws, this was not one. Davis resisted all attempts to wantonly accrue dictatorial power; what he did do was embrace the centralized states with greater frequency as the war continued, which, of course, ran counter to states' rights theorists. Even Wiley acknowledges that "far from being a despot, [Davis] exercised notable restraint," *Road to Appomattox*, 112; Lincoln was also accused of being a dictator—often—also not true, Donald, 564. Such were the passions of war. **he generally embraced a strategy:** On this rich subject, see *BC*, 337–38; Weigley, *American Way of War*, esp. 3–17; Williams, "Military Leadership of North and South"; and Potter, "Jefferson Davis and the Political Factors in Confederate Defeat," esp. 45–46, 108–10. **each state at first raised its own forces:** As did the Union, it could be added. **that nearly ruined George Washington:** At one point, a deeply frustrated Washington asked Congress to increase the number of allowable lashes from "the biblical 39 to 500," see Leckie, *Wars of America*, 139–46, esp. 123; for insights into Washington and comparisons to Lee, I am also indebted to Bob Parker; also Jared Sparks, *The Life of George Washington* (Little, Brown, 1839), 156–96. **Yet for all his considerable weaknesses:** See McPherson on this point, "American Victory, American Defeat," 38–40. Had he lost the 1864 reelection, or had the outcome of the war been different, Lincoln would have gone down in history as an also-ran and a loser, Davis as a great leader of a war for independence. **fanatical . . . all these men shared common traits:** For more on just two of these examples, see Tim Joyner, *Magellan* (International Marine, 1992), and J. Atkinson, *Martin Luther and the Birth of Protestantism* (Johns Hopkins University Press, 1968). **learned about Lincoln's assassination:** Davis himself knew of Confederate plans to kidnap Lincoln and was perfectly willing to consider the idea, largely because he believed there had been several Northern-inspired plots against his own life. See Donald, 677, footnote for 549 (*retaliation . . .*). He declined all plans because he believed they would lead to Lincoln's death, not his capture (because, as he said, it "Would probably involve the killing, instead of bringing away the captive alive"). Also, the South—and Davis—believed that there had been a plot to kill both him and his cabinet, when in 1864 they found documents on Union Colonel Ulric Dahlgren, who was killed in a failed mission to liberate prisoners in Richmond. The papers spoke ominously of killing Davis and the Confederate cabinet, as well as burning Richmond. The Union denied that the papers were accurate, but as Ernest Furgurson concludes, "though debates over the paper's validity would run on . . . the weight of the evidence suggests that they were indeed genuine." See his compact account in *Ashes of Glory*, 249–55; also Donald, 549. **Davis was captured:** He was released from Fort Monroe in 1867, without standing trial; see Foote for account of his captivity, 1034–39. **"virtually at an end:** However, the war was not formally declared over by President Johnson until August 20, 1866, see, for example, Trudeau, *Out of the Storm*, 396–97.

But for all to be at an end to April 1865 what it was: For this section on Booth, his background, his assassination plans, and his flight, I have extensively relied upon the following, from which all quotes are taken unless otherwise indicated: Donald, 585–88; Bak's excellent *Day Lincoln Was Shot*, 39–46 (Booth background), 47–62, 74–92 (flight and capture); Kunhardt and Kunhardt, *Twenty Days*, 31–37, 176–82; Reck, *A. Lincoln*, esp. 63–79 (conspirators and planning); Leech, 357–65 (background and planning), 389–90, 406–9 (flight and capture); Lewis, *Assassination of Lincoln*, 131–45 (background of Booth family), 131–45 (Booth biography), 144–78 (Booth planning), 175–86 (Booth flight). Francis Wilson, *John Wilkes Booth: Fact and Fiction of Lincoln's Assassination* (Houghton Mifflin, 1929), is still one of the best biographies. Also see portraits of Booth in Robert Donovan, *The Assassins* (Harper and Brothers, 1955), esp. chapters 9 and 10, and in Franklin Ford, *Political Murder: From Tyrannicide to Terrorism* (Harvard University Press, 1985), chapter 15. On the aftermath of the assassination, Turner, *Beware the People Weeping*, is very good, see 65–75, 100–11, for Booth and pursuit; also Philip Van Doren Stern, *The Man Who Killed Lincoln* (Random House, 1939). The literature on the conspiracy to murder and abduct Lincoln is too vast to list here, but William Hanchett's *The Lincoln Murder Conspiracies* (University of Illinois Press, 1983) remains an excellent and important guide to this maze of works; George S. Bryan's *Great American Myth* is still one of the best accounts of the conspiracy. Some older works are marred by attempts to link Stanton to the assassination, an interpretation that has been discredited by William Hanchett, "The Eisenschiml Thesis," *CWH* 25 (September 1979): 197–217. Other useful information, albeit somewhat flawed, can be found in Eisenschiml, *Why Was Lincoln Murdered?*, and the best-selling Jim Bishop, *The Day Lincoln Was Shot* (Gramercy, 1955), which nonetheless is a riveting read with much good information that properly conveys the feel of panic gripping the city. **were all seized and locked in double irons:** On the fate of the conspirators, see Roy Chamlee, *Lincoln's Assassination: A Complete Account of Their Capture, Trial, and Punishment* (McFarland, 1990).

Booth provided the sentry: Sergeant Cobb, whom he dealt with, later explained: "I thought he was a proper person to pass—and I let him pass."

Booth explained: This was in his journal entry, while on the run. **they arranged to be ferried:** This time it was by three former riders from Mosby's raiders, which had just been disbanded on April 21.

It is a paradox . . . the theater flourished: Donald, 568–70. **$297:** This figure is taken from Will Chasen, *Samuel Gompers: Leader of American Labor* (Praeger, 1971), 16. **he recruited a band:** For sketches of all the members of the plot, see Theodore Roscoe, *The Web of Conspiracy: The Complete Story of the Men Who Murdered Abraham Lincoln* (Prentice-Hall, 1959). **his traveling pass . . . Grant:** Booth laughed that the pass provided him with "freedom of range without knowing what a good turn [Grant] has done for the South," Bak, *Day Lincoln Was Shot*, 58. **Like all great mysteries:** Two newer accounts, William A. Tidwell, James Hall, and David Winfred Gaddy, *Come Retribution: The Confederate Secret Service and the Assassination of Lincoln* (University of Mississippi Press, 1988), and William A. Tidwell, *April 1865, Confederate Covert Action in the American Civil War* (Kent State University Press, 1995), are important works, authored (or coauthored) by a retired intelligence officer, that come close to linking the Confederate government with Booth's plot. Also see Tidwell's essay in Bak, *Day Lincoln Was Shot*, 63–69. **newer scholarship has reopened the debate:** For instance, found in the Library of Congress, where the papers of the Confederate States of America are housed, are sixty-three vouchers signed by Davis. They called for the allocation of gold to various secret service projects, involving $1.5 million, an immense sum, for the period of August 1862–March 1865. Tidwell points out that some $840,000 was for a secret service account to support a program of active sabotage and other clandestine operations, with the paperwork being handled by Secretary of State Judah Benjamin or a state department clerk. Thus, this opens the possibility of Confederate higher-ups being involved, according to Tidwell; see Bak, *Day Lincoln Was Shot*, 64. **would never have approved:** The American CIA is a vivid example of a secret servic carrying out numerours projects without authorization at the presidential level; even as late as the mid-1990s the CIA was carrying out activities without approval or even required congressional authorization. Given the exigent circumstances of the Civil War, it is far easier to understand the Confederate government, even Davis himself, looking to assassinate Lincoln, than John F. Kennedy seeking to assassinate Castro. See Victor Marchetti and John D. Marks, *The CIA and the Cult of Intelligence* (Dell, 1974); also author interviews with former CIA operative. **began concocting a fervid new role for himself:** See Albert Furtwangler, *Assassin on Stage: Brutus, Hamlet, and the Death of Lincoln* (University of Illinois Press, 1991), for discussion of the assassination in terms of the theatrical tradition of tyrannicide. Furtwangler contends that the theatrical tradition of tyrannicide helped shape Booth's actions. Also see Leech, esp. 358–65. **dwelling solely in hate-filled fantasy** to **process gone awry:** Or, one could add, if the blade had gone just a bit deeper into Seward's neck. **"April 1865 what it was":** Booth quote in Bak, *Day Lincoln Was Shot*, 114.

CHAPTER EIGHT: RECONCILIATION

South had wagered all: Brian Holden Reid notes that it was remarkable that the Confederacy "fought so long," an obvious testament to their passion for carving out a new nation, see "Why the Confederacy Lost," 40. **hate . . . most perilous:** Gary Gallagher points out that in contrast to the romanticized version, this was not simply a brothers' war, but one in which the hate was quite strong, as Southerners mourned the death of their four-year-old republic, *Confederate War*, 105, 64, also chapter 8. As Stephen Ambrose further reminds us, "Oh, how they hated each other!" (*Wall Street Journal*, book review essay, March 21, 1997, A21). Also see James McPherson's *For Cause and Comrades* (Oxford University Press, 1997), esp., 148–62. One Texas captain told his wife to teach his children "a bitter and unrelenting hatred of the human race." Another Southern soldier instructed his wife, "Teach my children to hate them with that bitter hatred." Confederates referred to Yankees as "fiends in human shape." McPherson finds that the desire for revenge intensified by 1864. He writes, "If soldiers' letters and diaries are an accurate indicator, bitterness and hatred were more prevalent than kindness and sociability," 152. Thus, reunion—and reconciliation—was that much more difficult a task. **"They left me"** . . . **"I have vowed":** Quotes from James Roark, *Masters Without Slaves: Southern Planters in the Civil War and Reconstruction* (Norton, 1977), 86; John Trowbridge, *A Picture of the Desolated States and the Work of Restoration, 1865–1868* (Martford, 1868), 577, reprinted in McPherson, *Ordeal by Fire*, 494. **"Hyena-like":** Quote in Catherine Clinton, "Noble Women as Well," *Ken Burns's The Civil War: Historians Respond*, Robert B. Toplin, ed. (Oxford University Press, 1996). **"Oh how I hate":** Gallagher, *Confederate War*, 79. **The hatred, the bitterness:** For more on this same argument, see Gallagher, chapter 8. **economic damage . . . without parallel:** Calculation found in Palmer and Colton, 532. **"We are scattered—stunned":** Quote in *MC*, 814. **widow Mary Vaughn** (quotes): See Clinton, "Noble Women as Well," 70. **Psychologists who have studied . . . incoherent with grief:** The best work on this phenomenon is by the Yale social psychologist Kai Erickson, *Everything in Its Path: The Destruction of Community in the Buffalo Creek Flood* (Simon and Schuster, 1976). While the whole book is worth reading, see esp. his "Collective Trauma: Loss of Community," 186–241; also 156–85. In discussing the "whole galaxy of miseries," he finds "chronic trauma," "loss of connection," "hollow feelings," feelings of "death," and the effects of a disaster "gathering force slowly and insidiously" overwhelming the "defenses." It is almost uncanny how much the words of the Buffalo Creek survivors in many places sound like those of Southerners at the war's end, including Mary Chesnut and the small sampling of others quoted here. **"They expected nothing":** Whitelaw Reid, *After the War: A Tour of the Southern States, 1865–1866* (1866; reprint, Harper and Row, 1965), 296; reprinted in McPherson, *Ordeal by Fire*. **"All over the Union":** Leech, 400.

everyone wanted a piece of it: For example, see Davis, *To Appomattox*, 390; Hendrickson, *Road to Appomattox*, 202–4.

Charles Lewis Tiffany: See Johnson, 582. **Walt Whitman:** Justin Kaplan, *Walt Whitman: A Life* (Simon and Schuster, 1980), 302. **Ralph Waldo Emerson:** Rusk, *Life of Ralph Waldo Emerson*, 427–28. **"It is simply maddening"** . . . **"I call that a warning":** Quotes in *MC*, 791. **By then though, Lincoln,** also section beginning with **After the mourning came pageantry** to **By day's end, at long last:** For descriptions and quotes of Lincoln funeral and return home, and review of the Union armies, I am indebted to the following, which I have drawn fully upon and from which quotes are taken, unless otherwise noted: *New York Times*, April 19–May 4 (a review of the *Times* reveals that it amply documented the feelings of grief in cities across the Union as early as

Sunday, April 16, encompassing Baltimore, Halifax, Syracuse, Pittsburgh, Providence, Ithaca, Newark, Brunswick, etc.); Kunhardt and Kunhardt, *Twenty Days*, 119–32, 140–73, 218–302 and Bak, *Day Lincoln Was Shot*, 131–40, are both outstanding; Kunhardt is especially vivid and thorough. Also Leech, 400–403, 415–16; Ward, *Civil War*, 386–96; further see Trudeau, *Out of the Storm*, 277–82, 313–23; and Oates, 434–36. **Theodore Roosevelt:** See the compelling discussion of the deeply divided loyalties of the Roosevelt family recounted in H. W. Fields, *T. R., The Last Romantic* (Basic, 1997), 3–9. **Grover Cleveland:** The twenty-eight-year-old Cleveland actually borrowed money to send a substitute soldier to fight in his place.

May 22: See Leech, 415–16.

on May 12 and 13, 1865 . . . one more sizable battle: See Stephen Oates, *Confederate Cavalry West of the River* (University of Texas, 1961), 155–59; also Trudeau, *Out of the Storm*, 299–310. **Sam Watkins:** Quote in Ward, *Civil War*, 404. **signs of healing** (church scene): Thomas, *Robert E. Lee*, 372; T. L. Broun, "Negro Communed at St. Paul's Church," *Confederate Veteran* 13 (1905): 360; Flood, *Lee*, 65–66. Did this scene happen? Or is it myth? I have discussed it with church officials at St. Paul's in Richmond, including church historian Calder Loth, who says the evidence indicates that it did indeed. As for his personal future, Lee lived in limbo for the rest of his life, never receiving citizenship or a pardon. He died in 1870.

EPILOGUE: TO MAKE A NATION

Jesse James: Frank Triplett, *The Life, Times, and Treacherous Death of Jesse James* (Sage, 1970), 19–24. **Sam Clemens:** I have used three sources here: Justin Kaplan, *Mr. Clemens and Mark Twain: A Biography* (Simon and Schuster, 1966); Margaret Sanborn, *Mark Twain: The Bachelor Years* (Doubleday, 1990); and Henry Canby, *Turn West, Turn East* (Houghton Mifflin, 1951). **A&P:** William Walsh, *The Rise and Decline of the Great Atlantic and Pacific Tea Company* (L. Stuart, 1986). **Henry Ford:** See the excellent treatment by Peter Collier and David Horowitz, *The Fords: An American Epic* (Summit, 1987), esp. 4–10. **Frank Woolworth:** J. K Winkler, *Five and Ten: The Life of Frank W. Woolworth* (R. M. McBride & Co., 1940). **John Roebling:** Alan Trachtenberg, *Brooklyn Bridge* (Oxford University Press, 1965). **Richard Warren Sears:** Borris Emmet and John Jeuck, *Catalogues and Counters: A History of Sears, Roebuck & Co.* (University of Chicago Press, 1950). **Thomas Alva Edison:** Robert Silverburg, *Light for the World: Edison and the Power Industry* (Van Nostrand, 1967). **The Nation:** See John Richard Dennett, *The South As It Is, 1865–1866* (LSU Press, 1965). **Samuel Gompers:** Two sources were employed here: Bernard Mandel, *Samuel Gompers: A Biography* (Antioch University Press, 1963), esp. 4–8, and Chasen, *Samuel Gompers*, 19–23. **John D. Rockefeller:** See Allan Nevins, *John D. Rockefeller: The Heroic Age of American Enterprise*, vol. 1 (Scribner's, 1940), esp. 129–226, and John T. Flynn, *God's Gold: The Story of Rockefeller and His Times* (Harcourt Brace, 1932), 110–24. **Andrew Carnegie:** Burton Hendrick, *The Life of Andrew Carnegie* (Harper and Row, 1932), esp. 103–30. **Henry Clay Frick:** George Harvey, *Henry Clay Frick, the Man* (Rudge, 1928), 1–43. **Albert Bierstadt:** N. K. Anderson and L. S. Ferber, *Albert Bierstadt: Art and Enterprise* (Brooklyn Museum, 1990). **Elizabeth Cady Stanton . . . Lucretia Mott:** On this fascinating subject, see, for starters, Mari Jo and Paul Buhle, eds., *The Concise History of Woman Suffrage* (University of Illinois Press, 1978), 1–44; Ellen DuBois, ed., *Elizabeth Cady Stanton, Susan B. Anthony, Correspondence, Writings, Speeches* (Schocken, 1981); Lloyd Hare, *The Greatest American Woman* (Negro

Universities Press, 1937), 210–89. **Hiram Revels:** It is tough to wrap one's hands around this historic figure's early days and motivations. See Julius Eric Thompson, *Hiram R. Revels, 1827–1901* (Arno Press, 1982), esp. 38–63. **Patrick Cleburne:** Symonds, *Stonewall of the West*, which is the best, and Buck, *Cleburne and His Command.* **P. T. Barnum:** That new career, of course, would be the circus. *New York Times . . .* **Henry J. Raymond:** Elmer Davis, *History of the New York Times* (J. J. Little and Ives, 1921), esp. 48–80; also David Halberstam, *The Powers That Be* (Random House, 1979); **in the future:** For more on post–Civil War America, see Paul Johnson's fascinating section "Huddled Masses and Crosses of Gold, Industrial America 1870–1912," 511–624.

 The Greek example: Brookheiser, *George Washington*, 189–90. **France . . . sixteenth century:** More precisely, of this time frame Palmer and Colton note: "Exact history distinguishes *no less* than nine civil wars . . . ," 130. **Farewell Address:** Smith, *Patriarch*, 280–83; also see Royster, *Destructive War*, 146. **Virtually unique:** See important essay by Murrin, "Roof Without Walls," 333–48, and the other essays in Richard Beeman, Stephen Botein, Edward Carter II, eds., *Beyond Confederation: Origins of the Constitution and American National Identity* (University of North Carolina Press, 1987), which is outstanding. *foedus . . . fides:* See Boorstin, 415. **was America a nation?:** Indeed, by design, it was no accident that the word "nation" appears nowhere in the Constitution, or for that matter, the Declaration of Independence. On the motion of Oliver Ellsworth of Connecticut, the Constitutional Convention dropped the word "national," instead referring to the new government as "the United States." All references to "national" were deleted from the Constitution accordingly. **The price of such ingenuity:** See Boostin's trenchant essay on this subject, "A Dubious Destiny," 264–74, which this paragraph is heavily indebted to. **scramble of . . . minor republics:** Palmer and Colton, 533. This also recalls to mind the immortal exchange between a Frenchman and Caleb Whitford, a British delegate, that occured in 1782. The Frenchman stressed the growing greatness of America, predicting that the "thirteen united states would form the greatest empire in the world." In turn, Whitford quipped with a scornful little laugh: "Yes, and they will all speak English." **fate of country . . . very much in doubt:** Even for the most optimistic in the Union, this weighed heavily on their minds. For instance, while stressing the theme of eventual if not hard-fought unification in areas across Europe, Edward Everett, in his obviously political address at Gettysburg, made the following poignant observations in discussing Europe's civil wars. While saying that the world avoided being "turned into an earthly hell" with "clans of furies and demons," each "forever warring with each other" (part 51), he observed the plague of ongoing strife that passed over the continnt before eventual reconciliation. His examples included Germany and the "contests entailed upon that country for more than three centuries"; England (part 53) in the "great rebellion," which suffered "years of discord, conflict and civil war; of confiscation, plunder, havoc; a proud hereditary peerage trampled in the dust, a national church overturned . . . and all the horrid circumstances of murder, devastation and parricide . . . "; Italy (part 54), where "society . . . resolved into hostile atoms, whose only movement was that of mutual repulsion. Ruthless barbarians . . . had covered the land with merciless feudalism. As the new civilization grew up . . . towns fell madly into conflict with each other . . . province against province, city against city, street against street . . . "; France (part 55), where there were "dreadful scenes throughout the kingdom . . . which in the name of revolution . . . commenced . . . seen the bloodhounds of civil strife let loose as rarely before in history of the world . . ." See Wills, *Lincoln at Gettysburg*, 243–44. Also see Boorstin, *Genius of American Politics*, 74–75, on the point of ongoing revolution, in which he says each historical episode ends on "a note of suspense." **bad endings:** See Ikle's classic work, *Every War Must End*. **Gladstone's memorable words:** He was chancellor of the exchequer. **the Union's task of reabsorbing an essentially hostile entity:** See also Carl Dengler on this point. "What the war represented in the end was the forceful incorporation of a recalcitrant South into a newly created nation nation," *Lincoln, the War President*, 109; Gabor S. Boritt, ed., *Why the Confederacy Lost* (Oxford University Press, 1992); also Gallagher, *Confederate War*, chapter 8. Indeed, this was what abolitionist Wendell Phillips feared from the very outset: "A Union is made up of willing states," he exclaimed. "A husband or wife who can only keep the other partner . . . by locking the doors and standing armed before them, had better submit to peaceable separation," *Speeches, Lectures and Letters* (Lee and Shepard, 1864), 350. For background, also see Don Fehrenbacher, who has drawn a comparison between Southern nationalism in 1861 and American nationalism in 1776 in his *Constitutions and Constitutionalism in the Slaveholding South* (University of Georgia Press, 1989), 59–60. Daniel Boorstin, *Genius of American Politics*, contends that in the absence of any real national identity at the founding, we might be wiser to call our Civil War "the second War of Independence," 21. **"I want peace":** Caldwell quote in Gallagher, *Confederate War*, 43. **war . . . engenders hatred:** for example, the prominent intellectual Ralph Waldo Emerson records that he was deeply troubled by Grant's generous terms and Lincoln's plans for reconstruction. As Emerson's biographer Ralph Rusk tells us: Emerson "found it hard to get the poison of hate out of his blood." And: "At the end of the conflict he could not refrain from writing down a list of atrocities he charged against the South," *Life of Ralph Waldo Emerson*, 427–28. **to mutual citizenship, not differences:** For criticisms, implicit and explicit, of the theme of reunification, see Eric Foner, "Ken Burns and the Romance of Reunion," in Toplin, ed., *Ken Burns's The Civil War*, 101–18, and also Leon Litwack, "Telling the Story," 121–40 in Toplin. Foner, for instance, stresses the need to highlight the complications of Reconstruction—including a view of it as a praiseworthy if flawed effort—and the contentious history of post–Civil War America, 112, and the question of racial justice. These are all valid and important points—but beyond the scope of this work, and covered amply in a number of important studies by Foner, Litwack; John Hope Franklin, *Reconstruction After the Civil War* (University of Chicago Press, 1961); and others. My point is quite different, referring to an essentially magic moment when a handful of leaders, inspired by Lincoln's vision in the North and Lee's dignity in the South, rose to the occasion to prevent a far greater, more raucous, more bloody, and even more civil war–ridden era, which would have made the Reconstruction period seem like a picnic. **In the fateful days:** These are the turning points of this crucial month of April 1865. McPherson has enumerated four turning points of the war (see, among other places, epilogue of *BC*). To that list this cluster of events from April could be added: Lee's decisive rejection of guerrilla warfare, coupled with Grant's generous actions at Appomattox, as well as the Union's orderly handling of Lincoln's assassination, thereby resisting its worst fears, including a possible coup by Sherman. **barbaric cruelty:** See Amos Perlmutter, *The Military in Politics in Modern Times* (Yale University Press, 1977), 166–205.

"It seems": Henry Steele Commager, *The Blue and Gray* (Crescent, 1995), vol. 1, 43. **"Strange . . . that battle":** Ward, *Civil War*, 393. Whitman biographer Justin Kaplan points out that for

Whitman, the war was "never about slavery," but "democracy and Union." The great thing, the poet said, is for "opposing elements" to "stick together," *Walt Whitman*, 300. **"the better class . . . All classes":** Quotes in Chester, *Black Civil War Correspondent*, 349, 359. **John H. Hinton:** Hinton, *History and Topography of the United States*, see introduction.

"Verily": Quote in Foner, *Short History of Reconstruction*, 34. **Litwack:** Leon Litwack, "Telling the Story: The Historian, the Film-Maker, and the Civil War," in Ken Burns's *The Civil War*, 119–40. **Eliza Scantling . . . Amy Lumpkin:** Quotes in Clinton, "Noble Women as Well," 76. **in the former slave quarters:** Litwack, "Telling," 132. **"I felt like a bird":** Holloway quote in Foner, *A Short History*, 35. **Booker T. Washington:** For this, see Harlan, *Booker T. Washington*, esp. 24–27. **In time, though:** For more on the transition of blacks from slavery to freedom, among the best workers are: Leon Litwack, *Been in the Story So Long: The Aftermath of Slavery* (Knopf, 1979), Joel Williamson, *After Slavery: The Negro in South Carolina During Reconstruction, 1861–1877* (University of North Carolina Press, 1965), and Barbara Fields, *Slavery and Freedom on the Middle Ground* (Yale University Press, 1985); also Kenneth Stampp, *The Era of Reconstruction 1865–1877* (Knopf, 1965), and John Hope Franklin, *Reconstruction After the Civil War*, both influential summaries of the revisionist position; for excellent documentary records, see LaWanda and John H. Cox, *Reconstruction, the Negro, and the New South* (Columbia University Press, 1973); for shorter overviews of Reconstruction, in addition to references already cited, one may also consult McPherson, *Ordeal by Fire*, 493–619, and Johnson, 498–507. **Andrew Johnson:** It is worth recalling that he called Reconstruction "restoration." **strands of reconciliation:** On this point, see Litwack, "Telling the Story," 136.

It could still be today: That ideas can be replaced is borne out by history: consider Germany's descent into barbarism during the twentieth century, just unimaginable a few years before, culminating not just in World War II but the Holocaust, an event on a scale no one would have even dreamed of predicting. However unlikely it is that future secessions could ever happen here in the United States, and however much fringe groups who opt out remain just that—fringe groups—one thoughtful commentator, Robert Kaplin, surveying the nation, suggests, "Future secession of regions and posturban pods will be far more subtle and therefore likely to succeed," *An Empire Wilderness, Travels into America's Future* (Random House, 1998); see also 296–338. As I write this, almost 135 years to the day after Appomattox, the *New York Times* is filled with headlines about Miami virtually "seceding" and carrying out an "independent foreign policy," Rick Brag, "Stand over Elian Highlights a Virtual Secession of Miami," *New York Times*, April 1, 2000, p. 1. Even if somewhat overwrought, the normally cautious *Times* begins: "The last time Floridians spoke fiercely about rebellion and secession, they left the Union. Now rebellion is happening again . . . But secession, say all manner of people here, has been going on for a long time. The battle over Elian [the custody case over the Cuban refugee child] merely shows how far it has come." And further: "To many people here . . . this is a declaration of independence for a part of the country that is, increasingly, a nation apart. People even . . . greet each other with, 'Welcome to the independent republic of Miami.'" Also see the report by the United States Commission on National Security/21st Century, "New World Coming: American Security in the 21st Century." In part it notes: "[T]here is nothing immutable about the present arrangements. The ties that bind individual or group loyalty to a state can change or even unravel, and the next 25 years portend a good deal of unraveling." (38)

In the fading light . . . to represent: This section, on Washington, is derived largely from Leech; also see Linda Wheeler's delightful "Bold Vision, Humble Start: In the Beginning," *Washington Post*, March 20, 2000, A1. **century's dawn:** A bit more relevant background: the population was 2,587 free inhabitants and 623 slaves, and shots fired near the Capitol in 1800 simply meant someone was hunting for dinner. The audacious city plan by Frenchman Pierre L'Enfant included a palatial President's House, influenced by Versailles, that was five times larger than what was actually built. L'Enfant himself, viewed as a temperamental artist, was fired, and died a broken man in 1825, long before his city was complete and still pressing the government for back pay of $100,000. Interestingly, at this time, in recognition of the support of the French Court, portraits of Louis XVI and Marie Antoinette hung behind the vice president's chair in the Capitol's Senate Chamber. At the first presidential address in the new capital, President John Adams said, hopefully one may add: "May this territory be the residence of virtue and happiness!" For her part, Abigail Adams complained about the President's House: "Not one room or chamber is finished in the whole. It is habitable [only] by fires in every part, thirteen of which we are obliged to keep daily, or sleep in wet and damp places." But Treasury Secretary Oliver Wolcott probably summed up the city best: "The people are poor, and, as far as I can judge, they live like fishes, by eating each other," see Wheeler, "Bold Vision, Humble Start," A8.

guns had fallen silent: Leech, 419.

ACKNOWLEDGMENTS

F or good reasons, the Civil War arouses a special enthusiasm in the American people. My first debt, at the outset, is to the extraordinary circle of Civil War scholars whose histories, biographies, and compelling essays have educated and inspired me. Their works provided a foundation for much of this project. I am especially grateful to Professor James McPherson, a scholar whom I admire enormously and author of the acclaimed *Battle Cry of Freedom*, who took the time to read an un-copy-edited manuscript by someone he didn't know, and offer not simply a blurb but warm words of support. My further thanks to the marvelous staffs of the Library of Congress, where I spent so much time; the Museum of the Confederacy; the Richmond Capitol and St. Paul's Church; Lee's Retreat and Appomattox Court House; Ford's Theater; and the keepers of all the Civil War battlefield sites I visited, too numerous to mention here, which are a national treasure.

Over the long course of writing this book, a number of friends, colleagues, and fellow authors sustained me in various ways—with tidbits of advice and humor, distractions, and an array of support: they include David Ignatius, Jim Denton, James Webb, Larry Smith, Chris Buckley, Erich Eichman, Rick Kahlenberg, Ken Adelman, Jon Karp, Richard

Perle, Leslie Barr, Mona and Bob Parker, Amos Perlmutter, and especially Steve Solarz, whose steady doses of encouragement and friendship were always invaluable. During the book's final stages, Steve also carefully read the manuscript from cover to cover; had he not been a distinguished member of Congress and foreign policy guru, he surely could have been a scholar and teacher of history. I also benefited from a complete read by Michael Humphries, doubling in his role as Civil War buff, and from the copy-edits of my father-in-law, Jim Wallwork. Professor John Murrin of Princeton was kind enough to provide me with his fascinating unpublished paper comparing the American Revolution and the Civil War.

Thanks also to my colleagues at the University of Maryland School of Public Affairs, Sue Schwab, Bill Powers, and Mac Destler, as well as to my research assistants, Jeremy Marsh, Andrew Morton, Mike Guerin, Max Grivno, and, particularly, Anthony Franzonella. My literary agent, Michael Carlisle, was always a great supporter of the book and there when I needed him. I owe a special debt to the Bradley Foundation, which provided crucial additional assistance for the project; notably, my thanks to Dan Schmidt and Dr. Michael Joyce, and also to William Schambra and Michael Uhlmann.

Through various gestations, HarperCollins couldn't have been more dedicated to this book. My initial editor, Eric Steel, brought endless energy and enthusiasm to this project, also helping sculpt its themes early on. When Eric left to help Scott Rudin make movies, Eamon Dolan plunged into the book with equal commitment and excitement. Later, when Tim Duggan took over the manuscript, I wondered what was left to be done; I was wrong. His careful edits and thoughtful questions and his support, attention to detail, and bulldog determination in shepherding this project have been equally invaluable. Sue Llewellyn was a most careful production editor. I am also grateful for the ongoing support of Cathy Hemming.

Above all, though, my deepest and heartfelt gratitude goes to my wife, Lyric. A gifted writer in her own right, from start to finish she has been selflessly and intimately involved with *April 1865*—from the first conceptualization to the brainstorming, editing (months upon months), and rewriting (more months upon months). Not a line appears that doesn't in some way bear her brilliant touch, discerning eye, and nuanced edits. Her contributions are immeasurable, and this book is what it is as a result. But more than that she is my rock, my best friend, the most special person I know. So this book is not just dedicated to her—but it is for her.

INDEX

About the author

About the book

Insights,
Interviews
& More...

Read (and visit) on

Meet Jay Winik

Carl Caruso

JAY WINIK was born on February 8, 1957. A preemie, his first weeks were spent in an incubator; he did not speak a word until the age of three.

He grew up the youngest of three boys on a suburban block in New Haven, Connecticut. They played touch football in the front yard, studiously avoiding the stone walk and the lamp post. His father sold paneling for dens and rec rooms; his mother took care of the kids. Winik's earliest literary passion was Marvel Comics. Starting at age six he would walk to the drugstore each Saturday morning to purchase shiny new editions of *Spider-man, X-Men, Avengers,* and other comic books. His artistic leanings were almost entirely visual—from a young age he painted, drew, and cartooned, making elaborate pen-and-ink creations well into his college years.

His parents believed in public schools, and Winik was one of the few children in his area to be bused to an inner-city junior high and high school. The experience taught him lifelong lessons and instilled in him a passion for giving back.

> " Winik was one of the few children in his area to be bused to an inner-city junior high and high school. "

Too small to play football, he turned to tennis, paying for lessons with his allowance, playing in tournaments throughout New England, and ultimately ranking as high as in the top five in the region. Although he dreamed of turning pro, he hedged his bets by going to Yale, where he played on the varsity team. (He once turned down a request to play doubles on a Saturday morning with a kid named John McEnroe, who had not yet made his surprise run at Wimbledon. Winik declined the invitation in order to "sleep in.")

By his junior year a pro tennis career looked increasingly unlikely, so Winik joined the *Yale Daily News* and discovered that he had a talent for writing. After graduating *cum laude* from Yale, he had, as he once put it, one goal: "not to become a lawyer." He didn't. He went to England to study at the London School of Economics and received a master's degree in international relations with distinction. "Back in those days," he told C-SPAN's *Booknotes,* "it was foreign policy, the great issue of the Cold War, that was one of the hot things to do and I was interested in it. I went to the London School of Economics, got my master's in international relations . . . and it sort of opened up a whole new world for me." He came back home hoping to work in government, but ended up entering graduate school in political science at Yale. About to begin his dissertation, he was plucked from New Haven to join the committee staff of Representative Les Aspin, the powerful chairman of the House Armed Services Committee.

Here Winik had a front-row seat to the momentous historic events of the day—the Cold War, the U.S.-Soviet standoffs, and the cruise missile debates. From there he went on to direct the first Blue-Ribbon Military Base Closure Commission, and then to work ▶

Meet Jay Winik (*continued*)

with the Senate Foreign Relations Committee. He traveled around the globe, meeting prominent dissident leaders, including Lech Walesa and Václav Havel, and numerous heads of state. His focus quickly became civil wars and regional conflicts, especially in Cambodia, which was lurching toward a second horrific genocide. Winik helped craft the United Nations Perm 5 Plan for Cambodia, which brought peace and elections. Despite fears that the aircraft could be shot down, he was aboard the first plane (a four-seater) to land in Phnom Penh since the United States severed relations in 1975.

With the Cold War over and Cambodia stabilized, Winik longed for a fresh challenge. He found it in his true passion, writing— books and history. Winik soon ventured back in time, choosing the Civil War.

He brings an athlete's discipline to his work. While laboring on *April 1865* he refused even to use e-mail. (He still doesn't give out his cell phone number and won't carry a BlackBerry; people looking for him end up calling his wife.) He eats the same breakfast each day and follows the same schedule, revising work from the previous day before sitting down to write. Except for the occasional movie, while at work he lives an almost monkish existence. (His vice is sneaking out during the spring, summer, and early fall for a periodic "nooner"—a noontime game of tennis.) Only Bogey, his Wheaten Terrier, intrudes to make his home among the books piled in the study.

April 1865 climbed to the top of the bestseller lists in 2001. Not least among its readers were three former presidents, as well as current president George W. Bush that

> 66 He traveled around the globe, meeting prominent dissident leaders, including Lech Walesa and Václav Havel. 99

September. "Here we were in the midst of a crisis of a lifetime, 9/11," Winik told the *Hartford Courant*, "and the president chose to read the book at Camp David and visibly carried it under his arm as he departed for Marine One (the presidential helicopter). Photos were taken which prompted stories around the world. . . . [T]hey did follow-up stories about the book and on me. . . . I was humbled and pleased."

April 1865 is one of those rare works to have spawned a new genre of history books; it was also honored as one of the New York Public Library's 25 Books to Remember from 2001, and received the first Walt Whitman Civil War Roundtable Award.

Winik makes frequent guest appearances on television and contributes regularly to the *New York Times* and the *Wall Street Journal*'s Leisure and Arts page. He serves on a number of boards of trustees for nonprofit organizations dealing with history and education, as well as battlefield preservation.

He lives outside Washington, D.C., with his wife, the writer Lyric W. Winik, and their sons, Nathaniel, born in 2002 and Evan, born in 2004. He loves tennis, art, the "great outdoors," family adventures, and playing with his kids.

He is writing a book about America and the age of the 1790s. ∽

" His vice is sneaking out during the spring, summer, and early fall for a periodic 'nooner'—a noontime game of tennis. "

Writing *April 1865*

IN A SENSE, a very small sense, writing books is a bit like going to war. No matter how well planned, you never know where it will take you. Spectacular success could loom around the corner, or, just as likely, dismal failure. Unlike those who engage in war, which is invariably a hateful, loathsome enterprise, writers write because they love to. Once drawn in by words you cannot look away. In my case, after years of government work pondering military strategy and national security policy—I had once advised two secretaries of defense, directed a blue-ribbon commission on military issues, and worked with the Senate Foreign Relations Committee—I woke up one day and decided that I wanted to write books. Not articles, not opinion columns, not clever essays, but books. I didn't care one bit for politics, nor did I see myself steeped in the issues of foreign or defense policy for the next two-thirds of my life. So I gave all that up, bought myself a computer, changed the lightbulb on my desk, sharpened my pencils, and got to work. I was also fortunate to have married a woman who cared about the craft of writing as much as I did. In her case, she was once the class poet at Princeton (her name is Lyric). So with such falling rocks do avalanches begin, or at least that was what I hoped.

Hope. What an emotion. But hope told me little about what to write, or how to write, or . . . well, you get the picture. And it was a frail guide for a topic as immense as the Civil War. At least this much I knew: Abraham Lincoln's prose was unlike any of his peers— his stamp was on everything he uttered. When short, simple words hit hard he used them.

> ❝ After years of government work pondering military strategy and national security policy, I woke up one day and decided that I wanted to write books. ❞

When soaring, rolling, pealing prose served his purposes he used it. And his feeling for the English word or turn of phrase was careful, rhythmic, even sensual—and so precise. As for me, well, that remained to be seen. What would sustain me, I hoped (again that word), was my love of books, literature, history, ideas and, above all, writing. So with that in mind I began.

But how to express the daunting nature of the enterprise? In truth, once I set out to write about the Civil War, this was a bit of a daring gambit. For starters, what did I have to add? This was territory well trodden by the likes of such immortals as Carl Sandburg, Allan Nevins, Shelby Foote, and James McPherson. They had written masterpieces, won Pulitzer Prizes, become celebrated historians, and devoted their lives to the subject. And as a friend, a Civil War buff, reminded me, more books had been written about the Civil War than any other topic, save for the Bible and Jesus, and by more talented historians than I can even name. Yet in countless ways I began to believe that *April 1865* was a book I was fated to write.

As it turned out, I did have something new to say, as well as a new way to say it. Fortuitously, during my years in government I had witnessed a number of civil wars firsthand: I had rolled through the blood-stained streets of El Salvador in armored cars; I had inspected troops in Nicaraguan jungles; I saw Yugoslavia as it was about to explode into malignant strife, dissolution, and chaos; and my heart nearly broke as I toured the desolate refugee camps and bullet-riddled cities of Cambodia. Cambodia, the home of the Killing Fields and quite likely the worst example of civil war in the twentieth century, was in the midst of yet another horrific civil war. Indeed, as I looked around the globe, ▶

> 66 Fortuitously, during my years in government I had witnessed a number of civil wars firsthand. 99

Writing *April 1865* (continued)

from Ireland to the Balkans, from Indonesia to the African continent, from Afghanistan to the republics of the former Soviet Union, it was clear that there was a tragic strain of history whereby far too many conflicts end quite badly, fostering a vicious cyclone of more violence, more death and instability, and more civil war.

It began to dawn on me that how wars end is every bit as important as why they begin and how they were waged. This was, of course, long before the profound turmoil that beset postwar Iraq. As I delved into the subject further, it occurred to me that from the very start the United States was a fragile entity, and that many of its fellow republics throughout history had collapsed into dictatorship, been overthrown by revolution, or succumbed to decades-long guerrilla war. How then, I began to ask myself, did a still young and embryonic America avoid the ghastly fate that has beset so many other countries embroiled in civil conflict in this and previous centuries? And it finally became clear that never were the temptations for an imperfect peace greater than in the final month of the war, in April 1865—the haunting specter of guerrilla war, the possibility of constitutional upheaval, or of vengeance-filled riot, retribution, and, in the end, national collapse.

So there it was. But then came the hard part, writing the book. How even to begin? In truth, while I had a rough sense that April 1865 was one of the most momentous months in this nation's history, I had no fixed agenda and no point I wanted to make. The fact is that any book done properly, especially a history, is a bit of a mystery once the author plunges into the mountains of research, letters, papers, and primary documents that become the basis for

> ❝ In truth, while I had a rough sense that April 1865 was one of the most momentous months in this nation's history, I had no fixed agenda and no point I wanted to make. ❞

what at some distant juncture will be a final product. You start at one point and invariably detour here and there as the bones of your story slowly take shape. New details are revealed and new epiphanies come to light. Ultimately, I saw my role as telling the story of this month, not as we see it now, but as experienced by the participants of the day. This meant envisioning and crafting the world as it looked to them, hearing their words and thinking their thoughts, and seeing the profound decisions they faced and how but for a quirk of fate events could just as likely have gone one way as another. I hasten to add that I didn't start out with any preconceptions of heroes or villains, which only would have hindered the process.

True, April 1865 was filled with men who often looked and acted like statues of cut marble and chiseled stone, but who, upon closer examination, had their own failings and frailties. Some were leaders of great courage, while others seemed to embody the intricacies of human nature. Some were uncommonly gifted, others were morbid or even mad, and all had their own unique roles and talents. As I relived Robert E. Lee's harrowing retreat and ultimate surrender, as I captured Abraham Lincoln's final days in all their exhilaration and heartbreak, or as I plunged into the fears of a nation unraveling either due to the president's assassination or the dire prospect of guerrilla war, I found myself day after day pacing in their heads and inhabiting their hearts. I felt as if I had been transported into the nineteenth century, and I was awed. When this happened, I believed in my gut that I was on to something. And if I was on to something, I thought the reader would be as well. ▶

66 As I relived Robert E. Lee's harrowing retreat and ultimate surrender, or as I captured Abraham Lincoln's final days, I found myself day after day pacing in their heads and inhabiting their hearts. 99

Writing *April 1865* (continued)

> 66 Language has its own music. There were points in the book where I slowed the narrative down, points where I sped it up, areas where I used thundering cadences, and other areas where I employed language in its simplicity. 99

Slowly I began to find the essence of my story. Along the way, the narrative was as important to me as anything else. I have often been referred to as a public historian, a title I willingly embrace. I was writing my book to be read by all Americans who love history, biography, or simply quality nonfiction, and not solely for ardent students of the Civil War. I often asked questions deemed heretical because they ran against the grain of prevailing orthodoxy. So be it. I read musty dissertations by Ph.D. students on the arcana of the war. I hunted down old photographs that could help me better see the world about which I was writing. I immersed myself in the study of leadership and the history of ancient and recent guerrilla wars. After a year (or maybe two) of sitting at my desk I came to conceive of the book as one long song. Language has its own music. There were points in the book where I slowed the narrative down, points where I sped it up, areas where I used thundering cadences, and other areas where I employed language in its simplicity. In each case, I chose whatever method I believed most adequately approximated the great events of the month as they unfolded. I also labored to capture the cliffhangers of the month, convinced that this more effectively captured the events and mood of the day.

Month after month, day after day, for more than four years I struggled with my subject. When the words came I was exhilarated; when I knew something needed to be improved I felt pained. There was scarcely a waking moment when in one manner or another I wasn't thinking about the book or living it. *April 1865* became a running dialogue in my head. About midway into the first draft I felt things really clicking. Professional athletes feel this. Writers do too. When the draft was done I read and reread it, and so did my wife. She knew what I wanted to accomplish and was never shy about commenting or proposing edits or rewrites, frequently making her own detailed suggestions. She helped me recast the first chapter, and though I was skeptical at first, it worked brilliantly. Then came the long hard slog; every page, every paragraph, every sentence, and literally every word and comma were scrutinized, dissected, and manipulated over and over until I knew the entire book by heart. I eventually became so meticulous about the narrative that if I made a change on one page, however small, I reread the two pages before it and the two after to gauge how the rhythm of the narrative was affected. I should also confess that the book was probably a hundred pages longer in draft. The Lincoln biography, for example, was twice as long, and so was Lee's. Both read quite well, but I felt at their current length they slowed down the story and led the reader astray. I reluctantly cut both. It was the right decision. My savvy editor, Tim Duggan, suggested writing more on the burning of Richmond. I was secretly peeved, thinking it was just fine, but once I took a step back I realized Tim was on the mark. This was a section I originally wrote when I was quite tired—don't let anyone tell you otherwise, writing a book is like running a marathon, and pacing oneself is quite important. So I added to it, and the section sprang magnificently to life. And on it went.

In the end, all I could hope for was that I would write the best book I possibly could. With fingers crossed, this I believed I had done. But I never could have anticipated the ▶

> 66 Don't let anyone tell you otherwise, writing a book is like running a marathon, and pacing oneself is quite important. 99

enormous response that the book would receive. C-SPAN's Brian Lamb surprised me, asking, "When did you know you had written a winner?" To my embarrassment, I found myself being compared to Barbara Tuchman. The book immediately climbed all the bestseller lists, becoming the top seller in the nation, and the reviews were raves. Almost inexplicably, to me at least, it was excerpted in not one but three places. The book was the subject of almost a dozen newspaper columns, including those in the *Washington Post,* the *New York Times,* and the *Wall Street Journal.* It became an award-winning documentary special on The History Channel, and I appeared on countless television and radio shows to discuss it. To my astonishment and delight it just kept going. One day I received a call out of the blue from ABC News anchor Peter Jennings, telling me he had heard me discussing *April 1865* on NPR's *Weekend Edition* and was moved to tears. He went out that afternoon and bought the book, then read it and felt the same way all over again. Justice Sandra Day O'Connor invited me to a private luncheon in her chambers to talk about the book; the chief justice asked to see me too.

And then my greatest surprise came less than two weeks after the horror of 9/11, when President Bush was seen carrying *April 1865* from Camp David to the White House. He told reporters it was a "great book." *April 1865* was subsequently written up in papers and discussed on television across the globe. An invitation followed for dinner with the vice president to talk about Lincoln's leadership and how lessons from history might apply to the War on Terror. Lest anyone think that the book was embraced by just one political side, I hasten to add that President Bill Clinton

> 66 Justice Sandra Day O'Connor invited me to a private luncheon in her chambers to talk about the book; the chief justice asked to see me too. 99

warmly informed me that he read the book when it came out, thought it was "terrific," and gave copies to friends to read. Senator John Edwards read it on the presidential campaign trail. The book was even discussed in secret meetings of the Blue-Ribbon Commission on Weapons of Mass Destruction and landed on the desk of the commanding general in Iraq.

But what touched me more than anything else as an author were the many gracious letters I received from readers all over the world: some were distinguished, like university presidents and foreign diplomats; some were glamorous, like Oscar-winning screenwriters; some were celebrities, like baseball superstar Mike Piazza or actress Jamie Lee Curtis; some were my heroes, like the many high school and university teachers on the front lines of history; and some were ordinary, like one senior citizen who informed me that he had been devouring history books for most of his eighty years and insisted he couldn't put down *April 1865*. Readers often told me moving stories about their family history and the war, said I had given them "closure" on the Civil War for the first time, or sent me keepsakes or copies of family letters. And just as often readers from all walks of life said *April 1865* was "the best history book I ever read."

When I sat down to write, this was more than I could ever have hoped. ᔕ

Author's Picks

To Read

Battle Cry of Freedom, **by James McPherson**
The best one-volume book on the Civil War,
by our leading Civil War historian.

The Civil War, **by Shelby Foote**
A rich and stunning saga of the Civil War
in a momentous three-volume set.

To Visit

For a walking tour of *April 1865* start
with some background, beginning with
Gettysburg. Set amid the rolling hills of south
central Pennsylvania, this is the most famous
and widely toured battlefield in the nation.
With the Union itself in peril, it was here in
1863 after a series of defeats that the Union
Army over three tense days was finally able
to stymie Robert E. Lee's vaunted Army of
Northern Virginia. The battle culminated in
the disastrous Pickett's Charge. This was a
crucial turning point in the war. It was also
here that Abraham Lincoln gave the most
famous speech in American history, the
Gettysburg Address. The tour guides are
excellent, and to this day, around the boulders
and wooded settings, if one pays enough
attention you can still hear the bugle's peal,
the cannon's boom, and listen to the ghosts
of the great American generals.

Antietam. The September day in 1862 on
which this battle was fought along Antietam
Creek in Maryland was the bloodiest in the
nation's history. Said one Northern soldier,

" If one pays
enough attention
you can still hear
the bugle's peal,
the cannon's
boom, and
listen to the
ghosts of the
great American
generals. "

"No tongue can tell, no mind conceive, no pen portray the horrible sights I witnessed." The losses were frightful for both sides. Go see the cornfield, the Bloody Lane, and the Dunkard Church. It is particularly moving to see Antietam in December, when 23,000 flickering candles are set out to commemorate the dead.

Lee's Retreat in Virginia. One of my favorites. In some corners, little has changed since Lee's army fled along these dusty roads and hills. Through a series of clearly delineated sites, you can follow Lee's harrowing, often courageous retreat with Grant nipping at his heels as he made his way from a burning Richmond to the gentle slopes of Appomattox in April 1865. You will need a car and a good pair of walking shoes, but it is well worth it. Fascinating guide tapes narrating the retreat are available . . . or you can bring along your dog-eared copy of *April 1865.*

Appomattox Court House in Virginia. On arguably one of the most momentous days in the nation's history, April 9, 1865, it was here that Lee rejected guerrilla war and surrendered to Union general Ulysses S. Grant. It was also a day of uncommon dignity, grandeur, and foresight, when these two great generals played the role of statesmen and set a tone for the postwar America to come. The McLean House, where the actual surrender took place, has been lovingly restored. This area is virtually unchanged from the time when Lee quietly said, "I have probably to be General Grant's prisoner on this day." No Civil War buff or lover of American history can afford to miss this site.

Ford's Theatre in the heart of Washington, D.C. Here Abraham Lincoln was assassinated by John Wilkes Booth on April 14, 1865, throwing the nation into sorrow and turmoil. The Presidential box has been faithfully preserved as it was on the night of the assassination. Lincoln died across the street at the Peterson House, lying diagonally on a seedy, four-poster bed.

Richmond. There are a number of often overlooked gems to see in Richmond, starting with the magnificent outdoor statue of George Washington on the capitol grounds. From there, begin at St. Paul's Church, go to the old Confederate capitol and Confederate White House, then spend time at the Museum of the Confederacy and the Tredegar Iron Works. Finish along historic Monument Avenue, to get a glimpse of the people and the period that almost split the nation North and South. ◠

Essays by Jay Winik

Jay Winik expands upon some of April 1865*'s themes in these varied, thought-provoking essays:*

"Beyond the Wildest Dreams of John Wilkes Booth," in *What Ifs? of American History: Eminent Historians Imagine What Might Have Been,* edited by Robert Cowley (Putnam Books, 2004).

"Abraham Lincoln," in *Presidential Leadership: Rating the Best and the Worst in the White House,* edited by James Taranto and Leonard Leo (Wall Street Journal Books, 2005).

"The Day Lincoln Was Shot," in *I Wish I'd Been There: Eminent American Historians Travel Back in Time,* edited by Byron Hollinshead (Doubleday Books, 2006).